DOMINION

OTHER BOOKS BY RANDY ALCORN:

Fiction:

Deadline

Nonfiction:

Prolife Answers to Prochoice Arguments
Christians in the Wake of the Sexual Revolution
Is Rescuing Right?
Money, Possessions, and Eternity
Sexual Temptation
Women Under Stress (with Nanci Alcorn)

Dominion

Randy Alcorn

MULTNOMAH BOOKS

SISTERS, OREGON

This book is a work of fiction. With the exception of recognized historical figures, the characters in this novel are fictional. Any resemblance to actual persons, living or dead, is purely coincidental.

To Nanci, Karina, and Angela Alcorn,

my Christ-centered and fun-loving wife and daughters.

Each of you has enriched my life in countless ways.
I respect you and your devotion to our Lord.
I treasure your friendship and thank God
for the privilege of being part of your family.

Wonderful as it's been here in the Shadowlands,
I look forward to greater adventures together
in our true home, which the Carpenter is preparing.
I can hardly wait.

I pray you'll keep investing your lives in eternity
and modeling for me the love of Christ.
I'm so proud of each of you.

Thanks for supporting me in everything,
including the long process of writing this book.
I love you.

ACKNOWLEDGMENTS

I'm indebted to many gracious people who helped me as I researched this book. (My apologies to anyone I inadvertently left out.)

Special thanks to three men who always went out of their way to answer my never-ending questions: Tom Nelson, Portland homicide detective; Jim Seymour, Gresham police officer; Sgt. Tom Dresner, Columbia Police Department armorer and inexhaustible source of firearms information.

Thanks also to homicide detective Mike Hefley, gang enforcement detective Neil Crannell, gang expert Madeleine Kopp, and police officers Bob Davis, Jim Carl, Dennis Bunker, Scott Anderson, Pete Summers, and John Cheney.

For giving of their expertise in everything from journalism to cars to medicine to gangs to science to art: Gene Saling, Dyrk Van Zanten, Rainy Takalo, Randy Martin, Leonard Ritzman, Doreen and Mike Button, Christy and Gordon Canzler, Mike Chaney, Matt Engstrom, Jim Anderson, Rod Gradin, Richard Brown, Jay Rau, Ron Noren, and Sheila and Jimmy Davis.

My heartfelt appreciation to Spencer Perkins and Chris Rice of *Urban Family* and *The Reconciler* in Jackson, Mississippi, Phil Reed of Voice of Calvary Church, as well as others I met in Jackson, including Ron Potter and Melvin Anderson. Thanks also to Don Frasier and Mel Renfro of Portland's Bridge Ministries and Jim Cottrell of Teen Challenge.

My deepest appreciation for the assistance and support of Nanci, Angela, and Karina Alcorn. Also, to Kathy and Ron Norquist and Diane and Rod Meyer for their encouragement and help.

I gained valuable insights on racial issues from Georgene Rice, Art Gray, Bruce Fong, Mike O'Brien, Jerome Joiner, Frank Peretti, Rakel Thurman, Ray Cook, Alex Marcus, Ron Washington, Dave Harvey, Barry Arnold, Bob Maddox, Steve Keels, and Stu Weber. Special thanks to my good brother John Edwards— your phone calls from across the country were always a special encouragement.

My heartfelt thanks to John Perkins, with whom I had lunch in Minnesota in 1987 and again in Mississippi eight years later. John, your example of love, forgiveness, and Christ-centeredness has touched my life deeply.

Thanks to NFL brothers, especially my friend Ken Ruettgers (you too, Sheryl), as well as Reggie White, Bill Brooks, and Guy McIntyre, men who spoke to me with honesty and great insight. Also, to former NFL player and current Antioch Bible Church pastor Ken Hutcherson, whose church is a powerful model of interracial partnership.

Thanks to those who opened their lives to me at Cornerstone Church in Chester, Pennsylvania: Arie and Marilyn Mangrum (and Arie IV), Jerome and

Leigh Burton, Ray and Dawn Jones, and Fred Catoe. Special thanks also to Wendell Robinson and Lynetta Martin of Portland's Mount Olivet Baptist Church, as well as to the church's youth choir.

I've benefited from the writings of some I've already mentioned, as well as those of Tony Evans, Carl Ellis, William Pannell, Raleigh Washington, Glen Kehrein, Thomas Tarrants, Glenn Usry, Craig S. Keener, Rod Cooper, Dolphus Weary, Harriet Beecher Stowe, Frederick Douglass, W. E. B. DuBois, Martin Luther King Jr., Marvin Olasky, Samuel Freedman, Ralph Ellison, Wellington Boone, Ron Washington, Alex Haley, Studs Terkel, Henry Louis Gates, Shelby Steele, Thomas Sowell, and Cornell West. On the subject of heaven, I'm indebted to C. S. Lewis, Peter Kreeft, and Joni Eareckson Tada.

My thanks to Bill McCartney and Promise Keepers, who have been raised up by God as a catalyst to racial dialogue, repentance, reconciliation, and partnership.

Thanks to the over six hundred readers of *Deadline* who have written kind and heartfelt letters to me. Your encouragement to write a sequel played an important role in *Dominion*.

Thanks to Rod Morris, my editor and friend, for believing in this book and bringing his wisdom and skills to it. Thanks to my brothers and sisters at Questar Publishers for being patient with me. After making my deadline on seven straight books, I was nearly four months late on this one. (I write a book called *Deadline,* and suddenly I can't meet one!)

I'm indebted to a faithful group of women at Good Shepherd Community Church, who diligently prayed for me during some challenging periods in writing this book. You know who you are, dear sisters—God will reward you for any impact this book makes for his kingdom. Thank you.

My deepest gratitude goes to El Elyon, God Most High. Thanks for leading me and sustaining me through the rigorous and enriching research and writing of this book. Please accept this, Audience of One, as an offering to you, for your glory. May the story cause readers to laugh, cry, and think—and in the process may you use it to change lives for eternity.

"Then the end will come, when he hands over the kingdom to God the Father after he has destroyed all dominion, authority and power."

1 CORINTHIANS 15:24

"He was given authority, glory and sovereign power;
all peoples, nations and men of every language worshiped him.
His dominion is an everlasting dominion that will not pass away,
and his kingdom is one that will never be destroyed."

DANIEL 7:14

The young man sat holding the .357 Smith and Wesson revolver, polishing its stainless steel with his mama's scarf until he could see in it his distorted reflection. He turned up the four-inch barrel and spun the cylinder, emptying all six shells on his bed. Staring blankly, he carefully reinserted one round.

He took out a bag of crack cocaine already packaged for the next day's delivery. He picked up one of the crusty rocks, smelled it, touched it with his tongue, debated whether to smoke it. Maybe it could make him forget what he could never tell his homeboys.

"They played me. Fools got it all wrong. Ain't their hood. Ain't their set. Can't tell my little homie, that's sure. What'm I gonna do now?"

He pointed the gun toward the pictures on the wall, setting his sights on people in the newspaper clippings, on one in particular. He slowly rotated his wrist, brushing the muzzle against the bridge of his nose, then pulling it back three inches. He peered deep into the seductive barrel, holding it so the light shone just far enough into the darkness to make him wonder what lay beyond. His trembling index finger fondled the trigger.

The barrel-chested man moved through the Gresham Fred Meyer supermarket aisle with surprising agility. He negotiated the aisles purposefully, pushing his shopping cart in and around the late Friday afternoon amblers, who seemed to have all the time in the world and nothing to accomplish.

His black tailored Givenchy suit and Cole Hahn dress shoes suggested he might be a CEO or corporate attorney. In fact, he was a columnist for the *Oregon Tribune,* where most of his colleagues dressed informally. But Clarence Abernathy calculated his dress for image.

Geneva had called him on his car phone and asked him to pick up a few things on the way home. He headed to the produce section to get the Granny Smith apples. "Granny Smiths are the green ones," she'd reminded him. As if he didn't know.

He headed toward the checkstand, bobbing and weaving just far enough down an aisle to snag a large box of Cheerios, when a loud angry voice invaded his private world.

"Shuddup! You hear me? I said shuddup! Keep your hands off!" The words spewed as if from a geyser.

A wiry man in his forties, about Clarence's age, stood fifty feet away at the far end of the aisle. He wore a tattered red-and-white Budweiser T-shirt. Clarence watched the man grab hold of the ear of a boy who couldn't be more than six years old. The boy's legs momentarily left the ground, his eyes dancing wildly.

The bloodcurdling scream pierced the store like a fire alarm. As the boy's tears flowed, the man pulled harder on his ear, then slapped his head.

"Shuddup, I said!" He cocked back his hand again, like a tennis racquet poised to serve. The arm came down powerfully but stopped just inches above the child's clinched eyes, stopped as if hitting a concrete wall.

The man in the Budweiser shirt looked at the big hand clutching his arm like a vice grip. The intruder had strewn five cereal boxes behind him in the moments it took to run the fifty feet.

"What the heck do you...?" The wiry man whirled to stare down the meddler, but he stared not into eyes but at an Adam's apple. The intruder was tall and thick, built like a redwood stump. He was the kind of man you'd grab hold of in a windstorm and run from in a dark alley.

"You're hurting the boy," he said, in a calm measured voice, deep and resonant.

The wiry man glanced to the side, suddenly aware of the gaping supermarket audience.

"Who do you think you are, you..." he sputtered, as if unsure what to say next.

"Doesn't matter who I am. Just matters you stop hurting the boy." He smiled broadly at the little man. But he didn't release his arm. "This your son?"

"Yeah."

"Then treat him like a daddy ought to treat his boy."

"It's none of your business."

"It's everybody's business. Now, tell me you won't hurt the boy again."

"I don't have to tell you nothin', you—"

"That's not the right answer," Clarence whispered, clamping his fingers harder, twisting the wedge on the vice grip. The man's arm throbbed, his eyes watered.

"Try again." The smile appeared nonchalant and unthreatening. The grip suggested otherwise.

"Okay," the man gasped.

"Okay, what?"

"I won't hurt the boy."

Clarence loosened his grip, removing his hand without the slightest twitch of uneasiness. He put the same big hand down on the little boy's head, covering it like a wool cap.

"Take care of yourself, son." The boy nodded, eyes big. Clarence turned to the father. "Have a nice day," he said, as if they'd just had a discussion about whether the economy size Cheerios was really the better deal.

As he walked back to his shopping cart, Clarence smiled reassuringly to the onlookers, some of whom nodded their approval, some of whom weren't so sure.

Clarence reached unconsciously to the two-inch scar just beneath his right ear.

It was a thirty-two-year-old scar, compliments of some teenage boys in Mississippi who'd pummeled ten-year-old Clarence and his six-year-old sister with a dozen beer bottles, most of them broken before being thrown. One of the jagged missiles cut the gaping wound that became the scar he now fingered.

He headed for the checkstand, still smiling pleasantly, the outward calm masking a raging storm within. Everyone gave him a wide berth.

The next morning was the second day of September, a sunny Oregon Saturday, the air fresh and exhilarating, suggesting an early fall. It was the kind of day people who live elsewhere think Oregon never has, just as Oregonians want them to think.

Clarence Abernathy rose early, grateful for the weekend. After reading a few chapters of *Biblical Keys to Health and Prosperity*, he put in two hours work on the yard, mowing and trimming and edging, getting it all just right. He always managed to have the best looking lawn on the block.

"Give Daddy a hug," he said to eight-year-old Keisha, proudly wearing her tights. She wrapped herself around him unreservedly. "Have a nice ballet lesson, okay?"

Clarence playfully punched eleven-year-old Jonah in the stomach. "And you have a good soccer practice. Use those Abernathy genes and fake 'em out of their socks!"

"Okay, Dad. Later."

Clarence grabbed a worn children's book from the shelf and put his tools in the car. Geneva came out by the car and hugged him. "Love you, baby," she said.

"You too. Have fun being the kids' taxi."

"What time you comin' home tonight?"

"Well, Jake and I won't be done tearing out Dani's carpet till late in the afternoon. Then playin' with the kids and dinner and hangin' awhile. Maybe ten or so?"

"Just make sure you're home by eleven, okay? I know how you and Dani get to talkin'." Geneva smiled. "I'll be waiting for you, but you know I can't stay up much past eleven."

"All right." Clarence said. "Maybe this time I'll bring you home some Granny Smiths."

"That's okay. The Golden Delicious are good eating. We didn't need a pie anyway."

Clarence took off in his bright red metallic 1997 Bonneville SSE, settling back in the plush champagne leather. He drove through the tidy suburbs toward the city, listening to oldies and dreaming about moving farther out to the country, which they planned to do in just another three weeks.

He pulled into a visitor's space outside the apartment of his friend and fellow

Tribune columnist, Jake Woods, who walked out the door as soon as Clarence came to a stop.

"Jake! How's my man?"

"Hey, Clabern." Jake called Clarence by his computer ID at the *Tribune*, a short form of Clarence Abernathy. "Beautiful Saturday morning, huh?"

The men talked shop as they drove toward Dani's, everything from the *Trib*'s changing editorial policy to the latest exploits of the multiculturalism committee to ideas for upcoming columns.

"Looking forward to finally meeting your sister," Jake said. "Tell me more about her."

"Dani's four years younger than I am. Thirty-eight now."

"Not married, right?"

"Not any more. Husband left her eight years ago. He took to drinking and doing drugs, freebasin', did some selling. Dani didn't tell me for the longest time. Finally she came to me when Roy was snortin' coke in front of the kids."

"So what'd you do?"

"I came over and flushed the crud down the toilet."

"The cocaine?"

"Yeah." Clarence didn't mention Roy's head had spent some time in the toilet too. "Next day he took off. Never heard a word from him since. Finally she admitted he'd hit her. We're close, really close, but she didn't tell me while it was going on. Said, 'If you go to the joint for killin' somebody, Antsy, make it for somebody more than Roy.'"

"Antsy?"

"Just a nickname."

Jake raised his eyebrows.

Clarence sighed. "When I was a kid, Mama would call us in from playin' ball. Of course, we never came after the first call. About the third time she'd yell, 'Clarants.' Dani was only three or four when she started thinking that was my name. She just turned it into Antsy."

"Thanks for sharing that with me, Antsy."

"Only Dani calls me that. And don't go telling anybody. I'd never hear the end of it."

"Your secret's safe with me, Antsy."

Clarence turned north off the Banfield Freeway toward Dani's house. After a few miles he saw a car with four flats, tires slit, windows broken, and insides stripped. He saw small businesses that had invested months of profit in steel bars so their merchandise would be there in the morning. They passed Sojourner Truth Middle School, with its heavy wrought iron fence surrounding the schoolyard. They had a metal detector there now to screen out weapons. He saw two teenage boys wearing T-shirts, both of which he'd seen in the suburbs. One said, "No Fear"; the other, "Life is short. And then you die."

"More gangbangers all the time," he said to Jake, looking at a young Crip strutting like a peacock and flashing his handsign, daring a Blood set to take on him and his homeboys. He watched obvious drug deals happening on two street corners. "Where are the cops when you need them?"

Clarence looked at the kids with baseball caps worn backwards, some tipped to one side, some to another, some with colorful bandannas. He knew it all had meaning, but he was a suburb dweller and tried not to think much about that sort of thing.

He saw boys dressed in gray oversized Dickeys and khaki beige work pants, sagging low. He noticed several black stretch belts with chrome or silver gang initials forming the belt buckle. White tennis shoes with black laces and black tennis shoes with white laces. Gold chains and black woven crosses around the neck.

Clarence looked at Jake out of the corner of his eye. His friend seemed to be studying the surroundings as a man would study the far side of the moon.

Clarence inhaled the smell of North Portland, the musty scent of aged buildings freshly baked in the last few weeks of summer sun. It wasn't the clean urban showpiece of Portland's renovated downtown, a stretch and tuck job done on the face of an aging movie star. This lacked even the appearance of a facelift. It had its highlights, its nice storefronts and well-preserved homes, but as a whole it seemed to Clarence a forsaken boneyard.

He glanced down the side streets at broken-down houses and lawns the size of pocket handkerchiefs. There on his right stood the rotting carcass of Zolar's shopping center, one of the last old-time mid-sized stores. Abandoned for at least fifteen years, the building still advertised bargains on faded colorless signs in the window.

"Thirty-nine cents a pound?" Jake asked. "Wonder what that was."

The numbers on the sun-bleached yellow tagboard were barely visible, the name of the product having long ago disappeared. Petroglyphs on glass, the remains of a civilization that once prospered, but now lay in ruins.

Clarence turned right on Jackson Street. About every fourth house was well kept, with flower gardens looking to Clarence like oases in the desert. But most of the houses on this street had sagging roofs, peeling paint, and weed-choked lawns. Some of the driveways were littered with junk—rusted sheet metal, rotting plywood, abandoned appliances. Clarence pulled up to number 920. He scanned his sister's house, noticing the dull gray duct tape on her bedroom window facing the street.

Something else I need to fix.

Felicia and Celeste, Dani's twin five-year-olds, ran out in synchronized fashion, yelling "Uncle Antsy, Uncle Antsy." Both forty inches tall and forty pounds soaking wet, they jumped into his extended arms and he curled them like dumbbells, holding one in each arm effortlessly. He lifted them up high like a shoulder press, while they clutched his arms, giggling hilariously. He proudly displayed the girls for Jake, who smiled broadly, nodding his approval.

Clarence waved to Dani, who was working on the left side of the house, tending her little rose garden, a stark contrast to her neighbor's, ramshackle and grown over with weeds. Though they'd reached their peak two months ago, under Dani's watchful eye the last of summer's roses still barely held on.

"Hey, little sister!" Eyes on Dani, Clarence passed the girls to Jake like two sacks of potatoes. Surprised, Jake grinned, and they touched his face with immediate familiarity. Any friend of Uncle Antsy's was a friend of theirs. Clarence made a bee-line for Dani.

"Hey, big brother!" Dani's girlish smile spread like a wave across her round moist face. Her skin was smooth except for one blemish on the right side of her throat, a discolored scar left by another jagged beer bottle that same Mississippi night.

Jake watched as Clarence lifted Dani off her feet, him laughing, her giggling. He envied Clarence for having this kind of relationship with his sister.

"Jesus is my best friend," Felicia announced to Jake, as if this was the most important thing he could know about her. It seemed to Jake only yesterday his own daughter Carly, now nineteen, was just this size.

When Clarence introduced Dani to Jake, she reached out her hand. "I've heard all about you," she said with a toothy grin.

"Not as much as I've heard about you."

They went in and sat at the kitchen table. Clarence wondered if she'd ever get a new one. He'd offered to buy her one many times, but she'd always refused. She poured them both a berry-red glass of Kool-Aid. The ice clanked against the glasses as they talked.

"Where's Ty?" Clarence asked.

"Who knows? I'm havin' trouble with that boy, Antsy. I know he loves me, but he's fourteen and he just won't listen to his mama. The boy needs a daddy."

Clarence nodded.

"I've put an ad in the *Trib* lookin' for one," Dani glanced at Jake with a dead-pan expression. "Course, maybe I shouldn't have included my picture." A low squeal of a laugh came out of Dani, rising to a crescendo. Jake smiled. He liked her already.

"You look great, Sis," Clarence said, despite the rapid aging of her face, the gray hairs and extra pounds.

Tyrone, wearing a blue durag, swaggered in the front door. His teenage sensors detected the presence of adults, and he made a quick turn toward his room.

"Ty, get over here—it's your Uncle Antsy," Dani called. "And his friend Jake Woods. From the newspaper."

Ty came out mumbling something under his breath, maintaining steady eye contact with the floor. An eighteen-year-old independence rose out of this fourteen-year-old boy, who disappeared immediately after his command performance. Clarence noticed the distinctive blue of his bandanna.

"What's he doin' wearin' Crip colors?"

"That's what I been tellin' you, Antsy. I just don't know. He says those colors aren't a gang thing any more. Some people say it's so and others say it ain't. Truth is, I'm losin' him to the hood. He's startin' to run with bangers. I think he's a wannabe. He's losin' his straight A's. Studies are slippin'. Boy needs a daddy, or at least a man he can look up to. Don't know what to do, how to stop it."

"We've been over this a hundred times, Sis. Move! Just get out of here. I'll set you up with a down payment. I'll find you a place out by us."

"Out in the burbs? They're not for me."

"You need to live someplace safe, that's all I'm saying. Doesn't matter where, as long as you can keep the kids away from the bad influences."

"Oh, no bad influences in the suburbs? Come on, Antsy. I've never lived in the burbs, and I don't think I could. Folks there don't know each other—you've said that yourself."

"And in the city you're likely to get knifed for pocket change by somebody you're on a first-name basis with, is that what you want? If that's what it means to know folk, I'd rather not know anybody."

"It's not like that, Antsy. Folks here look out for each other. We've got lots of problems, that's true, but it brings us together. Me, I just got to find a way not to lose my son."

"You want Ty to stay out of trouble, off drugs, out of the gangs? You're gonna have to get him out of here. Change his environment. That's the way it is."

"Things are gettin' better. Councilman Norcoast has a new plan." Dani ignored her brother's rolling eyes. "It's a *good* plan. I've been at the sounding board meetings. We can turn this thing around if we work together. Why don't you move in on my street, Antsy? There's some houses for sale."

"I'm surprised they aren't all for sale. Who'd want to live here?" Clarence saw instantly he'd hurt her. "Sorry, Sis. I didn't mean it that way."

"I really appreciate you comin' over every week and spendin' time with the kids," Dani said. "But if your family was nearer and Ty knew he could talk to you, watch you, maybe then…We need all the role models we can get, big brother. The community needs people like you."

"Stop thinking of the community and start thinking about yourself and your children. Don't you see, Sis? The city belongs to drunks and druggies and users and pimps and gangbangers. They've taken over. That's why your big shot Councilman Norcoast doesn't live in a hood like this. Why would he? And why would I move somewhere just to triple bolt my door every night and hope some lowlife with a sawed-off shot-gun or an Uzi doesn't blow open my door and rob me blind? What's the point?"

"The point is giving back to your people, helping the neighborhood, brother."

Clarence hated this conversation, as much as he'd hated it the dozens of times they'd had it before. He shook his head and kissed Dani on the cheek, as if to say "We're never going to agree, but I love you." He looked at Jake. "Time to go to work. If you think you're man enough to keep up with me, I mean."

Clarence and Jake started tearing out the badly worn living-room carpet. They followed with odds and ends chores, Jake fixing a leaky faucet while Clarence mea-sured Dani's bedroom window for a replacement.

At four o'clock Jake peered out the living-room window, watching the street. There she was. Janet, looking tentative and studying the street numbers, crawled up in Jake's lapis blue Mustang.

"See ya, Dani. Nice to meet you," Jake said.

Dani gave Jake an unexpected hug. "Bye, Jake. Thanks *so* much for your help."

"Come on out and meet Janet," he said to her. The women chatted a few min-utes, then Jake got in the driver's seat. As he pulled off, he rolled down the window and called out, "Later, Antsy."

Clarence glared. "Later, Jakey."

On their way back up the porch steps Dani said, "You can't give up on the city, big brother. You can get me out of here, but who's gonna get out the Hills up on Jack Street? And the Devenys over on Brumbelow? And Mr. Wesley and his children on Moffat? And old Hattie Burns right across Jackson? We need men like you, Clarence."

"Geneva tells me you've been talking about getting us in here. Well, you may be able to push her buttons, little sis, but not mine. My dream's the same as always. A house in the country, even farther out than where we're moving in three weeks—but hey, it's a start. Beautiful fields and trees and flowers and horses and peace and safety for my children, that's what I want. And I want it for you too, Sis. That's not such a bad dream, is it?"

"You and your dreams, Antsy," Dani sighed. "At least you could come to our church and teach a class or work with the youth. At least you could do that."

"It's a long way to drive for church."

"How 'bout I cut you a deal, big brother? Instead of Saturdays, you come out Sundays to church, spend the afternoon with my kids. That way we'd see Geneva and Keisha and Jonah. The girls would love to hang with 'em. And you'd have your Saturdays all to yourself and your family out there in your suburbs."

Clarence acted as if he didn't hear, turning to watch the commotion at the front door. Celeste and Felicia had arrived again, in tow from Hattie Burns. The old woman scowled at Clarence.

"Now, Clarence, these little girls say you been readin' them some stories. And they don't want to finish the video they been watchin' at Grandma Hattie's. They prefer your readin'. Now if that don't beat all!"

She gave him a big grandmotherly hug. Hattie always reminded him of Mama, soft and warm and cuddly, but with more authority than smart boys ever wanted to challenge.

"You goin' to read about Aslan?" Felicia asked wide eyed.

"And Lucy and Susan?" Celeste asked.

"And Peter and Edmund," Clarence said. "Don't forget the boys! Yeah, I brought the book along. When we finish it, there's still six more books to go! How does that sound?"

Both beamed ear to ear as he picked up *The Lion, the Witch and the Wardrobe*. He'd started reading stories to them two years ago. Back then Ty sat and listened too.

Clarence walked toward the big bedroom the twins shared with their mama. Meanwhile the girls ran to the living room to pick up the old brocade chair that had been Clarence and Dani's mother's prize possession. One girl lifted it on each side. Like throne bearers, they carried in the chair for Uncle Antsy.

Felicia's and Celeste's own beds were tucked in the corner of their mother's room. Three years ago when Clarence's daddy still had the strength, the two of them had built a paneled divider for the girls to give them that closed-in cozy feeling kids like. Dani said she shared the room with the girls so they wouldn't be scared at night. Clarence knew she needed the company too.

Felicia proudly showed off her new lunch bucket with a big-eyed giraffe. "Isn't it *fine*, Uncle Antsy?"

"Finer than frog's hair, Felicia." He picked her and Celeste up and swung them together effortlessly around his head.

"Have I told you how much you girls look like your mama when she was little?"

They both giggled—he told them that every time he saw them. He slowly brought them down from near the ceiling, depositing them gently on the bed. Uncle Antsy was the biggest, strongest man on earth. With him around, they never had to be afraid.

The girls took their place on Mama's bed. Clarence read to them for nearly an hour, then the family ate pork chops, potatoes, and collard greens, Uncle Antsy's favorite meal. Following the sweet potato pie and coffee, Clarence and Dani put the girls to bed. Brother and sister stayed up late talking about old times, growing up in Mississippi, the years in the Chicago projects, and the move to Oregon. Time got away from them. Geneva called at 11:20 to make sure Clarence was okay. He finally moved toward the door at 11:45, kissing his little sister good night.

"Antsy…promise me you'll pray about movin' in here, or at least comin' in for church. So you can keep in touch. I think it would do you a world of good too."

"You've got the tenacity of a pit bull, Sis, I'll give you that." Clarence suddenly shook himself loose, arms dangling, puttin' on a strut and lookin' like he owned the world.

"Yeah, you right, Mama, do me a *world* a good. I could smoke me some hubba, sip me a forty, do a few speedballs. I get draped, put on lokes and a durag, dress down, and put in some work, huh? Yo, whatchu think, little sis?"

He pulled his pants down low enough she could see the top two inches of his underwear. She slapped her hand over her mouth.

"I be one bad hoodsta, hey? I mean, why play tennis out in the burbs when you can fly yo' colors in the hood, grab a rosco, and go get dusted with the homies?"

"Very funny." Dani tried not to laugh, but she did. "Come on, Antsy. There's more to life here than gangs and drugs, and you know it. I want you to promise me you'll think about it." She looked at him with those big pleading brown eyes.

"Okay," he said, putting his hands up in surrender, almost touching the ceiling. "I promise."

"Great. I love you, big brother." She kissed him on the cheek and gave him a bear hug. He'd always enjoyed her hugs, even when they were children.

Clarence got in the Bonneville and drove down Jackson, the street now gleaming with a late summer sprinkle that cooled the night air to a pleasant chill. About every third streetlight didn't work. Some had burned out, others were shot out, target practice for gangbangers. The street gleamed, black oil drawn out by the light rain.

As he drove by houses, Clarence imagined residents going through the ritual of checking and rechecking the locks on their doors. Like tortoises withdrawing into their shells, many inner-city families withdrew into their houses shortly after dark to find refuge. He watched teenagers still on the streets, some on foot, some on dime-speed bikes, some driving, including a few he was certain weren't old enough. As he turned on to Martin Luther King, he saw graffiti tags everywhere, reminding him of wolves marking their territory.

He thought about Tyrone. He had to help Dani, to keep Ty from running with those young hoodlums. Yeah. He'd make sure of it.

Clarence drove past a police car with two uniformed officers in the front seat. His whole body stiffened, and he exchanged wary glances with them.

"Boom! Boom! Boom!" He winced, hearing behind him the muffled noise of successive backfires that seemed to go on and on. Or was it gunshots?

The cops pulled a U-turn and headed toward the sound. Clarence considered turning around himself. But why? If he turned around every time he thought he heard a gunshot in this part of town, he'd never get home. He drove a mile farther, heard a siren and watched another police car and then an ambulance fly by.

I don't care what you say, little sis. I'm going to get you out of here before it's too late.

Clarence turned to his favorite Christian radio station. He listened to the preacher say, "God wants his children healthy and happy. Claim his promises for you, and he'll send his angels to protect you. He'll make you prosper, and he won't let harm come your way."

Thirty minutes later Clarence turned into his driveway east of Gresham. Suddenly he hit the brakes, startled. A bluish figure paced frantically under the front porch light.

Geneva? It was after midnight.

He saw his wife's contorted face and shoved the Bonneville into park before it stopped. He jumped out of the lurching car and bounded up the porch steps.

"What's wrong? What's happened? Are the kids all right?"

"Oh, baby." Geneva sobbed. She hugged him tight, clung to him. She was trying to tell him something, but Clarence couldn't understand her.

"Calm down, Geneva! Tell me what's going on."

"I got a call. From Hattie Burns. It's Dani."

"What? What happened?"

"She's been shot. Dani's been shot!"

CHAPTER

2

"I'll stay with the kids. Call me!"

Clarence didn't hear Geneva's frantic voice. He'd already hopped in the car and jammed it into reverse as soon as she'd said, "Emanuel Hospital."

"Be careful," she begged as the hedge obscured her view of the screeching Bonneville. She prayed he'd make it to the hospital in his car rather than an ambulance.

Clarence drove toward Emanuel in a blur, immersed in a fog of thoughts and images and questions and pleadings to God. The farther he got into the city, the more the artificial lights bombarded him, on the one hand illuminating what was out there, on the other obscuring it.

The streetlights bounced off his car's metallic finish, creating a reddish glint. The SSE was sporty, expensive. More than they could afford. He thought of how meaningless the car was in the face of what was happening.

What is happening?

What was it the health and prosperity book said this morning? "Serve God and he'll always take care of you. Count on it!"

O God, take care of her. Please make her all right. Please.

He ran three red lights getting to the freeway. Holding it to seventy, he hoped to escape being pulled over by the police. When he finally got off at the hospital exit, he came to a stop and waited impatiently for red to turn green.

Why wouldn't she listen to him? Sure, the suburbs weren't heaven. True, half the time you didn't know your neighbor. He might be an embezzler or tax evader or adulterer. Maybe his kid smokes dope and cheats in algebra and his wife's in alcohol rehab. But at least they just gossip about you or at worst bash in your mailbox. They don't shoot you.

He drove up to the big red Emergency sign, ignoring parking instructions. He ran up to the double glass doors and into the waiting room.

The blonde receptionist, skittish at the sight of the intruder, held her finger over a panic button and said in her most commanding voice, "Yes? Can I help you?"

"My sister." Clarence struggled for breath. "She's here."

"Name?"

"Clarence Abernathy."

"I mean your *sister's* name." Clarence thought he heard condescension in her voice.

"Dani. Dani Rawls."

She looked over some papers, then pushed a few buttons on the computer, looking at the screen. "When was she admitted?"

"I don't know. Forty minutes ago, maybe. Where is she? What's happening?"

"We have no record of her. We do have a Rawls though. Felicia Rawls."

"Felicia? That's my niece!"

O God, not Felicia.

"Yes. She's...hold on, I'd better get a doctor. Please take a seat."

"I'm going in."

"No! You can't!" She pressed the panic button. As Clarence pushed open the emergency door a blue-coated doctor said, "Hold on. You can't come in here!"

"Where's Felicia? Where's Dani?"

A uniformed security guard rushed in from the parking lot. When Clarence turned toward him, the guard put his hand on his gun.

"Wait," the doctor said. He looked at Clarence. "Are you related to Felicia Rawls?"

"She's my niece."

"Okay. All right. I think we've got it under control, Freddy," he said to the guard. "I'm Dr. Brose," he said to Clarence. "Please sit down."

"I don't want to sit down." His eyes smoldered. "Tell me what's going on!"

"Your niece is in surgery."

"Surgery? Why?"

"To remove the bullets."

"Bullets? Felicia's been shot too?"

"I'm sorry," Dr. Brose said. "I thought you knew. Look, Dr. Mahmoud is doing the surgery. I'm not sure how long it will be." He craned his neck, looking through the door's glass window. "There's a surgery nurse coming out. Hang on, I'll be right back."

Clarence put his foot in the door, heard hushed whispers in the hallway, then watched Dr. Brose coming with another doctor. This one had blood on his blue scrubs, his brown forehead dripping with sweat.

"This is Dr. Mahmoud," Dr. Brose said to Clarence.

Great. They couldn't get an American doctor to treat a little black girl?

"Are you Felicia's closest relative?" Dr. Mahmoud asked Clarence.

"Besides her mother and…Yeah, I'm the closest."

"Your niece took two bullets."

Clarence's jaw trembled.

"One's not a problem. It's in her shoulder. We can get it later if…"

"If what?"

"If we can…take care of the one lodged in her cranium."

"Her head?"

"I'm afraid so."

Clarence sat down.

"I got the surgery started. We couldn't wait for the specialist. Dr. Deumajing took over for me, and I've been assisting."

Deumajing? What is this, a United Nations hospital?

"Was the surgery successful?"

"It's still going on."

"Then why are you out here?"

"I've been working ten hours straight, been in four surgeries. They pushed me out the door for a break. You don't want to get punchy. We've still got a ways to go. I honestly don't know how it's going to come out. It will be another hour at least."

"Do either of you know where my sister is? Dani Rawls?"

"No," Dr. Brose said, while Dr. Mahmoud shrugged. "Is she supposed to be here?"

"That's what I was told. She was shot too. Unless they got mixed up and meant just Felicia. But then Dani would be here. Where is she?"

"I don't know anything about her," Dr. Mahmoud said. "I've been with Felicia.

I need to get a cup of coffee then head back into surgery. You'll have to ask the receptionist."

"I did. She doesn't know anything." Dr. Mahmoud walked back through the door.

"Where did the shooting happen?" Dr. Brose asked.

"North Portland. Jackson Street."

"Maybe there were two ambulances. They could have taken your sister to Bess Kaiser."

"I'll call them," the receptionist said, dialing the number without having to look it up.

"Thanks," Clarence mumbled. He looked at her, wondering why she was on hold so long.

"Sorry," she finally said. "They have no Dani Rawls."

Clarence went to the phone and called Dani's number. No answer.

I can't do Felicia any good here. I've got to find Dani.

He ran to his car. He drove toward Martin Luther King Boulevard, praying for Felicia and Dani.

She's just a little girl, God. Just a child. And she needs her mama. So do I.

Clarence rolled down his window, needing to feel the fresh air and light rain on his face. He whizzed by the graffiti-marred street signs of Brumbelow and Moffat and made a sharp right turn onto Jackson Street, his tires squealing.

What the…

He threw on the brakes and skidded to a stop two feet short of a car parked crossways in the middle of the street.

Who's the jerk that left his car…

A thin muscular man with what looked like tools dangling from his belt stood stiffly. He'd popped up from behind the parked car and moved cautiously but swiftly toward Clarence's window.

Clarence jumped out, moving toward the man, his voice agitated. "I need to get to my sister's."

"Hold it right there." The man's arms were fully extended in front of him. Clarence looked at the gun in his hand.

"Show me both hands. Now! Get 'em up!"

Clarence raised both his hands. He knew the drill.

"Keep 'em up."

Clarence surveyed the scene, shrouded in semidarkness because of three shot-out streetlights. He now saw a half-dozen people, some of them in robes and night-shirts, gawking at Dani's house. He looked at the yellow police tape strung across the street behind the police car. He could barely read the bold black letters on the shimmering yellow tape: Crime Scene—Do Not Cross.

"Bend over. Hands on the hood."

Clarence leaned on his hands, turned his head to the left, and looked toward Dani's, three houses away. He could see a bustle of activity, at least four people standing on Dani's front porch, coming in and out the front door.

The uniformed officer patted him down. Though Clarence had never committed a crime other than speeding, this was the sixth time in some twenty-two years living in Portland he'd been patted down by police. He was counting.

The cop turned his neck to the left and mumbled something into a two-way radio microphone on his shoulder, with the curly black chord running down to his belt.

"Can we get this over with, officer? That's my sister's house. My name's Clarence Abernathy."

"Abernathy? The sportswriter?"

"Yeah."

And who are you, Elliot Ness?

"All right, take out your wallet," the officer said. "I need to see some ID." The cop seemed more relaxed now that the pat down had produced nothing more threatening than breath mints and a credit card receipt.

Clarence remembered his *Trib* press pass. He turned to lean back through the window and reach into the glove box.

"Freeze!" The officer's gun followed him like a homing beacon. "Keep your hands out of the car!"

"But my press pass is in—"

"Just show me your driver's license."

Clarence fumbled through the wallet and produced his license. The officer shined a flashlight on the picture, and then on Clarence's face. He made another mental comparison, perhaps to his profile sketch in the *Trib*.

"Okay, Mr. Abernathy. I'm sorry. But you should drive more carefully. And don't go jumping out of your car like that. With what happened here tonight I thought… It's a tense situation."

"What *did* happen here?" Tired of not getting answers, Clarence strode toward the yellow tape and stepped right over it.

"Wait. Stop! You can't go in there."

"I just did," he mumbled, not looking back.

Clarence marched toward the house, still sixty feet away, eyeing a second ribbon of yellow tape cordoning off the entire front of the house. If he had just walked into the holy place, he now headed toward the holy of holies. He expected the officer he'd passed to grab him, but instead he heard him talking on his radio in an excited voice.

Out Dani's front door barged a heavy-jowled, ham-fisted man in plainclothes, maybe six feet tall but an easy 250 pounds. He duck-walked to the top stair, then glided quickly down the steps. He stepped over the yellow tape beneath him and faced off with Clarence.

"Hold it right there, buddy."

I'm not your buddy.

"This is a crime scene. You can't come in. You've got to leave."

Clarence stood still, restraining himself and calculating his next move.

"I'm Detective Ollie Chandler."

Well, I'm the Prince of Wales. Wait a minute. Ollie Chandler?

The uniformed officer appeared from behind, looking back nervously at the assigned post he'd deserted in pursuit of Clarence.

"I warned Mr. Abernathy not to come in," the officer said.

"Look," Detective Chandler said to Clarence, "the yellow tape there—you might have read it as you crossed it—it's the one that says a kazillion times Do Not Cross? It's to keep the rubbernecks away from a crime scene that needs to remain undisturbed. So please, Mr. Abernathy…hang on. *Clarence* Abernathy? From the *Tribune?*"

"Yeah." Clarence felt a glimmer of satisfaction. Recognition had gotten him in a lot of places. Maybe now he'd get an apology.

"Well, then," Detective Chandler said, "you're especially unwelcome."

"What?"

"Nobody messes up a crime scene like a reporter. They think they're above all the rules. Guess you're a case in point, aren't you?"

"This is Dani's house. This is my baby sister's place."

"Dani Rawls is your sister? I'm sorry. I didn't know."

"I just came from Emanuel Hospital. My niece is there, but I can't find my sister. Did they take her somewhere else? Is somebody with her? What's going on?" The voice now sounded more pleading than demanding, and Ollie Chandler's defenses dropped. He looked down at the dark pavement, sighing deeply.

"I'm sorry, Mr. Abernathy. Your sister—"

"What? *What?*"

"She's…dead."

Clarence dropped down knees first to the sidewalk. Another man in plainclothes, a young Hispanic, moved quickly toward him, obviously concerned about Clarence disturbing evidence. Ollie waved the man off. "I'm really sorry," Ollie said to Clarence.

Clarence looked up, he and the Hispanic now eyeballing each other. "This is my partner, Manuel," Ollie said.

Clarence didn't hear the introduction. He stood slowly, in disbelief. He looked from the porch to Dani's bedroom. He gazed at the window that had the duct tape on it, the one he was going to fix next week. Wait, had someone already fixed it? He blinked hard. No, it only looked okay because the glass had been obliterated. There was barely a shard left hanging from the edges. All that remained were shreds of vanilla blinds hanging limply on the far side of the window frame.

The whole front right side of the house looked like a piece of meat that had been tenderized, then picked at with a filleting knife. It appeared an explosion within the wall itself had popped parts of it outward.

Clarence looked up at the porch, which extended three or four feet out from Dani's bedroom window. It was covered with yellow triangular markers, each with a bold black number. At first Clarence thought they must be some of the twins' playthings.

"What are those?" he asked weakly.

"Evidence markers," Ollie replied. "One for each shell casing."

The highest number he saw was forty. "But…there's forty of them?"

"Yeah."

Forty shells? It couldn't be.

"Did they take her away?"

"Not yet. They're waiting," Ollie said. He pointed past the yellow tape crossing the street eighty feet on the other side of the house. Clarence saw a beige paneled van with someone putting away a small box behind the driver's seat. "We have to finish a couple of things before we move her. We're using a laser unit to document the crime scene before anything gets disturbed."

"I'm going in to see her."

"I'm sorry, Mr. Abernathy. You can't. No way."

Clarence raised his foot above the yellow tape at the bottom of the stairs. Manuel stepped right in front of him, glaring up at his eyes, which had the effect of waving the red cape in front of a bull. Without lifting his arms Clarence moved forward, pushing the smaller man back.

A uniformed officer on the porch pulled a big .45 from his holster and said "Hold it." Manuel opened a fanny pack at his waist and smoothly pulled out a smaller gun, a nine millimeter, with his right hand and cuffs with his left.

"Hands behind your back. Now!"

"Hold it, hold it," Ollie said. "Back off, Manny."

"He's disturbing evidence. Interfering with an investigation. Assaulting a police officer."

"I'll handle it, Manny. I said back off."

Manny hesitated, then self-consciously gestured, a disgusted look on his face. His look seemed to say, "I followed procedure—we get in trouble for this and you're on your own."

"Look, Mr. Abernathy," Ollie said. "Trust me. You don't want to go in there anyway. It isn't pretty."

"I have to see her."

"I can't let you in." Ollie glanced around, assessing the situation. He looked at a few of the worker bees. "We've done all the work on the steps, right? You got that footprint, right Bo?"

A nonuniformed man carrying a little kit nodded.

"Okay, Mr. Abernathy. I'm not supposed to do this, but if you promise to stay right here, you can sit on the steps. If you let us finish our job they'll...wheel her out in a few minutes."

Manuel shook his head in disbelief. He pulled Ollie aside.

"We can't let him..." Clarence heard them arguing. At one point he heard Ollie say, "We're done with the steps. They're history. If it was my sister..." The voices trailed off, then he caught a few more snatches.

"The lieutenant hears this and he's gonna have a fit," Manny said.

"It's my case, my call. I need to talk to the medical examiner. Ken, watch Mr. Abernathy, okay?"

Ken, the uniformed officer up on the porch, stood in front of the door like a jackal guarding an Egyptian tomb. Clarence watched several bursts of light come from Dani's bedroom. A few minutes later he saw the police photographer through the open door, kneeling down to change film.

"Clarence!" The sobbing voice called to him from across the street, inside the outer cordoned zone. Clarence stepped over the inner yellow tape and embraced the big woman, Hattie Burns, who ran past another frustrated uniformed officer.

"I've got Ty and Celeste," Hattie said. "How's Felicia?"

"She's in surgery. They're trying to take out the bullet...," his face suddenly distorted, "from her head."

Hattie's arms surrounded him again. Clarence didn't know whether the moan that reverberated through him was his or hers. He pretended he was hugging Mama again, after all these years.

"What happened, Hattie?"

"It was an explosion that went on and on. I looked out the window. Saw someone up on the porch, hard to see with just the streetlights. Think I saw a big rifle in his hands. He ran to a car in the middle of the street, got in, and they were gone, just like that. Why would they do this? What's wrong with those gangbangers?"

Clarence wanted to ask her many questions, but not now. He stood silently, not sure of the whats, but certain he would never understand the whys.

He looked across the street and saw Ty standing on Hattie's porch, numbly looking over the situation. The air hung wet now, little droplets moving from mist to shower. He walked from Hattie and went toward Ty. Clarence hesitated as if there was something he needed to apologize for, then tried to put his arms around his nephew. Ty resisted, as though he was trying to be tougher than he was. Suddenly the raindrops on the boy's face were joined by tears.

"Why they do this to my mama?"

"I don't know, Ty. I don't know."

They stood in awkward silence for a few minutes, until Mrs. Burns joined them. "I'll take care of the children till...till we figure out what to do. Don't worry about them."

"Thanks," Clarence said, his face feeling as if it had been shot with novocaine. He crossed the street and went back up the stairs, scrutinized by Officer Ken. He started to sit down, then something caught his eye. The shredded blinds that had been hanging so precariously a few minutes ago had dropped out of sight. He could now see part of Dani's bedroom. He leaned to his right over the stair railing, trying to look in. Suddenly he went up the final stair and strode the eight feet to her window.

"Hold it. I don't think you're supposed to come past the stairs, are you?" Officer Ken sounded uncertain.

Clarence gazed into the room through the windowless window. His first sight was the familiar needlepoint wall hanging made by his mother, with a green lettered quote from Martin Luther King. "We must spread the propaganda of peace."

He squared up with the window frame and stared directly into the room. Glass and wood chips and chaos permeated it. Mama's prize brocade chair lay splintered, one leg ripped off as if severed by the jaws of a monster. He saw Detective Chandler leaning over what appeared to be a mannequin lying on the floor.

"O God," Clarence said. It was Dani.

He watched Ollie pointing to something, talking with Manuel. To the right he saw blood-soaked sheets on one of the two little beds tucked next to each other. It was Felicia's. There by her bed sat her little lunch bucket with zoo animals and that big smiling-face giraffe. Clarence stared at the twisted and misshapen box. He noticed the giraffe had a strange black spot on his head. No, it was a hole. A bullet hole.

Clarence buckled, falling to the floor of the porch, knocking aside three of the yellow evidence markers.

"Take me, God, but not Dani. And not Felicia. You can't have them. You can't!"

Officer Ken stood uncertainly over Clarence, then put his hand on his shoulder and led him back to the stairs. Clarence sat down, oblivious to the raindrops now pelting him.

A tall middle-aged woman walked out Dani's front door, gazing uncomfortably at Clarence. She wore a badge that said "Deputy Medical Examiner." She gestured down toward the man smoking a cigarette outside the beige paneled van. The man stomped out his cigarette, wheeled a collapsible gurney out of the van, lifted the outer yellow tape, pushed the gurney under it, and made his way to the front steps.

Everything moved quickly now. Clarence heard sounds of lifting in the bedroom. Then the gurney came out, covered with a white sheet, crimson stains already soaking through. The medical examiner led the way, peering nervously at Clarence.

He got up and walked alongside the gurney, ducking under the police tape, until it was at the back of the van.

The man attempted to lift part of Dani's body to better position it on the gurney before wheeling it up into the wagon.

"Let me move her," Clarence said.

"No, I got it. Do this all the time."

"She's my sister."

The man shrugged, looking at the medical examiner. "Okay."

Clarence lifted his baby sister. As an eighteen-year-old she had been barely 100 pounds, now perhaps 140, but still a light load for arms so big. He remembered as a ten-year-old lifting six-year-old Dani in his arms and carrying her across that little creek off the Strong River near their home in Puckett, Mississippi. She was so vulnerable. She always needed him to watch out for her, just as he needed her to watch out for.

"You can put her down now." The man's voice intruded, scattering the memories to the wind.

Clarence lowered the body slowly, moved to the side, and watched the man wheel the gurney up the ramp into the van. He and the medical examiner got in. The van rode off into the darkness.

Another uniformed officer came to Clarence and without a word escorted him across the cordoned-off area to his car. The driver's side window was still open. The soaking wet seat would normally have bothered him. He would have been concerned that the water might damage the plush champagne leather. Now it didn't matter. Nothing mattered. He sat down in the car. The heavy smell of wet leather assaulted him. He watched the water drops on the windshield join together and gather momentum, creating a hint of a rainbow from the streetlights. A cheap imitation of a real rainbow, with none of the hope.

Got to get back to the hospital. Got to see Felicia. Got to call Geneva. Got to tell Daddy.

How would he tell them? What would he say? He stared at his fingers, which felt strangely numb and, despite the moist air, dry like chalk. He studied them as if what he saw might bring an explanation, might bring order to a universe gone mad.

He remembered the timid young girl in her pink and yellow dresses, the diminutive sister, always his little shadow. She was as short and skinny as he was tall and stocky, as though they couldn't have come from the same genes. But one look at the face and everyone knew they did.

He remembered after they moved from Chicago to Portland, how he drove her to that party at Jefferson High when she was a freshman. How she peeked inside the doorway on her tiptoes to be sure there was someone she knew. How she looked back at him and said she'd decided not to go in. And how he made her go in because he knew that's what she wanted. She'd thanked him later. She'd been such a little mouse back then. And he had been her lion, her protector.

He relived the moments on that old Mississippi road where those white boys had thrown the broken beer bottles at him and Dani. He'd wrapped his arms around her to protect her, but it was an instant too late. One of them hit her and cut open her throat. He remembered her blood flowing out on his hands. Every time he'd seen that scar since, every time he'd looked at her, he'd wished he could get his hands on the ones who hurt her.

Suddenly a loud tortured voice erupted from within. "I'm sorry, Sis. I'm so sorry I wasn't there for you."

CHAPTER

3

The early September day, unusually hot and humid, felt more like Jackson, Mississippi than Portland, Oregon. The white-hot sun focused down relentlessly, as if some cosmic naughty boy held a giant magnifying glass to torment the dumb creatures below. The anticipation of relief that came with the previous week's milder weather turned out to be still another broken promise.

Clarence stepped into air-conditioned Emanuel Hospital, feeling physical relief but mental torment. He made his way to ICU. After an interminable wait, they finally let him in to see Felicia. He bent over the tiny girl, casting a shadow on her as he eclipsed the overhead light. He looked at her pint-size body, lying there defenselessly. Intrusive tubes ran into her. A white skullcap covered her head where surgery had been performed. She held to life by the slimmest thread.

Why did this happen? How can people hurt children like this? Why do you let them? Let her live. You *have* to let her live.

Clarence bargained with God repeatedly, as he had the last four days. He cited his books on God's promises of health and healing. He grabbed a Bible from the hospital chapel and turned from passage to passage, claiming every promise he liked and skipping over those he didn't.

"Ask and it will be given to you; seek and you will find; knock and the door will be opened to you. For everyone who asks receives; he who seeks finds; and to him who knocks, the door will be opened."

"If you believe, you will receive whatever you ask for in prayer."

He recited the passages as if they were mantras, as if every repetition might be the one to finally convince himself and God of what the Almighty must do. Clarence pushed aside every thought of the worst. He asked everyone he knew to pray. He claimed God's healing for Felicia.

"I'll let you have Dani as long as you let Felicia live. Don't let her die." He tried to cut a deal with God, speaking out loud, as if the one he addressed had turned hard of hearing and needed to be roused from slumber by a louder, more insistent voice.

The nurse came in, intending to tell him he should leave. She could see his eyes, smoldering coals ready to burst into flames. This man frightened her. She stepped forward, bracing herself, then whispered to him, "It's time to go."

He left the room feeling defeated, having no more power over life and death than did the little girl on the bed.

Geneva greeted Clarence with a hug in the intensive care waiting room. She held onto him as onto a redwood tree in a windstorm, but he gave under her embrace. He felt less like a towering redwood than a weak sapling, leaning in the breeze, tilting so far his wife wondered if his roots would hold.

A few feet away on a waiting room chair, stoop shouldered and leaning forward, sat Obadiah Abernathy, staring off into nowhere. Eighty-seven years old, he was the son of a sharecropper, the grandson of a Mississippi slave. He'd lived in Clarence's house the last two years, as mind and body had begun failing him. Clarence sat down next to him and looked into his father's deep-set eyes, eyes that had seen incredible changes and endured unforgettable conflict. Clarence wasn't sure if he should interrupt the wanderings of his daddy's mind. Any alternative to the present reality seemed welcome. He said nothing.

Clarence recalled the stories Daddy would read to him and Dani and their family, with the quaint vocabulary and beautiful inflections of a man who'd dropped out of school in third grade to pick cotton, and as a thirty-year-old had taught himself to read. He was the youngest of eleven children, he and his brother Elijah now being the last survivors of the brood. He'd played for the Indianapolis Clowns and nine other Negro League teams in the late twenties to late forties. At the age of thirty-three, he'd enlisted and served his country in World War II. He'd put his life on the line for a nation that wouldn't let him eat in most restaurants or sleep in most hotels or use the same drinking fountains or restrooms as white folk. He'd taken a bullet in his shoulder for a country that wouldn't print his birth announcement or wedding notice in its newspapers.

During and after his baseball years, to put food on the table this man had worked in mills, on assembly lines, as a library custodian, and a Pullman porter. He'd moved his family of eight from Mississippi to Chicago and finally to Portland in search of a better place, like Moses leading his people out of the wilderness in search of the Promised Land. This man who'd seemed so big to Clarence as a child had lost inches over the years, some because of the stoop of his shoulders and hunch of his back. His body had sagged, time and gravity digging the crags in his face ever deeper. But they had done nothing to remove his contagious smile and the sparkle of his eyes. It was as if his eyes and mouth drew their strength not from this world but another.

"We need to get to the funeral, baby," Geneva whispered to Clarence. "Harley picked up the kids fifteen minutes ago. They'll already be there."

Funeral. The word cut into him. He sternly reminded God of his bargain: "You can't have Felicia."

Clarence gently stirred his father and escorted him toward the car. Daddy was wearing his funeral suit, Clarence his short-sleeved white dress shirt, having kept his suit coat in the car. The air was so thick on his sweaty arms it felt like long flannel sleeves. He got in the Bonneville, which still smelled of wet leather, the scent reminding him of the nightmare that began four days ago and from which he had not yet awakened.

As he drove, Clarence prepared himself for a black funeral. With white funerals you'd get back to the office in an hour, in time to return your calls. With black funerals you were gone for the day. The white funeral preacher's job was to take away the grief. The black funeral preacher's job was to stretch it out. Right now he'd rather be going to a white funeral than a black one.

They drove up to Ebenezer Temple in North Portland, three miles north of the hospital and a mile from Dani's home, in the heart of "the black part of town." It was his third visit to the church. Twice he'd come with Dani, at her insistence. Today once more he'd come because of her, but this time without her. This time she was gone. Perhaps if he'd agreed to come to church she wouldn't have died. These and a hundred other irrational thoughts plagued him like bats swarming through the attics of his mind. He braced himself as he got out of the car in the church parking lot bustling with mourners.

"Clarence, oh my Lawd, Clarence."

"We gonna miss her so. Ohhh…"

Hugs and tears swarmed him from all directions. This wasn't a shake hands occasion, but a time for lingering embrace. Nobody could weep like black folk—they'd had centuries of practice. Clarence waded through the sea of people to the church entrance, not even seeing some who comforted him from the sides and behind.

"Hello, Clarence. I'm terribly sorry." This approach was different, a handshake, not a hug, surprisingly controlled. Clarence looked into the eyes of Reginald Norcoast, the popular councilman whose district included North Portland. Though he was white, he was known as a cutting-edge advocate of black concerns.

Clarence nodded to Norcoast, choosing not to say anything but wondering, What are you doing at my sister's funeral?

Like most in North Portland, Dani had trusted Norcoast. Clarence, on the other hand, saw him as a pretentious bureaucrat, self-packaged as Mother Teresa in a business suit. Except Mother Teresa didn't wear a Rolex, drive a Beemer, or smoke fancy cigars to celebrate political victories.

"Look at all these people whose lives your sister touched," Norcoast said. "You should be very proud of her."

"I am," Clarence said.

"Councilman Norcoast!" An excited commoner greeted the royalty. Clarence watched the public servant glad-hand the crowd. Of course. The explanation was obvious. This was a campaign appearance. Norcoast, the consummate opportunist. No wonder he was already the heavy favorite for Portland's mayoral race next year. At only forty-four and immensely popular, he had a likely future as senator or governor.

In tow behind Norcoast came his wife, Esther, a stately woman, prematurely gray but well preserved, with a few cosmetic tucks and rolls. A personal and political asset to her husband, ever graceful and elegant, she wore stunning jewelry, including the gold guardian angel pin always prominent on her ensemble.

Dani could have used a guardian angel. .

Geneva turned just then and saw her. "Esther!"

"Oh, Geneva!" Esther Norcoast threw her arms around Geneva Abernathy. The two had met several times before and felt a kinship.

"How kind of you to come, Esther. Thank you."

She came because her husband came, that's why, and he came as a campaign tactic.

Clarence watched the two women and saw tears flow from both of them. He felt a tinge of guilt, realizing this woman might be entirely sincere after all. Perhaps he had judged both the councilman and her too harshly. Geneva always said he was cynical.

A dark-skinned, white-gloved usher in a tuxedo presented himself with aplomb and seated Clarence and his family in the front row of Ebenezer Temple.

A passionate choir, rocking back and forth, sang an old slave song—"Soon I will be donna wid da troubles of da world, da troubles of da world; I'm goin' home to live wid God!" They built up to the chorus: "No more weepin' and wailin', no more weepin' and wailin', no more weepin' and a wailin', I'm goin' to live wid God!"

"I'm goin' to live wid God" sounded like a triumphant declaration rather than an unwilling acquiescence, and the apparent inconsistency bothered Clarence. Maybe that's why he never really liked the slave songs Daddy always sang under his breath. He couldn't be romantic about slavery, sharecropping, separate drinking fountains, beatings, hangings, hatred, and injustice. You don't look for the good in things like that. Clarence wasn't one to whine about it, never one to use it as an excuse. But he certainly wasn't going to pretend it was all some blessing in disguise. Like the brutality of slavery itself, Dani's death was a horrible tragedy, pure and simple. Nobody should try to make it anything else.

The pastor's wife led the choir in "Amazing Grace." They sang that song most Sundays in the black churches Clarence had been part of. The three white churches he'd been to out in Gresham sang it once in a while too, but never like this. In white churches you sang it quickly, crisply, without much emotion, and you always knew when the song was over. Here it was long and drawn out, half dirge and half joyous rapture, as if it had a life of its own. Black folk never sang it twice the same way, never knew when the song leader would stop until he did. Often it would last three times longer than in a white church.

Clarence didn't sing. He didn't want to sing.

"When we've been there ten thousand years, bright shining as the sun, we've no less days to sing God's praise than when we'd first begun."

I won't sing your praises for letting Dani die.

Clarence heard the sobbing all around him, the shaking, the low mournful wailing. It was a black funeral all right. He felt his father's hand on him. The old man's immense deep-set eyes watered, changing slightly their deep brown color, making them shine like polished rocks. The eyes held more tears than they should have been able to.

"Dani loved that ol' song," he whispered to Clarence. "Written by the old slave-ship captain, you know. God got hold of that boy, he did. Yessuh, Dani loved it wid all her heart. She there now, Son. Singin' God's praises. Wid yo' mama."

Those great eyes could no longer contain the water, which spilled down on the front of his old brown polyester church suit, purchased in the seventies.

Clarence put his right arm around his papa and his left hand on the patriarch's left hand. It felt something like it did when he touched it as a boy, callused and leathery from years of toiling at every form of work coloreds ever did in the South, from picking cotton to milling grain to shoeing horses to scrubbing floors. Except then it was so strong. Now it was so weak.

"A man shouldn't have to see his baby die," Obadiah whispered.

"I know, Papa. I know."

"Lord Almighty," Obadiah continued to whisper, "he know the pain of his child dyin' though. He had a reason for Jesus dyin'. Powerful reason. And he gots a reason for this too. I knows he does."

Daddy, stop looking for the best in the worst. It's not to be found.

Clarence remembered sitting out on their Puckett, Mississippi, porch as an eight-year-old, his father looking up at the sky and talking on and on about the man in the moon. "Yessuh, I see you's smilin' again tonight, ol' friend. What you got up yo' sleeve? What you know we don't? Look like you's ready to burst, ol' man." He'd laugh and laugh.

Young Clarence would ask him to point out all these happy features on the moon's face. But no matter how much his daddy pointed, all he could see was the craggy, lifeless desolation, a scarred and beaten surface on a tedious repetitive journey across the sky. It bothered him then and it bothered him now that his father saw with such different eyes than he.

"I gonna miss her, Son. Gonna miss my Dani terrible. Already do. Already do."

The congregation sang two songs about crossing Jordan. They sang "Swing Low, Sweet Chariot, Comin' fo' to Carry Me Home." These songs blended pain and joy in the strangest ways, as if written by those who knew one because they had seen so much of the other, as if the hope they expressed somehow meant much more because of the suffering that preceded it.

Clarence mouthed the songs as a lapsed practitioner of a faith mouths its creeds, more out of habit than conviction. His lips moved, but no sound came out. It wasn't so much that he disbelieved as that he resented what he believed.

I'm tired of injustice. I'm tired of evil winning. If you're God, why don't you just stop it?

A worship team came up front and sang a song he'd never heard. "Knowing you Jesus, knowing you; there is no greater thing; you're my all, you're the best; you're my joy, my righteousness, and I love you Lord."

Pastor Cairo Clancy stepped forward. A hush fell on the congregation. Dani had raved about Clancy over the years, but Clarence had only heard him preach once and wasn't so impressed. He knew enough to realize that, like politicians, not every minister was what he appeared to be.

"Welcome to Ebenezer, family and friends of Sister Dani Rawls." The pulpit looked like the bow of a ship, Cairo Clancy her captain. He gazed directly at the audience. Clarence could see no notes, nothing but a big black Bible.

"Sometimes I have to do funerals of people I don't know. On a few occasions I've had to do funerals of people I *wish* I didn't know."

Some snickers and laughs and lots of knowing nods.

"But this time it's someone I knew, someone I was *proud* to know." His voice broke on the word proud.

"Amens" and "Yessirs" and "Hallelujahs" rippled through the crowd.

Clarence braced himself. He took pride in his objectivity. He resisted the emotional buttons they tried to push in churches like this. He viewed emotions as the back door, a way of sneaking past the mind to manipulate the audience.

Nobody's going to manipulate me.

"Even as we meet right now, many of our minds and hearts are a few miles away at the hospital with little Felicia. Let's go to prayin' for her right now."

Without looking down, as if no transition were needed, he talked to God: "Lord, we love that little girl and we pray for her healing. We want her back, Lord. She's so young." His voice cracked. "If you have a reason to take her to be with you and her mama, we'll accept that—"

No we won't.

"But you know we want her healed. You're the great physician, Lord. You're all powerful. And you're all good. We commit Felicia to your care. We pray in the name of Jesus. Amen."

If you're all powerful and all good, you'll have to prove it. I won't let you off the hook.

"Most of you know Dani was an artist." The pastor pulled out a painting from behind the big wooden pulpit. Clarence saw the blue waves of an ocean.

"Dani painted this for me. It hangs in my office and always will. I don't think she ever spent much time at the ocean. But she knew how to dream, and her art was a gift from God."

He held up the oil painting and pointed. "Look at this water. Just the right blue, with a hint of green. Bright and dark colors mixed just right. Now I don't know a Picasso from a Grandma Moses—I'm no art critic. But one day Dani called me and Martha over, and we watched her finish up this beautiful painting. We saw her put her signature on the bottom. See, right here. Dani Rawls. And then she said to us, 'I made it for you.' Well, in the ol' days people used to give things to us preachers, but I tell you, this painting sure beats fried chicken, collard greens, and a pan of cornbread! And you're lookin' at a man who likes his chicken and cornbread!"

Everyone laughed, replete with some hoots and snorts. Part of Clarence questioned whether this was appropriate at a funeral, but an older part remembered that in his family and in the black churches of his youth there had always been a close line between tears and laughter.

Clarence gazed at the painting. He knew Dani's talent; she'd even sold a few paintings commercially over the years. In his home hung three she'd done for him and Geneva. One of his favorites was two old men playing chess. But the best was a painting of the Kansas City Monarchs, based on an old black-and-white photo of her father's. There in the front of all these Negro League players stood Obadiah Abernathy, eyes sparkling and body strong. Obadiah loved that picture. Clarence thought he'd seen all her paintings, but never this one of the ocean. It took his breath away.

"Well," Pastor Clancy said, "I've been looking at this painting, and I've been thinkin' about Dani—about how leaving this world was like signin' and framin' her own self-painted portrait. What she said and did before she died, it was the finishing touch, the final signature."

He took out a white handkerchief, slowly wiping it across his black face, the color contrast dramatic.

"Death's the signature, now isn't it? Till then our lives aren't open to final appraisal, because it isn't over till it's over. As long as we're alive, the painting's still in process and we don't know for sure how it's going to turn out. Well, I can tell you that Dani's life portrait was a masterpiece. It turned out well. She loved her family. She loved the church. Above all, she loved God."

Sobs and "Amens" filled the sanctuary.

Clarence felt a sudden compulsion to leave. He couldn't stand to stay in the auditorium another moment. He whispered to his father, "Got to go take an insulin shot." He whispered the same to Geneva. He could tell she didn't buy it.

He went out to the side aisle and walked to the back of the church, uncomfortable having everyone watch him. But it hurt less to leave than to stay. He didn't want to hear any more. There were Jake and Janet, near the back of the full auditorium, a little out of place sitting there in their white skin. Jake turned and looked at him, his eyes asking if he was all right.

Clarence nodded as if to say yes. He went into the bathroom and took out of his suit pocket the three-by-five inch blood test monitor and his little vial of tracer strips. He grasped the beige pen-like pointer that housed the blood test needle and pushed it down on the little finger of his left hand. The spring popped, the needle pierced, and the dark red blood surfaced. Clarence gathered it into a bead, letting it drop neatly on the quarter inch of exposed litmus paper. He pushed the button on the monitor to begin its count to sixty. While it counted he wiped his finger with a cotton ball and stuck the vial back in his suit pocket.

When it reached 57 the monitor started beeping at him. He neatly wiped off the tracer strip on the third beep. He then slipped it down into the slot to be read in another minute. It said 178. Could have been worse, but higher than he suspected, too high. He reached to his other coat pocket and pulled out the small, clear-colored vial of insulin with the white label. He untucked his shirt, took off the orange syringe cover, drew four units of R insulin, and injected himself in the stomach.

His need to take insulin or to consume sugar to combat too much insulin sometimes embarrassed him, but in cases like this it came in handy as an excuse to leave somewhere he didn't want to be. He knew he had to return now. Why had he consented to say something at the funeral? Reluctantly, he came back up the aisle and took his seat.

"God says it's appointed to men once to die, and after that comes judgment," Clancy said. "One day we'll each stand before God. And it'll take more than gold chains or lizard skin boots or fancy Easter hats to impress him."

"Amens" sounded everywhere. A woman behind Clarence said, "Yessuh." He heard the sounds of purses opening and closing and handkerchiefs unraveling and people crying. Though part of him resisted it, this black church brought up something in Clarence, something precious and long forgotten.

"Dani was a Christian," Pastor Clancy said. "Her name was written in the Lamb's book of life. God says because of what he did for her on the cross, she'll spend eternity with him in heaven. Well, she's there with him now. I'll miss her. But if I had the power, would I call her back here?"

Yes. In a second.

"I don't think so. It would be selfish. Once you meet Jesus on the other side, I have a feeling the last thing you'd want to do is come back here."

"That's true, pastor," someone said.

Clancy went on for another few minutes, then looked at Clarence. "Now, I want to call up someone many of you know, or at least you know of him. Clarence Abernathy. Maybe you read his columns in the *Trib*. I asked him if he'd say some words about his sister, Dani. Welcome, Clarence. Come on up here."

Clarence walked up front and faced the congregation. He saw the proud faces of the older women, glowing, beaming, ready to burst like they always were when a black man who'd made it stood up front before the community. He was never comfortable being shown off; it seemed to imply black men rarely succeeded. He felt particularly out of place standing behind a pulpit. If God wanted someone to speak for him today, Clarence knew he was a poor choice. He could think of nothing else to say, so he just looked at his notes for a prompting.

"Dani had that knack for fixin' up the food, even when she was little. She always wanted to be near Mama, and Mama lived in the kitchen. I remember them fixin' up possum, and Mama explaining to Dani you had to cook that possum till you could pull out the hair, nice'n easy."

Some made faces and chuckled, many smiled.

Without him realizing it, Clarence's diction had changed as he made himself at home in the community. "Dani and I did chores together. Went on adventures together. Snuck around and spied out raccoons and skunks and badgers and foxes. Sometimes we just spent the day watchin' the corn grow and talkin' about our dreams. We had lots of dreams, me and Dani."

His voice thickened. He paused for nearly ten seconds.

"One of the things about my little sis was her laugh, that delightful, hilarious, out-of-control laugh." Clarence had planned to say more about her laugh. He didn't.

"Summers were the best. Sometimes we hiked into the Bienville Forest, just the two of us, not far from our home in Puckett. Other days we moseyed down the Strong River and walked through the Mississippi mud. Dani loved to squish her toes in it. Then she'd skip up to Farmer Marshall's jade meadow and pick buttercups. She used to put them up to her face and the sun would hit them just a certain way, and I remember the reflection, the amber color it made on her skin."

Sobs of recognition and comfort and anguish filled the auditorium. Clarence no longer looked at his notes and found himself saying very different things than he'd written.

"I used to work the grease into Sissy's hair when she wanted to try something new with it, which seemed like about every week. One time in the Chicago projects, in Cabrini Green, some boys called her a name, made fun of her nappy hair. Next thing I knew my fists were bleeding, two boys were on the pavement, and I was on top of them. When I got home I caught it from Mama. Nearly knocked my head off, Mama did. I ended up hurtin' a lot worse than those boys."

Laughter erupted from the congregation, especially the men, many of whom had nearly had their heads knocked off by Mama too. Obadiah sat there nodding, as if to say, "My boy's tellin' the truth, now, this ain't no story, folks."

"Mama was so mad she told me to stay in my room for five hundred years." More laughter. "Daddy told me I shouldn't have done it, but he said he understood why. He said we had to protect our womenfolk."

Clarence looked at his daddy, both of their eyes watering.

"Later that night Dani snuck into my bedroom and told me, 'Thanks, Antsy.' Then she gave me a big plate of cookies she'd baked up just for me." He fought for control.

"She'd gone and baked cookies for me. That was just like Dani. Then she said, 'I know you'll always be there for me, Antsy.'" His face contorted as if in a wind tunnel. "Well…I wasn't there for her when those hoodlums came after her Saturday night. Nobody was there for her. Nobody."

Not even God.

He didn't say that out loud, out of respect for his daddy. But something inside him burned so hot he didn't trust himself to say any more. He had some concluding words written out, some thoughtful words people would walk away saying were profound, but he decided not to say them. He crumpled them in his fist and sat down.

Geneva hugged him tight from the left, leaving her wet makeup on the shoulder of his suit. His father put his frail, feather-light hand on Clarence's. He couldn't believe it was the same hand that used to throw a baseball to first without it dropping an inch, that used to swing a chopping maul for hours on end, that used to overpower him in arm wrestling even when young Clarence used both hands against him.

The pastor spoke on, but Clarence didn't hear him. He was in a Mississippi pasture, with Dani, watching the color of buttercups on her face. "Do I look high yella now, like Aunt Licia?" Aunt Licia, Mama's sister, was always so proud to be high yellow, the closer to white skin the better they thought in the old days, and if you could pass for white, that was the ultimate.

Dani. Oh, Dani.

The funeral procession snaked toward the graveyard. Clarence's mind traveled to another graveyard, thirty years ago, outside Puckett. They'd gone to bury Papa Buck, his mother's father, and he and seven-year-old Dani walked hand in hand. The funeral procession entered a beautiful cemetery. It was a peaceful, lovely, manicured plot with sculpted velvety grass and colorful arrays of flowers, growing wild and gathered in bouquets. He and Dani thought this was a fine place for Papa Buck.

But Uncle Elijah explained, "We's just passin' through the white section." Soon they came to an unkempt pasture where instead of beautiful marble tombstones, plastic covered notepaper marked the graves. Looking around, Clarence saw that after exposure to the weather, no names would be left visible. Even in death it was marble monuments for whites and thin, rain-soaked paper for blacks. Little Dani had cried then. He drew her close to him and told her it didn't matter, even though it surely did. He wanted to reach out and touch that little girl's face again.

The rest of the day—Dani's graveside service, family feast, all of it—passed for Clarence as if it were a television movie with bad reception going on in the background when your thoughts were somewhere else. When he got home, he withdrew to his office, withdrew from Geneva and the children and his daddy, the loved ones still with him, to brood about Dani, the loved one now gone. He kept thinking of that angel-like face, that face that looked just like…Felicia's.

"You can't have Felicia, God. You took my sister. But you can't take away that little girl."

He came out of his office and announced he was driving to the hospital. Geneva insisted she come with him. He relented.

"Let me inside, Clarence," she said as he drove. "I know you're grieving. So am I. Talk to me, please."

He wouldn't talk, not out of meanness but because he was afraid of what he would say, afraid he would frighten her. Besides, talking seemed so useless. What would it change?

Geneva tried repeatedly to fill the silence. But she couldn't penetrate the dark winter of her husband's soul.

"Felicia's condition hasn't changed," the doctor told them. "Obviously, it's a good sign nothing is worse. But she's not out of the woods yet." Clarence insisted on going into ICU to watch over Felicia, who still lay motionless on the bed.

Clarence stood at his bedroom doorframe, leaning back against the sharp edges, positioning the center of his back just so. Then he rubbed back and forth, up and down. Geneva always teased him about this, how he was her lumbering grizzly bear. She didn't tease him now.

He flashed back to college football days as an offensive lineman. The defensive man could try all day to get to the quarterback. If he made it through once for the sack, he was a success even though he failed nine out of ten times. But if an offensive lineman succeeded nine out of ten times yet failed to protect the quarterback just once, his day was a failure. It didn't matter how many times you succeeded. If you failed even once, everything could be lost.

His mind replayed sharp images of specific sacks he allowed twenty years ago, one at Alcorn State, a couple more at OSU. He could still see the enemy coming at him, feel himself getting knocked off balance, leaving his quarterback defenseless, vulnerable for the hit. He didn't remember those hundreds of times he'd done his job, hardly any of them. But he did remember every time he hadn't.

Spike, their English bulldog, marched into the bedroom, swaying side to side like an overstuffed sausage, walking like Charlie Chaplin. Spike looked up with his soulful eyes and tried to console his master. Dogs were so loyal, their lives so wrapped up in their masters, they could go days without eating until they were in his company again. Cats could take people or leave them, Clarence thought. It would be easier to be a cat than a dog.

After lying quietly in bed and having no idea what he'd spent fifteen minutes reading, he turned off the light. He rehearsed his last conversation with Dani.

"It's bad in here, Antsy. Children are dying, and they're killing each other. You've got to come help. We need men like you. You said you'd always be there for me, and you always have been, big brother. But we need you here."

"My dream is the same as it's always been. A house in the country. Peace and safety for my children. And for you too, if you'll only come join us. That's not such a bad dream, is it Sis?"

The dream was gone, replaced by this nightmare. Even the hope of moving soon to that country house five miles farther out wasn't enough to lift his spirits for more than a fleeting moment. How far from the city would a person have to move to escape the realities of sin and death?

Night covered the open bedroom windows like a grainy cloth. Clarence Abernathy became part of the impenetrable darkness that surrounded him. He felt like a bird shot from the sky, dying in the reeds below, no longer able to see the horizon.

In a moment's time, seemingly without warning, his grief began to transmutate, taking on a more powerful identity—rage.

Who killed my sister? And why? What makes him think he can get away with it?

For over an hour as he lay in the darkness, his mind filled with dozens of imaginary scenarios in which he tracked down and came face to face with the killer. Teeth clenched, he rehearsed in detail what he would do to him.

It was late Thursday afternoon, two days after the funeral. The temperature had dropped from the eighties to the sixties. Clarence returned from a hard bike ride and took an extra long shower. When he got out, Geneva joined him in their bedroom, shutting the door behind her.

"Dr. Newman called," Geneva said meekly.

"The shrink? What'd he have to say?"

"The *psychologist* felt it wouldn't be good for the kids to stay out here in the suburbs, at least not now."

"That's what he *felt*, huh? Why?"

"Too much change, too much stress. He said loss of a loved one was worth so many points of stress, and more for Celeste since she was in the room where it all happened. He said when you add moving and a new kindergarten and isolation from friends, it's too much, the stress goes over the top."

"So he knows how many points everything's worth? Smart guy. No wonder he costs a hundred twenty bucks an hour."

"Plus there's the racial pressure."

"Of transferring to a white school? How many points is that worth?"

"The kindergartens out here are decent, and Barlow's a good high school. But we're talking what, a dozen black kids out of sixteen hundred? Celeste would withdraw, and Ty would...Who knows what Ty would do? It would be hard to adjust."

"Our kids have adjusted," Clarence said.

"They've lived here since they were born. They've made friends. It still hasn't been easy. But Ty and Celeste would have to start from scratch, move from a black world to a white one. Dr. Newman thinks it's just too much after losing their mother. I agree."

"So what are we supposed to do?"

"I talked with Hattie," Geneva said. "She's like a grandmother to them. She'll keep them as long as we want her to. Since she's right across the street, it would be the closest thing to home."

"Closest thing to where their mom was murdered. The neighborhood's the problem, not the solution."

"I told Dr. Newman about Hattie's offer. He said given the limited options, the pros probably outweigh the cons."

"That's encouraging. If somebody else gets killed will he take responsibility for it?"

"You have another solution? I'm listening."

"Okay." Clarence sighed. "I'll talk to the kids." He walked down the stairs to the family room where Celeste was reading the Berenstain Bears with Keisha. Ty, looking like a caged animal, paced in the far corner, talking quietly on the portable phone.

Celeste seemed to be doing amazingly well, all things considered. With Ty it was hard to tell. Clarence sat down with them to explain the options.

"You could stay here with us or go back to your neighborhood for awhile, stay with Mrs. Burns."

"Don't want to stay here," Ty said. "Need to get back to my friends."

Celeste's big brown deer eyes, identical to Dani's, peered up at her uncle.

"What do you want, Celeste?"

"I want to stay at the hospital with Felicia."

"I know, but we can't do that. But we'll keep visiting her every day till she's better."

"We could move your house to our hood," Celeste said. "So we could still be with you and Aunt Geneva and Keisha and Jonah." She smiled broadly, having come up with the perfect solution.

"We can't do that either, sweetie. But we'll figure something out."

Clarence heard the doorbell ring, warning of an intruder. He listened from the bottom of the stairs.

"Jake!" Geneva exclaimed. "Hi. Come on in."

Clarence bounded up the stairs. "Hey, Jake. What's up?"

"Nothing, really. GI Joe's has a big sale going. Thought maybe we could check out fishing rods or tennis racquets or whatever."

"Sounds good. Let me change. Just take a minute."

"No need, Clabern. You look fine. It's not Club Med."

Truthfully, Clarence in his designer jeans and classy Green Bay Packers sweatshirt was almost overdressed for GI Joe's, especially compared to Jake in his faded Levis and stained gray sweatshirt. But that was one of Clarence's peculiar habits, Jake had noticed. They'd gone to a mall together a few weeks ago on a hot sweaty day and Clarence had dressed up like he was taking a brief to the Supreme Court.

"How is he?" Jake asked Geneva, knowing he'd get a straight answer from her he wouldn't get from Clarence.

"He's really struggling. But he's pretty good at pretending. I'm glad you dropped by. He came up those stairs with a spring in his step that hasn't been there since… everything happened. He needs a friend."

"Yeah. We all do."

Clarence reappeared in slacks, sweater, and a tie. As he walked past him and out the front door, Jake stared at him.

We're headed to a sporting goods store, and Clarence looks like he's going to close a deal with Bill Gates at Microsoft.

Jake looked back at Geneva for an explanation. None came.

Sunday morning Clarence's family drove to Covenant Evangelical Church in Gresham, where they'd been attending the last few months, their third church since moving to Gresham ten years ago. Ty had been painfully uncomfortable, the only black teenage boy in the church, the only black at all besides Clarence's family. Clarence insisted he go to the high school Sunday school class and peeked in to be sure he followed through. He saw him sitting sullenly in a corner, defying anyone to reach out to him. As far as Clarence could tell, no one did.

After steaks and salads at the Road House Grill, Clarence and his family took Ty and Celeste to Hattie Burns. Hattie showed Celeste her own little cot, miraculously missed by the spray of bullets, tucked up next to Hattie's big bed. The little girl stood there and stared at it. Hattie had prepared her sewing room for Ty. It once belonged to her two boys, one of whom was now a successful welder with a strong family, the other serving time for armed robbery.

Why did people growing up in the same home turn out so different? Clarence thought about his brothers, Harley and Ellis—Harley the professor at Portland State, Ellis having spent almost as many years in prison as out of it. He tried to tell himself it would work out, Ty living under Hattie's roof. But he wondered how she could possibly give him the discipline he needed.

"The boy needs a father, Antsy," a familiar voice said inside him.

While the children moved their things into their new rooms and Geneva talked details with Hattie, Clarence wandered out the front door, over to Dani's house. He stared at the riddled siding and the boarded up bedroom window. He looked down on the tattered porch where the bullet casings had lain, highlighted by those forty yellow markers.

He peered through a crack in the board and noticed much of the room's contents had been removed. Hattie had a key. She'd moved Celeste's cot. Maybe she'd taken care of the rest too. Lying in the corner was Felicia's cot, what was left of it. At least the blood had been cleaned up. He saw the little lunch pail and stared at the giraffe, focusing on the hole in its head.

Clarence made it to the *Oregon Tribune* building before seven Monday morning, an hour earlier than usual. He wasn't about to put himself on display by walking into a room full of people.

As always, he carried his brown soft leather briefcase, so habitually overstuffed that on a low-load day, such as this one, it looked like a relaxed trumpet player's sagging cheeks.

Clarence came up the elevator to the third floor, walked out briskly, and headed to the right, toward sports. He carefully avoided eye contact as he bypassed the southern fringes of the newsroom.

The place buzzed with motion, the harmony of steady routine punctuated by the melody, the excited bursts of breaking news. The air smelled of paper and ink, copy machines, fax machines, laser printers. Paper was everywhere. Pieces thumbtacked to corkboard, taped to computers, hung on walls. Blue, green, red, and gold paper, much of it in the form of little Post-it notes, desperately vied for attention.

Clarence glanced at the vast spread of 120 low-partitioned cubicles linked together—cookie cutter workspaces. All that distinguished one from the next were photos, knickknacks, and various degrees of disorder. A zoo with barless cages. Being a journalist required a practiced ability to ignore the commotion around you and preferably to feed on it.

His walk to sports made him wish for the old days when he worked for the *Oregon Journal*, before it was bought out by the *Trib*. Sports was its own self-contained world then, glassed off in a corner, on the north side, right by its own elevator. You could park, come up the elevator, go to work in sports, and never interact with a single non-sports person. The news reporters were just bodies in the distance, scurrying around dealing with inconsequential events such as assassinations and plane crashes and moon landings, while the really important stuff—whether the Portland Trailblazers were beating the Seattle SuperSonics—all happened in sports.

Back then, Clarence imagined one day his desk would be alongside the news reporters. He dreamed of writing stories about regular black people—good salt of the earth, hard-working, family-loving, church-going folk. Stories unrelated to sports, entertainment, poverty, discrimination, protests, or crime. He'd take one of those photographers, take him where he'd never been, and reveal to the people of Oregon black life as they'd never imagined it. He'd show them the black community had a whole different face, a much bigger one than the isolated and slanted glimpses they caught in news stories. That vision once fueled him, energized him.

Clarence finally arrived at the archipelago of partitioned desks that comprised the sports section. He sat down in his semi-private columnist's cubicle. It wasn't an office, just a self-contained space enclosed on three sides, with partitions rising three feet above the desktop, rather than the standard eighteen inches. He'd never felt comfortable with those eighteen-inch dividers any more than with those obnoxiously low partitions in some public restrooms. His work station was adjacent to the main maze of partitions. People could see his backside, but by journalistic standards it was private. He could almost ignore the hum of the newsroom, even if it required popping in his foam earplugs when deadline loomed.

Clarence settled into his desk, figuring he was somewhat safe. The guys in sports weren't the touchy-feely type, and there were just two women on the sports beat. Not that he didn't like women. Just that he didn't want to be blubbered over. The guys wouldn't know what to say, so they'd either talk business or stay away. Either was fine with him. The last thing he wanted was to have some sensitive man of the nineties come over and tell him he understood his pain.

He wasn't too worried about the women. Penny was a third-year reporter, still getting throwaway assignments. Laurie was a seasoned twelve-year vet who recently moved to sports columnist to take up some slack for Clarence's transition to general. He hoped they would act less like conventional females than jockettes and refrain from picking the scab of his grief.

Sure enough, for his first hour back at the desk it was just a few hands on the shoulder, a few "I'm sorrys," a few "Good to have you backs," and more hushed conversations than usual. But at least nobody sat down to walk him through the fourteen stages of grief.

On his desk lay expressions of sympathy, one signed by the marketing department, another by the guys down in production. He tried not to be moved by them, but set them carefully in his briefcase to show Geneva.

Clarence made a quick rendezvous with the sports section coffeepot, where the coffee was always stronger than anywhere else in the galaxy, as if sportswriters needed the extra kickstart since they'd probably gotten home from a late ball game the night before and stopped for a few beers after logging their stories. He poured in the creamer, swirling it into his coffee, the black and white disappearing into each other, producing a mellow brown.

The newsroom had a feel to it, a superior feel. From here you stood and looked down at the goings on of the world in a way that let you imagine you were above it all—until you got mugged or diagnosed with terminal cancer or your child died. Journalists are a cynical lot, Clarence long ago had decided, and over the years he'd become more cynical than most. It always surprised him how many journalists remained liberals, since liberalism's assumptions about the goodness of man were daily disproved in most stories you worked on.

Journalists had to pry beneath the surface of apparent goodness and show the corruption that usually lurked underneath. Thus, the vice they originally found repugnant became their bedfellow, especially as they tried to compete with television news. They seethed with righteous indignation but became addicted to that indignation as Type A's become addicted to their own adrenaline. Hence their consuming attention to the titillating morbid lives of the world's Amy Fishers, Lorena Bobbits, Menendez brothers, Tonya Hardings, O. J. Simpsons, and an endless parade of social misfits and afternoon talk show guests.

Like most seasoned journalists Clarence had long ago cast aside the idealistic notion he could change the world. If you couldn't change the world, the next best thing was to judge the world. To become its resident critic in a way that put it at arm's length, so you could imagine you weren't part of the problem. Whether you were a political writer, a sportswriter or a movie reviewer, you were first and foremost a judge, a magistrate who adjudicated the mortal multitudes.

Sports had always played an important part in his life. He remembered his first baseball mitt, how Daddy had taught him to oil the leather glove, how he'd worked it in, put a baseball in the middle, drawn it tight with a few lengths of twine to make the best pocket. He remembered how he and Daddy would throw and hit the ball for hours on end. He remembered watching Aaron hit it out of the park and Mays chase down a fly ball. He'd listen to his father's stories about the old Negro Leagues and wish he'd been able to see his father play. But Obadiah was forty-four when Clarence was born, and Ruby thirty-five. When she had her last child, Dani, she was thirty-nine, worn ragged by the years of sharecropping and the hard life of Jim Crow but with a fire in her eyes her youngest son had inherited. Yes, his parents were old when he was born. Old? His mother had been seven years younger than he was now, his daddy only two years older. How could that be? The notion struck him as too strange.

Clarence had lots of calls to make. He looked up Portland police in his Rolodex for the first and most important one.

"This is Clarence Abernathy at the *Trib*. I'd like to talk to a homicide detective, first name's Ollie. Forget his last name. Big guy."

"Ollie Chandler?"

"Yeah, that's it."

"Just a moment." As he waited, Clarence sorted through three-by-five cards, narrowing down ideas for his next column.

"Ollie Chandler."

"This is Clarence Abernathy. Dani Rawls is…was my sister."

"Yeah. I remember meeting you."

You don't sound too happy to hear from me.

"I was wondering what's happening with my sister's case. Have you guys just given up on it?"

"No, we haven't." Chandler sounded defensive.

"Then...what's happening?"

The detective sighed, then paused. "Tell you what, Mr. Abernathy. Why don't we get together and discuss it? Have any time tomorrow? Maybe one o'clock?"

"I could be free by one-thirty."

"One-thirty tomorrow it is. Justice Center. Fourteenth floor."

"I'll be there."

Careful not to look to either side or appear less than busy, Clarence sat quietly in his cubicle, the memories falling upon one another like dominoes. He'd been raised on his daddy's love for baseball, and when he felt drawn to a career in journalism, the idea of combining sports and writing seemed an incredible dream. Sports was about choosing sides, affirming loyalty to colors. It had the thrill of combat without its fatal consequences. It wasn't like when men gave their lives to hold up the colors in battle, to be riddled with bullets rather than let the red, white, and blue touch the ground. You could celebrate Packer green and gold, Dolphin turquoise and orange, Forty-niner red and gold, and it didn't require that anyone die.

That's what he loved about sports. Great passion without real consequence. You could love your team, cheer them on, rave about them, be disappointed in them, even boo them. You could leave them, but they would never leave you. Of course, with player free agency and especially franchise free agency, it wasn't like that now. When the Browns left Cleveland it proved even the most loyal fans couldn't keep the team in town. The players were changing teams year to year. The guy you cheered for last year comes in and you boo him this year. Pretty soon all you were loyal to was jerseys. Cheering for laundry. Rooting for colors.

Between baseball strikes and football franchise moves and basketball scandals, Clarence's idealism about sports, about the love of the game itself, had been tempered. Maybe it wasn't sports that had changed so much as he had. While he still loved a good game, especially football, maybe he'd just outgrown his unbridled enthusiasm, maybe he was less naïve about life. For years he'd wanted to make the jump to general columnist, to leave sports as a career behind him. He'd thought it would be impossible, given his conservative politics. But things had changed at the *Trib*. A year ago he'd been allowed to shift to one general column a week, keeping two sports columns. Just five months ago they'd moved him to two general and one sports.

Jake Woods had been the only non-liberal in-house columnist, coming down moderate or conservative on most issues. There'd been the predictable negative responses, but mainly positive ones to Jake. Many readers thought the *Trib* was becoming more balanced. Next thing he knew, Clarence stepped through the door Jake opened. In fact, Jake had lobbied to get Clarence in there.

As Jess Foley, managing editor, often reminded them, newspapers were fighting for survival all across the country. They'd once had a monopoly on the delivery of information; they'd been the gatekeepers and hadn't had to listen to their critics. But with fewer people reading news and more looking to the network tabloid fare, the trashy pseudo-news, the *Trib* had been forced to make sure it did less to alienate its constituency. The radio talk show phenomenon at both the national and local levels had bypassed the gatekeepers of the media elite and brought conservatives out of the closet. Many of them dropped their subscriptions to the *Trib*. As Jake put it, "That drew the attention of management like getting hit with a two-by-four draws the attention of a mule."

But what really paved the way for Clarence's breakthrough to general columnist, he believed, was the nation's slap in the face of the mainstream press in the fall of 1994. The vast majority of newspapers endorsed liberal candidates, but in all but a few cases the voters went against the papers. The American people didn't trust the press, didn't follow the press. And they didn't just send a message to Washington, D.C. They sent a message to the entire newspaper industry. Including the *Trib*. That's when Raylon Berkley and Jess Foley first talked to Clarence about the possibility of doing a general column. He now basked in the thrill he'd felt, this moment from the past a drug to kill the pain of the present.

Clarence opened mail and sorted through mounds of papers. It was good to be back at work, where a man could forget his problems, or at least paper them over with other ones.

"Clarence?"

"Yeah?" He looked over his right shoulder to see Tim Newcomb. Twelve years younger than Clarence, red headed and energetic, Newcomb had already proven himself in his first three years out of J-school. He was a solid reporter.

"I'm sorry about your sister," Newcomb said. "And your niece."

"Thanks. My niece is going to be fine, though."

"Really? So she's out of danger now? That's great."

"Well, not out of danger. But she's going to make it."

"I'm really glad. It's hard to get facts in a newsroom, you know. Somebody told me she was still in critical condition."

Clarence didn't want to discuss it.

"Anyway," Newcomb said, "do you want an update on stories we've been covering while you were gone?"

"Sure, Tim. Pull up a chair."

Actually, since Clarence was a columnist, he didn't really need the update to do his job. But he welcomed it. He'd read the sports page every day the last week, but the real story was in the newsroom, where reporters and editors and columnists bantered about what should go in and what shouldn't. Often the most interesting angles on the story never got reported, either for lack of attribution or in the interests of taste. Yes, taste was still an issue in journalism, even if the old standards of taste had gone out of style with bobby socks and saddle shoes.

Clarence looked around his workspace, comfortable as an old pair of bedroom slippers. Above his computer terminal were two rows of shelving, filled with about forty books, most of them on serious topics. He liked to think. He loved a good argument. He was serious about issues. Too serious, Geneva told him.

Posted on the cubicle walls to his right were a variety of typed or neatly written quotes and political cartoons, many of them lampooning the press itself. One clip was a 1995 snippet from the *Washington Post*. It read, "Correction: Yesterday's Post incorrectly identified a D.C. monument. The building pictured was actually the Lincoln Memorial."

Next to this was a group of actual headlines clipped from various major newspapers: "Asbestos Suit Pressed" and "Tuna Biting Off Washington Coast" were the *Trib*'s own. "Defendant's Speech Ends in Long Sentence" and "Man Held over Giant LA Brush Fire" came from the *L.A. Times*. A half-dozen comparable clips from other papers accompanied them.

Taped on the top of his computer was a quote from President John Adams: "Our constitution was made only for a moral and religious people. It is wholly inadequate to the government of any other."

Tacked up on the corkboard to the side was one of his favorite letters, which he made a point of showing everyone. "Please get off your soapbox on abortion and come to terms with some of the real problems out there. For instance, our continued serial killings of animals, our brothers and sisters. The cannibalism must stop. George Bernard Shaw asked, 'How can we expect peaceful conditions on earth, as long as our bodies are the living graves of murdered animals?'"

He loved getting letters like this. They made great fodder for columns. Besides, this one made him feel more literate. Whenever he ate a hamburger, he thought of George Bernard Shaw.

On the left side was a collection of some of his favorite leads, such as "NBC and the Titanic are the same, except the Titanic had an orchestra." He looked absentmindedly at one he'd once been impressed with—"In the beginning God created the heavens and the earth." Attention getting. Astounding. Right to the point. But for the first time he could remember, Clarence found himself wondering whether or not it was true.

———

Clarence punched numbers again, his tenth phone call in the last hour and a half.

"Bowles and Sirianni. How may I help you?"

"Grant Bowles, please. This is Clarence Abernathy." He waited, flipping through more file cards.

"Morning, Clarence."

"Grant—so what's the deal with Dani's house?"

"It's borderline as to whether her assets are sufficient to require probate. But since she didn't have a will, we can probably count on it going to probate."

"How long is this going to take? And how much is it going to cost?"

"Who knows? Months at the very least. You know my hourly fee. Depends on how many complications we hit."

"I can't believe she didn't have a will."

"When you had me meet with her a few years ago, to clean up things with her ex-husband and all, I gave her the papers. According to the file here, my secretary followed up with a call, but Dani never returned the papers. At the time I asked her what would happen to her kids if she died, and she said you'd take them."

"She said what?"

"I'm looking at my notes right here. She said she wanted you to raise them. Said they needed a man and she was sure you'd do it."

You might have mentioned that to me, Sis.

He felt guilty even thinking it. He'd promised to always be there for her. Of course he'd take the kids.

"We need to get that house up for sale, Grant. I want to get the money into that trust for Ty and Celeste."

"You can't sell the house until it goes through probate, Clarence. That's how it works. Sorry."

"So what do we do with it? We leave it sitting there and it'll be torn to shreds. You don't know that neighborhood."

"I'd recommend somebody live there until this is settled. Maybe it can be rented out."

"Yeah, and turned into a drug house or something."

"You'll have to think of something."

Clarence hung up, hating the legal system. It was like politics—supposed to help people, and all it did was make life harder for them.

The phone rang. "Hello, Mr. Abernathy. This is Sheila, Councilman Norcoast's secretary. The councilman wonders if you're available to speak with him."

"I haven't got much time. But I guess I could squeeze him in." Clarence smiled. It felt good.

"Clarence?" Norcoast spoke with a television anchor voice.

"Yeah?" Clarence tried to sound as unimpressed as he could.

"This is Reg. I know I said it at her funeral, but let me express to you again my deepest sympathy. Danita was a wonderful person. I'm so sorry about your loss."

Nobody called her Danita. Nobody would, unless pretending to know her when he didn't.

"Yeah, me too. Thanks for the flowers."

Paid for with our tax dollars, no doubt.

"You're very welcome. It's the least I could do."

"What's on your mind, Mr. Norcoast?"

"Call me Reg, please, Clarence. Well, I have an idea of something we can do for your sister and the community."

Aren't you a little late for that?

"We've decided to kick off our 'Fight Crime' campaign a few weeks early. We're thinking the best way to capture the public's imagination is to have victims of violence appear at the rally and press conference. So people can see that those getting hurt are real people."

Of course they're real people. What other kind of people would they be?

"My assistants are contacting the other families, but I wanted to talk to you personally so you'd know my commitment."

Yeah. So I can say nice things about you in my column or so people will think I support you. Forget it. Never happen.

"A lot of people know your name, Clarence. You're highly respected. A role model to the community. You being on the platform, that would be a real boost to what we're trying to do."

"I don't think so," Clarence said. "I'm not comfortable doing that. Besides, I don't think it's good practice for a journalist to make appearances at political events."

"Oh, no, you don't understand, Clarence. This isn't political. It's part of a concerted effort to reclaim our neighborhoods, to stop the violence, get kids back into school, say no to drugs and yes to opportunity."

An endless fount of political platitudes. You forgot a chicken in every pot.

"No thanks."

"But Reverend Clancy, your sister's pastor, he said he thought you would be perfect."

"Clancy said that?"

"Yes, he did. He's going to be up there, kick off the program. So are family members of at least a dozen different people who've been killed. This is for our children. Can we count on you to help?"

"I'll have to think about it."

"Well, please call me back by tomorrow. The rally is this Saturday, one o'clock at Woodlawn Park. Maybe you can say something?"

"I'm not saying anything."

"All right, no problem. But I do hope you'll be there up on the platform. I know it's something that would have made your sister happy. And it would be a big encouragement to our whole community."

To whose community? What are you, an honorary black person?

"I'll think about it."

"All right, thanks, Clarence. I'll look forward to hearing you say yes. And again, my deepest sympathies about Danita."

Clarence put down the phone and shook his head, his profound distrust for politicians reinforced again. Democrat, Republican, Independent, it didn't matter. He just couldn't believe these guys were doing anything more than trying to keep themselves in power, cutting deals and taking payoffs. They were notorious for sidling up close to journalists, getting chummy. Reporters joked about this, but Clarence had seen them succumb to political charm, usually without knowing it. He'd determined not to spend time informally with any politicians unless he thought he could get more from them than they could get from him. Politics. Patterson, the *Trib* reporter assigned to the state capital in Salem, had told him, "There's two things you don't want to see made. Sausage and laws."

Clarence was all for laws. It was lawmakers he didn't trust. He worked to get a jump on his next column, forcing himself not to think about what kept trying to hijack his mind.

Tomorrow's face-off with Detective Ollie Chandler.

CHAPTER

5

At six o'clock in the morning, Clarence sipped a strong cup of coffee to prepare for the ritual of shave and shower. He stood gazing into his saltwater aquarium, watching the glass steam up from the heat of the cup. The brilliant yellow tangs glided across in formation, while the red-and-white lionfish with its swirling, feather-like spines ominously patrolled what he clearly regarded as his dominion. Hard to believe anything so beautiful could be so deadly.

Clarence loved the order and beauty of the underwater world. It was a world where he controlled the temperature, the water purity, the vegetation, the food, the props. Even the inhabitants. A world he could govern. A world where he called the shots.

His prize possession Eli, the black-speckled moray eel, lurked in the darkness, waiting to scare one of the kids' friends who came by and tapped on the glass despite being told not to. Clarence chuckled to himself, realizing Eli was more terrified than the children to whom he'd become a legendary threat.

Clarence studied the glowing blue-and-orange Potter's angelfish and the green-

and-blue long nose bird wrasse. He watched as the orange-and-white two band anemone fish darted in and out of his makeshift home. He wondered sometimes how they could stand living in a world so small and artificial. He imagined they must long to live in the adventurous world for which they'd been made, rather than this confined one. Reaching to sprinkle food into the water, he felt certain they must yearn to see beyond the distorted glass, to make sense of the shadowy image they now saw from a distance, the caretaker who provided their food and maintained their environment.

He untucked his shirt and wiped a fingerprint off the glass. There. The world he governed looked perfect now.

You poor dumb creatures don't even know what you're missing, do you? You can't imagine the great oceans beyond. You can't even see past your little artificial world.

After his shower, Clarence performed the daily ritual of putting in his contact lenses. People wear contacts for different reasons, but Clarence Abernathy wore them because glasses emphasized a flaw. It was never good strategy to give visibility to a weakness. Which was why most people who knew him weren't aware he was an insulin-dependent diabetic. He took the blood test now: 132. Not bad. Barely above normal. He took two insulin bottles from the refrigerator and stuck a slender syringe into the bottle marked Humulin U, then withdrew twelve units. Next he extracted fifteen units of Humulin R. With his left hand he untucked his T-shirt and injected the insulin, then went to pour his breakfast cereal.

His only other physical liability was, as the doctor put it, anomalous trichromatism. A type of color blindness. He could see the whole range of colors visible to people with normal vision, but he matched colors differently than they. He especially had trouble with greens, often mixing up yellow and green. It was a source of irritation in little ways. Like bringing home Golden Delicious apples instead of Granny Smiths.

He would keep the chinks in his armor invisible. That was critical when you advanced into enemy territory, which Clarence felt he did nearly every day. Especially today, when after finishing his column he would march to police headquarters and demand some answers from Ollie Chandler.

Clarence was eager to get to the office. Still, he determined to read the Bible now, just in case God was keeping score and it would stack up on the side of healing Felicia.

"Name and claim the blessings of God," he remembered the preacher say in his former church. "Jesus wants you well," he'd said. "The only reason you don't have money and health is you don't ask for it. God takes care of his own."

The preacher hadn't quoted many passages, but Clarence looked up those he could remember.

"Well, God, I'm naming Felicia. And I'm claiming her. I'm claiming your healing for her. I don't know why you let Dani die. But I'm trusting you not to let Felicia die. I'm trusting you to keep your promises."

———————

Four miles from his house, Clarence pulled up to a stoplight at the corner of Burnside and Powell. His window rolled down and arm leaning out, he glanced at the snow-white Toyota Camry LE on his left, meeting the eyes of the young female driver. He heard a familiar sound—the decisive thud of power locks.

As he pulled across the intersection, he stole a look in his rearview mirror. What was it that terrified people? His skin was rough, weathered as if he'd endured more life and carried more burdens than a man of forty-two should have. But he didn't look like a killer or a mugger or a rapist. Did he?

He studied the backside of his dark brown hands on the steering wheel, his creamy-white fingernails making a striking contrast. He turned up one of his palms, surprisingly light. It was as if an artist painting his skin had used up all the dark brown paint and only had enough left to spread it thinly on his palms, with none left at all for his nails. If his whole body was the color of his nails, or even the color of his palms, how might his life have been different? Better? Worse? He would never know.

———————

Clarence walked into the *Trib* at eight o'clock, exchanging smiles with Joe the security guard and Elaine the receptionist. Things weren't as bad now. People were asking about Felicia, but that was okay. He hoped his optimism was infectious enough to influence God.

He went to his desk, sat down, and inserted his tan foam earplugs, preparing to write his column. But he had four hours before his noon deadline. Too much time. The incentive wasn't strong yet, the mood not quite right. As usual before starting the column, he revisited his inner world, walking through its vast interconnected corridors, picking up things along the way that would work themselves into the column.

In his first few years as a journalist, he'd carried his blackness like a heavy backpack. He wasn't ashamed of it, but he could never leave it behind. Just the moment he started to forget it, he saw someone staring at him, studying him as if he were a zoo specimen. Whenever he looked at them, their eyes immediately turned the other way. He felt as if some of the whites were overseers, standing and watching him, looking for him to slack off, to pause too long between pulls on the hoe. It was a few years before this feeling subsided.

When he'd worked at the *Oregon Journal* back in the late seventies and early eighties, they'd been curious about him, as his white friends at OSU had been. In a predominantly white college he had still hung with blacks almost exclusively, just as whites hung with whites. The white ball players talked about things utterly foreign to him—camping, hunting, surfing, skiing, even hang gliding. Only the occasional reference to fishing and tennis struck a resonant chord.

Both in college and at the newspaper he found most white folks awkward and self-conscious and over-polite. He supposed he understood them far better than they understood him. No wonder. He had to live in their world; they didn't have to live in his. White reporters in the newsroom thought they knew him, but they didn't. That was painfully obvious.

"Clarence," one of them told him, "you're the whitest black man I've ever known."

"Thanks, Lee. I suppose that's quite a compliment coming from you." There was no use trying to educate some people. He didn't even know where to begin.

An editor looked at him one day and asked, "You people spend a lot of money on clothes, don't you?"

"Not a dime," he said. "Us people shoplift all our threads."

He couldn't win. If he looked like a slob, like some of them, he'd be a shiftless black man. If he wore decent clothes, he'd be a materialistic superficial black clotheshorse on the make.

Socializing was a challenge his first few years at the *Journal*. White people tended to be old fashioned, apprehensive, constipated. "White tight" the brothers called it. White folk stood around, schmoozed, talked about current events, and told corny jokes. It wasn't bad, just a different world with different rules. White parties were weird. Lots of times there was no music. No music at a party? Kind of like no meat at a barbecue. Black parties pulsated with rhythm, throbbing beats, perpetual dancing. A black friend once said to him, "At white parties, nobody sweats."

Though he'd been tempted to quit more than once, in time Clarence had become more at home in the workplace with whites than he'd ever felt possible. But that's where it ended. His interaction with them started and stopped at the *Trib*'s front door. In his home, in his personal life, even out in the white suburbs, he didn't feel close to a single white man. Except Jake. He was still weighing and measuring his relationship with Jake. He knew too many black men who'd thought they had a good friendship with a white man, only to discover it wasn't what it seemed. A brother at the *Trib* warned him not to think Jake could ever be a real friend. He'd been stubborn enough to ignore the warning but guarded enough to keep his eyes open and let time be the test.

At the *Journal* Clarence had been the only black person in sports. He'd had to learn the white culture, as a missionary must learn a nation's culture in order to understand its people and not misread their intentions. At first he'd been offended when other reporters would brush by and not acknowledge him with a word or a nod. In black neighborhoods, you didn't do that unless you were sending a message of disrespect. Eventually he realized this was part of white culture, or at least part of the busy milieu of newspaper culture. What was rudeness elsewhere he came to regard as professional efficiency here.

In 1982 the *Journal* was absorbed into the *Tribune*. Going to work for the *Trib* meant starting over for Clarence, having to prove himself again. He worked long shifts and often came in on his day off. It had been tough on Geneva. He realized why the divorce rate was so high among journalists, as it was among doctors, lawyers, and pro athletes. In the newsroom it was harder than in sports—men and women working long hours with each other, creating a "let's go have a drink" synergy while their wives and husbands were off in their own world a million miles away. Given this reality, Clarence felt thankful to be holed up in the sports department.

This crew can bug me, but they sure don't tempt me.

Race was omnipresent, always there though rarely spoken of. It lurked in the shadows, just beneath the surface of words. It skulked around in Clarence as much as some of the whites, sometimes more. Occasionally he'd balked in those early years, thinking the white guys were getting the good assignments while he was covering double-A high school JV water polo.

In time though, he determined not to attribute it to racism, but to the seniority pecking order. Other young inexperienced journalists, white guys, also got the nonglamorous jobs. That came with the territory. Seniority should count for something, and when he had it he would want the best assignments and be glad there were younger guys to cover the dog races. After all, he reminded himself, he wanted to be treated like those other guys, no worse and no better.

Meanwhile, he always carried the burden of having to prove himself. While this burden drove some men to resignation, he'd managed to turn the burden into an edge by letting it drive him to excellence.

Excellence? He shot back to reality. There would be no excellence today unless he started writing. He pulled back his desk drawer and removed one of four large three-by-five card holders. He flipped through them and found the section labeled "Green Bay" and a subsection with a group of a few dozen cards labeled "Women in Locker Room."

Two of his best columns last football season had come out of his unforgettable visit to Green Bay. He'd gone back to legendary Lambeau Field. The names of Vince Lombardi, Willie Davis, Ray Nitschke, Bart Starr, and Jim Taylor were among those encircling the stadium. He visited the Packer Hall of Fame. He loved the place.

The sixty thousand plus fans generated an indescribable noise. They were knowledgeable about the game, not like the stupid fans in some cities who booed when coaches didn't go for it on fourth and two in the second quarter. But what really struck Clarence was their unique relationship with the fans. The way their wide receivers would jump into the crowd after scoring a touchdown. The way the fans would carefully catch them and congratulate them and hug them, then lower them back down to the field. He'd written a column contrasting the Packer fans to the thousands of ice-ball-throwing fans in New York who had pelted coaches and players on the field. In Green Bay they announced that any fans throwing ice would go to jail and their season tickets would be confiscated. Jail was the less serious threat. Losing your season tickets in Green Bay was worse than having your house burned down.

Among the many subjects of his interviews in Green Bay had been the controversy surrounding women reporters in the men's locker room. Clarence hadn't been able to squeeze in this column last year, but now its time had come. On Sunday another NFL coach had gotten in trouble for not allowing a female reporter into the locker room immediately after the game.

Clarence typed a tentative title: Women Reporters in the Locker Room. He'd change it to something snappy later on. As the first words came out, he experienced the rush.

An hour later Clarence pressed the word count button: 829. He'd have to cut twenty-nine words, and maybe another fifty to make room for names and specific quotes that would personalize it and give it authority. He'd get on the phone right now and go down the list of athletes and wives he'd interviewed before. Hopefully some of them would be available. If not, he'd use their old quotes.

Clarence thought of all the people, including the publisher and three or four reporters, who would hate this column. The thought energized him.

Now it was strategy time. Hugh, the sports editor, was sure to cut "jack-booted feminists" and make a half dozen other changes to placate irate readers. So Clarence began inserting other offensive phrases he had no intention of including. This way Hugh, like any editor with rifle butted against his shoulder, could shoot at these targets on the fringes of the herd while the main pack managed to get away. Hugh could say, "You think *that's* offensive, you should have seen it before I whittled it down."

Clarence took quiet pride in positioning himself so that what survived editing would be as close as possible to what he wanted in the first place.

After half an hour of phone calls, additions, deletions, and revisions, he pushed the "send" button to route the column to Hugh, who he saw at his desk drinking a Dr. Pepper. He would watch his editor's facial expressions as he read it.

Okay, Hugh, don't let it snort out your nose.

He looked over at Laurie, his main sports columnist competition. She was a veteran with a great knowledge of sports, but she was a flaming liberal. It was amazing how much of your agenda you could hijack even into a simple sports column.

You're going to be livid, Laurie.

He smiled. Like a sidelined quarter horse able to run against the competition once more, for the first time in a week Clarence felt really good, on an emotional high. If only it could last.

Clarence entered the Justice Center pretending not to be nervous. He walked directly to the elevators on his right, as if he belonged there. He got a nod of recognition from one uniformed officer and cold stares from two others. As usual, he was glad to be wearing a suit. There were probably at least a hundred other black men in this building. Eighty percent of them, however, were behind bars.

He stepped in the elevator, which gave him only five options despite the building's sixteen floors. Floors two and three were courtrooms, four to eleven were jail floors, both accessible only from the other side of the building and only by authorized personnel. Twelfth floor, his first option, was ID, Intelligence, Juvenile, and Narcotics. Thirteenth floor housed Internal Investigations, the DA's office and a hodgepodge of smaller departments. Fourteenth, the button he pushed, was the detective floor. Above it were the Chief of Police's office and the media room. He'd been to the media room only three times, all in the last few years. His first fifteen years on the sports beat never brought him into contact with the police. The last three years, with player scandals ranging from drunk driving to girlfriend beating, had changed that.

The elevator stopped at the twelfth floor. A young woman in a sharp business suit stepped on. She forced a smile because she knew she should, Clarence thought. But he felt her uneasiness. She looked educated. Maybe she told herself she shouldn't feel what she was feeling. But she felt it nonetheless, he was certain.

I'm only going up a few more floors, lady. No time to mug or rape you.

The acid of his cynicism burned deep. This woman had learned society's lessons well, he supposed. Black men are ruthless crooks and killers. If you had to share space with them on an elevator, put one finger on your mace spray.

Nearly everyone wore plain clothes on the detective floor, so Clarence didn't stand out, except his tailored suit was sharper than the shop-worn standard here. Unlike the other floors, which allowed free access to hallways, detective division had only one place the general public could go—the reception desk, with a thick bullet-proof window and no door that opened from the outside.

"I have an appointment with Detective Chandler," Clarence told the receptionist. Five minutes later Ollie Chandler came through the lone door on the far end of the floor, licking his fingers. This was Clarence's first daylight view of him. He sized him up. Ollie's stomach and chest were battling to occupy the same space. Clearly, his stomach was winning. Clarence's impression was of a man in no danger of being mistaken for a regular on *Baywatch*.

"Come on in, Mr. Abernathy." The raspy basement voice seemed even lower than Clarence remembered from outside Dani's. "Just finishing up a steak sub in chili sauce. From the vending machine. It's not Tony Roma's, but when you're stuck in the office it works. Hungry?"

Not anymore.

Clarence shook his head.

Ollie escorted him to his desk in an open area. It was reminiscent of the *Trib*, but much smaller and less segmented, with greater separation between desks and therefore a little more privacy.

"Hang on just a second," Ollie said, stealing a chair from an unoccupied desk and rolling it to Clarence. "Got to make a quick phone call."

Clarence looked beyond the desks, out the huge windows. He soaked in the breathtaking panoramic view of the city. It all seemed so tranquil from up here. So ordered and peaceful, the stately buildings testifying to man's ability to create beauty, the bustling shops and offices his ability to produce wealth. Ironic, since this grand view came from Homicide.

Jake said he felt more secure visiting Ollie than anywhere in the city. So why did Clarence feel so insecure here? Why did he feel as if he were standing there naked and every detective who walked by stared at him?

Ollie put down the phone, then walked eight feet and peeked into a window. "Let's meet in the lieutenant's office," Ollie said to Clarence. "It's empty. Give us a little privacy."

They sat down, Ollie behind the desk, Clarence on the other side. He studied Ollie's light-skinned Scandinavian features and blotchy cherry-tinted neck.

A red neck. How appropriate.

"Jake Woods told me you might be calling. So what's on your mind, Mr. Abernathy?"

"My sister's death is on my mind. It's been over a week. I want to know who did it. And why."

"You and me both, friend."

I'm not your friend. Don't patronize me.

"Jake said you told him once if a case isn't solved in the first two or three days, chances are it won't be."

"Hey, guess I trained Jake pretty good," Ollie lightened up. "But actually, it's thirty-six hours. Even the third day is marginal, and by the time you hit seventy-two hours, good luck. Most of your physical evidence is gone and people's memories deteriorate. That's if you're lucky enough to find witnesses. For the most part, we weren't."

"What about Mrs. Burns?"

"She's our one witness, but darkness and failing eyesight are the problems. She heard the shots—so did most of the neighbors. They all said it was like a series of explosions, had its own quick cadence, loud and long. Automatic weapon, obviously. But most of our potential witnesses were frozen in bed. Can't blame them. You hear forty rounds ripping a house to shreds and you don't want to stick your head out as a target. By the time they looked, the car was gone. From the first shot to the screeching tires was maybe less than ten seconds. Barely time to wake up and get to a window."

"But Hattie Burns saw something, right?"

Ollie nodded, looking down at his report. "Her head was on her pillow, just a couple feet from the window, which was open. Just had a screen over it. As soon as she sat up, she could see straight over to your sister's porch. Couldn't make out much but a shadowy figure holding a rifle. The noise level was incredible. Everybody's used to hearing gunfire, but this was another ball game. One of the neighbors described it as 'ear splitting.'"

"So, what else did she see?" Clarence had talked with Hattie too. But he wanted to test what the detective told him.

"Well, she saw a car. Of course, with a big assault rifle they're not going to be on foot. Neighbors heard the squeal when it peeled out, so the driver was pretty excited."

"What kind of car?"

Ollie shrugged. "Mrs. Burns doesn't know for sure what kind, how big, anything. We've showed her all kinds of pictures. Midsize or large. She thinks four-door sedan but can't swear to it. Maybe a light color, but not white. A couple of streetlights were out. That didn't help."

"They've been out for months," Clarence said. "If it was anywhere else, they'd have been replaced weeks ago."

Ollie hesitated. "Maybe you're right. I don't know. Anyway, artificial lights can really mess you up when it comes to colors."

"What else can you tell me, besides it being a drive by?"

"Well, technically it *wasn't* drive by. It was drive up, walk up, then drive off. The walk up is considered big time macho, especially by Hispanic gangs. It's just you, *mano y mano*. But the old drive by is more popular. It does the job and gets them on the road in a hurry. This was a combo."

"How many in the car?"

"Well, it was left running in the street, not parked. Mrs. Burns saw the shooter jump in the passenger side. So it wasn't a one-man job. At least two, shooter and driver. Could have been more in the backseat, who knows? No physical description of the perps. Don't know size, color, age, what they were wearing, nothing. It's frustrating."

"What about the weapon?"

"We've got forty .223 shell casings." He reached in his pocket, pulled out a casing, and handed it to Clarence. "Here's one of them. Haven't got the rest back from the technicians yet. There's a huge backup in ballistics right now—too many shootings. Presumably the casings are all alike, so having forty won't be much better than having one. We've got a partial left footprint coming up the porch steps. It matches perfectly a plaster cast of a full right footprint where the shooter stepped off the walkway onto the lawn during his retreat. At least we're pretty sure it was the shooter. It had been dry all week and just rained earlier that night. The print was fresh. Size eight and a half, Air Jordans. That's about it. Maybe narrows us down to a few million people."

"So…is this case going to be solved?"

"To be honest, I don't know. The initial window is gone. We're into the tough part—trying to beat the bushes and find any witness, any clue. But I won't give up. I've solved cases a week later, a month, three months, six months, two years. Some precincts have cold-case crews that have solved cases going back fifteen years."

"So…are you optimistic?"

"The truth? Not really. Problem is, the killings don't stop. If we could have one murder and just focus on it for however long it takes, it would be great. But we've only got five homicide teams. Manny and I already have three open cases, plus another dozen unsolved that can yank our chains anytime if there's a new development."

"So Dani's just number three?"

"No. She's still number one, but we rotate, go on call, and our number's up again. Next homicide and she'll drop to number two. That's how it works. But I have to tell you, your sister's case is really pulling my strings. I take it personally, the way it was done. Vicious. Mother and child. I want the perps. But I'm just being honest with you—the fact that we haven't got much now suggests a good chance we won't. The lieutenant's always talking about case load management. There have to be priorities. The new cases get priority because if we put them on the back burner, we miss our best chance at solving them."

"I've heard gang killings are low priority," Clarence said.

"Not low priority. It's just that there's getting to be more of them. Hard to keep up with. And hard not to move on when there isn't a quick solution. What can I say? We're overworked."

"So you're going to let my sister's murder fall through the cracks?" Clarence watched Ollie's red neck get redder.

One of the advantages of black skin. Easier to hide your emotions.

"Nope. Told you that already. I'm doing my best. See this?" He lifted up a half-inch stack of papers held together by a metal clamp. "Those are reports from the uniformed officers who first arrived on the scene."

He picked up another stack and pushed it toward Clarence. "These are inter-views with neighbors conducted by Manny and me."

He picked up a big bulging manila envelope. "These are the photographs from the scene, and the autopsy." He kept the envelope on his side of the desk, his hand on top of it.

"I've gone over it all three or four times, looking for anything." As Ollie flipped through the big stack of papers, Clarence saw yellow highlighting and red under-lining and scribbling in the margins.

"I'm just trying to help you understand why I can't give it my undivided atten-tion," Ollie said. "I've got other victim's families just as anxious as you are." Ollie's eyes went to the office window. He jumped up and opened the door.

"Hey, Manny, come on in here. Say hi to Mr. Abernathy."

Manny came over and nodded coldly to Clarence, flashing an unmistakable "what the heck is he doing here" look at Ollie. He didn't extend his hand. Neither did Clarence.

"We were just discussing his sister's case."

"Think that's a good idea?" Manny spit out the words as though they were stale chewing tobacco that couldn't spend another moment in his mouth.

"Don't know," Ollie said. "But I'm trying to be accommodating. I size up the person and ask myself how much I should say. A skill you need to learn, Manny. Now look at Mr. Abernathy. What strikes you about him?"

Manny sized up Clarence, as if at a loss to come up with anything. "He's big," he finally said.

"Good, Manny. The eyes of a skilled detective, picking up the subtleties other people would miss. Now, what impresses you about him? Something positive."

Manny paused, searching. "He doesn't speak ghettoese."

Clarence stared at him hard. Tacobender.

"You'll have to excuse my partner, Mr. Abernathy. He doesn't try to be offen-sive. It just comes naturally." Manny looked unrepentant.

"Now, Manny," Ollie continued, "what I see is a man who loved his sister and wants to see that the bad guys get caught. We can understand that, now can't we?"

"But we shouldn't let him get in our way. The time you spend holdin' his hand could be used on the case."

Ollie looked at Clarence. "Manny's a former gangbanger. Fresno, wasn't it? Still has that flair, don't you think? What he knows could come in handy on this case. He's like sixty grade sandpaper. He rubs on you, but he gets the job done. Right, Manny?"

"Speaking of the job," Manny said, "I've got work to do. Later." He looked at Ollie, not Clarence.

"Okay. Have a nice day. Try not to spread too much good cheer." Ollie smiled and waved as Manny shut the door behind him.

"Charming guy," Clarence said.

"Savvy guy. Glad he's on our side."

"Doesn't he get to you?"

"Occasionally," Ollie said. "He's not Mr. Personality, but he's fast, careful, and efficient. He hasn't been a detective long, still on probation. Everybody is their first year in detective division. I'm breaking him in. By the time I'm done, maybe he'll be as good as I am. But he'll never be as handsome. Wasn't gifted with a kisser like this one." Ollie patted his own cheeks affectionately.

"What was he before? A patrol officer?"

"Yeah. That's where we all come from. You pay your dues, emerge from the ranks. I recommended Manny. Saw him work uniformed in a few cases. His reports were clear and detailed. He's perceptive, vivid imagination on how to pull off a crime. Comes with the gangbangin'. Knows how to think like a crook. That's a gift for a detective, you know. Separates the men from the boys. Now, if we could just get him a personality."

"So, there's no other witness besides Mrs. Burns?"

"Not necessarily."

"But you said—"

"Truth is, there could easily be witnesses. It wasn't that late, and it was a Saturday night. In fact, I'm surprised they did it as early as midnight. Maybe they just got anxious and jumped the gun. People are out on the streets late in that part of town. I drove around same time last Saturday night, up and down the streets. I saw maybe eight people who could have easily seen something if it happened that night. You got this car squirreling off following forty rounds? My theory is there *was* a witness or two. Getting them to come forward is something else."

"They don't trust the police," Clarence said. "They come forward and they think they'll be arrested for the crime."

"You got it," Ollie said. "Irrational, but that's what they think."

Blacks are irrational, huh? Or maybe they're smart enough to learn from experience.

"Let's say you *do* find a witness," Ollie said. "Try getting them to talk. Try getting them to go all the way to the witness stand. Either it's a betrayal—they feel like they can't snitch—or they're afraid of retaliation. Sometimes the gangs fill the court when the witness testifies, and all of a sudden they forget their story. With gangs, usually we know who did it but we can't prove it in court and it's all a waste of time."

"What do you mean you usually know who did it? How?"

"With gang killings, word gets out on the street. Guys brag about it to their homies, somebody overhears, tells all his friends. The ghetto grapevine. Next thing you know, one of our gang officers catches the word. Often it's the girlfriends."

"Huh?"

"The homegirls, the gals that hang around the set. It's the latest gossip, bragging rights on whose man shot who. Usually within twelve hours everybody knows on the street. These guys are into building their reputations, and you can't build your rep unless people know what you did. A Blood wants people to know when he kills a Crip. He wants credit for it. Puts up the newspaper clipping on his wall. You do the work, you want the payoff, and the rep's the biggest part of it."

"What makes you think you know so much about gangs?"

"Used to work gangs for LAPD," Ollie said. "Before I transferred up here in '86."

Figures. LAPD. Racism capital of the world.

"Speaking of people knowing on the street," Ollie said, "that's what bothers me most about this case. Word isn't out on the street. Typically we hear who did it. Hearing isn't proof, but then we can focus in on the guy. If we can nail him on another charge, say shoplifting or possession, we can get a warrant to search him. We can do a ballistics match on his weapon, the whole nine yards. But this time, there's nowhere to begin. No word on the streets. Totally quiet. That's different. Really different. And that's not all that bothers me."

"What else?"

"Okay." Ollie stood up and paced, like a professor getting wound up for a lecture. "Why do gangbangers do drive bys rather than go face to face? Mostly to take them by surprise and avoid being shot back. And of course, to get recognition and send a warning. The Italian gangsters started it back in old Chicago, and the Irish picked it up. In the sixties, the Hispanic gangs perfected it, and all the gangs do it now."

Clarence took strange comfort in picturing Italians and Irish and other Anglos originating gangland drive bys.

"The difference is, in those days, the crooks shot each other. They seldom wasted women, children, or innocents. If they did, they got in trouble with the bosses, who conned themselves into thinking they were moral people. But today's drive by is looser. It's still aimed at an enemy, but it's more careless. They can hit bystanders, even babies, and they may just think of it as casualties of war. Not like the old days."

The good old days. When murders were careful, thoughtful, responsible.

"Okay," Ollie said. "I can see how they could go after someone outside your sister's house or even somebody they thought was inside, and your sister and niece could accidentally get shot. But that's not what happened. This was thought out. They had to know it was your sister's bedroom. But why your sister? I just can't see why they'd go after her. It doesn't make sense. Can you help me out?"

"I've thought about it," Clarence said. "I asked my whole family. I mean, Dani didn't greet the bangers with open arms, but there's lots of anti-gang people in the neighborhoods. She's just one among many. There's nothing about Dani that could explain what happened."

"Nothing we know about. The question is, what don't we know?"

"I know her…knew her better than anybody."

Ollie looked at notes in front of him. "No needle marks. No indications of drug use. No prostitution. Nobody she was sleeping with."

"Who do you think you are, talkin' about Dani like that?" Clarence was on his feet, leaning forward, his hands on Ollie's side of the desk, his face inches away, close enough for Ollie to feel the heat of his breath.

"Hey. Chill. I said she *wasn't* doin' any of that. My point is, she was a model citizen."

Clarence sat down.

"Maybe," Ollie said, "she knew something she shouldn't have and somebody wanted to keep her quiet. All I know is, it just doesn't fit the profile."

"What profile?"

"The kind of people who get hit. Lots of drive bys are just to scare people, warn them. If they get hit fine, but most people survive drive bys. But this was a make-sure killing, a big-time hit, one of the biggest we've ever had in Portland. By L.A. standards, no big deal, but in Portland at most you might have a nine millimeter spray from an AK-47 or a MAC 10, a Tech 9, maybe an Uzi. A dozen shots, maybe as many as twenty. But forty automatic high penetration rounds targeted into a single bedroom?"

Clarence stared at the back of his hands on the table.

"I could see it if it was a gang leader or somebody who raped the killer's sister or murdered his brother. Or maybe a baller or high roller who sold bad cocaine to your best friend, so it's personal and you want to take him out in a blaze. Here, the only remote connection we can make is that your nephew's been hanging with some Rollin' 60s taggers and wannabes."

"You're saying they were after Ty?"

"No, I don't think so. His room's on the other side of the house, in the back. They wanted him, they'd have shot up his room. But it's too much. Nobody would do this to get a fourteen-year-old wannabe."

"How do you know all this about my nephew?"

"It's my job to know. I interviewed a dozen people in the hood. Asked about your sister, your nephew, anything and everything. It's like panning for gold. You have to go through a lot of mud and rocks, and you don't know what's what till you sift it out."

Clarence stared blankly.

"Nobody pulls out that kind of weapon for a crime of passion."

"What kind of weapon exactly?"

"Still working on that. We know from the number of shells, the distribution, and how quickly it happened it was a fully automatic rifle. The weapon caliber is common—not as common as nine millimeter, but .223 is no big clue. The penetration was exceptional; .223 doesn't sound like an impressive caliber, but it's very high velocity, and at close range it had a devastating effect."

"That night, when I saw you at my sister's?"

"Yeah?"

"You said something about using lasers. What did you mean?"

"It's pretty new. Been using it less than two years. Called the total station. It sends out a laser beam, a light beam technically, which strikes a mirrored prism on top of a pole. In three to five seconds it measures horizontal distance, vertical height and degree of azimuth based on a compass point. Gets pretty technical."

I can understand. I'm not stupid.

"A handheld computer, less than a pound, interfaces with the station, and it screens plots with points and lines. Then you take it back to the office and download it to a bigger computer, like our Pentium here. Draws everything to scale. Accuracy is something like three millimeters per mile."

"What's the point?"

"Lets you study the crime scene exactly as it was, only a day later, a week or a month. I was just looking at it again this morning."

"Can I see it?"

"Doesn't tell you that much, really," Ollie said. "I don't know if it would be good for you to see it. I mean, with your sister and all."

"I want to see it."

"Don't know if I can do that," Ollie said. "Better talk to my lieutenant."

"She's my sister."

"Right. That's why I've been talking with you—and because Jake Woods vouched for you. But it's my case. Don't forget it."

"It's a free country," Clarence said. "I can nose around myself."

"Yeah, you can. But you better not get in the way of my investigation." Ollie caught the tension in his own voice, though he couldn't see the red splotches on his neck.

"Tell you what, Abernathy. You let me write your columns for you, and I'll let you take over my investigation. Deal?"

"I'm headed out to the trail."

"Okay. Be careful. Got some raisins?"

Clarence grunted and was gone. Geneva lived in fear of him having a serious insulin reaction when he was biking. He'd had a couple, which is why she insisted he keep a sugar source in his bike pack.

Clarence got on his eighteen-speed Cannondale and headed toward the Springwater Corridor Trail. Crossing the Mount Hood Freeway at Hillyard Road, he saw a McDonald's bag, then a Taco Bell sauce packet, then a Ben and Jerry's wrapper.

What's wrong with you people? Think you're the only ones living on this planet?

It frosted him to see what people were doing to his beloved Oregon. Dumping garbage by a roadside was once practically a capital offense in this state. You could be pardoned for armed robbery, maybe, but not for littering. Now he'd see high school kids throw their garbage out the window as if what they did just didn't matter. Once he even pulled some over and bawled them out.

After a quick left and a quick right, he was on the Springwater Corridor Trail, in another world. It was an escape from roads, litter, noise, crime, and congestion. He felt the tension draining already. The only people he met on the trail were fellow respectors of nature and wildlife and solitude. Trees surrounded him. He picked up the speed and kicked it into high gear but could still see minutia all around him. A huge, architecturally perfect spider web, the white froth of the stream as it swallowed big rocks.

He listened to the soothing sound of the gravel, like pouring milk on a huge bowl of Rice Krispies. He heard birds sing and crickets chirp and a bossy squirrel chatter at him. He thought of what people back in the Chicago projects, people even in Portland, would give to have daily access to a place such as this. It was a better world. Something inside told him he was made for a better world, and if this wasn't it, at least it contained hints of what he longed for.

He passed by the old brick factory just before crossing under Hogan Road. There was another squirrel. Two rabbits. A few days ago he'd seen a raccoon and a skunk. Two weeks ago, three coyotes.

The trail had been developed by removing old train tracks that connected Portland to Gresham. There were seemingly endless miles of trail hidden behind trees and invisible from streets. It afforded a chance for Clarence to work his body while resting his mind, a welcome change from the usual pattern.

He noted the waxy green of the leaves, the bulging black of the overripe blackberries, the penetrating purple of the faux paws. Colors thrived here, outside the destructive reach of human hands. What a stark contrast to the encroaching concrete jungle of the city, which like the Sahara seemed to claim more turf every day.

A low powerful growl erupted into a series of excited barks.

Ah, Hugo.

He looked at the Rottweiler he'd christened Hugo, who had the good fortune of living near the trail and challenging every rider who flew by. Clarence had gotten into the habit of bringing leftovers to make the dog's day.

"See you in thirty minutes, Hugo."

Twice he'd taken Dani out here this summer, and she'd loved it. "If you move out to Gresham, we'll find you a nice place near this trail," Clarence had promised her. Why hadn't she listened to him? Why hadn't she moved out here where it was safe? Why had she been so stubborn?

He pedaled toward Main Street Park. He looked carefully into the shadows on his left, down at the pond, looking for familiar faces. There they were. A mother doe and her fawn, drinking from the pond. He'd told Dani about these two, and she'd wanted to see them. He said he'd bring her out here again. It hadn't ever worked out.

He rode by the baseball diamond at the back of the park, today empty, but where white kids played summer baseball. White kids? Why had he said that in his mind? It was open to all kids in the community, blacks as well as whites. But he'd never seen a black kid out there. Nobody's fault. There were just so few black kids around. He winced at the fresh gang graffiti above a garbage can. Just a few years earlier there had been no gang presence in Gresham.

He came to the cemetery and zipped the windbreaker high up his neck. It was mid-September and the heat of just ten days ago was a fading memory. Why did everything feel like winter now? Many of the leaves seemed past their prime, dried out prematurely, giving up on life and ready to be blown away into oblivion.

After a few minutes of sprinting hard on the bike, he turned around and parted from the trail at Eastman, riding up across Powell. He headed to Coffee's On, by GI Joe's, to reward himself.

He locked up his bike to a bench. "Double caramel mocha." Clarence popped the chocolate bean in his mouth and set the coffee on a table to cool a little, went back and used the restroom, then sat long enough to drink the mocha and scan the *Trib*. Then he was off again, cutting back across Powell and tying into the trail.

As he headed back home, he saw the old house, hidden back from the trail, billowing forth the fall's first burn from the chimney. He'd seen the smoke from a distance, first black, then gray, then white, dissipating quickly into nothingness. Behind the ancient wrought-iron fence lurked Hugo the Rottweiler, who started to bark but, on recognizing his friend, suddenly stopped.

Clarence pulled over and unzipped his bike bag, opened up some aluminum foil, leaned over the Cyclone fence, and handed Hugo a gristled piece of steak, saved from last night's dinner.

"If he could see us now, Spike would think I'd betrayed him," Clarence confided in Hugo. "Of course, he had his share last night, but still, there's no talking to Spike when he's jealous. Hell knows no fury like a bulldog scorned."

He talked on and on the silly way people do to dogs and babies, knowing they will love them no matter how stupid they sound.

Hugo licked his hand through the chain-link fence. Clarence felt certain the dog saw every person the same. It didn't matter to Hugo that he was black. It neither irritated him nor impressed him. He liked that.

Clarence rode to the lonely park bench just past Hugo's. It had become part of his ritual to pull over, kick back, and stretch out on the bench before digging in again and climbing the big hill that would take him back toward the freeway and home. After five minutes of lying there, soaking in the world of dreams and promise around him, he got back on his bike and braced himself again for the real world.

It felt strange being at the *Trib* on Saturday, but he and Jake both wanted to get an extra jump on this week's columns, to free up time during the week. Jake had plans with Janet and Carly. Clarence had plans of his own.

He finished off his sports column—not a home run, but a triple anyway, or at least an off-the-wall double. He'd had only a few strikeouts over the years, but he remembered each of them vividly.

Clarence waited for Jake. He looked around the *Trib*, manned by a skeleton crew. He'd worked so hard for so many years to make a mark on this place. He thought about Daddy. When Clarence was a boy, Obadiah had told him, "Son, you has to work twice as hard as white folk to get half as far. I know it don't seem fair and I reckon it ain't, but that's the way it is. I know you can do it. I'll be in your corner whenever you needs me."

"Ain't no shame to be ignorant, boy," his daddy'd told him. "Only shame is to stay ignorant when you don't has to be."

Obadiah had been raised behind the plow of his sharecropper daddy, fighting weeds and drought and the boll weevil. In the years after Negro League baseball, he'd worked a dozen jobs, some two at a time, everything from short-order cook to custodian at a small black college. Administrators had let him sit in on classes after he finished his job. He loved it. He'd discovered the school library, a temple for the mind. He loved books, checked out hundreds of them while working there.

"Ol' books, they got the most wondrous smell, they do. Most wondrous." His eyes would sparkle, and at dinner he'd read aloud some precious fact or insight.

"Don't let your dinner get cold, Obadiah," Mama would say, but good as her cooking was, and it was the best, Obadiah Abernathy was always more excited to learn than to eat.

There was only one book, though, opened at every dinner. *The* book. God's book. Obadiah would read from it, voice trembling. "These are the words of the Almighty, chillens. You don't mess with God, you hear me now? You break his commandments, and they'll break you."

He wished Daddy had been given more of a chance. With his thirst for knowledge he could have been a scholar, a doctor, a teacher. He could have been anything. But when you worked fourteen hours a day to provide for your family, there wasn't much time for the scholarly life.

Clarence remembered Daddy lining up the kids like crows on a fence: Harley, Ellis, Darrin, Marny, Clarence, and Dani. More than once the lecture began, "Always pick you out a rabbit, chillens. Pick out somebody ahead of you in their schoolin'. Then try to catch 'em, and when you catch 'em, pass 'em. Better yourselves, chillens. That's what you gotta do. Always better yourselves, you hear me?"

I heard you, Daddy.

Clarence picked up the phone and dialed. "Hi, baby. Yeah, everything's okay. Can I speak to Daddy?" He waited.

"Well, hello, Dolly." His father surprised him with a beautiful imitation of Louis Armstrong's low gravely voice.

"Well, hello, Daddy." Clarence laughed. "Just lookin' in on you. Check your blood pressure today? Everything okay?"

"Shor nuff, Son. Why you askin'?"

"Just checking on you, that's all. You still feel up to coming out to the park for the rally?"

"Sure do. I ain't mulch on the flowers yet, you know."

"I know, Daddy. I'll see you at the rally then."

"See you there, Son."

Clarence hung up the phone, wiping his eyes. He went to Jake's desk and they headed from the *Trib* to what had been billed by Norcoast's office the "North Portland Fight Crime Rally." Geneva would be bringing Obadiah and meeting them there.

Clarence braced himself as they turned north on Martin Luther King Boulevard. He never drove on this street without remembering the bitter opposition to changing the old Union Avenue to MLK. It bothered him that some of the people who fought against it were conservatives. One of the contradictions of his life was that among the people whose beliefs and morals were most like his and who hated political correctness and big government and encroaching liberties as he did were some who didn't seem to ever want to concede anything good to those of his skin color.

"You remember when Martin Luther King was killed?" he asked Jake.

"Yeah, I do. I was fresh out of the army."

"You remember exactly where you were?"

"No. Not exactly."

"I was in eighth grade, still livin' in Chicago at the Henry Horner projects, just before we moved to Cabrini Green. I heard about it out on the street, playing stick-ball after school. Spider Edwards came runnin' up wide eyed and stuttering, 'They killed Martin.' I ran home to Mama. She was frantic—never remember her like that. Daddy came home from work early. He cried and cried. To us in the projects it was the end of the world."

"I remember when President Kennedy was shot," Jake said. "Exactly where I was, in high school my senior year. Gym class. We were playing basketball, and I'd just shot a free throw when the principal's secretary came in and told the coach, and he told us. It's like it was yesterday."

"Yeah? I've heard people say that. I remember too, but not as much as when Martin died." What Clarence really remembered from the day of the Kennedy assassination was his mama asking, with terror in her eyes, "It wasn't a black man who shot him, was it?"

Clarence decided not to say more. How could he expect Jake to understand why Martin dying was like the descent of the four horses of the apocalypse? It seemed like the end of hope for black people. Martin had his flaws, no doubt about it, but his convictions on equality and his dream of the races living in harmony was from God.

"Tell me about Chicago, Clabern. What were the projects like?"

"They were...like another planet. Alien nation. We thought everything would be great, man, comin' up from Mississippi to Chicago. I was ten; Dani was six. Blacks couldn't buy real estate in the outlying areas, so we all got pushed into the Southside. You know, just like in every city, though the truth is we felt more comfortable with our own anyway. My family was better off than most. Daddy and Mama worked really hard to give us kids an opportunity. But the gangs were going even in those days, and the racial tension was hot, you know, the sixties. Whites and blacks were from two different worlds. Still are, I guess. Back then we thought it would be different by now. But it isn't."

Jake nodded. He had a few more questions, but held off.

"You know what bugs me, Jake? And this is something Dani and I used to go round and round about. I was raised in poverty, so I want to put as much room between me and poverty as I can. Middle- and upper-class white kids can talk about identifying with the poor and all that noble-sounding stuff, but that's because they've never been poor. When you've known poverty, there's no mystique about it, no appeal. You just want more than anything never to be poor again. That's why I hate this part of town."

Clarence looked where the dry cleaner used to be, now a liquor store. Where there was a doctor's office, now a pawnshop. Where there was once a church, abandoned years ago for the safety of the suburbs, now a gang hideout and a drug-running station.

The broken-down store that had been a Rexall Drugs had an old RX sign from the fifties swaying in the wind and poised to fall and injure some passerby. The only thriving businesses seemed to be the little foreign-owned stores, plastered with signs for Lotto and Powerball. He watched people walking in, eyes full of hope they would win the big one and escape life's drudgery. Later the same people would feel fear and remorse and shame for having wasted money that could have bought school clothes for their children.

"I can't stand that stinking lottery," Clarence said. "State funded temptation for the poor. Makes people think you can prosper without hard work and discipline." He suddenly pulled over by a freshly painted red sign announcing "Kim's Grocery," one of a dozen Korean-owned stores in north Portland. "How about a soda?"

Clarence walked in, Jake behind him, and noticed a Korean woman immediately step into a back room. He sensed the other woman behind the counter gazing at him suspiciously, watching him out of the corner of her eye. For a moment he felt that ever-present tension, as if it was assumed he was about to pull out a piece or shoplift them blind.

"Nice day, isn't it?" he asked, as he handed her two dollars for two pops. She said a quiet yes and looked down, then placed the change not in his hand, but on the counter.

Clarence seethed as he walked out the door. "Won't even dirty her hand by touching a black man."

"What?" Jake sounded startled.

"All these Asian store owners are the same. Koreans, Japanese, Cambodians. They come into the black community, get rich off them, then think they're better than their customers."

"But…she seemed very nice. Quiet, but nice," Jake said.

"You notice she put the change on the counter? Didn't want to touch my black hand. Like I'm a leper or something. They're all that way."

Jake's forehead wrinkled, but he said nothing.

The streets were the color of soot, somewhere between black and white. Politicians such as Councilman Norcoast had set up photo ops and drawn up plans to restore, beautify, and renovate, to prove Portland was a city that cared about all its citizens. But like most tax money, it seemed to always fritter away in overhead and salaries and plans and discussions and never actually do much good. Clarence resented the politicians, but he also blamed the people, like his sister, who put too much trust and hope in government, expecting it to be a benefactor, to do justice, to take care of their problems.

"It's up to hard work and individual initiative, Jake," Clarence said. "The sooner black Americans figure out government just subsidizes and perpetuates their poverty, the better off they'll be. Government isn't the solution. It's a big part of the problem."

"Still, sometimes it helps, doesn't it?"

"Forty acres and a mule," Clarence muttered.

"What?"

"That's what the government promised all the freed slaves after the Civil War. You know, to help get them started."

"I'd forgotten that."

"Don't feel bad. The government forgot it too. No acres, no mules. What else is new? Lyndon Johnson did a lot of good on civil rights, but then he promised the Great Society's welfare programs would obliterate black poverty in a decade. Guess what? It's much worse now than it was then."

Clarence withdrew into himself. Jake wanted to know what was going through his friend's mind. But Clarence held his thoughts close to his chest like a poker player, as if he was afraid someone would see his cards.

———————

The two men appeared similar in many ways. Both dressed meticulously. Both were compulsively clean, wearing fashionably cut suits. Both sneaked frequent looks in mirrors. Two differences were dramatic, though—the build of their bodies and the color of their skin. One was thick and black, the other slender and white. One was Clarence Abernathy; the other, Reggie Norcoast. They were scheduled to sit near each other today, with only the Reverend Cairo Clancy between them, on the special rally platform set up in Woodlawn Park.

Clarence had wanted to bail out of this public appearance, but Geneva had talked him into it. She said she knew Dani would want it. That was a low blow.

As the crowds arrived, Clarence sat in his assigned chair, observing Norcoast's moves around the platform. He studied him as if they were the moves of a chess or tennis opponent, moves that might display both strengths and weaknesses.

With Norcoast, any contact, regardless of its purpose, was a political image meeting. The meeting began the moment he walked in, the agenda was whatever image-enhancing event or perspective was on his mind, and the outcome was whatever he wanted it to be.

Beneath the confident exterior, Clarence surmised, the councilman was nervous and insecure. He reminded him of a dog endlessly sniffing out the ground, trying to find where other dogs had been and, on seeing a new hound, overeager to get familiar with him.

You could see Norcoast's handshake coming a block away. He'd turned the common handshake into an art form. He clasped with the right hand, but that was just the beginning. His left hand searched out just the right place, sometimes the forearm, the elbow, the shoulder, sometimes the back of the opposite shoulder, making a partial embrace. Occasionally the left hand went on top of the other's right hand, creating a double-handed clasp signifying double sincerity. This was clearly a man who had a great deal of experience with his hands.

What his hands didn't do, his ears did. Clarence could almost see them grow as he leaned forward toward each individual he came to. They were vacuum-cleaner ears that sucked up every word, making the constituent feel Norcoast heard him and felt his pain and understood every nuance of his thirty-second gut-spilling, leaving the implicit promise the politician would take action on every word spoken, whether that be as a councilman now, a mayor next year, or a governor in five years. Everything about Norcoast shouted "I care, I *really* do; I am sincere. I *really* am."

Norcoast was a weather vane spinning in the wind. To Clarence he seemed another life form. The politician.

Walking around within a few feet of the councilman, as if to monitor the variables and make sure nothing got out of control, was his longtime aide, Carson Gray. Only in his late thirties, he was a savvy operator. Gray strutted around like a banty rooster, with quick steps and self-important motions. His skin was pale, with blue penciled veins. Despite his expensive suit, his anatomy resisted a tailored look. He was one of those bottomless men who hikes up his pants and tightens his belt an extra notch to keep gravity from embarrassing him. He was largely responsible for cultivating and watchdogging Norcoast's political success. Gray stood there, always keeping his finger on the pulse while Norcoast bubbled and smiled and effervesced.

Down in the front row Clarence saw Geneva, looking fine in that pretty emerald green dress. She stood face to face with Norcoast's wife, Esther, immersed in animated conversation. Geneva had remarked to Clarence several times how kind it was for her to come to Dani's funeral. They seemed to really be hitting it off. As he watched the two women thirty feet away, he saw the tears well up in Geneva and assumed they were talking about Dani. Esther Norcoast put her arms around Geneva. Clarence saw she was crying too, and he sensed the grief was real.

Well, maybe she hasn't been infected by politics. At least, not like her husband. Maybe she's the idealistic people-serving person her husband imagines he is.

Clarence felt guilty, as he often did when realizing his cynicism had led him to misjudge someone. His eyes now caught a familiar slow moving gait and brown polyester suit. He stepped down into the crowd and put his arms around his father.

"How you feelin', Daddy?"

"Well, when you gets as old as I am," Obadiah Abernathy said, "if you wakes up in the mornin' and nothin' hurts, it's a sure sign you're dead." He laughed hard, from deep within, with a delightful hiss that sounded like air escaping a balloon.

"I've been thinking about things today, Daddy. I want to thank you for all you taught me. For raising me like you did. And helping me through college. Thank you." He hugged him.

Obadiah looked at his son curiously, as if to say, where is this coming from? "Couldn't have done it without two people, Son. My sweet Jesus and yo' sweet mama." His eyes gleamed.

Clarence helped Obadiah into a folding chair. Jake came over to sit next to him.

"Hello, Mr. Abernathy. Good to see you again."

"Mr. Jake. Always a pleasure, sir, always a pleasure."

Clarence made his way back to the platform. After a few people came up to greet him, Clarence's eyes went back to Esther Norcoast. He watched her go up to her husband. Both were all smiles, when suddenly she halted. He thought he saw surprise and anger in her face, but he couldn't be sure. Words were exchanged. Norcoast looked intent on restoring her smile.

I didn't even see him say anything. What's she mad about? Well, she's a woman. Norcoast probably doesn't have a clue. Wish I could read lips.

Norcoast appeared to be giving her assurances in the universal language of men with their tail between their legs, with the added dimension of not wanting several hundred people to suspect anything was wrong. After twenty seconds of intense but discreet dialogue, the appropriate smile returned to Esther Norcoast's face, no doubt to the relief of Carson Gray, whom Clarence noticed was also watching.

Norcoast's a master. If I could get Geneva to smile at me again within thirty seconds of making her mad...wow. What if you could bottle that and sell it to men across America? You'd make Bill Gates look like a pauper.

Reverend Clancy gave the invocation and introduced Norcoast. He had no words of lavish praise, just a simple introduction—"Our Councilman."

Norcoast stepped up to the microphone with the familiarity of a drunk stepping up to the bar.

"It's been just two weeks ago since we lost an outstanding member of our community, Dani Abernathy Rawls. Murdered senselessly in her own home. And her daughter still courageously clinging to life in an intensive care unit, where I visited her just this morning."

He went to the hospital? So he could tell us he did. What a jerk.

"Up on this platform with me are the silent victims of crime in this city, victims who will remain silent no longer."

Clarence looked around at the faces on the platform, nearly all black, most of which he didn't recognize. But at the front of the crowd, down on one knee, Clarence saw a familiar figure, dressed casually and wearing a press pass. It was Carp, his favorite photojournalist. She was thirtyish, blonde, and infuriatingly liberal, but he liked her anyway. They sometimes took coffee breaks together. As she positioned herself for another shot, he caught her eye and they both smiled slightly.

"Now, there are those who take simplistic solutions to the problems of our community."

Like the people wanting to run against you for mayor?

"But I've brought on a new task force chairman to deal with these problems. A young man who's a success story from this community. A Howard graduate, Derrick Morton."

There was applause. Clarence had met Derrick. He was a nice enough kid, smart and talented. But it felt like tokenism. Norcoast was parading black faces to show how in touch he was with black concerns. It reminded Clarence of all the social gatherings where well-meaning white folks, or WMWF, as they'd been dubbed by blacks, would feel compelled to bring up that they had a doctor who was black or they knew a black stockbroker or used to live next to a very nice black family or had some "good friend" who was black, upon whom they would lavish unctuous praise. Of course, if they employed black house help, this never came up.

Norcoast went on and on, talking about the task force, how much progress was being made in the community. He proposed a ten-point agenda for fighting crime, most of which Clarence saw as the same old political drivel that gave the illusion something was being done just because something was being said.

"We have to send a message, my brothers, we have to send a message to the gangbangers. The message is, this isn't *your* hood, this is *our* hood!"

He noticed Norcoast even imitated inflections and rhythms of black speech. Perhaps it was because black voters were his ticket and he didn't want some black candidate coming along to take his district from him.

"The chief of police tells me there was only one witness to the murder of Dani Rawls. This witness wasn't sure of the race of the perpetrators. But it's possible this was a racially motivated crime. If it was, I promise you, I'll personally make sure the hate crimes division gives it top priority!"

The crowd applauded enthusiastically, the first clap coming from Carson Gray.

Racially motivated? Who said anything like that? When's the last time two whites did a drive-by shooting in North Portland? You're just stirring up the crowd, Norcoast. Being big white savior to your colored folk, that it?

"My office has approached businessmen inside and outside the community, and I'm pleased to announce we have raised a ten-thousand-dollar reward for any information leading to the arrest and conviction of whoever committed this horrible crime. I've donated a thousand dollars of that myself. I promise you, I will make sure these culprits are brought to justice."

You on the case with Ollie or what? Carry handcuffs in that fancy briefcase?

"So that as a result of our efforts done in their memory, as a tribute to their lives, Dani Abernathy Rawls and all the others, whose dear families you see before you today, will *not* have died in vain!"

Norcoast's voice cracked as he said the last few words. The applause surged, but Clarence's hands remained frozen on his lap.

Race-baiting opportunist. Exploiting tragedies to make your self-serving political statements.

He thought of what those on both the right and the left did with Waco and Oklahoma City. It nauseated him to see those political peacocks posturing in the wake of human suffering. He wanted people to mourn his sister's death, not capitalize on it.

A few follow-up announcements, a number from a black church choir, and it was over. Clarence detested himself for having said yes to sitting on the platform.

"Hello, Clarence." It was Barry Davis, from *Trib* city beat.

"Hey, Davis."

"Can I ask you a couple questions?"

Clarence didn't feel like talking, but he nodded.

"The councilman said this may have been a racially motivated crime. A hate crime. Do you believe it was?"

"No, I don't. But I really don't care."

"What?"

"I said I don't care."

"But how can you not care...she was your sister. I mean..."

"I care about my sister. I just don't care if the shooter was black or white or brown or yellow or purple. I don't care if he was a high school drop-out or a college professor. It doesn't matter—it all comes out the same. Don't you get it? My sister's been murdered. My niece is...lying there in the hospital with tubes in her. Norcoast is just looking for votes, and you're just looking for a story angle."

"But if it's a hate crime—"

"What? If murder's done black on black you think that makes it a *love* crime? Who cares? When you're dead, you're dead!"

Normally Davis would have pushed it, but he knew Abernathy's reputation well enough to realize that would be a mistake. Clarence sat on his platform chair with a scowl so noticeable, no one else approached him.

He looked at Norcoast, now thirty feet from him, down in front of the platform, immersed in the crowd. His smile looked to Clarence less like a facial expression than an implant. The politician's sparkling eyes made the journalist wonder if there was some new product called "Sparkling Eyes" and Norcoast was a beta tester. The man's right hand searched the crowd like a heat-seeking missile wanting, needing to make contact.

Carp moved in close to the councilman, one camera draping from her shoulder, a bigger one in her hand. She got still another angle on Norcoast.

"Hello, Lynn," Clarence heard him say, as if she were his favorite cousin.

Who else would know photographers by their first name but a baby-kissing glad-handing crowd-working politician like Norcoast?

"Say," he looked at Carp. "How about we get a picture with my good friend Clarence Abernathy?"

Carp stifled her smile. As Clarence started to wave them off she said, "Yeah, let's get you two buddies together here. Come on Clabern, shake the councilman's hand. Yeah, turn this way, hands clasped, big smiles."

Clarence let Carp's cajoling get to him, and when Norcoast reached out his hand he didn't slap it away like he wanted to. He did pull back his hand, but too late—Carp already took the picture in the micro-second their hands had clasped.

Clarence stood there, noticing for the first time Norcoast's tie. It was burgundy, very distinctive, but the material seemed inexpensive, not at all Norcoast's standard fare. It was covered with identical designs of various sizes, like irregular triangles, with the black line on the right side thicker than the other two lines. The whole effect was slightly lopsided. It was the sort of tie your aunt might give you for Christmas. You'd keep it at the back of the tie rack and wear it only if she was coming for dinner.

You're slipping, councilman. Dress isn't up to par.

This moment gave Clarence pleasure. He looked up at Norcoast's face and for a moment thought he saw his first sign of weakness. A nervous twitch of his left cheek. A tic.

Norcoast moved off toward Geneva, greeting her warmly. Geneva, Esther, and good old Reg seemed to be hitting it off. Clarence sat there sulking, staring at Norcoast with eyes that could drive a penny nail through a four-by-six.

Clarence's skepticism about politicians didn't stop at Democrats like Norcoast. He considered Republicans just as opportunistic. To him most elections were choosing between a suspected witch and a known devil. Politics were very important in the black community—too important in his mind—but he felt blacks were often used and exploited by politicians, both black and white. It irritated him to think Norcoast had used him today.

As the crowd dissipated, Carp came over again, this time to pay her respects. "Hey, Clarence. How you doin'?"

"Okay. Just not enjoying the company."

"Oh, Norcoast's all right—for a big old bag of hot air, I mean. He's a real hero, you know. Should have seen him visiting your niece this morning."

"You were there?"

"Sure. You don't think he would've done it without calling the *Trib* first?"

"A staged photo? Who sent you out? Betty?"

"Yep."

"I can't believe how he uses the *Trib*."

"Raylon's his bud, remember. Gets a lot of free PR from us, doesn't he?"

"Is Betty really going to use it?"

"I don't know. Hey, I'm just the photographer. I don't decide what goes in. I do what I'm told."

"Yeah, that's what all the Nazis said at Nuremberg," Clarence said, his voice so sullen it was comical.

Carp slapped him on the shoulder and giggled girlishly. "Well, here he comes now. I'll leave you two buddies to bond. I've had enough of Reg for one day." Carp walked off the other way, pretending she didn't see him coming.

"Bye, Lynn," Norcoast called out.

Nobody calls her Lynn. She's just Carp.

"Oh, bye, Reg," she said. "Nice tie."

"Clarence," Norcoast extended his hand again, "thanks so much for coming today. Your presence spoke volumes to the community."

This time Clarence rejected Norcoast's outstretched hand.

"Why the sudden concern for my sister, Norcoast? Was she one of the niggers on your plantation, that it? You lookin' out for your coloreds? Or are you just lookin' out for yourself?"

Norcoast's left cheek contracted and twitched. He looked stunned.

"Clarence, I'm shocked. My record makes clear I'm the furthest thing from a racist. I'm an advocate of your people. When I looked at your sister and when I look at you I don't see the color of your skin."

"What, you blind or something?"

"But…"

"I suppose when you look at your wife you don't see a woman?"

"Well, I…"

"When I look at you I see a white man. When you look at me you see a black man. Don't lie about it. What you're saying is that you won't hold my skin color against me. Well, why should you? Do you mean you'll forgive me for being black, or that you'll pretend I'm not black? Well, I don't need your forgiveness and your pretense and your condescension. You got that, Bwana?"

Clarence watched Carson Gray's expressionless face, as he stood five feet behind his flustered boss.

"I know Dani's death and your niece's condition have to be hard on you," Norcoast said. "I'll chalk up your comments to your grief. Let's leave it at that."

"Chalk it up to whatever you want, Councilman. I'm gonna get the dudes that killed my sister. And I don't care what color they are. They're going to bleed red."

Clarence walked the North Portland streets for two hours, starting a dozen different conversations. He asked all the older folks if they'd seen or heard anything the night Dani was killed. Nearly all of them heard, none of them saw, other than the smoke in the air after the car was gone. Most said they'd been talked to by the police. Some hadn't.

He waved to two boys eleven or twelve years old, about Jonah's age.

"Hi. I'm Mrs. Rawls's brother. Tyrone's uncle?"

They nodded suspiciously.

"What are your names?"

"Jeremy."

"Michael."

"Did either of you see or hear anything the night Tyrone's mama was killed?"

Jeremy shook his head, Michael nodded. "Lots a shootin'," he said.

"Did you see anything?"

"Nuttin'. I looked out the window, but I live on Moffat, next street over. Couldn't see nuttin'."

"Okay, listen, I'm asking you to do something. There's money in it for you. I want you to spread the word that if anybody was on the street or looked out their window and saw anything that night, before or during or after the shooting, I want them to call me. Here's my numbers at work and home."

He handed them both an important looking business card.

"What'd you say about money?" Jeremy asked.

"If they have anything for me, anything new, anything I don't know, I'll give them a hundred dollars. And whoever brings or sends them to me, he gets a hundred dollars too. That's you. Okay?"

They both nodded.

"Now, I don't want anybody foolin' with me. I'll know if they're making up a story. They'll be in big trouble. So will you. You hear me, Michael? You hear me, Jeremy?"

They nodded again.

"Okay, guys. Spread the word."

They ran off. He saw them stop the first two boys they saw. Word would be out in no time.

Clarence continued to ask questions on the street, giving the same offer to a half-dozen other boys. He'd gotten a similar offer thirty years ago in Chicago from a private investigator working a case in the projects. It was twenty dollars then. Inflation.

After a dozen conversations with people under twenty—many of them dominated by *ain't* and various obscenities—Clarence walked back toward his car.

He remembered a sociology prof at Alcorn State saying, "Whites talk white, blacks talk black. White's no better than black. You need to be with people who understand when you say 'ain't' it's because you're choosing to."

But a literature prof took the opposite tack. "Don't ever say ain't. It isn't proper grammar for anyone, white or black. You speak good English, you get the best jobs. People take you seriously. And swearing? You talk this garbage mouth stuff, you think people will want to be around you? It gets you nowhere. You want to go start your own country, okay. You want to succeed in *this* country, that's the way it is."

It was his literature teacher, not his sociology teacher, whose philosophy he followed. And it was a geeky speech teacher's enunciation lessons they'd laughed at in class that he secretly practiced every day for years. "Twenty dwarves took turns doing handstands on the carpet. Round and round the rugged rock the ragged rascal ran."

Nineteen years later, his diction long since perfect, he still rehearsed some of those sentences. He didn't speak in double negatives. No cotton in the mouth. No ghetto-speak for Clarence Abernathy. While his mind often traveled back to Chicago's Southside, he policed himself to not let his tongue go with it. Clarence had learned to clip the words as they come out, hardening every *d, t,* and *ing*. He spoke crisply. The exception was when he kicked back with his family and old friends, his guard down. When he relaxed, his childhood Mississippi twang came out. When he got angry, a Chicago Southside dissonant jive could take over. The old dialects weren't bad. They just wouldn't get him as far in mainstream society as he intended to go.

His enunciation had produced a lot of tense situations. After calling people and arranging interviews, Clarence was always ready for the first surprised look. Occasionally someone would say, "I thought you were white. I mean, you don't *sound* black."

"Oh?" Clarence always asked. "Just how does black sound?"

Clarence unlocked the door of the Bonneville, whispering, "Round and round the rugged rock the ragged rascal ran." He set out in rush hour traffic, mind immersed in his inner world, leaving only eyes and reflexes and instincts to take care of the outer one.

His daddy hadn't worked so hard to give him a chance so Clarence would blow it. He thought back to his two years at Alcorn State. He'd considered Howard and Fisk and Morehouse, the black answers to Harvard, Yale, and Princeton. Half the black doctors in the nation had graduated from Howard, and Daddy wanted him to go there, but there just wasn't enough money. Alcorn State in Lorman, Mississippi, was only fifty miles from where he grew up. He could live with Uncle Elijah and Aunt Emily, who'd moved to Red Lick, only a few minutes from the campus. That way he wouldn't have to pay room and board, and his scholarship covered most of the tuition. In those days you always adjusted your dreams to what you could afford.

After two years at Alcorn State, he wanted to try an integrated college. If he was going to succeed in a white world, he needed to see it closer up than he had in the all-black neighborhoods in Mississippi or the all-black projects of Chicago or the all-black classrooms of Alcorn State. His senior year of high school, his family had moved out to Oregon where Uncle Silas found a mill job for Obadiah. Oregon State University in Corvallis, south of Portland, offered him the transfer football scholarship he needed to move from Alcorn State. The bonus was it would bring him back less than two hours from his parents and Dani, by then a junior at Jefferson High in Portland.

He'd built on his transfer credits and gone through the journalism program at OSU, staying on for a two-year masters degree and entering the job market in 1978—the perfect year, since the 1968 Kerner Commission Report had concluded the media ignored blacks or portrayed them in a negative light, and the ten year follow-up report showed sixty percent of American newspapers still didn't have a single nonwhite reporter or editor.

So just as he was looking for a job came the rush to correct the imbalance. Newspapers tripped over each other to show who was the least racist. Affirmative action policies were implemented everywhere. Recruiters swarmed J-schools, searching for blacks. To Clarence it seemed a great opportunity. Still, the minority hiring frenzy made him feel as if he was being put out on the auction block, like his ancestors. He knew he was highly qualified—he'd worked hard and he was good. But he had the unsettling impression some newspapers would have hired him even if he wasn't. If you were black, could tell time, and speak an intelligible sentence, it was as though you'd overcome some genetic flaw and already exceeded the highest expectations of whites.

He remembered overhearing a white reporter say, "Yeah, Abernathy's okay for a quota boy." He knew he'd earned his job, but the affirmative action that helped some people get jobs also perpetuated the myth it was impossible for blacks to win jobs unless things got tilted their way. It troubled him then, and it troubled him now.

The *Oregon Journal* wined and dined him, especially fortyish and independently wealthy Raylon Berkley, who after the merger—by one of those strange quirks of business—had become a VP, CEO, and finally the publisher of the *Trib*. Berkley himself took Clarence to a Portland restaurant where he was one of three blacks, the other two busboys. It was far and away the fanciest dinner he'd ever had. That unforgettable evening Berkley made his big offer, and a few days later Clarence signed with the *Journal*.

When he got his first paycheck it embarrassed him. It was so much money, much more than his daddy had ever made, over twice as much as his janitorial job.

For a while he felt the token black, which was its own kind of slavery without the whippings. He learned that editors could lash out verbal beatings, but they did it to whites too. In time, he fit in, at least on the outside.

Looking back now, Clarence felt guilty he'd ever compared his experiences of racism to those of his ancestors. He felt he'd cheapened their ordeals, trivialized their sufferings when his were so much less. While he'd heard black people didn't have many opportunities, his experience in the workplace suggested otherwise. This was the beginning of his gradual fifteen-year swing from moderate liberalism to die-hard conservatism.

At a family gathering eighteen years ago, hearing he was going to work for a newspaper, one cousin warned him, "Stay black, man."

He'd thought about that exhortation often. If black was just a skin color, how could he *not* stay black? He knew the real message. Only white people succeed in America. If a black man succeeds, it means you're a porch nigger, an Uncle Tom, a traitor. The cousin who'd told him to stay black had deserted his wife and children, sold dope, and gone to the pen for armed robbery and grand theft auto. Yet Clarence imagined his cousin probably still took pride in thinking he'd "stayed black."

Clarence was no more comfortable with racial applause than with criticism. In North Portland, some people would read his columns and talk about them in diners and say to his parents or to him, "We're so proud of you." It was as if every column, every accomplishment struck a blow for equal rights, as if he were the Martin Luther King Jr. of the sports department. He was a success story, and it felt good. But something about it bothered him, as if any young black man off drugs and working and not knocking off a 7-Eleven was a regular Frederick Douglass.

I'm just a reporter, for crying out loud. Don't lay the world on my shoulders.

Still, he told himself something he'd heard many years ago. "Your reputation is all you have." Clarence Abernathy had worked painstakingly to build that reputation. He would never let it slide.

Clarence sat downstairs in the family room, turning upside down the front page of the *Trib,* not wanting to see again the two pictures of Norcoast, one at the rally, the other at the hospital.

He relaxed in his ancient recliner, stuffing oozing out the breaks in the brown Naugahyde. Geneva had wanted to toss it ten years ago when they moved in, but in a compromise it was demoted to the basement. As he sat back to experience the chair's friendliness, he smelled something familiar, something sweet, like the residual of an old perfume. He turned around. Right above him was the stitchery his mother had done for him fourteen years ago, a millennial scene with lion and lamb lying down together. Under it was the caption from Isaiah, "And the whole earth will be filled with the knowledge of God, as the earth covers the sea."

She'd worked on it for a year, finishing it not long before she died. Her hands and her heart had gone into it, and the countless hours had immersed it with her comforting fragrance. But the smell disappeared as suddenly as it had arisen. It was so elusive. He would never forget his mother, of course, but many of the details had been eclipsed by the passing of time, and that bothered him. He wanted to hug her again, look at that old cracked black skin, that beautiful skin that was now more of an impression than the sharp image it used to be.

It was even worse with his brother Darrin. It had been twenty-seven years since he'd died in Vietnam. He didn't seem real to Clarence anymore. He'd become an almost mythical figure, someone you sometimes talked about but who wasn't real, like Spiderman. He was no more than a bunch of old black-and-white pictures now, and the whole didn't seem any more than the sum of the parts.

He wondered about Dani. Even the features of her face once engraved so clearly in his memory seemed to be blurring in this, just the sixteenth day without her. He'd looked yesterday at picture after picture of her, but the soft contours of her face weren't there. Neither was the warmth of her touch.

First Darrin, then his mother, now his sister. All lost to him. And yet, even as he brooded silently, he had the odd feeling that something was going on beyond him, as if he, not those who were gone, was the odd man out. As if there was a party and he hadn't been invited. Or perhaps he'd been invited, but he'd have to show up late, after work. In any case, he felt left out, terribly left out.

His thoughts piled up as kindling in which a flame suddenly emerged.

She always talked about you, always put you first. And this is how you repay her? By having her blown away by gangsters? I wonder what she thinks of all those promises now.

Clarence twisted his big body into a semi-fetal position on the recliner, crying out to someone he wasn't sure was listening. He spoke out loud in case it might help.

"You took my brother and you killed him in a rice paddy. You took my mama with a cancer you could have stopped. And now you took my sister and shot her up, killed her like she was nothing. And you expect me just to forget it, to pretend it's okay? Well, it isn't!"

He sat quietly for a moment. Then he added, "If you're really there, you've got to save Felicia. You've got to."

———————

Clarence went out on a drive to no place in particular. He stopped at the Leathers gas station, just two miles from his house. He thought about the triple murder here that had rocked the community, and the double murder a week later, just up the street on Kane. It was three years ago now. Several times the nineteen-year-old killer had been featured again on *America's Most Wanted*. The station served as an endur-ing symbol of loss of innocence in the suburbs, the story of a quiet beautiful place invaded by the kind of crime people hoped to forever leave behind when they aban-doned the big city.

Tragedy has no suburbs.

He thought about local high schoolers who'd died in drunk driving accidents, children run over on the streets, kids who killed their friends playing with guns, the local high school valedictorian who died from hypothermia in a river, freaked out on LSD. Suicides, scandals, child abuse, and now gangs had come to Gresham. No place seemed immune anymore. The contamination of the suburbs was the death of a dream.

Clarence was just glad that soon they'd be moving farther out. He was expect-ing a call from the real estate agent that night.

Better get home.

———

"You signed on the dotted line." The real estate agent sounded adamant. "You've still got to move out by September 30. It's that simple."

"Simple for you. You don't have to move when there's no place to go!"

"Look, I'm sorry the Langley's deal fell through. But when you put down the earnest money the contract said you couldn't move in until they move out. They have until the end of the year."

"But they said they'd be out by September 22."

"I know, but what they said doesn't matter. The contract you signed is all that matters. That gives them until December 31. My guess is they won't be out till Thanksgiving, maybe not till Christmas."

"Two and a half months? Three and a half? What am I supposed to do?"

"Rent some place. Hard to do for a couple months, granted. A decent rental house in Gresham or Sandy doesn't come cheap. Sorry. If you'd had a disaster, your insurance would cover it, but—"

"It *is* a disaster."

"Any family you can live with?"

"No." Clarence put down the phone in disgust, sighing the heavy sighs that had become second nature in the last two weeks. Geneva walked in.

"What's wrong?" she asked.

"What we were afraid of. The Langley's deal fell through. We can't get into the house until the end of November."

"But we have to move out. What are we going to do?"

"Don't know," Clarence said. "Should have done the contracts differently. I knew it was a mistake."

"Can we find a rental?"

"That'll be tough. With the new car payments and everything else, this isn't a good time. There's not that much in savings. I'm just not sure we can afford this."

"Harley and Sophie would let us stay with them."

"No way. Not Harley. We'd kill each other off like two pit bulls with rabies. Of course, then you could use the life insurance money to get a place for you and the kids."

"Very funny," Geneva said. "Where will we go? With your daddy and Ty and Celeste there's seven of us."

"I can count."

"Well," she said it gently, "there's always Mama or my sisters."

"You think I'm going to listen to all their talk about what bums black men are and how it's a good thing black women know how to run the show?"

"Clarence, that's not fair."

"May I quote your mother? 'It's the rooster that crows, but it's the hen that delivers the goods.'"

"Okay, they've all three had some bad experiences with men who just wanted to jive around all day and sleep in and do drugs and make babies."

"Yeah. And black women just want money and jewelry and to take charge of the universe. Right?"

"I wasn't agreeing with the stereotype, Clarence! I was just explaining how they feel."

"Making excuses for them, that's what you're doing."

"Okay," Geneva said, her hands in the air, "now that you've ruled out every option, where's a place we can live for the next few months? I can't tell you anything, that's for sure. How about you tell me?"

Geneva sat quietly and looked at him.

"No." Clarence said finally. "We're not going to Dani's."

"I didn't say anything." She raised her hands again.

"You didn't have to. I know what you're thinking."

"So what are *you* thinking? What's the alternative?"

"I'll come up with something." Clarence groaned.

"This isn't easy for me either," Geneva said. "But we've had three neighbors robbed in the last six months. It's not like it's completely safe out here either. I don't want to drive our kids to school both ways every day. But we've both got family that have lived in city neighborhoods all these years, and Dani and Felicia were the first ones to get hurt bad. Come on. Living in the inner city isn't like living on the moon."

"No, it's not," Clarence said. "If it was the moon, I'd say let's go."

"Think about it," Geneva said. "We've decided to take in Dani's kids. The psychologist says they'd benefit from staying in the same school, same routine.

Meanwhile, we can't stay here, and there's no place else to go. Dani's house is just sitting there. Looks to me like God's providing it for us."

"Jake said if this happened we could move in with him," Clarence said.

"Okay. Fine. Eight people in Jake's two-bedroom apartment. No problem. You and I and Jake and Daddy could share one room. Sounds like fun, doesn't it?" She gave a half smile, calling his bluff.

Clarence knew she knew he wouldn't stoop to mooching off someone. It was irritating living with someone who knew him so well.

"It's only two or three months, Clarence. We've got to do something." She walked out of the room.

Without looking up, closing his eyes, or opening his mouth, he talked to someone with a great deal of experience being blamed.

You take my sister, Felicia's struggling for her life, and now you take my house out from under me? I've got to find a roof over our head, like some homeless person or something? Well, thank you, Lord. Anything else you want to do to show how much you care? If this is love, do me a favor and don't start hating me!

A rush of sound and fury awakened her, and she felt a panicked fear for the safety of her daughters. But in the next moment, Dani Rawls awoke again, this time not to a scene of agonized confusion but to a glowing quiet passageway. Behind her lay a land of shadows, a gray and colorless two-dimensional flatland. Ahead of her lay...something that defied description.

The departure point stood in stark contrast to the destination, a fresh and utterly captivating place, resonating with color and beauty. She could not only see and hear it, but feel and smell and taste it, even from a distance. The light beckoned her to come dive into it, with abandon, as cool water beckons on a blistering August afternoon.

"Wow!"

She sensed intuitively this place she moved toward was the Substance that cast the shadows in the other world. If that place was midnight, this was sunrise. Up ahead was the twelve-dimensional reality of which the two-dimensional flatland had been but a replica. A very poor replica, Dani thought, the closer she got to the real thing.

"It's fabulous. Incredible."

Though she had not yet stepped foot on it, already everything within her told her this was the Place that defined all places, the Place by which all places must be judged. It was the prototype, the master from which all copies were made. The place reached out to Dani, playfully grabbing at her, drawing her soul as a powerful magnet draws iron filings.

"The colors. So many colors!"

The transition reminded her of the *Wizard of Oz,* where the film goes from black and white to color. But this was millions upon millions of colors. In comparison to this, all the colors of earth she'd enjoyed so much had been no more than shades of gray. Now there was an infinite rainbow of colors, reaching as far beyond earth's rainbow as sunlight beyond a match flame.

"I'm getting stronger. I can feel it."

Only moments ago she'd been so weary, bone tired, the way she'd felt many nights caring for her sick children, alone without a husband. Not exactly alone. She'd often clung to the promises of someone invisible to be the Father of the fatherless. She felt now like the bride about to finally embrace the groom.

How was she moving so quickly while still feeling too drained to move? Wait. She was being carried. Carried in giant arms. How could she not have realized it until now?

She turned her head and looked up at a sculptured face, appearing semi-human, semi-marble statue. This giant of a man had a face like she'd never seen. A face chiseled from rock. Quarry stone features. She knew intuitively this was a warrior, a veteran of battles, one who had carried many wounded to safety.

"Don't know who you are, but you can carry a load, that's for sure!" She laughed that unbridled laugh, that contagious laugh which had served her so well in the difficult times. Not breaking his stride, Stoneface looked in her eyes and listened intently, the corners of his lips turning up just slightly.

Who was this? She stared at his arms, brawny and strong. The muscles were taut but not bulging, suggesting he wasn't taxed by her weight, that she was a light burden or that he was used to bearing heavy ones. Maybe like her slave forefathers. She was thankful for his strength and felt her own body infusing with energy.

She remembered her Bible. Lazarus was carried to heaven by angels. Was this an angel sent to carry her home?

He was dark—not quite as dark as she, more like pure-blooded Middle Eastern, a dark skin sun-baked to further darkness. She gazed at her own skin, the same yellow brown as it had been on earth.

Perhaps this wasn't heaven's threshold. She'd heard once that in heaven all skin would be the same color. But *which* color? Actually, she hadn't pictured skin at all. Maybe heaven would be a giant hanger for skinless spirits. But what she was moving toward wasn't ghosty; it was solid. Considerably more solid than the world she'd just departed.

The warrior's size and strength and rock hard features made her shiver involuntarily. He looked away from the far end of the passageway where they were headed and gazed at her. She saw in his eyes both resolute purpose and kindness. She could almost see the rock crack and a little dust fly off as a slightly unnatural grin broke across that marbly face.

"Hello, Dani."

"Well, hello to you, tall, dark, and handsome. You gonna tell me what's goin' on here?"

He smiled again, like one who hasn't smiled often but enjoys it when he does.

"Who are you?" she asked. "An angel sent to get me?"

"Not sent to get you. Beckoned to take you. I've been with you all along. We're both going home."

"Home? You mean…home, like in the Bible?"

"Just like in the Bible."

"I didn't hear a trumpet sound."

"The trumpet comes later, at the return and the resurrection. This is not that day. It is the day of your exodus from mortality to life."

She looked confused.

"Do not worry. You will understand more soon. Are you gaining strength now?"

"By the minute. It's like I had the best night's rest and I'm ready for the big day. I haven't felt this good since…since I was a child and it was my first day of school."

"Yes, I remember. I was there."

"But I've never seen you before. Who are you?"

"I am Torel, servant of Elyon Most High."

"But how—"

"No more talk of me. I am only the Bridegroom's servant. He awaits you. I must not delay. Do you feel strong enough to walk?"

"Yes."

He lowered her with a tenderness belying his great size. She tried out her legs like a newborn fawn. Immediately the voices grew louder, the calls and laughter intensified. Her heart surged toward the end of the passageway. Dani looked at Torel and grinned impishly.

"Catch me if you can."

She took off running. She was a child again, scurrying across the Mississippi fields, eyes upon home. The guardian behind her reminded her of Clarence, who pretended he couldn't catch her running across those fields, staying just a breath behind her. The enchanting laughter beyond made her want to run faster and faster, then leap carelessly into the wonder, losing herself in Joy.

"It's a birth," she cried, arms flailing in the air, gaining strength with each stride rather than losing it. It *was* a birth, she knew. Her own! She was about to thrust herself into heaven's birthing room. She realized in an instant that her entire life on earth had been but a series of labor pains preparing her for this moment.

As she was once born into a world of cold confusion and blaring artificial lights, she was now being born out of that cramped domain into a wide open realm of warmth and natural light, the place for which she was suited, the world for which she had been made.

"At last," she shouted. "The *real* world!"

At the doorway into life stood a shining being of natural radiance, but with the brightness of a million klieg lights. The radiance threatened to blind her, but somehow her new eyes could endure it. This was more than a man, yet clearly a man. She knew at once who it was. He who had been from eternity past, he who had left his home in heaven to make one here for her. He who spun the galaxies into being with a single snap of his fingers, who was the light that illumined darkness with a million colors, who turned midnight into sunrise.

It was he. Not his representative, but he himself. He put his hands upon her shoulders and she thrilled at his touch.

"Welcome, my little one!" He smiled broadly, the smile teeming with approval. "Well done, my good and faithful servant. Enter into the kingdom prepared for you. Enter into the joy of your Lord!"

He hugged her tight and she hugged him back, clutching on to his back, then grasping his shoulders. She didn't know how long it lasted. These same arms had hugged her before, somehow—she recognized their character and strength—but she enjoyed the embrace now as she'd never dreamed she could enjoy any embrace. It was complete, utterly encompassing, a wall of protection no force in the universe could break through. His was the embrace she was made for. He was the Bridegroom, the object of all longing, the fulfillment of all dreams.

"My sweet Jesus," she said.

She bowed to worship him and he delighted in her worship. Then he lifted her up effortlessly and gazed into her eyes. She studied his eyes through the blur. She saw in them things she had long known coupled with things she had never imagined and still others she sensed she would never fully grasp.

"You're crying," he said. He put out his hand and wiped away her tears. As the hand came close to her cheek a feeling of terror struck her, a feeling she'd assumed could have no place here in Joy itself. She cringed because she saw his outstretched hand was marred and disfigured.

"Your hand." She looked at the other. "Both hands. And your feet." He allowed her to contemplate what she saw.

These were the hands of a Carpenter who cut wood and made things, including universes and angels and every person who had ever lived. These same hands once hauled heavy lumber up a long lonely hill. These same hands and feet were once nailed to that lumber in the Shadowlands, in the most terrible moment from the dawn of time. The wound that healed all wounds could make them temporary only by making itself eternal. Hands and feet of the only innocent man became forever scarred so that no guilty one would have to bear his own scars.

She saw his pain. An ancient pain that was the doorway to eternal pleasures.

Understanding rushed upon her and penetrated her mind as the howling wind had penetrated every crack in her bedroom in that old ramshackle Mississippi home. She wept again, dropping to his mangled feet and caressing them with her hands. He put his fingers under her chin and turned her eyes up toward his.

"For you," he said to her, "I would do it all again."

She could not stop weeping. She was surprised she could cry here, one of the first surprises in an eternity that would bring endless ones. If some tears would never be cried again, she thought, then tears of love and joy and fulfillment were among heaven's pleasures.

She searched the Carpenter's face as one searches a face she has yearned for, which she has seen in her dreams as long as she can remember. On the right side of his throat, she saw another scar, a mark of discoloration, not prominent, only an inch long. The scar looked remarkably like... She reached suddenly to the side of her neck to feel the scar from the broken beer bottle. She couldn't feel it. Gone.

He smiled at her, rubbing his finger on his scar, which used to be hers, just as she had so often done on earth. That quickly the scar on his neck disappeared. But the scars on his hands and feet remained. She knew they always would.

They talked long, just the two of them, without hurry and without distraction. A circle of people surrounded them, waiting for them to finish. But she did not want to finish. She was held captive by one face. She asked countless questions, and she was surprised that he asked her some too, since she knew he knew the answers. He said to her, "I have a secret for you."

"A secret? I thought there were no secrets here." She'd always imagined she'd miss telling secrets to her girlfriends, not the gossipy kind, but the good ones.

"You were wrong," he said simply. "You'll find you were wrong about many things, and you will take delight in discovering the way things really are."

"But what is this secret you have to tell me?"

"It is a name, one which I chose for you long before I created you. It will be private, a name shared between us alone. Only I will call you by this name." He leaned and whispered into her ear, "Your name is ..."

Those in the surrounding circle saw her eyes grow big, her jaw hang open. They didn't hear her new name, but they remembered the feeling of hearing for the first time their own true name, which perfectly captured everything they were, all their loves and longings and gifts and character and personality traits. As he gave her the name, each heard in his own mind the name the Carpenter had once first whispered to him.

Her new name was her true one, now finally discovered after a lifetime of groping for identity in the dark world. Her name perfectly captured her uniqueness as his special creation. It perfectly expressed her nature as his beloved. And it testified in some unique way to one particular facet of his character.

She repeated the name within her. It was so beautiful and so perfect. As if it were the name that had always been hers, but which she had never known. She felt at the same time free of self, free of the burden of self-preoccupation. Yet she felt ten thousand times more herself than she had ever felt, as if all the convoluted scars that had buried and distorted the person Elyon had meant her to be were now gone. At last she was free to be who she was, who Elyon had made her to be.

The Carpenter looked in her eyes, nodding, understanding the liberating realization of this moment. "Those who spend their lives trying to find themselves never do. But you have lost yourself in me. In doing so, you have found yourself."

He squeezed her hand tightly and said, "Those who are wise will shine like the brightness of the heavens, and those who lead many to righteousness, like the stars for ever and ever. You are among them. This is the place I have made for you to shine."

She smiled, unaware of the radiance of her smile, knowing who she was and whose she was and having no desire to look in a mirror to approve or disapprove of what she saw.

"There are many who wish to welcome you." The Carpenter pointed to the crowds still holding their distance.

"Here she is," he said to them. "You can have her now!"

As he watched delightedly, friends and relatives swarmed to her. She put up her hands for protection before realizing she didn't need to. In a sea of faces, one pressed near with greatest urgency, a face and a fragrance she had never forgotten.

"Mama. Oh, Mama!"

"Dani. My little girl."

The hug was tight and long, and the two who had once been inseparable spoke to each other for the first time in fourteen years.

"Mama, I missed you so. Daddy misses you and Antsy and everybody. We talk about you all the time."

"I know. I've been listening." She grinned just the way she always had, but without the burdens that once pulled down on the corners of the grin. "You didn't think death was going to stop your ol' mama from keepin' her nose in your business, did you child?"

"Oh, Mama. I can hardly believe it."

"There's so much to show you, baby. But there's so many people who want to see you first." She looked up over Dani's shoulder and smiled broadly.

Before Dani could turn, two hands from behind gently covered her eyes. No one had done that for years. Not since her childhood when someone always used to come up and...Darrin!

She turned and stared up at the face of her brother who'd died in Vietnam.

"Darrin, it's you. Oh, my sweet Jesus, it's really you." Dani wept as you weep when reunited with those you never got to say a proper goodbye to. "Oh, Darrin. I yelled at you before you went off to Vietnam. I was so stupid. Do you forgive me?"

"Quiet, Dani. Don't talk about that. Of course I forgive you. We're both forgiven or we wouldn't be here. Let me just look at you. My little sister. I've watched you. I've prayed for you. I'm so proud of you."

Dani never remembered him crying. He and Clarence and Harley and Ellis were all tough on the outside. They could be called every name, kids would throw rocks at them, but they'd never cry. Now here was Darrin, crying unashamedly, but happier than she ever remembered him.

Dani saw her giant companion Torel looking on with others of his kind, studying the scene in front of them as if it were somehow beyond their grasp. Then her eyes again caught those of the Carpenter. She relished the look of recognition in his eyes. In her mind she heard him say to her two words as clearly as if he had shouted them.

"Welcome home."

CHAPTER

8

"I seen somethin'." The voice on the other end of the line sounded tense and determined. "I want that hundred bucks!"

"Who is this?"

"Mookie."

"That your gang moniker? What's your real name?"

"Just Mookie."

"Okay, Mookie, you know where old Mrs. Burns lives? Across from the Rawls place where the shooting was?"

"Yeah."

"Can you meet me there? Right after school?"

"Don't go to school. But I can meet you there."

"In an hour?"

"Yeah. A hundred bucks, right?"

"Right—but only if you're straight up with me, you got it? If you're foolin' with me, tell me now, because I'll find out and I'll be real mad. You don't want to see me mad. You telling me the truth you saw something?"

"Straight up, man."

"Okay. Then the hundred's yours. See you in an hour."

———————

Clarence pulled up to Hattie's house. A slender, sullen fifteen-year-old boy sat nervously on the porch. The boy wore a velveteen sweatshirt with a full breadth of loud shiny colors, reminiscent of one of those roadside-bought canvases of Elvis. His sleeves were pushed up to his elbows. Clarence wasn't sure whether this was a cutting edge urban style, an indication of Mookie's tackiness, or a fashion experiment gone awry.

"Mookie? Clarence Abernathy." He stuck out his hand, force of habit. Mookie brushed his fingers awkwardly. Clarence took him inside and sat him in the living room. Hattie Burns brought in milk and cookies, then disappeared as Clarence had asked her to when he called ahead.

"Okay, what did you see?"

"Was walkin' home on Jackson Street, 'bout midnight. Crib's on Dennis Lane, two streets past Jackson, but sometimes I walk Jackson and cut across the back way. I see this car drive up like a block away. Heard these big explosions, like an AK but louder. Then saw them screechin' down Jackson."

"You saw their car?"

"Yeah. I was duckin' behind a tree, but I saw 'em."

"What kind of car?"

"Big ol' lowrider, a bomber, maybe Impala or Caprice, late seventies."

Clarence jotted down some notes excitedly in the back pages of his pocket calendar.

"Color?"

"Gold. Weak paint job."

"Did you see anyone in the car?"

"Two guys. The driver was a Spic for sure, wearin' a white T-shirt. Had a light mustache. The other guy, I think he had a white T-shirt too. Another Spic, almost sure of that."

"You positive they were Latino?"

"Spics? Yeah. Positive on the driver, almost positive on the other dude."

"You're sure about the white T-shirts? And that you saw two guys?"

"Know what I saw, okay? Where's my hundred bucks?"

"Hold on. You see a license plate?"

"Oregon plates. The gold ones. Didn't catch the numbers. Where's the money?"

Clarence reached in his wallet, took out a hundred dollar bill, and put it on Mrs. Burns's coffee table, placing an oil lamp on top of it.

"It's yours as soon as I'm done asking questions. Not until."

Clarence talked with Mookie another half hour, asking his questions different ways to get more details and make sure the story held up. It did.

After he was satisfied, Clarence walked Mookie to the door, hugged Mrs. Burns, and marched off with a triumphant smile. He couldn't wait to tell Ollie Chandler he'd found a witness. Or to see the expression on Manny's face.

———————

"Hi, Daddy," Keisha said, with adoring eyes. She craned her neck up at her father, her dozens of cornrow braids dangling on her back, the colorful barrettes slapping against each other.

Clarence picked up Keisha and spun her around. "How's the cutest girl in third grade?"

"Fine. We made pictures today, like Aunt Dani. I painted leaves on a big tree."

"Good for you, sweetheart."

"Hi, baby." Geneva kissed Clarence and took the grocery bag out of his hand.

"Hey, Jonah." Clarence tackled him gently and they wrestled on the carpet. Keisha joined them.

"We're having lima beans," Keisha told her father, with a look of contempt. "I hate limas." She folded her arms and looked as utterly disgusted as an eight year old could.

"Well, you may as well save yourself some problems and stop hating them," her father said, "because you're going to eat them, that's for sure."

"But they taste so *gross.*"

Clarence picked her up in his lap and sat down on the dark blue living-room glider.

"Not everything that's good for you tastes good. Your father knows what's good and what isn't. You have to trust your daddy. Limas are good for you, even if you don't like them."

She grew quiet, knowing any further statements could mean dad and mom would call in a dump truck and bury her in lima beans.

"Where's Grampy?" Clarence asked.

"In his room," Jonah said. "Reading another baseball book he got at the library."

"I think I see some stories coming down." Clarence smiled. "He's been thinking about the old days again."

Some stories would be just fine. Being with his family was almost enough to make him forget about the world that filled the news, where folks hated each other for their skin color, where men grabbed children by the ear and hurt them, where innocent people got shot by two-bit gangbangers. This was his home, his castle, his family. And if the world went to hell in a handbasket, at least no one could take away his family. At least, that's what he'd always told himself.

"Daddy," Keisha said, "you promised you'd read from the Narnia book last night and you never did."

Celeste pulled the double team, taking her stand next to her cousin.

"Sorry, honey," Clarence said. "I got a call, somebody I had to talk to. I'll read it tomorrow night. I promise."

"What about tonight? Celeste and me wants you to read it tonight."

"Celeste and *I* want you to read it tonight."

"But I want *you* to read it, Daddy."

"No, I meant...never mind. Your mama and I are going out to eat tonight. Carly's coming over to watch you. We're going out with her parents."

"I like Carly," Keisha said. "Carly's a good baby-sitter. She's got her own baby," she explained to Celeste.

"She's bringing her baby with her, so you'll get to see him," Clarence said. "His name is Finney."

"That's a funny name," Celeste said.

"She named him after a good friend of her father's."

"But Daddy, you just *have* to read to us about Aslan the Lion. You promised."

"But, honey, I told you, I'll be gone tonight."

"Then read to us now, Daddy. Pretty please."

Clarence was about to tell Keisha begging wouldn't do any good when Celeste stepped out in the hallway from the bedroom, clutching in both hands *The Lion, the Witch and the Wardrobe* and pleading silently with her big brown Dani eyes.

"Okay. I'll read it to you now. But just one chapter. No more."

The girls shrieked and celebrated and headed toward the bedroom. "But we have to put on our jammies. I'll get Jonah." No sooner had she run out of the room than she screamed, "Jonah, Jonah! Daddy's going to read the Narnia book right now. Put yo' jammies on!"

Jonah walked out of his room. "Now?"

"Come as you are, Son," Clarence said. "No jammies necessary."

They settled in around Keisha's bed, with Keisha and Celeste propped up against pillows on top and Jonah sitting on the floor leaning back against the bedpost, not wanting to look quite as eager as the girls.

"All right," Clarence said, "you remember what happened last time we read?" Clarence couldn't look at Celeste without thinking of when he'd read this book in Dani's bedroom, six hours before the shooting.

"Edmund was bad," Celeste said.

"He betrayed his brother and sisters," Keisha added. "Peter and Lucy and Susan."

"And the White Witch says she has the right to kill him," Jonah said.

Clarence nodded, thankful that for once it was a *white* witch, not a black witch.
He read a few paragraphs that culminated in the White Witch's words to Aslan the
Lion:

> "You at least know the magic which the Emperor put into Narnia
> at the very beginning. You know that every traitor belongs to me
> as my lawful prey and that for every treachery I have a right to a
> kill. You know that unless I have blood as the Law says, all
> Narnia will be overturned and perish in fire and water."
>
> "It is very true," said Aslan. "I do not deny it."
>
> "Oh, Aslan!" whispered Susan in the Lion's ear. "Can't we—
> I mean, you won't, will you? Can't we do something about the
> Deep Magic? Isn't there something you can work against it?"
>
> "Work against the Emperor's magic?" said Aslan, turning
> to her with something like a frown on his face. And nobody
> ever made that suggestion to him again.

"Then Edmund really has to die?" Jonah asked quietly.

"We'll see," Clarence said. He'd never read the stories before and didn't know
what would happen next.

He read on, as Aslan talked to the witch privately and no one knew exactly
what was said. But Aslan came away and announced to the children, "I have settled
the matter. She has renounced the claim on your brother's blood."

All the children rejoiced and everyone was relieved, both in Narnia and in
Keisha Abernathy's bedroom.

Clarence then read about how deeply troubled the Great Lion was, sad and
lonely, and how the children could not understand why, since Edmund no longer
had to die. Then at night they saw Aslan plodding away and they sneaked out and
followed him to the Great Stone Table. There ogres and wraiths and hags and the
witch herself lay in wait, torches in hand and gloating their evil threats. Aslan
appeared and the crowd was at first terrified, but the Witch ordered them to bind
him. He permitted them to do so, "though, had the Lion chosen, one of those paws
could have been the death of them all."

The Witch ordered him to be shaved, and they cut off his beautiful mane. They
mocked him, called him names, and muzzled him. Then as the Lion lay quietly on
the stone table, the witch sharpened her knife.

Keisha and Celeste looked horrified; Jonah look perplexed. Clarence continued
to read. As the White Witch lifted up the knife over Aslan she said to him:

> "And now, who has won? Fool, did you think that by all this you
> would save the human traitor? Now I will kill you instead of
> him as our pact was, and so the Deep Magic will be appeased.

But when you are dead what will prevent me from killing him as well? And who will take him out of my hand *then?* Understand that you have given me Narnia forever, you have lost your own life, and you have not saved his. In that knowledge, despair and die."

With this she plunged the knife down into the Lion, killing him, to the roars and celebration of the spectators.

Clarence stopped reading, the chapter over. The children sat stunned and teary eyed.

"You mean Aslan *dies?*" Keisha said. "But I thought he couldn't die! Isn't he too powerful to die?"

"I thought Edmund was going to die," Celeste said.

"I didn't think anyone would die," Jonah said quietly.

"Keep reading, Daddy," Keisha pleaded. "Something has to happen."

"No. I've read too long already. I have to get ready."

He shut the book, wishing he could tell them life was different. That no one had to die. But that would be a lie.

She stared at the Cosmic Center, intoxicated by his character. This was her only king. This her only kingdom. The character of God defined the landscape of heaven. The Carpenter had prepared a place all right. What a place!

Her family and old friends had greeted her. Finally she had a chance to ask her mother a question.

"Did he give you a special name too, Mama?"

"Yes. He gives one to all of his redeemed. Wherever you go you will be a testimony to one particular facet of his character, that reflected in your new name. Everyone who meets you will see something of Elyon they have never seen before."

Torel, the giant warrior who had carried her to this country, said, "It takes all the redeemed together to paint the picture of his character. Even then, the multitudes of his followers are insufficient. The caverns of the knowledge of God each lead to another and another and another. Should any explorer exhaust them on one world he can simply move to the next. There will always be more to learn, more to discover about him and his universe and his people. The learning will never cease, the reverence always deepen, the symphony of worship ever build, one crescendo upon another."

"But," Dani said, "I thought we would know everything here."

"A common error of Adam's race, one I can never comprehend," Torel said, looking puzzled. "Only Elyon knows everything. Creatures can never know everything. They are limited. They are learners. *We* are learners. You have already learned much here, have you not?"

"Yes," Dani said. "For one thing, I've learned why America never felt like home to me. For a time I'd thought maybe Africa was my home, but somehow I knew that wasn't right either. I always sensed I was on foreign ground. Whether it was in the city, the suburbs, the country, or on a tropical island, nothing there could be a permanent home. And given all the injustice and suffering, who would want it to be? I never fit in there, Torel. Sometimes I thought it was because of my skin color. Now I realize it was because of the God-shaped emptiness within me, the void that could only be filled by being in his presence. By being here."

Torel nodded, listening intently, as if he was not tutor but student.

"While on earth I kept hearing heaven's music," Dani said, "but it was elusive, more like an echo. All that clatter, all those competing sounds, all the television programs and ringing phones and traffic and voices drowned out Elyon's music. Sometimes I'd dance to the wrong beat, march to the wrong anthem. I was never made for that place. I was made for this one."

The wild rush of Joy, the rapture of discovery overwhelmed her as if she'd just gotten in on the greatest inside joke in the history of the universe. Now she saw and felt it with stunning clarity. Her unswerving patriotism had been reserved for another country. Every joy on earth, such as the joy of reunion, had been but an inkling, a whisper of greater Joy. Every place on earth had been at best a rented room, a place to spend the night on a long journey.

She remembered the rough sketches she used to make before starting to paint. "Mount Hood, Niagara Falls, the Grand Canyon, the Oregon Coast, all those places on earth were only rough sketches of this place. The best parts of the old world were sneak previews of this one. Like little foretastes, like licking the spoon from Mama's beef stew an hour before supper." She smiled at her mother and grabbed her hand.

"I'm home," she shouted, first hugging her mother, then grabbing the angel's hands and dancing in a circle, turning around and around and around, taking pleasure in his unfamiliarity and awkwardness at the dance, while her mother clapped a beat. "Did you hear me, Torel? I'm really home!"

Clarence looked up Barnes and Noble in the yellow pages and called. "How late are you open tonight? Ten o'clock? That's great. I'm looking for some books on racial issues. You have a black literature section, don't you?"

"We have an *African American* section."

"Okay. Guess that'll have to do."

It chafed him to be corrected by a white woman, as if he wasn't entitled to say "black." He knew the woman assumed he wasn't black just because he pronounced his words clearly.

Geneva stood in the bathroom, looking in the full-length mirror that hung from the back of the door. Her five-foot-three slender build fell nicely within the mirror's borders.

When Clarence got six feet from the bathroom door, he started saying, "I'm walking toward the bathroom. I'm getting closer. I'm still coming. Hand on the door-knob now. I'm going to open it slowly."

Suddenly Geneva let out a blood-curdling scream.

"Clarence Abernathy! How many times do I have to tell you, don't sneak up on me!"

"I *didn't* sneak up on you. I tried to tell you I was coming. But if I'd spoken any louder I would have startled you. There's no winning, Geneva!" He laughed. Finally, she did too.

Clarence stepped into the bathroom. When he entered rooms, he didn't pass through doorways, he filled them. As tall men negotiate doorframes vertically, he negotiated them horizontally as well. He stood far back from the mirror, positioning himself three different places before he could see everything he needed to, and then never all at once.

"How do you get all of yourself into this mirror at the same time?" he asked Geneva.

"Just petite, I guess." She finally had her breath back. "Of course, you help my image, you know."

"How's that?"

"Standin' next to you, a rhinoceros would look petite." She smiled. "Maybe that's why I put up with you sneakin' up on me like a prowler."

"I pity the prowler who has to hear *you* scream."

Clarence looked sharp in his dark blue dress slacks, maroon sweater, and blue tie, overdressed for a dinner at a casual restaurant. He never dressed garishly, never with too much color, making sure no one thought he was a black man trying to draw attention to himself. No shiny Florsheims like black hustlers wore, but not the penny loafers of the imitation white crowd either. Years ago he'd read *Dress for Success*, underlined it profusely, made some alterations for his blackness, and used it as a flight plan.

"What would you do without me?" Geneva asked, as women do whose husbands don't ask the question themselves.

Clarence didn't hear her. He was busy leaning toward the mirror with the tweezers, zeroing in on a stray nose hair. He pulled it hard. His eyes watered. He put away the tweezers in the drawer without looking down, closely studying the white fringes of his short sideburns.

"You're goin' gray, old man," Geneva teased.

"Not sure I'm ready for all these white hairs."

"Well, it's not the same as a melon goin' bad, you know."

"Feels the same."

"Could be worse. Could be your skin turnin' white on you!"

They both laughed.

"Baby," she turned toward him and straightened his collar, "I declare you just get more handsome with the years."

She put her arms around his thick firm stomach, and he hugged her tight. She liked that. He enveloped her and it made her feel secure. She would have liked him to add how beautiful she still was too, but she'd take the hug.

When Clarence left the room, Geneva resumed her look in the mirror. She rubbed skin softener onto her face. Her skin was "maple syrup," her mom had always said in the many discussions of grades of skin color she'd heard growing up. She and Clarence were both "black" by popular description, but there was a stark difference between his deep brown and her sandy brown, a little lighter than Dani's skin, but with less yellow.

Geneva's eyes were called brown, but had just a touch of what sometimes seemed blue and sometimes green, depending on what she wore.

"Your eyes are most striking when you wear red," her mama used to tell her.

Geneva had always been intrigued by the hint of light colors in her eyes. It made her think of the European blood in her veins, presumably going back to slave masters and overseers who molested her great-great-grandmothers when they were slave girls. That's where the lightness in her skin came from, she knew, because none of her ancestors had ever married a white, not in the last three generations anyway, and before that, interracial marriage was almost unheard of. The thought made her tremble, and she felt uncertain and powerless about the forces that had shaped even the genetic code that made her who she was.

She continued to rub in the skin lotion, watching it disappear into the maple syrup brown. Her skin was soft, and she could have been mistaken for a college girl if not for the thin dark lines time had carved in her face.

Suddenly the bathroom door flung open and she barely escaped getting hit.

"What's this, elephant stampede on the Serengeti? How many times I got to tell you not to charge in like that?"

"Sorry, Mama," Jonah said. "Frettin' about your lines again?"

"I'm not frettin', boy. You want frettin', I'll give you frettin'. Now get yourself gone, you hear me? Just like your father, chargin' in on a defenseless woman! I swear."

She swatted him on the rear, good naturedly. She saw his smile as he left.

Clarence came back in, this time to get shoe polish. He looked at her gazing in the mirror. "You're just maturing. I don't want you to look like some high school cheerleader anyway."

"Thanks a lot! You made my day."

He smiled at her vanity, then took another look in the mirror to satisfy his own. The doorbell rang.

Jake, Janet, and Carly all stood at the front door. Geneva welcomed them in and everyone exchanged hugs.

"How are you, Carly?" Geneva asked.

"Oh, I don't feel that great, to be honest. But I've been growing a lot in my faith. I guess that's what matters most, huh?"

Jake put his arm around her, drawing her near. Carly looks tired, Clarence thought. He knew her battle with HIV had moved into the early stages of AIDS, with some sort of cancer starting, her immune system unable to fight it. Something about how she looked reminded him of his cousin Mack, who'd died of AIDS a year ago. Carly was only nineteen, her son, Finney, a year and a half.

Geneva helped Carly get Finney settled in Keisha's old crib, set up in their bedroom. Carly's life had changed dramatically in the last two years, outside much for the worse and inside much for the better. Through Jake and Janet, Clarence and Geneva had come to know and love her.

"Olive Garden or Red Robin's? I'm still going back and forth," Geneva said.

"Both sound good to me," Janet said. "They're just a stone's throw apart, so we don't have to decide till we get there."

In January Clarence and Geneva had gone with Jake and Janet to the Old Spaghetti Factory. They'd had such a great time, they'd gone out together at least once a month since, trying different places and establishing some favorite haunts. They rarely went to fancy restaurants, preferring to dine less expensively but more frequently.

"Mind if we stop by Barnes and Noble's just before dinner?" Clarence asked. "It's right by the restaurants. The coffee's on me."

Clarence drove to the bookstore and bought a round of mochas at Starbuck's Coffee, attached to the store. All four loved to read and enjoyed hanging around bookstores together—especially a store that encouraged you to drink coffee, browse, and sit back on couches and comfy chairs.

The girls hung out in fiction, domestics, and food while Clarence and Jake went to sports, military, and humor. While Jake was looking at Vietnam books, Clarence said, "Be back in a minute."

He headed around the corner toward the African American section. It was one of the largest and best he'd seen, with hundreds of titles. He looked at a few of the huge picture books, showing closeups ranging from Frederick Douglas, Booker T. Washington, and W. E. B DuBois to Muhammad Ali and Arthur Ashe. He found himself touching the picture of Ashe in childlike admiration. His eye caught a book called *The Rage of a Privileged Class: Why Are Middle-class Blacks Angry?* He picked it up and started reading.

Four pages later he felt someone close to him and whirled around.

"Hey, Clabern. What's wrong?" Jake saw the scowl on Clarence's face.

"Nothing's wrong. I was comin' back in a minute, just like I said."

"No problem. I finished up, so I was just wandering. What are you looking at?"

"Nothing." Clarence turned and shoved the book back on the shelf, his body shielding it from Jake's eyes. "Just checking out some racial stuff so I can get ready to debate Harley over the holidays."

"I'd like to meet your brother. I keep envisioning a Black Muslim version of you."

"We're nothing alike," Clarence heard the edge in his own voice. If Geneva were there she'd say, "You're a lot alike." He cringed every time she said that.

"Better find the girls and get to dinner." Clarence walked away briskly. Jake wondered if he'd done something to offend him. He had no idea what.

"Would you buy this for me, baby?" Geneva handed Clarence another one of those creative health-food books. He went up to the counter, choosing the college-aged black girl rather than the fortyish white woman who'd corrected him over the phone about the "African American" section.

"Did you find what you needed, sir?"

Clarence looked at the young black girl with surprise. The voice. It was the woman he'd talked to on the phone an hour and a half ago.

"Is something wrong?" she asked.

"No. I…I just recognized your voice. I'm the one who called and asked about a black literature section. You told me you had an *African American* section."

"I'm sorry. I didn't know…"

"Yeah. Me neither."

It embarrassed Clarence to realize he'd made the same assumption about her she'd made about him. While the clerk processed his Visa, he thought of when he first called a real estate agent looking for a home in Gresham. He explained he was want-ing to move out of Portland and asked if east Gresham had good neighbor-hoods. "Oh, sure," the man had said, "there's no blacks or Mexicans or anything." He'd hung up on him, but he was still angry at himself for not paying the man a visit, showing him the face behind the voice, and maybe putting the fear of God into him while he was at it.

The four walked out of the bookstore. Though Clarence tried to hide it, the other three knew something was wrong. They walked across the street to Red Robin's, attempting to make the best of it, Geneva and Janet walking close to each other and a little ways ahead of the men.

Geneva thought Janet and Jake made a cute couple and kept thinking of them as married. Actually, they'd been divorced five years earlier but had started a dating relationship in the last two years.

"When's he going to ask you to marry him again?" Geneva asked as they walked through the parking lot.

"Maybe when he's sure it'll turn out differently this time," Janet said.

After they'd been seated and had ordered, Clarence was still quiet.

"Geneva," Jake said, "Janet was telling me how you and Clarence met. I'd like to hear about it."

"Well, I grew up in Corvallis, one of just a handful of blacks. My parents came from Alabama. Daddy got a job as a custodian at Oregon State. It was his dream for me and my brothers and sisters to go to college there. Three of us did. Anyway, I loved football. I was at our first game when I noticed this big lug of an offensive line-man on the field. I checked his name on the program. I was down there real close to the sidelines and saw him take off his helmet. I memorized his face."

She squeezed Clarence.

"Tell them how you chased after me," Clarence said, his first words since the bookstore.

"The program listed him as a junior transfer from Alcorn State in Mississippi. Well, I was a junior too, and I thought, maybe he came out here to Oregon to meet some girls. Figured I might as well be one of the first."

Janet laughed and grabbed her arm. Jake and Clarence chuckled.

"I started visiting practices and watching from the stands. I even used binoculars. Can you believe that?"

"So when did you finally introduce yourself?" Jake asked.

"I had a girlfriend who worked in registration. She got me a copy of his winter term class schedule. I saw he had an English lit course, so I signed up for the same section."

"You didn't," Jake said.

"I did. And on the first day of class, I made sure he noticed me."

"That was pretty easy," Clarence said. "We had the only two Afros in the room. Oregon State was less than one percent black. Here I was, thinking I'd spontaneously bumped into the girl of my dreams, and all the time she was pulling the strings. Course, hard to blame her. I was a pretty studly young man."

"When did you find out it wasn't spontaneous?" Jake asked.

"Too late. She already had her hooks in me."

Clarence looked at Geneva. He always saw her as she was back then. Young and energetic, short but leggy and Bambi-like. Her neck was long, and she had big vulnerable eyes on top of high cheekbones. She took a positive outlook on life, the perfect foil for Clarence's cynicism.

"You both came from Christian homes, didn't you?" Jake asked.

"Yeah. We had strong convictions," Geneva said. "I had to beat off some white girls who kept putting the make on him, you know, hearing the myth about black male sexuality."

"What do you mean, myth?" Clarence asked, laughing.

"We kept our virginity," Geneva said, "but it wasn't easy."

"Good for you," Janet said.

"You made the right choice," Jake added. "Janet and I have talked about how much we wish we'd waited till marriage. I'm afraid it got us off on the wrong foot. And I take responsibility for that."

"Me too," Janet said.

"I'm just glad God forgives and we get another chance," Jake said. He put his arm around Janet and drew her toward him.

"Geneva, can I have your water?" Clarence gestured at her full glass sitting next to his empty.

"Just tell me the three little words every wife wants to hear."

"Pass the catsup?"

"No. I love you."

"Well, I do. That's why I married you." He grabbed her water.

"He's a hopeless romantic," Geneva told Janet. "Hey, I've got one for you. Why does it take fifty thousand sperm and only one egg for a new life to begin?"

Jake and Janet both shrugged.

"Because none of the sperm will stop to ask directions."

They all laughed hard.

"See why I married her?" Clarence asked Jake.

"Yeah, I sure do."

"Now if I can just survive her health food kick. She's been feeding me these slimy green drinks made in the blender. Seaweed specials."

"I just want you to live longer."

"That stuff makes me not *want* to live longer. I'd rather live shorter and die happy."

"Geneva," Janet said, "You have to tell Jake what you told me the other day about your great-grandmother. What you did for her."

"Well," Geneva looked at Jake, "when she was ninety-two and I was ten, I taught Great-Grandma to read."

"No kidding? Wow."

"I'll never forget it, the light in her eyes. She was like a little girl. She could read the Bible for the first time. She lived another five years and she read for hours every day. Sometimes she'd sit in her rockin' chair shakin' her head, and she'd say, 'I's readin', chile, I's readin'!' She never got over it."

"How come she hadn't learned earlier?" Jake asked.

"Well, she was the daughter of slaves. They didn't know how to read. When she started her own family after emancipation, she lived where they didn't let black kids go to school. The black school was six miles away and there wasn't any way they could get the children there, so my grandfather grew up not knowing how to read either. Great-Grandma just never had anybody to teach her. It was one of the biggest thrills of my life."

Geneva teared up, as did Janet. They sat quietly for a minute.

"I noticed some of those books in the African American section at Barnes and Noble," Jake said. "I really don't know much about black history and racial issues. I was thinking I should go back and do some reading. And maybe get your perspective on things."

"Race. You want to hear my food preparation analogy?" Geneva asked. "To whites, race is like a sauce. You can put on as much or as little as you want. To blacks, it's a marinade. It permeates everything. You can't take it or leave it. It's always there, no matter what."

"Being black in America is like wearing shoes that don't fit," Clarence said, his finger unconsciously running over the leathery patch of skin surrounding the scar beneath his right ear. "Some people will toss them off completely and go barefoot; some can adjust better, but their toes are always cramped. My mama used to say to me, 'Boy—' Now, if you ever heard a black woman say 'Boy' that was my mama! She said, 'Boy, you'll always be colored, so get used to it. Won't do you no good to fret about it. Just do your best and leave the rest to God.'"

Jake and Janet looked tentative, afraid whatever they might say would display ignorance or offend Clarence and Geneva, who were eager to talk, but only if their friends wanted to pursue it. The topic died an unnatural death.

"You know, I told you Detective Chandler is on Dani's case," Clarence said to Jake. "What can you tell me about him?"

"Ollie? Well, he's brilliant, for one thing."

"Brilliant? Are we talking about the same guy?"

"Yeah. Unorthodox, maybe. A few idiosyncrasies. Okay, more than a few. But he really knows his stuff. I've told you about what he did on the case when my buddies died. Remember, he's the one who saved my life."

"That counts for a lot with me," Janet said.

"Mormance, over at the *Trib*," Clarence said, "told me your Detective Chandler is into police brutality."

"Into it?" Jake asked. "There was only one accusation I know of, and he was cleared of all charges."

"But was he guilty?"

"No, I don't think he was. He did hammer on somebody, yeah, but the guy was resisting arrest and out of control, grabbing everything he could to use as a weapon. He was a danger to everybody."

"What color was the guy he beat up?" Clarence asked.

"Well...he was African American."

"You mean black?"

"Yeah, black," Jake said. "He was a criminal who happened to be black."

"Jake looked into it before he even knew Ollie," Janet offered. "He talked to some witnesses. That's how he formed his opinions."

"Those opinions weren't very popular at the *Trib*," Jake said. "Ollie got crucified in a couple of articles and an editorial. After a week of research and a half-dozen interviews, I wrote a column in his defense. Okay, he's a Nam vet, so maybe that's why I showed some special interest at first. But I don't believe he's a racist. And I don't believe he was guilty of police brutality."

"I've heard different," Clarence said.

"Well, maybe you've heard wrong. You've obviously gotten one side. If you want to get the other, you better talk to Ollie directly. If you've got that kind of prejudice, you're not going to be able to trust him."

What do you know about prejudice?

"I *don't* trust him," Clarence said. "And he hasn't told me as much about the case as I'd like."

"He doesn't have to tell you anything," Jake said.

"Clarence hasn't always had good experiences with cops," Geneva said.

"Ollie's had horrible experiences with reporters," Jake said. "Maybe you both need to trust each other more."

A few seconds of uncomfortable silence followed.

"Look, guys, could we talk about something else?" Geneva asked. "We were having a good time. Let's get back to it, okay?"

"Sorry, Clabern." Jake put his hand on Clarence's, white on brown.

"Me too, Jake."

When the food was served, Jake leaned toward Clarence and said, "One good thing. If you spend any time with Ollie, you won't have to worry about health food."

An hour later they ordered dessert, talking and laughing. Clarence seemed to be enjoying himself again.

When the waiter finally got a yes to, "Will that be everything tonight?" he brought the check to the table and set it in front of Jake.

Clarence reached over and grabbed the check. It was his turn to treat.

They walked over to Clackamas Town Center to look around for forty-five minutes before closing. Clarence had turned quiet again.

The two couples walked into Meier & Frank. After a few minutes, Janet glanced over at Clarence, who seemed to be pacing and looking over his shoulder. Geneva came up and said to her, "We'll just be sitting on the bench out in the mall. Take your time. No hurry."

"Clarence seems upset, and Geneva looks like she's about to cry," Janet said to Jake. "Did we do something wrong?"

"I don't know," Jake said. "Maybe it's a fight or something. Guess they need some space." Jake looked out in the mall at the couple sitting uncomfortably on the bench. He felt like he knew them well and yet somehow didn't know them at all.

"Clarence seems really angry these days, on the edge," Jake said. "I'm worried about him."

9

The English bulldog sat poised, his neck two-thirds the width of his colossal chest. His short stocky legs looked like thick pedestals supporting an oversized load. Spike was a fire hydrant on four legs, his head disproportionately sized, almost human in mass, stuck on the end of a short squatty body that looked like a giant bulging sausage.

"Oh, you're a fine lookin' boy, now aren't you?" Geneva asked Spike. "All the girls are crazy about you! See those cocker spaniels on their walk yesterday? Had their hair done just so? Tryin' to impress my little boy, that's what they were up to!"

His short tawny lion-like coat was bright, smooth, and brindled, flecked with dark spots and little streaks. His largely lion-brown face was divided by a streak of white that culminated in a coal black nose.

"Can you believe Daddy wanted one of those big ol' Rottweilers? Yeah, but Mama talked him into an inside dog. You were the only one studly enough for him. That's my boy!"

Spike's wrinkled gargoyle-like face left anyone who didn't know him ill at ease. His teeth bared and his lower jaw protruded sternly, at least two inches beyond his flat nose. His harness served the purpose of black leather jackets on fifties tough guys, giving an even more rugged look to the most solid forty-five pounds on four feet. His eyes were so wideset, people couldn't meet them both. Nervous folks glanced back and forth from eye to eye, wondering what the other was looking at.

"How's my little boy in a doggy suit? How you doin', Spikey, huh? Here's some pizza bones for you."

He was putty in Geneva's hands, rolling in that shuffling, sideways motion. Wriggling the half inch fold of flesh over his flattened nose, Spike took the pizza rusts gingerly from her hand, then devoured them, looking to her for more. Clarence walked in, startling Geneva.

"You're spoiling that dog."

"Spike? Spoiled?" Geneva laughed. "That's just part of the fun. You're not supposed to spoil children. But it's okay to spoil a dog."

Clarence put one knee to the floor, prompting Spike to do the doggy dance of joy. "Mama tryin' to make a sissy out of you? What happened to your nose? Been chasin' parked cars again?"

One glance at Spike's ferocious profile was enough to terrorize everyone from Jehovah's Witnesses to the UPS man. But behind the stern face and the intimidating physique was a kindness and loyalty to his family.

The only ones who needed to fear him were those who brought harm to his loved ones. And they were right to fear him. Given opportunity, he would tear them to shreds.

———————

Clarence stood outside the big window on the fourteenth floor of the Justice Center, eyed by the receptionist.

"Do you have an appointment?"

"No. But I've got some important information. Trust me, he'll be interested."

Three minutes later Ollie Chandler opened the door.

"Abernathy. What's going on?"

"Got somethin' for you." Clarence tried to look casual. "The car was a large gold lowrider, maybe an old Impala or Caprice, late seventies. There were two guys, both Hispanic, wearing white T-shirts. The driver had a light mustache."

Ollie stared at him, as if wondering whether this was a joke. "Come in," Ollie said. He pointed to an interrogation room and closed the door behind them. "Who told you all this?"

"I did my own investigating. Found a kid named Mookie who was walking home on Seventh Street, you know, a couple of blocks over from MLK. He heard the shots, then saw them screeching down Jackson. Right in front of him."

"I want to talk to this kid," Ollie said.

"Sure. I've got all the info." Clarence pointed to the yellow legal pad in front of him.

"How'd you find him?"

"I put out word on the streets."

"Yeah? So did we," Ollie said. "What word did you put out?"

"I offered a hundred dollars for information."

"You what?"

"I said I'd pay for information. I gave Mookie a hundred dollars."

"That's not the way to do it."

"Oh? And how many witnesses has your way uncovered?"

Ollie's red blotches started to expand. "Okay. I'll take whatever I can get. Don't kick a gift horse in the teeth."

"You mean, don't look a gift horse in the mouth?"

"Why would you want to look him in the mouth?"

"Never mind," Clarence said.

"Okay, so how do you know Doogie isn't conning you?"

"Mookie."

"Whatever. Sounds like an easy hundred bucks for makin' up a story."

"Look, it was all solid. I kept asking him questions, different ways. No contradictions. He sounded authentic. Didn't come across like he'd made it up."

"And you'd know the difference?"

"I'm a journalist, okay? I have to figure out people all the time. You get a feel for who's shooting straight and who's shooting bull."

"He didn't happen to see the license number?"

"No. Gold Oregon plates, that's all."

"He's sure on the racial tag?" Ollie asked.

"Like I said, two Hispanics. He's positive about the driver anyway. Window was rolled down. Got a clear view. Pretty sure on the other guy, the shooter. Positive on the car—size and shape and color anyway."

"Okay, write down his phone number and address for me. I'll get hold of your Mookie today. Nice job, detective. You maybe found us our best witness."

"Maybe?"

"Just being cautious," Ollie said. "I'm optimistic."

"I've still got the word out. And I'll keep nosing around."

"Just be careful, okay? Remember, it's not your case."

"She was my sister."

"You keep saying that. I've got a sister too, Holly, lives in Minneapolis. That's why I've been talking to you. Manny thinks I'm crazy, but maybe he'll change his tune with the info you dug up. Remember, though, I can't let you too far in. You've got too much at stake in the whole thing to stay objective."

"If some guy wasted your sister, what would you do?" Clarence asked him.

"Go after him."

"Think the Minneapolis cops would let you in on their case?"

"Of course not. I mean, not officially. Shoot, my own lieutenant wouldn't let me head up the case if it happened right here. You have to be able to keep your objectivity."

"So that would keep you from going after the guy?"

"I'm saying officially I wouldn't be able to—"

"I'm not talking officially. What would you do unofficially? If it had been almost three weeks and the cops hadn't caught anybody, you'd nose around, wouldn't you?"

"That's different."

"How?"

"I'm trained. I know what I'm doing."

"Guys don't go after people who kill their sister because they're professional detectives. They do it because she's their sister."

Ollie sighed. "But you still can't—"

"I'll do my part one way or the other. With you or without you."

"You can always tell a journalist," Ollie said. "But you can't tell him much. The last time I let someone in on a case it was Jake Woods. He almost bit the big one. And I got a reprimand. 'Keep civilians out unless they're essential.' That's what the lieutenant told me, as if I didn't know. And ever since Jake, I haven't let civilians inside. Bottom line, Mr. Abernathy, you're not essential."

"Yeah? What did you know about the guys who shot up my sister until I got involved? Maybe I've got more time and interest than you do. How long before this case gets buried? You have to care about the other cases, I don't. So maybe I *am* essential. Anyway, I'm not giving up."

"Just don't expect me to deputize you," Ollie said.

"I'm not asking you for anything, okay? Maybe I'm just asking you to keep me posted, that's all. What can I do to convince you? Besides offer you a Häagen-Dazs, I mean."

"You've been talking to Jake, haven't you? It won't work. I won't compromise my position for an ice-cream bar."

"I didn't think you would." Long silence. "How about a double burger, fries, and a blackberry shake at Lou's Diner?" Clarence asked.

"Now you're getting closer." Ollie got up from the desk. "Make it onion rings instead of fries and I'll think about it. Woods is dog meat." Ollie hesitated. "Before we hit Lou's, you still want to see the computer image of the scene?"

He went over to a centralized computer ten feet from his desk, entered a program, called up a file, and a schematic of Dani's room popped on the screen. The accuracy and detail stunned Clarence. Everything was labeled. Window, blinds, closet, big bed, little bed #1, little bed #2, all of them with enough reference points to form an outline of their shape. On the far wall were twenty-three dots labeled "bullet holes," numbered consecutively. There were also some small items. One of them said "lunch pail." There on the floor, points forming an outline, he saw two forms, the larger one labeled "dead body," the smaller "live body."

Clarence's heart raced. "There were forty shots though, right?"

"Yeah. Some pierced the floor, some the side walls. See here?" He reoriented the screen so Clarence could see the other markings.

"I'm still a little skeptical about this new-fangled computer stuff," Ollie admitted. "But it's the latest thing, huh?"

"Yeah, well, next month drive through dentistry may be the latest thing. Doesn't mean I'm gonna do it. But I'll give it a chance."

"Drive through dentistry?"

"No. The laser unit."

The phone rang. "Ollie Chandler. Yeah. Our turn again, already? Say it ain't so. Okay. Off Southeast 39th and Powell? What's the numbers? Got it."

He put down the phone and sighed. "We'll have to do Lou's tomorrow, but I'll hold you to it. Open case number four. Murder takes no holiday."

"Jake?"

"Yeah, Clabern?"

"Have you ever asked God to heal Carly?"

"Hundreds of times. We've asked everybody we know to pray for her. We've prayed God would take away the HIV. When the cancer started, we prayed he'd remove it. The chemo's been going pretty well, but the ultimate prognosis is the same. We're thankful for whatever time we have with her."

"You don't sound like you have much faith God will heal her."

"I go back and forth, I guess. My pastor helped me do some study on it. Paul said he prayed three times for God to heal him from some terrible disease. He called it a thorn in the flesh. And God said no. He chose not to heal him. Paul talks about one of his fellow workers he left behind sick, and he tells Timothy to take a little wine because of his stomach problems. If Paul and his coworkers didn't get healed, I don't think it was lack of faith, and I don't think we can assume all of us will get healed. If God always healed or didn't allow accidents, nobody would ever die."

"So, have you given up?" Clarence asked.

"No, of course not. I still ask God to heal her, every day. I know he can, but I don't know if he will. I guess that's up to him, not me. I don't want to lose her, that's for sure. I feel like it's been such a short time since I've found her again. Then I look at baby Finney, and I say, Lord, that boy needs his mother." Jake's voice cracked.

"When adults get hurt, that's bad enough," Clarence said. "But when it's kids, it just tears me up. Felicia's the sweetest little girl." He let out an unexpected moan. "And she's lost her mama, the best mama you ever knew."

Jake put his arm on Clarence's shoulder. Then he faced him and put his arms around him in a full hug. The two big proud successful men held on to each other, both realizing they had no control over life.

Clarence got special permission to bring the pastor from his old church into ICU to see Felicia. Though it had been a year since he'd left Pastor Turlock's church, Clarence swallowed hard and called him, asking him to come pray over her.

"Lord," Pastor Turlock prayed, "we claim the healing provided in the atonement of Jesus. 'By his stripes we are healed.' You healed lepers and gave sight to the blind and raised Lazarus from the dead. It's a small thing for you to heal this little girl. We believe you *will* heal her. We *know* you will heal her. We claim the promises of God for her healing. We claim the hundred-fold blessing you promise to those who serve you."

After praying the prayer numerous times in different ways, finally the pastor said, "Amen." Uncharacteristically, Clarence echoed his own loud "Amen." They walked out to the ICU waiting room, where Geneva and the pastor's wife had prayed and were now catching up on the past year.

"I'm sure the Lord's going to heal her, Clarence," Pastor Turlock told him.

Clarence nodded, attempting to be sure himself.

"God wants her well; we know that. He's going to heal her. He already has healed her. We just need to claim it."

"So, what about Dani?" Clarence asked.

"What do you mean?"

"If God wants all his children healthy, how come he allows them to die?"

"I guess she was gone before anyone could pray for her."

Clarence held the words that came to mind, afraid they would show a lack of faith.

"Have faith, Brother Clarence. Trust God that he'll raise this child up to health. Claim his promises."

After escorting the pastor and his wife out and trying to explain why they went to a different church now, Clarence and Geneva went back to Felicia's side.

He looked at her innocent face, so placid, and saw her mother's features. It took him back thirty-five years to when Dani was frightened one night and called him into her room to sleep nearby. Once she'd fallen asleep, Dani had looked just like Felicia did now, except no blue tubes and whirring machines.

Without warning, Felicia's face twitched. Her lips moved ever so slightly. Hope rose up in his chest.

"Felicia? Felicia honey? You're there, aren't you? You can hear me now, can't you?"

He saw what seemed to be a faint smile on her lips. She was coming back. He believed, he finally believed God was healing her. Her eyes opened slightly, like window blinds given a half turn. He knew she was looking at him.

"Oh, Felicia baby." He cupped her tiny left cheek in his big right hand. "It's so good to have you back where you belong!"

He was about to call the doctor, but his teary eyes locked on Felicia's droopy ones. Yes, he could see recognition in her eyes. She was seeing someone she knew. She was going to live!

Suddenly the eyes dropped closed and the lips fell limp. The machines started beeping. First a nurse, then a doctor came running into the room, yelling out orders.

Clarence stepped back. A whirlwind of activity followed, with blue and white outfits moving around the bed like medicine men performing a tribal dance. Clarence wondered if perhaps medicine men might have more power over life than these doctors did.

After a few minutes of chaos, calm returned to the room.

Felicia was gone.

———

Three days later Clarence stood at the graveside in front of the little white casket. The funeral had been worse than Dani's. Much worse. Pastor Clancy couldn't talk about what a full life Felicia'd had.

"Death is the destiny of every man," Clancy read from Ecclesiastes as he stood over the grave. "The living should take this to heart." He cleared his throat. "God had a wonderful purpose for this delightful child. Her life here was only five years long, but she was ready to meet the Lord—she always used to tell me Jesus was her best friend. Well, every one of us is going to die too. And God says we better take death to heart, to make sure we prepare for our own deaths. Felicia was ready to meet the Lord. The question is, are you?"

"A man shouldn't have to see his grandbaby die," Obadiah whispered to Clarence. "The Lord gives, and the Lord takes away." The old man's voice broke. "Blessed be the name of the Lord."

If you wouldn't do it for me, at least you could have done it for Daddy. Is this how you repay the people who serve you? Is this how you answer prayer? She was just a child. Just a little girl.

———

Another familiar face. The index cards of Dani's mind sorted themselves quickly and she remembered. Thirty-two years ago. The white woman who lived down the street from her aunt in Jackson. Diane McClure.

Dani and Antsy were visiting their aunt. Dani had been riding an unfamiliar bike, too big for her. Antsy wasn't with her on this ride. She'd strayed too far off the sidewalk and hit a mailbox, falling to the ground and crying. Mrs. McClure ran out of her house and fussed over her. "You poor darling."

She brought her inside. At first Dani was afraid; she'd never been in a white person's home before. Mrs. McClure gave her cookies and Kool-Aid. She sat with Dani and talked to her, asked her about herself as if she was genuinely interested. She was, Dani knew. Diane McClure had called her aunt to assure her Dani was safe and asked if she could stay and visit with her for awhile because her children were grown and Dani was such a delightful little girl.

The Carpenter had said that not even a cup of cold water given to one of his little ones would be forgotten in heaven. Mrs. McClure hadn't been forgotten, even though Dani hadn't thought much about her all those years. Now she hugged her tight.

"Thanks for the cookies. And thanks for loving me when I was so scared."

"It was my pleasure," Diane said. "Elyon used me to show his love to you. That's his way. There's no higher joy than to be used by him."

"That's true, isn't it?" Dani said. "On earth, it seemed like being used by someone was the worst thing. But the *best* thing is for Jesus to use you." Her eyes shone like a little girl safe and warm and eating cookies, and Diane McClure's shone like a woman helping a little girl in need.

Suddenly there came a rush of people with whom Dani had already been reunited. They ran past her and Diane, back toward the birthing room. What was going on? She followed them, finding Zeke and Nancy standing at the room's doorway from the other world.

"We have another arrival," Nancy said.

A tall dark warrior walked through the portal. Holding his hand, eyes wide with wonder, walked the most beautiful young girl Dani had ever seen. So beautiful that for a moment she didn't recognize her.

"Felicia! My baby!"

"What happened, Mommy?" Felicia asked. "I heard a loud noise and...where are we?"

Just as Dani started to speak, someone else stepped forward, the Answer to every question. Felicia stared at him, eyes full of wonder.

"Jesus is my best friend. You're Jesus, aren't you?"

"Yes. And you are my special friend too. I have a new name for you. But first, you have a question you want to ask me."

She scrunched up her face and asked, "Are you Aslan?"

The Carpenter laughed. "I have many names. Elyon. El Shaddai. Lion of Judah. Lamb of God. Jesus. Messiah. Ancient of Days. No one name is nearly enough. Yes, I am Aslan too. Would you like me to roar like a lion?"

Her eyes got big. He laughed and roared a playful but powerful roar. All those around saw the delighted face of the child peering deeply into the eyes of one both Lion and Lamb.

Dani hugged Felicia again. Though she hadn't been away from her long, she was eager to share this place with her.

"You can talk with her at the welcoming feast," the Carpenter said to Dani. "But now is my time with her. I have first claim on her, you know. You loved her for five years. I loved her before I created the universe."

Dani watched them walk off together: a child so small that every aspect of this place was a wonder crying out to be explored, a God so big that every relationship was unique, every conversation fresh, every destination tailor-made to each of his children.

Zeke and Nancy came up to Dani. "Finally I have a chance to ask you," Dani said. "I know I have a special link with you. But what is it? Who are you?"

"We are your great-grandparents," Nancy said with obvious pride. "Felicia is our great-great-granddaughter. We've watched you, cheered for you, prayed for you, waited for you to join us here in the great cloud of witnesses."

"I was your father Obadiah's grandfather," Zeke said. "He never knowed me. I died when my little Ruth, Obadiah's mother, was still young. They sold me and tore me apart from my Nancy and my Ruth. I never seen neither of them again till I comes here. I had plans to come get them one day, but then the hounds chased me down when I was goin' for the railroad. The Underground Railroad, you know? Some very fine white people. I'll introduce you to 'em soon and then—"

"Zeke, let the girl settle in!" Nancy said. "There's plenty of time for stories and introductions. We've got the welcome banquet ready, and as usual you're just jabberin' away."

Zeke and Nancy both flashed toothy smiles. "Looks like we've got a combined banquet, with two guests of honor," Nancy said. "That is, if you don't mind sharing the spotlight with Felicia?"

"Mind? That would be wonderful."

As they stepped out of the birthing room, a boy walked in and stopped Dani in her tracks. It was a face she hadn't seen since two years ago. But then it was a drained, troubled face and a shriveled body with plastic tubes running into it. He looked so healthy now, so much more healthy than anyone on earth could ever look.

"Bobby!"

She hugged the boy so hard she was afraid she'd hurt him, but hurting didn't appear to be a problem here.

"Aunt Dani! I heard you'd come. I'm so glad to see you."

"Me too, Bobby, me too!" She looked at Zeke and Nancy. "Bobby's my nephew, my sister Marny's boy. He died of leukemia two years ago. He—what am I saying? You know all this, don't you?"

They laughed.

"Oh, Bobby. Remember just a few days before you died when you told your mama you'd seen an angel? That meant so much to her. You said you'd seen a black angel. Remember?"

Bobby laughed and put his head against Zeke's chest, knowing his great-great-grandfather wouldn't pass up this chance to tell the story.

"The one he thought was an angel," Zeke puffed out his chest in mock pride, "was me! He saw me through the portal as we were praying over him." Zeke whooped as if this was the funniest thing.

"Elyon made a great promise to me and Zeke," Nancy told Dani. "He said to us, 'You were faithful to me. Therefore, in every generation that comes from you some will follow me, and it will be your honor to welcome them to my world.'"

Dani and Bobby had locked arms, and she kept staring at him. "Oh, Bobby. We prayed so long and hard for you. It was so devastating to lose you. I wish your mama could see you, just for a minute."

"I can see her," Bobby said. "And we'll be together again soon. Time here moves quickly because there's so much to do, so much to see, so much to learn."

"Bobby," Nancy said, "take your aunt Dani to her banquet. We'll be there soon. Just somethin' we need to do first."

Dani and Bobby walked away, reminiscing and laughing, while Zeke and Nancy bowed their knees to pray for one of their own, whom they now viewed through the portal. He was a huge man with huge pain.

———————

It was a pleasant fall day, blue and green and bright, the sun unobscured. But Clarence's soul was in late November, in cold wet dreariness minus the warm fires of Thanksgiving. What he could see ahead was only stark cold December minus Christmas, and a New Year minus hope.

Where was that hundredfold blessing Pastor Turlock always spoke of? "If you work hard and say your prayers and read your Bible, everything will work out fine." Clarence had. It hadn't.

The rules seemed crooked, the game tilted and rigged. Had a man done this to him, he could have come armed with lawyers to prove his case and demand compensation. But God did not let himself be accountable to men.

You move us like pawns on the chessboard. We suffer and you sit back and don't even care about our pain.

Clarence spent an hour with his father in the living room, the old man spinning his old platters, the crooners. Nat King Cole, Brook Benton, Ben E. King, Johnny Mathis. Music that made you feel sad, yet somehow good. There was a certain obscure joy and hope in melancholy. Clarence could see it in his father's eyes.

"Now them boys knowed how to sing," Obadiah said, "Lordy, Lordy, did they know how to sing!"

Clarence felt only the empty sadness with no sense of joy or hope. The music took him nowhere but deeper into the black hole. He put on Chuck Barry, and even he couldn't get him out. Clarence left his father in the living room and opened the front door.

"Where you goin', baby?" Geneva called from the kitchen.

"For a walk."

By the time she said, "I'll come with you," he was gone, the door shut behind him.

The world he had seen two weeks ago bore little resemblance to this one. It reminded him of the vacation he and Geneva had taken to Italy. One day they were in warm, sunny, musical, carefree Venice, in love and filled with laughter. They enjoyed it so much they planned to come back a week later, the day before heading home. But a week later it was different. Cold, dark, slimy. The semi-septic ooze of the streets stank dreadfully. The bright welcome byways had become menacing alleys threatening to swallow them up. Venice was both their most loved and most hated city in the world.

Clarence walked tonight in the second Venice, this time without even a companion to share the misery. He returned home an hour later, neither knowing nor caring how long he'd been gone. He retreated into his office.

Why are you silent, God? Is there something more I have to do? Do I need to work harder still?

The framed "I have a dream" speech on the wall mocked him.

That's all it was, just a dream, never a reality. Martin's gone. So's Mama. And Darrin. And Dani. And Felicia. So's the dream.

He emerged after an hour alone in his office. Everyone had gone to bed. He saw the Narnia books in their slipcase, lying outside Keisha's door. He resisted the impulse to dump them in the garbage.

He retreated to the dark lonely basement, the mirror image of his soul. Clarence sat down on his mother's old chair. For an instant her familiar scent comforted him. But in the next moment he flung his arm across the coffee table, knocking over a rack of coasters, a few magazines, and the family Bible. He looked at the Bible just lying there, propped open, misshapen and lifeless. He didn't move to pick it up.

He walked up the steps and out the front door, grabbing his car keys from the fireplace mantle. He left the house without saying anything, got in the car and drove away, while Geneva, wide awake, prayed for him in their bedroom.

He pulled up to a Gresham tavern. He'd never been in it before. Hadn't been in any tavern for ten years at least. He ordered a Jack Daniels on ice. Then he tried a bottle of Colt 45 malt liquor. It didn't work either. The sweat, the stale perfume and cigarettes of this shadowy place held no attraction for him. He didn't know why he was here unless it was to get back at God. He sat at the far end of the bar. A few times the bartender thought he heard him say something, but no one was there.

I thought you just gave the best to your children. All I wanted was a home in the country where I could enjoy my wife and kids and my sister and her kids, and they could be safe. Was that asking too much? Were my dreams too big for you, was that it?

In another place, the rough, eternally scarred hands of a Carpenter reached out toward one who pushed them away. No stranger to suffering, he heard the man's words as if they were the only words being spoken in the universe.

"No, my son. This is not the time. That is not the place. Your dreams were not too big for me. They were too small."

After a long day at the *Trib,* Clarence came in the front door and went straight to his home office again. He brushed by the kids and closed the door, ignoring the smells of pot roast.

Keisha came up to Geneva.

"How come Daddy's mad at me, Mommy?"

"He's not mad at you, honey. He loves you. This is just a real hard time for him. He misses Aunt Dani. And Felicia. He's...got a lot of things inside. You need to keep praying for him, okay? Right now Daddy's just mad at...the world."

An hour later Clarence came out of his office and surprised Geneva by coming to her.

"We need to talk."

"Good," she said. "I'd like that. Then you can eat your dinner."

"I've been thinking about what you said."

"About what?"

"About staying at Dani's place for a while," Clarence said. "Maybe we should go ahead and move there, just for a couple of months until we can get in the new place."

"Really?"

"Isn't that what you suggested?"

"Yes, but...I was sure you'd say no. I never gave it another thought."

"Well, I did."

"What changed your mind?" Geneva sounded suspicious.

"You did. We've got to live somewhere. We can't really afford to rent a place, and Dani's house is just sitting there. For a few month's rent we can fix it up a bit. If we leave it sitting there, it'll just get ripped up and turned into a drug house or something. Dani always wanted us in her neighborhood. Celeste and Ty can keep going to their school, like the psychologist suggested. Just for a few months. Maybe this is the best thing after all."

Geneva nodded, still not looking so sure, still wondering what was really going on in her husband's head.

"Clarence? Ollie. Sorry to call you at home. Listen, I talked with your friend Mookie today."

"What'd you think?"

"I don't know. It's a start, but he just didn't get a good enough look at these guys. No scars, no tattoos, nothing. I talked to gang division. How many Hispanic males with dark brown hair you think live in this city? Light mustache? It could be shaved tomorrow, or by now it's a heavy mustache. Lots of them wear T-shirts. What are we supposed to do, line up five hundred Hispanic males so Mookie can pick one out in a lineup?"

"What about the car?"

"Impalas and Caprices are the most common car type they've got. And low-rider? Would have been more distinctive if it wasn't. There's probably a hundred cars at least that fit the description."

"You going to follow up on those that do?"

"Doesn't seem real practical," Ollie said. "Needle in a haystack."

"A haystack that has only a hundred pieces of hay?"

"Good point." Ollie hesitated. "Something else you should know. Manny isn't so sure he believes Mookie."

"Why not?"

"He's just skeptical. Especially since you paid him a hundred bucks."

"Or is it that he can't stand the idea the killers were Hispanics?"

"Give him a break." Ollie sounded disgruntled. "He has his doubts, but we're still pursuing it, okay? I already fed Mookie's info into GREAT."

"Into what?"

"It's a computer system. Stands for Gang Regulation, Evaluation, and Tracking. There's some detailed gang information on the different sets and their homeboys. It's for cross-linking. You can search for info by all kinds of criteria. Quite a few police departments input their gang info. Problem is, our input is still pretty vague. But we might get something. Keep your fingers crossed. And one more thing. The police armorer looked over a shell casing from your sister's porch. He thinks he's got a lead on the murder weapon. I've asked him to walk me through it in detail. He's coming up tomorrow morning at nine. Thought you might want to sit in."

"Well, I have to work on a column, but...yeah, I'll be there. Thanks." Clarence hung up, glad he had a head start on tomorrow's deadline. He'd do some more work on it tonight.

He couldn't get his mind off Manny.

Don't want to work against your own kind, is that it?

"Were you always there with me, Torel?"

"Since you were a child. Elyon sent me to protect you."

"Children really have guardian angels then?"

"Did not the Carpenter warn you not to look down on little children because their angels always behold the face of my Father in heaven? We seek to protect them. And we also plead their case to the Almighty when injustice is done to any child—male or female, black or white, born or unborn. We call upon him to bring vengeance."

She trembled at the way he said this.

"I wasn't aware of you, Torel. Although...sometimes I felt someone was there. Not only God, but someone else."

"It was me you sensed. I was there every moment, never sleeping, always watching."

Suddenly earthly images appeared and Dani saw herself asleep in the backseat of an old brown Studebaker, her head resting on Clarence's shoulder. Marny was on Clarence's other side, Daddy driving, Mama next to him in the front. They'd been visiting Uncle Elijah and Aunt Emily and got a late start home. It was about midnight.

"I remember! Daddy missed the turnoff to Puckett that night, and it was an hour before we got turned around. He was really disgusted with himself. And Mama and Clarence and Marny didn't notice either. Of course, I was asleep."

She watched the scene and suddenly saw five huge forms, five guardians hovering inside and outside the car.

"Torel. I see you there!"

"Yes, and my comrades."

"The car's coming right to the junction where Daddy was supposed to turn."

She watched in bewilderment as all four angels seemed to cover the eyes of the waking passengers while Torel touched Dani's right leg. She cried out in pain.

"I remember that! It was this terrible cramp. I woke up screaming. *You* did that to me?"

"Yes. Keep watching."

Everyone in the car turned toward Dani, distracted by her panic, while they drove right past the junction. By the time she settled down and stopped screaming the junction was a quarter mile behind them. None of them had seen it.

Suddenly the view changed. She saw two cars piloted by drunk drivers racing down the road from Puckett, coming toward the junction they had passed. They occupied both lanes, drag racing at eighty miles an hour.

"You mean...?"

"This is what would have happened," Torel said.

She watched still another scene, a replay of the original, but without Torel touching her leg and without the other guardians closing the family's eyes to the road. Obadiah made the correct turn at the junction. Three minutes later he suddenly exclaimed, "What's goin' on?"

Four headlights abreast came at them. Dani felt she was right there in the backseat, suddenly waking up as Mama reached back to the children and cried out. Daddy flipped on and off his bright lights, swerved to the edge of the road, but couldn't get out of their way. One of the cars smashed into them head-on. Dani saw the old Studebaker crumple and roll and burn. She saw herself and her family tossed and battered. Mama and Daddy were killed instantly, as was Marny. She watched as Clarence died a few minutes later. She alone still lived, unconscious, lying in that mangled heap of burning metal, bleeding to death.

She watched the scene in stunned silence. Finally she spoke.

"Thank you for giving me that cramp," Dani said, her voice trembling.

"You are welcome," Torel said. "Your leg was sore off and on for a few days. You could not run the race at the county fair that Saturday. You were very disappointed."

"Yes, I was. But looking at it now...Torel, were there other times like this?"

"Yes. Many more."

"Will you show them to me?"

"If you wish. But now there is much we need to discuss. What do you think of your new home?"

"It's wonderful beyond belief. To have a body and soul free of the compulsion to sin. I can't understand how disobedience ever appealed to me when it always hurt Elyon, hurt me, hurt everyone. Sin never did good. Why did I do it? I'd no sooner commit a sin against Elyon now than I would have drunk a gallon of motor oil on earth. It has no attraction—it's just so repulsive. No envy here. No jealousy. I didn't comprehend the depth of the darkness either of that world or the darkness within me. They waged war against who Christ made me to be. I feel as though I was on the *Titanic*, sinking, and I've been rescued. Rescued by Elyon and by you, my friend."

Torel nodded his appreciation for the recognition of his role, belated as it was.

"I used to say that handicapped people would be especially glad for heaven,"

Dani said. "No doubt that's true, but I never realized until now how handicapped I was. Disabled by self-centeredness, self-preoccupation, self-pity, self-everything. Handicapped by the racial prejudice of others toward me, and mine toward others. Handicapped by reading in racial prejudice where there was none. Handicapped by indifference to many things that mattered to Elyon. Here I feel delivered from myself. Free to be the self Elyon intended me to be. Instead of the universe revolving around me, I am revolving around Elyon. He is my center of gravity."

"Well said, daughter of Eve. Some of your people have told me this realm is not what they expected. Is that true for you?"

"In countless ways. For one thing, I didn't expect I'd be able to go walking in the mud, squishing my toes in it." Dani laughed hard and long, delighted at the experience and looking forward to doing it again. "I've already walked in meadows and forests like nothing I ever imagined on Earth. But the truth is, I seldom thought about heaven there. It seemed too 'pie in the sky,' you know?"

Torel gazed blankly, as if he didn't know.

"Had I any inkling, I would have thought about heaven every hour. I see now that those whose minds are set on heaven serve Elyon most faithfully on earth— because they draw their beliefs and values and hopes from this world, not that one. Too often I thought of earth as the real place and heaven as something unreal. Now I see heaven is the real place, the substance. It is earth that seems intangible, shadowy, less real."

"Many of your people," Torel said, "seem surprised to find how earthly heaven is."

"Yes, it is earthly, but in all the good ways and none of the bad ones. Maybe that's why I love squishing my toes in the mud. I thought we would just be spirits here."

"Elyon created you dust and breath, body and spirit," the angel said. "That is what it means to be human. You do not become inhuman here, but fully human, all he intended you to be. You ate there, you feast here. You walked there, you run here. You snickered there, you laugh here. This is a physical world because it was made for you and you are physical as well as spiritual. If it is a place prepared for humans, as the Carpenter promised you, then it could only be a human place, both spiritual and physical. Your old body was destroyed by the ravages of sin and death. You will be reclothed in the resurrection body, but you now have a temporary body that allows you to experience this world, all the while awaiting the reclothing, the merger into your eternal body. You will not be complete until the resurrection. But you always have been and always will be human."

Clarence left home early. He decided to treat himself to breakfast, to mull over the events shaping his life.

As he drove, his mind drifted to that foreign planet, Mississippi of the fifties, which he so loved and hated, which would always and never be his home. That unforgiving landscape, forever frozen in his mind, that place of Third World conditions where many blacks and some whites had lived in illiteracy, malnutrition, windows without glass, no running water, no electricity. Trips to the outhouse were as routine then as selecting CDs was for his kids now. Many couldn't afford to take their children to the doctor.

In those days Mississippi was the slowest movin' place on God's green earth. When you went to the store and sauntered up with a Dr. Pepper and a dime, the friendly Gomer Pyle behind the counter would say something like, "Fixin' ta buy ya a soda, are ya?"

In Mississippi Clarence had come to believe something he would later labor to overcome—that the American dream was a white man's dream. For it was in Mississippi that the South drew its last line against the dreams of the uppity Negro.

Mississippi memories weren't all bad. Most of them were good. He remembered the rolling store, usually a step van or panel truck. The white driver sounded the horn to announce it was coming. Crowds of barefoot children materialized out of nowhere. They had no refrigerator at home, so the ice cream was especially welcome. His favorite was stage plank—slender, gingerbread-type cake with thinly spread icing, eight inches long and four inches wide. When you're poor it's quantity over quality. The bigger the better. They were two for a nickel. He and Dani would share one, then they'd save the other for later, sometimes in the middle of the night, devouring it over their whispers. Stage plank always tasted better in the dark.

Clarence pulled into the parking lot of Krueger's Truck Stop. The restaurant itself triggered more memories. When he was a kid, his father would never stop at a Stuckey's Restaurant because blacks weren't welcome there. Instead, they'd buy sandwich fixins at a store and eat in the car, then stop to "use the restroom" by the side of the road when no colored restrooms could be found. When they traveled overnight, usually for family funerals or weddings, they'd drive up to hotels that had big "Vacancy" signs. But Daddy would come back to the car and whisper to Mama, "They say there ain't no rooms left."

"Uh huh," Mama would say, knowingly, not wanting to discuss it in front of the children.

"It's all right, Mama," Daddy'd say, forcing that winsome smile. "Better folks than us been told 'no room in the inn.'"

As Clarence walked into Krueger's, a black man walked out, holding the door open for him. They exchanged knowing looks and nods. He remembered his father greeting black folk. There would always be the side glance, the slight nod of the head, the mutual recognition like foghorns blown by passing boats floating on a great white sea. The acknowledgments looked outwardly similar to what two white men might exchange, but inwardly they were very different. For two black men in America share a sense of camaraderie like two Englishmen in Saudi Arabia or two men in a foxhole. That's why, Clarence thought, black men often call black men they don't know "brother" and white men never do.

As he stood in the restaurant lounge waiting to be seated, he caught what seemed to be a scornful stare from the white trucker seated in front of a nearly empty plate. He had that look of a Klansman without the sheet.

Just when one nigger finally leaves, another one walks in to take his place.

The man didn't say that, of course. He might not have even thought it. The look of scorn might be because he had a thousand miles and an overdue load and a case of heartburn. A white man seeing the same look might think nothing of it. But Clarence was not white and he had seen too many similar looks later proven to be racist to assume this one was anything different.

A busy, blustering waitress, doubling as hostess, seated him. He knew what he wanted without looking at the menu. Like shells and seaweed, memories from his childhood washed up onto the beaches of his mind. Sometimes he could identify the winds and waves that carried them. More often he could not.

Now he was nine, Dani five. Vacations were mostly just for white folk, but this time Daddy added a few days to a family wedding and said, "We's gonna kick up our heels, what you think about that?" They thought it was grand.

The highlights of their rare vacations weren't the historic spots or natural wonders, but eating in restaurants. On this trip they went so far north that twice they were served by white waitresses. It seemed so strange. Clarence remembered how nervous he felt. Whites serving blacks. The very thought was incredible.

One particular day, they stopped to eat in the eastern part of Mississippi, past Meridian, he recalled, right on the verge of western Alabama. On this day, forever engraved in his memory, Clarence's family accidentally stepped into the wrong restaurant. They hadn't seen the "Whites Only" or "No Coloreds" sign. Maybe there wasn't one—in some places, smaller towns especially, this was simply understood. No sign was necessary, any more than a sign that said "Keep your hands off the grill."

The children didn't look for the signs, but the adults were always wary, on guard, watching for the posted signs and the unposted ones—the ones you could see in the eyes and body language of the white folk who turned and looked when you entered.

They strayed that morning, trespassed as commoners into the king's court. Harley, the oldest, followed his parents in, shadowed by Ellis, Darrin, Marny, Clarence, and Dani. As the children smelled the pancakes and syrup and looked at the tall glasses of orange juice, Obadiah and Ruby Abernathy were watching something else—the icy stares of customers and employees. But they weren't all icy, Clarence recalled. Some were pained and troubled. Maybe they thought of themselves as good people, and good people couldn't like what would happen next.

The waitress at Krueger's yanked Clarence back to the moment, laying in front of him a massive side of crispy hash browns piled high and his three eggs and three pancakes the size of Frisbees. Truckers demand not just good food but lots of it. Clarence came here because he was a trucker disguised as a journalist.

He went back to the entryway of that eastern Mississippi restaurant, smelling the delights, itching to be seated in one of those green upholstered booths. A Mississippi waitress—Clarence remembered her name tag said "Glenda"—stepped forward, in her white nurse-like uniform, only with a lower neckline and shorter skirt. Glenda looked like a lot of waitresses in small southern towns, about forty, made-up, flirtatious, efficient, and hardened to the wisecracks and local gossip.

Clarence had met eyes with Glenda at the very moment she looked over at the doorway where the Abernathys entered. She closed her eyes in what seemed a distressed response. In his peripheral vision Clarence saw people at table after table stop chewing, nudge each other, nod toward the doorway. People reacted like that toward two kinds of people—those above them, such as rich folk and professional athletes and Hollywood stars, and those below them, largely limited to niggers.

Glenda stepped across the center stage of his mind. She was strong—to this day Clarence could envision her pouring ice water in the lap of a customer whose advances weren't welcome. But she wasn't strong enough that day to keep from doing what she did.

"I'm sorry," she said to Obadiah and Ruby. "This isn't...I mean, there's a restaurant with a colored window down the way. It's called Dottie's. On your left just before you leave town."

She hadn't said, "No colored here," or "Whites only here." What she did say meant the same, of course, but she would sleep better having said it that way. Clarence always remembered how she seemed to choke a bit, to hesitate. She was one of many white southerners who would never defend burning crosses, lynching black men, riding horses with bed sheets flying in the wind. She wasn't one who invented the status quo. She was simply one who maintained it. A woman brave when it came to working hard and teaching her children to do right and telling off a man who didn't respect her, but cowardly or ignorant or both when it came to resisting a degrading system so long in place, so long assumed to be right.

Mama's eyes challenged Glenda, as they sometimes did when she sensed white guilt, when she knew a conscience was there. If it was a Klansman or a hardened racist, she never bothered. Partly out of fear, partly because it was just no use. "Don't cast your pearls before swine," she'd said to Obadiah when he tried to convince a dogmatic and self-assured white minister that coloreds really did have souls.

But as Mama's eyes tried to burn into Glenda the message, "We're people too, you know," the rest of Mama backed away. Daddy didn't nod, as if not wanting to bend, but by ushering out the children, their hopes for the meal suddenly dashed, he bent. They walked back out to the parking lot, Daddy's back straight as a board, as if to reclaim the dignity of which he'd just been stripped.

When they got in the car, Mama leaned over and laid her head down beside Daddy, as if her neck could no longer bear the weight. "Maybe that's why coloreds exist," Clarence heard Mama whisper to Daddy in a despairing voice. "So poor white folk don't has to spend their lives always lookin' up to others. So they can has someone to look down on too."

"Now, now, Mama," Daddy said and held her close with his right arm, his left on the steering wheel. Clarence heard what sounded like a deep moan, followed by deathly quiet. Though they'd never discussed it, Clarence somehow knew all his brothers and sisters could recount those moments as easily as he, whether or not they wanted to. He particularly remembered the silence.

"A colored window." Clarence's disappointment at those words was as palpable now as it had been thirty-five years earlier. It wasn't the disappointment of being told again he was inferior. He'd gotten used to that, so he told himself. It's that they wouldn't have the smells and sights that came from being inside a restaurant. They'd get food from the "colored window" all right, but they'd have to eat in the car, or at best a bench or sidewalk. After Daddy ordered through the colored window at Dottie's, he said, "These folks believes all money's created equal, even if all people isn't."

Funny what you remember.

Clarence looked around the room at Krueger's, at all the white folk, outwardly indistinguishable from those in that other restaurant, which it seemed like he'd been in only yesterday. Seeing those in this room here and now, he supposed he knew exactly what they too really thought of him.

Clarence's mind moved from Glenda to Mr. Spelling, the golf course owner, four years later, where Clarence and his brother Ellis applied for jobs as caddies but were turned down because—because of why they were always turned down.

"Now, I'm no racist," Mr. Spelling insisted. "Those are just the rules."

Well, you own the golf course don't you? You make up the rules. If you don't like 'em, change 'em.

Clarence realized now Mr. Spelling spoke of "the rules" in a broader sense. It was just the way life was. He was apologetic. This made him feel better, not as guilty. He knew he was fair and open-minded, even benevolent. That's what it was when whites thought it was okay for blacks to have more rights—it wasn't simple justice, but benevolence, as if it took a special virtue to believe other people shouldn't be treated as inferiors. Funny, people never thought of themselves as especially virtuous just for thinking stealing was wrong. But they thought a great deal of themselves for believing discrimination wasn't quite right.

Clarence pushed around the dwindling food morsels on his plate as if they were pieces of a jigsaw puzzle. As if by looking underneath the potatoes he'd find the answers to life.

Glenda and Mr. Spelling, Clarence reflected, were what Reverend Sharo at the black Baptist church called "little racists." Big racists were the KKK types, the cross burners, the ones that would call you "nigger" and spit on you and beat you up as long as there were at least three of them for every one of you. But Reverend Sharo always said they weren't the dangerous ones. Bad as they were, the devil only had so many big racists. But Glenda and Mr. Spelling were the nice people, the church-goers, schoolteachers, police officers, businessmen, mayors, milkmen, and mail car-riers. They made the community what it was, they made the wheels turn. The wheels of commerce. The wheels of benevolence. The wheels of oppression and injustice. They were the little racists.

Clarence recalled Reverend Sharo's sermon on how the midwives went against Pharaoh and protected the Jewish boys. He talked about the Jews and Nazi Germany and what was later called the Holocaust, while it was still fresh in people's minds. Sharo said it wasn't Hitler and the Nazi insiders who slaughtered the Jews. Dozens of the devil's men, even hundreds or thousands of them, couldn't pull off the mur-ders of all those millions. The key was normal people, those who thought of them-selves as decent folk. Those who wouldn't kick a Jew to death, but would look the other way when someone else did. It was the normal people who made holocausts happen, the "good folk" who tolerated unspeakable evil.

Mr. Spelling and Glenda were nice enough white folk. They seemed hurt and irritated, as if *they* were being victimized, as if the Negroes ought to be more sensi-tive and not put them in these awkward situations by coming into a restaurant or asking for a job. The tragedy wasn't so much the brutality of bad people as the silence of good people.]

Where were Glenda and Mr. Spelling now? Clarence wondered. It seemed yes-terday, but they'd be in their eighties or nineties or dead. If alive, what did they think now of what they had done? If dead, what was their perspective? Could they see their hearts and actions now through the eyes of eternity? Does moral blindness stop at the grave, or does it go beyond it?

"I'm no racist." Why was it so important to Mr. Spelling to say that? Who was calling him a racist but his own conscience? Perhaps it was the God he worshipped on Sunday morning, but whose truths didn't seem to make much difference week-days.

Clarence looked down at his empty plates. Where had all the food gone? He tried to recount the pleasure of the tastes, but he'd missed them while absorbed in the videotapes of his memory. He took his last sip of coffee, paid at the counter, then walked briskly to the restroom, occupied by two white men. They were rednecks, he assumed, who pretended not to notice he was black. He straightened his tie, checked to be sure his Ferragamo shoes were still shiny, then headed out the door to a world that had changed since his childhood days, much for the better and much for the worse.

Clarence drove downtown and parked his car in the all day parking garage on the fourth floor next to the elevator, then walked briskly toward the *Trib*. He was about to pass two older white women when one of them looked over her shoulder and saw him approaching. She stepped closer to her friend and clutched her purse tight. Clarence pretended not to notice, not to care.

Funny what you remember.

––––––––––

Ollie escorted Clarence to his desk in the midst of homicide, surrounded by other desks buried in a quantity of paperwork that rivaled even the *Trib*. Ollie's own desk looked as if it'd been rifled by a burglar.

"Manny's working on the new case. We're doing a juggling act." Ollie pointed at the piles of paperwork. "That murder last night? Ugly. Not our case, but Eisenzimmer briefed me on it. Really shook him up, and he's seen more homicides than anybody in this city. A fifteen-year-old boy shot in the head at point-blank range, execution style."

Both men shuddered.

"Get you some coffee?" Ollie asked. Clarence nodded. "Black?"

"Yeah," Clarence said. "But I'll have cream in my coffee."

Ollie looked at him, unsure whether or not he should smile. "The sergeant should be here any minute," Ollie said. After an uncomfortable silence, he asked, "Have you heard they're thinking about changing the name of the Washington Bullets?"

"For political correctness you mean?" Clarence asked.

"Yeah. They're tired of having a name that's synonymous with violence," Ollie said. "So from now on they're just going to call them the Bullets."

Clarence didn't smile.

"What's the difference between a journalist and a catfish?" Ollie tried again.

Clarence rolled his eyes. "I've heard it."

"So, Jake told you all about me? What exactly did he say?"

"He said you were brilliant. And that you didn't suffer from anorexia."

"Brilliant, huh? Anything else?" Ollie asked.

"That I'd never mistake you for Gandhi."

Ollie let out a belly laugh. "Here comes the sergeant now." He reached out his hand to the slender uniformed officer carrying a black rifle case.

"Sergeant Terry McCamman, Clarence Abernathy. Clarence is with the *Tribune*,

but don't hold that against him. I've invited him to sit in with us while you walk me
through the details. Okay with you?"

"No problem. First, I'm an armorer." McCamman spoke like a seminar leader
and looked at Clarence to see if there was a nod of understanding. There wasn't.
"That means I'm trained to repair weapons. Sort of like a gunsmith. I'm certified by
different manufacturers to fix their guns."

"Okay."

"Also, like most armorers, I'm a firearms enthusiast."

"He means gun nut," Ollie translated.

"Yeah." The sergeant laughed. "Anyway, the detective here gave a shell casing
to the SERT captain, then he passed it on to me just this morning."

"What's sert?" Clarence asked.

"You know, SWAT is Special Weapons and Tactics? SERT is Special Emergency
Response Team. They're just different names for the same thing. Anyway, as soon as
I saw this brass, I knew what it came from."

"Terry," Ollie said, "give me the explanation of how you know this, the one you
started on me yesterday when we didn't have time. Go slowly for us non-armorers,
okay?"

"Sure. Basically, there are three types of actions that drive automatic and semiautomatic weapons. One type is gas operation, where the gas created by the gun-
powder ignition is bled off a hole in the forward part of the barrel. That drives the
action. That's true of an M-16 or AK-47. The second type is a simple blowback, used
mainly in pistol caliber submachine guns. The round just drives the bolt to the rear
and cycles the gun. A MAC 10 or Uzi, for instance."

"Okay, I'm with you," Ollie said. "And the third type?"

"Delayed blowback. Some mechanical system delays the action cycle until
pressures are low enough to safely cycle the action."

"And what all this means as to our murder weapon is...what?" Ollie asked.

"Well, to jump to the bottom line, what it means is your weapon was manu-
factured by Heckler and Koch. It's almost certainly an HK53. I brought one up from
tactical so you could see it."

He took out of the case a black rifle, holding it like a mother holds a three-month-
old. The rifle was just under thirty inches long, a precision balance of solid steel and
durable black plastic. It wasn't quite rifle and not quite submachine gun. It looked very
sleek and solid, like something out of the future. Compact, with a telescoping buttstock
and a flashlight built into the forearm of the gun. Clearly this was no ordinary firearm.
It screamed quality from front to back, cutting a stark contrast to the mass-produced
weapons Clarence had seen, such as the AK-47. He could imagine it being hand-
crafted by a spectacled European artisan listening to Beethoven. Clarence didn't know
rifles very well, but he knew enough to be impressed with this one.

"Whoa," Ollie said under his breath. "Our perps are running around with one of *these?*"

"Germans are into quality," the sergeant said. Clarence could see the admiration on McCamman's face. He reminded him of a car mechanic pointing out the features of a brand new Mercedes. "Heckler and Koch leads the world in tactical weaponry for police and military."

"But I still don't see how you know that's our weapon," Ollie said.

"Okay. The HK system is very sophisticated and distinctive—it's called a delayed roller locking bolt. In order to reliably extract spent casings, the chambers of HK rifles and submachine guns are fluted. Look down this chamber and you can see it." He raised the gun, opening it up and positioning it just right.

"See that series of longitudinal flutes? They allow gas to come back around the case and prevent it from getting stuck in the chamber after firing. Once fired, the brass looks exactly like this." He held up the casing Ollie had passed on to him, pointing to the prominent black stripes dug into the brass, reaching over an inch down the one-and-three-quarter-inch casing.

Ollie and Clarence both moved in for a close look as McCamman pointed at the markings.

"The flutes in the chamber always leave these stripes. It's so distinctive that the moment I saw it I knew it couldn't be anything else. Go out to the range where the SERT team does target practice. HK brass is different from every other spent case out there. Very distinctive."

"And the magazines hold…how many rounds?" Ollie asked.

"The standard HK53 magazine holds twenty-five rounds. But there's lots of after-market magazines that hold forty."

"We had exactly forty shots," Ollie said. "A magazine change takes what, three or four seconds?"

"I can do it in two, no problem. But if you aren't as practiced, I'd say four seconds."

"Nobody reported a lull in the shooting," Ollie said. "It was continuous."

"Then you can pretty much count on the forty-round magazine. Even if you had the original twenty-five round mag, it would be easier and cheaper to buy a forty rounder at a gun show than get another twenty-five from HK. And gangbangers *do* shop at the gun shows—or send their girlfriends to shop for them."

"Plus the forty-round magazine would look a lot meaner," Ollie said. "And gangbangers are into looking mean."

"The HK53 fires seven hundred rounds per minute. So per second, that's what…?"

Both Terry and Ollie looked up in the air to punch one of those invisible calculators.

"Just under twelve rounds per second," Clarence said.

"I'm impressed," Ollie said. "So, Terry, what kind of noise would this baby make at midnight?"

"It would raise the dead, that's what it would do. This is thunder and lighting. It's a gangbanger's dream machine. It'll make any punk feel like he's God, for a few seconds anyway."

"More than your typical nine millimeter auto?" Ollie asked.

"No comparison. Much deeper, throatier, louder than a nine. If he kept the trigger down, the rounds are all gone in under four seconds. But that's the loudest four seconds you've ever heard."

"Why so loud?" Ollie said.

"The HK's got a rifle ammo, but it has this really short barrel." He held it up. "That means lots of noise. Did anybody see the shooter's face? It was probably visible with the muzzle flashes."

"What muzzle flashes?" Ollie asked.

"You mean nobody saw the gun actually firing?"

"Yeah. Mrs. Burns saw it. But she didn't mention any flashes."

"If she saw it firing she *had* to see muzzle flashes. I mean with an Uzi or an AK you're going to get little flashes, but with this baby we're talking flashes the size of softballs at least. I've seen them as big as basketballs. There must have been a lot of smoke, right?"

"Yeah," Ollie said, "a dozen neighbors saw the smoke, but by then the car was gone. The first patrolmen who got there said smoke was still hanging in the air."

"Sometimes just for fun," McCamman said, "we do hand loads to enhance the flash on this unit. Of course, from a tactical standpoint, flashes are bad. They nightblind the shooter and identify his position. But civilians aren't in combat, so they love all the flashes. Pretty macho stuff. You're sure nobody saw flashes?"

"Mrs. Burns wasn't wearing her glasses, and nobody else got to the window in time."

"Too bad."

"Isn't that much smoke unusual?" Ollie asked.

"Not with the HK53. It's this short barrel, just over eight inches. See you've still got unburned powder igniting after the bullet leaves the barrel. You know, in a longer barrel, the powder burns in the barrel with the bullet capping it, and there's just a little muzzle flash. I still can hardly believe it though."

"Believe what?" Ollie asked.

"That a gangbanger would carry an HK. I can count on a few fingers the crimes I've heard of committed with an HK. I mean, there was a California bank robbery where guys used HK rifles in their getaway to keep the cops back. And I think I heard a Missouri State Trooper was killed with one. But HKs are almost always used by the good guys. Certainly not by gangbangers."

"Why's that?" Ollie asked.

"Well, for one thing you're talking incredibly expensive. For the private citizen living in a state where automatic weapons are legal, over three thousand dollars. Police departments can get them for twelve hundred dollars, but that's a special deal. And even that isn't cheap. This is an uncommon weapon. You could buy four or five Uzis or AKs for the price of one of these. Now, Hollywood uses them. I've seen HKs in *Lethal Weapon, Die Hard*, Seagal's flicks, you name it. But on the street? Unheard of."

"Until now." Ollie scratched his chin. "All right, we know HK is the manufacturer. How can you be sure this one's the right model?" He nodded at the weapon now cradled in his arms.

"Well," Sergeant McCamman said, "HK makes a lot of rifles, but your shell casings are .223 caliber. That narrows it down to four. The HK G41 is extremely rare, I'd rule it out. The HK33, which is full-auto, but rifle sized, is possible. The HK93 is a civilian legal rifle, semiauto only. See this selector lever?" He pointed to a black switch on the side of the HK53. "This fire selector lets you choose between three different modes of fire. Semiautomatic, three round burst, or full automatic. You say the witnesses reported nonstop fire?"

Ollie nodded.

"Then you can eliminate the HK93, unless it was converted to auto, which I can't rule out. But I'd bet big bucks the HK53 is your weapon. Though I wouldn't have believed it if I hadn't seen the casing myself. And I still think somebody should have seen the flashes."

"Thanks, Terry. You've been a big help."

As McCamman took the weapon from Ollie, he said, "Your gangster found the full auto switch, and he's so impressed with himself he's dumping the entire magazine in a three second trigger squeeze. In a shoot-out, he'd be more accurate with the semiauto or three shot bursts. But when he dumps the load, I pity anyone who happens to be in front of this gun. They wouldn't have a chance."

McCamman left the room as Clarence fought off images of Dani and Felicia in a hail of gunfire.

"So, where does this put us, Ollie?" Clarence asked.

"It's a big break. We don't have the murder weapon, but we know the kind of murder weapon. It's uncommon, and that helps even more. Of course, maybe it was stolen that night to do the job. Maybe it was torn apart and buried. Maybe it'll never reappear again. But at least we've got something. Between your boy Mookie and the HK53, we've finally got something."

Clarence waited impatiently in the reception area outside Reggie Norcoast's office. His ten o'clock interview was supposed to have begun twenty minutes ago.

He watched Sheila, the receptionist, warm and transparent, friendly to a fault. In stark contrast stood Jean, the office administrator. Stiff suit, rigid posture, icily efficient. Colder than Duluth in January. Jean marched around the office making sure everything was just so, launching periodic darting glances to restrain Sheila's casual friendliness from its tendency toward dawdling.

Carson Gray walked into the room from his office. He gave out a series of rapid-fire orders to Jean and Sheila about calling people and canceling this and adding that and implying this was all the most important stuff since the dawn of time. Clarence noticed even the flowers outside Gray's office were lined up perfectly, mute soldiers to do his bidding. Suddenly Gray saw Clarence out of the corner of his eye and froze for an instant, caught by surprise.

"Mr. Abernathy." Gray didn't move toward Clarence. "What are you doing here?"

"My tax dollars pay for this office. Just thought I'd come and see what you're doing with them."

"Sheila, why is he here?"

"Mr. Norcoast told him he'd meet with him," Sheila said, cringing.

"Why wasn't I informed?"

"Maybe because," Clarence said, "you're not in charge of the universe."

"I don't have to take your insults, Abernathy. I *am* in charge of the councilman's schedule."

A lap dog, Clarence thought. A Chihuahua in a parked car, barking his brains out at anyone getting too close to the master's dominion. Clarence had seen his type before. Give him a little territory and he thinks he owns the world.

Clarence sat and stared icily as Gray and Sheila whispered, Gray expressing his displeasure in animated style. Jean stood in the background, her hands on her hips, posing for the female Carson Gray look-alike contest. If there was a not-a-happy-camper award to be given in this office, Carson and Jean were slugging it out for top honors.

Gray's pale skin highlighted blue penciled veins. There was something animal about his profile, lean and hungry. The sharp eyes, the slightly pointed ears, the dilating nostrils. And the thin lips. They were most striking. Clarence still had a habit of naming adversaries, as they'd always done in the projects. He toyed with several labels, including Chihuahua, Rooster Man, and Wolverine, but tentatively settled on Skinny Lips.

Gray came over to Clarence, now extending his hand, not in the promiscuous way of a politician, but in a reserved, street-smart way. Gray's forced grin detoured around a toothpick under his dark manicured mustache, revealing bad teeth that had been polished to make them appear normal to the undiscerning eye. The teeth and smile, infrequent and unattractive as it was, seemed sufficient to explain why this man was not a politician but his assistant.

Clarence didn't extend his hand back and Gray took it as the insult he intended. His expression changed.

"I don't know what your problem is, Abernathy. But you should know this. Reg Norcoast will tolerate you, but I won't. In politics, there are fights, and there are winners and losers. I choose my fights carefully, and I win them."

"I don't know who you think you're pushing around, Gray. I'm not Amos and I'm not Andy and I'm not here to entertain the plantation owner *or* his overseer. You got that?"

"I wonder what your publisher would think if he heard you talking like this."

"I don't know. Why don't you ask him?"

"Maybe I'll suggest to Reg he talk with Raylon Jennings about you."

"You do that, Gray." Clarence bit his lip. "Take your best shot, Skinny Lips." He said it before thinking.

Gray stared at him incredulously, then retreated to his office. As if on cue, Norcoast opened his door and drifted out of his own office, moving across the room swiftly and with dramatic flourish, like a woman dancing the tango.

"Clarence, Clarence, so good to see you. You've met my secretary, Sheila? And our administrator, Jean?"

Clarence nodded, noting Sheila's smile and Jean's glare. Norcoast shined his Norman Rockwell face, clean cut and ruddy, an Ozzie Nelson face from the fifties on a man otherwise born and bred for the nineties.

Despite making constant public photo-shoot appearances jogging and playing tennis, Norcoast was fifteen pounds overweight, five in the face and ten in his stomach, everything else being reasonably slender.

"Come on in," he said, motioning with his long right arm. Norcoast thought he was taller than he was, Clarence noted, as he slightly ducked his head walking through the doorway. Clarence, three inches taller, made a point of not stooping.

Just as they walked in the room, Sheila buzzed Norcoast.

"Sorry, Clarence," Norcoast said. "Real quick call here. No, you don't need to leave. Take a look at my art gallery." He gestured like a game show prize babe.

Clarence perused the wall. He saw Norcoast posing with the governor, senators, the president of the NAACP. Norcoast posing with children, teenagers, and adults in his own district. Norcoast with his foot on a shovel, breaking ground for a new community center. Norcoast with his arm on the shoulders of high school valedictorians,

Norcoast holding children in his arms, Norcoast and his wife and his teenage daughter hobnobbing with North Portland families. Norcoast, Norcoast, Norcoast.

The great white savior. General MacArthur of the projects.

Clarence recognized several pictures he was certain came from the *Trib*. A few looked like they had to be Carp's. Carp had her way with photos, cropping them just so. It was as distinctive as one columnist's stylistic differences from another. She was the best. He respected her work. Too bad these ended up on Norcoast's wall. Probably just asked his buddy Raylon, and he made sure these blowups got sent over.

Clarence came to one picture on the wall, shocked to see himself smiling and shaking hands with Norcoast. Of course. From the day of the rally. Carp's quick shot. Norcoast and his off-center burgundy tie, smiling like a schoolboy at a carnival.

Reggie Norcoast, Clarence believed, was a doer and receiver of favors. A man who used other people's money to endear himself to those who could further his ambitions. After serving a term as mayor, decades from now Norcoast would probably be one of those guys elected to his eighth term in Congress running on a platform of term limitations. To Clarence, anything short of drug dealing and grand theft auto would be a step up from politics. To Norcoast, everything else would be a step down.

Clarence took a seat as Norcoast got off the phone. He brushed aside the politician's attempts at small talk.

"Mr. Norcoast," Clarence began, "I want—"

"Please, Clarence. Call me Reg."

"Mr. Norcoast, I'd like to hear your perspectives on crime and gang problems in your district."

The councilman sighed. "Could you be a little more specific?"

"Okay, how about this? Is it true that in your last campaign you hired known gang members to pass out your literature, post signs, and take them down after the election?"

"Now wait a minute. That was legitimate work. I gave those boys a decent job, something good and constructive, an alternative to all the illegal stuff. They need jobs, Clarence. You know that."

"But gangbangers?"

"The fact that they haven't always made the best choices doesn't mean we shouldn't give them a chance. If they don't have the experience of a decent job, how can we expect them to say no to the temptations? I'm proud of hiring these kids, of giving them a chance. I wear it as a badge of honor."

"According to the records I'm looking at, you spent over twenty thousand dollars to put up and take down signs and pass out literature. Did most of this go to gangbangers?"

"I don't know the exact breakdown. You'd have to talk to Carson Gray about that."

"I don't want to talk to Gray," Clarence said. "I'm talking to you."

"Is this an interview or an interrogation?"

"Don't you think hiring gangbangers implies that gang life is okay? And isn't there potential for intimidating the public? Like if someone found out you voted for another candidate, you might have to answer to a group of young thugs?"

"This is America," Norcoast said. "We have secret ballots here, remember? People can vote however they want without fear of reprisal. There's no intimidation. This isn't Chicago, this is Portland, Oregon. You should know better than to even suggest that."

"I've lived in Chicago, and I've lived in Portland. Both are in America. And there's no problem in Chicago that can't become a problem in Portland."

"Clarence, please." Norcoast's voice turned into a plea, almost a whimper. "We've accomplished a great deal in this city. Your own sister was one of my supporters. I've always felt I could count on the *Trib* to show the positive side of my district."

"Well, you're right, Councilman, there has been a lot of positive press about your district, but this column isn't about the positive. It's about crime. Unless, of course, you can find a positive angle on gangs roaming the streets and people getting blown away in their own homes."

"That's a harsh and unbalanced perspective," Norcoast said. "Don't you think your own experience has clouded your ability to be objective?"

"You don't seem worried about objectivity when the *Trib* does a puff piece on you. Or when it endorses you every time you run for office."

"Now hold on, Clarence. Let's not take an adversarial tone here. We're both on the same side."

"And what side is that, Mr. Norcoast?"

"*Please* call me Reg. We're both on the side of progress. The progress of ideals, the promotion of diversity, the battle against racism, the commitment to opportunity."

"Well, I'm just on the side of reporting the truth and giving my opinion on it," Clarence said. "I don't care if it's positive or negative. I just want a piece that's accurate. I know politicians succeed in proportion to their skill at lying. You know better than to tell the truth to the press. But maybe today you could make an exception?"

Norcoast's left cheek twitched. Clarence heard something and looked under his desk.

Councilman. You're shuffling your feet like a four-year-old needing to go tinkle.

"Now, Clarence—"

"Please, Mr. Norcoast, just call me Mr. Abernathy."

After returning to the Trib and getting back to a half-dozen phone calls, Clarence put his fingers on the keyboard and started the next day's column. Like an extemporaneous speech that's twenty years in the making, his column came from deep within, having been forged in the fires of many years' thoughts and experiences:

> The slaveowners were pro-choice. They said, "Those who don't want to have slaves don't have to, but don't tell us we can't choose to. It's our right." Those who wanted to make slaveholding illegal were accused of being anti-choice and anti-freedom, of trying to impose their morality on others.
>
> The civil rights movement, like the abolitionist movement one hundred years earlier, opposed the exercise of free choice that much of society defended. It was solidly anti-choice when it came to racial discrimination. Historically, whites had a free choice to own slaves, and later to have segregated lunch counters. After all, America was a free country. But the civil rights movement fought to take away that free choice from them. Likewise, the women's movement fought to take away an employer's free choice to discriminate against women.
>
> Nearly every movement of oppression and exploitation—from slavery to abortion—has labeled itself "pro-choice." Likewise, opposing movements offering compassion and deliverance have been labeled "anti-choice" by the exploiters.
>
> In reality, the pro-choice position always emphasizes one person's right to choose instead of the other's. But what about the *victim's* right to choose? Blacks didn't choose slavery. Jews didn't choose the ovens. Women don't choose rape. And babies don't choose abortion.

He pressed the word count button. Only two hundred words, a quarter of the way to a column. He'd have to flesh it out, tie it to some current event of the last few days. He took some comfort knowing how many toes he would step on. But he also hoped maybe he would do some good. Maybe somebody out there would listen.

Clarence and Jake went out to a late lunch at Lou's Diner, which Jake called "the diner time forgot," a throwback to the fifties. The owner, Rory—Jake's friend—waited on them hand and foot, bringing them complimentary mochas after their burgers, as the jukebox played "Under the Boardwalk," "Stop in the Name of Love," and an endless parade of old hits. They talked and laughed for forty minutes.

"So, how's it going with Ollie?" Jake asked. "Sounds like he's gone out of his way for you."

Clarence shrugged. "He's okay, I guess."

"Okay? Is that all?"

Clarence sat stiffly, saying nothing.

"It's still the brutality charge, isn't it?" Jake asked. "Sometimes people get accused of stuff. It doesn't mean they're guilty."

"You think I don't know that? I'm a black man, remember?"

"Maybe you should forget you're black," Jake said, "and just think of yourself as a man."

"Easy for you to say."

"Yeah, maybe it is. But maybe it's still right. You taught me that, Clarence. You used to tell me how much it bugged you that people made skin color such an issue. But lately you've been doing it. It's as though you don't trust Ollie just because he's white. And frankly it makes me feel like you must not trust me either. I'm white too, you know."

"Really? I hadn't noticed." Clarence smiled.

"Look," Jake said. "You still haven't talked to Ollie about the brutality charge, have you?"

"No."

"Then do it. If you don't, I'll ask him to talk to you about it."

"It's none of your business."

"Yeah it is. You're my brother, Clabern. And Ollie's my friend. And I'm the one that linked you up—I mean, after you met at Dani's. It's my business, all right. You talk to him or I'll have to."

"Is that a threat?"

"It's a promise."

Clarence drove home brooding. It stung him that Jake didn't understand his skepticism about the police. Jake's father hadn't been beaten by police because of the color of his skin. Jake wasn't a suspect in every crime committed by someone of his race. He wasn't pulled over three or four times a year for no good reason.

Clarence recalled some of his tense conversations with Jake during the O. J. Simpson trial. On the one hand, Clarence hated the race-bating. He wrote a column taking on Johnny Cochrane for not just playing the race card but the whole deck. He'd been disgusted and embarrassed when Cochrane told the jury that to show opposition to LAPD's racism, they needed to acquit O. J. As if whether the evidence indicated Simpson was the killer wasn't the *real* issue. As if even if he was guilty of murdering two people he should go free because Mark Fuhrman was a racist jerk.

As if one man saying the word *nigger* was sufficient reason to acquit another man for two vicious murders.

Clarence couldn't buy the full-scale conspiracy theory against Simpson that would have involved forty police officers from seven different departments. But unlike Jake, he couldn't dismiss the possibility of racist conspirators at a smaller level, enough to raise reasonable doubt. Jake had seen it differently. To him, Fuhrman was just one bad apple. To Clarence, it was obvious there were a lot more bad apples in the barrel. Ollie Chandler might be one of them. And the fact he'd come from LAPD and was accused of brutality against a black man gave Clarence cause to believe he was.

Clarence understood Jake's world much better than Jake did his. When they crowded around their tiny black and white in the sixties, *My Three Sons, Ozzie and Harriet, Donna Reed,* and *Leave It to Beaver* allowed blacks to study the white world. All whites saw of the black world were the caricatures of Amos 'n Andy and Buckwheat and Stymie, and maybe Rochester on Jack Benny. This culture was a white man's culture, and blacks couldn't help but learn about white people, while whites could get by knowing almost nothing about blacks.

Just last week Clarence and Geneva had rented the movie *Out of Africa.* It struck both of them how Meryl Streep and Robert Redford were continuously surrounded by black Kenyans on the edges of the screen. The blacks were nothing but props, like the lions and wildebeests and trees. Clarence found himself thinking not about the white central characters, but the blacks in the supporting roles. Who were they? They were people, with families and inner lives and philosophies and theologies and joys and struggles, successes and failures. But they were portrayed as one-dimensional, like the natives surrounding Tarzan, who as one white man in the midst of a jungle full of blacks still managed to be the main character. Black Africans were no more than a backdrop for those at the center of the human drama—European and American whites.

Though he was less than ten in their heyday, Clarence remembered well the Clairol hair-coloring commercials, where they zoomed in for a closeup on a beautiful young white woman whose blonde hair rippled in the wind and captivated the viewer like a bleached version of a Greek goddess. Then a throaty voice affirmed, "Blondes have more fun." There was no such thing as a blonde Negro. People like him were destined not to have fun.

Clarence hadn't been around many whites in Mississippi, but he was aware that white people *did* have more fun for at least two reasons—the way they looked and the money they had. The only people in town with convertibles were white. The only blondes were white. The only rich people were white. Black men served the whites as hired laborers, black women as domestics, maids and cooks and house-cleaners and babysitters and such, getting up in the dark, catching two or three city buses to make it to the big houses in time to fix up breakfast. "Livin' large," that's how they described the white lifestyle, and all of them wanted it. Who wouldn't?

Clarence remembered Mama catching her buses to make it to the Haverstrom's to care for little Billy, Joseph, and Karen. When Mrs. Haverstrom decided to throw out their old clothes, Mama retrieved them from the garbage. They were Clarence's best clothes, white kid clothes, white kid jackets. It troubled him now that those clothes had meant so much to him.

He thought of how jealous he used to be of Billy, Joseph, and Karen when Mama showed him the picture of them with her, crowded up close to her as if she belonged to them. They had their own mother, yet all day they received the attention of his mother. Their gain was his loss. Did they ever ask to see a picture of him? He never met these kids. His mama crossed into their world every day. Not once did they cross into hers.

They probably thought she just disappeared at the end of her day, like an image in a Star Trek holodeck. When it was time again, she materialized from nowhere to serve them, a piece of scenery on the stage of their lives, a minor character in the drama of which they were stars, a drama in which coloreds, if they were lucky, only got bit parts as gardeners and maids.

Black people's hair was a silent testimony to their destiny. People who had fun possessed hair that blew in the wind. Black people's hair didn't blow in the wind. Black people's hair was steel wool. It couldn't be slung or tossed back out of their eyes— unless they imitated white people's hair, which dozens of hair care products encouraged them to do, thick greases to tame the nappiness as though it were a wild beast.

Maybe if they acted white and looked white and thought white, maybe then they could have fun. Maybe that's what he was thinking when he went to the old burn barrel out back and dumped it out and sifted through the white ashes and spread them all over his body. Clarence remembered looking in a mirror and feeling shame when he saw his black skin peeking out from behind the white.

Funny how he could forget the name of someone he met ten minutes ago, but he could never forget the flowing blonde mane of the white Clairol woman and the look and feel of the white ashes on his skin and the picture of the Haverstrom kids with Mama. His mama, not theirs.

He remembered Aunt Greta, his mother's sister, chastising him and his cousins for their mischief in the chicken coop. "Stop showin' your color," she'd said. Whenever they'd go out in public in a white area she'd say, "Don't go actin' like niggers, now."

He remembered how it angered him that when he got a little rowdy it was a federal offense, but it was fine for the white kids to act like niggers.

Lots of white people had called him nigger back in Mississippi and Chicago days. But not nearly as many whites as blacks. Clarence now believed the clearest sign his people had bought into the lie of black inferiority was that they called each other "nigga." How often would they say, "Get off your black rear end," as if black was the most demeaning adjective they could think of?

In the black pride days of the early seventies, black skin took on an almost religious significance. His skin color became his primary reference point. He was ashamed of the ash, ashamed he'd tried to look white even for that half hour. And that was the story of black people's lives, he thought. Ashamed because you're not white, then ashamed because you wanted to be white, and then ashamed because white people think black people are stupid and incompetent and immoral, and then ashamed because now so many black people believe the same myth about themselves. The immoral myth perpetrated by white racists was like radiation poisoning passing itself from generation to generation. Among many blacks, the effects of racism had become self-perpetuating.

There were two Americas, the white one bright with promise and unlimited opportunity. And the black one, dark with hopelessness. Clarence had fought against the system, overcome it, succeeded as a black man in a white world. He refused to bend either to racism or to the accusations that he was sleeping with the enemy. Yet here he sat, still feeling the shame of the Haverstrom throwaways, the hair grease, the ashes, and being called "nigger" by whites and blacks alike.

When it came to being black in America, Clarence had long ago realized, shame came with the territory. So did anger. He wished he could explain all of this to Jake, he *longed* to explain it. But how could he? Where could he find the words? How could he risk the humiliation and rejection? Some things you can't change. Jake was white. Could he ever understand a black man?

One voice within always said to him, "It's so much better than the days of slavery, so much better than sharecropping and Jim Crow." Laws had changed, opportunities had changed. Now a black person could be stopped only by the limits of his abilities and determination. That's what he always told himself, and usually he believed it. But not today, not here, not now.

As he was often reminded at stoplights, on elevators, and in department stores, no matter what he had accomplished, no matter who he really was, to some whites and to some blacks—sometimes even to himself—he would always be just one more nigger.

Dani continued studying her life on earth, reviewing obscure incidents long forgotten. She'd looked again at Bible passages she'd failed to live by, heard again the wise counsel of her parents she hadn't followed, listened to sermons she hadn't paid attention to, taken a fresh look at life experiences she hadn't seen from an eternal perspective.

"It's as if," Dani said to Torel, "Elyon is teaching me here all the lessons I failed to learn on earth."

"That is exactly right," Torel said. "He brings to his redeemed certain lessons he desires them to learn. If they are not learned on earth, they must be learned here to prepare you to serve in your appointed place."

Dani looked confused.

"Surely you have read in Elyon's book that you will reign with him, sit upon his Father's throne, even judge angels. That those who were his faithful servants on earth would be appointed leaders in heaven. That those trustworthy in small matters would be put over large ones. I know you read these things. I looked over your shoulder as you read them."

"To read is one thing; to understand, another," Dani said. "It seemed too fantastic to believe."

"Everything Elyon says must be believed. It is not for you to pick and choose."

"I realize that now. You speak of service, but heaven is a place of *rest*, is it not? I'm surprised how active I've been here, studying my life on earth, observing the dark world, interacting with others, traveling back in time to see history unfold, running and exploring and enjoying the incredible beauty here. I'm grateful for all the activity. I'd just expected there would be much less to do."

"Rest is a condition of the soul," Torel said. "You are at rest when you are where you should be and doing what you should be doing. At times you choose to do nothing here, just to soak it in and enjoy it—even here there is the Sabbath rest. But surely you didn't imagine you would sit around and do nothing? Good is multifaceted and deep; evil, monolithic and shallow—that is why hell is endlessly boring and heaven endlessly fascinating. As for activity, does not Elyon's Word say that in heaven 'His servants will serve him'? What is service but action and effort and duty and responsibility? These do not conflict with rest. Heaven is a place both for rest and for activity. But I am moving ahead to another lesson. Tell me something you have been learning."

"For one thing," Dani said, "all this study of my life on earth has been a surprise. I thought I would never look back. I find that what I experience in heaven is largely an outgrowth of earth. The two aren't disconnected. It's not a new and separate reality as much as an extension of the old reality."

Torel nodded, as if she had said something self-evident.

"My mind is the same mind, only sharper; my soul the same soul, only completely pure. My skills are the same skills, but less hindered in their expression. I was not a mountain climber on earth and do not have some sudden desire to be one now, though perhaps I will eventually. But I loved to paint and swim on earth, and I love to even more now."

"Of course," Torel said. "You are the same person. Earth leads directly into heaven, just as it leads directly into hell. Your life on earth was your running start into heaven, just as for those who do not know Elyon, it is their running start into hell. What you learned there you bring with you here. The treasures you laid up when you were there will be yours here. Elyon's gifts are irrevocable. He made you to be an artist not for time but for eternity. You learned to be an artist there to prepare you to be one here."

"Then in the coming kingdom will people have the same jobs as they did on earth?"

"Gifting and vocation are not the same. The doctor, undertaker, police officer, and paramedic will not have the same job here. But they will have the same gifts and new opportunities to use them."

"I expected heaven to be entirely different than earth," Dani said.

"Elyon is the same Creator, you are the same creature. It is the same universe. You have simply relocated to a better part of it. It is *you* in heaven, not some new creature that did not exist on earth. The same person who steps out of earth is the one who steps into heaven."

"I used to think heaven was an entirely new book, with a new cast of characters—a nice setting, but with no drama, no plot."

"On the contrary," Torel said. "It is the next chapter of the same book, or perhaps a sequel to it. A continuation. The viewpoint is more comprehensive, the setting more varied, the characters have more depth, the plot is more interesting, the anticipation more heightened."

"Will there be other characters in the drama?" Dani asked.

"Elyon is the Author," Torel said. "I am sure his cast of characters is not exhausted and never will be. My comrades and I have often discussed this very thing. We ask ourselves what creatures and what worlds he will create in the ages to come, and what adventures he will lay out for us, and what more we will discover about him in our journeys. This is the wonder of heaven—always more and always better as we move further in. Is it not compelling?"

"More compelling than anything I could have imagined," Dani said. She appeared eager to go, a smile of anticipation on her face. "I want to paint now, Torel. I want to paint something for the Carpenter, something beautiful, just for him."

CHAPTER

12.

The movers were coming Monday. Today and tomorrow the Abernathys would have to get everything ready.

Clarence began a final inspection of his orderly Gresham home, contrasting it to the ones he and Dani grew up in. Mama and Daddy had calendars on every wall. Real estate, insurance, and funeral calendars, all free, some decades out of date. Those who had little clung to what was free. They hung on to things the affluent would toss without thinking. Clarence had grown up a saver but was now a tosser. The thought of moving into Dani's house, the house of a saver, didn't excite him. There would have to be lots of tossing.

While Geneva still slept, Clarence looked at the clear bright morning, put on his shades, and went for an early walk. Probably his last walk ever in this neighborhood. He knew he would miss it.

He strolled down the less-traveled back streets. It had been a long time, he realized, since he took time for a walk. Geneva invited him often, but there was always so much work to do. There were a couple of new neighbors he hadn't even met, but this was the suburbs and no sense meeting them now anyway. Last time he'd been on this street, Anderson, the old curmudgeon, had been walking his half-breed pit bull down the narrow sidewalk the opposite direction. He hadn't budged an inch and clearly expected Clarence to step off into the wet grass or onto the street.

It was possible Anderson expected this because Clarence was the younger man, and that would not have bothered him in the least. But most likely, Clarence supposed, it was because he was black, and Anderson expected blacks should always move out of the way for whites. Clarence had deferred, stepping off the sidewalk to let man and dog pass. The ugly dog growled and the ugly Anderson may as well have. Clarence thought he saw a smug look on Anderson's face, the look that says, "Know your place, black man."

Clarence had reenacted the scene in his mind dozens of times since it had happened two months ago, coming up with all sorts of sarcastic comments he would make if it happened again.

Today he saw an unfamiliar face coming his way. Must be one of those new neighbors. The man walked out the driveway of the old Thompson place. He'd seen the "For sale" sign taken down a few weeks ago. The man was fiftyish and white as a cumulous cloud, walking his German Shepherd and wearing sunglasses. He and his dog occupied all the narrow sidewalk themselves.

Clarence determined that today he would not defer. He would gladly move for woman, child, or elderly man, but he would not move for a man just because he was white. He would not send that message or endure that indignity.

The two men wearing dark glasses in the bright morning sun walked closer and closer toward each other. As he got near, Clarence saw a blank expression on the man's face. He felt certain he was analyzing and dissecting him. "What's a black man doing out here?" Or, "So this is the nigger they told me about." The more he thought about it, the angrier Clarence got.

Now they were fifteen feet apart, and one was clearly going to have to step off the path. It would be the white man with the dog, not the black man walking by himself. Clarence would not step aside. He would not give a greeting. If the man wanted to be friendly—Clarence was certain he didn't—he would have to take the initiative.

They were now just eight feet apart. Clarence determined he would hold his ground if he had to walk right through the man. He walked straight forward, not hesitating, biting his lip involuntarily. It became obvious the man was not going to move off the sidewalk either. The dog squeezed by Clarence's left leg, but Clarence's wide left shoulder bumped squarely into the smaller man's, causing him to totter. He fell part way to the ground, sticking out his hand to catch himself.

Why didn't you just move out of the way?

"Pardon me," the man said. "So sorry. Not accustomed to this neighborhood yet. Barney and I are still getting used to each other. Narrow sidewalks, aren't they? Jensen's the name. Marty Jensen." The disoriented man stretched out his hand at a ninety degree angle from Clarence.

Clarence's ire turned to horror when he realized Barney had the harness of a guide dog. "Sorry," Clarence whispered, his voice trembling. Embarrassed, he quickly decided he didn't want the man to know his name.

Clarence walked away briskly, hearing the man apologize a second time and say, "Have a good day. Hope to bump into you again." The man uttered a self-deprecating laugh as Clarence retreated.

Clarence split wood after he returned home. There was no need to do it. It made no sense to be chopping wood as they were preparing to move out. But swinging the splitting maul had always been a way to express himself. It beat biting his lip.

After forty minutes, he sat on one of the logs, sweat dripping. He looked at his woodpile, seeing one tilted wedge in the otherwise Swiss-perfect symmetrical stack. He corrected the imprecision.

He looked at his yard, smiling, remembering Jake's comment when he'd looked in his garage a few weeks earlier: "Clabern, you've got enough lawn fertilizer here to get arrested by ATF." Clarence inspected the neighbors' lawns. His was still the best. It had to be. If a white man hasn't mowed his lawn lately, it's because he's busy. If a black man hasn't, it's because he's lazy.

Clarence came in the front door and settled on the living-room couch, straightening out the *Black Enterprise* magazine on the coffee table. It was the annual special issue, The Black Enterprise Largest 100 Black Businesses in America. He loved reading about legends such as Reginald Lewis, Howard Naylor Fitzhugh, Arthur G. Gaston, and John H. Johnson. There was a special feature on Berry Gordon of

Motown. He loved the ads, seeing page after page of successful, well-dressed black professionals. Even though the editorials could be infuriatingly liberal, he loved the magazine. Next to it was *Destiny*, a magazine for black conservatives. He'd decided *Ebony* and *Jet* and *Essence* had become drivel on the level of *People* and *Us* and were too superficial for guests to associate with serious black folk.

It was now just 9:15 A.M. He put on some late coffee and picked up the *Trib* he'd pulled from the paper box following his walk. He'd read his own column first, then immerse himself in the rest of it.

"What a beautiful day!" Geneva said from an oversized padded lawn chair on the deck just outside the living room. Had he looked up at her she would have struck Clarence as catlike, curled up, arms and legs overlapping, brushing the lint off one sleeve and then the other. But he didn't look up.

Geneva stared through the gray screen door at Clarence sitting in the living room, pouring over the newspaper like a four-point senior studying for his final exams. It was a guy thing, she'd long ago decided. She wondered what it would take to get his attention, and whether she was willing to pay the price.

"How did this garbage make it on page one?" he said.

"Good morning to you too, baby. Maybe we could go for a walk," she said.

"McNews. Polls, pie charts, scenery pics on page one? A lead article on 'hot movies'? It's like the *Trib's* been possessed by the *National Inquirer*. We don't just need new editors. We need an exorcist! Where's the hard reporting? Where's the news? *News*paper. Get it?"

"Spike wants to go for a walk. Maybe after you've read the sports page?"

"Look at the size of this headline. It's a no-news day and we've got fonts the size of a Mississippi cockroach. What are they trying to be, the *New York Post*? How's anybody going to know when war's declared?"

"Clarence?" Geneva spoke loudly this time.

"I'm reading the paper."

"I know. You're always reading the paper."

"What's that supposed to mean?"

"That...you're always reading the paper."

"I chopped wood this morning; I'm gonna work all day. Make the big move into the city, just like you want. Now let me relax awhile, okay?"

"*You* made the decision to move, remember?" Geneva said. "And I don't want you to work all day. I want you to relax. The kids need you more than the moving company does. How about we just kick back together a few minutes before we start packing up?"

Clarence sighed, picking invisible particles off his shirt sleeve. "You're saying

I'm neglecting the family again, right?"

"Stop getting defensive, Clarence. This isn't a putdown. I just want you to come with me and take the dog for a walk. You need to relax."

"I am relaxing."

"No you're not. You're like a bee trapped in a Mason jar. You're angry."

"I'm not angry!" He said it a little too loudly.

"Okay, you're just *acting* like you're angry. And you're a really good actor!"

"Sure. Fine." Clarence threw down the paper. "You were hinting at taking the dog for a walk? Well, I went for a walk before you got up. And I'm not a mind reader. Don't expect me to figure it out. Just come right out and say it, okay? It's called communication."

"Forget it. I'll walk the dog myself."

"Fine. Just don't make like it's my fault."

"Why does everything have to be somebody's fault?" Geneva shouted, jumping to her feet. "Look, I'm sorry you lost your sister, okay? But she was one of my dearest friends. And I'm sorry about Felicia. It rips me up too—you don't know how much. But I didn't just lose them. I lost you. Excuse me while I go grieve, okay?"

She charged to the door, then looked back at him.

"Not that it matters to you. You've been sitting around feelin' sorry for yourself that you're a black man? Well, let me tell you Mr. High and Mighty journalist. You try bein' a black woman. Black women are the mules of this world. And we get whipped by black men because they think everybody else is whippin' them. Well, I'm tired of bein' whipped by your mouth, you understand me?"

She grabbed the leash out of the front closet, hustled a salivating Spike out the door, and slammed it behind her.

Clarence sat stoically, listening to her pounding footsteps recede.

It was Monday, at Dani's. Between loads from the moving van, Geneva and Clarence crossed the street to see Mrs. Burns.

"Thanks for taking care of the kids, Hattie," Geneva said.

"Happy to. Always told Dani that. Lordy, Lordy I miss that girl. I want you to know I'll be here for these children. You ever need help, ever need someone to watch 'em, you call on ol' Hattie, you hear me now?"

"We really appreciate that," Geneva said.

"Celeste is quiet, maybe too quiet," Hattie said. "She misses her mama and her sister somethin' terrible. I've been teachin' her to bake, and she seems to like it. Don't know how much help I can be for the boy. He needs a strong hand. Needs a man to show him the way. I'm scared for him. The school called a few days ago. He's not doin' his homework, skippin' classes, doesn't seem to care."

"Ty's a four-point student," Clarence said.

"Used to be. Won't be this year. I think you better talk to him. I tried but he gave me that look boys have nowadays. Like what do I know about life and why should they listen to me."

"I'll call the school first chance," Clarence said. "Thanks again, Hattie."

"Well, my door's always open to you, hear me? We got to stick together here. It's our only chance."

The next morning Clarence stared at the headline on the front page of Metro. "Hispanic Gang Members Suspected in Murder." He read the article by Barry Davis.

> The fatal shooting of Dani Rawls and her daughter Felicia that stunned a north Portland neighborhood two weeks ago took on a new twist this week. A witness has come forward indicating that a car speeding away from the murder scene was a gold, late seventies Chevrolet Impala or Caprice. The driver and passenger were both young Hispanic males, perhaps in their early twenties, each wearing a white T-shirt.
>
> While refusing to identify the witness, police spokesperson Lieutenant W. C. Jannsen said, "The shooting had the earmarks of gang warfare." When asked if this is another example of growing racial tension in the greater Portland area, Jannsen replied, "Hopefully it was just an isolated incident."
>
> "The new eyewitness information confirms the shooting was probably racially motivated," Councilman Reginald Norcoast stated. "I have personally talked with the chief of police and asked that the department's hate crimes division take a closer look at this. I remind the community that the reward still stands, $10,000 for information leading to the arrest and conviction of the killers. I believe in this so strongly that my wife and I contributed the first $1,000 ourselves."

Clarence threw down the paper.

I've never known anyone to get more mileage out of a thousand dollars.

"In the next phase of your studies you'll learn about your family history," Torel said to Dani. "Your great-grandfather will be your guide. "

Zeke beamed, champing at the bit to get started.

"I knew my grandfather was a sharecropper," Dani said, "that his mama was born a slave and her name was Ruth. But that's about all I knew."

"Ruth was our daughter," Zeke said. "Nancy and I served the same massa three years, then we jumped the broom together."

A time portal opened and Dani watched the ceremony, just as it happened in old Kentucky.

"You literally jumped over a broom?"

"Yes'm! It was a combination of African and American wedding ritual. They wouldn't give us a Christian ceremony, but jumpin' the broom married us before God and the church."

"The church?"

"Well," Zeke laughed, "back then the church was just any of the slaves who loved Jesus and that was most of them. See those folks there?" He pointed to the portal. "That was Sam and Darla. They was good friends."

"And that little boy dancin' next to them," Dani said, "is that theirs?"

"Yeah, that was little Sam. The massas called him Sambo. They didn't want two slaves hassin' the same name. Said it was confusin'."

"He's so cute. And lanky."

"Sam and Darla loved little Sam," Zeke said. "Used to talk about their dreams for that boy. But then Massa Collins sold him. He sold away their only son."

A look of horror swept across Dani's face.

"Darla was never the same. Shriveled up after that. And ol' Sam, he heard his boy was at a farm outside Lexington, just a few hundred miles away. After two years he couldn't stand it no more, so he rans off to find him. Didn't get but forty miles 'fore they found him. Beat him, then cut off both his big toes so he wouldn't run again. He did run again. Just didn't get very far." Zeke's eyes misted up.

"I'm sorry," Dani said. "I didn't mean to cause you pain, Great-Granddaddy. I didn't think—"

"That there was pain here? Well, it's funny with that. You know, the promise is that God will wipe away the tears from every eye. But that doesn't happen until after the ol' devil's throwed in that ol' fiery lake. There's so much more laughter and joy here than tears—you seen that I reckon. But the joy isn't in forgetting what happened. It's in remembering and seeing the hand of God and how he sustains and heals."

"And if you didn't remember the bad things," Dani offered, "you couldn't experience God's comfort for them. Tell me about my grandmother."

"Well, 'bout a year after Nancy and I jumped the broom we had a boy. Named him Abraham. Then another year later Ruth was born. And..." Tears flowed again. "She was the most beautiful little girl on God's green earth."

No sooner had he said it than the portal showed the girl in her mother's arms, with proud young Zeke doting over her.

"Now look at her. Was I just braggin' or was I right?"

Dani was instantly taken with how much this child looked like her own baby pictures. "You were right, Great-Grandpa," she said, putting her arms around him and squeezing. He reminded her so much of her daddy. She could hardly wait to introduce them to each other.

"We had some happy years together, Nancy and me and Abraham and Ruth. Not easy years but happy ones 'cause we was free inside and we had each other. See, I hears people say in the Shadowlands that Christianity enslaved blacks. No, it was just the opposite. Knowin' the one true Master gave us dignity, that God made us, that Jesus died for us, that God gave us the same rights as other men even if nobody acted like it. We knew we had a home in heaven and we could keep our heads high even when our backs was beaten till our shirts stuck to them from the blood.

"Your great-grandma, bless her, rubbed on lard to grease my back, and it felt so good—see her doin' it right there now? The overseers was cruel, though our master was kinder than most. Still, ownin' slaves did somethin' to a man's soul and mistreatin' them did somethin' more, shriveled up that soul like an orange drained of its juice. But God kept the juice in our family, I'm here to tell you, Great-Granddaughter. And Abe and little Ruth, they was our pride and joy."

"And then?" Dani asked.

"Well, then it was the same ol' story. Mr. Collins had promised he'd never separate our family 'cause I was the hardest worker he had, and he was gonna do right by me. Then times turned hard and somebody wanted a field hand and house help. They had some older hands that could train younger ones to do it right, so they wanted chillens. Abraham and Ruth was nine and eight, and in those days you could do a lot of work by that age. So this man inspected the slaves and when he was lookin' at my little ones I could tell what he was thinkin'. Nancy stole them away into our shack and stayed with them, huddled up in the corner. She was so scared."

Dani saw it as it happened, the terrified look in Nancy's eyes, the frightened children clinging to their mother and each other in the dark far corner of the shack.

"I kept tellin' Nancy that Mr. Collins had promised us he'd never do that, and she reminded me what he did to little Sam and how Darla was never the same and big Sam's toes got cut off and I said, 'Mr. Collins made some mistakes, but he a Christian man. He gonna keep his promises.'"

Dani looked at him, anxious yet afraid to hear the rest of the story.

"Finally Mr. Collins tells me he's sorry, but he's gonna has to sell our babies. And I tells him, 'No sir, you can't.' He never heard me talk like that. Didn't slap me, just stared at me, tryin' to measure if there was a line you could cross even with a po' nigger. Well, he'd crossed that line. Finally he gave us a choice. He'd sell two of our family. But we could choose which two. So we gots one day to decide, and we wept all that day. We cried out to God Almighty and asked him to help us. We begged him to let our family be together."

"But…he didn't answer?" Dani said.

"Oh, yes he did, chile, he surely did."

"But—"

"Sure enough, we's all here together, just like we prayed for, now ain't we? You hasn't met Abe and Ruth yet, they been busy since you came, but they's here all right. What better place than this one? Now, the answer to my prayer took a tad bit longer than I wanted. But Elyon doesn't always do it our way, now does he?"

"No, he doesn't," Dani said. "So Mr. Collins sold off part of your family?"

"We chose to have Nancy and Ruth stay at the Collins place, because they'd be safer, I thought. At least nobody was rapin' the slave women there. Abraham and I was hauled off to an old plantation outside Louisville. Them peoples didn't seem to care much 'bout how us slaves grieved when they split up our families."

Dani watched Zeke and Nancy and Abraham and Ruth torn out of each other's arms and the man and boy pushed into the back of a wagon. It rode off leaving a trail of dust covering a weeping Nancy on her knees, huddling next to little Ruth.

"Knowin' we'd be parted," Zeke said, "we set up a meeting place not far from the Collins plantation. I told Nancy that one year later to the day I'd do anything to get me and Abe there."

"Did you make it?"

"Well, we made it to a different meetin' place. But it wasn't a year later I came, it was six. And then it was fifteen more years after that before Nancy made it. She always was one to run late!" Zeke laughed uproariously.

"You met again…here?"

"Yes'm, we surely did. Can you imagine a better place? And Abe and Ruthie met us too, in their own time." Zeke stared toward the throne on which the Carpenter sat. The liberated slave's eyes gleamed just like Dani's father's. "Come with me, Dani. I's gonna take you to meets some folk. For starters, Darla and Big Sam and Little Sam."

"And then?"

"Well, I think she's comin' back soon from Elyon's mission. And soon as she does, I'm gonna introduce you to somebody who looks a lot like you. Your great-grandma, my precious darlin' Ruth."

"Geneva? I'll be on the computer awhile. When Ty gets home, tell him I need to talk to him. Okay?" Clarence closed the door to his home office.

He surfed the Internet via America Online, checking out a half-dozen favorite Web sites, then moved over to the forums on CompuServe. He loved the Sports Forum, where he always called up the latest AP stories on the Packers. He scanned the African American Culture Forum, as always finding a few discussions of interest.

He especially enjoyed going into the Journalism Forum and interjecting his conservative commentary, then waiting for the hysterical responses. He'd spent long hours here arguing politics. He delighted in the debate format. He especially liked the fact that computers were colorblind. He could enter into the exchange of ideas without people thinking, "What do you expect, he's black," or "I wouldn't have thought that from a black man." Here he wasn't a black man. He was just a man.

He checked the responses to his last post about whites and blacks both needing to take responsibility for their lives rather than blaming others and looking for government to solve problems.

"Clarence," began the post from Bernie in New York City, "I wish you conservatives would have some compassion on those who weren't born with silver spoons in their mouths. I'd point out the racist assumptions underlying your comments, but they're all too obvious."

Clarence read the other posts piggybacked on his, as well as the comments on Bernie's. He was used to being called a racist by white liberals. Once in another forum he'd finally given in to the temptation to reveal that he was black. Those he'd been arguing with for months refused to believe him. He considered requesting their snail mail addresses so he could send them an autographed picture. It wouldn't have mattered. If he'd convinced them he was black, it would only have meant that by advocating black responsibility and self-sufficiency he was a rear-kissing Uncle Tom.

He recalled seeing police officers posting notes in the gang section of one of the Crime Forums. He composed a question about drive-by shootings and the HK53 and threw it out for response. He'd turn any wheels he could. What was it Ollie had said about panning for gold?

———

"Grab a chair, Ty. The vice principal and I talked today."

Ty hesitated, but seeing his uncle's glare he sat down, slouched back with both legs splayed out in front of him.

"Sit up!"

He didn't budge.

"I said sit up before I make you sit up."

Ty sat up.

"I called the school because I hear you're having trouble with your studies. And then I find out that's not the half of it. Why'd you hit that boy?"

"He was foolin' with me, dissin' me. He talk trash to me." His voice was low, as if speaking under protest or asserting his masculinity.

"So?"

"So I fixed to get some get back. I rearranged his face." His voice swelled with pride.

"That's not a good enough reason."

"Not fo' you. Good enough fo' me."

"Look, people are going to be jerks. You can't stop them."

"You can stop 'em if you packin' heat."

"You think a gun's the solution? Well, it isn't. I carried a gun awhile when I was your age, till your grandpa found out and thrashed my rear end till tomorrow. Thought I was one bad dude. I walked around shakin' dice in my hand like that really meant somethin'. Bangin' isn't new, you know. I was in the Chicago jets, man. I barely made it out with my life, and wouldn't have if it wasn't for Daddy. And that was before the hard drugs and the big money and the automatic weapons. You get in and you'll never get out. I see your strut, like you're the hot new rooster in the coop. You've got to get over this macho garbage. They'll kick you out of school, and school's your ticket out of here, boy."

"I don't want out of here. This is my hood. They ain't gonna kick me outta school. Just for swingin' on someone? Man, nobody'd be in school if that took you out. Shoot, Flash pulled hardware on a dude and he didn't get kicked out. They ain't gonna do it, no way."

"*Aren't.* I've never heard you say ain't. Don't pull this ghetto lingo on me. Your mama taught you better than that. I know you know better. What's happened to your English?"

"Nothin' wrong wich da way I talkin'. You want me talkin' white?"

"No. I want you talking right. Some whites talk right, some wrong. Some blacks talk right, some wrong. You use bad English and it's not going to make you cool. It's just going to make you poor. You say, 'Lemme ax you a question,' and you may as well burn up your résumé, bro, because they're not going to hire you."

"Teacher say it Black English. Jus' the way we talk. Don't need to talk white."

"Your teacher's wrong. It's not white and it's not black. It's American. It's the language of business and newspapers. That's the way it is. If you're going to succeed as a businessman in Kenya you have to speak good Swahili. In America, you have to speak good English."

"Teacher say it don't matter. If black folk make it to the top, they get pushed down by whites. Like the Surgeon General three years ago or somepin'. Teacher said they couldn't stand a black woman doin' important work."

"Jocelyn Elders? They couldn't stand someone doing *lousy* work, that's what they couldn't stand. Didn't matter what color or gender. Incompetence knows no color or gender. Neither does excellence. Look at Colin Powell and Alan Keyes and Thomas Sowell and Kay Coles James, that's where you should be looking."

"Don't push on me. I ain't no punk."

"I've never thought you were a punk. Until now. Because now you're talking like a punk and acting like a punk. I used to be a punk when I was your age. But your granddaddy wouldn't let me. And I won't let you. You hear me? There won't be any punks in my house. Ain't gonna happen."

"*Isn't* going to happen," Ty shot back.

"You got that right, boy," Clarence fired at him. He felt the pain in his lip and waited to regain composure.

"The vice principal said you were caught cheating. That you took a test from a teacher's desk."

"Wasn't cheating."

"Then why'd they think you were?"

"One of my homies, he put de tes on my des."

"Put the test on my desk. Say it."

Ty looked down.

"Say it!"

Geneva rushed to the door of Clarence's office, alarmed by the shouting.

"Test on my desk!"

"See, you *can* speak English. If one of your friends stole the test and put it on your desk, you're hanging with the wrong friends."

"They my homies. They straight. Righteous. We watch each other's backs."

"You better start watching your books, Ty."

"Cut me some slack, Jack. You don't know nothin' about nothin'."

Clarence grabbed Ty by the shoulders and lifted him out of the chair. Geneva peered around the doorjam, trembling.

"The name's not Jack. Got it? And I know more than your homies ever will. Because I work at it. And if you don't work at it, you'll end up nowhere, knowin' nothin'." He pushed Ty back on the chair.

"Are we done now?" Ty tried not to sound afraid, but the squeak in his voice gave him away.

"No. I'll tell you when." Clarence sat down, trying to come up with something that might get through.

"Look, Ty, the vice principal told me what I already know—that you're really a good kid underneath it all. But I want to tell you something. You stop going to class, neglect your homework, hang with the wrong kids, get into fights, and that's just the beginning. Next thing you know you'll be stealing and doing drugs and gangbanging and shooting people, getting a police record. Then it isn't going to matter. Good can't just be buried underneath. Good is how you live, what you do with your life. Good is the choices you make. You make bad choices and before long you won't be good anymore. You make good choices, and you can have a good life. Otherwise you're gonna end up in that chalk circle, boy. Nobody's gonna help you then."

Clarence looked at Ty, who stared at the floor, unresponsive to his uncle's words. Clarence's mind went back just a few years ago to when this same boy loved to talk with him, loved to hear his grandpa's stories, loved to hear his uncle read. He remembered his childlike excitement about winning the spelling bee at Tubman Grade School just two years ago.

Now he'd lost something. Innocence. Kindness. A sense of purpose and hope. He didn't seem like the same boy.

Where did the child go?

———

He looked at his watch. Two hours to finish his column. After that a half hour for lunch, and on to Ollie's, who'd asked him to meet again. Like most columnists, he knew how to hone his natural gifting with focused hard work. The reward was a flexible schedule, since you were paid by the bottom line, not successive hours at a desk. Clarence felt fortunate he could grab time most people couldn't.

This column began like most, with a grain of an idea that becomes an irritant. The same irritants that produce pearls in oysters produce good copy in writers. But a column also has to have fire. Some logs just smoke and smolder, some catch fire quickly and burn hot. That's what he was looking for. Before him sat three piles of three-by-five cards paper-clipped together, representing three column ideas. In keeping with the maxim "as goes the lead so goes the column," he was trying to write a lead for each, then let the best lead determine the column.

Looking for inspiration, a kick-start, Clarence pulled a file of clippings containing his best column leads. One article on Hollywood's adverse effects on America began, "According to my research, one in three Hollywood conservatives goes on to be president of the United States."

For another column, he'd interviewed a Mexican-born ranch hand from California who was a legal immigrant. He'd asked him what he thought about his children being taught in Spanish in their California public school. His response became Clarence's lead: "In the school they teach my children Spanish so they can grow up to be busboys and waiters. At home I teach them English, so they can grow up to be doctors and teachers."

He'd written some columns on abortion that were among his most controversial. He looked at the one in front of him, written after Susan Smith drowned her children in that Carolina lake:

> Susan Smith killed her two sons. Amid all the shock and dismay expressed in the media, I can only ask, What's the big deal? Why is everybody so upset? After all, people all over the country, including columnists at this newspaper, have for years defended her right to kill the same two children. Their only stipulation was that Susan Smith kill them when they were younger and smaller.

> Based on this I can only conclude that Susan Smith, exercising
> her right to privacy and freedom of choice, was not guilty of
> doing a bad thing. She was only guilty of bad timing. What she
> did to her sons was just a very late-term abortion.

He'd concluded the article, "It's time for abortion advocates to be honest and admit that Susan Smith is the poster child for pro-choice America."

He looked at the file folder full of angry responses to this column. Winston, Jess, everyone but Jake had tried to talk him out of it. But Clarence went to those upstairs and asked, "Are you going to censor your first-ever black columnist? If you do, I may have to file a complaint."

He'd played hardball and made some enemies. They toned down the column, but Clarence's lead and conclusion held.

"Hey, Clabern."

"Jake, my man!" He turned outward from his cubicle and slapped hands with his friend.

"Sorry to bother you," Jake said. "I know you've just got an hour before deadline."

"No problem," Clarence said. "What's up?"

"Just heard from Pam in Metro that the Portland Hispanic Coalition had a meeting. Apparently they expressed concern that police are harassing Latinos, questioning them about your sister's shooting."

"Nobody's accusing the whole Hispanic community of doing it. Just two guys."

"I know. Guess they think they're getting bad press and it's creating racial division."

"Sure it is. It always does. White guy kills somebody and nobody says, 'That's what white guys do.' Black or Latino does it and people think, 'Yeah, it figures.'"

"Well," Jake said, "apparently Raylon is considering giving them space for a guest opinion. They think the *Trib* has been more pro-black than pro-Hispanic."

Clarence shook his head. "It's like slicing up a pie. Everybody wants a bigger piece."

————————

Ollie took Clarence and Manny into an interrogation room, carrying the HK53 the armorer had showed them.

"I twisted some arms and checked this baby out from SERT just for the day. Thought maybe if I threatened you two with it I could talk you into kissing and making up." Manny and Clarence both stared blankly at him, neither amused. "Okay. Bad joke. Look, before we get going on the rifle, can I talk off the record Clarence, just between the three of us?"

"Yeah."

"Captain says there's been a backlash from the Hispanic community. Manny and I were poking around on this murder and word got out. They want to know who's making the accusation."

"They have a right to know," Manny said.

"Look, Manny, we've been through this," Ollie said. "We don't want Mookie intimidated into silence. I told him his name wouldn't get out for now so he and his family don't have to worry about the old witness elimination program. If we nail somebody, we'll worry about it when we have to put his name forward, but till then, why risk it?"

"It stinks," Manny said, "and they can smell it. Some black kid accuses Latino kids of doing a murder in the black part of town where the black gangs rule."

"You seem hung up on the word black, Junior Detective," Clarence said. "If you've got problems with blacks and you don't think Hispanics commit crimes, maybe you should get off the case."

"*I* should get off the case? I'm a detective. The only one who should be taken off this case is you, you..."

Go ahead and say it.

"Knock it off you two," Ollie stepped between them. "Let's be civil, okay? You don't have to like each other. But we're on the same side, all right?" Both men stared at each other. Neither blinked. "Now, Manny, tell Clarence who you've been talking to."

Manny hesitated, then finally spoke. "I've been with the leaders of all the big Latino gangs—from Nuestra Familia to the Mexican Mafia, to all the locals. They're all laughin' at us. They say if anyone from the barrios did a hit in North Portland they'd know all about it. To them it's a joke."

"So you're trusting the word of gangbangers?" Clarence asked. "You think they're going to confess to you they did it? Who's side are you on?"

"*I'm* trusting gangbangers, Mr. Bigshot Journalist? Who's the one that paid a black gangbanger a hundred bucks for a good story?"

"Mookie's not a banger." Clarence looked at Ollie. "Is he?"

"I was just going to tell you that," Ollie said. "I asked around, found out he's not a big name, but he's more than a wannabe. He's a Rollin' 60s Crip."

"I still say he's telling the truth," Clarence said. "Don't you think so, Ollie?"

"Yeah, I lean that way. His story seems solid enough. But I see Manny's point too. Anyway, the captain doesn't want us overstepping our bounds with the Hispanic gangs. We can't turn people into suspects just because they're male Latinos driving a lowrider. We have to move carefully."

Manny and Clarence glared at each other.

"Anyway," Ollie said, "I wanted to tell both of you what I did with our HK53 this morning. I took it to the range and flipped the full auto switch. I bought me one of those forty round after-market magazines McCamman mentioned." He pointed to the long impressive hardware extending from the rifle. "Emptied it in under four seconds, just like we figured."

"You take your work seriously," Clarence said.

"I'm a hands-on guy."

"So did you learn anything?" Manny asked impatiently.

"You always learn something. And anything you learn may pay off later. These boys have the full meal deal. This is major hardware. The good news is, this is no little piece somebody hides in their saggers or their pillowcase. If we get near the perps, secure a warrant for something else, drugs maybe, and they've still got it, it won't be easy to hide. If we find an HK53 in the hands of a bad guy, we've got him."

"And the bad news?" Clarence asked.

"Sort of the same thing. As far as we can tell, there's never been so much as a round fired from an HK53 in any crime in Portland or anywhere in Oregon. McCamman was right. This just isn't a typical banger's gun, not a street gun at all. Hope it appears somewhere so we can get a lock on it. On the other hand, part of me doesn't want it to show up."

"Why not?" Clarence asked.

"This gun's a score-settler. Packs a big-time power surge. Whoever used this baby once is going to be hard-pressed to keep from using it again. And any time it's used…"

"Somebody's liable to get killed," Manny filled in.

"Yeah." Ollie shook his head and started pacing, while Clarence reached out and picked up the HK53. He shouldered it and hit the forearm switch that turned on the flashlight. It lit up the wall. The front sight jumped out in the contrast created by the light beam. Clarence's pulse picked up as he felt the power.

"Mrs. Burns didn't see a flashlight," Ollie said. "The perp didn't want to draw attention to himself, I guess, so he didn't hit the switch. Either that or his unit didn't have a light." Ollie paced again, restlessly. "The whole thing still bugs me."

"What?" Manny asked.

"You want an AK, an Uzi, MAC 10, a Tech 9? Fine. Walk into any sleazy backwater tavern in Portland and start talkin' like you want one. Pretty soon somebody will whisper they know a guy who can get you one for five hundred bucks. Or you can just get them in the nickel ads."

"But fully automatics are illegal, right?" Clarence asked. He saw Manny smirk.

"Yeah, so's tax evasion and prostitution," Ollie said. "It's easy enough to buy and sell semiautos. Then convert them to fully automatic with a sear. Gun stores carry them for people authorized by a federal permit. Just get one off another weapon, buy it on the street, or steal one from a gun store. Whatever. Some guys make their own. But no way, even with a roll of crack money, are they going to buy this HK53 for five or six times what other automatics cost. Even if they could find one, which they probably couldn't."

"So what does this mean for the investigation?" Clarence asked.

"Well, if it really is a gang shooting, I figure it's a stolen weapon. Maybe bought after it was stolen, but not bought new by a gangbanger. I put word out on a police bulletin. Maybe that'll turn up something. The other thing is, I can't rule out that somebody with legal access to one could have used an HK53."

"Who?"

"I called Heckler and Koch. It's a short list, tell you that. First, the Navy Seals."

"You're saying a Navy Seal shot my sister?"

"Of course not," Ollie said. "Just sayin' they use them. So do SWAT teams. And possibly other police with access to department weapons."

Clarence raised his eyebrows. He was surprised Ollie would bring up the possibility. Police committing a crime. It wouldn't be the first time, that's for sure.

"But these guns are under lock and key," Ollie said. "You should've seen what I had to go through to check this gun out for the day. It's not like your nine millimeter you bring home at night and put in your dresser drawer. The access problem is big. Nah. Even a messed up cop couldn't pull it off."

Clarence sat quietly. Growing up in Mississippi in the fifties and sixties, he had a fertile imagination when it came to what messed up cops could pull off.

"So…the killer is either a gangbanger who stole it," Clarence said, "or he's a Navy Seal or a police officer who tried to make it look like a gang killing? What about Mookie's description? Two young Hispanic guys."

"He probably got it wrong," Manny said. "Or he just made it up."

"Protecting your own, is that it?" Clarence asked.

"It could be a Latino with a police or navy connection," Ollie said, trying to ignore the tension.

"Well, you two keep goin' on your theories," Manny said. "I doubt we'll ever get to the bottom of this one. Why don't we put an ad in the paper and offer a thousand dollars for anybody who can top Mookie's story? I'm outta here. I've got another interview on the Gailor case."

Ollie nodded, and Manny left, ignoring Clarence.

"Obviously, I think they were bangers," Ollie told Clarence. "But they got the gun somewhere—where? If you rule out Seals and police just because they're unlikely, it can hang you later. Remind me to tell you sometime about the case I solved based on an orangutan's prints. Anyway, I'm keeping an open mind."

"An orangutan?"

"I also called around to see if an HK had been stolen from a distributor warehouse. Nothing. I've run a trace on Oregon gun permit holders to see if one was stolen. Nothing." The phone rang.

While Ollie answered, Clarence looked at the pile on the detective's desk. He surveyed the interview records and the crime scene reports on Dani's case. Under them lay two manila envelopes. Ollie was engrossed in conversation, his back partially turned. Clarence retrieved and opened the top envelope. Three pictures of street signs, Jackson, Ninth, and Tenth; pictures of footprints, the shells scattered on the porch. He stiffened when he saw the next pictures, looking at them one eight-by-ten at a time. Dani. Felicia. Picture after picture, ten of them. He put them back, heart racing and stomach convulsing. He opened the other envelope. He looked at the autopsy photos, staring blankly. A dozen of them. Surreal images, like holocaust pictures that the mind keeps telling you must be mannequins because nothing so horrible could be real. And if it was real, you didn't want to live in the same universe ever again.

Ollie turned, still on the phone. Seeing Clarence, he quickly reached across the desk and jerked the envelopes and pictures out of his hand. Clarence offered no resistance.

Ollie saw his eyes, vacant eyes, the emptiness slowly filling with flames.

13

Clarence sat in Dani's workroom, where in the midst of the city's gray maze she had created such beautiful things with her mind and hands. On a round polished wood table full of dents sat her three wicker baskets containing maybe forty different colors.

He sat in the special chair, the chair he'd carefully repaired after the shooting. A brocade chair, the best heirloom of a poor family. Daddy had bought it for Mama back in Mississippi when Clarence was only eight. Thirty-four years ago. There it was again—the sweet, faint elusive smell of his mother, like from the stitchery in his basement, which he now had in safe storage, not wanting to hang it up in the city where it could be trashed or stolen.

Just a month ago he'd sat right in this room, in Mama's old chair, watching Dani paint. Dani said she often looked at that chair and imagined Mama watching her. The canvas was covered with a large cloth, just as it had been the last time he'd been in here the day she was killed, and she'd told him, "Don't peek." He still hadn't touched it, hadn't lifted up the cloth to see what she was working on. It was as if he felt that once he did, she would be gone forever.

He remembered her asking him about his color blindness. "You don't have total color blindness, where all colors are just different shades of gray. You just can't see some colors, or when you do see them, you get them mixed up. Right?"

He'd shrugged. "I guess."

"Colors tell us about God," she'd said.

"Tell us what?"

"That he values differentness and variety and beauty. That he's an artist. And that by giving us eyes to see all these different colors, he wants us to experience all that life offers."

"I don't know, Sis. Sometimes I think we'd all be better off totally colorblind."

"But then we'd only see shades of gray."

"So maybe red and yellow and brown wouldn't be so important. Solve our racial problems, wouldn't it?"

"It would be so dull."

"Better dull than dead, don't you think?"

"If we saw God as the Artist who made us all, there wouldn't be any killing."

"Yeah. And mankind would live happily ever after. But that's not the way it is, Sis."

Her idealism and romanticism, just like his father's, never failed to surprise him. Given the hardships she'd faced, he'd have expected more cynicism. Maybe he had enough for both of them.

He'd put it off long enough. He reached toward the canvas and slowly lifted the cloth to unveil her painting. It appeared perhaps 80 percent done, but he immediately recognized the subject. It was Dani. A self-portrait. And she'd left before the portrait was finished.

She'd already painted something on the bottom, in neatly constructed letters. He stared at them.

"To Antsy. Thanks for always being there for me, big brother."

———————

Sunday morning Clarence walked into Ebenezer, Dani's church, and heard the soft background soul music, sad and joyful at the same time. Bright colors fought for his attention, reds and blues and yellows and greens. He saw lots of jewelry, most of it inexpensive. The white-gloved ushers, dressed in sharp tuxedos, held up their right hands, their left hands behind their backs with military precision. Clarence smiled. At black churches even ushering could be an art form. One usher crooked his elbow for Geneva's hand and sat her down. Clarence could tell Geneva enjoyed Dani's church already. He wasn't so sure. He followed the usher and Geneva with his daddy, son, and daughter, as well as Celeste and a disgruntled Ty.

All around them sat elderly women wearing white hats. Clarence looked at the hands of the old woman sitting two over from him. He saw how rough and callused they were, perhaps from picking cotton and a lifetime of other menial tasks. They reminded him of his mother's hands. He supposed her knees were callused too, both from scrubbing floors and praying for her children.

Spread throughout the four hundred capacity auditorium were dozens of kufi-type African hats. Braids were everywhere, some of them laden with colorful berets. Here and there he saw Jamaican dreadlocks. The choir got up, wearing burgundy robes with yellow insets on flounced sleeves, their subtle stripes giving a distinct African look. They swayed and clapped, singing, "Thank you for the blood..." Their shoulders shook, as if their whole bodies, not just their mouths, were engaged in worship. The voices explored all the nooks and crannies of the vocal range. Clarence felt this same choir could sing this same song a hundred times and every time would be different.

An a cappella group started singing, "The blood that gives me strength from day to day, it will never lose its power." They sang unrestrained, holding nothing back.

The words were drawn out to emphasize the message, never in a hurry to end. Every number left the impression the singers would rather keep singing than quit. The solos—one baritone, one soprano—were magnificent. Like waves coming from and receding back into a great ocean, the solos made you feel the ocean was the thing, not the wave. In the front row, six- to nine-year-old boys and girls danced joyfully. "As pretty as you please," Daddy whispered to Clarence, nodding his approval. Clarence could tell Keisha wanted to go join them. Perhaps in another week or two she would.

Some hands rose high, though not all, which relieved Clarence since he wasn't the hand-raising type. Heads swayed, many eyes closed. The song leader led out with "Mighty is our God. Mighty is our King. Mighty is our Lord, Ruler of everything." This song went on and on—it seemed at least ten minutes.

Pastor Clancy rose from his seat on the platform. "Well, just this week Jefferson High School released its list of honored students based on last spring's achievement tests. Of the fifty who scored highest, we have fourteen students from our church!"

Hand clapping and "Praise Gods" and whooping and congratulations filled the air. As the pastor read the names, he asked each student to stand. Each received lengthy applause.

A man came up front, introducing himself as Jeremy, one of the deacons. "Angela Marie, how's your mama? Better? That's good. Karina Elizabeth, how's that back been doin'? Holdin' up? We'll keep prayin' for you, sister. Now, anybody have anything to say to God's people today?"

One brother stood up. "I want to praise God I got that job at the True Value hardware store. I start tomorrow."

Applause erupted.

"Hallelujah. Isn't that great news? Brother Henry, pray for Brother Jimmy here, will you?"

"God, we lift Jimmy up to you. This job's a real answer to prayer. Help him do a fine job, to work as workin' for you. Help him provide for his family. Help him to be a strong witness there. Thank you, Lord, thank you, God Almighty, thank you, Jesus."

"Amen."

"Hallelujah."

"Yes, Lord."

"Thank you, Jesus."

"Who's next?"

A man stood and gave a five-minute testimony about his deliverance from drugs and how he'd come back to his wife and children and was being discipled in the Ebenezer men's group. The applause rang out again, and Clarence found himself clapping harder than he would have expected.

"Are the Bensons out there?" Pastor Clancy asked. "Darnelle and Mary, you got that brand new baby with you, don't you now? A little boy named what? Cairo Clancy?" Laughter. "No? Kevin. That's almost as good. Let's pray for Kevin.

"Lord, we lift up Kevin to you. Help Kevin become a godly young man from the earliest age, dear Jesus." A chorus of *amens* and *yes, Lords* punctuated the request. "Help Sister Mary to be the mama she needs to be, dear Jesus." Another chorus of *amens*. "Help Brother Darnelle to lead this family spiritually and provide for them, sweet Lord." More *hallelujahs* and *thank you, Lords.*

The choir got up again, and by the time the first words erupted, feet everywhere pounded the floor to the beat. "He broke the chains of sin and set me free." The rhythmic, swaying movement was contagious, and Clarence found his own feet tapping.

Clarence watched Pastor Clancy starting to fidget like a bull waiting for the gate to open. This boy was ready to do some preachin'. When the choir finished, he sprang to his feet and spoke loudly into the microphone, "Do you *love* Jesus today?"

"Yes." Hundreds of voices united as one.

"I asked you a question. Do you love *Jesus* today?

"Yes!" The response was even louder.

"I'll ask it again. Do you love Jesus *today?*"

"Yes!"

Cairo Clancy moved back and forth on the platform with pronounced arm motions and hand gestures, looking like a boxer working the big bag. His voice was slow and measured at first, gradually building in intensity. Low tones developed into a high-pitched squeak as he made important points.

"What's wrong with you people? After all that awesome worship, some of you still look like you been baptized in pickle juice."

Laughter.

"You know what bothers me?"

"What's that, pastor?"

"This prosperity theology, this health and wealth gospel. Let me tell you a story, now. One day I asked the Lord, 'What's a million years to you?' He says, 'It's only a second in time to me, son.' So then I asked, 'What's a million dollars to you?' He says, 'It's only a penny to me, son.' So then I says, 'Okay, Lord, how 'bout you just give me a million dollars?' 'Sure, son,' the Lord answered me. 'But you'll have to wait just a second.'"

Laughter permeated the congregation, quick and spontaneous laughter, as of people wanting to laugh, just waiting for the opportunity.

Clarence remembered that growing up in black churches he'd gotten the impression God has some strict rules, but he also has a great sense of humor.

"Preach it, brother."

"Now the point is, God's gonna give us great gifts, treasures beyond our wildest dreams, but that doesn't mean he gives them to us here and now. Faith is trusting God that he'll come through later, in the world to come, there and then, not just here and now. If you think God promises great wealth and perfect health here and now, you need to go back to the Bible and let God pop you upside the head, you hear me?"

"Amen."

"Ain't it the truth, Lord?"

"Yessir, that's right."

"Now, what all this prosperity teaching shows me is that many people today care less about God than they do the benefit package. My daddy always said, 'He that serves God for money will serve the devil for better wages.'"

"Yes. Amen. Hallelujah. Say it again."

"This 'name it and claim it' business feels to me like we're pulling on God's leash till he comes our way. That's not how it works. We got to come *his* way."

"Yessuh."

"Well, well."

"That's true."

"You try to twist the arm of the Almighty, and you'll bite off a lot more than you can chew. You can wrestle with God, but you'll never pin him, that's sure. You won't even score a point."

"Amen. Hallelujah. Praise Jesus."

"You know what I think?"

"What's that, pastor?"

"I say when we tell God he has to take away this illness or handicap or financial hardship, we may be tellin' him to remove the very things he put into our lives to conform us to the image of Christ!"

"That's true!"

"See, I watch some of these television shows and listen to some of these radio programs. And you know what I think?"

"Tell us, pastor."

"I think they're trying to make God into a no-lose lottery in the sky. Like he's just a cosmic slot machine where you put in a coin and pull the lever, then stick out your hat and catch the winnings. It's like God's reason for existing is to give us what we want. Well, I got news for you, folks. My God ain't Santa Claus. He's the Lord God Almighty—and don't you forget for a moment he's on the throne and you're not!"

Enthusiastic applause overwhelmed the verbal responses.

"Now, there's some people that call God 'Master,' but they act like they're the masters. And God's the genie. Instead of rubbing a lamp, they just quote a verse or say 'Praise the Lord' three times, and presto, changeo, alakazam, the smoky God with the funny hat and big biceps does whatever they tell him to do! Like they're the ones that have dominion, not him. And that explains why people don't care about good theology; they don't care about God. I mean, who cares what the genie's like? Genies serve one purpose—to grant us our wishes, give us what we want. Then we can just say," his voice went high pitched and squeaked, to the laughter of the congregation, "You can go now, God. I'll call you back when I think of something else I want."

The man was moving, pummeling that big bag from every side.

"See, now, I've thought a lot about this prosperity theology. I've thought about it as I've read my Bible. I thought about it two years ago when I walked through the streets of Cairo's Garbage Village, shaking the grimy hands of the Christians who live there in poverty. I thought about it when I worshipped alongside faithful believers on a rough backless bench on a dirt floor church in Kenya. I thought about it some more when I met a pastor from China who lost everything because he stood up for Jesus. Well, this health and wealth gospel may look like it works sometimes in California, but it doesn't work in China or Haiti or Rwanda, now does it?"

"No, sir." Lots of heads shook.

"And hear me now, folks. Any gospel that's more true in California than in China is *not* the true gospel!"

Thunderous applause.

"Now I figure, maybe it's because they're hearing a false gospel that we got so many people that claim to become Christians and next thing we know we never see 'em again. You know what I'm sayin' now, don't you?"

"Yessir, pastor."

"Amen."

"You said it."

"My good friend Harvey Williams over at the AME church on Albina, he was tellin' me about all these bats he had flyin' around in the church attic. I told him, 'Harvey, we used to have that problem at Ebenezer. Then I figured it out. All I had to do was baptize those bats and then I'd never see 'em again!'"

Laughter.

"Now, Brother Daniels, down there, you're a computer salesman, aren't you?" The man nodded, obviously enjoying the recognition. "You'll appreciate this story. There was a computer salesman, a real smooth black cat, showing a video on the screen, called 'The sights and sounds of hell.' Well, it showed this handsome man and beautiful woman dancing and drinking and having fun, partying together, havin' a great old time. The man watchin' the video thinks this is pretty cool, and he just goes right on livin' like hell. But then he dies and he ends up going to hell, and it's horrible and miserable, with no relief. And then he asks the devil, 'Hey, where's all the fun?' Then the devil gives him this sly smile and says 'Oh, you must have seen our demo.'"

The brother three down from Clarence laughed so hard he almost fell off the pew.

"Well the truth is, the devil makes sin look fun and righteousness look boring. He tries to make hell look good and heaven look bad. But don't be fooled, folks. My daddy taught me something I never forgot. He said, our time on earth is just a dot. It ends not long after it begins. But our time in eternity, heaven or hell, will be a line that goes on forever. Every man has to choose whether he's gonna live for the dot or live for the line. You live for the dot and you're a fool. You live for the line and you're a follower of Jesus. Now you think about that. You think about that for a few million years!"

"Amen."

"Yessuh."

"Can I get a witness?" Pastor Clancy asked, unsatisfied with the feedback. Hundreds of *amens* and *uh-huhs* replaced the fifty or so from a moment before.

Men were wiping their brows, and women waving their bulletins like a flock of birds, but no one seemed to be looking at his watch. It'd been ages since Clarence had been in a church where time mattered so little. He realized the pastor hadn't turned to his Scripture passage. He wasn't to the sermon yet. He was just warming up.

"Now, last night I drove by Murphy's Bar down the road on MLK. And you know, there were lots of cars, and folk were hootin' and hollerin' and havin' a good old time. Well, here we are today, and Jesus is our Lord and gives us victory and made a place for us in heaven. We gonna let them have a better time at Murphy's Bar than we have at Ebenezer Church?"

Lots of heads shook. "No way. Never."

"I see some people come to church on Sunday. They wear their best glad rags and patent leather shoes. They come in with their curls adrippin'. And maybe they're thinkin' how sharp they're lookin' instead of how great God is. Now listen to me, folks! God doesn't just want people who dress up for him on Sunday. He wants people who obey him on Monday! When my daddy told me to do something, he wasn't askin' a favor. When God tells us something, he's the same way—doesn't want discussion, doesn't want negotiation, wants plain old obedience. So don't just amen the sermon with your lips. Amen it with your life!"

"Hallelujah, sweet Jesus."

"Uh-huh!"

"That boy sho' can preach."

"Now we're takin' an offering for the poor today. Because truth is, I don't think you can worship a homeless Man on Sunday, then ignore one on Monday."

"Amen."

"Say it again, now."

The plate came by and Clarence took out a twenty dollar bill, leaving another seventy or so in his wallet. He passed the plate to his father, knowing what would happen. Obadiah opened up his wallet and dumped all his money into it. Clarence knew he'd cashed his Social Security check, and it was still early enough in the month that this might be hundreds of dollars. He'd tried to tell him God didn't expect him to do all that, but the stubborn old man wouldn't listen. Clarence looked at the delight on his father's face and realized this was something that couldn't be bought. It provoked a longing within him for what this old man had.

After a powerful hour-long sermon full of Scripture and illustrations and a lot of laughter and some tears, Pastor Clancy reminded Clarence of a pilot starting to lower the landing gear.

"I want you to say this after me: We're gonna *learn* God's Word."

"We're gonna *learn* God's Word."

"Who am I talkin' to, the dead in Christ or what? I want to hear you. We're gonna *do* God's Word."

"We're gonna *do* God's Word."

"We're gonna *share* God's Word."

"We're gonna *share* God's Word."

He went through a dozen more expressions, all of which were repeated enthusiastically.

The choir got up and sang, "Knowing you, Jesus, knowing you. There is no greater thing. You're my all, you're the best, you're my joy, my righteousness, and I love you Lord."

Pastor Clancy got up to close in prayer.

"Set us free, Jesus. Your Word says you came to set us free. Our people were slaves for centuries, but you set us free. But there's an even greater freedom. Freedom from drugs and booze and gangs and violence and divorce and abuse and immorality. O God, set us free from bondage to sin. Set us free by the power of Jesus. In his name we ask it, amen."

"Amen."

"Hallelujah."

People hugged and greeted each other and slapped each other on the back. Clarence looked at his watch.

Two and a half hours?

"Hey now, you're Clarence Abernathy, ain't you?" Clarence shook the old wrinkled hand extended toward him. "I's Harold Hadaway. Seen you over at the councilman's office t'other day."

"Really?" Clarence asked. "What were you doing there?"

"I'm the chief custodian." Harold pushed out his chest. "Takes care of three offices in that building—the councilman's, a law office, and an accountant. I read your columns, son. Like what you has to say. I surely do."

"Thanks, Mr. Hadaway. Glad to meet you."

"Call me Harold. Proud to know you, Clarence Abernathy. Miss your sister, Dani, I do. Yessir, she was always good to me. Always good."

Clarence introduced Harold to his father. He watched the two instantly connect, as old black men who shared the same struggles and the same faith always do. There was something about this church, this place, Clarence sensed. Something in it that reached way back and way deep.

The family sat around Dani's big dining-room table, Obadiah at the head, Clarence and Geneva on one side of him, Keisha and Celeste on the other, with Jonah and Ty at the far end. Ty was there under protest. As usual, he wanted to be doing something with his friends.

Obadiah sat straight as his eighty-seven-year-old back would allow. As always, he chewed his food over and over, as if stretching it, savoring it, trying to draw extra nourishment. He ate like a man who hadn't always had enough to eat. At Sunday dinner he held the family reins, and in the last year or so with Obadiah, you never knew where the conversation would go next.

"Fine message, fine message," Obadiah said. "I like that Pastor Clancy."

"So do I," Geneva said. She passed Obadiah a big piece of huckleberry pie.

"Much obliged, Daughter. Looks wondrous. Looks wondrous." After one long bite and lots of head shaking, he resumed his commentary. "Good chu'ch. I likes that chu'ch. Good chu'ch, isn't it boys?" He eyeballed Jonah and Ty.

"Yes sir," Jonah said.

Ty looked down and grunted, "Yeah."

"Been to lots a churches in my day," Obadiah said. "One time went with Cousin Jabal to a church in Louisiana. They put whites on one side and blacks on another. Then they had this big ol' rope goin' down the middle aisle, just to make sure no one forgot what color he was. Funny thing, pastor was preachin' through Colossians, and the text was how race don't matter and we's all one in Christ Jesus." He chuckled, eyes dancing. "I don't know what more that pastor said. I just sat there thinkin' about how we're all one in Christ Jesus and lookin' at that rope!"

Obadiah laughed long and hard, shaking his head. "You remember Jabal's boy Rabe, don't you Clarence?"

"Yeah, Daddy. He stayed with us a few weeks until...until the polin'."

"What's polin?" Jonah asked. Clarence glanced at his daddy as if to say, "You're the one who brought it up."

Obadiah sighed. "Polin' was where people would get in their cars, drink enough beer to gets them up some courage, then drive down roads settin' to whack blacks in the back of the head with two-by-fours. It happened to Rabe. Hurt him pretty bad."

"Why are white people so mean, Grampy?" Celeste asked.

"They're not mean, honey, not all of 'em, not even most of 'em. Just some of them, chile, just some of them." He looked around the table. "Jabal always used to say, 'Never trust a white man,' and he said it more than ever after Rabe got poled. Well, Jabal was wrong. I told my chillens then and I'm tellin' you all now. Never trust a man with bad morals and a weak character, that's what Jabal should have said. Skin color don't matter, 'cept to people with small brains. There's good blacks and bad blacks. There's good whites and bad whites. You can't never tell a book by its cover. And you can't never tell a man by his color."

Obadiah measured the silence at the table before continuing. "The problem ain't white folk. The problem's just folk—black, white, or purple, it don't matter. Bible calls it sin, and sinners is what we all is." He seemed to be reaching for a story, and his eyes glowed when he found one.

"When I was a boy, my grandpappy on my daddy's side was visitin'. It was a hot day and we was fishin' down by a lake—prettiest little lake you ever seen. Well, Grandpappy, he took off his shirt. And I saw the marks all over his back. I came over and ran my finger over them. They was all healed, but you could still see the pain in his eyes. I asked him, 'Who did this to you, Grandpappy?' I knew he'd been a slave, but the stories never made much sense to me till I saw the marks.

"He said, 'A cruel man did it to me. I've asked Jesus to forgive him. I hope he asked Jesus to forgive him too.' See, he never said it was a white man. He said it was a *cruel* man. I never forgot that."

Obadiah looked around the table, and Clarence could almost hear an abrupt gear change in his daddy's head. "You know what's missin' in churches these days?"

"What's that, Daddy?" Clarence asked.

"The mourner's bench. 'Member our old church in Puckett? They had a mourner's bench. That was back in the days when you didn't need no theologian to explain away the Bible. We just believed it. And tried to live by it. 'Member ol' Reverend Charo, Clarence?"

"Yes, Daddy."

"Now that was a preacher. Man had more points than a thornbush." Obadiah smiled broadly, his white teeth looking like piano ivories. "The Reverend used to say from the pulpit in this big loud voice, 'It's no disgrace to be colored.' Then he'd pause and lean forward and wink at us and whisper, 'It's just awfully inconvenient.'"

Obadiah laughed and laughed, mostly on his own, though Geneva managed a few chuckles herself.

"Sunday was the finest day of the week, I reckon. We'd leave behind those cotton fields, that ol' ramshackle house, and come to the house of God. Without Sundays, we woulda shriveled up and died, worked ourselves to the grave 'fore we was fifty years ol'. We'd put on our Sunday best. Mama, she'd put wheat starch in my collar to glue down the threads on my one white shirt. I'd pick the trousers with the fewest holes. We'd walk the four miles to Sunday school, rain or shine. And we had fun walkin'. Ol' Elijah and me, we was always cookin' up mischief along the way."

He looked right at Jonah and Ty and nodded, as an old man who's never forgotten what it is to be young. Everyone's eyes focused on Granddaddy. Frail as Obadiah's body had become, his eyes were strong and he still carried the indomitable authority of a senior black man.

"Pastor served four churches, so he'd be there once a month. We'd take a break after Sunday school, then have a big service. Preacher go up there and say, 'Remember your mama? How she used to hug you and tuck you in? But she gone now. Can't tuck you in no more.' And he'd carry on and on, till we was all snifflin' and sobbin'. He'd keep remindin' us of our grandmammies and all our kin that died until we was almost in a frenzy. Then he'd shout, 'But someday you goin' to see yo' mama again. Some day you goin' to heaven, if you loves Jesus, and there she be— arm's awide open, waitin' fo' you. How many o' you can hardly wait for that day?'"

Obadiah's voice had taken on the strength of the preacher's from seventy-five years ago. "People, they be shoutin' and clappin', twitchin' and tremblin.' Not like some churches where it's just a lecture and they has to stop at an hour so you don't falls asleep. Now, your churches today, they don't preach about heaven no mo', not like that anyways. Not like that. Maybe nowadays we thinks this world's our home. Maybe that's whys we's in so much trouble."

His deep-set eyes surveyed the table as if it were a poker game and he was trying to read in the faces each player's hand.

"Then there was revival week. Relatives would come back from all over. Church and family was the same, wasn't one without the other back then. Lots of eatin', singin', preachin', and lots of offerin's, sometimes two or three in a service if we didn't collect enough for the poor."

"I thought *you* were poor, Grandpa," Jonah said.

"Well, compared to most folks we was. But there's always people poorer than you, and you always gots to help them. You remember that now, chillens."

He scanned the children to decide which to light his eyes on, and this time chose Keisha.

"We'd come together and focus on a better life—the life to come. Always read the Scripture that said we was strangers and aliens and pilgrims. Slave stock understood that. Property owners never did. See, Keisha, black folk couldn't own property back then. A few did, but very few. We was sharecroppers; our pappies was slaves. We knew this wasn't our home. It's harder when you think you own things yourself. 'Cause then you starts actin' like a big shot owner instead of a tenant. This here is God's world, chillens. No man owns anything. We's all just sharecroppers on God's land. But he never cheats us—come harvest time, he'll give us the rewards of our labor."

"Doesn't seem that way sometimes, Daddy," Clarence said. Geneva looked startled. She didn't remember him ever taking issue with his daddy in front of the children, at least not on spiritual matters. "Lots of bad things happen in this world. Seems like sometimes our labor doesn't pay off."

"That's because it ain't harvest time yet, Son. You jus' wait. You jus' wait."

I'm tired of always waiting.

"You trust him, boy, and yo' sweet Jesus ain't gonna let you down. These television preachers make it sound like today's the harvest. Give a bunch o' money and next thing you know there's a big Cadillac in your driveway. Show me the chapter and verse fo' that one, will ya? God say at the proper time we'll reap a harvest, if we don't give up. Proper time ain't here yet. Don't give up, Son. Just don't give up."

The old man's eyes started to glaze. His mouth kept moving, but he was in transition. "I remembers those ol' songs, songs black as night, black as the raven. 'Steal away.' 'Swing Low, Sweet Chariot.' 'I'll Fly Away.' 'Just Over in Glory Land.' 'In the Sweet By-and-By.' We always sung about 'one day acomin'.' We knew this weren't the day."

Obadiah was somewhere else now. Was he thinking about his mama? Clarence wondered. His wife? His daughter? Little Felicia?

Suddenly, so low and quiet you could barely hear, he began singing a song Clarence vaguely remembered from childhood. "I does not know why all aroun' me, my hopes all shattered seem to be. God's perfect plan I cannot see. But one day, someday, he'll make it plain."

Clarence envied for a moment the simplicity of his father's faith. But in another moment, he pitied the old man who clung to promises made to slaves who were beaten and raped and ridiculed and sold like cattle.

"I don't understand," the old man continued to sing, "my struggles now, why I suffer and feel so bad. But one day, someday, he'll make it plain. Someday when I his face shall see, someday from tears I shall be free, yes, someday I'll understand."

It was awkward at the table. Nobody knew quite what to do when Grandpa edged off into his other world.

———

Zeke and Torel left Dani alone to observe through the time portal a great ancient civilization in northern Africa, near modern Sudan. She viewed with fascination the coal black people who called themselves Kushites, whom the Greeks called Ethiopians, which meant "dark skinned." She watched them develop their own alphabetic language, build pyramids, masonries, ironworks, and complex waterways. She marveled at their excellence in architecture, education, and the fine arts. They were one of the most vigorous and advanced civilizations the world had ever known. Suddenly she saw the writing of the psalmist, and it thrilled her: "Ethiopia shall soon stretch our her hands unto God."

She watched as Jeremiah was rescued by a black African, then as Simon—from Cyrene in Africa—carried the cross of Jesus. By the time of Christ, this black people group was sending ambassadors to Arabia, India, China, and to Rome. She saw a number of Africans gathered on the day of Pentecost, converted to faith in Christ. She saw the church at Antioch, among the chief leaders Simeon, called 'Black Man,' and Lucius the Cyrenian. She watched the Antioch church send out Paul and Barnabas to evangelize Turkey, Greece, and Italy. It inspired her to see black church leaders sending missionaries to reach pagan white Europeans with the gospel. She wished Harley could see this. She wished she'd learned about it back in the Shadowlands.

She watched, intrigued, as one man came to the fore in this ancient drama, a man born just before Christ. He was the chief officer in charge of Ethiopia's treasury.

Something inside this man—Dani recognized it as the voice of Elyon—told him there was more than the petty ethnic-centered gods of races and nations, such as the three-faced Kushite lion or the Egyptian ram god. There must be a true God who made all races and nations and reigned over all. This Ethiopian sought to know that one true God. He'd heard of a God who brought justice and redemption to a band of slaves, delivering them from the Egyptians a millennium and a half earlier. This was a God who could not be manipulated, who did not exist to fulfill the agenda of any man or nation.

The Ethiopian welcomed the opportunity to travel to Jerusalem. After a few weeks of observing Jewish worship and faith, he began his long journey back by carriage through the Sinai desert to Egypt, from which he would travel another eight hundred miles to his home. Along the way he studied the Hebrew Scriptures, of which he had obtained a scribal copy for his queen at great price. As Dani watched him riding in his chariot, she felt the longing, the ache in his heart to know the truth. It thrilled her.

Suddenly a man appeared on the scene, Philip, a Jewish Christian convert. He had already gone to reach the Samaritans, who had been hated as half-breeds but whom he knew should be embraced because all racial barriers had been broken down in Christ. Now, sent by God's Spirit, he went to the Ethiopian.

Dani listened as the black African asked questions, and Philip, the brown Jew, explained how God's Son had suffered and died and risen for all men that they might be forgiven of their sins and spend eternity with him, along with brothers from all nations and tribes and languages.

The Ethiopian listened in rapt attention, sensing this was the missing piece to life's puzzle. The man came to faith in Christ as he sat in his chariot. He asked Philip to baptize him in water by the road. Dani wept at the sight of this baptism, feeling as if she were there. It moved her more than any she'd ever witnessed.

Dani watched in excitement as this black national leader continued to study and grow in his faith on the journey home. Back in Ethiopia he became an outspoken witness for Elyon's Son. She watched many in that nation come to Christ, knowing the descendants of these people would migrate to west Africa and seventeen hundred years later many would be taken to the new world as slaves. She realized her roots for the first time—she and her family were descended from the very Ethiopians she now observed. Churches were established, thriving churches. She watched the decades become centuries as some of the greatest theological minds of early Christianity—including Augustine, Tertullian, and Origen—came out of the black churches of North Africa.

As she watched the courage and conviction of the first African Christians, the strongest bulwark of early Christianity, she swelled with wonder and the right kind of pride. The spiritual heritage of her people, she realized for the first time, did not simply go back a few hundred years to American slaves. Many people of her race embraced the Christian faith before the first white churches were born, before the gospel traveled north to Europe or spread to Asia, and fifteen hundred years before it came to the new world.

She marveled too, as she followed the timeline of history, that the Christian church was solidly grounded in North Africa over six hundred years before Mohammed lived and Islam began. She watched the flourishing ministries of over five hundred bishops in the African church, then grieved as she witnessed Islam's military conquest and persecution of African Christians. She wondered why she had never before heard this part of history. But she thrilled at the vibrant Christian faith and perseverance of her ancestors, even amid the suffering and enslavement by Muslims.

Dani wept at length, feeling pain eclipsed by joy. Finally she felt a hand on her shoulder. Thinking it might be Elyon's Son, she peered up at the broad smile of a coal black face she immediately recognized. It was the Ethiopian man, baptized by Philip, now in the full-time service of the King of the universe. Dani and the man walked and talked and exchanged stories. He introduced her to many of his family and old friends, who became her new ones.

On Wednesday, Clarence sat through his third funeral service in the past four weeks. He didn't want to come, but Geneva talked him into it. The boy killed in a knife fight Sunday night was Robby, a thirteen-year-old who lived just two blocks away. Geneva told Clarence he'd met him the day after they moved in, but he didn't remember.

Clarence looked around in the funeral chapel at the number of blue bandannas around heads and knees, and clothing accents of every kind, from blue shoelaces to blue yarn on belts. Whoever this kid was, he obviously claimed Crip.

It was an open casket. Often teenage funerals weren't anymore. When someone is shot at close range, it doesn't lend itself to viewing the body.

The funeral was impersonal compared to Dani's and Felicia's. The minister didn't know the boy. Apparently they didn't go to church.

A young woman with a face aged more than her body stood up and said, "My Robby was a good boy. He jus' hung with the wrong crowd. Some of *you* the wrong crowd!" She pointed defiantly at some blue-accented teenagers. "I know you his set, but you took my baby from me. Won't never forgive you for that. Never." Her lower lip quivered.

"I told Robby ten times if I told him once, 'You tied your shoes this morning— maybe the funeral director's gonna tie 'em for you tonight.' Well, one of *you's* gonna be next, you hear me now?" She pointed menacingly at certain faces in the crowd. "I know whassup. I know whatchu thinkin'. You boys thinkin' no good. I see it in your eyes. You thinkin' revenge. Don't do it. Don't go kill somebody else's baby tonight. Let it end here. Let it rest. Just let it rest!"

She pled with them, as other mothers sitting in the crowd said quiet amens.

After the short service, Clarence watched as teenage boys and girls walked by the coffin, many of them dropping in blue flags. The girls cried openly, while the boys brushed off tears quickly, pretending they were reaching for their hair or swatting a fly. Some of the older boys looked grim and thoughtful. Their eyes suggested something was brewing. Clarence thought Robby's mother might be right. Revenge. He shuddered at the thought. It was like the old feuds, but much worse—the Hatfields and McCoys with Uzis.

Clarence and Geneva were among the last to walk by the boy's body. In the casket lay three of his favorite stuffed animals, most prominent a green camel with red balls hanging around its jaws.

He was just a little boy.

Geneva walked over to Robby's mother, whom she didn't know except for a brief conversation at Kim's Grocery. She put her arms around her and hugged her and cried with her. That was Geneva.

After Geneva rejoined him, Clarence looked back at Robby's mother one last time. She removed the blue flags from the coffin, handling them quickly as if they contained an airborne virus. She threw them on the floor, then kicked them for good measure. She looked at her baby, hugged the body that had once contained his spirit, and cried loud and long, as only a mother does who has lost her little child.

Meanwhile, on the streets outside the funeral chapel, the Rollin' 60s Crips passed the word that at nightfall they'd gather at Boyle Park. They'd be puttin' in some heavy work against the Woodlawn Park Bloods and the Loc'd Out Piru Gangsters. The Crips would make them pay for what they did to their homeboy.

CHAPTER

14

The Rollin' 60s Crips met at the fringes of Austin Park, adjoining a Northeast Portland cul-de-sac where there were three R6C houses. They gathered with two sets of Bloods on their mind—the Woodlawn Park Bloods and the Loc'd Out Piru Gangsters. Crip intelligence knew Robby, a Rollin' 60s baby gangster, had been put away by two Bloods from one or both of these allied sets.

The drums had been beating ever since the funeral, word passed everywhere about the meeting at Austin Park. The Rollin' 60s Crips convened here when there was a gang infraction, discipline problem, or when Bloods needed to get kicked. They'd plan moves, hit tactics and strategies, and pump each other up. They'd choose a riding party, a group of shooters to invade enemy territory, to mount up, embark on a mission of revenge.

Forty or so homeboys had showed. Tyrone recognized most of them, though he'd never seen them together at once. He gazed in awe at the fashions, studying them as if he were a freshman girl on her first day of school.

Two homies wore baseball caps backwards, another tipped to one side. He saw three dudes with hairnets and others with a variety of bandannas, most of them blue with white swirls, some covering heads, others wrapped around knees. Some of the homies had long hair combed straight back into a tail or braided at the neckline, oth ers wore pageboys, others "fades," highly styled flattops with geometric designs etched into the sides.

Several guys wore huge Le Tigre knit shirts buttoned to the top and hanging loose, others pin-striped baseball shirts, still others oversized plaid Pendleton long sleeves. Ty could see many tattoos, most of them R6C. Footwear was all-white athletic shoes with black shoelaces or all-black athletic shoes with white shoelaces. Some sported Crip-blue shoelaces, mostly unlaced.

Black Raiders jackets were everywhere. Some homeboys wore overalls, partly unfastened. Others wore black, brown, or gray oversized Dickeys, khaki work pants, or starched and creased Levi's. Most of the pants were worn low, sagging or dragging on the ground.

Serious soldiers dressed in combat black. Black leather, black shoes, black everything, to blend into the night and to confuse rivals and 5-0s. They knew homeboy blues made an easy target, so they weren't flagged out. Even though it was almost dark, most of them wore shades.

The girls, outnumbered two to one, wore variations on guy clothes, leaning heavily to the darker colors and favoring jackets with fancy cursive or Old English lettering. They wore heavy makeup, with excessive dark eye shadow.

Blasters were everywhere, playing the latest rap, the latest funk, along with songs of sex and violence and cop-killin'. There was a Geto Boys song about women being whores, and raping a girl because she left her curtains open. The song ended with, "Then slit her throat and watch her shake till her eyes closed."

The boys seemed to enjoy it, with no thought that the woman degraded and raped and murdered in the song could be their mothers or sisters. While some girls drifted away from this music, others stayed and gyrated to the beat. Ty glanced sidelong at his friend Jason, another fourteen-year-old wannabe, eyeing the Crip girls. Both felt tense, but tried to look cool.

Gangster Cool, GC, head of Portland's Rollin' 60s, was a transplant from L.A. His father had been an Original Gangster, an OG Crip with a bad rep, still serving hard time at Folsom. GC had seen him face to face as a six-year-old at a jail visit and never since. GC himself had gone to juvy for armed robbery at fourteen but was back out in a year and became a Ghetto Star by eighteen, earning OG status just like the daddy he'd never known. Now he was twenty-one, a streetwise veteran with charismatic charm, a high roller entrepreneur with a thriving crack cocaine business.

GC wore his hair in a g-ster do, with rows of skinny french braids secured with blue barrettes. A turkish rope, a thick gold chain, hung around his neck. He had the sculpted good looks of a movie star, a Denzel Washington image, with an unshak-able street-smarts confidence. Ty stared at the most prominent feature of GC's face, a four-inch scar he'd gotten in L.A. in a knife fight with Eight Trey Gangsters. GC started talking, and the homeboys listened in rapt attention, like they never did at school.

"Yo, 60s. Ready fo' some action? Ready to be down fo' yo' hood?"

"Yeah. We ready, man. We down."

"We kings of da turf," GC said. "This *our* dominion."

One of the homeboys was Mookie, who'd received a recent promotion. Behind him stood Shadow, GC's lieutenant, minister of defense. He wore gray work gloves for handling weapons and doin' work—which usually meant beating people up.

"Soldiers watchin' fo' Po Po?" GC asked Shadow, who nodded. Po Po was one of the nicer gang names for the Portland Police. "First," GC said, "we got to do some discipline."

Shadow yanked a young boy up by his collar. Ty recognized him. His name was Pete.

"Somebody say you snitchin' on us, boy," GC said to Pete.

"No way, man," Pete said, voice trembling.

"Cops been talkin' to you," GC said.

"They talkin', but I ain't listenin'."

"Well, maybe you talkin' and maybe you not. We not so sure. So we gonna give you a reminder of what happens if you do." The gang responded with grunts. Ty watched in fascinated horror as they beat up the boy and kicked him until he was almost unconscious. This was one of the cardinal gang rules, one step beyond pledg-ing for a fraternity—you join and you have to submit yourself to any mistreatment the older gang members care to dish out. Ty noticed his friend Jason was nowhere to be seen.

"You next?" GC looked at Tyrone. "Sup, little man? Hey, I seen yo' family's car. Bumper sticker say 'Proud parent of honor student.'" They all laughed. "Well, honor student don't count for much here, boy. Street smart's what counts. That's what gets you your green and the homegirls, the best little Cripalettes. Don't matter about math—'cept you know how to count up yo' money!"

GC slapped hands with several of the homies, including Mookie. Shadow, the hard-faced enforcer, stood guard.

"Hear you been claimin' us, honor student," GC said to Ty.

"Well, uh…"

"You sound stupid, honor student. Claimin' us or not?"

"Been doin' some wallbangin'. Just strikin' up the hood a little."

"Advertisin' the set, huh?" GC seemed impressed. "You just a toy or what?"

"I seen his piece on Miller," one of the older boys said. "He fresh."

"On Miller? Seen it too. That yo' work, nigger? Nice piece. Def. So you wanna kick it with us? Wanna be mo' than a tagger?"

"Yeah," Ty said.

"Know how big this set is?" GC asked Ty. "Hundred of us. We stick to our own hoods unless a war's on, then we join up, help each other."

A hundred. Ty was impressed. It never occurred to him GC might be exaggerating.

"Hey, I'm a 60 from L.A. Set's over a thousand deep there. Big sets join as nations for a major war and we could take the city apart. You should see the East Coast Crips. Go from 1st Street out to 225th. Harbor City! One set, takes five divisions of cops to invade their turf. Crips lots bigger than LAPD!"

More low whistles and hand slapping, like the punctuated *amens* at Ebenezer that encouraged Cairo Clancy to keep driving home his points.

"There be hood and there be N-hood," GC said. "Take all the sets in N-hood, and man you got power, big time. Portland way behind—it's L.A. twenty years ago. But our sets be gettin' deeper every day!" He stared at Ty, as if trying to read what was inside him.

"Why you claimin' us, boy?"

"Sixties is the main set in my hood."

"That all?"

"Gangsters kill my mama and my sister. Maybe Spics or Bloods."

"Heard about that. Nobody know who did it, huh? Hey, we kill somebody, we proud, don't hide it. But we don't just kill somebody's mama wid no reason. They scum, Bloods are. Spics too." He looked at Ty. "You ready to get jumped in?"

Ty swallowed hard, then nodded. GC slapped him to the ground, and the rest started hitting and kicking him. After thirty seconds, with blood flowing into his eyes, he started fighting back and got in a few good licks himself. They pushed him around for five minutes, and though he was bleeding badly, he'd drawn blood on a couple of them too.

"Okay, you all right, little homie," GC said. "You fight back. Won't be beatin' on you anymore. Unless we bored and need a tune up for the Bloods." GC put his arm around him. "You pretty low right now, what wid yo' mama and all. But you want to show us you down? Wanna make a rep? That be good. You long way from OG. You just a baby gangster, a tiny. But you in now, you been jumped in. You a homie, a 60. It's 'Do or die, Crip or cry.' But you want to be OG, you gotta build your rep. You gotta go head up on slobs. And you gotta do it with this set so when they speak yo' name it's like speakin' the Rollin' 60s Crips. You gotta promote the set, recruit for it, buy and sell for it, live for it, be willin' to die for it. But you gotsta prove yourself, man. You down fo' dat, honor student?"

"Yeah," Ty said, filled with pride and terror.

"You strapped, little homie? You carryin'?" When Ty shook his head, GC said to Shadow, "Get me a gauge, road dog." Shadow, in charge of munitions, pulled out from a military-green canvas bag a sawed-off shotgun, a twelve gauge missing most of its eighteen-inch legal minimum.

"This yo' first time, cuz?" GC showed him how to handle the weapon. "Sawed-off's easy to carry and sprays fast so you don't have to be too accurate. It's got double-aught buckshot. Only problem is, if you has to shoot more than fifteen feet, it's a spray and you not gonna get a funeral out of it. But you can still do some damage, man. Understand?" GC spoke with the calm reassurance of a tennis pro instructing a child in the proper forehand grip.

Tyrone felt the shotgun, awkward in his hands. He'd never held a gauge before, much less fired one. He'd never shot any gun. He looked at GC.

"You got the gauge now. Make you a man. Go spray some Bloods, little homie." GC held his hands up in the air like he was holding his own gauge. "'Booyah! You dead.' You wit' me?"

"Righteous, man. I wit' you." The words sounded much more confident than the cracking voice that spoke them.

GC looked out at the group. "All right, cuzzins, we been clockin' dese Bloods three days since they waste our little homie. We know right where they is tonight. They celebratin' our tiny's funeral. And we gonna pay 'em a visit, get some get back. For our homeboy. For the 60s."

Skin slapping and numerous exclamations of "down" and "righteous" and "def" filled the air. Ty felt the anticipation.

"Remember," GC said, "it's all about droppin' bodies. It's all about Blood funerals. They been woofin', the slobs. They dis you, they call you Crabs or Smuzz or Ricket. You gonna take that?"

"No way, man."

"This our mission tonight, homies. You show 'em. Watch the sentries now. You get Pretty Boy, that big black cat, you ring up points! You see that nigga, you shoot him, hear me? You don't see him, you shoot him anyway. You don't get them, they get you. Got it?"

It felt like NBA players breaking from the huddle and heading out on the court. Ty felt the intoxicating surge of power, the sense of being part of the Rollin' 60s dominion. Instead of being a victim, waiting for life to beat up on him, he could seize control.

They took five cars, all loaded up and lights off. Ty trembled as he found himself sitting right next to Shadow. He could smell the nuclear waste, the pungent grease in the defense minister's cornrowed hair. Shadow was R6C to the core, tough as they come. They cruised up to a house on Loc'd Out Piru Gangster turf, where the Bloods were hangin' and slangin', a dozen on the outside and at least as many inside. GC was first to jump out of a car. With quick aim, he shot out two street-lamps with his gauge. Booyah! Shadowy forms ran in confusion in the front yard. Glass fragments rained all over GC, and it seemed to exhilarate him. One gangster let loose with what sounded like a cannon. BOOM! BOOM! BOOM! Ty heard some-one yell "Sixties!" but wasn't sure if it was friend or foe.

The big bass of a .45 sounded off. Ty heard a Booyah. Another shotgun. The enemy flew off like starlings charged in the park, one screeching "Rollers!" Ty stood up close behind a Crip car, leaning over, terrified. One Blood turned and shot toward the car. The Crip next to Ty shot his nine-millimeter Beretta and the Blood dropped to the ground.

By now the Crips were all spread out, and only Ty and the banger with the Beretta—he didn't even know his name—were by the car. The other boy shot again, but his gun jammed. He saw Ty holding the shotgun and yelled, "Shoot it, fool!" He looked like he was about to grab it from him, so Ty turned it toward the house and blindly pulled the trigger. Booyah! It exploded, a surge of power going through him, seducing and terrifying him at the same time. The buckshot fired toward two Bloods, both with their backs turned. One hit the ground, the other kept running but pulled up limp.

"Move in," the nameless 60 told Ty, who panicked, trying to stick the sawed-off shotgun into his pants like he'd seen GC do once. Ty burned his skin and cut himself with its jagged metal edges.

While the other boy ran ahead, Ty stopped where the boy lay face down, totally still. He turned his head and in the dim light recognized him. He was a year older than Ty, but they'd gone to the same middle school. His name was Donnie. They'd had a math class together. Donnie had given Ty some chocolate chip cookies one day.

Ty spread his hand on Donnie's back and felt the blood. He ran back to the car and got in the backseat and shrunk down low. He wiped the blood off his hands onto his jeans and started crying. Sweat, blood, and tears soaked his shirt.

After a few minutes the car suddenly filled up again. In the panic no one noticed Ty had run from the scene. All the Crip cars seemed to take off at once. Tires screeched as Ty's car pulled out. Ty saw Shadow still standing by a telephone pole, with his nine-millimeter gun pointed at the house.

After a few moments, the Bloods, thinking all the Crips were gone, began mov-ing around outside the house. Two Bloods got up and brushed themselves off, just in time to be targeted cold by Shadow. He shot three times and knocked them both down. Then he ran up close. Ty watched in horror as Shadow put the gun close to one head and fired. Boom! Then he pointed at the other. Click! Click! Click! Shadow ran full speed toward the getaway car, which had stopped and backed up toward him.

One of the Crips in the car laughed hilariously. "That Shadow, he down. He get mo' points after the hit than in it! Those Bloods, they always fall fo' screechin' tires. You leave one soldier and he do de cleanup!"

Shadow jumped into the car, and the excited comrade slapped his hand. "Shadow, you one sprung nigger."

When they got back to their turf, less than two miles away, the set retreated into an old abandoned church building to celebrate and tell war stories, which got grander as time went on and lids broke out and bottles were passed. Ty snuck out and went around a corner. He threw up. Some of the boys laughed at him.

"You hurled, honor student, but at least you didn't bail!" It was GC. "You down, boy. You halfway down, at least! Heard you got you some get back on a couple slobs." He slapped Ty on the shoulder.

"Cuz be with us—he blasted slobs tonight, hey?" GC looked at Mookie. "Now move yo' black rear end and open up some tall ones. Let's drink some forties!"

The forty-ounce bottles of Olde English beer gave the feel of pirates drinking their ale after seizing a ship on the high seas. GC let Ty drink out of his forty. Ty loved the weight of the bottle in his hand. He loved being a part of something important, something bigger than himself. Being with these guys had been scary, but now it was feelin' better, feelin' real good.

"How's the brew, little homie?" GC asked.

"Great, man. Righteous." He lied. It tasted awful.

"Beats Night Train. Gangsta juice," GC laughed. He was so cool.

After the crowd dispersed, GC took Ty aside.

"Bend the corner here, cuz. GC gonna talk wid you." GC looked at Ty like a veteran pitcher might a promising rookie. He seemed almost tender. "You dropped bodies tonight, tiny. That puts you in all the way. Bangin' ain't no part-time thang. It yo' life now, hear me? I 'member seein' yo' family at the church—Ebenezer? Well, it's like that pastor used to say, everybody has a callin'. This yo' callin'. Nothin' matters like bein' a Crip. Love yo' set; hate yo' enemy. Hear me now?"

"Yeaaah."

"Homeboys is yo' family. We yo' daddy and yo' brothers. Crip women yo' mama and sisters, and they more than that too. They give you some fine action, you see. You get 'em big, that be okay. Show you a man. Bring 'em a lid or jewelry once in awhile, you keep 'em happy. Daddy Welfare take care of de rest." GC laughed. "They ig you or dis you, jus' find another one. Know what I'm sayin'?"

Ty nodded, though for the most part he didn't know at all. But his education had begun.

"Now on, you go out, you go out g-down, hear me? Here some decent locs." He handed him his dark glasses. Ty couldn't believe it. He had his own shades, from K-Mart, but these were from Gangster Cool himself. He'd won his approval.

"Don't want you lookin' like some fool Blood or somethin'." GC reached down into a bag. "Got sumpin' else for you. Yo' own strap." He handed him a big black nine-millimeter handgun, a Taurus PT 92AF.

"A nine?" Ty's eyes got big, admiring the cheap knockoff of a military sidearm Beretta 92F, as if it were a work of art.

"Whatchu think, I give you one of those .22 pea shooters?" He laughed. "Man, I took a deuce-deuce round once and thought it be a mosquito bite!" He slapped hands with his little homie.

GC showed him the fifteen-round magazine. "It's a virgin, not a hot one, not like mine," GC said, meaning no murders had been committed with it yet. GC kissed his own gun, a nine-millimeter Glock, identical to the ones used by many police officers. Some said he'd gotten it from a cop he killed. GC never challenged them on it. "You a cop-killer, you got juice." It made for a good rep. He treated his gun a lot better than his girlfriend. He had an extended magazine good for eighteen rounds without reloading.

"Now, little homey, you got to keep yo' piece loaded all the way. Bloods, they got one mo' round than you and you be sorry, you be dead. They don't know you now, but they will soon. And you can't just be slippin' down these streets. Got to have yo' eyes open. You hear me?"

"Yeeaah. Eyes open."

"Pretty soon you feel naked without yo' piece. The gat's part of the dress code. You ain't strapped and it be like one of them downtown boys in his monkey suit, like your uncle, goin' around without a credit card. Don't leave home widout it." GC thought this was extremely funny, and the pot made it funnier. He handed another lid to Ty, who laughed too, though the weed was making him sick.

"Now, yo' mama—sorry, I forgot they killed her, those dirty…Spics." He was obviously used to blaming Bloods for everything, so "Spics" didn't come out naturally. "Yo' uncle and auntie, now they ain't gonna understand why you need a piece. They jus' civilians. So hide it good. You got it?"

"Got it."

Ty went to GC's house to get cleaned up and spend the night. He'd told his aunt Geneva he was spending the night with his friend Troy Knopf, one of his few friends his mother had approved of. Geneva had called Troy's mother to make sure it was all right. At the last minute Ty told Troy he couldn't come. He hoped his aunt hadn't checked up on him again. He especially hoped his uncle wouldn't suspect anything.

Ty slept in GC's room on an extra mattress in the corner. It was almost three o'clock before he and GC stopped talking, nearly four before he fell asleep. Images flashed through his mind as he slept, feeding his dreams. Flashes of light, tumultuous sounds, and grotesque body shapes fought for dominion over his mind. Some of the haunting images came from earlier in the evening, some from another world. He lay there trembling. Now he watched the beautiful gruesome way the buckshot tore through the enemy's clothes and into his flesh, like piranha ripping into their prey. He saw a terrified look on the face of the Blood, unarmed, just fifteen. Donnie from math class, who gave him cookies. His tossing and turning became moaning and writhing.

He saw Shadow dropping those two boys and moving in to finish them off. The horror of it drew him out of sleep. He lay there wondering if he knew them. Maybe one was an honor student. Maybe his mama had one of those bumper stickers too.

He felt a lump in his throat. He lay there feeling proud, exhilarated, alive, terrified, guilty, and ashamed.

Tyrone fell back asleep, exhausted. He dreamed the sounds of magazines being rammed home, shotguns pumped, tires screeching, surreal blasts of gunfire. He saw twisted, lifeless bodies, a crippled boy trying to run or crawl away. He saw the blasts piercing the house. He saw his mother and sister riddled with bullets. He screamed.

"Mama, no, Mama, I'm sorry. I'm sorry."

GC came to Ty's side, not knowing what to say, remembering years ago when he used to have bad dreams too.

"It be okay, little homie," GC said to him. "Everything be okay."

Surrounded by people of every color and nationality and language, Dani squinted as she joined them in gazing at the four living creatures in the midst of the burning fire of Elyon's holiness. The creatures looked somewhat like men, but very different, with four wings. They stood upright, legs straight, but their feet were calf-like and looked like polished bronze. They each had four faces on four sides of their heads, faces which Dani did not dare to look upon.

Whirling disks bisected each other at right angles. The wheels within wheels made her think of Elyon's omnipresence; the eyes she saw everywhere, of his omniscience. In concert with millions around her, both men and angels, she fell on her knees and trembled at a terrifying holiness beyond comprehension.

"Behold, the cherubim who surround the throne of God." The voice was Torel's, but it sounded muffled and feeble, in stark contrast to the clear confident voice with which he normally spoke. She turned to see his face pressed against the ground.

She finally looked up at the four faces of the cherubim. Man, facing forward, he who had dominion over animals, king of the earth. Lion, king of wild beasts. Ox, king of domesticated animals. Eagle, king of the sky. They all spoke of Elyon—King of all the universe, he who exercised dominion over all.

Their human-like hands reached upward and outward, as they chanted "Holy, Holy, Holy is the Lord God Almighty."

Dani recognized this as the sound she'd heard from a distance from the moment she entered heaven, just as she'd once heard Niagara Falls from far away. But now she was at the base of the waterfall, a waterfall of holiness that made Niagara seem like drips from a kitchen faucet.

The cherubim were connected in a square and could travel straight in any direction at immense speed, able at a moment to change direction without turning. On the one hand it seemed to defy natural laws, yet on the other it seemed to be the ultimate expression of mathematical and geometrical precision. Dani remembered having once thought of mathematics as a distinctly secular subject, without spiritual dimension. Now it seemed the opposite, that mathematics was in its essence spiritual not secular.

In a universe handmade by Elyon, she thought, under his dominion, there's no such thing as secular, nothing that lacked a spiritual dimension.

Dani shook, bordering on dread. Her visceral instinct was to run from the terrifying holiness as from a tidal wave. But her mind reminded her emotions that this was the essence of the same Carpenter she loved, the Bridegroom himself. And if she would be forever swept away by this galactic tidal wave, then so be it. She lost all thought of self, including self-preservation, and let the tidal wave engulf her.

She felt for a moment vulnerable to the anger of the Almighty. But she was suddenly immersed in the reality that his holy anger against her sin was taken out on the Carpenter, and because she had accepted that provision, God had no anger left for her. Elyon's anger was there, all right, anger stored up for a day of judgment. But she would survive that day, for she was no longer an object of his wrath.

It struck her now as amazing that the Carpenter could talk and laugh and tease and relate so easily, even casually, to her. For that which the cherubim surrounded was the essence of Elyon, who was the Carpenter himself.

After time immeasurable had passed, Dani and Torel rose, and in concert with the congregation of millions, they slowly backed away from the cherubim, then dispersed to the corners of an ever-expanding universe, one that seemed bigger after each encounter with the Lord of the cosmos.

"The cherubim are so powerful and so…beautiful," Dani said, voice still trembling.

"Yet their power and beauty," Torel said, "is but a faint reflection of the infinite power and beauty of Elyon. His is a beauty so great that to those with corrupt eyes it is a more hideous ugliness than the mind can imagine."

"Hideous? Ugliness?" Dani said.

"Did you not feel the terror?"

"Yes, but—"

"Then you felt only a hint of what the inhabitants of hell feel about heaven, what the ungodly feel about God. The terror they feel is unmitigated by solace and reassurance. They feel the burning fire of his holiness without his hand-piercing love."

"How horrible," Dani said.

"Yes. And how unnecessary. For everything essential for their redemption has been done. The price has been paid. The blood has been shed. Only their stubbornness keeps them away. To the cleansed, beauty is beautiful. To the unclean, it is ugly beyond imagination."

Dani shuddered. "Who are the cherubim, Torel?"

"They are the highest order of created being. They defend the garden of God against the intrusion of sinful men and guard Elyon's throne against all that is unholy."

"But Elyon needs no guard," Dani said.

Torel looked at her curiously, as one does when he hears the obvious stated as if it were a dilemma.

"Of course he needs no guard. He is self-existent, independent, needs nothing and no one. But for the sake of those he created and out of love for them he *chooses* to use them. Did he need you to raise your children or share your faith or be his ambassador? No, yet he *chose* to use you, to rely upon you, and in that sense to *need* you to do all of these things and more. Did he need me to guard you day and night? Of course not. Yet he chose to use me in this way so that I had a vital role in your life and in his kingdom plan. He does not need the cherubim, but he has chosen to use them for the most sacred task. They are immersed in his presence. They serve as conduits for his attributes."

"For a moment I was overwhelmed," Dani said, "and my impulse was to bow before them. Then I remembered they are creatures and the bowed knee is reserved for Elyon himself."

"You see the dilemma faced by my kind," Torel said. "When men bow before angels to worship us we respond in panic. It is unthinkable."

"I used to have people come to the door," Dani said, "and argue that Jesus was the greatest of the angels, the highest created being."

"I was there to hear this blasphemy," Torel said, "and even now it burns deep within me." He paced, and she saw fire in his eyes.

"I knew those people at the door were wrong," Dani said, "and I'd quote a few verses to show that Jesus is God, but—"

"I tried to whisper to you the greatest proof, but my whispers were lost in the competing noises of your world."

"What proof do you mean?"

"The one we are discussing. Angels are God's servants, and one thing is more deeply ingrained in us than any other—we must worship *him* and him alone. Under no circumstances can we ever worship anyone else. To do so is unthinkable, repugnant above all else. We worship the Carpenter not because he is the highest of our kind, but because he is *not* of our kind—he is God, the world maker, the Alpha and

Omega, beginning and end."

"I understand," Dani said. "There's so much I see now that I wish I'd seen then, so many answers I wish I'd been able to think of."

"It was there for you to see, much more than you ever realized," Torel said. "You did not have to wait to die to know how you should have lived or what you could have said. Elyon's Book contains the answers you needed, and his Spirit gave you the power you required."

"At times," Dani said, "I fall to my face before him. Yet when we walk together, it is so intimate, sometimes even casual. He is my Lord, but he is also my Friend."

"What you say appears very strange to my kind," Torel said. "Yet it seems to please Elyon, and what pleases him can only be right. On earth people spoke of him with such ease and familiarity, without first being leveled by his holiness and terrified by his power. It was blasphemy. Yet when they feared him first, *then* responded to his invitation to be their friend, it was different. We of Michael's race do not experience him as friend. To us he is a benevolent Master, but always Master." He paused. "And perhaps there is something else we fear."

"What?" Dani asked.

"The memory of Morningstar and his betrayal of the Almighty. He desired to make himself like the Most High. He became intoxicated by the esteem of his fellows. Instead of deflecting adoration to Elyon, he craved and solicited it for himself. He claimed dominion and in doing so tried to steal it from the One who alone has dominion. The creature usurped that which is only the Creator's. That was the birth of sin, the beginning of hell, the seed of every injustice and evil the universe has ever known." He seemed to choke for a moment. "Many of my comrades were lost in that rebellion."

Torel turned and walked away, overwhelmed by recalling those painful events. Dani left him alone. She looked back at the cherubim that surrounded the throne of God and listened to their words, which she realized to be the perpetual background sound of heaven, like waves crashing at the seashore.

The face of the eagle said, "Dominion and awe belong to God; he establishes order in the heights of heaven."

The face of the ox shouted, "Dominion belongs to the LORD and he rules over the nations."

The face of the lion roared, "How great are his signs, how mighty his wonders! His kingdom is an eternal kingdom; his dominion endures from generation to generation."

The face of the man cried out, "You are the living God and you endure forever; your kingdom will not be destroyed, your dominion will never end."

Clarence stopped for breakfast at Barney's, a North Portland diner. It needed renovation, but he'd heard the food was good.

He parked his car and walked toward the diner, his stylish dark suit sticking out among the street clientele. A young woman noticeably pregnant and with the eyes of a druggie tried to act sexy, attempting to turn a trick this early to support her drug habit. Clarence felt disgust and pity. Two guys, both with the profiles of drug dealers, studied him head to toe. One sported a beeper on his belt.

Dealing drugs in the morning? The early bird catches the worm, huh?

"Whas it like, dancin' wid da man?" one of the dealers asked Clarence. The brothers from the hood slapped hands with each other. "That yo' wheels over there?" He pointed to the Bonneville. "Thought you'd have a pickup truck." They slapped skin again and laughed heartily.

Clarence didn't answer them, pretending the opinions of two no-account, shiftless, Jim Beam lovin' dope pushers meant nothing to him.

"I think he's one of those double thick Oreos, know what I'm sayin'?"

"Have a nice day, Monkey Suit Man." The dealer said it in his best imitation of a white accent. "See you, handkerchief head," the other added. As Clarence kept walking to the diner's front door he heard one say, "Man, that cat be whiter than white!"

It took all the self-restraint he could muster for Clarence not to dive for their cuffs and show them he hadn't forgotten the streets.

He sat down at the counter, recalling the jibes he'd taken from blacks. He'd never imagined the degree to which getting inside the professional world would alienate him from those he'd grown up with. It angered him to know that if he'd fathered children outside marriage and abandoned them to the care of mother and welfare, if he was a drug addict or spent his days stumbling the sidewalks and drinking malt liquor, he would be fully accepted by some of the same people who rejected him for succeeding. They ascribed his success to something other than his hard work and determination. They ascribed it to kissin' up to the white man.

The unpardonable sin wasn't killing your own people with drugs and guns, it was successfully competing with whites on society's playing field. These guys would never stoop to work at Burger King or a dry cleaners or the Fred Meyer warehouse. To them the supreme humiliation was to put yourself under whites. And because they'd never take an entry-level job, they would never be in the job market, never become qualified to work over whites instead of under them. They weren't at all like the backbone of the black community, the stalwarts such as his daddy and Dani and Mrs. Burns and most others, solid people who did right and lived responsibly and never made the newspapers until they died.

His daddy's words came back to him, as they often did. "Street hustlers, they ain't your heroes. A man who gets up every morning and does an honest day's work and takes care of his family—that's a hero."

———————

After breakfast Clarence drove south on Martin Luther King Boulevard. Suddenly he saw in his rearview mirror the swirl of red and blue and white. The colors eerily bounced around the car's interior as if they had a life of their own.

Clarence looked at his speedometer. Right at the speed limit. He hadn't run a red light. He figured it must be "one of those" stops.

The cop strode forward. Clarence watched him in his sideview mirror. He noticed the officer's hand on his gun, the holster unsnapped.

"May I see your driver's license please? And your registration and insurance information?"

Clarence removed the license from his wallet, trying to appear calmer than he was. He reached to the glove compartment to get the other papers. An orange-capped needle dropped to the floor of the car.

He handed the papers to the officer, who stared at the needle.

"I'm an insulin-dependent diabetic," Clarence explained.

The officer looked at him as if to say, "Right."

"Okay, Mr. Abernathy. I'll be back in a minute." Clarence knew the drill. He realized he was being checked for outstanding warrants, parole violations, possible auto theft, you name it. Having seen the needle, the officer was probably expecting a few drug convictions would pop up on his computer screen.

Clarence kept looking at his watch. He had an interview and he was already cutting it close. Five minutes later the officer returned with his papers and his license.

"Everything checks out, Mr. Abernathy. You're the sports guy aren't you?"

Clarence nodded. "Yeah, I'm the sports guy." Who are you, Robocop?

Clarence looked the officer in the eyes. "Why'd you pull me over? I wasn't speeding. No traffic violation, right?"

"No, it was just…at roll call this morning they described a suspect in a couple of crimes in this area. Similar car color. When I saw you, I thought maybe you fit the description."

"What's the description?"

"Male, driving a nice four door."

"What color car?"

"Maroon."

"This isn't maroon."

"Well, you know—red, maroon, some people get them mixed up."

"What color was the suspect?" Clarence knew the answer, but he wanted the cop to say it.

"Black."

"How old?"

"Oh, twenties maybe."

"I'm forty-two."

"Well, I guess you take good care of yourself. You looked a little younger when I saw you." He laughed. Clarence didn't.

"What size was the guy?"

"About five eight, 170 pounds. That was just approximate, of course."

"I'm six four, 285 pounds." Clarence stared hard. "Doesn't sound like I fit the profile, does it? Except that I'm a black man. Is that why you pulled me over?"

"Look, sir, I'm sorry. You're sitting in a car. I couldn't tell your size or age. I was just doing my job."

Clarence stared at him.

"Have a good day, Mr. Abernathy. Be careful around here."

He didn't add, "It's a dangerous part of town." He didn't have to.

Celeste's hair felt like the tassels of woolen rugs she used to unravel on her living-room floor. Geneva loved to touch black hair in its natural state—the way it sprung up, just inviting you to lightly bounce your hand on it. But Celeste wanted her aunt to straighten her hair. Geneva understood.

She scooped up a dollop of VO-5, worked it into the strands of hair, spreading it evenly with a brush. Then she applied the heated iron. Geneva loved the beauty shop smell of hot hair. It brought back so many childhood memories.

"We used to have a favorite way of doing a process. You don't know what you're missin', girl." Geneva talked to Celeste as if she were older, an equal. The little lady ate it up. "We'd mix mashed potatoes, eggs, and lye, then smear it on our hair with a paintbrush. Took the kink right out."

"Mashed potatoes?" Celeste's nose scrunched up.

"Believe it, girlfriend. Would I make up something that weird? I remember when your Uncle Antsy's hair was as high as it was wide. He was about six inches taller back then."

Geneva thought of Janet's long brown hair. Yesterday they'd gone out for a walk and were suddenly caught in a shower. They ran and laughed. Geneva had stared at her friend's rain-soaked tendrils glopping down her back. Even when it was messy, there was something about white girls' hair. She wanted to ask her what it felt like. She didn't ask because she was afraid the question would sound envious. She didn't realize Janet was thinking about Geneva's hair. Thinking how beautiful it was even when wet.

Geneva thought about the white blood in her veins. Only a few years ago her cousin in California told her his study of the family roots uncovered that their great-grandmother, a slave, had borne two children by her Irish master—one of them their grandfather. At first no one in the family could believe they had Irish blood, especially the darkest ones, but recessive and dominant genes made it work. That's where some of the family's "high yellows" had come from. It still bothered Geneva, thinking about how her great-grandmother had been raped. She tried to make light of it, asking Clarence, "If I'm going to have white genes anyway, why couldn't I get the hair genes?" She also made good use of her cousin's discovery. When she was filling out a credit application form, after "Race" she put "Irish," then watched the clerk scan the page and suddenly look up at her with dropped jaw.

Geneva's mama had told her, "God blessed black women with low maintenance hair; all you gots to do is wash it, and the wind and rain and sun won't hurt it." Well, in her experience black hair was *high* maintenance. It took a lot of foolin' to get it just the way she wanted.

She thought nostalgically back to the hair products of her childhood, like Sta-Sof-Fro. The billion-dollar-a-year black hair-care business now reigned over by Revlon and other companies was once dominated by black businesses—Soft Sheen, Johnson, M&M, World of Curls, Luster's, D-orum, and Bronner Brothers. She'd used all their products and more, searching for the perfect hair product as if it were the holy grail. She laughed at herself, then turned Celeste around and looked her right in the eyes.

"Let me tell you somethin', girlfriend. There's some good white folk around, but they don't know nothin' about hair. We black folk know how to keep it nice and nappy. We know how to straighten it, part it, fry it, conk it, wave it, texturize it, shave it, hot-iron it, cold-wave it, jheri-curl it, dreadlock it, Afrotique it, activate it, oil it, braid it, and we're just gettin' started, you hear me? We have our own black hair-care shows because white folk just don't understand our hair. But that's okay, little girlfriend. Daddy used to say the reason God gave black people their hair was so we could have a business all our own!"

Clarence sat outside the office of Raylon Berkley, publisher of the *Tribune*. He'd already been waiting fifteen minutes. The plush furniture and original paintings on the wall, even Mimi the white-haired secretary who looked like British royalty, made him nervous. It all reminded him of his first encounter with Berkley twenty years ago, the night he wooed him to the old *Oregon Journal*, taking him to that incredible restaurant.

He suspected he might have been the establishment's first black customer of the year, and it was June. He had the distinct impression that if he'd walked in by himself, the management would have called the cops. He'd sat there and smiled all evening, trying to be respectful and appreciative, yet not to look ingratiating like an Oreo.

They'd started in a reception area with crystal punch bowls and a silver tea service and fancy little this and that. He'd never had hors d'oeuvres before, unless potato chips and onion dip counted. Here there were tiny finger sandwiches, rose-shaped radishes, olive-topped cream cheese delicacies, polished cherries, and endless sprays of parsley. It reminded him of anything but food.

They'd talked softly as white people always do in such places, not like he did at his family gatherings. When they finally sat down to a table to actually order a meal, the menu featured a myriad of delicate foreign items, nothing sounding remotely close to collard greens, black-eyed peas, or a pig-ear sandwich. The waiter recited the menu as if it were a love sonnet.

The music was something he didn't know, except that it wasn't Chuck Barry, the Temptations, or the Supremes. Later, when he went to his parents' house in North Portland to spend the night, he turned on Aretha Franklin and Otis Redding and even some Louis Armstrong to wash down the evening's aftertaste and remind himself he was still black.

It was that night Raylon Berkley had said the magic words he remembered to this day. "Clarence, we're offering you a beginning salary of twenty thousand dollars, plus expenses, and some decent benefits." In 1977 that seemed a great deal of money to do anything, much less to get free admission to ball games and write about them.

Behind Mimi, the door to the inner sanctum of Berkley's office burst open and Clarence sat up.

"Clarence! How are you?"

Berkley's words filtered through his perfect mustache, which never seemed to grow or shrink. Raylon was a compact man, short, medium weight, deliberate and purposeful, characterized by an economy of movement. This economy carried over to both his smile and his frown, which were strikingly similar, capable of their slight alterations with the least amount of warning. A perfect poker face. Behind it was the belief system of an atheist and the fervor of a missionary.

"I'm sorry, Mr. Berkley," Mimi said. "Congressman Thomas is on line one. Says it will only take a minute."

"Excuse me, will you Clarence? You know how persistent the congressman can be." Raylon laughed as if this were funny, and Mimi chuckled too, in the dignified way of royalty.

"Sure," Clarence said. You pay my salary.

Berkley wasn't one of those publishers who wanders around looking over the shoulders of reporters, like a domineering mother or a team owner who prowls the sidelines when the coaches and players wish he'd stay up in the owner's box, drinking martinis. He took pride in giving his editors and writers the widest berth. Still, everyone knew they were *his* editors and writers and the *Trib* was his. This came out most clearly at election time when the paper's endorsements were handpicked by Raylon.

As Berkley chatted with the congressman, Clarence stood close to the wall, perusing framed front pages of the *Trib* and the *Journal* going back thirty years. He thought about the favor and disfavor you could fall in and out of under Raylon's dominion. The publisher had distanced himself from Jake Woods the last few years. The scuttlebutt was that Jake's change to more conservative values or perhaps his embracing of a "fundamentalist" Christian faith had been viewed as a betrayal of the man who'd hired him. Since then, Raylon had redoubled his efforts to get closer to Clarence. He supposed this was because of his skin color, which Raylon considered a political asset, not entirely canceled out by Clarence's irritating conservatism, which in fact exceeded Jake's considerably. Things had improved, Clarence had to admit. At the *Trib* ten years earlier the same conservatism would not have been merely irritating, but intolerable.

In the early days, Clarence had been paraded into Berkley's office to meet VIPs as if he were a champion show dog or a carefully cultivated prize rose. "See, we're progressive. Meet our black man." In subsequent years, Raylon had hired dozens of other blacks, nearly all of them liberal, so Clarence was rarely brought in on the dog and pony shows. He didn't miss them.

Berkley reappeared with a friendly but efficient gesture. "Okay, Clarence, come on in." After fifteen minutes of small talk, name dropping athletes he knew personally and asking Clarence how he liked the transition from sports to general columnist, Raylon finally cut to the chase.

"I was talking recently with Reg Norcoast."

"Oh?"

"He said he's confused. He's taken a real interest in your sister's…situation."

It's called murder.

"And your niece, of course. He was really shook by this thing. Went to your sister's funeral, I hear, and named a memorial fund after her to improve North Portland. Even contributed his own money to the reward to find the killers. Is that right?"

"Yeah."

"Well, he tells me that on two occasions you've been…let's say, very angry with him. He said you lashed out at him and he doesn't understand why. Seems to think you have something against him. You've done a couple of articles critical of his district. Some folks have said they feel like it's coming across as a little racist."

"My main criticisms were of Norcoast's policies," Clarence said. "What's racist about that? I'm a black man criticizing a white man because I think his policies and programs are counterproductive."

"Yes, but his district is predominantly black."

"I know that. I'm living in it."

"Right. Well, then I'm sure you'll want to be sensitive to the community concerns."

"I'm not sure the community's concerns and Norcoast's are always the same. My main criticism was Norcoast's history of hiring known gang members, young thugs. Twenty thousand dollars to put up and take down signs, pass out his literature. Think of the potential for intimidation and legitimizing gangs. Are you saying you disagree?"

"Not exactly," Berkley said. "I don't know. It's being done in the larger cities, you know. Some people feel it's a good gesture, hiring kids to do legitimate work, maybe get them interested in something meaningful, politics and all. These gang summits have established some positive relationships both directions."

Clarence decided not to argue his case. This wasn't the time or the place, and Raylon certainly wasn't the person.

"Anyway, I know you and Reggie, and respect you both. I wondered, is there anything I could do to help patch up this rift between you?"

"Not that I know of."

"I realize you don't trust politicians, Clarence. And I know you're pretty adamant about your conservatism. I'm just asking you to give the councilman a chance. He's a good friend. A good man. Don't judge him without getting to know him. I've got an idea." He said it with the confidence of a man used to fixing life's problems. "I mentioned it to Reg. I know you both play tennis. Why not get together and play a few sets? Get to know each other as people."

What is this, *Fiddler on the Roof?* You the matchmaker or something?

"I'm not going to order you to do it, of course. But I've tried to give you every opportunity here, Clarence. I've let you in the door as a second conservative on-staff columnist, which is a major change. Very few papers have done that. So, call it a favor if you want, but I'm asking you to give Reg Norcoast an opportunity. I'd like to see you have a civil relationship. Does that sound reasonable?"

"Yeah, okay," Clarence said, hating himself for saying it. He felt as though he'd just been set up for a prom date with the most obnoxious girl at school.

Raylon walked over, put his arm around him, and asked him about his family, asked if he needed anything. Clarence told him everything was fine, though he knew that wasn't true.

————

Geneva walked out of Kim's Grocery on MLK with a paper sack containing a half gallon of milk, a loaf of bread, and a tub of margarine in one hand and her purse in the other. It was only a four-block walk back to her house, but it was almost evening.

The darkness was creeping in. She trembled involuntarily, less from the cold than from the idea of not being able to see clearly what was happening around her. She drew in her red mid-length fall coat and buttoned the top button.

After walking briskly two blocks, she saw some shadowy figures to her left and heard a whistle.

"Now there be a bumper kit," a male voice said loudly.

"I feel like gettin' me somethin', don't you?"

Geneva tensed up and walked a little faster. She wished she was wearing her Nikes instead of her pumps. Half a block later she heard footsteps behind her but decided not to turn around. One more block and she'd be home.

The footsteps seemed to be gaining on her. She considered running all out, but whoever was behind her probably didn't know she was close to home. It might be better not to turn it into a chase she was certain she'd lose. She looked to see if any neighbors were out who she could go up and talk to. There was nobody.

The footsteps kept coming, and she could hear breathing now. She hoped it was just her own. Only thirty feet from the walkway to her house.

She felt a hand on her neck, and she turned and screamed. The stocking-capped figure pressed up close against her. He grabbed her purse and pulled. She held tight to the strap, but heard the stitching rip and felt it slip out of her hands into his. She fell backward to the sidewalk, hitting her head, groceries tumbling. Frank, the next door neighbor, ran out of his house as the teenage boy in the Air Jordans sprinted off in the other direction. Frank chased after him about twenty feet, then shouted at him.

"Run, punk. Come back and see me, you want some trouble, boy. I'll make you wish you was sittin' barebottom on a short order grill, you hear me now?"

Hattie Burns charged across the street like a rushing linebacker, running as fast as her queen-sized body would let her. She plopped down on her knees over her fallen neighbor, just as Frank reached her.

"Geneva!" Hattie cried, desperation in her voice.

"You okay, Mrs. Abernathy?" Frank asked.

"Yeah. I think I'm all right." She sat up, rubbing the back of her head. "Thanks."

Hattie comforted Geneva, making a bit more fuss than Geneva liked, but she appreciated the concern. Frank picked up the loaf of bread, milk, and margarine and wadded up the torn grocery sack.

"You have any mace?" Frank asked Geneva. "Or one of those pepper sprays? You know, the ones you can carry in your coat pocket or on your key chain?"

"No. I don't." She'd never thought she needed one.

"Well, I get 'em for my wife and daughters. Got an extra. I'll bring it over later."

"Thanks." She heard the shakiness in her voice.

Hattie and Frank escorted Geneva, arms still trembling, up the stairs.

"Didn't have no church buildin's," Zeke told Dani, "but that was all right because we was the church, and that made us feel powerful important. We'd meet in our slave quarters or outside. The mens would rise up and tell Bible stories. Ol' Zachariah, he'd always say, 'The day's acomin' when negroes will be slaves of none but God Almighty.' We'd look at him big-eyed and didn't believe him. That was when no black man dared to think of freedom except by runnin'."

A man appeared in the portal. Dani could sense his meanness.

"That's Daniel," Zeke said. "They called him the nigga driver, the overseer. He'd sooner beat the breath out of you than draw one of his own. We was scairt of Daniel, I won't deny it. We'd set on the floor and pray with our heads down low and sing soft. But when you're praisin' the Master, you just can't stay quiet too long, and next thing we knew, Daniel he'd come and beat on the wall with the stock of his whip."

Dani watched Daniel do this very thing and heard him threaten, "I'll come in there and tear the hides off your darky backs."

"Now ol' Daniel," Zeke went on, "besides likin' his liquor, he took special pleasure in whippin' coloreds. He'd strip us to the waist and take a cat-o'-nine-tails and bring up the blisters to where you'd pray God would take you home then and there. And then he'd bust the blisters with a wide strap o' leather fastened to a stick handle. You'd be all blood from the neck to the waist.

"Sometimes they'd strip us naked when they beat us, and that was the worst, the women and the children seein' you humiliated like that. Wasn't enough to break your skin; they tried to break your spirit, and sometimes they succeeded and black folk lost their self-respect. Womenfolk would git us a sheet and grease it with lard and wrap us up in it, and sometimes we'd wear it under our shirts for three or four days after a bad beatin'.

"Ol' Daniel, one day Isaac sassed him, and Daniel he took Isaac down toward the pond. We knowed that was terrible bad 'cause he usually whipped us in front of each other to teach a lesson. Well, an hour later he come back without Isaac, and Isaac's wife was wailin' 'cause we all knowed what it meant. A few days later somebody found Isaac's body floatin' in the pond, and some folk said, 'That ol' nigger just didn't know how to swim.' Course, Daniel got away with it, but just for a little while. 'Cause we knowed God would get him one day and do worse to him than we ever thought of. And sure enough, he did. Once I seen him through the portal, like Lazarus seen the rich man. Just for a moment, but I saw him in hell and he saw me here, which must have made hell even worse for him."

Dani shuddered. "Daniel. Ironic that he had a biblical name."

"There was men that beat me named Peter and Timothy, and the meanest woman I ever knowed, that was Martha. Always thought it strange to hear those Christian names of folk who didn't understand what bein' a Christian meant. Always felt sorry for them, knowin' that unless they repented, Elyon's avenging angel would take 'em down to the pit."

"I'm surprised you could live under that kind of oppression," Dani said.

"A man can live under anything long as he keeps his eyes on the prize, on what will be instead of what was and what is. I'd think about the ol' ship Zion takin' me across the Jordan, away from Egypt and Pharaoh, into that land of milk and honey. I'd think about Jesus and how he suffered so much more than I did because of carryin' the sins of me and ever'body else, includin' ol' Daniel. And I thought to be punished for my own sins, much less Daniel's, was more than any man could take. Sufferin' ain't all bad, you know. That's one of the lessons I learned since bein' here and watchin' what goes on in the Shadowlands—faith falters where it should thrive and thrives where it should falter. Most God's chillens fail the test of prosperity but pass the test of adversity. How's that for some lessons?"

Dani nodded her approval. "I look forward to learning them myself."

"Sufferin' shouldn't surprise God's chillens, that's for certain. Peter say, 'Do not be surprised at the fiery trial you are suffering, as though something strange were happening to you. But rejoice that you are partakers of the sufferings of Christ.'"

Dani watched through the portal of the past as another scene materialized.

"Ol' Master Jacobs, now he was a religious man, but only as it suited him. You know that ol' Negro spiritual, 'Everybody talkin' 'bout heaven ain't goin' there'? Applies to blacks and whites and every color folk, and sure did apply to Master Jacobs. He'd have the traders come in and he had this big ol' stump, and after selling off hosses and cattle, he'd parade up the slaves. He'd take their scars from beatin's and fix 'em up with some brown tar he'd put on hot, burn right into your skin 'cause the higher price come with the smoother skin. He'd strip 'em to shows off their muscles."

"Did you think much about trying to escape before you finally did?"

"Thought about it every day—a man wants freedom not just in the life to come, but in the life he's livin' now. If it was just me, would've been easy, 'cause it was either get free or die and be with Jesus and be really free. I even thought of takin' a few of the meanest overseers with me—I don't deny it—but I didn't. I was heaven bound and I knew they wasn't. Besides, when I still had Nancy and the chillens, I knew I couldn't escape with them, and I wasn't gonna leave them or has them get beaten 'cause I runned off. I'd never leave my family. Sooner die a thousand times than do that."

Dani looked at Zeke with admiration, seeing so much of her daddy in him. She treasured this Christian heritage going back two generations before her father. She wished she'd known more men like Zeke and Daddy on earth.

"But after Nancy and Ruth was gone and Abe growed up, I didn't have to wait no more. Wanted to be free. Free in Ohio, free in Canada, or free in heaven."

Dani looked through the portal and saw a man come to Zeke, a well-dressed man, the master.

"Now, Zeke, I know you's happy livin' here with me. And you know I takes good care o' yous, don't I now, boy?"

Dani realized the man was talking down to Zeke, talking poor black slang, but not knowing quite how to do it.

"Yessuh, Massa Jacobs," she heard Zeke respond, "I was jus' sayin' to the niggas what a good massa you is. Thanky, thanky so much fo' bein' such a good massa. Yessuh, I thanky."

The man seemed to hesitate, as if he wondered whether Zeke might be working in a little sarcasm at his expense. He seemed to dismiss the thought, as if Zeke's mind were incapable of such craft and subtlety.

"Well, Zeke, I just want to be sure you'd talk to me if you ever got wind of this Underground Railroad nonsense. You ever hear anything about that, you'd tell me, wouldn't you?"

"Sure I would, now, massa, sure I would. I heard stories of course. Underground Railroad? Now if that don't beat all. Can't believe some a dem darkies would play with such foolishness. Don't realize how good they got it, that's what I says. No suh, must not be a brain in dose dark heads."

Dani looked over at Zeke next to her, surprised at his words. He had a big smile on his face. They both listened as Jacobs spoke again.

"All right, there'd maybe be some reward in you tellin' me, specially if we caught a few runaways. Maybe give you one of my old silk shirts to wear for your own. How would you like that, Zeke?"

"Yessuh, yessuh, massa, you can count on Ol' Zeke. One of your silk shirts, you say? Now, wouldn't that be somepin' fancy? Yessuh. Ol' Zeke be the first to tell you, massa. Silk shirt, you say?"

The master nodded his approval, slapped Zeke on the back, and sent him on to his work. "Yessuh, yessuh, I'd tell you all about it iffen them fool slaves tries to run," Zeke said as he turned to shuffle off. Then under his breath he added, "The day I start ridin' a pig sidesaddle."

The master stopped short. "What was that you said, Zeke?"

"Oh you know me, massa. Jus' mumblin' mah fool black head off, that's all. Said the day's gettin' on and I gotta feed them pigs and polish yo' saddle."

"Oh, yes, of course, Zeke. Good boy. You're a credit to your race."

"Yessuh, kind o' you to say so, thanky massa, thanky."

The scene shifted to that night. Dani saw a big plantation party. It was getting late, and the house slaves were finally done with all the serving and washing. They'd gathered outside with the field slaves, away from the party. They were singin' and dancin' up a storm. One of the masters peered out the window and joked, "Look at them nigger fools hoppin' around to their darky music!"

Dani felt disgust at this scene. It troubled her and she looked to Zeke for answers.

"You has to keep watching, chile. I should explains we learned to communicate to each other in codes. Like, we'd be out in the fields and start singin', 'Steal away, steal away to Jesus.' That meant an hour after sundown we'd be havin' chu'ch. Havin' chu'ch down at the swamp, so the slaves should steal away to get there."

"The swamp?"

"Had to go somewhere the masters wouldn't go to at night. Guess you could call it 'First Fire Baptized Church of the Swamp' or somethin' like that." Zeke laughed. "Then the next day, all us slaves would wonder if we was in trouble, if the massas had heard us. Once somebody found out fo' sure everything was all right, they'd start singin' 'I couldn't hear nobody praying.' We'd talk with each other through the songs. But the 'Steal Away' song, one night that had a special meaning. It was the most thrillin' and scariest night of my life down there."

Dani started to ask him to elaborate, but he pointed to the portal where she could see her answer just as it happened.

The slaves sang and danced, Zeke playing on his harmonica and a Jew's harp. "Steal away...steal away to Jesus." The slaves' eyes fired up with fear and hope. It was the message they'd been waiting for, the message from Zeke telling them this was the night. The Underground Railroad was going to steal some of them away, either to death or to freedom. It was a farewell party. "We's prayin' for you, Zeke," Dani heard an old woman say. "I'll sees you in the north or I'll sees you in heaven."

Dani watched as Zeke and five others met some white folks down by the swamp. They put them on a wagon, overloaded and slow moving. All seemed to be going smoothly until back at the slave quarters the overseer discovered they were gone. Men on horses and others on foot with hound dogs launched out into the night, chasing them. With Zeke was a family, a man, a woman, and two children, a vulnerable group to attempt escape. When the search party got closer, Zeke jumped out of the wagon, hoping they'd follow him instead of the others. The driver quickly told him he'd meet him in a day and a half at a prearranged place six miles away.

Zeke ran off into the woods, running with his arms outstretched to fill the air with his scent, hoping to attract the dogs away from the wagon. Dani noticed his bulging pockets. After he jumped in the river and swam to the other side, he took out two onions from his pocket, broke them open and rubbed them all over his body.

"Nothin' messes up a hound like onions," Zeke laughed. "That was some night. I crossed that river like it was the Jordan itself. Ran like that through the night and into the next day. I heard them hounds abayin'. Elyon went before me and my guardian Zyor, he protected me from the rear. There was a pack of dogs and six men after me, all carryin' rifles." Dani saw it in the portal. "Should have caught me long before, but I got them clean away from them other runaways."

Dani watched with horror as a rifle fired and the bullet exploded in Zeke's right shoulder, the blood spilling on the thick leaves as he continued to run. Despite his injury, he made it to the rendezvous point and was taken away in a buckboard, laid in the back, supported by a pillow and concealed with blankets. A white woman tended to him while her husband, the driver from two nights before, drove the wagon.

Dani watched as the white family in the buckboard wagon was stopped by the men chasing Zeke, led by the overseer Daniel.

"Lookin' for a runaway nigger. Winged him good," Daniel said.

"Haven't seen him," the soft-spoken man said. "The Misses and me, we're just taking our daughter to the doctor."

"What's wrong with her?"

"Scarlet fever. You can take a look at her if you want. She's wrapped up in the blanket back there."

"Uh, no, got to be goin', find them darkies." The slave chasers backed away from the wagon and disappeared.

Zeke looked at Dani and laughed loud and long. "Scarlet fever, can you beat that? You never seen them boys move so fast. Those peoples in the railroad, they knew what they was doin', I tell you. They loved Elyon and loved their neighbors, just like Elyon told them to. The Footwashers, Quakers you know, they was like angels of mercy to us. Helped slaves escape all the way to Canada. See, up in Canada black folk could be free and not has to worry about bein' stole back to the south. Heard it was cold up in Canada on the outside, but always wanted to go there, 'cause freedom's always warm."

Dani watched as the Footwashers tended his bloody right shoulder, got him to a sympathetic doctor, gave of their time and money, and risked years of imprisonment to help him. Dani looked on as Zeke died in the arms of the Quakers. They wept over him and gave him a Christian burial.

"Never supposed I'd see my own burial, but I watched it from heaven. They said kind things about me and read Elyon's Word. And I knew I'd be seein' them again up here someday. Jacob and Alexandra Marcus. As fine a folk as you've ever met. They rescued my friends and took care of me, with other kind white folks, until I left that world for this one."

"I'd like to meet them," Dani said.

"Jacob and Alexandra? I'll take you to them now."

"Please. I want to thank them for taking care of you." She put her arms around him. Then they turned and walked, arms on each other's backs, Dani leaning her head on her great-grampa's strong right shoulder, no longer bleeding, no longer scarred, no longer in pain.

"How's Geneva?" Jake asked.

"Still a little shook," Clarence said. "Hattie Burns is keeping an eye on her. So's Frank, next door."

"The shotgun's in my car," Jake said. "You sure you want it?"

"Positive. Can we get it now?"

Clarence had never kept a gun in the house. He'd thought about getting one, but Geneva wasn't comfortable with it. She said she was afraid he'd use it. "That's the point of having it," he'd told her. But he remembered the seductive draw of the gun he'd had in Cabrini Green. He'd never pressed the point.

Things were different now. When he got home after she'd been accosted, he fixed her a cup of hot chocolate and let her cry on his shoulder. He told Geneva he was getting a gun, maybe a couple of them. He was ready for her to argue. This time she didn't.

Jake opened the trunk of his Mustang in the parking garage, and took out a shotgun, a Mossberg twelve gauge with a pistol grip. He handed it to Clarence, giving him two different types of shells.

"Like I said, I've got another shotgun, a Remington, so you can just keep this one. I don't need both."

"I'll buy my own eventually," Clarence said. "But it's nice to bring something home today. Thanks."

"If it's a home invasion," Jake said, "and you want to stop them in their tracks, use these double-aught shells." He handed him a full box. "Twelve .33-caliber pellets in each shell. At close range it's lethal."

Clarence took out and fingered one of the shells.

"You have to be sure, though, Clabern. Once you pull the trigger, there won't be much left of them."

Clarence pumped the shotgun there in the public parking lot, not noticing a businessman forty feet away ducking for cover behind his car. Clarence put the shotgun in his trunk, and he and Jake walked back to the *Trib*.

After writing his column, Clarence walked down the street to the nearest gun store, with its barred windows and security cameras.

If jails were this secure, nobody'd ever escape.

"Can I help you?"

"Looking for a handgun."

"What's it for? Target practice? Home defense? All purpose?" The man behind the counter talked like a vacuum cleaner salesman wanting to select just the right model for just the right job.

After a dozen options, the man showed him a nine-millimeter Glock 17. The boxy gun with a flat black finish had a polymer frame, steel slide, and a steel barrel and internal parts. Clarence held it.

"How does that feel?"

"Pretty good."

"It holds seventeen rounds. That's a lot of ammo."

Seventeen rounds. If he had to, he could shoot up a whole gang before reloading.

"Yeah, the Glock's a winner," the salesman said. "It's popular on the streets. But not many are equipped with this baby." He took out another Glock 17 from behind the counter and pressed his hand against the back of the gun. A ruby red light projected a bright dot on the chest of a man in a picture on the wall.

"A laser?"

"Yeah. The Glock's one of very few handguns with a laser inside the slide. I mean, there's been lasers on handguns for years, but they've always stuck out under the gun or from the front of the trigger guard. But in the Glock, the laser replaces the full-length recoil spring guide rod."

Clarence didn't understand all the terminology. He figured Sergeant McCamman and this guy could probably be best friends.

"How's the laser powered?"

"You put these batteries back in the rear of the frame behind the magazine well." He pointed. "The laser's activated by a pressure switch here, right on the rear of the grip. Go ahead. Try it out."

Clarence held the gun and targeted different objects in the store with the laser. It gave him a power surge, like holding the HK53. It took him back to that first .22 pistol in Cabrini Green. He remembered how disenfranchised he'd felt back then, how alienated from the mainstream of life. The gun had made him feel differently, as though he had the power to alter fate, to give life or take it. To step out from under the control of other people and take control himself. The power to be god. He walked up to a mirror and stood six feet away and centered the ruby red beam first on his forehead and then in the center of his chest, the bright dot glowing, inviting him to pull the trigger. He did. Again and again and again.

"That gun's a shooter and a half," the man lobbied.

"I'll take it," Clarence said.

"Okay, great. We've got a little paperwork here, just a little background check." He handed him some papers that asked about committing felonies and being hospitalized for mental instability.

"All you have to do is come back in fifteen days and it's yours."

"I really have to wait that long?"

"That's the law."

At least I've got Jake's shotgun, and Geneva's got her pepper spray. That's a start.

"While you're here, can I talk you into a knife? Big sale. Forty percent off everything. Best prices in town." He pointed to the display case.

A knife. Why not?

Clarence perused the display case, featuring a small sampling each of nine different manufacturers—Colt, Hibben, United, Case, Western, Sog, Buck, Ole Smoky, and Schrade.

"We can special order anything you want. Don't have room to carry any more."

"These are too big. You got something that doesn't make me look like Daniel Boone?"

"Sounds like you want a boot knife."

"Don't wear boots."

"No problem. The clip on the sheath can go inside your belt. Here, try one." He reached into the display case and grabbed a rosewood-handled knife labeled "Classic Western boot knife." He handed over the black leather sheath and showed Clarence how to put on the clip and conceal the knife.

"Hang on. Your hand's too big for this one." He stared at Clarence's hand, as if it were a catcher's mitt. "I've got a bigger handle here." He reached in and snatched up the knife's bigger brother, the handle and blade each an inch longer. "Okay, this baby's eight-and-five-eighths inches, a little big for a boot knife, but it looks about your size. It's a 440 stainless steel blade, full-tang construction," he said, as if he were Einstein explaining relativity, only with a greater sense of importance. "The sheath uses a compression spring band for an easy, smooth draw. How does that feel?"

Clarence gripped it. He put it into the sheath and clipped it on the belt on his left front. He crossed over his right hand and drew it out a few times. "Feels good. I'll take it."

"Can I interest you in anything else?" The salesman scanned the store, looking for other weapons he might sell him, thinking that if he had a basket of hand grenades he could probably peddle Clarence a few of those too.

"No. That should do it."

The thought of the shotgun, the Glock, and the knife brought Clarence strange comfort. He wouldn't shoot to injure and go to court and get sued for hurting some poor criminal who'd be out of jail in a few months if he ever went at all, free to hurt other innocent people. If anyone would sue him, it would have to be the criminal's relatives. Because the next guy who attacked anyone in his family would die.

He walked out of the store, reaching to the knife and drumming it with his fingers.

Clarence walked into Lou's Diner and nodded at Rory, the manager. He saw Ollie in the far corner, looking at the menu like a marksman at a bull's-eye.

"Clarence," Ollie said. "Hey, how can you tell when the Saints are going to run the football?"

"Don't know."

"The back leaves the huddle with tears in his eyes."

Clarence smiled.

"What's the difference between the New York Jets and a dollar bill?"

Clarence shrugged.

"You can still get four quarters from a dollar bill." Ollie's forehead wrinkled as he reached back for another one. "Did you hear Tampa Bay's offensive coordinator does the work of three men?" He paused. "Larry, Moe, and Curly."

"Ollie," Clarence said, "you leave me speechless."

Rory took their orders with an earnestness greater than any sandwich deserves.

"Day before yesterday I finally got that full ballistics report I've been waiting for," Ollie said. "Can't believe how backed up they are. But I think we're on to something important. See, the night of the murder I looked at maybe ten of the cartridge casings, and they were all the same. Not that I expected those stripes would lead us to the exact weapon—McCamman gave us that. Anyway, I assumed the other casings were the same as the ones I looked at, and I got distracted while the criminologists bagged everything up for ballistics. So yesterday I finally get the report back, along with the shell casings. Brought along two of them for you. They're clean, so you can handle them." Ollie passed him two brass-colored cartridge casings.

"They both look like what you showed me before," Clarence said.

"One's the same, the other's different—look here at the case heads." He pointed to the back of the casings. "Different manufacturer, different year. Now, that's not so uncommon. I mean you can load some of your rounds from one box and some from another. Our lab ran tests on the bullet fragments. Turns out two rounds were completely different from the rest—they were frangible ammunition."

"Frangible? What's that mean?"

"It's a highly specialized ammo, designed not to overpenetrate. See, one of the big problems with using the .223 round in a civilian context is the danger of over-penetration. The small caliber makes people think it's like a little .22 fired with a slingshot or something. Well, it's not. I mean, this is the same round fired by the M-16 Jake and I carried in Nam. Wish we would have had one of these HKs. It's a lot smaller, a lot smoother than our old M-16s. Jam-o-matics, that's what we used to call them. Anyway, this .223 stuff is great for fighting wars, but it's risky on the streets."

"Because it travels too fast?"

"Yeah. I met with McCamman again and took some notes." Ollie looked down at a yellow legal pad. "The fifty-five grain bullet coming out of the HK53 travels faster than three thousand feet per second. Pretty good chance the round will go right through the person shot. Plus you may miss him in the first place, and that's even worse. Remember how McCamman said the SERT team uses HK53s rather than the nine-millimeter alternative?"

"Yeah?"

"The main reason is to penetrate perps wearing body armor. But for a general police weapon, chasing guys down streets, this baby packs too much wallop. So, they've got the option of the frangible ammo, for situations when there's no body armor you need to pierce and you're exposed to the public. You can still use your same weapon of choice, but you minimize the penetration danger."

"But how do you know for sure when to use them and when not to?"

"You carry several identical magazines, except a few are clearly marked with a different color tape, say green, those are the frangibles. If there's civilians in range, you pop it in. It's that simple."

"Okay, I can see why police might use them. But why would gangbangers?"

"They wouldn't."

"But you said—"

"That's the whole point. Perps don't care about overpenetration. Conscience isn't their strong suit. They're not going to shop around for frangibles. Pay extra money to get less fire power? When hell freezes over."

"So what are you saying, Ollie?"

"The manufacturer traced the lot from the headstamp. They confirmed they sold that whole lot of frangibles to a dozen different police departments around the country. Without a doubt two rounds of this ammo—at least—came straight from the police."

———

Clarence peeked into his father's room as the old man sat staring at one of Dani's paintings. He sang under his breath. "Soon I will be donna wid da troubles of da world, goin' home to live wid God. No mo' weepin' and awailin', I'm goin' to live wid God."

Clarence wasn't sure the move to Dani's had been best for his father. There was so much to remind him of her. One song moved into the next, and though the voice was thin and weak, Clarence remembered vividly the strong and hearty voice he'd heard from his father thirty years ago singing the same songs with more gusto then, but more anticipation now.

"Git on board, li'l children, git on board. De gospel train's acomin', git on board."

Clarence could barely hear him, the haunting melody almost imperceptible to human ears. He felt empty as he looked at his father. Every day the old man appeared to be drifting more from the present and into the past or future. He seemed more and more out of touch with reality.

Dani watched as English and American ships docked in West Africa. She was aghast as she witnessed them capture and pile onto their ships children, teenagers, and young adults. She looked at the names of the slave ships. Among them were Jesus, Mary, Liberty, and Justice.

The portal of the past showed her 150 slaves crammed in the bottom of a filthy ship, chained and living in their own excrement. Only forty survived the crossing of the Atlantic and made it to America. She watched one young woman in particular. She saw her cleaned up and sold as a slave. She saw her taken advantage of by the master and giving birth to mulatto children. She watched one of these children grow and become the father of Zeke. There it was. She had white blood in her, slavemaster blood. She'd always thought it, but she'd never known for sure until now.

The ability of a man, in this case the slave owner, to ignore his children repulsed her. She saw how the lighter-skinned black children were despised by the plantation mistress, the wife of the master. Dani saw white women weeping late at night as their church-going husbands took their late evening strolls. The wives knew where they were going and why. To lie with another woman. The black women hated it, the white women hated it, and the black men hated it too. The children of blacks and whites alike suffered the shame in silence. It corrupted the souls of the white men who succumbed to it, though many did not. Dani saw how slavery brought misery not only to black families but also to white ones.

"Ironic, isn't it, Great-Grandpa?"

"What's that, child?"

"It seems to me," Dani said, "that maybe the greatest proof of slavery's immorality was the mixed blood of blacks and whites. If these were animals or subhuman, they couldn't breed together. You can only have children with your own kind, and though there are many kinds of animals, there's only one kind of human. The fact that blacks bore the children of whites proved they were the same kind. And therefore equal."

Dani watched the scene change. Slave women exchanged knowing glances, and excitement filled the air. What was this? They were going down to the creek to fetch water. They gathered by some sassafras trees and strung soaking wet quilts from the limbs. She watched as they filled the water pots two-thirds full, then got on their knees in a circle, each head hovering over its own water pot. Were they sick? What was happening? Dani didn't know. She looked at Zeke, who watched intently.

Suddenly they opened their mouths and in beautiful melody and harmony began to sing a song Dani had never heard. "I'm comin' home, sweet Jesus, comin' home sweet Lord…"

They repeated the words, each line louder than the previous, most of the sound absorbed into the water. The song built on itself, grew off itself like cells dividing. It was music of the soul, something deep and penetrating, something that touched deep sorrow and joy. She heard in the voices of these slaves the sacred roots of rhythm and blues, the music her father had played on that old scratchy phonograph.

"God gave Noah the rainbow sign, no more water, the fire next time."

"Steal away, steal away, steal away home—I ain't got long to stay here."

Dani listened to the haunting echoes of the songs as they bounced muted off water and blankets. She saw the unrestrained joy of the singers, watched as their bodies swayed and once in a while one's head lifted and the full sound of unbridled worship broke out just for a moment before she would quickly lower her head again and project her voice into the pot of water one inch away.

"What wondrous memories, my child." Dani looked beside her and saw Great-Grandma Nancy. "I watched you on earth," Nancy said to Dani, "and sometimes I longed for you to know your spiritual heritage. Now you're watchin' me on earth. See that little girl singin' into that pot with her mama?" Dani saw her. "That's me, chile. We hung those wet quilts and sung into those pots to deaden the sounds of praise, so the massas couldn't hear us, but the Master could. They didn't want us to sing, no ma'am, for singin' the songs of Elyon was lightin' candles in the darkness, and when there was enough light it scairt the darkness away. The massas could takes away a lot, but they couldn't takes away our music. Singin' reminded us and them that we was people. Animals don't worship and they don't sing. They couldn't take away our music and they couldn't take away our Jesus. Like Paul and Silas singin' at midnight in prison, we sang. O sweet Jesus, did we sing." The tears ran down her cheeks. She didn't wipe them away.

"I've listened through the portal to slaves whispering their songs," Dani said.

"Yes'm, we did that too, but we tired of singin' so soft. Sometimes the song burns through every inch of your bones, and it has to come out like smoke has to rise from fire. Sometimes you couldn't hold it back. Sometimes everything in us cried out to sing the unchained praises of Elyon, even if it meant a whippin'. The quilts and the waterpots allowed us to sing unchained. We longed for the day we could sing the songs of praise without ever holdin' back, without them wet quilts and waterpots, bless 'em. That day come all right. The day the midwives delivered me into the new world."

Nancy put her arms around Dani and Zeke. The three began to sing. "God of our weary years, God of our silent tears…" They sang softly at first, but the volume rose with the momentum of the song. Then they sang, "I'm comin' home, sweet

Jesus, comin' home sweet Lord. I'm comin' home, sweet Jesus, comin' home sweet Lord…" Zeke pulled out his harmonica and made music with it he could never have made on earth. He beckoned to his good friend Finney to join Nancy in a celebration dance.

The song spread as people from far and wide gathered around them, people of every color, circling Nancy and Finney and now Dani, following their lead. They turned toward the throne where the Carpenter listened in rapt attention to their voices. It was just as it had happened on earth, but this time the voices were no longer absorbed into wet quilts and water pots. Now they flooded the far reaches of heaven itself, absorbed into the fabric of Elyon's country. Songs were the molecules of heaven. The one who sat on the throne smiled his pleasure, just as he had when the songs were sung into water pots and quilts so long ago in that other world.

"Clarence? Winston. Get to my office."

Working with Winston for two columns a week had been a challenge for Clarence. Jake had warned Clarence what a sourpuss Winston could be, but he'd understated it. The man's wrinkled face looked as if it had been left in the dryer too long.

"Sit down."

Clarence sat.

"I've seen a lot of changes in my thirty years at the *Trib*," Winston said.

"And I'll bet you were against every one of them," Clarence said.

Winston raised his eyebrows. "Actually, I *was* against most of them, and with good reason. Anyway, I still don't know about you doing two general columns and one sports. Seems unnatural. Like we should fish or cut bait."

"I'm willing to go all the way as a general columnist. Whatever you and Jess and Raylon think is okay with me."

"I've heard talk they might put you back in sports," Winston said.

"Why?"

"You're the most popular sports columnist we've ever had."

"And some people don't like my general columns, is that it?"

"Yeah, that's true, I don't deny it. And something would be wrong if everybody *did* like them. I'm not telling you anything official. God knows I don't have any control over this paper, I'm just an editor." He sounded for all the world like Eeyore, Winnie the Pooh's melancholic donkey friend.

"Should I talk to Jess?"

"Your choice. If I were you, I'd focus on my general columns. Just make 'em good enough, keep carving out a loyal audience, and they won't dare throw you back to sports."

"Thanks, Winston." Clarence walked out wondering if "good enough" meant content, style, or a certain ideology. Something else bothered him. He'd seen Winston gruff and irritated at everyone he worked with, seen him yell at most of them. With Clarence he'd been a little surly at worst. But Winston had never once yelled at him, and he couldn't help but think other reporters had to notice this. Clarence didn't feel treated the same way as the other columnists, all of whom were white. It told him he wasn't on the same plane with the others, and that bothered him. But what really bothered him was the idea of losing his general column. Raylon would make the ultimate call on that one.

Clarence went back to his cubicle. He picked up the phone twice but put it down each time. He drummed his fingers on the desk. Finally, he picked up the phone again and dialed.

"Councilman Norcoast's office," Sheila said. "How may I help you?"

"Clarence Abernathy from the *Trib*. Is Mister Norcoast available?"

"He's very busy today."

Yeah, and the rest of us are eating bonbons and playing solitaire.

"But hold on. I'll see if I can interrupt him."

Clarence waited for a minute.

"Clarence! How's your family?" The campaign voice was unmistakable.

"We're surviving."

"Glad to hear it. What can I do for you?"

"I hear you're a tennis player," Clarence said.

"Yeah. Love to play. You too?"

"Oh, I've played a bit. Not much lately." Actually, Clarence had played twice already this week and three times a week all summer.

"How about coming over to Westside Racquet Club and playing me? I'll buy you dinner afterward. They have a great restaurant. What do you say?"

Clarence thought about Raylon. "Sure, why not?"

"How about Tuesday afternoon? Four o'clock too early?"

"No. Perfect." Clarence jotted down on his to-do list, "Prep for tennis against Norcoast."

———————

Clarence and Jake walked out the Trib's front door, pulling their coats in at the neck as the rain trickled down. They headed to their favorite nearby hangout, the Main Street Deli, two blocks down and across the street. They staked out a table and hung their coats over the chairs. Jake was about to get in line at the counter when he caught the expression on Clarence's face and decided to sit down.

"How are you, Clabern?"

"I've been better."

"Dani and Felicia?"

He nodded. "It's all so…senseless."

"Yeah. I've been feeling that with Carly."

"How is she?"

"Taking it one day at a time. Physically, she's not good. Getting weaker. They say the cancer shows it's full-blown AIDS now."

"I'm sorry, Jake."

"These aren't pleasant times for either of us, are they buddy? Well, God's still on the throne. It's all under his control. If I didn't believe that, I'd go nuts."

Maybe I'll go nuts then.

"How's your grandson, Jake?"

"Finney? He's just fine. Here's the latest picture." Jake pulled a photo out of his wallet, and Clarence studied it with genuine admiration.

"Skin's a little light, but he's still a beauty." Clarence smiled. "You must be really proud of him, Gramps. How's Janet?"

"Good. We're still communicating, still dating, talking through the past. Rebuilding. We've even talked about…getting married again. I don't know."

"Geneva told me that might be in the works. She and Janet are always chatterin', you know." Clarence paused for a moment, looking uncertain whether he should say something. Finally it came out. "Do you ever get tired, Jake? Just tired of life?"

"Sometimes. But…what exactly do you mean, Clabern?"

"It's like I told you before. Sometimes I just get tired of being black."

"But it's fine to be black. That's the way God made you."

"Yeah, I know. And it's easy to say that…when you're white. Don't get me wrong. I'm not ashamed to be black. It's just that it's so draining."

"What do you mean? Tell me—I really want to understand."

Clarence sighed, weighing how much he should say. Finally, he jumped in. "Growing up, I thought about my skin color every time I saw a white person. Every time I watched *Sky King* and *The Lone Ranger*, looked at all the billboards, paged through *Life* and *Look* and *Saturday Evening Post* and *Boy's Life*. Everybody was white. Everybody. The politicians, the astronauts, everybody but the janitor, the street sweeper, and some of the athletes. If I was away from home and forgot about my skin color for a few minutes, when it was time to find a restroom I remembered."

"But it's different now. Isn't it?"

"What? Mississippi?" Clarence laughed half-heartedly, running his index finger beneath his right ear. "No more colored restrooms, if that's what you mean. Racism wears different clothes now. It's less overt, more subtle, more disguised. But laws change more quickly than hearts do. Thing is, you know how I've said I want people to be colorblind? Well, it's not realistic. They're not. I'm not. Things constantly remind me of my color. I can't get away from it. It haunts me, dogs me, forces me to spend so much time and energy." He sighed. "Anyway, no use talkin' about it. Doesn't change anything. Let's order. There's already a line."

They walked up to the line, six people ahead of them. After a minute of silence, Jake said, "Okay, Clabern. I'm not dropping the subject this time. What reminds you of your skin color right now?"

Clarence moaned, pretending he didn't want to talk about it. He looked around the room. "How many people in this place?"

"I don't know, three dozen? Maybe forty?"

"How many blacks?"

"Counting you? Three."

"There's the first reason. When you're in the majority, you don't have to think of your skin color. When you're in the minority, you do."

"Okay, but I see what, two or three Latinos? And that guy looks American Indian. And there's maybe four Asians—Japanese or Korean or Chinese. Are they thinking about their race?"

"Probably. I don't know. Now the Hispanics, maybe their great-grandfather's land was stolen by the U.S. Or maybe they just came to America in the last twenty years, and hey, it's a lot better than Mexico, even if you can't buy a decent tortilla here. But you don't have a lot of Latinos who were forced to live in this country at gunpoint. They could cross the border if they wanted to. The Asians, they came to succeed in business. They can get a loan from the bank; they're considered good credit risks. And above all, they're here because they want to be."

"You're not?"

"I want to be here, Jake. But is that *why* I'm here? No. I'm here because some of your ancestors decided to put chains on some of my ancestors, kidnap them, throw them on a slave ship, and bring them over here for cheap labor."

Jake looked startled, wondering if this was the payback for wanting to listen.

Clarence held up his hands. "I'm not as bitter as I sound. And I don't hold it against you personally, bro. *You* didn't put chains on my ancestors, march them to those ships, starve and humiliate and rape them, steal their families and their culture from them, beat them down until they'd submit to white dominion. *You* didn't put my ancestors on that ship. And *you* didn't preach from a Christian pulpit that black men had no souls. I know that. But it still hurts; it hurts more than I can ever tell you.

"So I'm just saying, the Asians here may be a little self-conscious, but it's different. The Hispanics are feeling out of place, but it's different too. The American Indian, well, he may feel the most like I do right now. This whole land used to be his, although as bad as it is to have your land stolen, I think it's even worse to have your body stolen. But one thing's for sure. Of the thirty white people in this room, none of them are thinking about being white. They don't have to."

"Okay," Jake said. "That makes sense. And you're saying always having to think about race wears you out."

"Well, sure, but that's not all. You get the looks. People treat you different. Like a couple months ago when we went to the car dealers and those two salesmen came up to you and I got boxed out of the conversation like I didn't exist. As if black men don't buy cars, they just steal them."

"I didn't realize what was happening until you pointed it out. I'm sorry for that."

"I know. And I didn't blame you. I wouldn't expect you to notice. I mean, it isn't happening to you. *I* probably wouldn't notice either if it was happening to someone else."

Jake looked at the five people standing in front of them. "Man, this line's taking forever."

"The girl who's taking orders. Recognize her?" Clarence asked.

"She's been here almost every day since Marcia quit two weeks ago. Don't really know her yet."

"How would you describe her? Friendly?"

"Super friendly. Why?"

"Okay, Mr. Veteran Journalist, let's do a little research here. Watch how she relates to the two guys in front of us."

"Okay." Jake watched and listened.

"Will that be all, sir?" she asked. "Thank you. Hope you enjoy it." The customer said something to her, and she laughed delightfully. The man in front of Clarence and Jake stepped forward.

"Yes, sir? Managing to keep dry today? What can I do for you?" Same enthusiasm. She rang up the order, took his money, and said "Thank you, sir. Have a great day."

"Watch closely," Clarence whispered to Jake as he stepped forward.

The girl looked down as if she were reading something off the register. "Can I help you?" she asked Clarence. Jake noticed the warmth and enthusiasm were gone. So was the "sir."

Clarence ordered. They didn't engage in small talk. She handed him his change, saying nothing. Clarence stepped away, and she looked at Jake.

"Afternoon! How can I help you, sir? Can I talk you into our special? Turkey on rye with cream cheese."

Jake looked stunned.

"Are you all right, sir?"

"No. I don't think I am. My friend who was in front of me. Why did you talk to him like that?"

"Like what?"

"You were…different with him."

"Different? I'm sorry. I didn't mean anything." She looked around as if fearing a supervisor would overhear this.

"Drop it, Jake," Clarence said.

"No, I won't." He looked at her. "My friend here—"

"I said drop it."

Jake set his jaw and ordered the special, even though he hated cream cheese.

They got to the table and put down their plastic number. It reminded Clarence of the evidence markers on Dani's porch.

"Clabern, why did you tell me to drop it?"

"I was just making a point, not trying to solve the world's problems. It sounded like oversensitivity. She probably doesn't even know she's doing it. Just the way she was raised, I guess."

"But she did treat you different."

"Of course she did. This is the third time I've been here since she started working. It was just like this the other two times."

"Well, I don't appreciate how she acted. It isn't right."

"Yeah, and most of the world is right, is that what you're saying? Hey, you're not going to change this woman," Clarence said. "No telling what she's been through. Maybe some blacks beat her up once. Who knows?"

"Well, that doesn't justify how she treated you."

"But if I hadn't told you to pay attention, you wouldn't have even noticed it. That's why when you ask whites—my fellow conservatives, anyway—if there's still racism, they'll say maybe a little, but not much, and they'll go on and on about reverse racism. I don't really blame them. They can only see what happens to them. They can't see what I see, because they don't live inside black skin."

"It bothers me, Clabern. I want to do something about it." Clarence thought he saw a tear in the corner of Jake's eye. It surprised him.

"You did the best you could. You saw it. You didn't tell me I was just oversensitive, that I imagined the whole thing."

"It was so obvious," Jake said.

"Only if your eyes are open to it. Same thing happened when we were in here last week. You didn't notice then. It's no different than what I get a dozen times a day."

"Really?"

"Really. Well, maybe not a dozen any more. But a couple anyway. Remember a few weeks ago when Geneva and I were out to dinner with you and Janet?"

"At Red Robin's?"

"Right. When the waiter brought the check, do you remember me being a little irritable? Later Geneva told me it showed."

"Yeah, I *do* remember. You seemed upset. Janet and I couldn't figure it out."

"How many times have we been out to dinner together, the four of us?"

"I don't know," Jake said. "Over a dozen."

"Pop quiz. Every single place we've been, every single time when the servers come up with the check, what have they done with it?"

"Put it on the table."

"Well, yes, but who do they put it in front of?"

Jake looked bewildered, then the light turned on. "Me?"

"Every time. No exceptions. Do you know how that makes me feel?"

"No, I guess not."

"Like the white man has to pick up the tab for the black man. Like black men don't make money, or if they do they spend it on drugs or fancy cars. I know the dance, Jake."

"You always want to pick up the tab," Jake said. "I have to arm wrestle you so I can pay my share."

"Usually I don't let it bother me like that. But I've just been fed up lately. Geneva says I'm under stress. Anyway, that's what happened that night. Then we went over to the mall, to Meier & Frank, remember? Well, we hadn't been there five minutes before the security guard was on me like white on rice. Finally, Geneva and I went and sat on a bench. It just takes the fun out of shopping."

"I knew something was wrong," Jake said. "But I had no idea what."

"You know how you're always trying to get me to go to that IHOP over on Burnside?"

"Yeah. I've never been able to figure out why you won't meet me there."

"Because one evening I dropped by there late. A waiter mistook me for a trouble-maker who'd walked off a few days before without paying. He was giving me a hard time, brought over the manager and the whole deal. I explained he was mistaking me for someone else; he said he was sure it was me. I got up and walked out. Never been back since. This waiter just couldn't live with the inconvenience of having to distinguish one black man from another. Could have happened anywhere, but it left a real bad taste in my mouth. And bad tastes and restaurants don't go together."

"Why didn't you just tell me?"

Clarence shrugged. "Sounds like whining, doesn't it? Like I'm another over-sensitive black man. Besides, it's a little embarrassing."

"Still, I wish you'd told me. It makes sense now, but I was in the dark. Clabern... I didn't realize stuff like this still happens."

Clarence shrugged. "Did you hear what happened when I dropped by Hugh's house a few weeks ago?"

"What?" Jake didn't know Hugh well, only that he was the ex-all-American sports editor.

"We go into his house and his phone rings. I'm standing right there when he answers, and I can tell he's uncomfortable. He says, 'No, everything's okay. Thanks for calling. No, I understand.' So I'm standing there trying to get Hugh to tell me who it was."

"So who was it?"

"The neighbor lady. One of those neighborhood watch communities, you know. She was calling to tell Hugh there was a black man on his porch. When Hugh told me, I busted out laughing."

"But it really wasn't funny, was it?"

"No." He looked deadly serious now. "Sometimes you laugh because you're tired of getting mad. Sometimes it doesn't bother me, I'm so used to it. But when I'm at a low ebb, it gets to me. The thing is, at my last two churches in Gresham, I was the only black man. People think they know me, but they don't. They don't describe me as the smart guy or the friendly guy or the guy that loves his family. I'm 'that big black guy.' I don't blame them for that. But my skin color doesn't say anything about what's inside, good or bad."

"To be honest," Jake said, "a few times I've thought maybe you were reading in racism when it wasn't there. But I'm starting to see it differently."

"I'm sure sometimes I *do* read it in. But when you know it's real with some people, it's hard not to assume it's there with others. Like when I was working part-time as a chauffeur when I was in college. All the guys would tell what they made in tips every day. And I always made the least, even though I swear I worked harder than any of them. There's no way I can prove white people wouldn't give me decent tips because I was black. But I'll always believe that. Maybe it's my own fault. I put my expectations too high. Now my dad, he learned not to expect too much, so he's usually not so disappointed."

After several seconds of silence, Jake reached across the table and squeezed Clarence's hand. "Thanks for telling me this, friend."

"Thanks for listening."

"How about next time we come to your house for dinner, Geneva fixes up soul food? Sometimes you talk about the stuff you eat, and I don't even know what some of it is."

"Like what?"

"Collard greens or chitlins, for instance. Never had 'em."

"You don't know what chitlins are, do you?"

"Nope."

"Tell you what, you promise me you won't look it up in the dictionary, and we'll have you over this weekend. We'll serve chitlins out the wazoo. I'll talk to Geneva tonight."

"Great." After the conversation went a different direction Jake said, "Have you talked to Ollie yet?"

"A couple of times."

"About the brutality charge?"

"No." Clarence felt his shoulders tense.

"When you do, ask him about Bam Robie."

"What about him?"

Jake told Clarence a story he wasn't sure he believed. He jotted down the name Bam Robie on the back of a business card. After another few minutes, the two men headed for the deli's front door. As they walked out, Clarence heard a friendly voice twenty feet away talking to someone else. He wondered if Jake heard it too.

"Good afternoon, sir. Keeping dry? Seen our special? What can I do for you?"

Clarence checked his e-mail back at the Trib. Eight messages. One was from Raylon Berkley. He selected that one first.

"Clarence, Jess tells me you're headed to Chicago to do background for a column. I have an old friend, Sam Knight, who owns the Chicago Ritz. He's always saying come and stay and he'll pick up the tab. I've never had time to take him up on it. Well, I called Sam yesterday, and it's all set. You'll be staying there all three days. Contact Mimi for details. P.S. Who says the Trib doesn't treat its employees first class?"

Clarence sighed with mixed anticipation and frustration. He'd planned on staying at his cousin Franky's, in the old hood at Cabrini Green. Not that it was a nice place to stay, but there was a certain nostalgia, and besides, it was part of his research for a feature article related to inner-city life, and a few columns to boot. Oh, well. The Ritz would be a lot nicer and a lot safer.

Not that I have much choice. You don't turn down Mr. Raylon Berkley's generosity.

Just as Clarence was packing up his briefcase at four-thirty, Sid Grady stopped him. "Mount Hood courts tomorrow morning at eight, right?"

"Right," Clarence said. "See you there, man."

"Hey, look out, big guy. I feel my luck changin'. Beat Ekstrom a couple days ago, 6-3, 6-2."

"Wow. Wish I had time to get ready for you."

Grady was a sportswriter who'd played singles in high school and a year or two in college and was still a good athlete. Clarence headed to his car, smiling to himself, feeling slightly guilty he'd misled Grady. He wondered what Grady'd think if he knew Clarence's racquet and sports bag full of tennis balls were in the back of his car and where he was headed now. It wasn't just Grady he was gunning for. Sid would be a tune-up for Norcoast.

Clarence did what he'd done twenty years earlier, in college. He went to the local courts to hit against the wall. He wouldn't leave until he hit a hundred forehands, a hundred backhands, fifty volleys on both sides, and fifty good serves each to the deuce and ad courts. It didn't matter if it took him thirty minutes or two hours. He would stay until he accomplished his goals. He always did.

Clarence had taken up tennis his junior year of college, a strange sport for an offensive lineman and even stranger for a black man. A white teammate, Greg, a wide receiver, introduced him to the game. But what really turned him on to tennis was Arthur Ashe.

It was 1975, and for the first time ever Clarence watched Wimbledon. He witnessed Arthur Ashe, toward the end of his career, bobbing and weaving his way to the final against Jimmy Connors, the number one player in the world. The commentators congratulated Ashe for making it so far. To be number two at Wimbledon was nothing to sneeze at. Everyone knew Connors would win.

It wasn't just that tennis was a game of upper-class suburban privilege. It was that Connors was quicker and stronger and hit harder than Ashe. Clarence watched that day, hoping Ashe would surprise them all and maybe take it to four or five sets. But something happened that day, and as he watched, something happened inside Clarence. Ashe out-thought Connors, strategized, refused to play into his power game. He didn't give him anything to tee off on, nothing to let him establish his rhythm and take over the game. Clearly, Connors should have won. But he didn't. The gold Wimbledon trophy landed in the hands of a black man, and the favored white man held only the silver tray. Clarence screamed and hollered in front of his television set as if he'd won the match himself.

That afternoon Clarence had gone out and hit against the walls and practiced serving for three hours. The next day when he played his teammate Greg, he beat him for the first time.

Almost every day back then he'd gone out and hit against those walls. He played hard through his junior year, meeting players on the tennis team and getting their help. His senior year he went out for the team. Incredibly, he made it, first as a backup player, then as fourth doubles, and by the end of the season as third. The tennis coach told him he'd never seen anyone take up a sport his junior year and make a major college varsity team his senior year. It was unthinkable. But Clarence did it. His coach told him it probably helped that he took up so much space on the court his opponent couldn't hit it where he wasn't.

A hundred forehand ground strokes.

Clarence habitually beat players born and bred in elite racquet clubs. He once whipped a guy who paid more for his tennis racket than Clarence had for his car, that 1967 Hillman Minx that he filled to overflowing. He loved the discipline of readiness, physical and mental. He loved every facet of the game, from his crushing serve, to rushing the net, to hitting the hard topspin passing shot or the lob four inches from the baseline. He watched his opponents swear and kick the court and occasionally throw down their racquets in frustration, wondering how this guy was beating them. In contrast, he always smiled and acted the gentleman.

A hundred backhand ground strokes.

What drew him to tennis was strategy. It was a thinking man's sport. Clarence belonged to Cascade Athletic Club in Gresham, a great facility where he could play through the winter. But on any nice weekend, he played outdoors if he could. He looked forward to facing off with Grady. He knew the face he'd see on the other side would be Norcoast's, not Grady's.

He hit the ball over and over against the concrete wall. He never liked the theory that blacks are naturally superior athletes. It implied they could get away with being lazy, undisciplined, or stupid, whereas white guys could make it only because they'd overcome their genes by being smart and working hard. One of his favorite football players, who he'd personally interviewed once, was Jerry Rice, the all-pro Forty-niners receiver. No one worked as hard as Rice. He always came to practice early, always stayed late, always studied the game films over and over. Rice wasn't the best receiver in NFL history just because of black genes. He was a hard worker, disciplined, smart, and studious.

Fifty forehand volleys.

In college Clarence had chosen for a course project to do a study of all the arguments for keeping blacks out of professional sports, articulated in the newspapers of the thirties and forties. The sportswriters reasoned that blacks lacked the mental discipline, the brains, the ability to focus that athletics demanded. Now, fifty years later, blacks had carved out a dominant role in many professional sports, and did anybody credit some of this to discipline, smarts, and ability to focus? No. It was just the luck of good African jungle, plowboy, cotton pickin', bail liftin' genes. In the ways that mattered to Clarence, blacks didn't get any credit before, and they got little now.

Fifty backhand volleys.

When Joe Louis whipped Max Schmeling, when Jesse Owens won the gold to the dismay of the lily-white Hitler in the stands, it sent a message that would later open the door for Jackie Robinson and finally burst the floodgates. Whites had so many heroes, from presidents to the Wright brothers, from Einstein to Schweitzer, from Superman to the Green Hornet, from movie stars to Miss America, from Red Grange to Joe Dimaggio. As a child, Clarence had clung to every black hero he knew, including his father. Maybe that was why it was so hard for so many to let go of O. J.

Fifty good serves to the deuce court.

Fifty good serves to the ad court.

After an hour of hard work, soaking with sweat, Clarence headed home, feeling ready for his match with Grady the next morning. Clarence would be lying in wait for him and for Norcoast. Grady had never beaten him. Tomorrow would be no exception.

CHAPTER

"Accosted right out in front of your sister's place?" Ollie shook his head. "You got protection?"

"She's carrying pepper spray when she walks," Clarence said, "but she's not walking alone any more. If no one's with her, she's driving. I borrowed Jake's shotgun and ordered a handgun. Familiar with the Glock 17?"

"Sure. That's the hardware that caused all the 'plastic gun' hysteria in the eighties. You know, supposedly wouldn't trigger the alarm in airport metal detectors? Ever see *The Fugitive*? Tommy Lee Jones carries a Glock 17. Then he uses its little brother, the Glock 19, for backup. You know, the gun he pulls out of the fanny pack in the storm sewer."

"Interesting what different people notice in a movie," Clarence said.

"Cops notice cop stuff. Like, every time Jones puts the Glock 17 in his hand, he racks the slide to chamber a round. Truth is, there's not a cop in the country who carries his gun with an empty chamber. The slide rack makes for good Hollywood, I guess. On the street it could get you killed. 'Scuse me, Mr. Armed Felon, but see, I haven't chambered a round yet, so could you hold off pluggin' me till I do it, just to even the odds?'"

"I got one with a laser on it," Clarence said.

"No kidding? Why?"

"I don't know. Haven't fired a gun in years. Guess it could help my accuracy."

"Maybe. Cops tend to shy away from lasers. They can make you dependent and overconfident. Then you get out on a bright day, you can't even see the thing and you freeze. And you can imagine the confusion of a room full of laser equipped SWAT cops. You don't know whose dot belongs to who. A friend with DC Metro police told me about some officers who got in the habit of playing laser tag around the station. Well, one of the guys forgot to unload. He tagged an officer with a round to the stomach. He lived, but it was all pretty embarrassing. The moral is, be careful with your laser gun. It's not a toy."

"If it was, I wouldn't have bought it."

"The really cool lasers are the infrared ones," Ollie said. "They're only visible with night vision equipment, so the subject doesn't know he's being tagged. Talk about stealth. Some of those lasers can go three hundred yards. Can you imagine? Wonder how long before the gangs get them."

"Are you serious?"

"Sure. Some gangs have started using explosives. Dynamite, bombs, Molotov cocktails, military weapons. The fully automatics. Look at our HK53. It escalates. Morals and respect for human life are all that would hold you back from using that stuff. Otherwise, it's just, 'If I can get my hands on it, I'll use it.' All it takes is money, and drugs bring in plenty of that. You just spend your illegal money to buy illegal weapons. It all adds up to a war zone with lots of casualties."

"Let's hope it doesn't come to that."

"Already has. Unless things turn around, it'll get worse. What's going to stop it? It's all a battle for dominion. Who's going to rule the turf? Who's going to have the final word?"

They both sat quietly, sagging under the weight of the topic.

"Ollie?" Clarence wondered if he looked as uncomfortable as he felt. "What was the deal with your brutality charge?"

Ollie stood and walked slowly. "I vaguely remember that. Let's see, wasn't there something about it in the *Trib*?" The sarcasm wasn't sufficient to mask his pain. "Kept thinking you were never going to bring it up." Ollie sighed. "It's a long story. Can we talk over lunch?"

"I've got the time," Clarence said. "Lou's?"

"Yeah. The world may be going to hell in a handbasket, but at least there's Lou's."

They small talked during the five-minute drive. They both bypassed the usual cheeseburgers for a corned beef on rye, Rory's special he begged them to try.

"Okay," Ollie said. "So you want to hear the story? Well, it was 1987. All started when this dude robbed a 7-Eleven, you know the one over on MLK and Jack?"

Clarence nodded. It was less than a mile from Dani's house.

"He was flipped out big time. Later we found out it was crack and PCP. Bad combo. Coming up from L.A., I was still a uniformed, before I got into detective division. I was driving on routine patrol. My partner sees this guy in the store facing off with the cashier. He can't see a gun, but she looks terrified. He says pull over, so I did. My partner, Rick Campbell, he got out of the car just as the dude was comin' out. The guy looks at Rick out of the corner of his eye but doesn't run. Smart move. Rick walks in and sees the cashier on the floor, her face smashed up. Turns out the perp pistol-whipped her with a Browning automatic, but she was still conscious. Rick makes sure she's calling 911, and he's back out the door chasin' the guy on foot.

"The perp cuts across a field, my partner chasing him, while I called 911 too, to make sure the girl gets help. I take off in the patrol car thinking I could head them off on a back street. Sure enough, I come around this corner and there they are, both still running, forty feet between them. I pull up, my partner hops in, and the perp suddenly jumps in a car himself. He leads us on a high-speed chase. We go about twenty miles; he dents up three cars along the way, almost hit half a dozen pedestrians. Amazing no one else got hurt. I still have nightmares about it."

"And then?"

"After a fifteen minute chase out the Sunset Highway past Hillsboro, we finally pull him over. He shoots at us; we pin him down and run him out of ammo. Then we come after him, hopin' he isn't saving a magazine for us. We try to cuff him, but he's absolutely crazy. Has the strength of five men. We'd handled guys like him with a net before, and no one got hurt, but the ACLU made sure we couldn't use nets anymore because they're degrading. Truth is, the nets let us subdue a perp without having to hit him. We can't just shoot them, of course, unless lives are endangered. Chemical sprays don't work on the guys flyin' high on crack, so if they keep fighting, the only thing we can do is hit them with our fists or nightsticks. Which gives bad cops an excuse to do what they want and puts good cops in a position where they have to do what they don't want to. The bottom line is far greater physical harm both to criminals and cops. All compliments of the ACLU."

"So what happened then?"

"Well, I didn't want to shoot the guy, and cool reason wasn't real effective. He was resisting arrest, hammerin' us with his fists, and grabbing for our hands and holsters, trying to get hold of our guns. He was dangerous to himself, to us, to everyone, so as a last resort I used the nightstick on him. Hit him a half-dozen times in the shoulders to get him to stay down so we could handcuff him. After the bad publicity in the *Trib*, there were three or four witnesses who got together and decided I beat him because he was black. Truth is, I didn't think about what color he was. I just thought about getting him under control and keeping him from hurting anybody."

"But that's not what other people thought."

"Well, the front-page article in the *Trib* did the real damage. It started something like, 'White Portland police officer Ollie Chambers, a transfer from LAPD, outraged a North Portland community by his brutal beating of a mentally handicapped black teenager.'"

"You think it came across that bad?"

"Just about. Check it out yourself."

"I did."

"Was I right?"

"Not word for word, but pretty close."

"The funny thing was, the guy was nineteen, but he could have passed for twenty-nine. Besides, when a guy pistol-whips and robs a woman and empties his gun at you, your first thought isn't to ask him when his voice changed or how long he's been shaving or whether his neighbors think he's a nice boy. And mentally handicapped? I didn't stop to do an IQ test. I'm sure the girl he pistol-whipped felt better once she knew he had a handicap. She had to have reconstructive surgery on her face."

Clarence nodded, his feelings tearing him two different directions. "I did some homework on your case. I'm curious about something. You didn't mention just now that your partner Rick was black. Or that the girl at the 7-Eleven, the one he pistol-whipped, she was black too."

"Didn't think it mattered. They were people, and they got hurt. Who cares what color they were?"

"Well, people seemed to care about the color of the guy you beat on."

"Yeah, you got that right. Isn't it funny? I was concerned about the victims. But some people, all they cared about was the guy who made them victims. They didn't care about the victim's skin color, just the perp's. Weird. I'll never understand how criminals get turned into heroes."

"I was surprised you had no comment at the time. You should have explained yourself."

"I was under department orders to say nothing. Our attorneys wanted a press blackout. Well, the problem was the press just took it and treated my silence as if it were an admission of guilt."

"I can understand that," Clarence said.

"If I had it to do over again, I'd violate the gag order. Probably would've ended my career, but maybe it would've been worth it to stand up for my reputation."

"So looking back at it, you still feel you were just doing your job?"

"Yeah. I thought so then and I think so now. Internal Affairs thought so too. But after Councilman Norcoast turned the screws on the DA, everybody wanted to take me down."

"Norcoast?"

"Yeah. You don't remember what the paper did the next few days? The *Trib* made the perp and Norcoast both look like heroes. And I don't have to tell you what they made me look like."

"Did you complain about the coverage?"

"Complain to who?"

"To the *Trib*. Or, I don't know, anybody."

"Well, sure, I groused about it. But who do you complain to? Who has the money to file a slander suit against a newspaper? My attorney thought about it, but he said we had a snowball's chance of winning. We'd have to prove malice, and how could we do that? We'd probably have to pay the *Trib*'s lawyers' bills. On a street cop's salary? Right. It's bad enough to have a newspaper make your wife cry through the night for six months and your kids ashamed to go to school. But to pay them and their lawyers for the privilege? Not me."

"Did you contact the *Trib*?"

"I tried to talk to the reporter, but it didn't do any good. I saw the photographer's name, so I called her, left a message. Got a call back from somebody else, telling me she was unavailable, and if I had a beef I should contact the publisher's office. I thought great, now maybe we'll get somewhere."

"Berkley has an open-door policy. What kind of response did you get from him?"

"I'll let you know if he ever calls me back. Yeah, I heard about the open-door policy too. Only I think it was the back door and he sneaked out when he saw me coming. His pit bull secretary told me to have my lawyer talk to his lawyer. I said hey, this isn't about a lawsuit or something. I just wanted to talk man to man, tell him my side, and what it was doing to my family. He never returned my calls.

"His secretary said something about the First Amendment and, 'The *Tribune* stands by the story.' I thought that was pretty funny. If today's *Trib* headline was, 'World will end at noon,' tomorrow's follow-up would say, 'We stand by yesterday's story.' Captain told me something I've never forgotten: 'Messin' with the media is like wrestling with a pig. Everybody ends up getting dirty, but the pig likes it.'"

"I was at the *Trib* when it all happened," Clarence said. "I remember it, but I think it got mixed up in my mind with a few other police brutality cases."

"Yeah. One cop deserved to be fired for what he did—I just wasn't the guy. There's a lot of people who still think I hit the perp in the face with the nightstick, that I sprayed him with pepper mace after he was under control, that I even wailed on him after he was unconscious, which he never was, by the way."

"You didn't do any of that?"

"No, I didn't. Look, I'm not saying I haven't ever gotten in an extra lick that maybe wasn't absolutely necessary, but it's subjective, you know? Every cop realizes the people you lock up tonight are out tomorrow. The justice system is like a merry-go-round, minus the merry. So sometimes maybe the cop tries to get in a little justice figuring the courts won't. What I'm saying is, I'm no saint. But the pepper mace and the nightstick were both last resorts. I only used them because he was still out of control and nothing my partner and I did was working."

"You use mace often?"

"Maybe four times in fifteen years as a uniformed. Nightstick less than a dozen times. See—and I'll talk slowly because you people in the press don't understand this—some of these guys won't come with you to police headquarters if all you say is, 'Pretty please.' Truth is, I went to the hospital too. The guy bit me. See this?" He showed him an inch and a half scar on his left hand.

"That's from this guy? No kidding?"

"No kidding. I could show you all my scars and tell you the stories, but I don't disrobe for journalists."

"Thanks, Ollie. You have no idea how much I appreciate your restraint. So what happened next?"

"The DA's office came after me. They needed a scapegoat. The *Trib* and Norcoast made me out to be this brutal racist cop. They described the perp as a 'mentally handicapped motorist' and a 'possible suspect' in a robbery. Didn't mention we'd seen him do it, that he pistol-whipped this girl, that he was out of his mind on drugs, trying to kill us and bystanders, that he'd taken us on a high-speed chase, he was resisting arrest, bit me in the hand, and so on. No mention that he was a convicted drug dealer, and who knows how many kids had turned to crime and gangs and died or become killers because of him. None of that mattered. He was a victim. Then the next thing you know they did interviews with him, and he was a hero, a martyr talking with this peaceful childlike voice about how he wished people could just love each other."

"You sound bitter," Clarence said.

"Maybe I am. You know the worst part? See, my mom was from Idaho and my dad from Arkansas, so I grew up bilingual. My dad was no racist, no matter what you might think, but I had some uncles and cousins that were the worst, like rejects from the Klan, the kind that used to tell stories about how black kids were born with tails and they had to be cut off by the midwives. Psychos. Next thing I know they send me a postcard and say, 'We're on your side, cousin—we're glad you beat the crud out of that nigger.' One of them said that to me at a family reunion, and I just lost it. I slapped him silly. Hurt him worse than I hurt the perp. Thought my cousin was going to press charges. Oh, well. One less Christmas card to send." Ollie pretended it didn't matter. "Did you see the front-page picture they ran of me, the closeup?"

"Yeah. Barely recognized you."

"Nobody recognized me. This scuffle went on like fifteen minutes. I guess someone at the *Trib* was monitoring the police band, and this photographer was already out in Hillsboro, so she had time to get to the scene. This gal keeps getting in close while the perp is swinging these big meathook arms. I was afraid he was going to take her out. She wouldn't back off. Anyway, she takes these photos, and I swear, I come up lookin' like Hitler on a bad hair day. My wife said she'd never seen me look so mean. I didn't know it was possible to make this beautiful mug look that ugly."

The photographer was a woman? Must have been Carp. "So you blame the *Trib* for what happened?"

"Jake told me, 'The press goes to scandal like a buzzard to entrails.' They crucified me," Ollie said.

"You're seeing the media through the lens of your own bad experiences," Clarence said.

"Sure. Isn't that the same lens you see cops through? Whose experiences do we operate by if not our own? What bothered me is that I became a cop not to bust heads, but to do some good. I didn't mind risking my life, but once I was accused of this, suddenly all those years—my career, my record—none of it mattered. I believe to this day if Jake Woods hadn't done his own investigation and found out the other side and written it up in the *Trib*, I would have gone to jail."

"Must've been tough."

"The worst part was when my youngest daughter, then she was sixteen, kept getting harassed by kids and teachers at school who believed the newspaper. One day she comes and asks me, 'Daddy, did you really do those things to that black boy?'" Ollie's eyelids got heavy. "That's when it hurt. Sure, police brutality happens and sure, there are racist cops. I'm not one of them. But I was made to pay for their sins."

Clarence thought about how often he'd been made to pay for the sins of black criminals who were the exception to the rule. "One last question. Jake told me something, but I want to hear it straight from you. Tell me about Bam Robie."

Ollie looked surprised, as if he hadn't heard the name for a long time.

"Prostitute. Crack fiend. Arrested him a half-dozen times. One night, this was maybe a couple months before the brutality charge, I was bringing Bam in for soliciting johns. Suddenly, right outside the police station, he drops down on the street. Stops breathing."

"And…?"

"I did what I was trained to do."

"Which was?"

"CPR. Then mouth-to-mouth resuscitation."

"What happened?"

"He revived. The paramedics worked with him awhile. He ended up okay, brief stay in the hospital, and later that night, at the end of my shift, they brought him in and we booked him."

"Did you know he had AIDS?"

"Yeah, I knew. Bam was high risk, to say the least. You get to know a lot of these guys on the streets, the regulars. He'd lost a lot of weight, was pretty scrawny by then. Everybody knew he had AIDS."

"And you gave him mouth-to-mouth anyway?"

"I was just doing my job. Was I supposed to let him die?"

"I'm not sure I would have done it," Clarence said. Silence. He cleared his throat. "You didn't mention Robie was black."

"You keep bringing that up like it's important."

"To me, it is important."

"You'd think even if I didn't win points with the black caucus, I would have been a hero with the gay lobby or some AIDS group. Don't know if there's a prostitutes or cross-dressers union, but they could've given me a medal too, I guess. No awards. Got a lot of razzing from the guys, though, for doing a mouth-to-mouth on Robie. I figure, hey, it's not like I married him."

"Why do I see the events on earth in succession?" Dani asked Torel. "Why do I seem to experience the passing of time? Doesn't the Bible say, 'And time shall be no more'?"

"You are quoting a hymn, not the Bible," Torel said. "Have you not read Elyon's Word where it says, 'There was silence in heaven for half an hour'? For finite beings, there is always time, wherever they are. As fish live in water, the finite live in time. Timelessness is for the infinite. Only Elyon exists outside of time, and to interact with his creatures, even he enters into it. Time is measured in the succession of events. One thing happens first, then another. There is a before, a during, and an after. That is time. Christ came once to earth, he rose and ascended, he will return again. The inhabitants of heaven eagerly await that day. In that sense, heaven is on earth's timetable. Consider the music you have heard in heaven and the music you make here. Does it not have meter, tempo, and rests? All these require time."

"There's something else," Dani said. "I thought we would forget the things of earth here. True, some things don't come to mind, but they haven't been erased, just eclipsed. I have such vivid memories of earth. Not only that, but I can still see what's happening on earth. I always thought that for heaven to be heaven we couldn't be aware of pain on the earth."

"Heaven does not make your mind duller, but sharper. You are aware of the rebellion on earth and the ugliness of hell. Happiness here does not depend on ignorance of reality. It depends on having God's perspective on reality. Elyon and the angels know there's evil and pain on earth, but heaven is still heaven for them. Your joy can be full even though there is evil in the universe, since you know that soon evil will be destroyed and the Carpenter's just dominion established forever."

After a long plane flight with a connection in Denver, Clarence walked into the Chicago Ritz around six o'clock, feeling more like a tourist than a customer. It dripped with class. He couldn't help but feel a little self-important walking around here. He was wearing his best suit, a Nick Hilton, and Alden shoes, usually reserved for only the most important occasions. But here, just walking in the front door was important.

The bellhop, a young black man, led the way to his room. Clarence looked at the sculptures and artwork all around him. Even the ashtrays looked straight out of an art gallery. He tipped the bellhop and wandered around his room. Incredible. A mammoth king-sized bed, a lavish flower arrangement and fruit basket, and a personal note of welcome from Mr. Sam Knight, Raylon's friend. A bar, a kitchen, a living room with beautiful sofa, two TVs. Geneva would love it here. Why hadn't he thought to invite her?

His bathroom looked like something out of a magazine. Ivory-like washbasin with what looked like gold-plated handles. A private Jacuzzi! Clarence felt on top of the world. After exploring every feature of his suite, he walked out in the hall, passing by other well-dressed occupants.

He pulled in his stomach and pushed out his chest a bit. He could think of worse ways to spend the evening—like in Cabrini Green, where he would go first thing tomorrow morning to his cousin Franky's. Clarence felt excited about doing this inner-city feature article, especially since most *Trib* columnists got a feature assignment maybe once a year, if that. As he walked to the elevator, a service cart came around the corner in front of him, ramming into his thigh.

"Oh, sir, I'm so sorry." The silver-dollar-sized eyes looked even more frightened and apologetic than the voice sounded. The nameless black woman, about Clarence's own age, seemed terrified, as if she had offended royalty who at a whim could command her beheaded.

"No problem," Clarence assured her, aware of the patronizing tone of his own voice—kind, magnanimous, the sort royalty uses with inferiors to remind themselves of their philanthropy.

"Forgive me, sir."

He didn't know what he saw in her eyes, and it bothered him. Was it mortification at having done a terrible offense? Or was it that she felt wonder or envy that one of her kind had made it to Clarence's station in life, that he could actually stay in such a place, not just be a bellhop or cleaner or candy machine supplier here? He sensed she had expected a white man and had been surprised to see him. Were blacks who had "made it" even more insufferable than whites, who take their privilege for granted?

He took the elevator down to the lobby and looked the place over. He saw a sign that said, "Ritz restrooms for guests only." Outside of it stood a tall young black man who had pumped his share of iron. He wore a tuxedo.

A restroom bouncer? In a tuxedo?

Clarence wandered into the plush restroom, which had a huge lounge area with chairs and paintings, then inside it another section with washbasins, and finally beyond that the facilities people actually went to bathrooms for in the first place. He remembered the Mississippi outhouse he visited a few times a day until he was ten years old and they finally got indoor plumbing.

He didn't really need to use the Ritz restroom; he was just exploring. The works of art hanging on the wall made it seem an ivory-colored museum. He wondered if artists considered it a great honor to have their paintings hanging in a john.

Opulence knows no boundaries.

Clarence turned the corner to the room with washbasins, then stopped in his tracks. There, in a fancy antique chair, sat an old man, maybe fifteen years younger than his father but looking remarkably like him. He was dressed in a starched white smock that cut a stark contrast to his leathery old sunbeaten black skin. He was working, if it could be called that, as an attendant, waiting to hand a towel to any hotel guest who'd washed his hands. He sat listlessly. In front of him, propped on an ornate pedestal, rested a shiny silver plate for tips. In it were some dollar bills and a fair stack of assorted change.

The man seemed frail and sad-eyed. A white man moved from a washbasin as if looking for a hand towel rack or a blow-dryer. He realized there was only one recourse—the old man who was guardian and distributor of the hand towels. As the white man walked toward the black man, the latter looked up with puppy eyes, handing him the towel with all the devotion of a loyal spaniel. Without saying a word, the white man wiped his hands, placed the used towel in a neat receptacle that somebody—maybe this attendant himself or maybe a black woman—would wash and fold. He reached in his front pocket and found no change, then into his wallet and pulled out a dollar bill.

The old man smiled weakly and nodded his thanks. As the white man walked away, the attendant's eyes caught Clarence's. For a moment the two stood there gazing at each other. At first Clarence thought the old man was silently asking if he could serve him a towel, but the eyes had something else in them, something he recognized immediately because he'd seen it so often in his life. Shame.

Clarence turned and walked out. He went straight to the elevator, directly to his room, changed his clothes, and packed his bags. He left a note for Mr. Sam Knight saying his plans had changed, but thanks for the room and the nice fruit and flowers.

He went out to catch a taxi. After three empty cabs passed him, the drivers pretending not to see his waving hand, he went back into the hotel and asked the concierge to call him a cab. One drove up immediately to the hotel's front entrance, and he climbed in.

"Where we goin' today, sir?" said the old black driver, an American, rather than the usual Nigerian, Ethiopian, or Sudanese.

"Cabrini Green."

The driver's eyebrows raised a moment. He hesitated, then said, "All right then. Know just wheres it is. My youngest daughter and her kids lives right there."

Clarence remembered a certain texture to the air at Cabrini Green. After all these years it was still there, palpable. It felt like a steel mill on a hot day and left a sulfur aftertaste.

The sagging tenements leaned like drunkards. Here in the "jets" was a higher infant mortality rate than in much of the Third World. Here televisions were often on twenty-four hours a day to fool prowlers into thinking someone was up, and to fool residents into thinking their lives had purpose. Many of the apartments didn't have curtains, half the appliances didn't work, cabinets were made of rusted sheet metal, sometimes riddled with bullet holes. Every back walkway smelled of urine. Daley's dilapidated plantations hadn't changed that much in all these years. For the most part, they'd just gotten worse.

The projects were their own world, with their own rules of conduct. Many of the children here had never traveled more than a half mile beyond. Some people were born, lived, and died in the projects, having never seen the parts of Chicago in the movies.

Clarence stayed up late with Franky, outlining some of the things he wanted to do the next day, what kinds of people he'd like to interview. Franky showed him to a bedroom. It smelled stale. The noise kept him up till three o'clock in the morning. At four he woke up to the sound of two gunshots. Just before five he woke up again to yelling and screaming. He suspected Franky and his family slept right through it all.

"We got smash 'n grabs goin' on all the time," Franky told Clarence. "Bangers jump a car at a stoplight, break out the windows with a baseball bat, and grabs jewelry right off the driver."

"What's it like for the kids nowadays?" Clarence asked, remembering his own childhood here.

"All the little brothas has a couple a.k.a.s. They never gives their real names to cops or strangers. The kids go down to the stadium, and the attendants keep them away. They say no neighborhood children allowed, to keep out the Horner kids right next door. Cousin Albert, he still at Horner, you know? You say you goin' there tomorrow? You look him up. Ol' Albert Lyin'stein, 'member how we called him that? Ax him about it. Just ax him. Says the kids all make money by guardin' cars at the stadium. Rich folks pays 'em to not smash their cars. Told me his own boys was paid five bucks to do the chicken wing."

Clarence recalled the chicken wing well and the memory knotted his stomach. Black boys would mimic a squawking chicken, and a white man would laugh at the frenzied dance and give them a few dollars. He felt his temperature rise. He'd never done the chicken wing. Even as a child, he would have died first.

"Things have changed, Cuz," Franky said. "In the ol' days everybody was mad at injustice. Thought they could do something about it, make the system work. Not any more. People's given up. Now they just looks out for themselves, gets the next paycheck, the next hit."

"What's the attitude toward cops?"

"The man? Yesterday some dumb cop left his patrol car for two minutes, and Swirl and Stumpy, they up on the third floor and drop a bowling ball right on it." He laughed. "Best was last spring. Couple o' brothas, Looney and Docta Doo, they push out an old refrigerator from the top floor. Landed three feet from a pig witch. Shoulda heard her scream!"

"She could have been killed."

"So what? Brothas gettin' killed all the time. Cops don't care about us."

"But they're better than the criminals, aren't they?"

Franky shrugged. "At least the criminals is our own."

Clarence wrote it down in his notes. "Does that apply to drug dealers?"

"There's a drug dealer, Bad Rod, he's big in the Vice Lords. Smart dude. One of the papers, they interviewed him, and the brotha say he recruits kids to sell just to get 'em enough green to give 'em a chance to be doctors and lawyers if that's what they wants. Dealers ain't so bad, not all of 'em."

"Yeah, right. And Al Capone did soup lines. What a humanitarian. You prey off people, then turn around and make yourself out to be a hero. Who's this pusher making a doctor and a lawyer? All he's doing is making drug addicts and gangsters that'll kill or die or go to jail before they can vote."

Franky gave him a look that said, Forgettin' who you is, Cuz?

Clarence asked Franky about the justice system. He said the courts were just a white good ol' boys club, with all the players—from prosecutors to public defenders to judges—their own white-collar gang, getting in their beatings on black folk by sending them off to jail.

"I got a neighbor," Franky said, "who tells his kids, 'Someday we be outta here. You has a nice backyard and your own garden and a good life and stuff.' I tells him quit lyin' to his kids."

"Lyin'?" Clarence said. "They finish school, work hard, save up their money, and they can do it. That's not a lie."

Franky looked at him as though he just didn't get it.

"Mrs. Stout," Franky called out to an elderly lady walking their direction. "Sup?

Hey, you hear about ol' Mrs. Watson in 395?" He pointed down the way.

"No. What about her?" The woman's face fell limp.

"Died last night."

The old woman shook her head. "Who shot her?"

"Wasn't shot. Woman was eighty-five years old. You know. Jus' died in her sleep, that's all."

"That's what I hope happens to me. Don't want to get shot."

In the afternoon Clarence interviewed two gang members, then asked Franky to drive him through the projects and point out some highlights. As they drove, he noticed two boys no more than fourteen cross their arms, close their fists, and throw the dramatic sign of the Black Gangster Disciples. Everywhere Clarence looked, he saw baseball caps of various pro teams from around the country.

"What's with the L.A. Kings hat?" Clarence asked Franky.

"Kings stands for 'Kill Inglewood Nasty Gangsters.'"

"How about that one, the Orlando Magic?"

"You know the Maniac Latin Disciples? Magic stands for Maniacs And Gangsters In Chicago." They drove a little farther.

"What about UNLV over there? Don't suppose it means University of Nevada Las Vegas?"

"Have to read it backwards, VLNU. Vice Lords Nation United."

Clarence stopped and interviewed a Black Gangster Disciple named Moff, who bragged his set was the biggest and toughest, that their dominion went far and wide. His brothers Sogs and Mile proudly showed Clarence their crossed pitchfork tattoos and six point Star of David, which he'd seen spray painted all over the city on public buildings and El platforms.

"Is that a sign of support for Jews?" Clarence said, unable to resist asking.

"Whatchu sayin' man?" Moff's dis-detector went off.

"That's the star of David," Clarence said. "It's a Jewish sign."

"No way, joker. That be the Gangster Disciple sign. We don't let no Jew boy steal it."

Clarence moved on, noting sides of buildings that looked as if they'd been strafed.

"Them drive bys can be messy," Franky said. "Sorry about Dani," he added, catching himself. "Thought maybe things was different out in Oregon."

"I guess people are the same wherever you go," Clarence said.

They got back in Franky's old car and drove toward the far edge of the development. Clarence recognized some old landmarks and suddenly started feeling clammy.

"Turn around," Clarence said.

"There's more I wants to show you," Franky said.

"No. Turn around. Now."

This part of Cabrini Green dug up a memory he was determined to keep buried.

Clarence flew out of O'Hare a day early, skipping his planned interviews at Henry Horner. After Cabrini Green, he'd had enough.

The images of the projects haunted him. Not so much the physical conditions—by American standards they were very poor, but by some Third World standards they were enviable. What troubled him most were the hurting people, most of them living for the moment and not for the future because the future held no hope or promise. One of the few oases in the desert were the students from nearby Moody Bible Institute. Led by a black student who'd once been a gangbanger in the Green, they had started Bible studies and provided tutoring. They brought over many children from Cabrini Green to their campus athletic facilities. Still, as much as he tried to focus on the hopeful aspects, an overall sense of despair overwhelmed him.

The hotel's opulence had accentuated the contrast between the two Americas. But it wasn't the gold faucets that plagued him. The image he couldn't shake was the man in the Ritz restroom.

Why did they have him there? Did the hotel get some percentage from his tips? Would any white man do this job? Clarence remembered counting twelve shoeshine men once in the Detroit airport. All twelve were black. He tried to imagine an elderly white man passing out towels in the Chicago Ritz restroom. He couldn't.

Handing out towels served no useful purpose. What was the old man's *real* job? To serve as a symbol of black inferiority? Were wealthy whites supposed to put a dollar in the plate to absolve themselves of guilt? To do an act of kindness to the man's race? Was it like those who don't need to think about the poor at Christmas once they drop two quarters in the pot of a Salvation Army bell ringer?

Clarence still couldn't shake the feeling he'd sensed in that old black man in the starched white smock and straight-backed chair. The feeling of humiliation. The feeling of shame.

GC was born Raymond Taylor. He'd been dubbed Gangster Cool as a fifteen-year-old and had always treasured the name change as his defining moment. Where else in the universe but in a gang could you be given a new name, and such a powerful one? He was determined to live up to it.

His relationship with his mother had changed along with his name. She opposed his lifestyle but loved him and hoped for his reform. He and Mama had resorted to hard stares at each other. GC had what was known on the streets as a thousand-yard stare, the kind that others can't hold. The only person who could ever hold his stare was Mama, and now she'd given up.

She'd been so close to losing him she didn't deny him much now. But one thing she could never forgive him for was what made her move to Portland from L.A. Her older son, Jesse, had become a Christian five years ago. He'd opted out of the gangs—no easy task. He was going to the university, active at church, leading Bible studies in the neighborhood, being a big brother to some of the boys without fathers. One night the Bloods had come for GC and shot up the house. GC didn't get hurt—he wasn't even home—but Jesse had been killed. Despite his mother's pleadings, GC had gone after the Bloods, killing the sixteen-year-old triggerman in Jesse's death, though the cops could never prove it. Meanwhile his mama's life got sucked out of her. Having lost Jesse to death and Raymond to the gangs, she'd begun to shrink from human touch. Just recently she'd said to Pastor Clancy, "I don't worry so much about the prison. I jus' worry about the cemetery."

GC's room was a command post. One poster said "Almighty Crips." Next to it was an eight-by-ten photo from Lloyd Center Glamour Shots. He and his homeboys posed in full flag, blue to the baddest. They held guns, aimed at each other. The photographer had said 'no way' when they pulled out the hardware, but when they pointed them at him, he relented and took the pictures. One guy, Ace, sat in a wheelchair. He'd been gunned down by Bloods but still hung with the group. A soldier. Righteous.

He looked at two other pictures of homies, both of these laid out at their funerals. He didn't have pictures like that of some of his closest homies; you take a shotgun to the head and it's a closed casket. It angered him. But he consoled himself that in the retaliation, with a few shots to the face at point-blank range, he'd helped make sure those dead slobs couldn't have open caskets either.

His left shoulder ached a little. Maybe he still had a bullet in there. He'd been shot in five different battles, taken a total of eight or nine bullets. Once an X ray showed a bullet he didn't know was there. He took pride in that.

His mama had moved him up here from L.A. because Portland was safe. In L.A. she'd seen house after house, neighborhood after neighborhood overrun by Crips, gobbled up like a plague. She called it the blue plague and the red plague. The only

L.A. she knew was a war zone. It would have been safer living in Beirut. Portland seemed her last chance. Her son's last chance. But he'd gone from an average gangster there to big fish in a small pond here. The highest he'd gotten there was assistant to the minister of defense. Here he was a general from day one. He'd tell his homeboys stories of glory, stories about the Crip sets, the Park Village Compton Crips, Nine Deuce Hoover, Main Street Crips, Sho-line Crips, and the Eight Treys, with whom his Rollin' 60s Crips were mortal enemies.

GC spent jail time in L.A.., where senior gangsters served as tutors. He'd done a little jail time in Portland too, the perfect place to recruit and scope out gang members. Gang life never stopped in jail. Any kid who wasn't in a gang prior to jail became part of one in jail, ethnic gangs defending themselves against each other. Portland was a land of opportunity for dope peddlers and gangs. The soldiers had lots of experience against L.A. cops, the enemy's best troops. Portland was L.A. waiting to happen all over again.

Raymond missed L.A., but he didn't miss the police helicopters ripping through the air. They didn't use them to fight gangs in Portland. Not yet. The day would come, of course, and when it did, maybe he'd move to Pocatello, Idaho. America would never run out of smaller cities to occupy once the larger ones were too glutted with drugs and gangs and cops to make it all worthwhile.

GC took out his blue notebook. Most of the pages had color photos and newspaper clips, primarily from the *L.A. Times* and the *Oregon Tribune*. Several *Times* articles used his given name, Raymond. Nobody in Portland even knew that name but the cops. Since coming here he'd been arrested for assault in a knife fight, for robbery, and for a murder they couldn't prove, where he cut a deal for a lesser charge, giving him just a few months in jail. The scrapbook looked like it was kept by an athlete or an author or a politician.

"Why you collectin' this stuff?" his mama asked. He shrugged his shoulders. Most of his crimes didn't make the papers with his name next to them, but some did. He valued those, every one of them. He wanted to get the credit, like the guy who catches the winning touchdown wants it. He knew the price of getting the credit publicly—sometimes jail, more often gangland revenge. Still, that was how reps got built, and his rep was already Portland's biggest.

He looked at a recent *Trib* article that mentioned a few names, none his own. Jimbo's name in particular was repeated. He might do the time, but GC had done the crime. Funny, Jimbo had done enough already to get life in prison if cops could just pin him on it. But he'd had nothing to do with this crime. Anyway, that was justice. In the end, you get what's coming to you, GC thought, applying it to everyone but himself.

"Fools say Jimbo did it, then Jimbo did it." GC snorted aloud.

GC fondled his old deuce-five auto, with which he'd killed his first Blood at age fourteen. He picked up his Smith and Wesson that he'd used to rob a convenience store after he'd been on the outs just two days. Next he fingered his trey five seven. He used to call the .357 his three hundred fifty-seven homeboys.

Raymond's mother watched him bring over the young kids, and somehow it struck her as dirty. She knew he wasn't a pervert, but it felt like that. It felt like he was taking boys into his bedroom to pervert them. And he was, though sex wasn't the weapon of perversion. It was something else, something just as deep, just as deadly. She'd given up now, and that was the hardest: to have no father for the child and to know she wasn't enough to control him. She'd lost her boy to the hood. Lost him to the Crips. Lost him from the church. Lost him from Jesus. It made her weep through long lonely nights when her baby prowled the streets.

Raymond didn't like his mother's church, Ebenezer. He liked that church in Los Angeles, where Pastor Henly assured them folks were good by nature, that it was only bad circumstances that caused bad behavior, that the fire and brimstone message of the Bible fundamentalists was not from God. Pastor Henly told them that because God was love there couldn't be a hell. He liked the reassurance of that message. In contrast, Pastor Clancy made him feel uncomfortable.

Raymond loved his mother. He told himself she must be proud of him. She saw his name advertised with blue and red paint alike, revered by Crips, hated by Bloods. He had the rep.

GC turned on loud gangsta rap, immersing himself in the pounding rhythm. He resurrected one of his favorite classics, Ice-T's *Body Count*. He listened to the "Cop Killer" song, singing with venom in his voice when it got to the chorus, "Die, die, die pig, die! _____ the police!"

I need my sounds. The beat was as real as angel dust. It put him in a trance. *That's one bad jam.* He fingered his old Smith and Wesson, picturing himself placing it against a policeman's temple. He slowly squeezed the trigger, relishing the moment. What a rush.

He reached for his journal and picked up a pen. Since seeing several gangster memoirs published, he thought maybe he'd write his own. He'd been a decent student once, an honor student, though he'd never admit that to his homies. "Po Po asked me today about a robbery three weeks ago," he wrote. "I say no. Not stupid. But done so many jacks, can't remember which was which." Then his style abruptly changed. "Some days it's not death that scares me as much as life."

He looked at what he'd written and liked it. He wasn't one of those dumb gangsters. He was a ghetto philosopher. Plato of the Crips. He'd once considered Plato for his moniker, but guys kept calling it "Play dough" and "GC" had a better ring, so it stuck. Yeah, *A Gangsta's Memoirs.* Some progressive white lady editor somewhere would get him published. He could use the money to get a grenade launcher or something serious.

He looked in the mirror on his wall and ran his finger over the R6C tattoo on his chest.

I got the rep, man. I got the rep.

———

Clarence wandered past city desk over to the photographer's corner, where he saw Lynn Carpenter. In her relatively short twelve years of experience, she was the *Trib's* most respected photojournalist. Carp was a pit bull who against the odds always came back with the most captivating shot. The type that might pull off a Pulitzer, as when the *Trib* sent her down to cover the L.A. riots and she caught a smoldering Korean store with the ominous graffiti on the concrete wall behind it, threatening "It's not over yet." Almost certainly she would be gobbled up soon by an eastern paper or at least the *L.A. Times.*

Carp was a loner, a quiet tomboy. Clarence liked something about her—certainly not her politics. They'd struck up an odd sort of friendship. She was upper thirties, about Dani's age.

"Hey, Carp."

"Hey, Clarence. Pull another fast one on Harman? Need me to make a blowup for you?" She referred to Clarence and Jake's series of practical jokes on one of the reporters.

"Nah. After the last one, we're being nice to Pete. I'm sure it'll wear off soon, though. What's up on the photo beat?"

"Not much. Same old stuff. Chasing everywhere. Hoping to stumble onto some human tragedy I can capitalize on." Carp spoke with the exaggerated cynicism common among seasoned journalists. But Clarence knew it stemmed from her decency, coupled with the regretful irony that most of her award-winning pictures were of crimes, accidents, rescues, and the aftermath of natural disasters.

"Glad you stopped by, Clarence. Read your column on media bias."

"Yeah? I'm considering doing a follow-up, but Jake thinks I should get a bullet-proof vest first."

Carp laughed. "Sounds like Woods." She shrugged. "He may be right. Listen, you know how I feel about your political persuasions."

"Me? Political?"

"Yeah, somewhere to the right of Attila the Hun," Carp giggled. Clarence liked her giggle. He also liked the fact that as often as they disagreed, he never felt from her that superior liberal contempt.

"Okay, m'lady. I'm not in the mood to argue. I've got something to ask you."

"What's up? Gonna tell me you're really a liberal and you need my support to come out of the closet?"

"Not quite. Do you remember a story back in '87 involving an officer accused of police brutality?"

"I remember a couple. Refresh my memory."

"This was one where you caught pictures of the arrest in process."

"That one? How could I forget? AP picked up a couple of my photos. Lucky to get there while the action was still hot."

"The officer you photographed," Clarence said, "the one charged with brutality? He's now a homicide detective. He's in charge of my sister's case."

"No kidding? You think he's doing a bad job?"

"No, not really. Just heard some stuff about his past, and I've been checking into it. Read the old papers in the morgue. I was curious about the pictures."

"Want me to look them up?"

"Look them up?"

"Yeah. I keep a master file of all my negatives and usually the proof sheets. Want to see them?"

"Great. Never occurred to me you'd still have them."

Clarence looked over her shoulder, noting her files were labeled year by year from 1984 on.

"You said '87? What time of year?"

"August."

"Right. It was still muggy, even though it all happened after dark. I remember my sweat dripping on the camera." She kept rummaging. "Okay, got it. Filed under Officer Chandler/Police Brutality, August 1987. Here's the clip from the paper…and here's three proof sheets. I shot three rolls. About a hundred pics."

Clarence saw the yellowish, file-aged story he'd already looked at in the morgue, then took a look at the proof sheets with their tiny photo images.

"Wow. That's a lot of photos."

"It's like the lottery," Carp said. "The more tickets you buy, the greater your chance of winning. The more pictures you take, the better your odds at making page one."

Clarence looked at the pictures the *Trib* had printed. He was struck again by Ollie's angry face juxtaposed with the look of helpless terror in the eyes of the man he was beating. It was a side of Ollie he hadn't seen in person. But pictures didn't lie. His original hostility toward the detective began to rekindle.

Carp looked over the proof sheets. "Out of the hundred or so shots, maybe fifty were usable, twenty pretty good. Bad lighting, quick action, a few out of focus. The editor decided on three shots. Two facial closeups and the one in the center, where he's swinging the night stick."

"Looks like it's coming down on the guy's head."

"Yeah, it does, doesn't it?"

"Was it?"

"On his head? No. He kept hitting him on the shoulders. It had a dull sound, like soft flesh absorbing the impact, know what I mean? No cracking sound like a hit to the head."

"Sure looks like it's going for the head. Not in the other pictures, just this one." He pointed at the main page-one photo.

Carp shrugged. "It's the angle. Creates an illusion. You don't have the depth of field in a two-dimensional medium."

"So…they just happened to choose the only one that creates the illusion he was hitting him in the head?"

"You sound surprised."

"I am, a little."

"You've never seen a reporter or editor slant a story or headline?"

"Of course I have. But a picture?"

"It's no different. Happens all the time. Want a magnifying glass? Helps with those little proofs."

"Thanks." Holding the glass, Clarence went picture by picture through the thirty-five-millimeter proofs.

"Wait a minute." Clarence pointed to the proof's original from which one of the *Trib* photos had been taken. "On the left side of the picture, this is the other officer. Right?"

"Right."

"This black cop. He's waving his nightstick. He looks pretty agitated."

"Sure. He got in a few licks too. Like I said, it was a tense situation."

"He's in your original picture but not in the picture the *Trib* carried."

"Story editors cut out words. Photo editors cut out images. It's called cropping."

"I know what it's called. I just don't think it's appropriate here. It communicates the wrong message."

"What message?"

"One white man beating up a black man. Instead of two officers, one black and one white, together dealing with a black man." Clarence studied the other proof pics. "In fact, several of these pictures are really good, the ones that show the black officer with his night stick. So why wasn't he included?"

"It wasn't my call, but I suppose because the story wasn't about him."

"So, you're saying that what constitutes the story isn't what actually happened but what the *Trib* wants to do with what happened?"

"Obviously. Isn't that the nature of journalism, or did I miss something? You want what happened, watch a videotape start to finish. You want the *Trib's* take on what happened, read the *Trib*. That's our business, Clabern. Better get comfortable with it."

The more he looked, the more agitated he became. "These pictures of the criminal—in most of them he's clearly out of control, almost vicious looking. This one's kind of neutral, hard to interpret. But in this one he looks like a nice guy frightened for his life."

"That's the one they printed, right?" She looked at the clipping. "Yep."

"And the pictures of Ollie—"

"Ollie?"

"Detective Chandler, Officer Chandler. Most of them are pretty calm and in control, don't you think? A few of them, after the scuffle, I guess, they even look pleasant. Almost jovial."

"Yeah, it's amazing how calm he looks, given what was happening. Of course, my job's just to take the pictures. I never get to choose what they print."

"But the one they put in, the third picture, the closeup of Ollie, it's this one." He pointed to the proof. "It's the only one where he looks wild-eyed, really angry."

"I remember that one. He thought I was in too close. He warned me to get back. Told me the guy was going to hurt me."

"What did you do?"

"What any journalist would do. I ignored him."

"So…"

"So, he got really mad. Yelled at me to get back. I turned and shot the picture. The flash was way too close. It bleached out his face, changed his features, don't you think? I was kind of embarrassed they printed this one. It was one of my worst shots."

"He was mad at *you*? Did your editor know that?"

"Yeah, I told her. I'm sure I must have."

Clarence stood up, his face animated. "Let me summarize. Correct me when I'm wrong, okay? Out of a hundred pictures you took, the *Trib* chooses to use three in its feature story. None of the pictures show the three people involved in the scuffle, only two of them. The one with the black cop edited out also happens to be the only one where Officer Chandler appears to be hitting the perp in the head with the baton, even though he wasn't. Right?"

"Right."

"One is a closeup of the criminal—"

"*Alleged* criminal."

"Okay, alleged criminal, and it happens to be the best take in the whole bunch, one of just a few, maybe the only one that makes this guy look like a choir boy. Right?"

"Right."

"And the third is a closeup of the officer—"

"The offending officer."

"The *alleged* offending officer—and of all the pictures of him it's by far the worst, artistically speaking. It's also by far the most intimidating, the only one that bleaches out his features, makes his eyes look wild, the one that shows anger and hostility. And to top it off, you're telling me the anger and hostility wasn't at the criminal but at a photojournalist refusing to back off when he ordered her to?"

She shrugged her shoulders. "Right."

Clarence sat back down dumbfounded, looking over the pictures and shaking his head. "There was a hearing about this whole thing, wasn't there?"

Carp nodded.

"Well, you were a primary witness, weren't you? Weren't you asked to testify?"

"Yeah. But I was at the scene as a member of the press. So I asked to be exempted from testifying. Raylon Berkley stood behind me."

"Did Berkley ask you what you saw?"

"Yeah, he did. Called me into his office. He asked what evidence of brutality I saw. I told him I wasn't an expert. It was brutal, but then the guy was screaming every profanity in the book at both cops, wrestling with them, threatening to kill them. I'm no expert. I don't know if it was brutality or not."

"What did Berkley say?"

"Just that he had a few phone calls to make and he'd get back to me about whether or not I should have to testify."

"Who did he call?"

"He didn't say. The *Trib* attorneys I suppose, maybe a judge or two? He knows everybody."

Maybe his old friend Norcoast.

"Anyway, bottom line, they excused me from testifying, even though the officer's attorney was really upset."

Clarence sat quietly.

"You look like you need some fresh air, Clabern," Carp said. "But when you feel up to it, you need a short course on photojournalism—what happens on our end of the biz. Words are only part of the story. Pictures are the rest. One picture is worth a lot more than a thousand words."

Clarence nodded, then walked off, hoping the fresh air would make him feel better about what he did for a living.

"She's back," Zeke said to Dani, voice bouncing with enthusiasm. "My little Ruthie, your grandma. Home from her mission. Want to meet her?"

"Yes! Please!"

Zeke and Dani began walking, but Zeke was in a hurry, so he turned a corner in space. That skill was still new to Dani, but with her hand in Zeke's she turned the corner with him, arriving immediately at a distant place she'd not yet been to, the terrain very different, calling out to be explored, to be painted, to be studied to learn more of Elyon's character. She made a mental note, adding it to hundreds of other places she wanted to come back to, each filling her with promise and expectation.

Now she saw a white-haired woman, appearing as old as Zeke himself, but she sensed he saw her differently, still as his little girl. Zeke ran toward her and she toward him, arms wide, laughing and longing for embrace. He spun her around, they touched each other's faces, she whispered words giving a teasing hint of the places she'd been and the tasks she'd done and the wonders she'd witnessed. Zeke grabbed her hand and the two ran over to Dani, as if they were six-year-olds.

"My Dani," Ruth said, framing Dani's face with her hands, hands so old and so young, so callused and so soft. "Sorry I couldn't be there to greet you in the birthin' room. Elyon had me workin'. I watched you in yo' mama's womb, watched you born and growed up. I's so happy you finally here."

"So am I, Grandma." The two embraced, clinging to each other. After they talked awhile, Dani started asking her questions about her life on earth. Ruth pointed to a portal, illustrating her stories with the people, places, and events themselves.

"That's Marse Kelly's place, right there in Taliaferro County, Georgia. We lived in the shotgun houses, long log houses. They had three rooms, see, one behind the other. All us chillens slept in one end room, and the grown-ups, they slept in the other end room. The middle room, that was the kitchen where us cooked and et. There was five of us chillens: me and Dicey and Hamp and Annie and Shang. We wukked in the field when we was old enough, started when I was four."

Dani was amazed at Ruth's dialect. She had no trouble understanding her, nor did her speech send the message it might have on earth. She'd expected Ruth's speech to be more refined than Zeke's, but apparently Grandma had even less exposure to books and standard English than Great-Grandpa. The richness of Ruth's voice, speaking now as it had spoken on earth, struck Dani as delightful. It was so unpolished and unsophisticated, yet so authentic, rich, and credible with Ruth's own kind of eloquence. Perhaps, Dani thought, language reflected the unique character and history of the communicator. That explained all the languages and dialects of heaven. There was no one heavenly language, nor accent, nor grammar, nor vocabulary, just as there was no one color. Every dialect was there, each given over to the praise of Elyon.

"Us chillens slept on pallets. Them wheat straw mattresses was mostly for growed folks 'cause they was too heavy to sleep light, and they was the ones wukkin' their fingers to the bone in the cotton pickin's, so it was only right they got somepin' softer. Us chillens, we could sleep on anything, and we shore enough did. Mostly slaves jus' wukked till they died, but sometimes they'd be around as old folks, and the marses, they'd try to make 'em useful. Ol' man Jasper, all he done was set by the fire all day wid a switch in his hand and tend the chillens whilst their mammies was wukkin'. Chillens minded better them days than now. Mama, after wukkin' all day, she'd still fix us up the best suppers in creation. See, Mama was a bird woman. When she saw a chicken, she saw dinner. When she prowled the barnyard, everything with feathers took to confessin' their sins 'cause they had visions of bein' dressed out by corncake, dodgers, and hoecake." She laughed hard and long.

"Tell me about the meals," Dani said.

"Now ain't that jus' like us peoples, to want to know about food?" She laughed a squeaky laugh that reminded Dani both of Obadiah and Clarence. "Well, chile, we done used to cook in the fireplace. It was one shore enough big somepin', that fireplace, with all kinds o' pots and skillets hangin' round it. We'd go out bar'foots down to the river to fish, and we'd catch the biggest mess o' fish you ever seed. We'd clean 'em and puts 'em in a pan and fries 'em in butter, and bless yo' sweet life, Dani chile, it was sumpin' if there ever was sumpin'."

Dani laughed contagiously along with Ruth.

"Now, the Master, the *real* master I mean, the Carpenter, he caught his share o' fish down there too. We's had some feasts up here that make everything that was somepin' back there seem like nothin', and I keeps bein' told we's gonna has lots mo'. So I axed the Master heaps a times, it's like a joke 'tween us now, 'Sir, is we *ever* gonna have catfish fried in butter?' And he keeps tellin' me I'm gonna have to wait and see, and he says he's got some surprises just for me, but he's not gonna spoil it by tellin' me everything now. That's just like him, the Master. Always watchin' out for us, always plannin' to make what's to come even better than what we gots now."

"What else did you eat, Grandmother?"

"Well, back then eatin' was somepin' real big to us, and from watchin' yo' family gatherings I know that's still true, girl. When we did the corn shuckin' all day, we'd think about eatin' some of that corn end of the day. And Christmas. What a time we coloreds had then! There was such doin's and goin's on. I'll has to show you through the portal, but not till I tells you my stories, if you don't mind."

"Mind? I love it," Dani said. "It's part of my heritage I've never known."

"Well, we'd has cake of all sorts, all kinds of geese and wild game. We'd eat lightbread, pecans, dried peaches, and apples. Had stores of everything we raised—corn and peas and cane and taters and goobers. Et hominy grits and red-eye gravy. And what vittles we had on Christmas! We'd roast those taters in the ashes—nothin' like that. And we'd talk about Jesus and tell the stories from the Good Book. And when I was little, no one knowed nothin' about Santa Claus, never heard o' him till after the war. Christmas was jus' Jesus back then, and that's all you wanted. We brung out the fiddles and guitars, and I was plenty biggity myself and liked to cut a step or two."

Dani laughed, putting her arms around Ruth, as the two watched her dancing through the portal.

"I'd dance bar'foot usually 'cause shoes was the worstest trouble them days. They jus' never seemed to fits. When I gots up here I asked my Jesus, 'Could you tell me one thing? Am I gonna *ever* again has to put up wid shoes that don't fits, 'cause if I is jus' tell me right now, straight out. I can take it.' He just laughed and laughed and promised me, 'Never again, Ruthie, never again.'"

Dani saw through the portal Ruth first as a child, then as a young mother with her slave family. As she watched, she saw the children sick one night.

"How did you care for a sick family? It must have been hard without modern medicines."

"My mammy, the first thing she always done for sore throat was to make us up a tea of red oak bark with alum. In the springtime, scurvy grass tea cleant us out. There was all sorts of remedies for miseries they don't even has no more. The po' little chillens would tote hoes bigger than they was, and they little black hands and legs bleeding where they was scratched by the brambledy weeds. But our mamas and daddies would care for us, make up some medicines from roots and such, and paste 'em on us. Some folkses hung the left hind foot of a mole on a string round their babies' necks to make 'em teethe easier, but not Mama. She said that was plain foolishness.

"Ol' Marse Kelley, James Kelley—not his son Donald, who was a right stupid man—ol' James Kelley now he was somepin', that man, all the time hasin' them 'portant mens up at the big house, talkin' 'bout the business of this and the business of that. There was bankers and lawyers and pol'ticians and all these mens that thought they was mo' important than the angel Gabriel, and I's sorry to say there's not many of 'em even made it to this world."

"Did you ever learn how to read, Grandma Ruth?"

"Heavens no, chile, what you think I used to be back then, white or sumpin'?" She laughed. "There wasn't no schoolin' for none of us negroes. We wasn't no eddi-cated people, that fo' shore. And the marses, lots of 'em would whips you if dey caught you tryin' to read. Them days we was taught to be more scairt of books than snakes."

"Your father learned to read," Dani said, looking at Zeke.

"Yes, he did. Some of them negroes learned to read without the marse knowin', includin' my daddy, Zeke. He's a fine talkin' man, now ain't he? But I was separated from him too early. Didn't gets to know him for long in that old world, but I sure has here. I's so proud of him."

Ruth, glowing with respect, reached out her hand to Zeke's beaming face. Dani wondered how many slave families were united here and how many relationships uprooted on earth had now blossomed.

"One of the first things I learned when I got to heaven was how to read, and guess who taught me. My daddy Zeke! I been readin' ever since. After the war I went to a farm where I'd heard Daddy'd been buried. They said he'd tried to escape on the railroad and a kind footwasher gave him a Christian burial. We couldn't find his grave though—somebody'd dug it up 'cause it was next to white graves and they said that was wrong. I cried 'cause I didn't know where he was buried, but I looked up to heaven and said, 'Someday I's gonna see you again, Daddy.' And sixty years later when I left that world for this one, the first face I sees, after the Master himself, says to me, 'It's someday now, darlin',' and he throws his arms around me and picks me up and I realize who it is and I cries out, 'Daddy! Daddy!'"

Dani watched as daughter and father gazed into each other's eyes, reliving the joy of their reunion as if it were this very moment, speaking volumes to each other without saying a word.

————

Clarence awoke suddenly. The red digits told him 3:37 A.M. He heard someone working stealthily on the front-door lock. He got up and grabbed Jake's twelve-gauge shotgun from the closet, fumbling in the dark for the box of double-aught shells. He popped in five of them by feel, just as he'd practiced. He knew if he had to shoot it, he'd destroy half the house. But even if the intruder managed to shoot Clarence, he'd make sure he wouldn't get back up to take on the rest of the family. One shot from the gauge, and no liberal judge would help this criminal. He'd be lawn fertilizer.

Clarence sneaked carefully out of the bedroom where his sister and niece had been killed, barrel out in front of him, pointing slightly upward. He rounded the corner from the bedroom to the hallway, to the fringes of the living room. He hesitated a moment before rounding the next corner. He heard the front door quietly open.

"Who's there?" he yelled, pumping the shotgun with the quick sliding motion, then applying slight pressure to the trigger. Geneva heard both voice and weapon and screamed from the bedroom. "Clarence!"

The shrill sound of her scream tightened his trigger finger another millimeter. He felt the trigger pushing back against him, inviting him to squeeze just a little harder. He heard the footfalls stop and a slight groan maybe four feet away in the darkness. He pointed the gun at what he figured was chest level.

"Stop where you are or you're dead," Clarence yelled.

"Don't shoot! Don't shoot!"

He held the gun steady at the voice.

"Who are you?" Clarence demanded.

"It's me."

"Ty? What the...?"

Ty said nothing. Clarence lowered the gun and rushed to a light switch.

"What you think you're doin', boy? You almost got your head blown off!"

Clarence's voice squealed with adrenaline. "What's wrong with you, anyway? I ought to…"

Suddenly he heard the frightened whimper of a fourteen-year-old boy. He laid down the shotgun and put his arms around Ty. They hugged in the stillness, now joined by Geneva, she under Clarence's right arm, Ty under his left. Clarence reached his hands to each of their faces. He could feel hot tears flooding both hands.

CHAPTER

19

"Jess has a column idea," Winston told Clarence. "I thought it was pretty good."

The old curmudgeon opinion page editor rarely thought any idea was good, even coming from the managing editor, so Clarence listened attentively.

"White kids attending mostly black schools."

"Hmm. Interesting," Clarence said. "We've done blacks and other minorities at white schools. This would show how white kids respond to being the minority, huh? Probably just like black kids."

"Probably. But maybe we'll learn something."

"Good. I like it. How about I call the principal at Jefferson? What's his name, Fielding? Yeah, Jay Fielding. Maybe they can help me recruit some volunteers for the interviews."

"Yeah. Then better contact their families for permission. Can't be too careful these days."

"I'll get on it."

Clarence went back to his desk and called Mr. Fielding, who'd always struck him as the kind of black educator the cities needed more of. Compassionate, yet firm and disciplined.

"Sounds like an interesting idea, Mr. Abernathy," Fielding said. "How about I talk to our junior and senior English teachers? They could pass out a sign-up sheet in class, and we'll get you some volunteers. All right?"

"Great. Thanks for your help."

"Don't mention it. I'll have my secretary call you back in a day or two. You can come interview them on campus, if you want to."

"I'll look forward to it."

"Oh, you've talked with our vice principal about Tyrone, haven't you?"

"Yeah. Is there another problem?"

"Just more of the same. Doesn't seem like he wants to be here. I'd encourage you to spend some time with him, establish open communication."

"Okay. Thanks."

What am I going to do with that kid?

Clarence walked into the *Trib's* multicultural committee meeting, in the big glass-enclosed editorial office.

"Well, if it isn't Clarence Incognegro." The voice with the dismissive tone belonged to Jeremy, a light-skinned black who was arts and entertainment department editor. "Just heard one the other day that made me think of you. What do they call a black man at a conservative dinner?"

"What? Smart?"

"No. Keynote speaker." Jeremy slapped his thigh, accompanied by several guffaws from the five others at the table.

"That's pretty funny, Jeremy. At least you thought so. Okay, I got one for you. What do they call a forty-five-year-old liberal with a teenage daughter?"

Jeremy shrugged.

"A conservative."

"And you know what they call a liberal who's just gotten mugged?" Clarence asked.

"Let me guess. A conservative."

"You're catchin' on, Jeremy. There's hope for you yet. Next election I'll get you an Alan Keyes bumper sticker to paste over your faded Jesse Jackson!"

Three more people walked in, one of them Jess Foley, who as managing editor chaired this meeting. "Okay, gang, let's get down to business," Jess said. "We have a letter here from Matt Engstrom, over in Metro. It concerns last week's diversity training seminar. All of us were there, right? Okay, here's what Matt has to say:

> I appreciate and agree with the *Trib's* continued efforts to understand and respect minorities. However, at the diversity training session last Thursday the speaker made continuous attacks on the character and credibility of white males. I don't consider myself defensive, but the cumulative effect of these references took a toll on me. Here are just two examples. I took notes and I believe I got both of them word for word.
>
> "Being born a white male in America is like being born on third base and imagining you've hit a triple." And, "White men

have so long enjoyed being in the position of power and privilege that they resent having to compete with women and minorities."

That's painting with an awfully broad brush. Seems as if we're teaching people to assume white men are always jerks. My thought is this—if color and gender shouldn't matter, why don't we stop kicking around white males?

"Okay," Jess said. "I think Matt deserves a reply. Comments?"

"I agree with what the speaker said," Myra volunteered.

"Engstrom's just being defensive. Both quotes are right on target," Jeremy said. "If you ask me, they didn't go far enough."

Everyone looked at Clarence, ready for his comeback. He just sat there, looking preoccupied.

"Clarence, I assume you have an opinion on this?" Jess said, looking concerned, as if Clarence's failure to start an argument suggested he might be seriously ill.

"I confess there's something else on my mind today," Clarence said.

"Something we can help you with?" Jess said.

"Well, I've been giving a lot of thought to this. I guess it's time to tell you this committee has helped change my mind on something. This is going to be a surprise, I suppose, but…well, you've moved me over to a pro-choice position."

"What?" Looks of shock and disbelief spread around the table. Clarence didn't sound as if he was joking.

"I've decided it's a civil rights issue. I believe a person has the right to do whatever she wants with her own body. It's none of our business what choice she makes. We have no right to impose our morals on others. Whether I personally like someone's choices or not is irrelevant. She should have the freedom to make her own choices."

"Clarence, I'm shocked. But really pleased," Pamela said.

"Well, it hasn't been easy to change, but I've given it a lot of thought. I guess I'm just tired of being anti-choice. I want to be more tolerant."

"Wow. Are you considering a column on this?" Peter Sallont asked.

"Well, I've thought about it. But I was asked not to do any more columns on abortion, remember? So I better not."

"Well, I imagine this would be an exception," Peter said.

"Do you think so?" Clarence asked.

"Definitely," Myra said.

"Clarence…," Jess measured his words, "are you shooting straight with us?"

"Of course. I do feel a little embarrassed I've been so blind. I mean, people have the right to do what they want with their own bodies—it seems so obvious now." They sat there staring. "Yeah," Clarence went on, "and that's why I've also finally realized now that every man has the right to rape a woman if that's his choice."

Several gasps didn't keep Clarence from continuing. "After all, it's his body, and we don't have the right to tell him what to do with it. He's free to choose, and it's none of our business what choice he makes. We have no right to impose our morals on him. Whether I personally like the choice of rape or not, he should have the freedom to make his own choices. Now, I'm not saying I'm pro-rape, mind you, just pro-choice about rape. So, do you really think I should do a column on this? Maybe I will."

The committee members stared at him, displaying everything from outrage to extreme disappointment.

"You look so shocked," Clarence said, appearing genuinely confused. "Did I say something wrong? I mean, you've held this position a lot longer than I have. Have I misstated it? Is there a problem?"

"Of course there's a problem," Myra said. "You're talking about the man's body but you've forgotten there's another body—the woman's! One person's right to choose ends when another person's rights begin."

"Oh, I see. So you're not really pro-choice, is that what you're saying?"

"Well, yes, but not about rape."

"Because there's a second person's body involved?"

"Right."

"And that second person has to agree to the first person's choice or it's morally wrong, is that it?"

"Yes," Myra said, "of course."

"Okay. I see. So if I could show you medical and scientific proof that abortion involves a second person's body and that abortion hurts that innocent person, and the second person isn't agreeing to the abortion, then you wouldn't be pro-choice about abortion either, is that what you're telling me?"

"Well…"

"I can see I'm going to have to reconsider this," Clarence said. "Maybe we all are. Yep, I think I'll do that column—abortion and rape: why we should be pro-choice about both or neither."

"We're not amused, Clarence," Jeremy said.

"Neither are the women who get raped or the children who die in abortions, I imagine. I keep hearing some people say these are real babies that are dying and other people say they're just blobs of tissue. So I was thinking, maybe alongside this column you want me to write, we could put in a few pictures of abortions. You know, like that picture of the heart we had in the heart transplant article? Then people could look at the actual evidence and decide for themselves whether this is a baby or blob of tissue. What do you think?"

"You're disgusting," Myra said.

"What do you mean?"

"Wanting to show those pictures. They're sickening."

"Oh, I see. It's sickening to show pictures of killed children, but it's commendable to support killing the children in the pictures? Is that it?"

"Clarence, this discussion is over," Jess said. "And you did *not* get permission to do another column on abortion. Is that clear?"

"My misunderstanding," Clarence said. "You remember how the *Trib* endorsed the mandatory seat belt law instead of defending people's right to freedom of choice about whether or not they wore seat belts? I get it. You *don't* have the right to choose to risk your own life by not wearing a seat belt, but you *do* have the right to choose to kill an innocent child in an abortion. Makes sense to me. You know, when I first came to the *Trib* we were a lot more pro-choice than we are now."

"What do you mean?" Jess asked.

"Well, you used to be able to smoke in the lunchroom, remember? The *Trib* was pro-choice about smoking. Now there's signs all over that say you can't choose to smoke."

"But that's because cigarette smoke hurts others," Mindy said.

"Right," Clarence said. "And abortion hurts the baby, don't you think?"

"Well, I..."

"Forget it, Mindy. You're only encouraging him," Myra said.

Jess sighed. "Okay, the room temperature's rising. Let's take a five-minute break, and we'll get back to Engstrom's letter."

"Yeah, take a break Mindy," Clarence said. "Maybe go somewhere and have a smoke—I mean, if you can find some place in this building that's pro-choice about anything besides killing babies."

GC and Ty drove up to the 7-Eleven, where on the side facing the road, the boys were chillin' and kickin', everyone from original gangsters to tinies.

"Hey, homes, sup?" The brothers slapped skin all around.

"Yo, GC, what it *is*, baby!"

"Who da man now, locs?" GC asked.

"Who da man? *You* da man, cuz."

"Ghost! How you be, my brotha?"

GC and Ghost embraced, patting each other on the back, showing the respect of officers in the presence of enlisted men. Ty had never been this close to Gray Ghost, and now that he was he took the opportunity to look at the outer corner of the Ghost's left eye. He'd heard he had five teardrop tattoos. Sure enough, he saw them. Some said each stood for a year spent in prison. Others said each stood for a rival gang member killed. Either way it put Ty in awe.

"Well, here de boys," GC surveyed the group, "hangin', bangin', and slangin'!"

"Hangin' and bangin' anyway. Not much slangin'." Ghost pointed to a dealer a block away, peddling product to two customers. "Punk there, he doin' the slangin'. He sellin' me cheap, and all the cluckheads goin' to him. He use more than he sell, but he costin' us today, cuz."

"He didn't buy from me," GC said. "Gettin' his product somewhere else, huh? Undercuttin' my homie? We gotta pay that boy a visit tonight, Ghost. What say?"

"Say right on, homes. We maybe smoke dat nigger. Righteous." The two gave each other a knowing look, slapped skin, and said no more about it.

"Daddy, you have to read to us," Keisha begged.

"Not now. I'm too tired."

"Mommy, can *you* read it to us? The first Narnia book? About Aslan the lion? It's almost to the end, but Daddy hasn't read it to us for the longest time. We want to know what happens."

"Your daddy's the reader."

"But he never has time."

"Clarence, do you want me to read it to them?" Geneva felt trapped.

Clarence shrugged. "Whatever."

She didn't want to, she wanted him to. But looking at the eyes of her children, she decided it was better Mom than nobody. She watched Clarence walk to his office, shoulders slouching, and close the door.

Celeste handed Geneva the book, as if passing her a royal scepter. "This is where we left off. They just killed Aslan."

Geneva read about Susan and Lucy coming to the dead lion. "And down they both knelt in the wet grass and kissed his cold face and stroked his beautiful fur— what was left of it—and cried till they could cry no more."

"This is very sad." Geneva looked at the children. "Are you sure you want me to keep reading?"

"Yes!" Keisha said.

"Yes!" Celeste echoed.

Jonah nodded.

Geneva read how they took the muzzle off the lion, how they tried to untie him, but the cords were drawn so tight they could do nothing with the knots. The girls grew cold; the sky gray. Hours later they walked away, feeling nothing good could ever happen again. After a time they heard a great thunderous noise where they'd left the lion's ravaged body. They ran back to discover "the Stone Table was broken into two pieces by a great crack that ran down it from end to end; and there was no Aslan."

The girls mourned that the body had been taken. Despairing, they suddenly heard a voice behind them. "They looked round. There, shining in the sunrise, larger than they had seen him before, shaking his mane (for it had apparently grown again), stood Aslan himself."

"Aslan's alive?" Keisha asked, eyes wide. Geneva saw the light in Celeste's eyes and the smile on Jonah's face. She continued reading.

> "Oh, Aslan!" cried both the children, staring up at him, almost as much frightened as they were glad.
>
> "Aren't you dead then, dear Aslan?" said Lucy.
>
> "Not now," said Aslan.
>
> "You're not—not a—?" asked Susan in a shaky voice. She couldn't bring herself to say the word *ghost*.
>
> Aslan stooped his golden head and licked her forehead. The warmth of his breath and a rich sort of smell that seemed to hang about his hair came all over her.
>
> "Do I look it?" he said.
>
> "Oh, you're real, you're real! Oh, Aslan!" cried Lucy, and both girls flung themselves upon him and covered him with kisses.
>
> "But what does it all mean?" asked Susan when they were somewhat calmer.
>
> "It means," said Aslan, "that though the Witch knew the Deep Magic, there is a magic deeper still which she did not know. Her knowledge goes back only to the dawn of Time. But if she could have looked a little further back, into the stillness and the darkness before Time dawned, she would have read there a different incantation. She would have known that when a willing victim who had committed no treachery was killed in a traitor's stead, the Table would crack and Death itself would start working backward."

With shouts of joy and roars of exuberance Aslan leapt high over the girls and landed on the other side of the Table. The girls chased him. He tossed them in the air with his huge velveted paws and caught them again. It was a great romp. A celebration of resurrection.

> And Aslan stood up, and when he opened his mouth to roar, his face became so terrible that they did not dare to look at it. And they saw all the trees in front of him bend before the blast of his roaring as grass bends in a meadow before the wind.

The children in the Abernathy home seemed connected with the children in Narnia. They wouldn't let Geneva stop reading, and she didn't want to stop either. She read of Aslan going to free the people who'd been turned into statues by the White Witch. Finally, she read of the great battle and the defeat of the Witch.

"Aslan is not a tame lion," the book said several times.

No, Geneva thought. He is not.

"Come on, Clarence. Stop whining, will you?" Geneva spoke to him from the passenger seat as he drove through North Portland.

"I'm not whining." He almost smiled in spite of himself. "I'm sulking. There's a difference."

"It's only a Bible study. Two hours a week. What's the big deal?"

"I just don't like to feel pressured. I choose my own friends."

"Pastor Clancy hand-picked the people for this group, and for some reason he chose us."

"Didn't ask to be chosen. Sunday's one thing. Wednesday night, that's something else."

"Clarence, you've been readin' the Bible for years. You and Jake talk about it all the time. You used to read it to the kids." The "used to" stung Clarence. "So what's your big problem with havin' a Bible study with some church folk?"

Clarence sighed. "It's not my church. Just don't think I'm gonna get much out of this group."

"Well, with that attitude I'm sure you won't. Maybe you need to stop thinking about getting and start thinking about giving." Clarence stared straight ahead, saying nothing. "You know what, Clarence? Every time you start to lose an argument you just shut your mouth and get sullen." She sighed. "Come on, baby, give it a chance. A group of mixed nuts, that's what Pastor Clancy called it. A sampling of blacks, whites, Hispanics, Asians, and an American Indian—every ethnic group in the church. A little experiment in racial harmony. What's the worst that could happen?"

"The experiment could blow up in our faces. I just don't think you can force a racial mix."

"Who are you, George Wallace? With that approach schools would still be segregated. Besides, nobody's forcing it. They're just trying it. You work with whites and Asians and Hispanics and God knows what else at the *Trib*. Why can't you do it in a Bible study?"

"I want my private life to be relaxing, you know? You can talk about racial harmony till you're blue in the face, but it never seems to do any good."

"So we just give up, is that it?"

Clarence retreated into silence. He turned on the overhead light just a moment to look at the directions Geneva had gotten from Pastor Clancy. He turned onto Weber Road, swerved around a broken beer bottle, and pulled up in front of the Edwards's house.

Geneva reached over and squeezed his hand. "Just give it a chance, baby. That's all I'm asking."

Clarence nodded. "Well, at least it's a potluck. Where there's food, it's never a total loss." He squeezed her hand back. He got out, went around, and opened her door. They headed up the cracked, rough-edged sidewalk to the front door, Clarence carrying the fried chicken in a Tupperware bowl.

"Welcome, Abernathys!" John Edwards extended his hand. "Come on in, you and your fried chicken both. Glad you made it."

"Glad to be here," Clarence said, avoiding Geneva's glance.

The other couples were already there, milling around the living room, engaged in small talk. Clarence noted the women hovering over the table, laying out the food. Two white men and an Asian stood on the other side of the room. It sounded like they were talking business and high finance. John Edwards had resumed a conversation with another black man Clarence had never seen. A Latino man and the person Clarence figured must be the American Indian had formed their own group of racial leftovers.

Typical. This is going to be an experience all right.

John Edwards got the group's attention. "Welcome to the United Nations Bible study group." Nervous laughter rippled over the room.

"We've got just about everybody but Arabs and Jews, and if any went to our church, I'm sure Pastor Clancy would have invited them too."

John introduced everyone by name, led in prayer, then said, "Let's eat." Clarence moseyed on up, engaging in small talk and answering questions about working at the *Trib*. People seemed genuinely interested.

"So, what do you do?" Clarence asked Ray, the Indian.

"I'm a PI. Private investigator."

"No kidding?"

"Yeah, I was a Detroit cop for fifteen years. Last five as a detective. It's that Indian blood in me, you know—fingers in the dirt, ear to the ground, listen to the train tracks, you've seen the movies." He laughed. "I'm pretty independent, so four years ago I took an early retirement from the force and set up my own business."

"What brought you out here?"

"Family. Kathy's parents live nearby. She wanted to be close, and I was ready for a change. Took a year or so to build the business. Now I've got more work than I can handle."

"Know any Portland police?" Clarence said.

"Sure. Quite a few. You?"

"Some. Ever meet Ollie Chandler? Homicide detective?"

"Big guy? Always eating?"

"That's him."

"Yeah. I helped him out once, and he's thrown a few things my way. Cops—especially detectives—aren't big fans of PIs, but it's different when they're ex-cops, like I am. That gives you credibility, opens the door."

"What kinds of cases you working on, Ray?"

"You name it. Missing persons. Deadbeat dads. Suspicious people having me trail their spouses. That's the worst kind. But, sometimes you can't be as picky as you'd like. You see some of the seedy side of life. That's why church and Bible study are a breath of fresh air."

Clarence grabbed two pieces of Geneva's fried chicken, a slice of ham, and some turnip greens. He didn't know who brought the greens, except he could narrow it down to the Edwards or the black man named Sal, who was married to Diane, a white woman. He looked at some vegetarian and fruit dishes and gourmet health food. Health food, he was convinced, was thought up by some bored white person wanting to make everyone miserable. He reached for a pork rib.

"Clarence," Ray jabbed, "I notice you're passing by all the stuff that's good for you. What's the problem?"

Clarence looked at Ray's plate. "I see you're doing the same. My theory is that high cholesterol is God's way of saying, 'This is real food.'"

"Indians are a disenfranchised minority," Ray said. "We figure, you can take our land, but don't take our food."

They sat around the room eating, talking, and laughing. After a half hour, John asked each person to share something unique about themselves.

A lot of interesting stories surfaced. Keo had been a champion skier, an alternate for the Japanese team in the 1968 Olympics. Duane, one of the white guys, had been with the Peace Corps two years in India. Karen, Duane's wife, said, "My ancestors came over on the *Mayflower.*" Jarod said his family immigrated from Sicily. He relayed his grandfather's stories about coming toward Ellis Island and catching his first glimpse of the Statue of Liberty.

Sal was next. He looked at Jarod and Karen and said, "Well, my ancestors came over on a big ship too. But they didn't come on the *Mayflower,* and they weren't welcomed at Ellis Island. They came in chains—kidnapped, beaten, and starving, to be sold like animals."

Sal's wife put her hand on his thigh and squeezed hard.

He looked at her. "I'm just tellin' the truth. That's the way it was."

Well, at least this group isn't going to be boring.

After everyone had shared, John took the floor. "Pastor Clancy and I have talked about doing a Bible study like this for a long time. Sharla and I are from Jackson, Mississippi, and we were involved in Voice of Calvary Church down there. We built some great interracial relationships and got really excited about reconciliation. We really want to get to know each other in this Bible study, to learn from each other. To get us going, I want to throw out a question: What needs to happen for Christians of different races to be reconciled to each other?"

"I think we're starting it right here tonight," Karen said. "To tell you the truth, all my friends have always been white. I'm looking forward to making new friends."

"I know what you mean," Sharla said. "Before we got involved in Voice of Calvary, all our friends were black."

"One thing we have to do is admit there's a problem," Sal said. "I guess Diane and I are aware of it all the time, with this chocolate and vanilla marriage."

"We call it Neapolitan," Diane said.

"Do you get hassled about it?" Duane asked.

"Sometimes you hear it up front," Diane said. "More often you just hear the whispers. We always see the looks, get the vibes. Neither of our families ever accepted our marriage. We don't even spend the holidays together anymore. It's just too hard." Diane's eyes looked heavy.

"Our kids aren't fully accepted as blacks or whites," Sal said. "I mean, we're glad we got married. Wouldn't have it any other way. But it hasn't been easy."

"We found that out eight years ago," Duane said, "when we adopted two black children."

"You've got black kids?" Sal asked.

"Yeah. They're the best. But you get the looks. Some white neighbors thought it was terrible. A black social agency stepped in and tried to take them from us and put them back in foster care because they thought no parents were better than white parents. Then there was my father. He wouldn't even hug them for the first few years. Finally I said, 'Dad, I love you, but if you can't accept my children, I can't be around you anymore.' In time he fell in love with them. Now you can't find a prouder grandpa."

"Maggie," John said, "you've been kind of quiet. What do you think about all this?"

"I grew up in Atlanta in the fifties and sixties." Maggie spoke with a deep southern drawl. "Talk about a racially charged atmosphere. My parents didn't blame blacks as much as white Yankees."

"Liberal civil rights agitators from the north, right?" Clarence asked. She nodded.

"Yeah, I've been in Georgia," Sal said. "I visited the capitol building in '85, and they were still flyin' the Confederate flag. I couldn't believe it. Remember, baby?" He looked at Diane. "Somebody should tell them they lost the Civil War. It was in all the papers."

Diane moved her hand to Sal's arm as if she were a pilot ready to press her copilot's eject button if a crash seemed imminent. Right now, it did.

"On the Fourth of July," Maggie said, "Mama used to hang out a Confederate flag. I've never thought it was wrong to be proud of my heritage. Do you?"

"Well, it depends on your heritage." Sal looked at her incredulously. "If you'd won that war, I'd still be pickin' cotton for you. When you fly that flag, it says to me you wish I was still your slave."

Maggie teared up. "I don't think that. Not for a minute."

"The white Southerners I've known," Sal said, "watch *Gone with the Wind* and long for the good old days when white folk owned everything and black folk were subservient nincompoops."

"That's enough, honey," Diane said.

"Sal," John said, "Stop beating around the bush—we all want to know what you *really* think." Everybody laughed, including Sal. "Okay, let's call a truce," John said. "It's a good discussion and I'm sure we'll get back to it. But let me throw out another question: Are race relations getting better?"

"In the sixties I was one of those northern agitators," Bill said. "A liberal ACLU civil rights boy, the kind Maggie's dad blamed for the problems. Back then I had dozens of black friends, good friends, at least I thought so. With all the laws changing, all the civil rights victories, I really believed in another twenty years we'd have a racial utopia. But from my perspective, things are worse. Maybe opportunities for minorities are greater, but instead of a racial melting pot, this country is more like a pressure cooker, ready to blow up. The irony is, and it really hurts to say this, I had many more black friends in the sixties and seventies than I have today."

"Several years ago," Clarence said, "for an hour or two I thought racial relations had really turned around. I was in Detroit, doing some interviews, going to some ball games, writing some columns. The last day I was wiped out. I just laid back in my room and did some reading. Didn't watch television or anything. I get up the next morning, catch a cab, and the cabdriver was a white guy, real friendly, extra nice. I thought, this is different. Then I get to the airport and there's no place to sit in the terminal, and a white guy sees me looking and gets up and offers me his seat. I go, wow, things really are getting better. Then I get on the airplane and the flight attendant offers me a pillow and a blanket. She's a white gal, but she's oh so sweet. The guy sitting next to me, he's really nice too. I think, hey, what Dr. King dreamed about, it's really happening.

"Then the plane takes off and I see the guy in front of me reading the newspaper. The headline says 'LA Blacks Erupt into Violence.' See, it was the morning after the police who beat up Rodney King got acquitted and the riots broke out. Then I realized what was up. All these white folk figured they'd better be nice or I might pull a tire iron out of my briefcase and beat the livin' crud out of 'em!"

Everyone laughed.

"Well, next week," John said, "we'll start our Bible study. But I think it was good getting to know each other. And raising some issues too."

Clarence and Geneva stayed another hour, chatting with new friends. They walked hand in hand to the car. "That was fun, wasn't it?" Geneva asked.

"Yeah, it wasn't that bad," Clarence said. "Aren't you glad I talked you into coming?"

"You had some awfully hard times on earth, Grandma," Dani said.

"Terrible times. The worst was when the marsers and overseers would come at night, force themselves on me. And other times when I'd jus' think one of the mens was comin', even if they didn't. I'd lay there and weeps. Of the eleven chillens I bore, three was fathered by marsers, the first when I was thirteen years old. But I tell you I loved those chillens as much as the others. And don't you ever tell me it's a chile's fault what his father done and that the chile don't deserve to live or that he's any less precious to God. You know, if we hadn't had those chillens and loved 'em, lots of our precious grandchildren and great-grandchildren, some of them powerful servants of Elyon, they wouldn't never have been."

Ruth sounded stern for the first time. Dani remembered herself arguing on earth that it was all right to abort children conceived by rape. She wondered if Ruth had been listening. Of course she had.

Ruth looked through the portal of current events on earth with an expression of distaste. "I swear, there's mo' folkses bein' fools down there now than ever. I tells the Master he should just close up shop and get on with the kingdom. Things ain't gettin' better down there, that's fo' shore. But Master, you know, he gots a mind of his own, and I gotsta admit he always be right. Stands to reason, he bein' the Almighty and all."

Dani and Ruth observed through the portal pictures of injustice, including those who gained their wealth from the suffering and unrelenting toil of the poor and needy. She saw people beautifully dressed, warm, and celebrating, other people shabbily dressed, cold, and shivering.

"Does it make you bitter?" Dani asked her.

"Bitter? No. The story don't never end in that world. Ends on the other side." She looked at Dani. "The brightest days in that world always had their sunset. The darkest nights in that world always had their sunrise. Those who live in hell's eternal night can't hardly remember the bright days on earth—only enough to torment them, so I's told. Those who lives in heaven's eternal sunrise can remembers the dark nights enough to fill their hearts with gratitude for the sunlight of this world. We live in the sunrise, chile. Ain't it wondrous?"

"Tell me more about your family—my family," Dani begged.

"Well, I jumped the broom with yo' grandpappy just before the war was over, when I was fifteen years old. He was a kind man and a powerful good father. It was hard bein' a man those days, the only rest bein' sneakin' a good leanin' on a hoe when the overseer was liftin' a whiskey jug or somepin'. Wasn't easy bein' a woman neither, but I was always glad that's what the good Lawd made me. Besides havin' three of marse's, eventually we had eight more chillens, Elijah and yo' daddy the last of them. Miracle babies I called them, 'cause God gave them to me ten years after I should have been barren. Now, when my first babies was young, they brung the marser's and mistress's chillens to suck with me. I loved 'em like my own, their color never mattered one way or t'other. But I always thought it strange marser never admitted three of my babies was his, even though they had his eyes and nose. Never could understand how I wasn't good enough to step foot in the big house but I was good enough to bear his chillens and nurse and mother the chillens of he and his proper wife. Seems like raisin' chillens be a lot mo' important than where you puts down yo' foots."

Dani sensed someone coming up behind them. Together she and Ruth turned, both delighted to see the favorite face of heaven.

"How are my sisters? I'm glad you've finally met." The three of them hugged.

"Want to tell you about my mission, Master. But before I does, I was just about to tell Dani one mo' story, and you knows which one."

"Yes. Tell her. I know she'll want to hear it. So do I."

"Well, I was just sixteen years old and Marse Henry, he say to us, 'You niggers been seein' the Federate soldiers comin' by here lookin' purty raggedy and wored out, but that no sign they licked. Them Yankees ain't gonna get this far,' he say to us, 'but iffen they does, you ain't gonna get free by 'em 'cause I'll line you up on the bank of the creek and free you with my shotgun, you hear me?'

"Well," Ruth said, "we never thought we'd get freedom till we comed home here. But one day a few weeks later, Granddaughter, we was all out in them cotton fields and then a kitchen negro come out on a hoss from Mistress, and he tell the overseer he should come right up to the big house. Well, he did and we wondered what was brewin'. Then the old bell rung, and we didn't know what to do 'cause we never broke from work this time o' day, and we was afraid we'd be whipped if we comes in. Well, finally one of the main negroes, ol' Samuel, he says, 'We best go on up.' So we did, but we let Samuel go first!

"Well, sittin' up there on the porch was a man we never seen, wearin' a big broad black hat like the Yankees wore. Now, I'm a thinkin', that's it, we all been sold off in a bunch. But this man has a funny smile on his face. And he say to us, 'Do you darkies know what day this is?' We didn't know, 'cept it was Wednesday, which couldn't explain the bell ringin'. Then he says to us," Ruth's voice got low, "'Well, this the fourth day of June, 1865, and you always gonna remember this day 'cause today you is free. Free just like I is, just like all the white folk is. The war's over and you's free. You don't need no passes to travel no more. You yo' own bosses. You free as birds.'

"We stood there in shock, hopin' this wasn't no cruel joke and wonderin' if those who danced a jig and sung a song was gonna get shot or whipped. But somehow we knew it was true, and all of a sudden there was whoopin' and hollerin' and dancin' like you never seen."

Dani watched through the portal and there it was, happening just as Ruth described it.

"I's heard a lot greater whoopin' and hollerin' here, hasn't I, Master, and seen a lot better dancin' here, but not back there, not never."

Ruth looked first at Dani, then at the Carpenter, and said, "Slavery was a terrible burden Elyon took off his black chillens, and I praise you for it. The years ahead wasn't easy ones, but we was free. We kept talkin' 'bout how Jesus of Nazareth come to set the captives free. And we laughed and shouted and cried and hugged each other. Because we was *free*. And I thank God always I saw that day, June 4, 1865. The only day better was October 8, 1924."

"What happened that day, Grandma?"

"That's the day the prison door swung open." She gestured at the portal, where Dani saw Ruth old and shriveled, lying on her sickbed. "That's the day I walked out of the world of pain and sufferin', the world of bondage. That was the day I walked into the arms of my sweet Jesus. And then I knew, then I knew shore enough for the first time what it *really* meant to be free."

The glow in her eyes penetrated Dani's heart. The Master put his arms around them both, and from nowhere Zeke and Nancy appeared, worming their way into the group hug, punctuated by sobs of joy.

"Welcome, Mr. Abernathy. Jay Fielding. Good to see you again." The principal extended his hand, which Clarence shook warmly.

"Thanks, Mr. Fielding. And thanks for setting things up for me."

"Glad to. How's Ty doing?"

"Not that great. We've got a curfew on him, try to watch the crowd he hangs with, but it's awfully hard."

"Yeah. Nothin's easy anymore. His grades have been slipping."

"Got him straightened out there. They won't be slipping from now on."

Fielding looked at him with uncertainty. "Well the students are going to meet with you right here in my office. I've got plenty else to do in other parts of the building. Sorry only three signed up, but they don't like to call attention to themselves. You know what it's like being a minority—exposure can make it worse for you. They should be here any time. Oh, here's Rachel and James. James Broadworth and Rachel Young, this is Mr. Clarence Abernathy from the *Tribune*."

Nods and nervous handshakes followed. Rachel and James were obviously a couple.

"The other student is Gracie Miller. Here she is now. Gracie, this is Mr. Clarence Abernathy." This handshake was warmer, more confident. Gracie was an attractive blonde, dressed as Clarence had always thought he would never let his daughter dress. After a few pleasantries, Mr. Fielding left.

"Just to let you know," Clarence told the students, "I was one of ten blacks in a white grade school back in Mississippi. So our skin color's different, but I can understand what it means to be the minority at school. Okay, so, what's it like for you here?"

"Teachers and students around here are always blaming white racism for everything," Rachel jumped right in. "But then they treat me the same way they say whites always treated them. I'm tired of high school. Just want to finish up. James and I are getting married after we graduate, and we want to get as far away from the city as we can."

"I feel a little different," James said. "I mean, I understand what Rachel's saying. Sometimes it's a hassle. But I guess it's a good education. I think I'll always be more understanding of minorities because I've been one."

Gracie, blonde with three earrings on each side and wearing a crop top that revealed a garish ring in her navel, appeared to be a classic sixties rebel with a nineties cynicism. Attitude seeped out of every pore.

"Mainly, it's the black girls I have problems with," Gracie said. "They're always pickin' fights with me because they say I flirt with their men, like they own them or something. Most of the guys here are black, so what am I supposed to do? That's their problem. I like being with black guys."

The discussion led to interracial dating, whites in sports at a black high school, educational quality, segregated tables in the cafeteria, "the white corner" of the locker rooms, and a host of other subjects, all the color-reversed image of what Clarence had always known. At 2:20 the bell rang.

"School's out already? Thanks for your time. The column should be out next Wednesday or Friday. Appreciate your honesty." James and Rachel walked out, grateful to have missed their last two class periods.

Gracie lingered. "Clarence, can I say something to you?"

"Uh, yeah, I guess so."

"I heard your sister was murdered. I'm sorry." She seemed surprisingly thoughtful, defying his first impressions of her being self-absorbed.

"Thanks."

"I heard they haven't found the dudes who did it, huh?"

"No. Still looking."

"Some of the guys talk to me. Bangers, I mean. If you want I could ask around, see if anybody knows anything."

"Uh, well, the police department is conducting the investigation, of course."

"Sure. But they haven't found anyone, and it's been, what, five weeks?"

"Six."

"Well, if you don't want me to, I won't ask. Just offering."

"No. Actually, what could it hurt if you asked?"

"Should I call you if I find out anything?"

"Yeah, please do. Here's my card." He pulled it from his wallet. "That's my number at the *Trib*."

"Okay. I work at Lloyd Center every afternoon till six. So I'd have to call you in the evening. Are you at this number then?"

"No. Here's my home phone." Clarence scratched it out on the front of his business card. "If you find out anything, please call."

"I will. Really nice to meet you, Clarence." She put out her hand, and he shook it, but her hand lingered on his. He pulled it back in surprise. He could see why the girls thought her a flirt. But he would take whatever help he could get.

She still stood close to him. He started to back away as the door suddenly opened. "Oh, excuse me, I thought you were done," Mr. Fielding said.

"We are," Clarence said, sounding defensive. "I was just leaving."

"Clarence and I were just talking about some personal things," Gracie said.

Why does she have to call me Clarence? And "personal things"?

Mr. Fielding forced a smile and reclaimed his office. Clarence followed Gracie out the door a full four feet behind her, determining that whichever direction she was going, he would go the opposite.

CHAPTER

20

After stopping at the usual drop-off points and distributing product to a half-dozen dealers, GC cruised by Ty's house in his Coup de Ville. As planned, on seeing his car, Ty ran down to the end of the street and met him around the corner. He jumped in the car.

GC had held his post much longer than the previous high rollers. Prison and death had a way of cutting short the reigns of most local drug kings. Pearly, Ba-ba, and Brain had all bit the dust in a few months. Capone was a legend for lasting over a year, and Li'l Capone who followed him went down in a month. GC picked up the mantle then, and he'd had it now for almost two years, making him the street equivalent of an eight-term senator.

Ty sat in the front seat fingering GC's special brass knuckles with their built-in switchblade. The power and deadliness of it enticed him. GC drove down a wide section of MLK on the inside southbound lane. In the outside lane two boys, maybe eighteen year olds, drove up beside them.

"Watch this, cuzzin," GC said to Ty. "I give 'em my crazy nigger face."

GC looked across Tyrone to stare them down, narrowing his eyes in a way that transformed his face from the pleasant Denzel Washington demeanor to that of a serial killer. Tyrone trembled at the monstrous hatred in his eyes and wished GC was watching the road. Ty looked to the side at the boys in the other car, preparing himself to hit the floor if lead started flying. But their eyes went down, and they turned right, away from GC. They knew if they returned his stare for more than a moment, they had to be prepared to kill or die. Today they weren't prepared to do either. Maybe next time.

GC looked at Ty and said, "Yo, got to teach you that stare!"

"Yeeeah," Ty replied, stretching it out like he'd heard some of the homeboys do.

"Takes heart to kill fo' yo' set. Makes you tall. You know? They kill our homies, we kill them. What go around come around. And some that comes around comes around quick, so you got to be ready, you know."

"Yeeeah."

They drove up to the next light and GC tried his stare again, moving to the right lane and looking to his left. This time the teenager in the passenger seat of the car stared back. GC rolled down his window with his left hand and with his right reached down to the piece lying beside him on the front seat. He lifted the gun and pointed it at the boy. Ty watched in horror as the red beam appeared on the boy's forehead. The kid's eyes almost popped out of his head. He ducked low, and the terrified driver stepped on it, running the red light. Cross traffic dodged and honked as the car screeched through. A police car popped out of a side street a block away and pursued the driver.

GC laughed and laughed. "Hey, Li'l GC. I like it! I got to get me one of these!" He tossed the Glock 17 into Ty's lap. Ty picked up the gun, handling it gingerly, afraid it might go off on its own. He'd make sure he got it back in his uncle's dresser before he got home from work.

———

Clarence drove up to the Westside Racquet Club. It was an exclusive club, much more elitist than the one he belonged to in Gresham. It looked like something Norcoast would be part of.

They hit strokes back and forth for the warm-up. After the third hit, Clarence knew he was in trouble. Norcoast was a 5.0 player, strong and consistent, heavy topspin, hitting every ball deep. Clarence studied his opponent's practice serves—hard, deep, with a variety of spin. Norcoast's service routine was the same. He'd rub his left sweatshirt cuff across his open mouth, perhaps to wipe off sweat or excess saliva.

Then he'd bounce the ball twice, go into his high toss, and bring down a commanding serve.

Norcoast took the net and volleyed powerfully, putting away balls with sharp angles and solid overheads, beating Clarence 6-3 the first set. Clarence adjusted his strategy, trying more passing shots low over the net. He'd underestimated his opponent coming into this match. He wouldn't do it again.

The second set was a dogfight, neither player losing his serve. At 6-6, it came down to a twelve-point tiebreaker. Clarence lost it 5-7, ending the match, which had gone eighty minutes, the most demanding eighty minutes he'd played in years.

They shook hands at the net, Clarence pretending he wasn't tired.

"Nice effort, Clarence," Norcoast said. "I'm impressed. We had some great rallies, terrific points. I'm ready for a shower and dinner. How about you?"

"Yeah. Sounds good." Clarence acted as if it didn't bother him to get beat by Norcoast. "Let me ask you something, Reg."

"Yes?"

"Do you play chess?"

"Used to play quite a bit, in fact. My father was a champion. I've got a hand-crafted chess table in my office at home. Do you play?"

"Yeah, occasionally. Maybe we could pull out a board sometime."

"I'd like that. You know, my father always told me what I learned in chess would pay off in politics."

"I'll bet it has."

———

Clarence and his family, including Dani's kids, arrived at his brother Harley and Sophie's house at 4:00 P.M. It was their annual fall family-wide gathering. Harley's family didn't celebrate Thanksgiving, so this late October get-together was the last before December.

Harley opened the door, greeting them with, "Here they are, black by popular demand!" His face was framed by Malcolm X style glasses. He often wore his suit and Black Muslim bow tie, but tonight had on a striking brown and yellow kente cloth. Clarence couldn't help but admire it, even though he sometimes made fun of his brother's Africa fixation. Black triangular designs fanned out across the kente cloth, each with one line thicker than the other two. It struck Clarence as familiar. Where had he seen that design?

"Hey, Harley. What's happenin' bro?" Clarence reached for his brother's hand and each tested the other's strong grip. Though Clarence was two inches taller, Harley—at 6'2," 250 pounds—was an imposing figure himself. Clarence hugged Sophie and the rest of the family. He listened to the music. Harley had put more money in his stereo system than almost anything he owned. It played black music, the kind that turned every holiday into a soul holiday. It was a refreshing change from dentist office music. Clarence didn't know how people could stand that stuff. This was the music he was nursed on. He'd never been weaned from it.

Soul music was flowing, swinging, the rhythm enveloping and hypnotic. Lots of bass, pulsing, antiphonal. Spontaneous and innovative. The syncopation and pulsating beat made you want to clap and keep time, as he found himself doing with his right hand as he sat on the couch. The vocalists responded to each other, someone calling, someone answering. It wasn't monologue, it was dialogue, it wasn't just performance, it was experience. It wasn't a commentary on life as much as it was life itself. A jazzy, emotionally intense song, where the women bordered on screaming and the men on shouting, would be followed by something soft, drifting up out of the room like a child's prayer to heaven. It wasn't all nice and neat, processed and packaged, timed to the second. You didn't know when most songs would end. And when they did end, often abruptly, the song continued inside you. That was black music, so central to black culture—full of depth, permeated by sorrow and joy.

"Hey, Marny. How's my big sister?" Clarence asked.

"Don't you ever call me *big* sister, Antsy Abernathy! If I ever get to be half your weight, I'm takin' out a lifetime membership with Jenny Craig!"

Clarence smiled at her. She was two years older than he. He'd never had as close a relationship with her as with Dani. Marny still hadn't gotten over losing her son Bobby to leukemia two years ago. He listened as Marny drifted back into the kitchen and resumed an argument with the women that *this* was the way Mama used to cook that turkey. Dani wasn't there to end the arguments now. Clarence peeked into the spacious kitchen as they put ham hocks in the pot and Geneva poured in some bacon grease. She'd threatened to stop this to keep the men from dying of heart attacks, but Clarence had said if she did, she just might as well kill them outright. She warned him about the problems with hypertension among black men. Maybe, Harley had suggested, it was another white plot to exterminate blacks.

Aunt Ida washed the greens, a ritual designed to get out every stubborn worm that might be clinging to the leaves. While Ida cut up the greens, Cousin Flora mixed up the cornmeal. Then Ida added the greens to the pot of ham hocks and bacon grease. Water drops sizzled, the grease started soaking up, and the scent was heavenly, taking Clarence back to Mississippi. Just about everything he loved, short of breakfast grits, would be served up tonight. Obadiah poked his head in beside Clarence, eyes closed, nostrils flaring, breathing in the aroma with conspicuous delight. Harley stood behind both of them, trying to lean in too.

"I swear, brother," Harley said, "you stand in a doorway and it's a total eclipse." The women turned and gave mocking looks at the men.

"Now you manfolks jus' get away from this kitchen, you hear me now?" Aunt Ida shooed them off as though they were stray cats. "Go on in and discuss yo' politics and solve the problems of the world so we can do what's important—fix up dinner!"

After forty minutes of small talk and lots of laughter, the family sat down for the meal. Mama's dressing, loaded with onions and peppers and celery, positioned itself for the center of attention. Big plates of greens filled the table—collard greens, mustard greens, turnip greens. There was a big side of macaroni and cheese, candied yams, a mixture of butter beans and peas, and the crowder peas along with the ham hocks. Though Harley's family didn't celebrate Thanksgiving, most of the family treated the fall gathering as an early Thanksgiving, so turkey was served, and as Daddy always said, "You don't want that bird gettin' lonely." A heaping plate of catfish, fresh from Marny's husband's recent trip to Mississippi, raised eyebrows, while a huge bowl of succotash and servings of okra and corn and peas, and a few spices the menfolk couldn't identify, vied for attention. All the dishes laid out next to each other reminded Clarence of a favorite soul food smorgasbord in Jackson, where the sign said, "When You Can't Go to Mama's, Come See Us." Mama. How he missed her. Nothing would bring her back for an evening quite like the smells and tastes on this table.

There was fried chicken, fried okra, fried potatoes, deep fried pork chops, and Clarence's favorite, fried green tomatoes. "Just fry it up and you can't go too wrong," Mama always used to say. Clarence wasn't a seafood fan, especially not oysters, but Aunt Ida would deep fry 'em up every year along with the gizzards, and every year he'd eat 'em. Clarence still couldn't abide the smell of chitlins, but it brought back a flood of memories, as did each of the dozens of competing aromas. He took just one slick rubbery bite of chitlins, for nostalgia's sake. The eye-watering Cajun pepper and hot sauce served as a recourse in case something objected to being eaten. It was always easier to ingest anything than to have to explain to the aunts why you didn't. This family was southern, and when a southern woman, black or white, goes to the trouble of fixin' up a meal, you eat it till it's comin' out your ears and you enjoy every moment of it and when she asks if you want more you say, "Yes, ma'm," and that's all there is to it.

Clarence looked at the plate in front of him, mostly fry brown with generous green and a spattering of yellow. You could look at the old black-and-white family photos of the little Mississippi house and fields, hear a sound that reminded you of a mockingbird, but nothin' took you back home like the smells of fried channel catfish and Baluxi shrimp and the tastes of ham hocks and collard greens and about everything else on that table. It was enough to get the Mudcat goin', to drudge up the deepest memories, sweet and sour, of Yazoo Basin, Black Prairie, the Bluff Hills, and the Flatwoods.

Clarence's mind drifted to the magnificent antebellum mansions of which most whites were so proud and which generated such sadness, distance, and anger in blacks. In his mind's eye he could see the palace of Jeff Davis at Biloxi and see the old Mississippi flag that still ushered up calls for the Confederacy and all it represented. He thought of the Bible study discussion about the Confederate flag.

Mississippi. Dusty towns with overdressed old men sitting on the town porches, plucking their suspenders and pronouncing judgment on all that didn't suit them. Corn-whisky stills. Backwater towns where the women spent their school years looking for a man to marry, then the rest of their lives wondering why they'd married such a fool. He remembered a big banner someone hung up in town with the acronym NAACP: Niggers, Alligators, Apes, Coons, and Possums.

No matter how he remembered the simple beauty of Mississippi, even longed for it, these somber memories always colored his appraisal. No matter what he heard of how much progress had been made there, to him Mississippi would always be that backwoods state where coloreds were hounded and beaten and lynched. It was his home, yet could never be his home.

Clarence picked up cornbread and mixed it with his fingers into the collard greens. The salty, grease-soaked greens attracted stray crumbs like a magnet did iron filings. He licked his lips. This was eatin'. He looked up instinctively to catch Dani's eye and maybe kick her gently under the table. The moment he looked up, reality slapped him in the face.

The laughter was loud, and as the talk branched off in different directions around the table it got louder and louder, each conversation competing with the others. Clarence stopped a moment just to listen. White gatherings he'd been at always struck him as so self-aware, the tones hushed and reserved. This high decibel, high energy family gathering was what he'd always known and loved.

Clarence savored the pungent taste of fried green tomatoes. "These are serious vittles, ladies." He winked at Geneva, who smiled back at him flirtatiously.

"This is livin', that's sure," Obadiah said.

"Just keep that pig meat on the other end of the table," Harley added, and for the first time the air filled with tension.

"You always have to get that in somewhere, don't you brother?" Clarence said. "This family isn't Muslim, and 'pig meat' is as black as coal at midnight. So if you have all that black pride, just join us or be quiet about it. Truth is, you know that deep-fried dish there you been eatin' from? Bet you thought it was chicken, didn't you? Truth is we bought it just for you, at Bits O' Pig!"

Most of the family laughed, but not Harley. "I take my religion seriously," he said. "Guess you wouldn't know about that, brother."

Harley's voice grated on Clarence. It sounded like an out-of-tune guitar. It didn't help that his brother was brilliant and one of the few people who could keep up with Clarence in an argument. The dinner continued in more hushed tones before regaining its carefree exuberance.

"Let's retire to the family room," Marny said after everyone was done. "Time for the menfolk to work off their dinner tellin' stories."

"Powerful good dinner, ladies, powerful good," Obadiah said, voice weak but energized by having his family together. "Menfolk gotsta come up with some pretty big whoppers to match this!"

Soon the stories flowed like melting butter on steaming okra. As usual, Obadiah was right in the thick of them. "We was crossing through Kentucky on horse and buggy, round about 1915 or somethin', my daddy, Freeman Abernathy, a drivin' proud as you can imagine. We comes to a car—nicest Model A you ever seen—but this white man had run it off the road. He was standin' there with his three chillens and one in the pantry, wife pregnant as you ever seen. It was gettin' dark, five miles at least to the next town.

"My daddy stopped, of course, like any Christian would. He offered to pull it out with our wagon. We had two strong horses, could've done it sure. This fellow looks at Daddy and says, 'I don't need no help from the likes of you, nigger.'

"Daddy just climbed up in the wagon and shooed off them horses. We looked back and the man's wife started cryin' and the chillens looked so bewildered. Mama said she felt sorriest for the chillens 'cause of the way they was gonna grow up. She said, 'You raised up in the garbage and you can't help but stink.'"

They laughed, but the laughter was restrained, held in check by pain. As usual, Obadiah's stories were a string of pearls without the string. There seemed no logical connection between them.

"Your mama's daddy, he went from being a Kentucky slave to a Lincoln Republican livin' in N'awlins. When he heard people say, 'Lincoln freed the slaves,' and such hullabaloo, he'd always say to us, 'No man gives freedom, not even Honest Abe. God gives freedom. He's the one who delivered us out of bondage like he did his people Israel. Ol' Abe just had the good sense to agree with God.'"

Obadiah looked at the children, most of them huddled on and around three big beanbag chairs.

"Did you know," Obadiah said, "Mr. Lincoln was good friends with ol' Frederick Douglass, the former slave? After the president gave a speech once, they wouldn't let Frederick in to see him, so Abe sent word to let that black man in. And ol' Abe says to him right in front of everybody, 'Mr. Douglass, there's no man whose opinion I respect more than yours.' That's the kind of man Mr. Lincoln was. And that's the kind of man Mr. Douglass was. Don't let nobody tell you different."

"Tell us more about Frederick Douglass, Daddy," Marny said. "For the children."

"Frederick, well he born a slave in the early 1800s. He taught himself to read at age twelve. He got his freedom by runnin' away, always feared maybe they'd lock him up and haul him off yet. You know how many books he had when he died?"

"A hundred?" Keisha asked, wide eyed.

"A hundred would have been a lot those days. Books hard to come by then. But Mr. Frederick Douglass, he had more than ten thousand books."

"Funny you should mention Frederick Douglass," Harley said. "I was just quoting from him this week in my African American literature class. He was talking about hypocrisy in the Christian churches. See, Douglass rejected this Christianity of yours."

"Just 'cause there's counterfeit money," Obadiah said, "don't mean real money's no good. You ain't paintin' the whole picture, Son. Frederick Douglass was an ordained AME deacon, a church man. I may not have your degrees, boy, but I've read his autobiography a half-dozen times. You get me a copy, and I'll read *you* somethin'."

Sophie went to the bookcase and took a book off the shelf, bringing it to Obadiah, who opened it eagerly and started searching.

"Here it is," Obadiah announced. "This is what Mr. Frederick Douglass said." He cleared his throat, with the look of pride that came over him whenever he read aloud. "'Between the Christianity of this land, and the Christianity of Christ, I recognize the widest possible difference—so wide, that to receive the one as good, pure, and holy, is of necessity to reject the other as bad, corrupt, and wicked. To be the friend of the one, is of necessity to be the enemy of the other. I love the pure, peaceable, and impartial Christianity of Christ: I therefore hate the corrupt, slaveholding, women-whipping, cradle-plundering, partial and hypocritical Christianity of this land. Indeed, I can see no reason, but the most deceitful one, for calling the religion of this land Christianity. I look upon it as the climax of all misnomers, the boldest of all frauds, and the grossest of all libels.' See, Son, he rejected the perversion of Christianity, but he embraced true Christianity. You need to see that difference—don't throws out the baby with the bathwater."

"Tell us another story, Grampy," Celeste said.

"Well, let's see now. Here's a story. Colored folk used to drive through Mississippi, comin' or goin' from Louisiana or 'Bama or Arkansas. One day this preacher was travelin' and had to go through Ol' Miss. He prayed loud and hard like black preachers do, 'O God, help me make it through Mississippi!'

"Well, there was a few moments silence and then the preacher heard a voice from heaven. It was God himself and he says to the preacher, 'You don't know what you're askin', son. Even *I* don't go through Mississippi!' Now, that's just a story, chillens. The Almighty's in Mississippi just like everywhere else, and don't say your grampy said otherwise, you hear me now?"

"Tell us about the Klan, Granddaddy," Jonah said.

"Well, my daddy explained the Klan to us one time after they rode up on their horses and put a burnin' cross in front of our ol' shanty. Daddy said that when God was makin' peoples, there was some folk at the very back of the line, and he ran plumb outta brains to give 'em. He felt bad he didn't have no brains left to pass out, so he decided to give 'em white sheets instead. That way they could cover up their heads and nobody could see their brains was missin'. That's how the Klan started."

Laughter and knee slapping and howls filled the room. Then Harley gave a serious explanation of what the Klan was. Clarence liked his daddy's explanation better. Harley started telling about the freedom rides and the battle against segregation in the South. Imitating their drawls, he made fun of white southerners who couldn't comprehend why blacks rose up in opposition to segregation:

"I dawn't unda-stay'en what's goin' awn. It's like some'mm dun jumped inta allda nigras ova'night." The older family members laughed and laughed, including Clarence, while for the most part the children didn't get it. It was true, though. White folk could talk so funny.

"What was it like living in your ol' shotgun house, Grampy?" Keisha asked.

"Well, let's see now. At night we chillens slept with each other, cuddlin' up to stay warm."

"Yuk," Jonah said.

"No yuk about it. Sometimes my ol' nose was so frozen, don't know what I would've done if brother Elijah hadn't been there and let me snuggle it into his back. They was hard days, but good ones." His eyes teared up. He looked up at the ceiling as if trying to peer beyond it. "I miss eatin' sowbelly and corn pone and slicin' up the catfish fresh out o' the river and sittin' on the porch those warm nights— Elijah and me and Daddy and Mama and the rest—jus' listenin' to those hound dogs bark and lookin' up at heaven's stars and seein' the face of God."

"I wish Uncle Elijah could come for Christmas this year," Clarence said.

"Not as much as I wish it, I reckon. But we both slowin' down, Elijah and me. We both slowin' down." He looked at his oldest son. "Harley, you still got that music me and Elijah loved? Count Basie, Lena Horne, Duke Ellington? Now *that* was music, um, um. Elijah and me, we'd listen to 'em till the cows come home."

Harley went over and put on the music while Daddy moved on to another story. Clarence watched Harley. He remembered when his brother had won a statewide essay competition for Mississippi high school students. But when they tried to make arrangements for him to stay in a local hotel, they couldn't because it was segregated. Harley had never forgotten that, just as Clarence had never forgotten the teacher at the integrated school who thought his paper was so good he must have plagiarized it. Clarence could never convince her he hadn't.

"Where we meeting for Kwanzaa this year?" Harley asked.

"Don't know where you're goin' for Kwanzaa," Clarence said, "but *Christmas* is at our place, right Geneva? Maybe we'll be moved into our new house by then."

Harley shook his head. "You celebrate an independence day that didn't consider blacks worthy of independence. You celebrate a Thanksgiving of people who came and stole America from its natives. And you celebrate a Christmas about a white man's religion that oppressed your ancestors."

Clarence held his tongue, letting it ride. Everyone seemed grateful.

"Well," Marny said, "Dani and Felicia sure had nice services, didn't they?" Her voice quivered. It seemed a strange topic nearly seven weeks after the fact, but this was the first big family gathering.

"Nice if you can overlook Dani's Uncle Tom preacher," Harley said.

"Brother," Clarence said, "to you anyone who makes a living outside of a government agency or a black studies department is an Uncle Tom."

"I'm an African first, an American second. That's why I celebrate Kwanzaa, not Christmas."

"Well, brother, I got news for you. Kwanzaa wasn't invented in Africa. It was invented in Los Angeles. By Americans!"

"It was invented to commemorate what Africa is about. Which you've obviously forgotten."

"To say our ancestors came from Africa is one thing. To say we're African is another. If our kids are going to make it in America, we've got to quit telling them they don't belong, they can't fit in."

"What chance do they have as long as whitey keeps 'em down? Racism's the disease. You don't deal with that and it's like wipin' a runny nose—messin' with the symptoms doesn't cure the cold. You know Dr. Ibrihim? He's lived in Africa and he's lived here—and he sees the racism everywhere in this society."

"He's been *taught* to see it," Clarence said. "Yeah, I've heard Dr. Ibrihim speak. I've heard him denounce America as this horrible oppressive racist country. Ironic, isn't it, that if he was back home in his own country and criticized it like he does America, they'd lock him up and probably torture him. Why'd he come here, tell me that, brother? To get a superior education so he could go back and help his people, right? But he never went back, did he? The standard of living was too high, life was too good, freedom was too precious. Well, if America is so terrible, why doesn't he just go back to Africa? And if it's all so great over there, why don't you just go back with him?"

"Sure, brother, I hear you," Harley's voice broke and went high pitched. "Now that the wood's all split, the water's all drawn, the cotton's all picked, and the rails reach coast to coast, now that the ditches are dug and there's just a few shoes left to be shined, now they tell us they'll give us just as much opportunity as they got. Well, they've been liars all along, and they're still lyin'! So excuse me if I don't join you in shufflin' for 'em anymore, Tom!"

Clarence got up and left the room, seeking sanctuary in the kitchen. Right about now, he knew, Dani would have come in to talk to him, cool him down, remind him how he and Harley used to be so close.

Dani watched her family. She enjoyed the gathering, relished the conversation, felt concern at the conflict. She needed to make periodic adjustments to sort out the principal parties. The dominant images were of great warriors in postures of defense and attack, guardians and enemies hovering over and around various family members. She took special pleasure in seeing the warrior guarding Celeste.

"How could I have been so blind?" she asked. "How could I have not seen these warriors? How could I fail to sense the spiritual battles surrounding me every moment?"

"I often wondered that myself," Torel said. "Now you see with new eyes. Eyes of eternity."

She looked now at the angel standing guard around Clarence. "He's magnificent."

"Your brother keeps Jartakel busy," Torel said. "My comrade guards against the attacks of the fallen ones from the outside, but many of your brother's attacks come from the inside. We do not have the luxury of doing battle on only one front."

"So, do you know well my brother's guardian? This Jartakel?"

"Yes. He is a great advocate of justice, far greater than even your brother. I did not know Jartakel until I was sent to guard you. He had been assigned to your brother at his conception, as I was to you at your beginning. Even as I guarded you in your mother's womb, Jartakel briefed me on your family. We became very close. I miss serving beside him. Heaven promises reunion not only for the redeemed, but for their guardians. Jartakel and I walked together many Mississippi hillsides and Chicago streets and stood by one another in your Portland home."

Dani looked through the portal and saw four images walking among the buttercups, one small, one medium size, and two huge. "I thought Clarence and I were alone on that hillside."

"You were never alone. The Carpenter promised you he would be with you always. And for extra measure he appointed us to stand beside you, never sleeping, always watchful."

Dani smiled at him. "Thank you, my friend. Thank you for all you did for me."

"To serve Elyon and to serve you was my pleasure, for I was made to serve."

She hugged him. He was struck by the warmth of her skin, she by the strength of his embrace. "Thank you for helping me understand," Dani said. She looked at her family in that living room, so very near. "I pray each of them may come to understand."

Still hiding out in the kitchen, Clarence reflected on his turbulent history with Harley. His brother had gone on the freedom rides and marches of Martin Luther King Jr., following his teachings of nonviolence and moral transformation. In time, though, hearing the voice of Malcolm X, Harley saw integration as acquiescing to white power and surrendering what it meant to be black. Eventually he followed the Black Power of Stokely Carmichael and was moved by the rhetoric of H. Rap Brown. Adopting the belief that police were an occupying force invading the black community, Harley became part of the Black Panther movement of Bobby Seale, Huey P. Newton, and Eldridge Cleaver. Clarence didn't know all his brother had done, but he knew he'd carried heavy hardware and he'd used it. In time Harley moved from the streets to the classroom, graduating with honors from the University of California at Berkeley and coming to teach at Portland State. He'd never lost his militancy. And while Clarence disagreed with him, he respected his brother's courage of conviction.

In his early twenties Clarence had admired Harley and for years echoed much of his thinking. He remembered with both sweetness and bitterness their late night intellectual discussions, reading first W.E.B. DuBois, then later Alain LeRoy Locke and other architects of the Harlem Renaissance. They discussed the writings of Marcus Garvey, who believed blacks could never find justice in white America and engineered a wave of immigration to form a black nation in Africa. With Harley, Clarence studied a host of black thinkers and social activists.

In the mid-seventies, brand new at the *Journal*, Clarence hung with Harley's crowd, most of them professors and students from Portland State. They'd smoke their spliffs, listen to tunes, and rap into the early hours of the morning about the evils of "Babylon," the white man's corrupt civilization. They spoke of their pilgrimages to the Gambia, Ghana, and Nigeria. The discussions about Babylon and the endless conspiracy theories fueled Clarence's anger and increased his suspicions. But he found it demotivated him, made him feel no matter how hard he worked, he couldn't change Babylon. He found himself torn apart, and after a few years decided he had to either leave his career or leave this group of friends. He left the friends, including Harley. He realized this would label him a black court jester, a puppet, a pawn of Babylon. But then, all of them got their financial aid and salaries from Babylon.

When Harley converted to Nation of Islam and changed his name to Ishmael, neither his parents nor his siblings bought into it. He would always be Harley to them. On the other hand, Clarence saw some positive changes in Harley. He admired his brother's discipline of memorizing the words of Malcolm X and Elijah Mohammed and the Qur'an. Harley acknowledged that it had helped him off drugs. He stressed education and studied the Qur'an, learning to speak Arabic. He prayed five times a day and made regular trips to the masjid. Black Muslims were committed to self-help, and at least that part jived with Clarence's conservatism.

Clarence came back in the room, just in time to see his father shake his head and say to Harley, "Nossah, Son, that's poppycock, pure and simple. Not all white people is like that. Many of them's good folk. Yes, some racists—white *and* black—

gots it so bad they'll never change, and you just got to let them go. Like my daddy used to say, 'Don't ever try to teach a pig to sing.'"

"What?" Geneva asked.

Obadiah grinned. "It wastes your time and it annoys the pig." Everybody laughed, including Harley and Clarence.

"We're in the second slavery, Daddy," Harley said, not one to give up an argument. "It's a myth that things have gotten better."

"Don't tell me about myths, boy." Obadiah spoke sternly, with more strength than Clarence had heard in months. "I was there when it was worse than you ever dreamed of, and my daddy was there when it was worse than I ever dreamed of. So don't tell *me* it isn't better now."

"Daddy," Harley implored his father, "Malcolm said you don't stick a knife in a man's back nine inches and then pull it out six inches and say you're making progress. Look around. The only way you can avoid being a slave is to sell out to white businesses. All the black businesses in America combined are less than Bill Gates's empire. One white man bigger than all black men combined. You think that's fair?"

"Equality don't mean it's the same for everyone, Son," Obadiah said. "Black folk got a late start—I knows that better than anybody. But this is America, and all men are created equal."

"You say that as if it meant something. When they wrote that they didn't even consider black men to be men. The whites loved to quote the Bible—'Slaves submit to your masters.' And what about you, brother?" He looked at Clarence. "Have you told your children the same Supreme Court that said Dred Scott had no rights opened their session with prayer and had a Bible sitting on their bench? That's how Christianity treats the black man. Always has, always will." Harley looked back at his father. "I wish you'd change your mind, Daddy. I wish you'd come to the true faith of the black man. It's not too late."

Obadiah sucked in air and sat up straight. "Hear me on this, Son, and hear me good." The voice was clear and firm. "I *knows* the true faith of the black man, the brown man, the red man, the yellow man, the white man. Every man. It's a faith in Jesus, who said, 'I am the way, the truth and the life; no man comes to the Father but by me.' I won't sit here while you attack the faith that's been the foundation for this family, for your mama and my mama and my daddy, and their mamas and daddies before them. You hear your daddy talkin', Harley?"

"It became their faith only because white slaveowners indoctrinated them with their Christianity. And my name is Ishmael Salid."

"Don't tell me what yo' name is, boy." Obadiah stood up, shaking his finger. Clarence hadn't seen such fire in his eyes for longer than he could remember. He felt like Daddy was about to bring out a hickory switch from the back room. "I'm the one that gave you yo' name. Me and yo' sweet mama. I love you, Son, but you'll always be Harley. Now, somebody else can call you Kareem Abdul Jabbar or the Ayatolah Khomeni or Sister Souljah or whatever they wants to, but *I* gave you yo' name and I's gonna call you Harley till the day I die and then some, and nothin' you say's gonna change that. You hear me, boy?"

"Yes, Daddy," Harley said quietly. "But no matter what you say, there's only one true religion of the black nation—Islam. The Christian missionaries tried to impose their white culture on Africa. And what did they do to stop the slave trade? Malcolm said, 'Christianity is the religion of oppressors.' Christianity teaches passivity. It's an opiate to put black people in their place. Can you tell me with a straight face that isn't true?"

"Sure," Clarence said, "*some* whites perverted Christianity, but that's not what it's really about. Read about Christ in the New Testament and tell me he was passive. Or John the Baptist or Paul or Peter. They didn't have a passive bone in their bodies. And don't forget David Livingstone and lots of other Christian missionaries spoke out against black slavery."

"There's a sura in the Holy Qur'an that says brothers everywhere must unite. We are warriors, not to kill each other, but we are in a jihad till death against our oppressors. We have to help our young men learn the ways of Elijah Mohammed. We must tell them, 'As you kill each other, the real enemy kills you. You kill each other and you do his job for him, and meanwhile you're less of a threat to him.'"

"So you don't tell our kids to stop killing," Clarence said. "Just to point the gun toward someone else?"

"Islam doesn't make black men passive or weak. It makes them strong and wise. When you've been emasculated by white Christians for four hundred years, you want to do something that affirms your *black* manhood. Islam is Afrocentric; Christianity is Eurocentric."

"Baloney," Clarence countered. "Both of them started in the Middle East, and there were black Christians in Africa six centuries before Mohammed. You can wear your bow ties and quote the Honorable Elijah Mohammed and Louis Farrakhan all day, just like you used to quote Mao and Ho Chi Minh and Castro and all your other liberators. But none of it changes the facts of history."

"Minister Farrakhan is right," Harley said. "White people are just tools of the devil."

"So are black people, Son," Obadiah said. "Farrakhan is right to think white people are sinners. He's just wrong to think black people aren't."

"Minister Farrakhan is the black people's hope. But you wouldn't know about that, would you brother?" Harley glared at Clarence. "You wouldn't even come to the Million Man March."

"I didn't go because I can't follow Farrakhan. I've read Minister Farrakhan and your Nation of Islam theology. It says the black man used to inhabit the moon, but then a scientist caused an explosion that blew blacks to the earth, who were the original Tribe of Shabazz, have I got that right? Then Yakub, a mad scientist with a big head, created the evil white race from the blacks, and the white satans were allowed by Allah to rule the earth for six thousand years, which ended in 1914. And now Minister Farrakhan is like the Grand Pubha or something?"

"Look who's talkin' about myths," Harley said. "How about, 'Blackness is the mark of Cain'? Or, the descendants of Ham are under the curse of Canaan, when in fact the great majority of blacks aren't even descendants of Canaan. The Christian myths make anything else pale in comparison."

"Why do you conveniently forget what I documented for you, brother, that a ninth century *Muslim* first came up with the myth that blackness was the curse of Cain, and he did it to justify the fact that Muslims enslaved blacks. I've showed you the reports, that today in Mauritania there are ninety thousand black tribesmen enslaved by the Moors, but do you or your intellectual colleagues who railed against apartheid ever speak out against slavery when it's *Muslims* who do it? Or what about the tens of thousands of children of black Christians in Sudan enslaved by Muslims? Why are you so selective about justice? Why doesn't Minister Farrakhan speak out against Muslim injustices instead of fraternizing in the palaces of tyrants and taking money from their bloodthirsty hands?"

"Minister Farrakhan has done more for our people than Martin Luther King ever dreamed of."

"Is this the same Minister Farrakhan who preaches whites are 'sub-human,' that they're all devils, that Judaism is a 'gutter religion'? What would Martin Luther King think of that, Martin the *Christian* minister? You think I want to take my son to hear that kind of bigot? Farrakhan isn't just a racist, he's a crazy racist. His numerology and his UFOs and his conspiracies? Napoleon shot off the nose of the Sphinx to destroy the proof that blacks created Egyptian civilization? AIDS was invented by white men to kill off blacks? Give me a break. The man's a Looney Tune."

Harley stood up and leaned toward Clarence, the whole living room cringing at the exchange. "What do you think it says about your precious Christian church that it took a Muslim to inspire a million men to come to Washington? Minister Farrakhan called on men to accept responsibility for themselves, their wives, their children. They vowed not to raise weapons against each other. He called on blacks to take responsibility for their behavior. I was there, brother, me and my sons. It was peaceful, it was positive, and Farrakhan was only a part of it—yet all the white media could do was tear it apart."

"The white media was handcuffed," Clarence countered. "They wore kid gloves. If this had been a white man preaching racism and malarkey like Farrakhan, they'd have crucified him."

"How come no *Christian* leader ever got a million black men together, tell me that. Minister Farrakhan is restoring patriarchy to black America. Paternal authority and responsibility—haven't I heard you say that's what we need, brother? Well, Minister Farrakhan was saying it long before you did. I saw two young boys stand up on that platform and ask black men to be their fathers and their grandfathers, to love them and discipline them. They came to show the nation black men aren't just drug dealers and wife abusers and drive-by shooters and child deserters. But all white America could do was scoff at them and mock them."

"I'm not scoffing at them, but—"

"Instead of applauding black men for standing up at the march for what's right, they denigrated them. Minister Farrakhan is a prophet of God."

"Minister Farrakhan is David Duke with darker skin!" Clarence saw the hurt in his brother's eyes, and while Harley's anger didn't bother him, the hurt did. Clarence felt empty, less because he was attacking a religion he believed to be false than because he was defending a religion he was no longer certain was true.

"Let me ask you just one thing, Daddy," Harley said, turning away from Clarence. "After all you've said about Mississippi and all the black folk lynched, all the suffering, how those white police nearly beat you to death, what does it tell you that the place was full to the brim with Bible believin' church people? I want you to tell me now, did you ever, even *once*, hear any white Christian church leader stand up and say to the community, to the black churches, to the newspaper, to anyone, 'This is wrong. I'm sorry. We will not tolerate the lynchings and the beatings and the humiliation and the cruelty anymore! We will kick the Klansmen out of our churches and stand up for justice for people of all colors.' Did you *ever* get that from a white church leader, Daddy? I want the whole family to hear your answer."

Twenty-seven family members sat in breathless silence in the crowded living room, all of them looking at the patriarch. Obadiah sat silently for a long time, his eyes down, slowly filling with moisture. Finally he lifted his eyes and spoke.

"No, I never did hear that. And I wish to Jesus I would have." He fought to gain control of his voice. "But that's not God's fault. And my faith is in God, not men. Not white men, not black men. My faith is in a God who isn't black or white but who made both and who died for both and for people of every color."

Obadiah looked around the room. He had the floor now and not even Clarence or Harley would dare try to take it back. "You two boys, you hear me now. It grieves this old man to see my sons fight like this. I don't want yo' mama or my Dani to look down here and have to see it either. I'm old as dirt, but I ain't mulch on the flowers yet. I's still your daddy. When you was boys 'member how I read those Proverbs to you over and over? 'Member how whenever you crossed the boundary, I always sided with the boundary? Still do, 'cause God made the boundary and the boundary always wins. Now I got just a few things to say, so shut up yo' mouths and listen to the boundaries, both of you."

The rest of the family sat amazed at his strength and attentive to his words. "Clarence, you should show more respect for your brother's beliefs. Yeah, you knows I disagrees with him too, but sarcasm and venom ain't the way to convince him. I wish I heard more love in your voice, more kindness to your brother. Yo' mama would want that. You knows the words of the gospel, boy. But you's missin' the music."

Clarence looked down, rebuked and ashamed.

"And now you, Harley," Obadiah said. "You better read Revelation, the last three chapters. And you better realize God ain't gonna adjust it all to fit your beliefs or Minister Farrakhan's or mine or anybody else's. If you're gonna get on the right side, you'll have to change your faith because God isn't gonna change his. He's stubborn that way, but then he's God and that's that.

"Now, the rest of you, hear this old man and hear me good 'cause I don't know how much longer I's gonna be here to tell you nothin'. There's bad Christians and there's good Christians; there's phony Christians and there's real Christians. The devil can go to church once a week. Nothin' to it. It's livin' it that matters, and the people that live it, those are the real Christians—not just the ones that mouth it. Now I'm not college educated like some folks in this room, but I was near the top of my class when I dropped out in third grade." His eyes gleamed. "And the way I reads my Bible, anybody who hates a man for the color God made him isn't filled with God, he's filled with the devil. So jus' because somebody say he a Christian, it don't mean he is. And even those that *is* Christians is still just people, and people's gonna always lets you down." He'd been talking fast, but his speech now slowed to a crawl.

"But my Jesus, he won't never lets you down. *Never.* Yessir, my Lord tooks my daddy and mama, my Ruby and my Bobby and my Dani and my Felicia, he tooks them all away from me, and all my brothers and sisters 'cept ol' Elijah, but he never *once* tooks away himself from Obadiah Abernathy, and that's the gospel truth. The Lord gives and the Lord takes. Blessed be the name of the Lord."

A hush permeated the living room. Clarence and Harley, both ill at ease with the tears now flowing down their father's cheeks, bowed their heads in chagrined silence.

21

Clarence arrived home early from the *Trib*. As he pulled into the driveway, Ty and three friends came walking out the front door. He sat in his car a moment and listened. Ty was animated, like Clarence hadn't heard him in a long time. His voice cracked, oscillating between child and adult. Ty was fourteen years old, all elbows and knees, not yet grown into his ears. His body was awkward but lean and strong. As Clarence watched, Ty pulled out of his pocket a blue baseball cap and put it on. On the front was a capital B with an X drawn over it, followed by the number 187.

Clarence recognized only one of the boys, Jason, a kid Ty had hung with for years. Jason looked different now. He didn't like the way any of these boys dressed. They had the look of bangers. But then, so did most the kids around here. Who could tell?

"Hi, Ty. Jason. Hey, guys," Clarence said, trying to sound friendlier than he felt.

Ty barely acknowledged him. His friends grunted, making eye contact only long enough to send an unmistakable message—"Outta my face, old head."

Clarence came inside and Geneva greeted him. They kissed. "I've had some of Ty's friends over after school the last few days," Geneva explained. "I figured if he's spending time with them, we should know what they're like. The key seems to be food. The more I put out, the more they come back."

"They're teenage boys," Clarence said.

"It's like the descent of the locusts. I put it out and it's instantly devoured. The grocery bill's goin' crazy. Ty's got the metabolism of a wolverine. I thought you ate a lot—you *do* eat a lot—but Ty leaves you in the dust. Jonah's catching up too."

"He's growin' up—almost twelve now. I still don't think this is the place for him."

"His place is with his family," Geneva said. "You know, when Ty was with his friends, I actually saw him smile. It shocked me. I hadn't seen him smile for months. Certainly not since the funerals. He's got this big lopsided grin, you remember? He only seems to be happy when he's hangin' with his friends. I'm afraid we're losin' him, Clarence."

"I don't think we ever had him, did we? But we've got to help him. I won't be beaten by a gang of young thugs."

Geneva started to say something, but thought better of it. Clarence went to the telephone and punched a number.

"Ollie? Listen, you used to work gangs in L.A., right? I've got a family problem—you know, my nephew? I need some info on gangs. Would you mind walking me through some things? Yeah? That'd be great. Thanks."

Maybe if I can understand his world better I can reach him before it's too late.

"Read to us, Grampy!" Keisha demanded.

"Grumpy? Who you callin' Grumpy?"

"No, *Grampy*."

"Okay, then, that's better, yessuh, that's better fo' sure! Yeah, ol' Grumpy, he'll read to his grandchillens any day. Readin's a joy if ever there was one. But first I's gonna play you some of my old music, just to set the mood."

Obadiah Abernathy moved slowly toward the stereo. On top of it sat the old turntable that he alone used. While the rest of the world had graduated from tapes to CDs, he'd never graduated to tapes from records. His music was engraved on platters. He played for Keisha and Celeste a sampling of jazz and jitterbug music. He played Duke Ellington, Nat King Cole, and Louis Armstrong. The children weren't old enough to know they weren't supposed to like it.

"You know why music is so important to black folk, chillens?"

"Why Grampy?"

"Because it lifts you up; it takes you somewhere else. It's a way of gettin' out from under the rock. Music gives you wings." He said it with great energy, and though he only said it once, the children would always remember it, as if he'd said it a hundred times.

"Now you think *that* music's somethin', you jus' wait for heaven's music—choirs of angels and all God's chillens there's ever been. They gonna make Nat King Cole sound like scratchin' fingernails on a blackboard."

"Will black people and white people live in the same part of heaven?" Celeste asked.

"Yes, darlin', I believe they will. Ol' Jim Crow won't be in glory. Maybe there'll be segregation in hell, but not heaven. Same eatin' places and drinkin' fountains for everyone in God's kingdom. Black people, white people, every color people. Some whites in heaven, some in hell. Some blacks in heaven, some blacks in hell. That's how it goes. God made all colors. If he don't care, we won't." He coughed from deep inside, hard and long.

"You okay, Grampy?" Keisha asked.

"Ol' Grumpy's all right, now. Don't fuss yo' nappy little heads none over me. I ain't mulch on the flowers yet, you know. Nothin' wrong with this ol' boy that couldn't be fixed by a good resurrection. For now, I'd settle for a mess o' cornbread and black-eyed peas. You tell yo' mama that, hear me?"

His eyes sparkled, and his contagious spirit worked its magic on the children. He then broke into song with as much gusto as his old lungs allowed. "Go tell it on the mountain…

"Oh Freedom, Oh Freedom, Oh Freedom over me. And before I'll be a slave I'll be buried in my grave, and go home to my Lord and be free.

"Swing low, sweet chariot, comin' for to carry me home, swing low sweet chariot, comin' for to carry me home. I looked over Jordan, and what did I see…

"O Canaan, bright Canaan, I'm bound for the land of Canaan."

Obadiah's mind returned to the living room as suddenly as it had left. "Let's see now. Which book you want your ol' Grumpy to read to you today? More of them Narnia stories?"

"Why'd you leave L.A.?" Clarence asked Ollie.

"It was turning into a madhouse. A fourth of the city's homicides were gang related. Now I hear it's close to a third. Kids killing kids. Everybody's goin' to the mission."

"The mission?"

"Gang-slang for dying. The L.A. morgue's on Mission Street."

Ollie handed a list to Clarence, printed on paper with a police department logo. "Okay, I got this from gang enforcement. These are the fourteen major gangs in North Portland, not counting odds and ends. Of course, there's dozens more gangs in Southeast, Milwaukee, West Side, you name it."

Clarence looked over the list. "Forty-Three East Coast Crips?'"

"First lesson. It's Four *trey*, not forty-three. Three is pronounced trey. Two is deuce, one is ace."

"What's with East Coast? They from Jersey or something?"

"No. Los Angeles. East Coast just means the east side of L.A.'s Harbor Freeway."

"So…these guys are from L.A.?"

"Nope. Maybe the originals, but most these kids have never been outside Portland."

"And the four trey means…?"

"Four trey is just an L.A. street number, forty-third. It means that's the center of the set turf, the area of their dominion." Ollie looked down at the list. "Most of our locals are named after L.A. gangs, but some are original with Portland. Like this one." He pointed at the paper.

"Forty-Seven Kerby Bloc Crips," Clarence read. "So, is this the 4700 block on North Kerby?"

"Exactly."

"This a typo? 'B-l-o-c'? No k?"

"Nope. There's a reason for everything. If you're a Crip you never put a *k* after a *c*. CK is Blood dialect for Crip Killer. So you don't follow a *c* with a *k* unless you're a Piru, a Blood."

"No kidding? The Hispanic guys that killed Dani—what local gangs could they be from?"

"Well, there's the CVTF, for one—Compton Vario Tortilla Flats, from Compton in L.A. They're a Southeast Eighty-Second gang, down in Johnson Creek, Clackamas. Usually they just go by TF. They've got the belt buckles with the M."

"Why M?"

"Thirteenth letter of the alphabet. After their home base, Thirteenth Street in Compton. Then we've got several gangs affiliated with the EME, also called Mexican Mafia. It's more than just another gang. It acts as overseers of the regular Hispanic street gangs, forcing them to pay 'taxes,' ordering hits on uncooperative gangs or members. A 'green light' is put on any gang that doesn't comply, meaning they're open to being hit. EME killed a movie consultant when the movie didn't portray gangs the way they liked."

"Sounds like the Gangsta Disciples in Chicago."

"You know them? That's right, you're from Chicago. Yeah, the Disciples were one of the first gangs, besides the EME, to really get organized, almost like Capone during prohibition. They've actually sent representatives out to cities all over the country, channeling profits back to the mother group to fund more crime and drug dealing and weapons purchases."

"What about white gangs?"

"We've got 'em. There's the Oak Grove Posse, a bunch of white thugs. Then there's the skater gang in Southeast, the Toaster Strudels."

"The what?"

"Pretty intimidating name, huh?" Ollie's voice got even tougher and raspier. "'Hey, man, we gonna rumble with the Strudels tonight.' It's weird, but hey, they're skaters." Ollie stood up. "Listen, I've got an hour. Let's take a drive, and I'll show you some things. Maybe something will strike us related to the case, who knows? You want to visit white supremacist territory? You up for that?"

"Yeah."

They went down to the bottom level of the Justice Center, into police parking. They hopped into Ollie's plain precinct car, where he reassumed the role of a presidential aide giving a briefing.

"Remember back in 1988, the Ethiopian student Skinheads beat to death with a baseball bat?"

"Who could forget?" Clarence said. "Led to the conviction of that White Aryan Resistance guy from California. What's his name?"

"Tom Metzger. His conviction date is a holy day on the white supremacist calendar, did you know that? Portland is known around the world as the place he became a martyr. The murder of the Ethiopian kid was my first homicide case that was clearly racially motivated, start to finish. I interviewed dozens of Skinheads. Eye-opening, to say the least."

"I'd like to interview some of them myself," Clarence said.

Ollie looked at him as if he were crazy. "Most gang members are from families that don't want them in gangs. The Skinheads, a lot of them, are from families that encourage it. It's scary. Okay, we're moving onto their turf now."

"There's a couple of serious dudes," Clarence pointed to his right. "Pull over. I want a closer look."

Clarence eyed the two young men, one with a brownish green flight jacket, the other with a tight fitting, wide open Levi's jacket, accentuating his bulging biceps. Both wore brown military-style shirts with white suspenders and white T-shirts showing from underneath. One wore plain black pants that highlighted the stark white of his suspenders and shoelaces; the other had on camouflage pants. The flight jacket sported an American flag; the other a swastika.

"Why are they called Skinheads? Most of them don't shave their heads."

"They used to," Ollie said. "A lot of them don't now because it makes them an easy mark for law enforcement. They want attention from other people, but not us. It all goes back to England in the sixties. The original skinheads shaved their heads to protest the hippies, who they saw as worthless, drug-using long-hairs. They were right about that, but not much else. Now you've got white supremacist groups all over Europe. The neo-Nazi movement in Germany has really taken off."

"See the Doc Martens?" Ollie pointed to their heavy workboots with steel-tipped toes. "Notice that punk has white laces—that's about white supremacy, white power. The other dude? Red laces for blood—that means he's shed blood for his cause. Okay, check out that pasty looking guy leaning against the wall, with the iron cross. See the 88?"

"Yeah, I've seen it before. What's it mean? A street number?"

"Nope. Each eight stands for the eighth letter of the alphabet, H. So 88 is HH—as in Heil Hitler."

Clarence stared harder. They were close enough to see the larger tattoos, ranging from Swastikas to hooded Klansmen to Viking symbols and a small circle with a cross in the middle. Most of the tattoos had three or four letters. "What's WSU?"

"Not Washington State University, unfortunately. White Student Union. SWP is Supreme White Power."

"Look above the swastika behind them," Clarence said, pointing. "Does that say what I think it does?"

Ollie strained his eyes and read the words slowly. "Hitler didn't finish the job. We will."

"Incredible," Clarence said. "Why doesn't someone just wipe out those tags?"

"Maybe they will. Then a few hours later they'll come up again."

Clarence scanned the walls and the gangsters. "The creep in the Levi's jacket has a tattoo that says BBKS. What's that?"

Ollie hesitated. "Stands for Black Boy Killers."

Clarence stared at the gangster, locking his eyes, then gazed at the graffiti on the wall behind him, the most prominent messages being "White Pride" and "Niggers Beware."

The two boys now noticed Clarence. They glared at him with palpable disdain. The younger boy stared at Clarence, then grew uncomfortable to see the black man in the business suit staring back, eyes not blinking. The boy lost the battle and looked down. The other young man, the muscular one, held steady. He met Clarence's gaze and poured out hatred through his eyes. He spit on the ground.

Clarence rolled down his window. "Somethin' you don't like?"

"What's it to you, nigger?" The boy's grimace shifted to an infantile grin.

"You punks are really tough, aren't you?" Clarence said.

"Tough enough to take you, shoeshine boy."

In one fluid motion Clarence hopped out of the car. The younger boy turned and broke into an all-out run. The muscular boy held his ground, reaching down to his boot. He pulled out a knife.

Clarence considered reaching for his own knife, but ruled it out when he remembered Ollie. Besides, he didn't need a knife for this punk.

"You say you can take me," Clarence blurted, moving closer to the boy. "I say yo' mama raised a fool!"

Suddenly Clarence felt a firm grip around him and saw two hands join together below his diaphragm, squeezing painfully hard. It felt like a professional wrestler administering the Heimlich maneuver.

"Clarence! Get back in the car." Ollie had never sounded so commanding. Clarence obeyed, reluctantly backing away.

The young man took a sudden step toward Ollie. "You come an inch closer," Ollie warned him, "and you're goin' down little man. You'll be breakin' the fall with your face."

"This is our turf. Don't want no nigger-lovers here."

"That's *officer* nigger-lover. Portland police." Ollie flashed his badge. "You own the whole city or just this corner?"

"We're gonna own the country, man."

"Not as long as I live here, you won't." Two other Skinheads walked closer, including the one who'd run off. Clarence opened the door and started to join Ollie.

"Stay where you are," Ollie yelled back at Clarence, only turning his head slightly, keeping an eye on the gangsters crowding in close.

Emboldened by the presence of his homeboys, the muscular Skinhead stepped toward Ollie with his knife. With lightning speed, Ollie thrust his right hand inside his suit coat and pulled a SIG-Sauer .38 Super from his shoulder holster. He pointed it at the boy's forehead, now only six feet away.

"Don't try growin' a brain on me, punk," Ollie said. "Okay, which of you junior

Nazis makes the move? I've got nine rounds here, three for each of you. I take requests—who wants his first?"

They all backed off, two of them raising their hands, the other lowering his knife.

"Now, I'm not going to make an arrest as it stands," Ollie said, "but anybody tries anything, and I change my mind real quick. Got it?"

They nodded. Ollie backed up and got into the car. He drove off slowly, he and Clarence both sitting silently and peering over their shoulders to keep an eye on the Skinheads.

"Why didn't you arrest them?" Clarence asked.

"More hassle for me than them. Take me longer to do the paperwork than they'd spend in jail. What's the point? Besides, you started it."

Clarence's eyes dropped.

"This isn't a game, Clarence. If I'm asking too much of you to not pick fights with gangsters, just let me know, okay? Criminy, cool your jets, will you?"

"They're a bunch of racists."

"Duh…well, *of course* they're racists. That's the whole point. Wake up and smell the coffee, Mr. Abernathy. Most gangsters are racists. It comes with the territory. But just because they're morons doesn't mean you have to compete with them for the head moron prize." They sat quietly as Ollie drove back toward the precinct.

"Hey, Ollie," Clarence finally said. "You surprised me. You're strong. You move fast. Seemed like I was just out of the car when you grabbed me."

"I'm so tough I do my own dental work," Ollie said. "When I was born and the doctor slapped me, I gave him a head butt. Learn your lesson, Abernathy. Messin' with me is like wearin' cheese underwear down rat alley."

"What's with the girls?" Clarence pointed to a group of a half-dozen girls, several in short skirts, a couple in camouflage clothes, wearing iron crosses, 88s, and swastikas.

"They're scary. Flakier than Mama's piecrust. Girl gangbangers are a mystery to me. They want the attention of these guys—they're impressed with their macho image, I guess. But the guys just pass them around like a bottle of cheap wine. Girls are much more active in the white supremacist groups than most gangs. They say it's their duty to fight beside their men in the coming race war. They claim the race war will be on us either in 2000 or 2020."

"Not much time left, huh?"

"They claim the L.A. riots were a warning to get armed and ready. Years ago when I interviewed them on that Ethiopian case, they kept calling their jailed members prisoners of war. And their dead members martyrs. A lot of them work out and stay in good shape because they're prepping to be soldiers. It's no joke—they're dead serious."

"What gang were those guys with?"

"White Power. Then there's Americans White Pride, 100% Honkey, the Swastikas, the Lightning Bolts. The KKK and White Aryan Resistance and Aryan Nations are more traditional groups, but they recruit and take advantage of all the skinhead gangs. There's a few so-called Christian groups—Church of the Creator and another church or two. Check out the gangsters over here." Ollie pointed to several Asian young men, leaning against the walls under graffiti. "We're going right by Red Cobra territory now. L.A.'s got all the Asian gangs—Korean, Filipino, Vietnamese, Cambodian, Samoan, you name it. Portland's getting more all the time. The Asian gangs are generally tougher than Hispanics and blacks. Once you're in, good luck gettin' out."

"I never drive this part of town," Clarence said. "Seems like the gangs are everywhere now."

"They just keep multiplying," Ollie said. "The worst thing is, now they're normal. To people in the cities they're a given, an accepted way of life. Like you can't stop them. Best you can do is maybe placate them, stay out of their way. You see that when politicians call these gang summits to ask the gang leaders how they can control the violence. The gang leaders get respect and esteem and financial bonuses from city government. In L.A. and Chicago, you've got politicians hiring gangs to get signatures for petitions and get voters out to the polling places. In Chicago there was even a gang leader elected to office. I read your column about Norcoast hiring bangers for his campaign. I'm telling you, it's making them look respectable."

"I hung out with the wrong guys for a while when I was Ty's age," Clarence said. "I was on the fringes of gang life, but I never got sucked all the way in. It's amazing these kids join the gangs when it's so obvious it's going to mess up their lives."

"They don't see it that way," Ollie said. "To them, joining the gang isn't a problem, it's a solution. For a kid without a dad, a gang gives him male figures to bond with. Gives him a feeling of belonging. It's a family thing. Lots of these kids don't feel like they have options. The gang gives them a sense of purpose. Kids who feel like they're nobody suddenly feel like they're somebody."

"Pastor Clancy was talking about that in church Sunday. He said the gang gives them support and companionship they aren't getting at home or church or school. Even the names are family names—Homeboys, Brother, Blood, Cousin. These kids are looking for something bigger than themselves, something to believe in, something to be loyal to. That's all good, but they're looking in the wrong places. That's why I'm concerned about my nephew. There's a lot of bad stuff out there."

"There's a lot of *weirdness* out there. Take that guy." Ollie pointed. "Hairdo looks like an inflammation on a baboon's rear end. You know what I think the root problem is?"

"What's that?"

"Guys wearing earrings."

"That's cultural, don't you think?" Clarence asked. "Not exactly a root problem."

"No? Well, did you notice the same time men started wearing earrings, women started wearing tattoos? Think about it." Ollie cringed.

"Good point."

―――――――

"You one o' my peeps now, Li'l GC. Want to prove you a true 60s?"

"Yeeeah."

"Okay. Check out dis piece, man." GC reached under his bed to one of several old cardboard boxes that contained his gun collection. He pulled out a .357 Smith and Wesson revolver, stainless steel.

"Four-inch barrel. One o' my homies got this for me in L.A.. Had it with me ever since. I don't take it out on the street 'cause I don't want Po Po to get it."

"Cool." Ty handled it nervously.

GC turned it barrel up, spinning the cylinder until all six rounds fell out. Then he picked up one of the shells off the bed and said, "Here's the one that proves your manhood."

GC slipped the single round in one of the chambers and spun the cylinder again, like *Wheel of Fortune*. He put the gun first to his forehead, then his right temple, finger on the trigger.

Tyrone jumped up off the bed. "No, cuz, don't do it. Don't do it!"

"Hey, little homie, you can't get scared or it might tag you. If you know it won't fire, it won't." GC smiled, looked right into Ty's eyes, and pulled the trigger.

The hammer pinged against an empty chamber. Tyrone shook, terror in his eyes. He slumped back on GC's bed.

"Hey, I was scared the first time too," GC said. "Not any more. No Fear. Go ahead. Try it."

"No way."

"Come on, cuz. Thought you wanted to be an OG. I bein' straight up. Gotta do stuff to get there."

"Yeah, but…"

"Everybody else do it." Actually, most of the 60s hadn't, though GC had persuaded five homies to play the game over the last year. There had been no casualties when GC was present, but one when a couple of his 60s had played the game on their own.

"You still a baby gangster till you do this," GC said to Ty. "Just a wannabe. That all you are, a wannabe gangster?"

Tyrone heard the contempt in GC's voice and it hurt him, goaded him. Finally, he reached out and picked up the gun. He spun the cylinder. He wouldn't go through with it, he told himself, but he'd play along, buy a minute. He hoped for an interruption, that GC's mom would knock on the door or something, anything.

"Come on, tiny. It's Crip or cry, do or die. You be all right. Show yo' stuff now. Show you a 60s."

Ty trembled, slowly raising the barrel to his right temple, praying for help, praying the nightmare would end, that someone, anyone, would rescue him from this. When the muzzle touched his temple he pulled it away, pointing it down at the floor. He wiped the heavy beads of sweat off his brow with the cuff of his long-sleeved Pendleton shirt. He saw GC's disappointed look.

He moved the barrel back to his temple and hesitated, looking at GC, his eyes pleading with him to let him stop. GC's vice-grip stare didn't release him. The fourteen-year-old boy tensed his trembling right index finger. Then he slowly pulled the trigger.

"Ty told me after school he was spending the night at Jay's," Geneva said at ten o'clock that evening. "Well, I just called to check up on him, and Jay and his parents don't know anything about it. He's sneaking around again. Should you go out looking for him?"

"I've tried to hunt him down three times before. I can never find him, but he always turns up. Soon as he does, I'll straighten him out," Clarence said.

He sat down in his old recliner, now in Dani's living room. Clarence contemplated Ty and kids and gangs. He remembered himself as a fourteen-year-old, as insecure on the inside as he was cocky on the outside. In his day, the putdown humor endemic among all American youth reached an art form among urban black kids. "Playin' the dozens" was his favorite sport. The continuous litany of bad mouthing went as far beyond conventional putdowns as Rembrandt beyond finger painting. By Clarence's time the more popular term was "jonin'" which required a sharp tongue to dish out and a thick skin to take.

When it came to the dozens, your rep was on the line, and kids would crowd around to listen and learn and laugh at the humiliation. The putdowns ranged from your tacky clothes to your questionable parentage to the company your mother kept to your distinguishing physical imperfections. "You high water, Picway-shoed, long-nosed, cucumber-lipped, zit-faced, rat-headed, Dumbo-eared, black nappy-headed sister-kisser."

They called it "disrespectin'" years before it got shortened to "dissin." Maybe they'd been disrespected by the culture for so long, Clarence's daddy once told him, they decided at least they wouldn't let another black disrespect them. Every action, whether with brass knuckles, a switchblade, a lead pipe, or a gat, was justified the same way. When asked, "Why you do that to Jimmy?" the answer was always, "He disrespected me." End of explanation.

Clarence became a jonin' king at Horner and Cabrini Green. His natural wit had been sharpened by a critical and cynical attitude that helped him succeed as a joner.

The worst part of getting joned, Clarence remembered, was being singled out. So Clarence learned what was hip, how to dress. They called it "gettin' clean." You got clean by wearing the latest styles—in his day starched, high-collar shirts, shark-skin pants, and Stacy Adams wingtips. The tags on your clothes proved you frequented the hip places.

Chuck Taylor Converse All-Stars were the Air Jordans of Clarence's teen years. You wore P.F. Flyers and everybody knew you were one lame dude. Chuck Taylors came in two colors, black and white. He remembered fondly the distinctive track they left in the dirt.

He also remembered the pimp—the proud, defiant stride, where one leg sort of hopped or dragged. You could twist your body a little, and it was style, man, cool and tough. You bounced down the road and nobody was gonna mess wid you, 'cause you was bad, man. Clarence recalled working to get rid of his pimp at college, where he saw it no longer as an asset but as a liability. Several times he stumbled while trying to retrain himself to walk straight.

Clarence remembered wearing his hat backwards, letting his belt buckle dangle unfastened, and walking around with his shoelaces untied, lookin' cool but causing the occasional fall on his face. He laughed out loud as he thought about it, realizing for a moment Tyrone and the boys in this hood weren't much different than he'd been. They just had more time, more drugs, more weapons, and fewer fathers.

But the hangin', that's what he remembered most. There was no identity as an individual. You were part of a group. Your life had no meaning unless you hung with someone. Your mama prayed to God that you'd hang with the right group, but you rarely did. "Who he hang wid?" was the defining question. "Man," the answer might come, "he hang wid Bulldog Turner and Li'l Ratface, the one that pulled the piece on Capone Man over on Fourth."

They slap boxed, like wannabe gladiators, prepping for their day on the coliseum floor. They shot hoops, "hawked ball," they called it. At both Horner and Cabrini, full-court basketball went on all day, with Chuck Taylor All-Stars worn to a frazzle. They learned to sneak a man, shoot cuffs, blindside, and coldcock. Clarence remembered that gold-colored bullet shell he worked around his tooth so it looked like a gold cap. Until Daddy saw it one day and took him over his knee for what he called "an attitude adjustment."

There was safety in the group. You weren't exposed and vulnerable. When guys would double bank you—one shooting your cuffs, the other jumping on you to stomp your face—you needed comrades or you were history. It wasn't your family you protected; it was your gang. It wasn't your house you protected; it was your turf.

Not owning much, they claimed ownership of streets that weren't theirs. "Whatchu doin' here? This be our corner."

He thought about all those boys on the street without a father. He thought about peers and peer pressure and how every kid's gonna hang with other kids. The only question is which kids, and which values, drive the group.

Clarence thought how close he'd come to an entirely different life. He'd gotten into shoplifting at a corner store owned by whites. Why should white people make profit from blacks? That's all they'd ever done, wasn't it? And if a black boy was lucky, the best he could do was carry their golf clubs or spread manure in their flower gardens. Telling himself this, Clarence pocketed some Butterfingers and Baby Ruths, some odds and ends. When the storekeeper called after him as he left, he and his buddies ran the maze of backyard escape routes any Green Beret strategist would envy.

But Daddy had found out and whipped him good with his belt. Afterward, that big strong man, a giant in those days, stood there crying and said to Clarence, "Son, I jus' don't understand. We taught you better than this. We reads you the Bible, takes you to church. I tries to be an honest man and work hard. We ain't poor, not dirt poor anyhow, and you ain't never gone hungry. Why would you steal? Can you just tell me why?"

Clarence still felt the lump in his throat as he heard his daddy's voice as clearly now as then. He especially remembered how when the discipline was done, Daddy put his arms around him and ran his soothing fingers through his hair and tucked him into bed that night, even though he was a teenager.

To disappoint his father, that had to be the worst thing he could imagine. Every boy lives to hear his father say, "Well done," and dies at the thought of his father's disapproval. Clarence had never forgotten his father's broken heart that day. He still thought of it every time he saw a Butterfinger or Baby Ruth bar. He couldn't explain to Daddy that he stole not because he was hungry and poor. It was about proving something, doing something risky alongside the guys he hung with. But in the face of his daddy's pain, no reason was good enough.

Clarence learned later it was that day his daddy determined he was losing his son and had to get him out of there. Obadiah made new sacrifices in a life that had known endless sacrifices. He took an extra job and saved up every dime. He put a strict curfew on Clarence to reel him in. He determined his boy would not get away from him, that he would not get away from God. Only years later did Clarence come to understand and appreciate what his father had done for him. Even as he thought about it, he wiped tears from his eyes.

He got up and went to Daddy's bedroom and knocked.

"Yessuh, Grumpy's home." Clarence opened the door.

"It's me, Daddy. I just wanted to see how you're doin'."

"Ain't mulch on the flowers yet, Son."

They talked about nothing in particular, mostly baseball. They laughed and told stories until Obadiah was too tired to keep his eyes open. Clarence helped him change his Depends, putting on fresh absorbent diapers, as Obadiah had put diapers on him forty-two years earlier. Clarence wrapped his arms around his daddy, and the old man ran his hand through his boy's nappy hair. Clarence tucked him in, said good night, and left the room.

Clarence went back to the living-room recliner to compose himself before joining Geneva in bed. In the darkness he choked back his emotions. Without warning his mind flashed back to that afternoon at Cabrini Green twenty-eight years ago, to something his father had never known, something he could never tell him, something he'd tried to forget but never could.

He remembered that white boy on the bicycle, the one who'd wandered into the projects. He remembered, with frightening clarity, what they had done to him.

CHAPTER

22

"Hear 'bout the dude who blowed his brains out playin' Russian roulette?"

"Nah. Who dat?"

"Young kid, Rollin' 60s tiny. Word is he learned the spin from Gangster Cool."

"GC could spin that cylinder a hunnert times and never take a round. Never seen any dude so cool at doin' the spin."

"That fo' sure."

"The tiny not so lucky, huh?"

"Yeeeah. Guess when you gonna die, you gonna die."

"I don't know if this is the right place to ask this question, Jess," Susan Farley said at the multiculturalism committee meeting. "But I've heard rumors lately that a few stories have been spiked from upstairs. Is that true?"

Jess Foley cleared his throat. "In the ten years I've been managing editor there have been only a few occasions where…the *Trib* management has expressed their concerns to me about…how we pursued a story."

"So…it *has* happened, then?" Susan looked genuinely shocked, as did several other committee members.

"I haven't been ordered to do anything, if that's what you mean."

"But you've been asked not to do something?"

Jess nodded. "But not very often."

"Asked by whom? Raylon Jennings?" Susan asked.

"It's not appropriate to say. It's very rare that there's a request to outright spike. Usually it's not *if* we pursue a story, but how we portray it."

"So…we're being told what slant to take?" Susan asked.

"To a degree, yes, but only in exceptional cases."

"I'm uneasy here, Jess," Susan said. "Can you give an example?"

"I'm not sure I should."

"You can't trust us?" Susan asked. Clarence felt gratified to see someone else on the committee generating the conflict for a change.

"It's not that, it's just…all right, I'll give one example, but don't ask for specifics. One of you knows this already, but some weeks ago I went to a reporter and her editor on behalf of Mr…on behalf of someone upstairs. There was a story, not a big one, with some elements to it that would have brought needless embarrassment to a family and a minority community. We did the story, but stuck to the basic facts."

"Meaning…you left out the embarrassing facts?" Susan asked.

"Yes."

"And how would you distinguish this from censorship?" Susan asked.

"One, it was voluntary—it was a request, not a demand. Two, it had a redeeming purpose."

"So, every time we could protect someone by withholding the truth, why don't we?" Susan asked.

"We've always believed ordinary citizens have a greater right to privacy than public figures," Jess said. "And that the newspaper must be sensitive to minors. And exercise compassion for the grieving and respect for diversity."

"That all sounds great," Susan said. "But we're *always* reporting embarrassing things about people, including minors. We printed the name of the boy who accidentally shot his friend with the rifle, the name of the girl involved with that schoolteacher, the name of the high school football player who sold drugs. And even though it might have bothered her grieving parents, we told the truth about the high school girl who got killed last week, that she'd been drinking. As far as respecting diversity, we report these stories whether they happen to whites or blacks or anybody else. Don't we?"

Jess cleared his throat again. "Okay, look, I wasn't comfortable with it. Neither was the editor or the reporter. But we make editorial decisions all the time. This committee has spiked whole stories, remember? Maybe the brass has a right to make a judgment call once in a while. It's their paper. We wouldn't have jobs without them. Look, if this happened often I'd be out of here. But it doesn't. Okay? Let's just leave it at that."

"So," Susan couldn't resist one last question, "what makes us decide whose privacy we protect and whose we don't?"

Clarence surveyed the room. All eyes looked at Jess. Except Mindy's. The meeting deflated like an untied balloon.

Clarence went back to his desk to pack up his briefcase before meeting Ollie for lunch. The phone rang. He listened to the recording and prepared to tune out the voice. "Clarence? It's Geneva. It's about Ty. Pick up if you're there." She sounded agitated, as if she'd been crying.

Clarence grabbed the phone. "Hey, baby, calm down. What about Ty?"

"There was an…accident last night. They found a body."

"Whose body?"

"Ty's friend Jason. You know, he's been hangin' with him off and on. Looks like he shot himself—maybe an accident, maybe suicide. Can you imagine? Fourteen years old, Clarence. There was that twelve-year-old in Gresham, and the ten-year-old on the west side. Kids killing themselves. What's happening any more?"

"How's Ty?"

"He's taking it real hard. He came home from school. He's in his bedroom. You need to talk to him."

Clarence sighed. "Maybe I'll take him to Jason's funeral. Maybe it'll be another lesson to stay away from the wrong crowd."

"What do the Denver Broncos and a possum have in common?"

"I don't know, Ollie," Clarence said.

"Both play dead at home and get killed on the road."

Clarence grinned despite himself.

"Did you hear the Saints quarterbacks have been asked by the United Nations to move to Iraq?"

"And why's that, Ollie?"

"So they can overthrow Saddam Hussein."

"I'm just going to assume you're done, okay?" Clarence said. "Something's bugging me about the whole gang scene. Crips and Bloods are mortal enemies. But there's a lot of in-fighting among Crips, right?"

"Well, there's something like seven times more Crips than Bloods," Ollie said. "Crips always used to stick up for other Crips, but with so many of them, they began to turn on each other. In the early seventies a Rollin' 60 and a Hoover fought over some girls, somebody got killed, and boom, different Crip sets took different sides and the conflict goes on. Thousands of people have been killed since, Crips killing Crips. More Crips have been killed by Crips than by Bloods."

"How did all this gang stuff get up to Portland anyway?" Clarence asked.

"Goes back to 1986. An L.A. Four Trey Crip got tired of all the fighting and the drug glut and came to Portland because he saw virgin territory for crack cocaine. Other bangers followed, and some mediocre gang members in South Central became overnight ghetto stars in Portland. They took on leadership roles, organized the locals. Next thing you know, kids in Portland are emulating the gang stuff, it was cool to them. The money, girls, and guns came with the drugs."

"So, these gangsters were just opportunists?"

"Entrepreneurs. You can take a pocketful of rock cocaine that might get you a few hundred bucks in L.A. and it'll get you maybe eight hundred in Portland. Or you can get on a Greyhound bus, take the same stuff to Nebraska, and sell it for a few thousand bucks. Anyway, once the gangsters brought in the rock, it was just a matter of time before the killings started happening here. First gang homicide in Portland was 1988. Now, we've got forty-three cops on gangs. Budget's over two and a half million dollars, all to monitor gangs, follow up on gang crimes, patrol gang-dominated neighborhoods."

"I see the gang graffiti when I ride my bike in Gresham," Clarence said, "and I still can't believe it's reached out that far in the suburbs."

"They're everywhere. You've got Angelitos Sur 13 in Hermiston, Crips in Madras, Gresham gangs, Hillsboro gangs, you name it. In 1988 we had less than a thousand gang crimes in Oregon. By 1994 we had over ten thousand. I haven't checked since then, but you get the drift. It's not just a city problem anymore. The gangs are coming to a neighborhood near you. Used to be it was all New York, Illinois, California. My brother lives in Omaha. Now half the homicides in Omaha are gang related. We're talking *Nebraska*."

"That's hard to believe."

"Hey, look at Cabot Cove."

"Cabot Cove?"

"Yeah, Cabot Cove. You got this small town in Maine where for twelve years someone got murdered every week. It's safer to live in a war zone than Cabot Cove. I mean, everybody Jessica Fletcher ever knew is dead. Frankly, I think she was the perp all along. Bein' a homicide detective, you get a little suspicious when the same person's in near proximity to three hundred homicides. Good thing that program went off the air. Cabot Cove was almost out of people."

"Mindy, how are you?" Clarence said, dropping by her desk in the late afternoon.

"I've been better, I guess. What's up?"

"I noticed how uncomfortable you seemed at the committee meeting this morning."

"Oh?" Mindy tensed up.

"When Jess was talking about censoring that story, it seemed to hit a sore spot with you."

"Pretty perceptive of you, Clarence. And here I thought all men were insensitive louts."

Clarence laughed. "Louts maybe, but not always insensitive."

"So…what do you want from me? Probably not to be my therapist."

"If I promise not to tell anybody, would you let me in on the story that was spiked?"

She looked surprised that he'd pieced it together. "I like you Clarence—please don't tell anybody that; I've got a reputation to uphold. But you're a lightning rod. I'm afraid you'd use anything I tell you as a wedge with the committee or the *Trib*."

"Even if I promise I won't?"

"Reporter's honor—is that it?" Mindy laughed sarcastically. "Well, since you're the only one asking, maybe I'll tell you, even if it's against my better judgment."

"Thanks…I think."

"There was a girl in North Portland, an African American, named Leesa Fletcher. Went to Jefferson, graduated in the spring, 4.0 student, was just starting University of Portland, full ride. Great girl, fine family. She'd been chosen for Portland's Black Future Leaders of America, the whole deal."

"Yeah, I remember. She died, right? A heart defect or something?"

"Right. Well, sort of. She *did* have a congenital heart defect. But what caused her heart to stop was a drug overdose. Crack cocaine."

"No kidding? I never heard that."

"*Nobody* heard that. The doctor ordered an autopsy, but the results weren't released. Nobody knew anything until two weeks after the story was cold. I followed up, just to confirm cause of death, didn't expect anything different. That's when I found out from the coroner's office about the crack cocaine. I wrote the story, turned it into Cecil, and next thing I know Jess is talking to us both, telling us to stick with the basic facts—congenital heart defect. 'That's the truth,' he kept saying, and yeah it was, but not the whole truth. Of course, as you no doubt picked up today, Raylon was behind the scenes, twisting Jess's arm."

Clarence shook his head in amazement. "What was Raylon's logic?"

"Well, of course I got it through Jess, but it was, Why unnecessarily hurt the family? Why feed into the racist stereotypes? Here's a girl who's been touted as top notch, outstanding student, the hope of black America, and she's tarnished with drugs. The *Trib* has an obligation to protect the image."

"What was Raylon's interest in this story?"

She shrugged. "That's what bugs me most. If we're going to protect minority images, okay. But let's face it: we've made every minority look bad one time or another, and we've made whites look bad—men, women, everybody. So why single this one out? It makes you wonder, is there something more to it?"

"If you can color a story one way for some supposedly legitimate reason," Clarence said, "what keeps you from having another reason but using the legitimate one as your cover?"

"Exactly, Clarence. For once, we're on the same wavelength."

"It's been more than once, Mindy." He put his hand on her shoulder. "Thanks for telling me. I won't mess you up."

"Thanks. I probably shouldn't, but I feel better talking about it."

"On the one hand I feel so fulfilled, so satisfied," Dani said. "This is Joy—every experience of joy on earth was the stab, the pang, the inconsolable longing for this place. Yet, in a strange way, I feel my desires, my yearnings, my thirst is greater than ever. How can this be?"

"You are experiencing what you were made for," Torel said. "There is thirst because there is water; hunger because there is food. There is spiritual thirst because there is the water that is Elyon, the one for whom you were made. It is a thirst fully satisfied in him, yet which reoccurs in order to draw you back to drink ever more deeply from him."

"Strange, though," Dani said. "I would have thought there would be no thirst here."

"And without the thirst, where would be the pleasure and joy? Without the desire, how could the desire be fulfilled?"

"But...I guess I thought there could be no need in heaven."

"No injustice, no suffering, of course. But no need? Elyon's creatures will always need to know him, to worship him, to serve him. Heaven's joy is not the absence of needs and desires but the continual fulfillment of them."

"Yes, I see that. My desires and thirsts never leave me depressed but fill me with joy and excitement in the anticipation of their next fulfillment. Like thirst that is satisfied but develops again that it may be satisfied again."

"Those who are never thirsty are never refreshed," Torel said. "Those who do not hunger are never filled. That is the beauty of heaven and the horror of hell. For in hell need never dies, but it is never satisfied. Desire never ends, but the ultimate object of every desire is forever absent—Elyon himself."

"What a horrible existence—to have no hope. Desire and need without possibility of satisfaction would be an unquenchable burning, an eternal fire."

"What do *you* long for now, Dani?"

"For the consummation of Elyon's plans on earth. I'm delighted with this place, yet I find myself anticipating, thirsting for the Carpenter's reign on earth. I'm not dissatisfied—how could I be dissatisfied with a place beyond my wildest dreams? Yet I yearn for God to make right all the wrongs, to make earth no longer what it is, but what it should be."

"When you cooked special meals for your family, did you wish them to hunger for them?"

"Yes," Dani said.

"So Elyon desires his children to hunger for righteousness. What else do you long for?"

"I long to serve," Dani said. "I've enjoyed the rest from my labor, but I also yearn to work for the Carpenter in the place he will appoint me to. When I hear Great-Grandmother Ruth talk about her missions and service for Elyon, it makes me eager to serve him. I've been very active here, of course; there is so much to do, I've barely scratched the surface. But I do long to serve him."

"When you are weary, as everyone is when he first comes here from the dark world, rest is very inviting," Torel said. "But rest is only one dimension of heaven. Another is work. For those who long for productivity, there is no greater promise than that of serving God for eternity. Elyon's book says that in heaven his people will always serve him. His Word says you are his workmanship created in order to do good works. Surely you didn't think those works would end when you left earth? You were made for eternity, and his purposes for you extend into eternity. That is why Elyon promises that in keeping with your service for Christ on earth, you will reign with him in heaven. You will have responsibilities delegated by Elyon himself. You will rule over the world and you will rule over angels. Tell me, Dani, what does service involve?"

"Well, responsibilities, duties, effort. Goals, planning, strategy. Service requires the creativity and the resources to do work well. Since Elyon does nothing without design, it must be work with purpose and significance."

"And how does such work relate to rest?"

"Well, it could be refreshing work. Like Adam and Eve did in the garden before sin brought the curse, with its weeds and thorns."

"Yes. Kingdom work with lasting accomplishment, unhindered by decay and fatigue, enhanced by unlimited resources. Heaven's labor is refreshing, productive, and unthwarted, without futility and frustration. The work itself is rest, just as rest is itself productive."

"I have still another longing, Torel. To hug my Celeste and Ty again. And Daddy. And Antsy."

"They long to embrace you as well," Torel said. "And in the right time, both your longing and theirs will be fulfilled."

Dani walked to the portal. Her guardian beside her, she fell on her knees, filled with both longing and satisfaction, overflowing with both contentment and desire.

Clarence and Geneva got in the car to head toward the Irvington area, a few miles south and a little east of their home. Reggie and Esther Norcoast had invited them for dinner. The councilman was also taking up Clarence on his challenge to a game of chess. Clarence had said yes both to satisfy Raylon and to avenge his loss at tennis.

To prepare for his match Clarence had played against Chessmaster 3000 on his computer at the highest setting. His Uncle Elijah had taught him the basics as a child. He in turn had taught friends and faced off with cousins, quickly and instinctively learning the game. Chess had a regal dimension, a Camelot character in which opponents jousted. Good players could approach the game either as brainy contemplatives or as street fighters. Clarence prided himself at being able to do either. He loved chess. It was sheer mind, no body. He enjoyed setting up opponents as though they were tin cans on a fence. Then he'd shoot them down one pawn at a time. In tennis, someone could think Clarence's physical skills had beaten them. But in chess, everything was mental.

Clarence had never been to Norcoast's home, but Geneva had driven by it once after she and Dani had shopped at the Lloyd Center and Dani had wanted to show off her councilman's estate. Clarence drove slowly now, as he and Geneva compared the increasingly stately houses, and remarked what a dramatic change there'd been in the space of a half-dozen blocks. This northeast fringe of Irvington was the far southwest fringe of the councilman's district but was a vastly different world. Property values appeared to have doubled about every other block in the last half mile.

"That's it," Geneva said, pointing to a beautiful white mansion, lushly landscaped. Clarence pulled forward slowly, then came to a stop. He turned off the engine and stared at this corner estate, which occupied two lots on one street and two more on the intersecting street. A beautiful iron fence surrounded the manicured front yard. Clarence and Geneva looked at each other, raising their eyebrows at the same moment, then laughing. They got out of the car and walked up to the entry gate, sixty feet from the front stairs. Clarence jostled the gate, but it was locked. Geneva pointed to a white button above a speaker, surrounded by several decals warning of a Brinks security system. Clarence pressed the button.

They heard a stately female voice say, "Geneva and Clarence! Hello. Welcome!"

The bolt snapped back loudly, prompting Geneva to gasp, then cover her mouth. Clarence laughed and pushed the gate open, beckoning her to enter the grounds. Clarence was tempted to leave the gate open, but its mammoth springs insisted on closing itself. They proceeded down the concrete walkway, lined with flowers. Clarence and Geneva both walked forward cautiously, instinctively looking behind trees for security guards, as if this were a scaled-down governor's mansion.

"He's a shoe-in for mayor next year," Clarence whispered. "I'll give him six years before he's governor."

"You really think it will take that long?" Geneva whispered back.

Esther Norcoast opened the front door and hugged them as though they were long lost kinfolk. "Reggie's in the den. Let me take you there. He thought you'd want to play chess before dinner. Maybe that's okay," she said to Geneva. "If we could get it out of the way, we could all chat after dinner and the menfolk won't have to be thinking about doing battle!"

As they walked into the spacious, richly decorated den, Clarence saw Norcoast quickly replace a book on the shelf. He noted it was a brownish clothbound, third book in on the fourth shelf. He stood too far away to identify the title.

"Hello, Clarence and Geneva. So glad you could come." The councilman's long arms filled the room, his half handshakes, half hugs surrounding first Geneva, then Clarence.

Clarence eyed the hand-carved oak chess set, beautifully displayed on an oak chess table, the squares ornately painted on the polished surface. As the councilman rehearsed the history of his estate, Clarence worked his way over toward the books. He noted the third one in on the fourth row—*Classic Chess Openings*.

"Oh, is that Katie? She's so pretty." Geneva pointed to a professional photograph of Reggie and Esther with an older teenage girl in front of them.

"That's our girl," Esther said. "She's back at Radcliffe, doing great. Adjusting. Just called yesterday. I made sure she's wearing her angel necklace. She needs all the protection she can get. And Mom needs to know she's getting it." She laughed, and Geneva smiled.

After they chatted awhile, Norcoast pointed to the board and asked Clarence, "Want to see how far we can get before dinner?"

"Sure," Clarence said and pulled up a chair on the black side.

"Don't you want to draw for white?" Norcoast asked.

"No. I prefer black. Even if white has the advantage."

"All right."

Clarence loved the order, the precision, the geometrical symmetry of chess. In the real world everything seemed bent. Chess was an ordered world, one that made sense. One where there was no guarantee of winning, but at least you always knew you *could* win. Nothing was rigged against you. The rules never changed on you like they seemed to in life.

There might be white history and black history, white literature and black literature, but there was no white math and black math, no white chess and black chess. This game had a mathematical quality to it. Sure, white always moved first, always got the initial advantage. But black could overcome it, and often did.

Norcoast pretended to consider carefully his move, but Clarence was certain he had made his choice already. Finally, Norcoast's manicured fingers wrapped firmly around the head of his king's pawn, thrusting it forward. Clarence responded instantly, boldly, moving his pawn as if his hand would now slap a time clock, which it often had during speed play in Chicago parks. Norcoast looked surprised at the abrupt move. He studied the board carefully, thoughtfully.

Clarence's strategy was to unnerve Norcoast with his confidence, a tactic his Uncle Elijah had taught him in his drafty Mississippi shanty. He'd used it on the weekend tables in Chicago parks and against his geometry teacher, Mr. Hardin, at Jefferson.

Clarence planned to attack in his street fighter persona, flailing away until his opponent was spent and prone for the kill. Brilliance and blunders abound in such games, and he suspected risk-taking would throw off the steady predictable politician. But as the game moved on, Clarence hesitated to follow his plan with the women watching, fearing an irretrievable blunder that would cause embarrassment. He started moving predictably and for the first twenty minutes, like two wary boxers, they slid into pawing at each other.

After half an hour Clarence became frustrated he'd confined himself to playing Norcoast's game. He determined to become aggressive, to try to seize the center of the board, the chess equivalent of the high ground. They had traded a knight and a bishop, and he considered which of the remaining pieces he would brazenly send to the center. He chose his knight, moving him with more confidence than he felt. Norcoast countered by sending his knight to face him, attempting to subdue and contain his lateral motion. White knight against black knight.

In a series of bold moves, lines that seemed to lead to a win appeared with stunning clarity, only to disappear like apparitions at sunrise. When the smoke cleared, fifty minutes into the game, Clarence was down a pawn. He could see Norcoast relax, and he felt his own nervousness. The pawn was a small advantage, but unless he regained the balance, it could be enough to beat him. He searched the board for any chance at retaliation.

Clarence laid a trap for Norcoast on his kingside. Perhaps he wouldn't notice. No such luck. Norcoast nimbly danced around the snare. By the fiftieth move Clarence could no longer prevent Norcoast's extra pawn from reaching his end of the board and transforming itself into an omnipotent queen. He looked down and considered the humiliating option of prolonging the game. Instead, he toppled his king and surrendered.

"A fine match, Clarence. Some brilliant moves." Norcoast extended his hand.

If mine were brilliant and I lost, guess yours were really brilliant, huh?

"Oh, yes. Both of you were brilliant," Esther Norcoast said.

Geneva cleared her throat and added, "Yes. Very brilliant." Geneva still called knights "horses" and rooks "castles," so her assessment was not particularly reassuring to Clarence.

He'd been intimidated into playing Norcoast's game, adopting a cautious defensive posture that failed to utilize his strengths. He'd lost to Norcoast twice now, both in tennis and in chess. He determined he would not lose to him again.

———————

"What's with this hat?" Clarence asked Ty, as he held out the blue baseball cap. "I saw you wearing it the other day."

"Thought my room was private."

"You thought wrong. Show me I can trust you and I won't have to go in your room. Now what about the hat?" Clarence pointed to the black B with an X drawn over it, followed by the number 187. "What's this supposed to mean?"

"Nothin'."

"It's gang stuff, isn't it?"

"Jus' means nothin'."

"You sure?"

Ty gave a contemptuous one-shoulder shrug, as if giving a full two shoulders would demand more energy than his uncle was worth. Ty grabbed the cap and rushed past him out the door. Clarence turned and started to grab him, but he saw Geneva out of the corner of his eye. He stopped, not trusting himself to lay a hand on the boy.

———————

The next morning Clarence poised himself over his computer, holding chair and whip against words, as a lion tamer against a lion.

> "It takes a village to raise a child." That was a fine old African proverb until liberals commandeered it. It meant extended family, friends, neighbors, and community should support and reinforce parents, who were the actual child-raisers. I experienced this growing up in Mississippi—neighbors and teachers and church folk often hugged us, but they also had Daddy and Mama's delegated authority to swat my bottom when they saw me do wrong, which was more often than I care to remember.
>
> Now liberals have hijacked this proverb and ruined it. They've redefined "village" as big government instead of family, neighbors, church, and community. An example of this village in action is

classroom sex education, which for three decades has brought America's children everything from handfuls of condoms, to phone numbers to call to get an abortion, to gay lifestyle advocates who inform our children many of them are really homosexuals who just don't know it yet.

It takes two parents to raise a child. It takes a village to get out of the way and quit trying to take over Dad and Mom's child-raising authority and responsibility.

It takes a village to raise a child. It takes a village idiot to believe government knows how to raise a child.

———

Clarence entered the Main Street Deli to meet Ollie. He saw him in the corner, sitting alone, munching on an elephant ear.

"Mind if I interrupt," Clarence asked, "or should I leave the two of you alone?"

"No. Join us."

"You would have made a good black man, Ollie."

"Why? Because I'm so athletic and sing so well?"

"No. Because you eat all the stuff you're not supposed to. How's the case going?"

"We seem to be caught in a quagmire of ambiguity." Ollie smiled. "Learned that from the captain. I think it means we don't know what we're doing. Manny and I went over it again, step by step. The key is motive. Motive is everything. Why did they hit your sister? That's been the question all along. Okay, your sister was outspoken against gangs, but no more than a lot of people in North Portland. I mean if they're going to take someone out, why not Reverend Clancy or one of the other pastors or the guys at Teen Challenge or Bridge or Gang Outreach? They've done more to put a dent in the gangs than anyone. Putting a hit on Tyrone because he's a tagger? This was way too big to get a baby homie. So, I tell Manny, no matter what we do, the puzzle pieces still don't come together."

"You expect killing to make sense?"

"Gangs operate by rules, just like we do. They have their own logic, their own way of doing things. This is obviously a gang hit. And yet, no retaliation. There's been no retaliation because the homies don't know who to go on. *Nobody* knows who did it, because nobody knows *why* they did it. Motive. It all comes back to motive."

"Okay," Clarence said. "So what are you thinking?"

"I'm thinking about a case I was on in L.A., back in '84. You remember Kermit Alexander?"

"Played for the Forty-Niners? Sure."

"You remember what happened to his mother?"

"Vaguely. Something bad."

"Yeah. It was South Central L.A. A couple of Crips entered the front door of Mrs. Alexander's house with a .30 caliber M-1 carbine. When they came out a few minutes later, everybody inside was dead, blown to a pulp. The perps ended up at San Quentin on death row."

"You've got a good memory."

"I should. I was the first officer on the scene. Mrs. Alexander had been in the kitchen preparing Sunday morning breakfast before getting the family off to church. Her youngest daughter and two grandsons were killed in their beds." Ollie shuddered. "It wasn't much later I put in for a transfer to Portland, though it didn't come through for two years."

"Why are you telling me this?"

"Because the Alexander case didn't make any sense either. There was no motive for killing this woman and her daughter and grandsons. None. Nobody could figure it out. But I was at the trial when suddenly the truth came out. It was so simple, nobody'd thought of it. The perps had intended to murder the people two doors down. They just got the wrong house number."

Clarence shook his head at the senselessness of it all.

"So I've been thinking about your sister. Same situation. Nothing makes sense, no possible motive. As Sherlock Holmes used to say, once you eliminate the possible, whatever's left, no matter how improbable, is the truth." He looked at Clarence. "Holmes was a great detective too."

"I know who he was, Ollie. I'm wondering what your point is."

"My point is, the killers got the wrong house. They were gunning for someone else."

"Who else?"

"Don't know. But I'm doing background checks on the houses on both sides and across the street. If we can figure out who they were really after, it's the key to solving this thing. If I know the real target, I'll find out who the perps were."

They talked another five minutes, then Clarence said, "I need to ask you more about gangs—for personal reasons."

"Okay. Shoot."

"Gang clothes," Clarence said. "Hats and stuff. I know the schools have dress codes. Can't wear gang threads."

"Right. But the kids just get creative. They write little things inside their baseball caps and on their undershorts which show up when they sag."

Clarence halted, deep in thought. "Ollie, how much time do you have?"

Ollie looked at his watch. "Don't have to be back for another hour."

"Can we run by my house? I need to show you something."

"Okay. Sure. Let me grab something to go."

They drove quietly, Clarence tense the whole way but noticeably tenser as he drove up to Dani's house. Clarence startled Geneva with the unexpected visit. He kissed her, introduced her to Ollie, and led the detective into Ty's bedroom. He opened up his bottom drawer and showed him some plastic tips, some cut glass, a glass drill bit, and some small pieces of sandpaper.

"What's all this stuff, Ollie?"

"Tools of the tagger. Your nephew's a graffiti artist."

"You saying he's doing vandalism? I've never seen any spray paint."

"Probably keeps it hidden in the garage or at a friend's or something."

"Look at this." Clarence flipped through the pages of a notebook filled with sketches.

"It's a piece book," Ollie said.

"A what?"

"Taggers use them to practice their graffiti style or plan murals or record pieces they've done." Ollie pointed at a page in the book. "The R6C means he's tagging for the Rollin' 60s Crips. Looks like here they were planning a bombing run, where they saturate an area with the names of the crew or the gang. And here they did a slash run—see where they cross out the names of rivals? These are Blood sets, and Frog is one of the names they were going to slash. Also serves as a scrapbook. Your nephew's got talent. Too bad he's using it to deface property."

"Well, he's not going to get away with it. You think I should get the police involved?"

"What can the police do? If we don't catch them in the act, it's secondhand, old news. This has to be community enforced. If the neighborhood didn't tolerate it, it wouldn't happen. We've got our hands full with beatings and robberies and murders. Spray painters aren't real high on the priority list. This is something that needs to be handled by parents. Or in your case, guardians. At least this book tells you what to look for. I'd go find it on some walls, then make him buff them. Make him clean them up. And make him apologize to the property owners."

Clarence went over to Ty's dresser and picked up the blue baseball cap. "This is Ty's. I told him he couldn't take it to school. I assume this is gang stuff, but he won't admit it. What does it mean?"

Ollie looked at the crossed out B, followed by the number 187, and whistled. He examined the cap, inside and out.

"B is for Blood."

"But…you said he's been taggin' for Crips, right?"

"Right. That's why the B's crossed out. It's a way of…dissin' Bloods."

"But what's the 187 mean? A street in L.A. or something?"

"Nope. It's a reference to the California penal code."

"Huh?"

"It's the code number of a particular crime."

"What crime?"

"Murder."

Clarence stared in disbelief.

"You see the same thing inside the cap here," Ollie pointed. "This B/K? That's Blood Killer. The P/K here is Piru Killer. This is worse than graffiti, Clarence. It's beyond wannabe. Your nephew's telling everybody he's a Blood killer—that he'll do a 187 on any Blood he can."

CHAPTER

23

Clarence heard Ty rustling around his room. He opened the door.

"Lookin' for your cap? It's history. I tossed it."

Ty shot him an incredulous how-dare-you look. "Ain't got no right."

"I know what it means, Ty, the 187. You're saying you want to kill other kids, just like somebody killed your own mama and sister? What's wrong with you, boy? You're never wearing a cap like that again, you hear me? Never!"

Ty looked at him with disdain.

"And I don't want you wearin' those saggers with your underwear hangin' out."

"Everybody do it."

"You're not everybody. And talk right, would you?"

"Ain't talkin' like dat no more."

"You mean the guys you're hangin' with make fun of you, say you're talking white?"

Ty nodded, surprised his uncle understood.

"I got that all the time too. Well, now the dudes that made fun of me are dead or jailbirds or cluckheads, and I've got an education, a job, and a family."

"GC say you can get an education from the streets."

"Yeah? And you can get a vocabulary from a bathroom wall too, but it won't get you very far. Who's GC?"

Ty shrugged as if it wasn't important.

"I hear you've been taggin', Ty. Don't deny it."

"We killed a few walls. Not too many."

"One is too many."

"You don't get it."

"Then help me. get it."

"I got the rep. They say I fresh. Like my style. I def."

"You're deaf, all right—you're not hearing a word I say. I'm going to take you with me, we're going to find your artwork, and you're going to apologize to everybody whose property you've messed with. And you're going to buff it all off. You understand me?"

Ty looked down, knowing his uncle would follow through with the threat.

"And that's just the beginning. I want you to straighten up—stop getting in fights."

"Ain't gonna be no hook. Not gonna do dat no mo'."

"Speak English, will you?" Clarence said. "What's a hook?"

Ty rolled his eyes, as if his uncle were an ignorant fool. "An easy mark. A coward. The kinda dude dat lets 'em jack yo' lunch money and give you a fat lip and never does nothin' to get some get back."

"Sometimes you've *got* to take it," Clarence said, "because you want a better life than they do. Look where you're headed, Ty. You're on a road. That road will take you somewhere, one step at a time. Unless you get off the road soon, you'll be flyin' colors, wearin' your durag, doin' the pipe, hangin' with cluckheads, maybe slangin' and takin' people down, then where will you be? Doin' big time with Uncle LeRoy, that's where. That's not the life you want."

"Maybe it is the life I want."

"Yeah, and what kind of girl do you want? A base freak? A crack queen?"

"Girls want the guys with gold chains and hot cars and nice clothes. They don't hang with some dude workin' for nothin' at McDonald's. Losers work for minimum wage. You can't make a decent livin' workin' for whitey."

"Minimum wage jobs are a wrung in the ladder you climb up on. You'll never get higher on the ladder unless you're willing to step up from the bottom, one rung at a time."

"There be all kinds of guys on the street wid nice threads and cars and stereos that's never worked for no minimum wage."

"That's because they're making their money off stuff that's illegal—peddling drugs and shoplifting and burglary. Don't you get it? That's no life! Who's filling your mind with this garbage?"

"Ain't gonna be a victim no more. GC say you let yo'self be a victim, and people learn to keep comin' after you."

"Who's GC?" Clarence asked again.

"Somebody. Never mind."

"Look, if anybody hurts you at school, you've got to let the school authorities deal with it, not strike back yourself."

"Authorities?" Ty laughed. "You kiddin' me? This stuff happen ever' day. You don't deal with it, nobody does."

"Okay, you can't make it in this school? I'll get you in a private school or transfer you to some other public school."

"You mean an American school?"

"What?"

"You know, *white*."

"White and American aren't the same thing," Clarence said. "You're an American."

"I'm an Afrikan."

Clarence could tell by the way he said it he was spelling it with a k. He raised his hands in frustration. "This is your country; this is your life. With that kind of attitude you'll never make it to college, never make it in business or anything."

"Ain't got no chance of makin' it anyway."

"*Now* you're sounding like a victim."

"It's true, ain't it?"

"No, it's *not* true. Don't pull this sob story on me. You're not trapped by racism, you're not trapped by poverty, you're not trapped by gangs. You go down it's because you *choose* to go down!"

"You never been one to just take it. Why you tryin' to make me a hook?"

"I'm not. Ty, you've got to stand up for what's right without breaking the law. You can't always get justice, you know."

"Why not?"

"I don't know why not. But sometimes you have to be patient."

"Be patient while they dis you and mess wid you and hit you and shove you and call you names, call you an Oreo, steal yo' money and yo' jacket?"

"Yeah, that's right. You have to choose when to fight back and how. Otherwise it escalates, until you've got people killing each other, like two-bit gangsters, like Crips and Bloods."

"Crips and Bloods ain't the same."

"They're *exactly* the same. They wear a different color, but color doesn't make the man. Character does. And Bloods and Crips don't have any character."

"Crips be righteous."

"Righteous? How come Crips kill more Crips than Bloods do?"

"Whatchu mean? That be a lie."

"No it's not. My friend's a cop and he knows."

"Cops? Man, 5-0 don't know nothin'."

"*You* don't know nothin'. You stay away from gangs or you'll throw away your life. Like Darryl and Robby and what's his name, the kid in the wheelchair they crippled for life. Every time a kid in the hood went down, your mama cried on my shoulder. Don't do this, Ty. Don't break your mama's heart."

"Mama's gone."

"She's somewhere else, that's all."

"Mama don't want me beat up all the time." .

"Of course not, but—"

"Got to be connected," Ty said. "Got to be in a gang or you got no protection."

"There's other ways to be connected. Like the youth group at church."

"Yeah, right." Ty glared at Clarence. "They gonna protect me from the Bloods?" Ty seemed emboldened. He looked at Clarence. "They say you white on the inside, Uncle Antsy. That what you is, huh?"

Clarence watched the back of his right hand slap Ty on the face. The teenager's head hit the wall behind him. "You watch your mouth boy, hear me?" Clarence felt the explosion of rage subside just enough to realize what he'd done. He reached out and put his hands on Ty's shoulders, firmly but tenderly.

"I'm sorry, Ty. I'm really sorry. I didn't mean to hit you. I know you don't want to get pushed around. But violence isn't the answer." Clarence sighed and out of desperation took a page from his father's book. "Maybe justice won't come now, but it will eventually. You have to have that faith."

The young man's eyes filled with anger. He stalked out the front door, turning around just long enough to fire a last round. "Yeah, right—my mama had that faith. And where's she now?"

Dani looked at the Carpenter, Torel, Zeke, Nancy, Ruth, and Felicia. She couldn't imagine a better group to make this journey with. They'd traveled to the far reaches of the universe, galaxies away. In the process they saw countless wonders that moved her heart to worship. Each planet, each star, each nebula unveiled some new aspect of the multifaceted greatness of Elyon.

Dani particularly reveled in Felicia's childlike expressions of wonder. "I'm writing a song for Jesus," Felicia whispered to her, as if she didn't want to spoil the surprise by letting the omniscient one in on the secret. "I'm making a painting for him," Dani whispered back, feeling every bit as delighted as Felicia.

Eventually they arrived on a world more beautiful than Dani could fathom— cascading waterfalls, rainbows of a hundred colors, mountain peaks five times higher than any on earth. Oceans with blue-green water, and waves crashing upon rocks the size of mountains. Grassy meadows, fields of multicolored flowers—colors she had never seen before. This place seemed somehow familiar to her, yet how could it, since it was like nothing she'd ever seen? Still, she felt profoundly at home.

"Why hasn't anyone told me of this place until now? I'd think it would be the talk of heaven!"

The Carpenter smiled at her. "They did not tell you because they do not know of it. They've never been here."

"What do you mean?"

"You are the first to visit this place."

"No," she said, then her face flushed. "How could that be?"

"This is your place. As your father once built you that tree house, I fashioned this place just for you."

Nancy beamed. "He gave us our own worlds too," she said. "Beautiful as this is, mine seems the perfect one for me. The Master tells me each world he gives is tailor-made to the receiver."

"This is all for me?"

"Yes," the Carpenter said. "Do you like it?"

"Oh, I love it. And I haven't even begun to explore it! Thank you. Oh, thank you." She hugged him tight.

"This is not the ultimate place I have prepared for you, my daughter. But it is a pleasant beginning, is it not?" He seemed to take delight in her delight. "I brought some of your family and your guardian with you, so they could enjoy it too. Pleasure is deepest when shared with those you love."

"I'm so glad to have them here with me. But I thought we'd no longer have family in heaven."

"No family?" The Carpenter laughed. "Family is what heaven is about. Earthly fathers were an imperfect shadow of Father Elyon. Earthly brothers were an imperfect shadow of brother Christ. The richest family relationships on earth offered just a taste of what is here. Relationships extend beyond blood family, of course. There is no marriage as you knew it, for all of you are one bride. My bride."

"But there are still such special relationships with family and friends from earth."

"Of course. You would expect this if you understood your life on earth was not disconnected to life here but the prelude to it. Those who loved each other and stood by each other in the old world developed a special bond. Heaven is not the end of earth's camaraderie but the extension of it."

"I often felt as though I'd just scratched the surface with some of my friendships on earth," Dani said. "I wanted to develop them, but there never seemed enough time."

"There are many new friendships of course, but relationships there continue here. Grandparents whose grandchildren grew up on mission fields and wished they could spend more time with them, have that time now. The bad things of that world are gone from here. The good things are made better here. Family is not eliminated, it is expanded. Marriage is not destroyed, it is fulfilled. Look at Zeke and Nancy," he said with a smile.

Dani gazed at the two of them, their love for each other so evident. "I am in awe of this place, Master," Dani said, eager to see what lay beyond the mountains and beneath the surface and within the waters. "Are there other places like it?"

"This place is as much unique in my creation as you are unique. I never paint the same picture twice. There are colors here that exist nowhere else."

"Colors unique to this world? I knew I hadn't seen them before. But you're saying these are colors you've only used once? That seems incredible."

"Do you think it is hard for me to do such a thing?"

"No. I mean…of course you wouldn't be limited to the colors of earth, or even to the new colors I've already seen in heaven. There's just so many, it seems like you'd run out."

The Carpenter laughed, touching the back of his scarred hand to her delighted face. "I can no more run out of colors than I can run out of worlds or people. I can simply make more, new ones as unique and beautiful as any I've made before. I am an artist, Dani. Your artistry was a gift from me."

Dani looked around, soaking in the incredible wonder of it. It grew darker, the sun setting with a brilliant cold blue. She looked at two of the three moons, one eclipsing another, sending a hue the color of…of what? There was no name for this color.

"Call it what you wish, my child," the Carpenter said. "It is yours to name."

Dani gazed at the face of her great-grandmother and saw the beautiful brownish shade with just a hint of red that suggested this particular hue. "I'll call it Nancy's color." Nancy beamed with delight.

"You are eager to explore your world, little one," the Carpenter said. "Go. Enjoy discovering its riches with your loved ones."

Her eyes sparkled with delight. She remembered her brother's words in the Shadowlands: "My dream is the same as it's always been. A house in the country. Beautiful fields and flowers and horses and dogs, and peace and safety for my children. And if you'd come join us, for you too, Dani. That's not such a bad dream, is it, Sis?"

Not a bad dream, Antsy. Just a short-sighted one.

Now *this* was a place worth dreaming of. It looked faintly familiar precisely because she *had* dreamed of it. This was the place for which she had been made. Her eyes said thank you again to the Carpenter as she felt the excited hands of family tugging her to come explore Dani's world.

Clarence ransacked Ty's room. He discovered a purplish blowpipe with a few seeds of unsmoked marijuana still in it. Under the mattress he found a little packet of white rock. He stared at it, his eyes burning, as if it were a living evil thing.

Clarence had seen almost daily the drug dealer who set up shop in his cherry red El Camino just four blocks away over on MLK, a block south of Jackson.

Georgie—that was his name. Georgie was decked out in flashy jewelry, the gold rope around his neck, the beeper on his belt, the stylish clothes. He figured Ty must have gotten the dope from Georgie.

Clarence went out on the street and found Ty hanging with some buddies. He grabbed him by the arm and dragged him into the house, under protest. Clarence showed Ty the blowpipe and the bag of rock, silencing his complaints.

"You and I are going to take a walk down the street, boy. And I'm going to tell that pusher he isn't putting drugs in your hands ever again. And you're going to tell him too. Got me?"

"No, Uncle Antsy. Please. I can't." Ty still had vivid memories of the humiliation of being forced to buff his tags off the walls.

"You can, and you will." Clarence turned to walk. When Ty didn't follow he grabbed him by the earlobe, as Obadiah had done to him to take him down to the schoolhouse when he'd put that mouse inside little Heather Brine's desk.

"Ow! That hurts," Ty said.

"So call the 800 number. You don't want to get hurt? Then walk—you got the legs for it. You fall behind, and I'll drag you by your big toe if I have to. Now get movin', boy!"

They marched toward MLK to the parking lot of a run-down motel known for its porno videos and prostitution. There sat the red El Camino, with several cool dudes hanging around it. Georgie, the head dealer, serviced six different neighborhoods. Most kids could get crack in their own hood, but Georgie was a high volume distributor, like a big car dealer who can sell for less. Georgie was one of Gangster Cool's best wholesale customers.

Georgie had converted hundreds of kids into users and dozens of the more promising ones into dealers. Clarence had been outraged to learn that as prominent as Georgie was, he'd never spent more than a couple months in jail.

Clarence eyeballed the man, the high roller himself, standing there plain as day in the same Ralph Laurens and Georgio Armanis, the gold jewelry dangling like oversized fishing tackle. Near Georgie stood three Rollin' 60s bodyguards. They also served as fall guys who kept the drugs on themselves so the big fish wouldn't get fingered if an undercover cop pulled a sting. These dudes were cool, their eyes giving the thousand-yard stare, telegraphing, "Don't mess wid me."

As Clarence and Ty approached the car, a teenage girl walked away. She looked as if she'd once been pretty. She had a short skirt and worn-out eyes. Only three weeks earlier she'd given birth to a seven-pound, eight-ounce drug addict.

Clarence grasped Ty by his wrist to assure he wouldn't bail. He marched toward the El Camino. When he was fifteen feet away, he began shouting at Georgie.

"You been selling to this boy, scum. I'm here to tell you you'll *never* do that again."

The three bodyguards weren't sure what to do. One reached in the weighted down brown paper bag he was carrying. Georgie held up his hand and shook his head at the soldier with the bag. He'd lasted this long because he was smart enough not to do his shootings in plain sight. If there was someone to be shot, it would be done in the dark.

"Easy, old head." Georgie looked at Clarence's front pockets while one of his guards checked around back. No bulges. The old head wasn't packin' a piece.

"Now, what be yo' problem?" Georgie asked. "You trippin', man?"

"It's simple," Clarence said. "This is my nephew, and you're not going to sell him drugs ever again."

"And what do the boy himself say?" Georgie looked at Ty, who shuffled his feet and peered into the sidewalk cracks, saying nothing. "Tyrone, isn't it? GC's little road dog. Whatcha say, Ty-man? You wanna keep buyin'? Or you wanna be a model citizen, a drug-free poster boy?" His friends snickered. "Whatchu gonna do when you go through the jonesing? Maybe take up Lipton tea?"

Clarence grabbed the thick gold chain around Georgie's neck and yanked it violently. When Georgie's head lurched forward, Clarence's head was there to meet it. Georgie's knees buckled under the crushing head butt. His glazed eyes now stared at Clarence's belt buckle.

Clarence yanked him to his feet by the chain and peered down into his eyes. One man's eyes were full of rage; the other's, fear. Clarence glanced to his right and left and told the three soldiers, "You take one more step toward me or the boy, and I'll break your main man's little bird neck. Open your hand and take it outta that bag now," he said to one of the henchmen, "or you're gonna hear his neck snap before you pull the trigger."

Georgie's homeboys saw the fear in Georgie's eyes. If this wasn't enough to convince them, one look around them was. The sidewalk had crowded up. Already there were a dozen eyewitnesses, some of them old heads. They could probably trust the young ones not to break the hood's honor code and talk to the police, but these older folks, the ones who hated gangs and drugs, they couldn't be trusted. The boys could shoot this dude hassling Georgie, but with all these witnesses, they'd be doin' hard time for sure.

"You're kid killers," Clarence said to Georgie, keeping alert to the three others. "There's nothin' worse. Well, we lose Ty and you're gone, man. You're history, you hear me? He turns into a cluckhead, and I'm coming after you. This is personal, Georgie, you hear me? I come for you, and you're gonna wish you were never born. You understand what I'm saying, punk?"

Georgie nodded his head slightly. Clarence pulled tighter on the gold chain. "I said, you understand me?"

"Yeah." His raspy voice was barely audible.

"And you tell all your dealer buddies the same. Anybody gets this boy drugs and I'll get you first, then them. You got it?"

"Yeah. Got it."

Clarence looked at Ty and said, "Now you tell these punks you're not a druggie. Tell them you don't want drugs ever again. Say it!"

Ty stared wildly. "Uh…I's not a druggie. Don't want no more crack." Hard as it was, it was easier for him to say it to the weak-kneed, bleeding, overpowered Georgie than the strutting, on-top-of-the-world Georgie he'd always seen before.

"You heard him, didn't you?" Clarence said. Georgie's glazed eyes stared forward. "Didn't you?" The gold chain was now a noose.

"Yeah," Georgie managed to sputter.

Clarence released the chain, and Georgie dropped back to his knees. He swayed and fell sideways, head bouncing on the pavement. Clarence grabbed the gray beeper off Georgie's belt. He dropped it on the ground and stomped on it as if it were a mechanical insect.

The homies gave Clarence dirty looks, then crouched down to help their main man regain his dignity.

Clarence grabbed Ty's hand and turned to leave the parking lot. He was surprised to bump into the crowd of bystanders who now numbered over two dozen. The teenagers, some of them gangsters, stared at him, not sure what to think. The older folk looked at him with respect, wishing they had the courage or the power—or maybe the temporary insanity—to do what Clarence had just done.

The kids under twelve looked at him wide eyed. It was the first time they'd seen Georgie get his comeuppance. Even when he was arrested, they'd watched him bad-mouth the cops, calling one of the black cops nigger. These children, especially the little boys, had come to believe the dealer was above consequences, that with his nice clothes and nice car and the jewelry and girls hanging off him, his was a life to be envied and emulated, a man who demanded respect. But not here. Not now.

Staggering to his feet, a humiliated Georgie swore and with a hoarse voice whispered, "Dat dude needs to chill." Suddenly he turned and vomited on the ground. His friends backed away in disgust.

Gangsters and wannabes and children pointed at Clarence and whispered, "That's Ty Abernathy's uncle. He one crazy dude." They'd watch out around this guy. He didn't understand how the hood worked. After dissin' Georgie like that, no way this dude was gonna live very long.

24

Clarence and Geneva walked through the hood an hour before sunset, chatting with Frank and several other neighbors, swapping stories, laughing, and exchanging good news and bad. In these six weeks on Dani's street, Clarence had already had as many conversations with some neighbors as in ten years out in the suburbs.

"Some nice people in this hood," Clarence said.

"Real nice," Geneva said, smiling. "I love to take walks with you. No problems, no issues, just a pleasant evening's walk."

Out on MLK they stopped to read a window-posted menu at a soul restaurant.

"There be a babe," a voice called out from across the street. Standing with another young male, he looked like a dealer or a pimp.

"I'll give you my beeper number, sweet sister," the second man yelled to Geneva. "Call me day or night. Lady, you'd give eyesight to the blind."

Clarence checked traffic, then charged across the street. As the two men ran off, one tripped momentarily over his unlaced sneakers. Clarence yelled, "Yeah, and I can qualify you for the Vienna Boys Choir faster than you can call for Mama." He stopped chasing them and shouted, "She ever gets touched by anybody and I'm comin' for *you*, hear me, boys? I'll know where to find you!" He re-crossed the street, walked back to Geneva, and took her arm in his. He said nothing, waiting for his pulse rate to drop.

"Yep," Geneva said to Clarence, with a sigh. "Mama always said, there's nothin' quite so nice as a pleasant evening's walk."

"Wanna see yo' crib," GC said to Ty. The boy felt privileged an OG wanted to spend time with him. He didn't realize that like any gang general, GC wanted to check out all possibilities for hiding dope and arms. Every new recruit meant more resources, more possibilities, more dominion.

Ty and GC came over in mid-afternoon, Ty thinking his uncle would be at work. But Clarence had arrived home early. He watched them coming up the front walkway. GC's swagger was smooth, well-established. It fit him like old jeans. Ty's swagger, in contrast, seemed forced and self-conscious. Clarence eyed GC's glistening jheri curls, early Michael Jackson.

"Hey, Ty," Clarence said as he opened the front door, trying to be friendly but startling his nephew. "What are you doin?"

Ty shrugged his shoulders. "Jus' hangin'."

"Who you hangin' with?" Clarence and Ty both looked at GC.

"We road dogs," GC said smoothly.

"Road dogs?"

"Best friends," GC said.

"Does my nephew's best friend have a name?"

"Name's GC," Ty said.

"Hi, GC. Good to meet you." Clarence extended his hand. GC passed his fingers lightly over Clarence's. "What's GC stand for?" Clarence asked him.

"Gangster Cool," GC said, eyes not flinching.

"How'd you get that moniker? Choose it? Or earn it?"

"Earned it."

"Well, if you're going to hang with my nephew you better change your name. Gangsters aren't welcome here."

While Ty's face contorted, GC just smiled, looking cool, as always.

"The gang's got nothing but death for you," Clarence said. "Today you're GC, tomorrow you're GD."

"Say what?"

"Gangster Dead."

GC glared at Clarence, testing him with the thousand-yard stare at a one-yard distance. He looked like a lion eyeing a zebra and trying to decide whether he's hungry enough to bother. Clarence stared back, gaze boring hard into GC's. The dynamic began to shift. For a moment, GC felt more like the zebra in the gaze of the lion.

"Never mind, Li'l GC," the gangster said to Ty. "Let's go."

Clarence put his hand on his nephew's shoulder, but Ty shrugged it off. Clarence wanted to hold him back. He wasn't sure what this gangster had mumbled to Ty, but it sounded like he'd called him "Li'l GC." Clarence's heart sank as he watched the two walk down the sidewalk.

"Whassup, cuz?" GC called to two teen boys coming their way.

"Hey, cuzzins." The two boys raised their fists high and signaled back something to GC and Ty. GC threw up a salute to his head with the cupped right hand that showed the Crip "C" and a clever turn of the left hand fingers that represented a six for 60s. Ty followed suit, flashing a more awkward Rollin' 60s sign.

If he'd had any doubts remaining, as he looked at the boys now, Clarence knew with certainty he wasn't watching three gangsters, but four.

On Wednesday afternoon Clarence finished his Thursday column, packed up his briefcase, and left the *Trib* at one. He'd been there since five-thirty, and his bones ached for the country. He dropped by the house in North Portland, changed to his sweats, affixed his bike rack to the car, strapped on his mountain bike, and jumped in the Bonneville's driver's seat with spring in his step. He drove out toward Gresham. When he'd lived in the suburbs, he'd ridden the Springwater Corridor Trail three or four times a week. Now because of the driving time, that was down to just once a week, Wednesday afternoons. But it was a ritual he looked forward to, rain or shine. These days, it was one of the few oases in the desert of his life.

———————

Thursday evening the violins, trombones, trumpets, french horns, drums, and cymbals permeated the living room at high volume. The two men sat next to each other, soaking in the music. In front of them were the rich blues, the deep reds, the black backdrop, and the white pinpoints of a distant part of the galaxy where their minds traveled, though their bodies sat in Jake's apartment. It was the introduction to television's *Deep Space Nine*. For the next hour they bantered through commercials and watched the show attentively right to the credits.

"*DS Nine's* getting better," Clarence said. "It's nearly as good as *Voyager* now, maybe *Next Generation*."

"It's not that good," Jake said.

"Well, Sisko's the best captain."

"Better than Kirk, sure. Better than Janeway? I don't know. I really like her. But nobody's better than Picard."

"Picard? He's a cold fish. Sisko's my main man."

"He kind of reminds me of you," Jake said.

"Because he's black and studly?"

"No. Because he's cute and lovable."

"Cute and *what?*" Clarence said. "Hey, Jake, you remember when Captain Kirk kissed Lieutenant Uhura in the original *Star Trek*? Did you know that was the first interracial kiss ever on television?"

"No, I didn't."

"Yeah," Clarence smiled wistfully. "It was less than thirty years ago, and we were still watching it on our black-and-white TV, Harley and Ellis and I. Mama saw that white man and black woman kissing and got right up and turned off the TV. She said, 'I don't want you boys gettin' no ideas.' She said, 'Don't you forget Emmit Till,' then she pulled out that old picture."

"Who's Emmit Till? What picture?"

Clarence looked surprised Jake didn't know. "A fourteen-year-old boy. He was visiting family in Mississippi. They say he made a friendly comment to some white woman in a store. They found him three days later in the Tallahatchie River, wired by his neck to a big old metal fan. He had a bullet in his skull, eye gouged out, head crushed. His mother insisted on an open casket so the whole world could see. *Jet* magazine printed a picture of his corpse. Mama cut it out. Even though we were just babies when it happened, a couple times a year she'd pull it out of a drawer and show it to us boys—to scare us into staying away from white girls."

"Who killed him?"

"The woman's husband and his brother, as I recall. There was an eyewitness who identified the two of them as dragging Emmit into their truck and driving off. The all-white jury deliberated one hour and found them not guilty."

"No kidding? I didn't remember that." Jake felt tentative, wondering whether to step into it or not. "Can I ask you something, Clarence? You obviously think a lot about…racial issues. That's fine, and you've helped me understand a lot of things. But sometimes I sense you're…angry. I can see it in your eyes."

"Harley says any black man who isn't angry is either stupid or dead," Clarence said. "Not that I agree with Harley. I usually don't." Jake noticed Clarence running his finger underneath his right ear.

"I guess I usually assume the anger is racial," Jake said, "but I'm not sure. Sometimes you're hard to read. I really do want to understand you better. We're friends. We're brothers. Talk to me. I want to know what's going on inside you."

Clarence sighed and sat silent for thirty seconds. "Where do I begin? Which of a thousand stories do I tell? How about this one? Once down in Mississippi I was with my cousin Rod and my aunt Charlene. A teenage white boy walks by and glares at us with these dagger eyes and growls under his breath, 'Niggers.' Aunt Charlene turns around and looks at him and a light goes on. She says, 'That's Jarod Smith. I used to take care of him. I raised him. I wiped that boy's nose and his bottom, and I dried his tears. All so he could grow up and call me and mine nigger?' She was mad as a wet wasp," Clarence laughed. "Can you blame her?"

"No," Jake said. "I can't."

"Or how about last night? Geneva and I rented *The Color Purple*. Hadn't seen it since it was in the theaters, years ago. Everybody loved *The Color Purple*. The book got a Pulitzer; the movie got Oscars. Well, can you look through that book or watch that movie and show me *one* black man who had any redeeming qualities, unless it was the fact that he eventually died? The worse the men, the more holy the women who had to suffer them. Used to be that the worst villains in movies were aliens, but now half the aliens are good. The only bad guys left are Nazis and black men, and maybe an occasional Hispanic or Arab."

"But wasn't *The Color Purple* written by a black woman?"

"So? You think it feels better for black men to be humiliated by black women than white men?"

"I've done a lot of thinking about the talk we had at the deli," Jake said, "about people being conscious of their skin color. Looking back, I grew up almost never giving a thought to it."

"We *had* to think about it," Clarence said. "With segregation, busing, voting, separate drinking fountains and restrooms and schools and what have you, we didn't have the luxury of not thinking about it. I first went to integrated school in fourth grade. When I sat down, the chairs around me emptied like I was a pipe bomb. I was the brunt of jokes, was spit on, called names. Even the kids who weren't cruel were always whispering about me. Most of the teachers weren't really hostile, but they tolerated the meanness and that just encouraged it. The color of our skin chased us everywhere. You could never outrun it. We had no choice but to take it personally. It shaped us. It had to. Maybe that's what you see in my eyes."

"Since you were a kid, how often have you really thought about the color of your skin?" Jake asked.

"Honestly?"

"Yeah. Of course."

"Don't say, 'Of course.' White folks think they want blacks to be honest with them, but usually it turns out they don't. How often have I thought about the color of my skin? Try every waking hour of every day of my life."

"Are you serious?"

"Dead serious. Did you ever look through those black magazines I gave you?"

"Yeah, I did. It was really amazing. Every picture was of blacks—every subject of a feature, every writer, every advertisement had people with black skin. I don't know if I saw a single white, except a few in *Urban Family*."

"Now imagine," Clarence said, "if when you grew up *every* magazine was like that, every television commercial and every billboard showed only people of another skin color, not yours. How do you think it would have made you feel?"

"Marginalized, I suppose. Out of it. Like maybe something was wrong with being white."

"Exactly," Clarence said. "That's just how it was when I grew up. I'd look through all those magazines and the Sears and Monkey Wards catalogues and wonder what was wrong with being black. Now if I was white, I wouldn't think about it either. When you're in the driver's seat, you don't think about conditions in the backseat. When you're born into a privileged class you just take it for granted. The people who think about it are the ones who *weren't* born privileged. It's a birthright thing. Kids who have plenty of food don't think about the fact they have food. But when you're hungry, it's always on your mind."

"I guess I don't think of myself as being privileged," Jake said. "I mean, I've worked hard for what I've got."

"I'm not saying you didn't. And I'm not blaming you for anything, Jake. It could just as easily have been me born white and you born with my good looks. But that's not how it happened. Didn't you tell me once your grandfather ran a hotel?"

"Yeah, in Colorado. His father built it. He worked with him from the time he was a boy. They did the building and maintenance and my great-grandmother did all the cooking and cleaning, then passed that on to my grandmother. Nothing came easy for them."

"I'm sure it didn't. But you're telling me your great-grandparents established their business back in the 1800s and they passed skills and resources and economic experience and training from their generation down to yours. Right?"

"Right."

"So you're the beneficiary of generations of hard work and education and opportunity and freedom. But see, while your great-grandparents were doing all that, my great-grandparents were forced to till the Mississippi soil and pick cotton until they couldn't straighten their backs. And *none* of it benefited their children or grandchildren. It all benefited the next generation of *white* children."

Jake sat there, not sure how to respond.

"So you see," Clarence continued, "*your* ancestors worked to pass on advantages to you, and *my* ancestors worked to pass on advantages to you. I'm not trying to lay á guilt trip on you. But you have to realize that's the way it was."

"But my ancestors weren't slave owners," Jake said.

"Are you sure?"

"Well, I'm pretty sure, at least going back to my great-grandparents."

"But it's not that easy. See, the whole country, south *and* north, benefited economically from the work of the slaves and the sharecroppers. Your ancestors worked hard. Mine worked even harder, but with one big difference. Yours worked hard as free people, choosing the kind of work they'd do. They experienced the rewards of their work. That's capitalism at its best. But mine worked hard at the bloody end of a whip, and they didn't receive the rewards of their work. Their white masters did, the white plantation owners did, and during sharecropping the white landowners did. With the dirt pay during Jim Crow days, the whole white community benefited at the expense of black folk, who just scraped by. Didn't you tell me your daddy went to Harvard?"

"Yeah, he did."

"I'm sure he worked hard to get there. But my daddy dropped out of school in third grade to work fourteen-hour days on land owned by white folks, to help feed his family. Your daddy was born with an opportunity my daddy wasn't. Your daddy's opportunity and your ancestors' opportunity came, at least partially, at the expense of blacks."

"I've never thought of myself as privileged—certainly not at somebody else's expense."

"Privilege is like being born tall in a world that revolves around basketball," Clarence said. "If you're a seven footer, basketball's going to come easier than if you're five foot six. Now a seven footer can say, 'I had to work hard to become a great basketball player.' Yeah he's right, but he'd be a fool not to realize he was born with advantages that helped his dream come true. There's no substitute for hard work. But your daddy's hard work and my daddy's hard work didn't bring them equal advantages, not financially or educationally. Now character, that's something else."

"Your father didn't come up short on character, that's for sure, Clabern. I'm sorry to say mine did."

"To compensate for his disadvantages, my daddy had to do extraordinary things to make it possible for Harley and me to go to college. In a lot of white families every kid has the opportunity to go to college, but in black families just one got that opportunity, if any. In my family it was two, Harley and me. There wasn't enough money for the rest. Your father had the benefit of working in a family-owned business. Not that long ago black folk couldn't own any property or businesses. We're in the race now, all right, but you have a several-hundred-year head start. Black folk were helping your ancestors get that head start while white folk were keeping my ancestors out of the race."

"Maybe I've gotten used to privilege and it feels like I earned it all," Jake said.

"Well, if some white folk are too slow to see their advantages, some black folk are too quick to see their disadvantages. I'm the first one to admit that, Jake. See, my daddy never let his disadvantages rob him of hope or keep him from working hard and building the best life he could. I hear some black folk whining all the time, when the truth is they've got all these advantages Daddy never dreamed of. The whining makes me sick. But when I hear some white people born with the silver spoon in their mouths talk about how everybody just needs to pull themselves up by their bootstraps, well that makes me sick too. Truth is, black people have had freedom such a short time, we haven't gotten real experienced at using it. Then there was the whole welfare thing and all those freethinking white university professors in the sixties that pushed this me-first family-destroying lifestyle that cut us off at the knees. I don't even want to talk about that, it makes me so angry. I've never been happy with liberals *or* conservatives on racial issues. Anyway, next time you think maybe I'm angry, there's a good chance you're right."

Jake nodded. He seemed unsure what to ask next, but Clarence didn't need more prompting.

"Tom Skinner used the example of a baseball game. The game starts, and one team—lets call them the White Sox—takes the lead. Next thing you know they're up 10-0. The other team, Black Sox, has been trying to get their attention that something's wrong. Well, come the seventh inning the White Sox finally notice the Black Sox have been playing the whole game with one hand tied behind their back. So, they say, 'Okay, we'll untie your hand. Batter up.' Well, by now the score is 20-0, and we're in the bottom of the seventh inning. The White Sox have mastered the skills necessary to play the game. The Black Sox are now able to play with both hands, true enough, but they're used to playing with one and they don't have the experience yet and their one arm is really sore, some of their shoulders are dislocated, and they've still got the rope burns. Given all that, and the score being 20-0, who do you think is going to win the game?"

"Yeah," Jake said. "I hear you."

"And by this time, some of the Black Sox are going to give up trying because who can overcome that lopsided score? They've gotten so used to being disadvantaged that even when they're untied they don't think there's any hope of catching up. Some of the black team adjust and excel, yes, but some just feel despair and anger, and some just give up and sit on the bench or throw rocks at the privileged team or fight with each other in the dugout."

"I see what you're saying. But am I wrong in thinking the score's not 20-0 anymore?"

"Harley's always telling me how things are so bad, worse than they've ever been. He'll give me a statistic about many more whites per capita graduating from college than blacks. Then I'll say, yes, but the percentage of blacks graduating from college is six times higher than it was thirty years ago. He'll point out all the blacks living in poverty. It's true, but the black middle class is much bigger than it's ever been—ten million people. Blacks work at blue-collar jobs for the same hours, wages, and benefits as whites. Black doctors, attorneys, professors, journalists—you name it—all at institutions that used to not allow blacks in the door. Colleges that didn't used to permit black students now actively recruit them. African Americans are in thousands of local and appointed offices around the country. They're mayors of some of the nation's largest cities. They're governors, senators, congressmen. They chair major congressional committees. Colin Powell was appointed head of the most powerful military machine in the history of the planet. A lot of the most popular and highest-paid television performers and athletes are black."

"What does Harley say to all that?"

"Harley will only talk about oppression of minorities. I tell him that in every country in history where people have been oppressed, they've flooded the borders attempting to leave. In America, almost no minorities are trying to leave, whereas a tidal wave of minorities are desperately trying to enter. Are they coming here to get oppressed? Of course not. They know America's the land of opportunity for minorities. But to Harley, and to a lot of black folk, it will always be a land of injustice. Blacks will always be helpless victims, and whites will always be malicious oppressors."

"Racial problems really aren't getting better, are they?" Jake said, voice weighed down in defeat.

"For some people, they are," Clarence said. "For others, it's pretty much the same as always. And for a lot of folks, it's just getting worse."

"I'm embarrassed to say I never used to understand all this talk about racism. But lately the lights have started to turn on. Race is a burden for you it's never been for me."

"*Burden* is a good word. More than anything else, I just get tired of it all. I'd like to put on white skin for a few weeks, not because I want to be white—I *don't*—but just so I could take a break, have a vacation. Just get the hay bales off my back awhile, that's all. So I wouldn't have to face the issue again and again every time I walk by someone at the supermarket or see a police officer looking at me or drive up next to someone at a stoplight. Some days I'm just so worn out by it all. I can leave my brief-case at home, but I can't leave my skin at home. Being black is a full-time job. Every class I was ever in, every white church I ever went to, I was expected to be the black voice, as if all blacks think alike. Somebody's doing a story and they need to talk to a black man, they call me. You know Jake, if you ever get dog-tired at the *Trib*, you can put your head down on your desk and snooze a few minutes. I've seen you do it. I can't do that."

"Why not?"

"Because when you do it, you're just a man taking a snooze, probably because you stayed up late working hard. If I did it, I'd be a black man—lazy, indolent, prob-ably up late partying or taking drugs. Cheating my employer by stealing his time. Proving black men are as bad as everyone thinks."

"Come on, Clabern, you're overreacting. Nobody would think that."

"Maybe not everybody. But some would. That's just a fact, Jake, whether or not you believe it. Dr. King used to tell the story of a man walking past ten drunk men, nine of them white, the other black. The man shook his head and said, 'Just look at that black drunk, now would you?'"

"I don't know what to say, man. I…really feel bad."

"Look, Jake, I don't want to make you feel bad, and above all I don't want your pity. Truth is, I went through a phase in the seventies, a phase my brother Harley's still in. I took delight in manipulating remorseful whites into flagellating themselves with guilt. I'd either make them admit their racism—in which case they were guilty—or deny their racism, in which case they were even more guilty."

"Like it was impossible for a white to be innocent?"

"Exactly. I, on the other hand, was part of the oppressed race, and that brought an innocence with it. Racism could go only one way. Whites could never be inno-cent; blacks could never be guilty. The whole thing was just self-indulgence. I was capitalizing on my ancestors' suffering. I came to realize they didn't give up, they labored hard to pass the baton to my generation, and now that we finally have a level playing field, we finally have a great chance to make it, a lot of us were sitting around smoking dope and whining about injustice and engaging in self-pity and excuses while we let opportunities slip away. I decided no more of this for me. I wasn't going to play the race game anymore. For several years I wouldn't even talk about race."

"Why not?"

"Because discussions about race always took place either in shouts or whispers.

I hated both. Especially the whispers. All the walking on eggshells. All the dishonesty where people's main goal is to not sound racist rather than to communicate what's really on their mind. I hated it, that's all. And as a middle-class black professional, I hated not being accepted by whites *or* blacks."

"What do you mean?"

"It's darned if you do, darned if you don't. I hear the pleas to 'give back' to my community. By living in the suburbs I've supposedly lost touch with my people and my cultural roots. Right. Like all blacks are supposed to live in constant danger in drug-infested, crime-infested neighborhoods, and both whites and blacks resent it when they don't. Any white person who lives in poverty and a crime area, when he earns enough money, what does he do?"

"Usually, he moves out," Jake said.

"Obviously, and that's perfectly fine with most people. But when I moved out, it was like a betrayal, like I wasn't being black. Hey, I was just being human. I want my kids to grow up safe and have a good education. What's wrong with that? Dani and I used to go around and around on this. She wanted in the world's worst way for me to move in to her neighborhood. Ironic, isn't it? I'm there now just because she isn't. You know, I've never known anybody sweeter than my little sis. But it was still real hard for her to trust white people."

"I feel like *most* blacks don't trust whites. Am I right?" Jake asked.

"Well, let's face it, the track record's pretty bad. How would you feel about black people if you knew your great-grandmother had stood on an auction block, stripped to the waist, while black men bid for her and the highest bidder got to take her as a slave and rape her whenever he felt like it? That's a lot to overcome, don't you think? My grandma, my mama's mama, she never trusted a white person. Some people thought she was bitter. But she'd seen her brother killed by the Klan. And she saw her father waste away in the cotton fields. And she saw her house taken away by the landowners when her daddy got too sick to work. Trusting white people doesn't come easy after what she saw. And the stories get passed on. For every bad thing you ever heard about a black person, I've heard five more about whites. Daddy wouldn't stand for too much of that talk, but it didn't stop my uncles and aunts and cousins and neighbors from filling my ears."

"I understand why they're suspicious," Jake said. "I guess I would be too. But if blacks gave white people a chance, I think they'd find a lot of us are different now."

"But that difference has to be proven over the long haul before there can be trust. You remember when we were sitting together at Promise Keepers down at Civic Stadium, and the Indian guy, the Navajo, next to us joked about the irony of a group of white American men calling themselves 'Promise Keepers'? I laughed like crazy. As I recall, you didn't think it was that funny. But I knew exactly what he was saying. All the promises to the Indians, all the promises to the blacks, those promises were never kept. Now you know how I love Promise Keepers, and I know they're serious about racial reconciliation and they've given me some real hope. But still, a lot of blacks are holding back, giving it time, watching whether all the talk is for real, whether it's going to pan out, translate into a long-term track record."

"I can appreciate the reservations," Jake said. "I just hope more and more black brothers keep putting their feet in the water."

"So do I. But a lot are going to stand out on the riverbank until they're sure the gators aren't biting. See, some of us have trusted white Christians before and ended up getting burned; we've told ourselves we'll never do it again."

"For example?"

"Okay," Clarence looked as if he were mentally sorting through dozens of dominoes and deciding which one to draw. "When I was at OSU I got linked up with a campus Christian group, all whites but me. I had some great times with them. But then one day I was walking across campus with a group of black friends. I see these four Christian white guys coming and I know they see me and I'm going to introduce them to my friends, maybe make a link to invite my black friends to the group. But all of a sudden these guys are headed across the lawn so they don't have to walk by me. I start to go after them, but then I realize what it's all about. I can be their friend on their turf, in their white world, but they won't cross over to my black world. I talked to them about it later. They apologized, but it was never the same after that. The friendship faded. I stopped going to the meetings. Too bad, because I needed them."

Jake looked at Clarence like a student listening to a professor, in over his head, but struggling to understand.

"Have you ever figured out," Clarence asked, "why I dress up when we go to a store?"

"Beats me. Just thought you like dressing up. It's always struck me as weird, I admit."

"I love to go casual. Jeans and a sweatshirt, that's what I really like," Clarence said. "But I also want to shop in peace. I get tired of the salesclerks saying, 'Can I help you?' every five minutes."

"What?"

"I don't like being watched."

"Clabern, what are you saying?"

"That I'm a black man," Clarence's voice thundered, "and black men are expected to be shoplifters! There. Can you understand that?"

"Sorry, man. Didn't mean to upset you."

"It wasn't you. Sorry." Clarence raised his hands and waited to regain his composure. "If you're a white man wearing jeans and a sweatshirt, you're just another customer. If you're a black man wearing jeans and a sweatshirt, you're just another suspect. Dressing up makes me look successful. So it helps compensate for my skin color. Sometimes it's enough to keep store security from breathing down my neck all the time."

"I had no idea," Jake said. "Are you sure—"

"That I'm not overreacting? Hey, I've got friends who are doctors and attorneys, and they do the same thing. If they dress comfortable, they're a suspect. It gets really old."

Clarence and Jake talked for another hour.

"Got to get home, bro," Clarence said. He hesitated, then added, "Hey, thanks for asking me about this stuff. And thanks for listening to me. I feel better just talking about it."

Jake put his arm around him. "Thanks for talking to me, brother. It gives me a lot to think about. And it helps me know how to pray for you." The two friends walked to the door.

———

Friday morning Ollie spent two hours driving up and down streets within a mile radius of Dani's house. He drove north on MLK, looking at every street sign. Switzer, Doolittle, Mormance, Moffat, Brumbelow, Jackson, Arnold, Skeets, Dennis, Jack. At Jack he turned right, driving out to tenth. He was about to turn right again when he looked up and suddenly threw on the brakes. He gazed hard at the street sign, which had been graffitied. He stared at it, wheels turning.

"Of course," Ollie whispered. "That's it." He picked up his cell phone. "Yeah, hey Margaret, how you doin', beautiful? Ollie here. Listen, find me a name and phone number, will you? City of Portland. I want the head of whatever department's in charge of fixing and replacing street signs. Call me on my cell phone as soon as you've got it." He flipped the phone shut.

Eyes still on the street sign, Ollie crossed his fingers.

CHAPTER

25

Clarence returned to his desk at 10:00 A.M. He reviewed his three new phone messages. The last one was a thin raspy voice that made him want to clear his throat.

"Clarence? Ollie here. Found something that'll interest you. I'm tied up all day—you won't be able to reach me—but I'll be leaving the office about 5:00. How about I meet you at 5:15 at the Taco Bell on MLK, near your place? You buy me a Burrito Supreme and I'll show you something big. I think it's the break we've been looking for."

And I have to wait seven hours to find out what it is?

Clarence tried to stay focused on his column. At least he was off to a strong start.

> What causes crime? For years Americans have bought into the liberal notion that poverty is the root of crime. There's only one problem with this idea—it is demonstrably false.
>
> If poverty were the cause of crime, there would have been more crime in the past, when people were poorer. But there wasn't more crime then, there was less. When the Great Depression set in, incomes dropped dramatically, poverty was widespread and guess what? The statistics show the crime rate not only failed to go up, it actually went down. The moral, spiritual, and familial foundations of this country were intact in those days, and held us up through an economic crisis.
>
> Over 70 percent of all juveniles committing crimes come from female-headed single-parent homes or from foster or group homes. USA Today surveyed 250 juvenile judges, who cited the breadown of the family as the number one reason for youth delinquency. Study after study shows that children born into single-parent families are much more likely to pursue a life of crime than children born into intact families. The root cause of crime is not poverty but illegitimacy, the defining aspect of which is the absence of a nurturing father.
>
> All the money we've poured into the 'poverty problem' has not only created a permanent underclass; it has also helped spawn the breakdown of the family, the *true* cause of crime.

The casually dressed man stood on the manicured eighteenth green of the PGA Senior Professional Championships at West Palm Beach. He stood fifty feet from the pin, determined to get to the hole in two strokes, tie for the lead, and force sudden death. He walked toward the hole, picked up a pine needle off the green, talked with his caddie, and positioned himself for the putt. The crowd watched in breathless silence. He let loose with a strong steady stroke. By the time the ball went thirty feet, it appeared it would make a serious run for the hole. The crowd readied itself for a moan at the near miss and polite applause for the valiant attempt. But the ball headed straight for the hole and wavered on the lip like a basketball on the rim. Suddenly it fell into the cup.

The champion dropped to his knees, looked upward, and extended both hands in exultation. The roar from the crowd ripped like thunder. People applauded at the wonder of the achievement, at the excellence of the man, at the magic of the moment. They would tell this story for years to come. They were there, in the presence of the master.

Most of them never considered that they were being observed from another place, and their experience served as an object lesson sketched on the blackboard of heaven.

"Do you see it? They are experiencing just a taste, just a faint shadow of something for which they were made. They stand on the periphery of boundless praise and energy."

"Yes, I see," Dani said to Torel. "It's like a glowing sunset that seems a doorway into another world. You want to hang on to it before it disappears, but then it's gone, replaced by drab gray twilight. The thrill of earth's greatest sporting victories is just a faint echo of the Joy for which we were made—a consuming participation in the worship of Almighty God, a celebration that never fades or disappoints."

The heavenly temple stood before them, the temple for which that built on earth was a small-scale model, suggestive of the real thing as miniature cars from a cereal box are suggestive of real ones. The courtyard of this temple seemed countless millions of acres, and the numbers of the throngs far exceeded even Dani's heightened capacity to estimate.

Here were teeming millions gathered to worship the One who has dominion over all.

Everything good on earth was seed to which this was the flower and fruit. The shadow was substance here. Dani realized in a way she never had that those on earth who did not believe in the substance could never appreciate the shadow. To them the shadow was all there was, something to be grasped and captured and fashioned into their own liking, rather than something which testified to that which was greater. Only those touched by the world of substance could truly find joy in the world of shadows.

Voices everywhere merged into a single hum of excitement. A sense of intimacy pervaded this huge group, a closeness Dani had never experienced among large numbers, though she'd caught occasional glimpses of it in church worship services.

She heard all the voices in different languages and enjoyed the distinctive tone of each. She was particularly drawn to Swahili but also loved Norwegian, Aborigine, Hmong, Assyrian, Tagalog, Greek, Hebrew, and Arabic. People from every nation, tribe, people, and language stood before the throne, in front of the Lamb. She'd read about it, and now she was living it. She chided herself that when she'd read the words in the dark world she'd never even tried to envision them, thinking of them as myth or metaphor.

Elyon's diverse creation reflected his internal diversity, the paradoxical interplay of his seemingly contradictory but always complementary attributes. He had built the unity of the universe, Dani saw now, not on the unwilling conformity of identical components but on the voluntary yielding to one another of diverse components. On earth this meant not only two different genders, but many different races and cultures and languages. She realized that despite what happened at Babel, from the very beginning Elyon's genetic blueprint had contained all that allowed this diversity to finally blossom.

She looked at Torel. "I once thought that in heaven every race would somehow be the same, every language the same, every outward appearance the same. Now it seems such a ridiculous notion. To strip people of their uniqueness would be like taking all the varied colorful vegetables and cramming them into a grinder, then churning them into a pasty gray puree. The beauty would be gone, the taste gone, the color gone, the vegetables themselves gone. In hell, perhaps such bland sameness exists. But certainly not in heaven!"

"You see it clearly now," Torel said. "There are different races, but all with one unifying center of gravity, the glory of God. In the Shadowlands the dark lord tries to commandeer for himself a perverted notion of diversity, just as he tried to ruin the beauty of sex by legitimizing sexual perversion. Of course, the beauty of diversity is in its perfect harmony with God's created order, not in a cacophony of violations of that order. Heaven's diversity has placed itself under Elyon's lordship, creating a unity that transcends the diversity. The Creator gives symmetry, order, and magnificence to the diversity of his creation. This diversity, not the diversity of sin, is what should be celebrated."

Dani watched as a short and unimposing man with dark face slowly ascended a huge platform beneath the throne on which the Carpenter sat. An angel, tall and straight, reverently handed the man a Bible. The two seemed intimately familiar with one another, as if they had fought side by side in a great war. The Bible's pages began to turn, apparently by sheer force of the little man's thoughts, until his eyes fixed on the passage he wanted to read, very near the end of the Book.

"Hear the eternal words of Elyon that tell us what is to come. This is what Elyon showed me on Patmos, that all men might know what awaits them."

John. The apostle John!

> "Then I saw a great white throne and him who was seated on it. Earth and sky fled from his presence, and there was no place for them. And I saw the dead, great and small, standing before the throne, and books were opened. Another book was opened, which is the book of life. The dead were judged according to what

they had done as recorded in the books. The sea gave up the dead that were in it, and death and Hades gave up the dead that were in them, and each person was judged according to what he had done. Then death and Hades were thrown into the lake of fire. The lake of fire is the second death. If anyone's name was not found written in the book of life, he was thrown into the lake of fire."

A shudder rose from the crowd. When it subsided, John continued. "Elyon is the gracious rewarder of those who seek and obey him. We whose names are written in the book look forward to the day of rewards. Listen now to his promises. Rejoice at what awaits you."

The pages turned again, and John spoke slowly and emphatically the words of Elyon's Son: "I tell you the truth, anyone who gives you a cup of water in my name because you belong to Christ will certainly not lose his reward." Wondrous rumblings of assent filled the air.

John launched into prayer, gazing at the glowing throne and him who sat upon it. Dani and the rest of the crowd followed John's gaze, turning in unison toward the object of his devotion. Their new eyes were able to tolerate a brightness that would have blinded mortal eyes.

"Elyon, God of Abraham, God of our fathers, we thank you that you are the judge of all men and your judgments are always just. We thank you that you keep careful track of all things, that you ignore no deed, whether righteous or evil. We tremble yet rejoice that nothing escapes your notice."

Countless praises rose from the crowd. Dani heard many languages but readily understood them all. In the distinctive rhythms and accents of every language she felt the very textures of the different cultures from which these people came.

"We pray for those in the dark world," John continued, "who live day after day with no sense of what is to come. We intercede for those who try in vain to fill the emptiness of their souls with violence, immorality, greed, self-importance, and every other form of rebellion and self-destruction. Show them, Elyon, that the holes in their hearts can be filled only by you; that they have no hope except in you; that apart from your redemption they cannot and will not stand on the terrible day of judgment. As the dark world races headlong toward that final judgment, may your Spirit enlighten many, teaching them to see with the eyes of eternity."

The intensity of his voice suddenly increased. "Embolden Michael's warriors who fight valiantly for the souls of men. Defeat your enemies who followed Morningstar in his rebellion."

What seemed like an electric current—Dani could hear arcs of energy surging and crackling—moved like lightning between the tallest beings in the crowd. The longing of humans for Elyon's final victory, great as it was, seemed eclipsed now by the more ancient yearning of Michael's hosts.

"We grow impatient, all-wise Elyon, for the kingdom of our Christ to be established on earth. We long for all things wrong to be made right. Yet you are patient, enduring every indignity and accusation cast upon you by rebellious men. You wait for one and then another to come to faith in you."

Expressions of agreement rose from every corner of the great assembly. As John concluded, a loud chorus of voices, perfectly timed, cried "Amen." Dani's voice was among them. On the platform a man began singing with a lighter-than-air voice that became steadily stronger and more focused with every verse. The voice was as clear and audible to those in the back of the crowd, hundreds of miles away, as to those only feet from the front.

At first she thought it was a new song, so original and penetrating. Then she realized she knew the song. "Amazing grace, how sweet the sound, that saved a wretch like me." The singer—of course, he was the writer of the song. The old slave-trader, repentant of racism and oppression and injustice, eternally cleansed. "I once was lost, but now am found, was blind but now I see."

He continued to sing, many in the crowd joining him, others just listening to his voice, contemplating the drama of redemption embodied in the man. All heaven joined together as he sang, "When we've been here ten thousand years, bright shining as the sun, we've no less days to sing God's praise, then when we'd first begun."

Many of Michael's legions seemed to appear from nowhere—some striding forward, some coming down from above, some appearing to come from beyond the far side of the throne. There were untold thousands of them, ten thousand times ten thousand. They encircled Elyon's throne and sang in a loud voice, "Worthy is the Lamb, who was slain, to receive power and wealth and wisdom and strength and honor and glory and praise!"

Suddenly an explosion of sound pierced the air from behind and around Dani. Everyone sang now with an impetus that pushed her forward toward the throne. Surrounded in sound, resonating as if she were a tuning fork, she both absorbed the sound and produced it. She felt like a leaf swept along in a raging river, a river that both came from and led to Elyon Most High.

The worshippers sang many songs. Now a little girl walked across the platform and began to sing. She looked so beautiful, she reminded Dani of...Felicia! She had written her song for Elyon's Son, and he wished all heaven to hear it. The song was so beautiful, Felicia's voice so wondrous. Dani swelled with the right kind of pride, realizing this was her girl, yet even on earth she had never owned her. People could own things, but only Elyon could own people. Felicia was and would always be Dani's treasure, for she had invested so much in her. But the girl was Elyon's treasure first and last and above all. Dani looked to the throne so far away and yet so very close and met the eyes of the Carpenter. For an instant, they shared an intimate joy over this little girl.

Dani could barely hear the million singing angels up front, for the voice of the multitudes overwhelmed them. The angels had at first seemed the largest choir ever assembled but now proved to be only the small worship ensemble that led the true choir of untold millions, now lost to themselves, lost to all but Elyon, singing at full voice, "To him who sits on the throne and to the Lamb be praise and honor and glory and dominion, for ever and ever!"

"Hey, Carp," Clarence said, standing over her desk. "I'm doing a column on bias in photojournalism. It's your fault. You're the one that opened my eyes. I'll leave you out if you want me to. Or if I quote you I'll let you see it before it goes to print. Will you talk to me?"

"As long as I can look it over before anyone else sees it, including Winston. Okay?"

"It's a deal. You know what I'm looking for. Talk to me about photojournalism." Clarence had yellow pad and pen in hand.

"Well, it's a world of its own, and people don't understand it. They understand misquotes, at least once they're the victims. But they don't understand photojournalism enough to realize what it's about. Of course, we've been altering still photos for decades. Like you saw with the police officer, we do cropping all the time, selecting what the viewer or reader will see and what he won't."

"That's not new to me, but when I saw what it did to Ollie, I admit it threw me."

"Well, that's just the beginning. Welcome to the computer age. We can load in a picture and do pretty much whatever we want to with it. It's like wire service stories. You take what you want and leave out what you don't want, right?"

"Yeah, but—"

"Sunny day but we want the picture to feel overcast? No problem. We can shade it. With the new technology, all the computer imaging and enhancing, we can edit reality more effectively than you can with words. Years ago *National Geographic* had a shot of the Great Pyramids outside Cairo. They couldn't all fit in the same picture and still be as big as the editors wanted them, so they just cut out the space in between. Squeezed them together. They figured, hey, it was just editing out sand."

"They really did that?"

"Sure. And I know photographers who defended it. It served the purpose and it looked great. But it wasn't real. I mean, it took 200,000 workers and what, over a hundred years, for the Egyptians to build those pyramids. But the editors at *National Geographic* moved them without breaking a sweat."

"How'd they do it?"

Carp pointed to the computer screen next to her. "This graphics software gives us the ability to manipulate images. Remove or add them, separate images or combine them. With computers you can do it seamlessly. The final product looks as good as the original. No, it looks *better*. Used to be if reality didn't look good enough, tough luck. Now you can edit reality." Carp reached in her top desk drawer and pulled out a photograph of a desk.

"Here's one I use in my photojournalism class over at Portland Community College. You've got a photo of this classy looking oak desk, and there's this can of Coke that ruins the ambiance." She pointed to the can in the picture. "The old question used to be, Is it okay for the photographer to *move* the can before she shoots in order to set up a better picture? Now the question is, Is it okay if she removes the can *after* she takes the picture?"

Carp showed Clarence a second photo, identical, but with no Coke can. "That's what was done with this photo. When it got published there wasn't anything to indicate the alteration. I ask my students, 'Who thinks this is wrong?' Almost none of them raise their hands. So I ask them, 'Where do you stop? What's the difference between removing a can and adding it?' I could put all kinds of things on this desk. It's called reverse cropping, and it's done more than you think. Thing is, unless you've got some incredibly observant eyewitness that was there when the photo was taken, nobody will notice."

"Amazing."

"I've got photo CDs with tens of thousands of pictures. I could put the crown jewels or a *Playboy* magazine on that desk. I could incriminate someone or I could exonerate them by what I add or subtract. Say you've got somebody you like, and he's wearing a T-shirt with an offensive slogan or his gut is hanging out. Used to be you had to use it as is or crop around it. But now you can just remove it."

"The slogan or the gut?"

"Either. Both. In fact, you could change the slogan to something more positive or just wipe it off the T-shirt. You could put six-pack abs in place of the soft gut. Whatever you want. It's like taking steroids in body-building or football. As long as you don't get caught, you're a hero."

"Have you ever done it, Carp?"

"Take steroids?"

"No. Manipulate photos."

"Off the record? Yeah, I've done it, just a few times. I'm not proud of it. I console myself with the fact that I didn't hurt anybody and that I feel guilty. Means I still have a conscience, I guess."

The radio scanner on Carp's desk suddenly settled on a channel where an excited voice was saying there was a fire at the Heathman Hotel, with people trapped inside. Carp grabbed her camera and car keys.

"Speaking of ethics, this is where I try to discipline myself to hope they all get out okay and I don't end up with an award-winning picture of somebody burning or jumping. Later, Clarence."

"Thanks for your time, Carp. Don't get too close to the fire."

Clarence drove into Taco Bell at 5:05 and waited impatiently for Ollie. The detective pulled in right at 5:15. He hopped out and beckoned Clarence to join him in his car.

"We'll leave your car here," Ollie called, "so you can't welsh on the Burrito Supreme."

"What's going on, Ollie?" Clarence asked as he got in the passenger seat.

"You'll find out." Ollie drove slowly down Jack Street and pulled over at Tenth. He put the car in park.

"Okay," Ollie said. "Class is in session. Look at the street sign. Tell me what you see."

"It says 'Jack.' How'm I doing, Sherlock?"

"So far so good, Watson. Tell me more."

"Well, looks like some tagger's messed with the *k* at the end of 'Jack.' Put a *c* over it."

"Right," Ollie said. "And who would make that kind of change?"

"A Crip. Bloods like the *ck*, you said; Crips hate it. Stands for Crip killer, right? So some Crip just put a *c* over the *k*." He looked at Ollie. "Do I pass the test?"

"With flying colors." Ollie U-turned back toward MLK and headed south. He drove down to Jackson, turned left, and pulled over immediately.

"Okay," Ollie said, "get out of the car and tell me this street name."

Clarence opened the door, stood on the sidewalk, and looked over the car top at the sign across the street. "Jackson. Ollie, this is my street. The sign just says Jackson. No graffiti. Nothing. Am I missing something?"

"Nope. But suppose just for a minute that some Crip decided he didn't like the ck in Jackson. What would he do?"

"Same thing as the other, I guess. Turn the *k* into another *c?*"

Ollie reached under the front seat and pulled out a green street sign with white letters. He held it up on top of his car for Clarence to inspect.

"Where'd you get that sign?"

"Never mind," Ollie said. "Tell me what you see."

"Well, it says Jack, except somebody painted a white *c* over the *k*. It was a neat job. Let me see it." Ollie handed him the sign. "Yeah, okay, they used a green paint on the edges of the *k* so the white *c* covers it nicely. That green paint's a perfect match for the sign. And there's some letters on the end, covered with green: *s-o-n*. Okay, I got it, this was a Jackson Street sign."

Ollie took the sign back, walked across the street, and held it up to the street sign post, just below the Jackson sign. "What does it look like?"

"Jacc. Okay, it looks like Jack Street."

Ollie bounced back into the car, put it in drive, and pulled off, Clarence barely getting in on time.

"Ollie, wait a minute, are you saying…?" Clarence didn't finish the sentence. Ollie continued to drive three blocks, past Dani's house, and turned north. When he got up to Jack Street he turned left, back toward MLK. Then he pulled over and this time shut off the engine.

"See this house? How many blocks down from MLK?"

"Three and a half, I guess. So?"

"Look at the house numbers."

"Nine twenty. Wait. That's Dani's house number."

"What color is the house?"

"Blue. Same as Dani's." Clarence hesitated. "Ollie, are you saying this house was the one the killers meant to hit?"

"Can't be sure yet. But I'd lay big bucks on it."

"Where did you get that sign?"

"When I saw the Jack sign graffitied, I thought about all the Crips and all the tagging around here. I figured, if one sign gets a *ck* tagged out, others do too. I thought, just suppose someone spray painted a Jackson sign the same way. So I called the city. If it's minor defacing they leave it or clean it up. But if it's a thorough job, they replace it. They keep records, and they've got a big bin full of old signs— save them for recycling or something. I got into the bin, and after ten minutes I found this sign. Turns out they ordered a replacement August 24. Put up the new sign September 5, three days after the murder."

"So…?"

"So the little gray cells," Ollie tapped his head, "tell me to go back to Jack Street. I drive up to 920. Same number, same side of the street, same color, same basic floor plan."

"I never noticed this Jackson sign when I visited Dani." Clarence looked transfixed at the piece of green metal in his hands.

"Why would you? You know the area. You know where to turn. You wouldn't look at her street sign. Neither would anyone else from around here."

"So you're saying—"

"The perps weren't locals. Couldn't have been. If they were, they'd know Jack *and* Jackson—no way they'd get them mixed up just because of a sign. I say they were from out of town, just following directions. They had a street name and house number, maybe the house color to make absolutely sure. They saw what looked like Jack Street and didn't go any farther north to the real Jack Street."

Clarence looked at the blue house. "Who lives here?"

"That's the sixty-four-thousand-dollar question. So far I've just got a name. The Fletchers. Manny's running a background check right now. After we do our homework, I plan on knocking on the door and introducing myself. I especially want to know whose bedroom is on the front right side of the house. And who might have reason to want them dead."

26

Clarence and Geneva drove into Janet's driveway, Jake's Mustang cruising in right behind them. All three came to the door together.

"Hi, you guys," Janet said, smiling but sounding frazzled. "I'm warning you, it's kind of a zoo around here. Carly and I've been watching kids all day. My friend Sue Keels and her daughter, Angela, took a little two-day retreat, and we've got Angie's baby, Karina. And we've also got—"

"Hi dere, Unca Jake!" the familiar but other worldly voice rang out. Jake had just stepped in the door when he was surrounded by young gangly arms.

"Hi dere, Little Finn," Jake said with obvious delight. He picked up the Down's syndrome boy and hugged him tight.

"Finn," Jake said to the boy six inches from his face, "this is my good friend, Mr. Clarence Abernathy."

"Hi dere, Mista Abernassy!"

"Hello, Finn. I've heard all about you." Finn reached both arms out to Clarence, the possibility of being dropped never occurring to him. Clarence embraced him gently, touched by the realization Finn didn't know how to hold back—he kept nothing in reserve. The boy trusted Clarence immediately and completely, like someone accustomed to trusting. Clarence wondered if he had ever exercised that kind of trust.

"Boy, Unca Jake, Mr. Abernassy is *really* big!" Little Finn almost shouted the words, stretching out the "really." Everyone laughed.

"And this is Geneva Abernassy," Jake said to Finn, "big Mr. Abernassy's lovely wife."

Finn and Geneva grinned at each other. Still in Clarence's arms, he rubbed his pale white hand against Clarence's face, studying the difference with obvious fascination. When he touched Clarence's hair, Finn said, with wonder in his voice, "It's just like a brillo pad!"

"Yeah, I guess it is," Clarence said, his smile even broader than Little Finn's.

"My dad used to say dat God made people of every color 'cause all colors need each other fo' da world to be what he wants it to be."

"My sister used to say something like that too," Clarence said.

"Unca Jake told me your sister's in *heaven* with my dad! Maybe they're watchin' us right now, huh?"

"Maybe so." Clarence wanted to believe it.

"So dere's at least two colors already in heaven!"

"Yeah." Clarence turned away, not wanting to show his eyes. What was it about this boy that reminded him so much of Daddy? They both seemed on the inside track, as if they knew something the rest of the world didn't. They had one foot here and one foot somewhere else.

"Have you seen Carly's baby, Mr. Abernassy? He was named after my dad and me!" Little Finn slipped out of Clarence's arms and tugged him toward the child's room, Geneva following. Geneva and Clarence hugged Carly and fussed over baby Finney.

After a few minutes Janet announced, "Okay, Carly, we're ready to take off. Are you sure you can handle everybody?"

"Positive. As long as I've got Little Finn to help me." She put her arm around the beaming boy. "He can entertain Karina and Finney both."

"Bye, Mista Abernassy!" Finn yelled at Clarence.

"Bye, Mista Finn!" Clarence said. "You behave yourself or I'll rub you with my brillo pad." He lowered his head and rubbed his hair on the side of Finn's face as the boy squealed with delight.

The two couples drove to Dea's in Gresham, since everybody felt like eating hamburgers. Clarence and Jake claimed a booth, while Geneva and Janet made one of their long journeys to the restroom.

"How's it going with you and Janet?" Clarence asked.

"Good, I think. We love each other. We love the Lord. We're rebuilding. Doesn't mean it's all easy, of course."

"Most things aren't." Clarence thought about Jake's faith, realistic yet idealistic at the same time. It was still fresh and new. Jake had a touch of Little Finn in him, an ability to see through the eyes of a child. Clarence's own faith felt cynical and jaded, blunted by years of abrasions and injustice.

"You know, Jake, sometimes I envy you coming to faith later in life."

"Strange to hear you say that. I've often thought how wonderful it would've been to grow up in a home like yours, with parents who loved the Lord."

"Sometimes you take it for granted," Clarence said. "Like it's more of a family thing than a personal thing."

"Still, to have Christian parents. I can hardly imagine. As for coming to faith later in life? Well, I look back at my first fifty years, and I think so much of it was wasted. Every day I've got now, I want it to count for eternity. Funny, I say something like that and I think of my old buddy Finney and how I never understood it when he said those things. He's been gone two years. Janet says sometimes I remind her of Finney. Sue, Finney's wife, she says the same thing. I can't think of a higher compliment. But I have so far to go."

"You've already come a long way, bro. My faith seems stagnant. Like I've lost my first love. Don't know what to do, really. Geneva says I'm angry with God. I guess she's right. It's hard to trust somebody, to put yourself in his hands when I look at…"

"What happened to Dani and Felicia?"

"Yeah."

"Still, what's the alternative?" Jake asked. "We're not God. You think things are a mess now, can you imagine what would happen if *we* were in charge of the universe?"

Clarence thought he'd like to have a shot at it anyway.

"Seems like," Jake said, "it doesn't take much faith to follow God when it's going the way you think it should. Maybe faith is learning to trust God even when it looks like everything's going wrong."

"Uncle Antsy?" Ty startled Clarence. He hadn't initiated a conversation with him for weeks, and he never called him by that name anymore.

"Hey, Ty. What is it?"

"I know you've been talkin' with the cops. What's happenin'? Are they gonna find the killers?" He even sounded like the old Ty.

"I hope so. Don't know for sure." Clarence debated how much to tell him, but he was so eager to talk, he decided to chance it. "Detective Chandler thinks the shooting was a mistake."

"Mistake? The house was shot to pieces."

"No, I mean they meant to kill somebody, but they got the wrong house."

"How could they do that?"

"He thinks they didn't know the streets around here. See, somebody painted over the Jackson Street sign on MLK, trying to change the *k* to a *c*, you know, because of the Crip killer thing? Well, the way the paint was sprayed on, it covered up the rest of the word. So *Jackson* ended up looking like *Jack*. Possibly they were going for a house over on Jack but got the wrong street."

Ty sat quietly, shoulders hunched. Suddenly he got up and walked to the door.

"Ty, wait. Come back. I—" Before he finished the sentence, Clarence heard the screen door slam shut.

At Keisha and Celeste's insistence, Clarence began reading the third Narnia book, *The Voyage of the Dawntreader*. Jake had given him a copy of *Mere Christianity* by C. S. Lewis. After reading it twice he'd passed it on to Dani, who devoured it and started reading other Lewis books. Even though he was a Lewis fan, this was Clarence's first trip through Narnia.

The children laughed after Clarence read the opening line: "There was a boy called Eustace Clarence Scrubb, and he almost deserved it." Hearing the name "Clarence" helped set them off.

"Eustace Clarence liked animals, especially beetles, if they were dead and pinned on a card." The portrait of the surly, arrogant Eustace continued. He thought things and did things that were selfish and hateful. Eventually Eustace Clarence's inner condition transformed his appearance. The boy turned into a hideous pathetic dragon.

For some reason this frightened Clarence.

"I want to introduce you to someone," Torel said to Dani. She looked at the man Torel towered over. He appeared very pleasant, with an impish twinkle in his eye that reminded her of her daddy. He smiled with polite reserve, but his eyes shined. Though she'd never seen him, she instantly felt as if she knew him.

"Welcome to Elyon's world, daughter of Eve," the man said brightly. She enjoyed his delightful British accent and his deep drawn-out, Hitchcock-like voice.

"Dani," Torel said, "this is C. S. Lewis."

"Lewis!" she exclaimed, wide eyed. "Oh, I *loved* your books. They're wonderful. My family's reading through Narnia right now in the Shadowlands!"

"Yes, so your guardian told me," Lewis said. "Torel spoke to my own advocate, Eldil, and asked if I might come and help tutor you for part of your orientation. That is, if you wish it."

"Wish it? I'd die for it!"

"Well," Lewis said with a smile, "there's no need for that, is there? You already have."

Torel seemed to enjoy Dani's obvious delight. "Those who impact Elyon's children on earth," the angel said, "often take a role in orienting them to heaven. Sometimes that includes people you knew on earth, other times ancestors you've never known, such as Zeke and Nancy. It may include someone whose writings Elyon used in your life. Lewis is one of those, and since he still speaks to your family in the Shadowlands, it seemed appropriate to seek him out."

"Appropriate? It was a *wonderful* idea. Thank you, Torel!" She threw her arms around him. He hugged her back with angelic reserve. "How like Elyon to surprise me with a treat like this!"

"Yes," Torel said. "Does not his Word tell you that he delights in the well-being of his servant and that in his presence there is fullness of joy?"

"Come," Lewis said, extending his hand to Dani. "Walk with me—I know just the place, one that stimulates both mind and body. As we walk, I will ask you questions and learn all about you. Before class begins, I must discover exactly who my pupil is!"

Shadow stood at the door of the abandoned church doing pig watch while eight bangers gathered for business inside.

"Hear you did the burg over on Mason," GC said to Pharaoh. "Nice crib. Got you some money to buy my stuff, make you up some rocks?"

"Burg? Me?" Pharaoh feigned innocence. "Man, I straight as an arrow. But I did win Lotto, so yeah, I got some green, if you got some white."

"Got some fine white." GC pulled the cocaine out of a baggy inside a McDonald's sack. Pharaoh looked at it skeptically.

"Best stuff in town," GC said. "Special blend. Sweet." It all came from the same source, but he was a salesman. He would have succeeded in a hundred legal occupations as surely as he did in this one.

Pharaoh, who'd excelled in science classes before he dropped out of high school, examined the powder with the detailed eye of a chemist. He poured some powder into a test tube, then dropped in a pinch of baking soda to harden it. He measured just the right amount of water and added it carefully.

Pharaoh's four companions watched respectfully, one hungrily picking up tips he could emulate when he graduated to high roller. The other three, less entrepreneurial, eyed the product itself and hungered only for it.

Pharaoh took out of his coat pocket a small butane lighter, an inch and a half wide and six inches long. He held the flame under the test tube, cooking it just so, like a finicky French chef. He added a few drops of cold water. He shook up the sticky substance until it hardened. He jounced the tube just so, and the newly formed rock clattered around like a single die in a Yahtzee cup.

Pharaoh placed the rock neatly in the middle of a piece of brillo stuck in the broken-off bottom of a car antennae, in a neighborhood where many cars no longer had antennas. He lit it. The moment the rock got hot enough, he took a long, hard drag, with the finesse of a wine taster. Pharaoh took advantage of the small window of opportunity and got his one vapor, his quick hit.

The four junkies were getting restless, like starving men watching the line go through a smorgasbord. Finally one of them took over for Pharaoh and produced more rocks. Another took out a shiny mirror and chopped up the cocaine powder with a razor into four fine lines, each an inch and a half long. He passed out tooters,

McDonald's straws cut into two- or three-inch lengths. The first guy inhaled, sliding the straw steadily up the line, snorting it up his nose, the powder absorbing into the membranes.

One other junkie didn't want to smoke or snort. He used the butane lighter to heat up water in a bottle cap, mixed in the cocaine, then drew it up a syringe. He injected a third of the syringe contents into his arm, then passed the needle to another shooter.

They all sat back, glassy-eyed, each going where no man had gone before.

"Which way you want to do it, little homie?" GC asked Ty.

Ty pointed at the mirror that had two lines left.

"Nah. Try the rock. You can do it." GC took an extra rock, positioned it in the brillo at the antenna's end, and told him, "Wait till I tell you, then suck it in."

He held the fire up to the rock and suddenly said "Now." Ty drew it in, got the full vapor, rocking him back.

Ty had smoked dope, but never crack. The bag of cocaine his uncle had found under his mattress had been entrusted to him to deliver to someone at school. He'd never done the stuff till this moment. He'd studied the others as tinies always do, not wanting to look the fool when their time comes. Ty was an amateur in a room full of veterans. He watched through changed eyes as one of the junkies studied the counter, then gathered a few white particles onto a piece of paper, as if they were the shavings off cut diamonds.

GC didn't touch the stuff himself, not when he was on duty. "Never get buzzed when you doin' a deal, or they run you up." He was armed with his nine, and a tiny back-up derringer in his jeans pocket, as well as a knife. Every drug dealer's dread was to get "run up on," to be robbed in a sneak attack. Such an attack had only been successful on him once, back in South Central. It had been tried twice in Portland, leaving him with a bullet and a sore back from a baseball bat. But he'd left two attackers in the hospital and one laid out in a casket. Word was out that if you wanted to run up a high roller or a baller, you'd better pick someone other than Gangster Cool of the Rollin' 60s.

"Don't smoke the co-caine," he'd advised Ty, "sell it." Yet now he'd introduced him to it. As Ty moved in and out of reality, he remembered GC's tip on how to tell if you're approached by an undercover cop trying to bust you. "Look at their eyes. If he be a crack smoker, his eyes all red. If his eyes white, he be a cop."

After a while, Pharaoh's head started to clear enough to do business. He looked at GC. "How much for a teener?"

"A teener?" GC looked horrified at the thought of selling only a sixteenth of an ounce. "Hundred dollars, but you make me mess with a teener, I charge you another fifty for the samples. I thought we'd do a Z, minimum."

"How much for an eight ball?"

"One eighty. You a dealer or just a doer? I'm sellin' the Z today. If you can't afford it, I got the plain stuff, I sell you an ounce for six hundred. You want a rep for havin' the good stuff, it's nine hundred for the best Z in town."

"How 'bout eight?"

"How 'bout nine and the samples be free, like I always do for the big sellers? You can break it down in dimes, make your rocks, sell it for three thousand dollars."

"Maybe twenty-six hundred."

"Still be a big profit."

"And lots of risk."

"You a business man. You rewarded for risk."

Pharaoh handed over nine hundred dollars cash, mostly in fifty-dollar bills, for an ounce of cocaine. After five more minutes they left, like business partners following a two-martini lunch. Now that Shadow was off duty, he fired up a rock himself.

Tyrone left the abandoned church a different boy. Already his body was developing an addiction to this new substance. Even now, though he didn't yet know it, he was chasin' the bag.

───────────

"Clarence, did you take some money from my purse?"

"Nope. Not guilty."

"I could have sworn I had two twenties," Geneva said. "Now I've just got a couple of ones. I can't remember buying anything." She hesitated. "This isn't the first time this has happened. I don't want to accuse him, but I'm wondering about Ty."

"You think he's a thief?"

"I don't know. I just know I'm missing some money, and this is maybe the third time in the last few weeks. Considering what else he's done, I admit I suspect him."

"I've got to talk to him about the drug thing again. I'm not sure the confrontation with that crack dealer was enough. He looks spacy, eyes are red. I think he's using. I've got to do more to convince him. I just don't know what."

Clarence walked to Ty's bedroom and knocked. After a while he heard a faint groan. He opened the door. Ty looked utterly detached, as if his uncle's presence had no meaning.

"Have you been taking money from your aunt's purse?" Clarence asked. Ty shook his head unconvincingly, then covered guilt and fear with a sullen look, teen code for "go to blazes."

"I want you to take a walk with me, Ty."

"Where we goin'?"

"We're going on a tour. And don't make me pull you by the ear this time."

They went out the front door and walked three blocks while Ty looked around frantically, hoping his homies wouldn't see him marching around with his uncle again.

"I'm gonna show you what drugs do to you." They walked past two addicts leaned against the wall. They looked like zombies straight out of *Night of the Living Dead*. A third to a half of their teeth were missing. Ty felt like heaving. He'd seen them before, but never got close to them, never looked at them like this. They sat there scratching, as heroin addicts do. Crack and methamphetamines were the younger generation's drugs of choice, but heroin still had a market with the older addicts. The pitiful men had scars everywhere from being beaten and robbed who knows how many times. Their skin looked ashen and sickly. It seemed contradictory to see black men so pale. In the midst of four blacks sat a white man and a Hispanic.

"Drugs are multicultural," Clarence said. "They're nondiscriminatory. They take down everybody." He gestured at a man with vacant eyes and a face as expressionless as a mask. The man wrapped up a tissue paper speedball, a combination of heroin and cocaine.

For most citizens, walking by these men was like driving past an accident. You wanted to look and not look at the same time. So you sort of half looked and half listened to their whispering whimpering testimony to a life not lived. Clarence was determined Ty would look and listen.

Two of the cocaine addicts appeared to be having a conversation, except neither could understand the other. They seemed oblivious to Clarence and Ty. A couple of times they glanced their way but looked through them as if they existed on another plane, as if their world was its own reality incapable of all but momentary intersections with the real world. They not only couldn't see legions of warriors surrounding them, they could barely see the people around them.

"See those old men, Ty? They're probably no more than forty. They're not old, just ruined. See what drugs have done to them?"

"Don't plan to live that long," Ty said.

"Well, that'll be a self-fulfilling prophecy if you mess with drugs. Crack will take you out. You'll be dead or wish you were. Maybe make somebody else dead. Is that what you want, son?"

"Don't know what I want. Just want to hang with my homies. That's all."

They went farther, nearing the corner liquor store, one of a dozen in a two-mile radius. Two old men sat with hands extended, looking like beggars on the streets of Delhi.

"See these guys? They all started by just hangin' with their homies too. Most of them don't have a life outside three blocks from this liquor store. It's their church, their synagogue. It defines the boundaries of their lives. They were nickel-and-dime hustlers. Now they beg for money. No self-respect. They eat rock and breathe liquor, that's all they do. Take a good look, boy. That's where you're headed."

Clarence stared at Ty's face, seeing the determined look of a boy who doesn't want to listen. "Hey, Petey." Clarence waved to a man who looked as though he could be anywhere between thirty and seventy. He sat on the cold sidewalk, gazing suspiciously at Clarence.

"See that guy? Name's Petey. I interviewed him for a column a few weeks ago. He doesn't remember me. Doesn't even remember how old he is. He just hustles for chump change, begging off little old ladies that come by. He's still trying to be hip, shirttails out, hat on backwards. Permanent adolescence. Ugly, isn't it? Like a twelve-year-old still wearing diapers. Anybody offer you so much as a toke, this is where they're sending you. Remember that, boy."

Ty stared at a crack in the concrete.

"In one of his clearer moments, I asked Petey what he thought of his life. Know what he said? 'I may not be in hell yet, but I can see it and smell it.' That what you want, boy? Answer me now."

"No. But don't want no white man pullin' my strings neither."

"Question is whether you're going to pull your *own* strings. You really think the Man is making all this happen, putting the liquor stores everywhere, floodin' the streets with crack? The white sheets aren't smart enough to pull off this kind of program. This is straight from the devil. It's right outta hell."

"But it's honkies that brings in the drugs and make the big money. They're the ones that wants us to kill each other."

"Well, boy, if you're right, then you're doing just what they want, aren't you? Are you really that stupid? Come on. People taking the drugs and shooting the guns, they only got themselves to blame. You want to take on the Man, fine, go slug it out, get smarter than he is, beat him at his own game. But don't hide in the ghetto and whine about injustice while you smoke the vapors. When white boys went to the moon, these brothas here were doing just what you're starting now. Well, take a good look, Ty, because if this is the life you want, here it is. If you're lucky, I mean. If you don't end up in a casket before you're twenty. They're losers, man. Their big prize is when somebody drops a cigarette with a half inch left on it. Then they suck that baby down to the filter, and it's like they repaired a car or taught a class or fixed a roof. Like it was some big deal. All the gangbangers, they're losers just like these dudes."

Ty glowered.

"Don't care what you think of them, they're still losers. They whine about how white folk treat black folk, then what do they do? Kill black folk. Break up black families. Steal black kids from their parents. Turn smart kids like you into stupid ones." Clarence searched for the words that might get through. "Our ancestors were slaves, Ty. Their hands and feet were chained, but they learned to use their heads. Your hands and feet are free, but you're going to be a slave, a prisoner, if your mind doesn't get back on track. You know why blacks kill blacks, boy? Answer me. You know why?"

"No."

"Because they hate the color of their skin and they take it out on anybody that looks like them. Is that how your mama taught you to think?"

Ty shook his head. Tears started flowing. Clarence hugged him. "Let's go home, son." As the two walked past the liquor store, an audience of curious addicts watched a fight for purpose and dignity, a fight each of them had lost years ago.

Clarence pulled Ty close. "I want better for you, son. With your mama gone, somebody's got to be her voice. That's why I hammer on you, boy. Not because I don't care about you. Because I do."

———

The next day Clarence walked into the Main Street Deli and saw Ollie sitting at the far corner table, reading the front page of the *Tribune*. His eyes squinted at the words under the headline "Economic Problems Plague Country."

"I thought you didn't read the *Trib*," Clarence said, taking the seat across from him.

"It's not that I don't read it. It's just that I don't believe it. There's a difference." Ollie flashed Clarence a serious expression. "There's a real economic crunch, huh? I hear it's so bad in New York City that the Mafia's had to lay off five judges."

"Ollie, before we get to anything else, I want to thank you for all your hard work on this case."

Ollie looked surprised. "It's my job."

"You didn't have to include me, and I really appreciate it." Clarence cleared his throat. "Listen, I got some great seats for the playoffs—the Mariners and Yankees on Saturday. I was wondering if you'd want to go up to Seattle with me and my daddy and Jake?"

"Wow, no kiddin'? I'd love to. Count me in!"

They went to the front counter. Clarence noticed the girl taking his order seemed friendlier to him than usual. The two men settled back at their table.

"What's the word on 920 Northeast Jack?" Clarence asked.

"Okay," Ollie said, flipping through his notes. "Solid family. Father Bob Fletcher, he's a mechanic, hard worker, well respected. Mother Georgene—housewife, used to be a third grade teacher before they had kids, but she's been a full-time homemaker. She's a gem, everybody says. Four kids. The youngest is six, then ten, then thirteen. All good kids, well behaved, not runnin' with the wrong crowd. But here's where it gets sad. They had an eighteen-year-old daughter."

"Had?"

"Yeah. She died about six weeks ago from a heart condition. Really tragic."

Clarence's throat felt scratchy. "Her name was Leesa, wasn't it?"

"Yeah. How'd you know that? You read about it?"

"Was her bedroom on the front right side of the house?"

"Yeah. How'd you know *that*?"

"Check the autopsy report. Talk to somebody about her real cause of death."

"What do you mean *real* cause of death? What are you telling me, Clarence?"

"That's all I can say. Just check into it."

Clarence drove Ty an hour south to the state penitentiary in Salem. They went through high security, including a metal detector, into the visitors room. The guard took an extra long look at Clarence.

They'd arrived half an hour early. Clarence sat quietly, tired of trying to engage Ty in conversation. He hoped this place would make an indelible impression on the boy.

Ellis was only two years older than Clarence. In 1972, the year Clarence graduated from high school, Curtis Mayfield's song "Superfly" blared everywhere among black youth. In the movie of the same name, the main character, Priest, was a slick drug dealer out to make a million dollars so he wouldn't ever have to work for white folk. Priest succeeded, riding off in his shiny El Dorado. To Ellis and thousands of other young black men, Priest became an instant cult hero. Ellis and his friends had been bouncing around like pinballs for years. Now they had a role model. And an opportunity—the drug trade was urban capitalism.

A grieving Obadiah had confronted Ellis time and again. "You're breaking the law, but what's worse you're gonna hurt kids with this dope stuff. Work for an honest livin'. Don't break your mama's heart, boy. Learn you a trade and go into business for yo'self—a good honest business. I'll help you, Son. I'll do anything to help you."

Ellis was smart. He knew all the arguments. He pointed out the Kennedys got their money bootlegging liquor during prohibition, and nobody cared about that because they were white. So why shouldn't a black man get his foot in the door, since everybody was trying to shut him out anyway?

"Your sins will find you out," Obadiah warned him. "When you cross God's boundaries, there's always consequences."

Ellis became the prodigal son. He started by selling reefer, learning all the tricks, such as padding it with oregano to maximize his profits. Soon he graduated to aluminum foil packets of cocaine, with a much greater profit margin. He dabbled in acid, mescaline, Quaaludes, and speed. He dressed like a Priest wannabe, down to the platform shoes and crushed velvet outfits, wide-brimmed hats and maxi coats. He hung a gold coke spoon around his neck. He carried a piece. He cruised around in a red Cadillac. He and his buddies, several of them dealers, did the dap, a handshake greeting consisting of a series of syncopated motions, slapping each other's palms, wrists, and elbows and playing out from there according to the improvisations of the moment. Ellis became all style, no substance.

For years Ellis got by. He spent nine months in jail and came out a stunning figure. He'd pumped iron three hours a day, his muscles bulging so he couldn't button his shirts, his biceps unbelievably thick. He could curl one-hundred-pound dumbbells fifteen times as if they were paperweights.

Three months after he got out, Ellis was a seller again and got taken down on a big bust. Some white kid had died of an overdose, sold to him by a black who fingered Ellis as the original dealer. The white boy's daddy was a politician and put pressure on the DA. Clarence was there when they arrested Ellis. He still remembered the clicks of the handcuffs, the wince on Ellis's face that told him they'd closed on a fold of flesh, the awkward motion of his brother into the backseat of the police car. He remembered the officer's hand on top of his brother's head, pushing him down with an extra shove of contempt. Clarence vowed to himself he'd never get arrested, never go through that humiliation. Ellis was sentenced to ten years for three felonies—selling a controlled substance to a minor, armed robbery, and assault and battery. Still cocky he boasted, "Ten years—man, I could do that standin' on my head."

The lawyer said the ten years would mean he'd be out in three or four easy. But that isn't what happened. In prison, he got into more trouble. He swore to Clarence he was just protecting himself with a shank against a guy who was going to rape him. His time had been extended for that, extended again for attempted escape and for attacking a guard, extended five times. The time had added up. He'd now been in twenty years. He'd lived nearly as many years inside prison as outside.

Clarence thought about how smart Ellis was. For years they'd played chess through the mail. The brother who once joned on Clarence for wearing last year's rags now had worn the same thing every day for nearly twenty years. He hadn't been allowed out even to go to his sister's funeral.

Clarence loved his brother, felt sorry for him. But he also felt sorry for all the kids hooked on the stuff he'd sold them, for all the kids who ended up stealing from their own families to support their addictions.

Suddenly on the other side of the glass came Ellis in his faded greenish-blue prison uniform. His muscles bulged, not quite as thick as Clarence's, but much more defined. He still worked out a few hours every day. What else did he have to do? But his skin was dull, a prison pallor created by a world of fluorescent lights and drab prison colors.

"Hey, bro," Ellis said to Clarence. "Good to see yo' mud-ugly face." He put his big right hand flat on the glass. Clarence matched his even bigger left hand to it on the other side.

"Hey, Ellis. I've missed you, bro. Remember Ty?"

"This my nephew? Hey, Ty. What's happenin'?" Ellis put his hand up to the glass again.

Ty shrugged, looking as awkward as he felt. He put his much smaller hand up on the free side of the glass.

Ellis looked at Clarence, tearing up suddenly. "Wished I coulda been at the funerals, man."

"I know." Clarence had visited Ellis twice since the funerals, and he'd said the same thing.

"Dani and her baby too? It ain't right man. Musta been Bloods. Had to be."

"A witness says it was two Latinos."

"Spics? What they doin' in that hood? Lot of guys in here that knows the streets, what comes down in Portland. I put word out to see if anybody knows anything. Nothin' yet."

"I'm poking around myself," Clarence said. "Let me know if you find anything."

"Count on it, bro."

"You been goin' to the Bible study?" Clarence asked. He'd heard there was a great Prison Fellowship chapter here, a fine chaplain, and some growing Christian inmates. He always made a point of encouraging Ellis to get involved.

"Nah," Ellis said. "Heard all that stuff when we was kids. Didn't do me much good, did it?"

"Maybe you didn't apply it. It's not enough to hear it, you know."

"That's for sure, bro, that's for sure. But I been talkin' with some of the brothas, Nation of Islam, you know? Harley told me to look for 'em, said they're in every prison, even in Oregon. He's right. These guys are clean. Tough. And they don't take no crud. They tell it like it is. Talk about bein' black and proud, not lettin' whitey push us around. Massa, that's what they call these white prison guards totin' around their shotguns."

Ellis went off on a familiar litany, a scenario in which he was just a political prisoner rather than a hood who robbed a store, nearly killed a man, and wasted who knows how many kids through drugs.

You sold the dope, you robbed the store, you pulled the trigger, you stabbed the guy in the pen. White man didn't do that. It was you.

"Malcolm was a prisoner, just like I am. And he made something of his life. Maybe I can too."

Clarence thought about Malcolm X. Well, his faith in Allah and the moral standards of Islam had certainly redirected his life. But Clarence reflected on the power of the cross to not just change you from the outside in, but the inside out. He wanted that for his brother. Yet he felt guilty that these days he seemed to be drawing on it so little himself.

Clarence looked in his brother's eyes and saw the pain, the vacancy, the regrets, the hopelessness. He'd heard of prisons where they learned skills, where they could work their time off, subtract days from their sentences through hard work and restitution, get ready for the outside world. As far as he knew, Ellis had experienced none of that here. The state pen was a place to sit and stare and do nothing but think of yourself and loathe yourself and others and learn criminal skills to bring back to the outside world and hustle and hang with gangsters and look at pornography and watch shoot 'em up videos and pump iron to get ready to fight the pigs when you got out and be angry and lonely and think about knifing somebody or cutting your own wrists to get out of this hell.

"Ellis, Tyrone's been hanging with some gangbangers. He's been doin' some dope. Anything you want to say to him?"

Ellis looked at Ty long and hard, his face first soft, then stern. "How old you now, Ty?"

"Fourteen."

"Two years younger than I was when I got started. All I can tell you is, get clean while you can. I told myself I was gonna get clean, but I never did. You can be somebody. I got a stack of letters in my cell, letters from yo' mama. She used to brag about your grades, what a good boy you was. Don't throw it away. That's what I did. And now look at me. I haven't been out there since before you was born, six years before. Life here is hell. No privacy, always noisy, always television and radio. Threats and fights and hits. Guys drop their soap in the shower and they don't dare bend to pick it up. It's no life. Whatever you do, little bro, stop now."

Even as he said it, Ellis saw in Ty's eyes what fifteen years ago he'd seen in all the eyes around him, including those that looked back from the mirror. But he was determined to get through anyway.

"They talk big time, like 'three hots and a cot man, that ain't so bad.' But you get in here and they forget about you, just like I forgot about my buddies in jail, my stickman Big Freeze and my homie Trig. The letters come at first—you get a few visits from yo' girlfriend till she finds someone who can touch her. But except for Daddy and Clarence and Harley and yo' mama, nobody stay in touch. I had a big rep, means nothin' here. You mess up bad and get the double digits, you lose hope, boy, you lose hope. You do time alone, nobody there to help you. You think they yo' friends, but they ghost on you. You get in trouble inside, they put you in solitary. I went three weeks not seein' a human face. They take the staples out of magazines so you can't use them as weapons. Every few years you dress up like a choirboy, spit shine and lotion yourself down, button yo' top button, and try to convince that parole board you're ready for the outside. And then you watch 'em look at the papers, the fights you've had and the drugs you've traded for and the time you popped a guard, and they close those folders, and you know they ain't gonna forgive your sins, no way. Nobody gonna give you another chance."

He stared straight through Ty, as if trying to find in him the one thing he might successfully hook on to. "When you see the sunshine out there, havin' to stay in here, it's like sittin' on the electric chair at low voltage, dyin' a little every day. I see the red in yo' eyes, boy. I know you been doin' the coke. Not too long though, huh? You not a cluckhead yet, but you be headed there. You listen to me, little bro, hear me now?"

"Yeah, I hear you, Uncle Ellis."

"You tell da brothas in da hood, I'd rather be the geekiest guy on the street than the coolest sucker in prison. I'd rather be fryin' the Big Macs any day than heatin' up the cocaine, 'cause that's what gets you here. Some folks say at least the black man rules in prison. Well, he don't. No way. We don't hold the keys. We don't carry the guns. We don't set the rules. It's all a lie. You know how long it's been since I seen the sky, boy? You know what it's like to never see the stars for twenty years? You know what it's like to live in a world without women? Ain't natural. No mamas, no aunts, no sisters, no girlfriends, no wives. Most the guys here dealt drugs and robbed stores to impress the babes. Well, there's no babes here. And guys start losin' their manhood, and if you do, they'll break you down, they'll flip you sure as—"

Clarence shot Ellis a don't-get-into-the-details look.

"Well, anyways, little bro, it ain't normal. It ain't a good scene." He hesitated. "Make yo' mama proud of you, boy. Make me proud of you." The tears flowed freely now down the rough leather-brown face. "Don't end up here spendin' every day like I do, wishin' I would have made *my* mama proud."

The guard put his hand on Ellis's shoulder and said "Time's up." Before Ellis stood up, he said to Clarence, "See you, bro." He put his hand back on the thick glass, and Clarence matched it, wishing he could touch his brother's skin, even for a moment.

Ellis looked at Ty one last time. "Stay outta dat chalk circle, little bro. 'Cause if you run wid the bangers, chalk circle or this place is all you gots to look forward to."

CHAPTER

27

"Sure do wish Tyrone and Jonah was comin' with us to the ball game," Obadiah said to Clarence as they packed the car Saturday morning.

"Ty wasn't interested. And Jonah's in soccer all day. Maybe next time."

They drove to Ollie's, where two passengers got in the back. "You're gonna love these seats," Clarence bragged to his guests. "Front row, halfway between third and home. Perfect. There's some payoff to all those years as a sportswriter."

Jake had called and said Carly wasn't feeling well, she and Janet needed him, so he had to cancel. When Ollie heard it, he asked Clarence if Manny could go in Jake's place. Clarence had reluctantly agreed, and now Manny sat in the back next to Ollie. Obadiah occupied the passenger seat beside Clarence, absentmindedly humming spirituals under his breath.

"We've got some things on the case, Clarence," Ollie said, as they pulled onto I-5 north. "Want to talk now or later?" Ollie looked at Obadiah, not sure how it might affect him.

"Now's fine. What's up?"

"Well, turns out Leesa Fletcher died from a cocaine overdose. But you knew that, didn't you? How?"

"Confidential source."

"I reread the *Trib* articles," Ollie said. "All they mentioned was congenital heart defect. Proves you can't trust newspapers. I've done some calling around. I talked to Jay Fielding, the principal at Jefferson, and a couple of other people who knew her well. Everybody swears Leesa wasn't a user."

"So what are you thinking?" Clarence asked.

"One, I think she was the original target. Two, I think we've got another murder. They tried the drive by and blew it. They couldn't do that one again, so somebody gave her bad crack."

"Or good crack, just too much of it," Manny said. "If they forced it on her, it wouldn't be crack, probably an injection of cocaine and water. It's a lot easier to inject someone than try to make them inhale crack at the right moment. Either way it shows up as cocaine in the bloodstream."

"Was there a needle mark?" Clarence asked.

"Several in the left arm, but she took allergy shots," Manny said. "Nothing definitive."

"Where does this leave us?"

"Years ago I investigated a counterfeiting operation," Ollie said. "I learned a bad counterfeiter always circulates these crisp new bills fresh off the press. People look them over real close and often they figure out they're counterfeit. But a good counterfeiter doesn't do that. He soaks his new bills in a bottle of crème de menthe and some india ink, then dries them with an electric fan. Nobody takes a close look because they see these bills that look well-circulated. That way they blend in. The crime goes unnoticed."

"Your point?" Clarence asked, knowing Ollie well enough by now to suspect there was one.

"Suppose the gang thing was a counterfeit, a cover for something else. I mean, it may have been bangers who pulled the trigger, but what if someone hired them, someone who figured we wouldn't take a good look at it because gang crime is too common. The best cover is the one that looks most like something else, the one least likely to be thoroughly investigated over the long haul. Let's face it, when gang stuff isn't solved immediately, it tends to get buried under the avalanche. They weren't counting on our persistence. Or yours," he added, looking at Clarence.

"I'm still working on a profile of the Fletcher family," Manny said. "Should finish it up Monday."

"Anything you can tell me now?" Clarence asked.

"No. I need to put it all together first," Manny said—rather stiffly, Clarence thought.

"Mariners and Yankees," Ollie said. "Well, I'm pumped. I haven't had a day off in three weeks. And I haven't gone to a baseball game since I was a kid."

"Where'd you grow up, Mister Detective?" Obadiah asked.

"Milwaukee. I was a Braves fan. Back then everybody talked about Mays and Mantle, but Hank Aaron just kept hitting those balls out of the park. Got his autograph one day. Biggest day of my life."

"You knew him, didn't you, Dad?" Clarence asked.

"Knew who?" Ollie asked. "Hank Aaron? No way!"

"Yessuh, I knowed the Hammer. He come into the league as a rookie my last season."

"You played pro ball? The majors?" Manny asked.

"It was pro ball, all right," Obadiah said, voice animated. "But not the majors. Not what the record books call the majors anyway. It was the Negro League. Shadow ball, folks called it. Henry Aaron spent his first year with us. So did Willie Mays."

"You knew Willie Mays?" Ollie asked, slackjawed.

"Sho 'nuf. I introduced Willie to Mama's pork rib sauce, and we was friends from then on." Obadiah laughed like a little boy.

"What was the Negro League like?" Ollie asked. Both he and Manny leaned forward to hear the old man's soft voice. Clarence could see Obadiah's eyes sparkle. He had an audience.

"We was barnstormers. Played three games a day, travelin' on our bus. Couldn't stay in most hotels. Wrong color. But we was so tired we didn't have energy to go where we wasn't wanted. Lots of peoples come to see us. In the big cities it was mostly coloreds. The whites had their Major Leagues, but lots of white folks come to see us too. Out in the sticks everybody came, more whites than blacks. We was the only pro teams come to play there. They cheered us and wrote us up. Still got some o' them old newspaper clippings. Played every city. They'd hitch up the team to come see us. If they didn't have a buggy, they'd ride two to a mule. If they couldn't find a mule, they'd ride an armadillo."

Ollie laughed. Daddy was just gettin' warmed up, Clarence knew.

"So who'd you play with?" Ollie asked. "I want some names. And some stories."

"Well, in those days we changed teams a lot, so half the peoples I played against I ended up playin' with, somewhere along the line. One year I'd be with the Kansas City Monarchs or the Indianapolis Clowns, next year the Birmingham Black Barons. You want names? How about Cool Papa Bell?"

The name drew a blank with Ollie and Manny both.

"Never seen a man so fast as Papa, and I seen 'em all, including Cobb. Only man who could hit himself with his own line drive. I watched Papa Bell run from first to third on a bunt, maybe a dozen times. They'd throw the ball to second thinkin' they'd catch him, but he was already headed toward third. The second baseman throws to third, and Cool Papa Bell's already standin' on the base, brushin' off from his slide. He always slid, that way he never had to decide whether it was necessary. One game I saw him hit three inside the park homers."

"No joke?" Manny asked.

"The Lord is my witness. His roommate swore Cool Papa Bell could flip off the light switch and be in bed before the room got dark."

Everybody laughed again, revving up Obadiah's engines.

"You want pitchers? Early on I played with Smoky Joe Williams. Six foot five, and in those days nobody was six five. Whoa, boy, um um. Smoky Joe had a cannon. He threw so hard we had to change catchers two or three times a game. They's hands would swell up the size of a melon." Obadiah flexed his big loose-skinned left hand as if it were throbbing. "When ol' Smoky joined our team, he was already a legend. I was just a rookie first baseman, just sittin' against a fence, no dugouts for us, usually. I hears one of our catchers whinin' about his achin' hand. I thinks, with all that padding in his glove, he has to be puttin' on. So I says, 'Lets me catch Smoky an inning or two.' In those days we always knew a couple of positions just in case. Anyways, the catcher, he's lookin' at me like I was crazy and hands me the mitt.

"First I calls Smoky a curveball and it curves all right, but it was the speed of a fastball and it really smarted. I thought, hey I'm not gonna call him a fastball. I was young, but hit me wid a two-by-four and I don't ask you to come back and take a swing at me with a fence post! So I calls another curve, and he shakes me off. I calls a four-day creeper, and he shakes me off. I went through every pitch known to God's angels, and finally I gives up and calls a fastball and Smoky just smiles, kind of like the dentist before he drills your teeth. Before I saw him wind up, that ball was in my glove. I heard thunder before I saw lightning. I don't know how I caught it. Never saw it. I screamed and threw off the mitt, and the umpire and the batter laughed their fool heads off. Ol' Smoky laughed so hard he was layin' on the mound poundin' the dirt. That was the end of me catchin' Smoky Joe."

Obadiah shook his head, chuckling from deep inside. Then he looked back at Ollie. "I faced Christy Matthewson and most the great white pitchers. Even young Warren Spahn. But none of them threw like Smoky Joe Williams."

"You hit against Spahn?" Ollie asked. "But how did you play against him and Matthewson and Cobb if you weren't in the majors?"

"We'd play exhibition games. Sometimes we'd go down to Cuba and play a long series against a Major League All-Star team. I remembers Ty Cobb's Detroit Tigers and Pop Lloyd's Havana Reds played against each other in a five-game series. Cobb batted .370; Pop hit an even .500. Cobb was the best base-stealer in the majors, and he bragged he was gonna 'steal those darkies blind.' Well, those darkies caught him every single time he tried. Cobb was an ol' sourpuss. You could put his face on a buffalo nickel and nobody'd notice the difference. They used to say, 'Nothin's wrong with Cobb that couldn't be fixed by hittin' him upside the head with a skillet.' After the last game in Cuba, Cobb announced he'd never play against blacks again. Well, we never blamed him for that. Cobb was ugly, but he weren't stupid!"

Now Manny joined in the chuckles. Clarence hadn't heard most of these stories for years. The pride in his chest showed on his face.

"You want a slugger? Josh Gibson. Hit more five-hundred-foot home runs than Ruth ever did. Only man ever to hit a ball clean out of Yankee Stadium. One season Josh hit seventy-five home runs."

"So how come I've never heard of him?" Manny asked.

"Well," Obadiah shrugged, "he was colored. I reckon it's that simple. Nobody wanted to think a black man was as good as Ruth. But he was. Except Ruth struck out 110 or 120 times a year. Josh, maybe fifty. If Josh had been allowed in white ball, he would have had Ruth's home run record. When Hammerin' Hank went for the record, it would have been held by a black man. And Josh would have been so far ahead of Ruth, even Hank like to never catch him."

"If this Gibson guy was playin' in the majors today, what do you think he'd hit?" Manny asked.

"Oh," Obadiah paused, "maybe .280, with thirty home runs."

"That all?"

"Well, you has to understand," Obadiah said, "he'd be over eighty years old."

Ollie convulsed with laughter, slapping Manny on the leg.

"They tried a lot of things to get us coloreds in the majors. They'd paint a black man's face light and make up the craziest stories. One team was called the Cuban Giants. They was mostly black waiters from a Brooklyn Hotel. Used to speak gibberish to each other on the field so people would think they was Cuban. Ol' John McGraw tried to sneak Charlie Grant onto the Baltimore Orioles by claiming Grant was a Cherokee named Chief Tokahoma. But they figured it out. White people do catch on after a while!" Obadiah grinned.

"McGraw went on to manage the New York Giants. One of the best pitchers in baseball was a colored named Rube Foster. The size of a barn, old Rube, black as coal, black as Clarence and me. Rube musta been twenty years older than me, and he was runnin' the colored league when I was playin'. McGraw hired Rube to teach Christy Matthewson how to pitch a screwball. That's the closest Rube got to the majors. If they'd let him in, I guarantee you woulda heard his name."

"Was Gibson the best you ever played with?" Ollie asked.

"No, Josh was great." Obadiah's eyes sparkled and Clarence knew what was coming next. "But one man was the greatest there's ever been." He paused, savoring the moment.

"Satchel." Clarence said. Obadiah nodded vigorously.

"Satchel Paige?" Ollie said, voice cracking. "You played with Satchel Paige?"

"I's not just black as coal," Obadiah said, "I's *old* as coal! Yeah, I played with Satch on two different teams, and I played against him more than I cares to remember. Satchel was older, but he was really somethin'. He was an inch shorter than Smoky Joe, but he towered over everybody else. And he was skinny—all arms and legs. No man never pitched like Satchel. He'd go into a game sayin' he'd strike out the first nine men he faced. And usually he did. First baseman didn't touch the ball for three innings. We used to clown around. Once we put a bat boy out on first base for two innings 'cause we knew he wouldn't have to do anything. Another time all us infielders sat down around second base and played poker till somebody finally got wood on the ball. It was the fourth inning. When I was with the Clowns, the catcher would bring out a rocking chair and sit in it. Yessuh, we knowed how to has fun!"

"I've read about Satchel Paige," Manny said. "And I saw his picture in the Hall of Fame in Cooperstown."

"You been there? Always wanted to go," Obadiah said. "Always thought I'd go with my son the sportswriter. Maybe someday we'll make it there still, hey Son?"

No way you'll ever see it now, Daddy. Time isn't on your side anymore.

"Ol' Satchel, he could pitch a greasy pork chop past a hungry coyote. He'd throw a no-hitter and be grumpy about it 'cause too many batters grounded out!" Obadiah's eyes glazed off to bygone days, his memory of the distant past incredibly sharp. "A showman, Satchel was. Used to call in the outfielders and have 'em sit on the bench. Then he'd finish the inning with just the infield—sometimes sat down the infield too. You know what that does to a batter to have a pitcher so sure he's got your number he sits his whole team on the bench? Well, I know. 'Cause when I was playin' in Kansas City and Satchel was with the Pittsburgh Crawfords, he did it to me. Big ol' smile on his face. I was hittin' .320 that year, so I wasn't exactly mulch on the flowers. But ol' Satch, he calls in the whole team. And it takes 'im three pitches to get me. Got me on an outside fastball, a four-day creeper, and a Satchel pitch."

"What's a Satchel pitch?" Ollie asked.

Obadiah shook his head and laughed. "Can't tell you to this day. Never seen another pitch like it. Called it a bat dodger, Rube did. That ball did things no ball is entitled to do. You know, after the war ol' Satchel finally got to pitch in the majors. He was somethin' like forty-five years old by then, though he claimed to be younger. Oldest rookie there ever was. Pitched for the Cleveland Indians. Chosen Rookie of the Year, can you imagine? Course he'd lost most his stuff by then. Still had enough that he only lost one game that season, though."

"Forty-five and he lost *one* game?" Manny asked.

"Yeah, he was 6 and 1. He felt terrible bad about that one loss too," Obadiah chuckled. "We changed baseball, you know. Changed the majors even though they didn't let us in."

"How do you mean?" Manny asked.

"Buntin' and slidin' and base-stealin'. They all come out of the Negro Leagues. And sign stealin', that was perfected by Judy Johnson. Called him Mr. Sunshine 'cause he was always so happy. Ol' Judy, he'd watch the other team's hand signals a few innings and break the code. Then he'd whistle his own coded message to let us know what was gonna happen next. The Pittsburgh Crawfords, now that was a team. One of the best I played on. Gus Greenlee owned the Crawfords. He was a black businessman. Most stadiums wouldn't let coloreds use the locker rooms. Ol' Gus, he asked 'em, 'What you afraid coloreds gonna do in those urinals that white men aren't doin' already?' I gots me a Crawford team picture in my room."

"No kiddin'? I'd love to see it," Ollie said.

"Well, come on over and take a gander, Mr. Detective. You too, Mr. Manny. No charge. Got some other stuff you might like to see. By the way, ol' Gus decided to build his own stadium so we coloreds could be at home. First stadium ever built for a black team. Then he bought us a topflight bus. Got a picture of that too."

"You seem like such an even-tempered guy, Mr. Abernathy," Ollie said. Clarence suspected he might be contrasting father and son. "Did you ever get mad at anybody when you played ball?"

"Well, one time I was battin', and it was a full count. The ball was way low and outside, so I drops the bat and trots off to first for the walk. Then behind me I hears the umpire call, 'Strike three, you're outta there.'"

"What did you do?" Ollie asked.

"Well now," Obadiah said, "I went right up to that umpire and looked him straight in the eye. Then I proceeded to thank him sincerely for doin' such a difficult and thankless job." He held a straight face, but when he finally broke out into a grin, Ollie and Manny laughed out loud.

"We're here, gentlemen," Clarence said, pulling into the stadium parking lot.

"Already?" Ollie sounded disappointed. The three hours had flown by.

"Mr. Abernathy, did you know Jackie Robinson?"

"Yessuh, I knowed Jackie. Knowed him well."

They got out of the car, Obadiah proudly putting on his Mariners cap Jonah got him last Christmas. Ollie and Manny walked on each side of Obadiah as if they were his escorts.

"Tell us about Jackie," Ollie said.

"Got to knows him three years 'fore I left baseball. Jackie was the grandson of a slave. See, those days, some of our parents was born slaves, like mine was, and nearly all our grandparents was slaves. Anyways, Jackie growed up in an all-white neighborhood in Pasadena. The white kids threw rocks at the Robinson boys until Jackie and his brothers said enough of this and threw rocks back at 'em. That stopped it real quick 'cause them Robinson boys, they knowed how to throw! Then he went to college and he was a star in everything—football, basketball, track, baseball. Set a national record in long jump. Then he went to the war. One good thing comin' outta that war was the signs coloreds held up at the baseball stadiums. They said, 'If we can stop bullets, why not balls?'"

Obadiah was breathing hard, and Clarence was about to suggest he stop talking till they got inside, but he didn't want to take away his father's moment in the sun.

"After the war, Jackie come straight to the Kansas City Monarchs, where I was playin'. I roomed with him a couple of months. He'd last been stationed in Texas. A military bus driver told him to sit in the back of the bus. He refused. They told him they'd arrest him. He still refused. He was court-martialed, but they found him innocent. He got an honorable discharge and come to the Monarchs. Mr. Branch Rickey saw him there. He was lookin' for the right man to be the first colored in the majors. The time was right, and Jackie was right."

As they walked slowly through the parking lot, Ollie asked, "You have any idea what it was like for Jackie Robinson?"

"At first the fans would yell, 'Nigger' and 'Go back to the cotton fields.' It hurt Jackie bad. Almost had a breakdown, he told me later. Once some fans started in on Jackie, and ol' Pee Wee Reese come over and put his arm around Jackie's shoulder and looked at the crowd. Pee Wee was a favorite, and most of the fans shut their mouths. See, there was a lot of good whites in baseball. Pee Wee was one of 'em. Now, when the Dodgers come to Cincinnati, coloreds would pile into a train in Norfolk, Virginia, six hundred miles away, just to see Jackie play. They called that train the Jackie Robinson special, and they say colored folk never had so much fun as on that train. Jackie made us all proud."

The sparkling eyes glistened with moisture. Obadiah stopped walking to wipe his brow. Clarence put his arm around his daddy's waist.

"Mr. Rickey told Jackie he had to agree for two years not to talk back at all the namecallin'. He kept his word. But after two years he started demandin' to stay in the same hotel as the white players, and it worked. Jackie and Roy Campanella, Ernie Banks, Aaron and Mays and Curt Flood. It wasn't easy for any of them. Campy had a hard time 'cause the catcher calls the pitches and that meant white pitchers was takin' directions from a black man. That didn't sit well with some of 'em. Curt Flood once said, 'I'm glad God made my skin black, but I wish he'd made it thicker.'"

"You know," Ollie said, "I was in high school rooting for Hank Aaron to break Babe Ruth's home run record. He ended the season with 713, one short of Ruth. Everybody knew he'd break it easy next season. I thought, he must be feelin' great. Then years later I saw an interview with Aaron. He talked about how horrible it was. About the hate mail, people calling him names and threatening to kill him. I never knew. I never understood."

Obadiah's eyes looked like a hound dog's. "I phoned Henry once a year in them days. He told me all about it. Letters would start, 'Dear Nigger Scum.' They'd say, 'You're an animal, not a human being,' and 'The only good nigger is a dead nigger.' All of us who'd been called every name in the book, we knowed a lot of white folk wouldn't tolerate Babe Ruth being toppled by a colored. It was so bad the FBI started reading his mail before Henry did. I remember sayin' to my Ruby, 'I don't think Henry will live through the summer.' I really didn't think he would. Sure glad he did. Sure glad he did."

They showed their tickets to the gatekeeper and slowly walked in, Obadiah's pace restraining the rest. "But Henry came through. Ended up all-time leader in homers, RBIs, *and* total bases. One of the greatest ball players that ever lived. Still say ol' Satchel was the best, though."

They made their way to their seats, Obadiah huffing and puffing. Clarence started to sit by his dad, but Manny and Ollie both positioned themselves to sit by the old man. They were about an hour early.

"Look at this stadium, will you now?" Obadiah said. "Never seen nothin' so big. But baseball's still baseball, I reckon. We used to joke playin' baseball was the only time a black man could wave a stick at a white man and get away with it." He laughed. "I almost made the big leagues. Born fifteen or twenty years too soon, that's all. But that's all right. Shadow ball suited me fine."

"Why'd they call it shadow ball?" Manny asked.

"Well, let me set it up for you, Mr. Detective," Obadiah said, tilting his baseball cap to the side and putting on his announcer's voice. "The Indianapolis Clowns take the field for warm-ups. The hard throw from first snaps back the second baseman's glove. He hurls the ball to third, for a quick peg back to the first baseman who dives to catch it, rolls a somersault, and heaves it to the catcher. He tosses it back gently to the pitcher, Satchel Paige, who watches for the catcher's signal, then winds up and throws the curveball." Obadiah flailed his arms. "The batter swings and hits. The second baseman leaps to his left, throws to first. The low throw kicks up dirt just before the first baseman catches it. The umpire calls him out. The crowd roars."

They all laughed at Obadiah's antics.

"But only those sittin' real close understand what's goin' on," Obadiah whispered. "See, there's no ball on the field. It's all an act. It's shadow ball."

"No kidding?" Ollie asked.

"Sometimes we'd play a couple innings that way," Obadiah said. "The fans way up in the stands could never tell. The ones close enough to see there was no ball were just smilin' and laughin' along with us. That was shadow ball. The name stuck, I guess, maybe 'cause we was all dark as shadows."

The warm-ups finished, and someone sang the national anthem. Obadiah stood straight and tall, gazing at the flag with his hand and his baseball cap on his heart. The umpire called "Play ball," and Clarence saw the moisture in the old man's eyes.

Why didn't I ever carve out the time to take him to Cooperstown?

Clarence finally asked Ollie and Manny to stop asking his father questions so they could all watch the game. It went quickly, punctuated with Obadiah's stories. The Mariners were up 4-3 at the seventh-inning stretch. Ollie escorted Obadiah to a bathroom, leaving Clarence and Manny in the seats. After two minutes of silence and pretending to read the program, Manny said to Clarence, "You're lucky to have a father like that. I wish I did."

If you'd had a father like mine, it would've made you a nigger.

Clarence caught himself, feeling guilty. "Thanks, Manny."

The Mariners won 6-5 in the tenth inning. Obadiah's entourage went out into the parking lot. This time Clarence asked Ollie and Manny to let Daddy get to the car before extracting any more stories from him.

As Clarence pulled out into the darkness for the three hour drive home, it brought back cozy memories of long drives after dark with his daddy—only in those days it was Daddy doing the driving. He'd always felt secure with his father there. As long as Daddy was close by, everything in the universe would be all right. In a strange sort of way, he felt that tonight.

Before Ollie and Manny could start quizzing him again, the old man turned to the backseat and said, "Tell me about yo'self, Detective Manny."

"Well, I grew up in Santa Fe. Most of the town was Mexican. Everybody belonged to a gang."

"Did you?"

"Yeah. Those were the days of switchblades, bicycle chains, and zip guns, mostly."

"Who'd you fight?"

"Black gangs and white gangs."

"What got you out of the gangs, Mister Manny?"

"One day I came home and my mama asked me, 'You gonna kill all the blacks and whites in Santa Fe? Then what?' She told me the real revolutionaries use ideas and words. She said I should get out of the gangs and concentrate on my studies, and that way I could really do something to fight injustice."

"A smart woman, your mama. And you followed her advice?"

"Yeah."

"You decide then to become a policeman?"

"I saw cops always hounding my family. I wanted justice. So I thought, what better way than be a cop myself? You can't do much from the outside. I thought maybe I could do something from the inside."

"What was your daddy like?" Obadiah asked.

"He was a veterano. He still hung around the gangs, even when I was growing up. Finally one day he got beat up and run over. Almost died. Wasn't able to walk again. Passed away five years later, when I was thirteen. Never found out who did it to him. Blacks, I think. Maybe whites. Not sure. Both of them used to gang up on my raza."

"Don't really matter, does it?" Obadiah asked.

"What do you mean?"

"The color of the hoodlums that beat him. Good matters. Bad matters. Color don't matter."

"Before they crippled him," Manny said, "my dad always told me he'd take me fishin', but he never did." Clarence looked in the rearview mirror. He saw Manny's hand on his face.

"My daddy took me fishin' all the time," Obadiah said. "Even if the fish lost their enthusiasm by ten o'clock, we wouldn't lose ours till midafternoon. Clarence don't has much time for fishin' no more. If you ever needs a fishin' partner, Mr. Manny, and you ain't in too big a hurry, this ol' man would love to tag along with you."

Manny stared at Obadiah. "Thanks."

As they approached Vancouver, still ten miles north of Portland, Clarence saw the cherry top spinning behind him and pulled over.

"I wasn't speeding, was I?"

"I'd give you 69 in a 65, but not worth pulling you over," Ollie said from the back. "Okay, Clarence, when the cop comes up, just don't look at the speedometer."

"Why?"

"You pull people over for speeding—I did it for years—and they sit and stare at the speedometer, which is pretty dumb since it always says zero miles per hour. Surprise this cop. Don't look at your speedometer. Maybe it'll throw him off."

Clarence watched in his side mirror as the officer approached. "I need to see your license, registration, and insurance papers," the gruff voice said. The officer pointed in his flashlight, looking through the car at the other occupants. Of the four, only the old man appeared pleasant.

"Stay right here," he said. While they waited, another patrol car pulled up behind the first.

"He called for backup," Manny said. "Can you believe it? He actually called for backup."

The original officer returned and said to Clarence, "Can I check your trunk please?"

"Why do you want to check his trunk?" Manny asked.

"I'm talking to the driver, not you."

"Unless you've got a good reason for asking, he's not opening the trunk," Ollie said.

The officer's eyes shot back at Ollie, and he pointed his flashlight at him. "We've had a lot of drugs and robberies between Seattle and Portland. Just checking."

"You can't detain a man," Manny said, "and call in a backup and check his trunk just because he's going four miles over the speed limit."

"Well, now, what are you?" The officer stared coldly. "Some kind of attorney for wetbacks or something?"

"Watch your language, officer," Ollie said, pushing Manny back in his seat. "Don't be calling my friend an attorney. We're cops. He's my partner."

Ollie reached to his back pocket to pull out his wallet, and the officer's hand moved instantly to his holster. Ollie slowed down his hand, clearly showing the wallet and removing his police ID, passing it behind Clarence's neck to the officer.

"Detective, huh?" the officer said. "Well, Detective Chandler, I'll leave you to detective work and you leave me to highway patrol. How's that? Stay right here. I'll be back."

The officer went to consult with the backup cops. After ten minutes, he came back and returned Clarence's license and papers.

"I'm not going to get you on the speeding this time. Just be more careful. All of you, *have a nice day now*, all right?" He aimed his sarcastic words to the backseat in particular.

As they drove off, Ollie said, "In all the times I've been pulled over, and there's been a fair number, I've never once seen such a rude jerk of a police officer."

"How often have you ridden in a car driven by a black man?" Clarence asked.

"Other than with my black partner in a cop car, not very often," Ollie admitted.

"I get the same thing when I'm with my Hispanic friends," Manny said.

"It could've been a lot worse, gents." Obadiah sounded eager to look on the bright side. "In the ol' days, dem boys might've just taken us out and lynched us."

———————

"I'm worried about Ty," Geneva said to Clarence Sunday evening. "He still hasn't come home. I told him to be back before dark."

Clarence looked at his watch—8:30 P.M. "You know how he forgets about the time. Maybe I'll have to ground him again. But don't worry. He'll be okay." Clarence wished he believed it.

"You had a message on the machine from some girl named Gracie. I rewound it."

"Gracie?" Clarence didn't know why he felt guilty.

"Yeah. Why'd you give her our home phone? Isn't that why it's always been unlisted? And why we gave up Dani's number for a new unlisted?"

"She couldn't call during the day. And she goes from school to work."

"No pay phones at school? No lunch? No breaks at work?"

"Come on, Geneva. What did she say?"

"Said she wanted you to call her. Left her phone number. What's this about?"

"I hope it's about Dani. I'll explain later."

He went to the phone in their bedroom, shut the door, and dialed the number. A male voice answered the phone—her father, Clarence assumed.

"Yes, may I speak to Gracie please? This is…Clarence. A friend of hers." Identifying himself as a *Trib* reporter might set off some alarms.

"Gracie," the gruff voice yelled, "it's one of your bum boyfriends. Says his name's Clarence."

"Hello, Clarence?" Gracie said. "Look, I asked around, you know, like I said I would. At first there was like nothing, but then this guy met me for a break over at the mall. We had a burger and fries. And a chocolate shake."

I don't care if you ate deep-fried mouse droppings, girl, what did he say?

"Anyway, he knows something about what happened that night. I can't really talk to you now. My parents don't want me on the phone. I should really tell you in person."

"Can you just give me a quick summary?"

"No, I really can't."

"Okay. Can you meet me at the *Trib* tomorrow?"

"No. I don't have a car."

"All right. I'll come over to the school. I'll ask Mr. Fielding if we can use a room again."

"No way. This guy goes to my school. If he saw me like talking to you, I could be in big trouble. Look, maybe this isn't a very good idea. Let's just forget it."

"No. Wait, it'll work. Where can we meet?"

"Well, my uncle owns a restaurant just six blocks from Lloyd Center, on Grand and Estep, just before it merges with MLK. It's called *Miller's*. When I got in trouble once and had to meet with a social worker, he let me use it. I can walk over there after work. He's got an office in the back he'll let us use. I'll call him to make sure. But if you don't hear back from me, he'll be expecting you. I'm off at 6:00 so I can be there by 6:15."

"Are you sure we can't meet at the *Trib* or your school?"

"No way. I'll take some risk for you, but this is plenty. Should we just forget it?"

"No. I'll be there 6:15 tomorrow."

He got off the phone and walked into the living room.

"What's up?" Geneva asked.

"Nothing."

"What did she say?"

"Nothing much. I'm going to talk with her more later."

Before Geneva could ask when, he'd walked into his office and closed the door. He worked for over an hour, then came to bed. It was 10:30 and still no word from Ty. Geneva was buried in a book and didn't even look up when he came into the room.

Her inattention got his attention. He craned his neck over to kiss those warm and inviting lips, only to discover they'd turned cold and immovable. She was as kissable as jagged granite.

The phone rang. Clarence grabbed the bedroom extension, tensing at the late call.

"Mr. Abernathy? This Mr. Kim, from store?"

"Yes?"

"I so sorry to call you this late, but just close up my store. This about Tyrone, your nephew?"

"Yes?"

"I see him shoplifting from my store yesterday afternoon. I try to talk to him, but he run out. Meant to call you yesterday, but got busy. Do not want to call police. But if happens again..."

"I understand. What did he take?"

"Pop, candy bars, magazine, beer."

"All right. Let me check into it. I'll get back to you."

Clarence hoped it was a case of Asians who couldn't tell one black boy from another. He went into Ty's bedroom. He searched his closet and drawers. Nothing unusual. Then he crawled down flat on the floor and reached way back under the bed. He found three candy wrappers and two unopened bottles of beer.

Clarence sat up and sighed, wanting Ty to come home soon, but also dreading it. It's almost eleven o'clock and he was supposed to be home by dark. And he's shoplifting now? What will it take to teach that boy his choices have consequences?

CHAPTER

28

Lately I've been talking to boys on the street and asking them what they plan to do with their lives. Most of them aren't thinking beyond age eighteen. Of those who do have plans, nearly half told me they're going to be pro athletes, most of them basketball players.

Here's the dream-shattering truth. Each year 300,000 kids play basketball. About a thousand of those get college scholarships. At the end of their four years in college, 57 of those are drafted by the NBA. Of those, 27 make an NBA team. Of those who make it, the average stay in the league is three years.

Even among those who do make the pros, many end up failing miserably in life. One of the great athletes of this century was Joe Louis, heavyweight champion of the world. He ended up penniless, a doorman at Caesar's Palace in Las Vegas. J. R. Richard was one of baseball's dominant pitchers in the seventies. In 1993 he was found homeless under a freeway.

The good news is, if you develop a strong character and a solid work ethic and get a good education, you can succeed in whatever you do. I used a football scholarship to help get me through college. Use sports, but don't ever let sports use you. Go to school, do your best, get your degree. Don't ever skip your homework to shoot hoops. Skip hoops to do your homework.

After pushing the key to send his column to Winston, Clarence went down to the newspaper morgue and dug up the stories related to Leesa Fletcher. He read the account of her funeral, juxtaposed with a picture of her grieving father—embraced by a teary-eyed Councilman Norcoast.

Clarence left the *Trib*, headed east on the Morrison bridge, turned north, and exited toward MLK. He'd stayed late at the office, and his thoughts now focused on how he should deal with Ty, who hadn't gotten home last night until after midnight and never called to say where he was. Clarence had confronted him on that and the shoplifting, which he denied at first, then finally admitted in the face of the evidence. Clarence had taken him to the Kims' store this morning before school, where under his uncle's eye, he apologized and promised he'd never do it again. Clarence told him they'd need to have a long talk tonight about the consequences. Geneva would be gone all evening at a community bazaar, which was just as well, since Clarence thought she tended to go too easy on Ty.

The drive home was dark and wet. When he was a half mile from Jackson Street, Clarence pulled up at a stoplight next to a lowriding gold Impala. He looked over and saw the driver, a young male Latino. In the passenger seat sat another Latino, also a young male. Clarence's pulse raced. When the light turned green, he changed lanes to follow them. He slipped open his briefcase, grabbed a pen, and scratched down their license number on a file folder: Oregon plates, TAH 755. He stayed behind them until they pulled abruptly into an ARCO station.

Driver and passenger both got out of the car as the attendant put the pump nozzle into their gas tank. Clarence approached them. "You guys pay a visit to 920 Northeast Jackson Street around midnight back on September 2?"

The two looked at each other, then turned and sprinted to their car, hopping in and screeching out of the station, the pump nozzle spraying gas on the ground.

"Hey!" The station attendant yelled. Clarence ran back to his Bonneville and pulled out on MLK. He saw them two streets ahead. They made a sudden right turn into what he knew was a neighborhood.

Don't let there be any kids in the street.

After the Impala turned, it went only forty feet before the driver slammed on the brakes. Two cars pointed opposite directions idled in the middle of the road, drivers jawing. The Impala's driver laid on the horn. Neither of the offending drivers moved an inch. One got out and stared. Suddenly Clarence whipped around the corner, coming to an abrupt stop right behind the Impala. He jumped out of his car and rushed the driver's door. He beat on the window. The driver jammed it in reverse, appearing as if he might ram the Bonneville.

Clarence looked for something hard, saw nothing, then thought of the handle of his knife. He pulled it from its sheath, then with a backhand motion slammed it against the window, breaking it open enough that he could reach in with his left hand and pop up the lock. Now the two Hispanics lay low in the front seat, covering their heads.

Clarence opened the door and pulled the driver out by the scruff of his neck. He reached in and grabbed the keys out of the ignition. He waved at the two dudes blocking traffic. "Call 911," he yelled. "Or the cops. Tell them there's two murder suspects at this address." They looked at him as if to say, Call the *cops*? They'd faced a lot of cops before, but they'd never *called* them. Finally, one shrugged and reached in for a car phone. Clarence heard him give the street name.

Clarence secured the driver in a headlock and instructed the passenger to stay in his seat and keep his hands on the dashboard. Five minutes later a patrol car drove up. The officers got out cautiously, one pulling his gun at the sight of Clarence's bleeding right hand holding the knife, while his left arm surrounded the driver's neck.

"Drop the knife," the cop said to Clarence.

"These are the bad guys. I just caught 'em."

"Drop the knife and we'll talk about it," the cop said. Clarence dropped the knife on the street.

"Okay," the officer said, "who are you?"

"I'm Clarence Abernathy."

"The sportswriter?"

"Yeah."

"And who are these two?"

"The lowlifes that killed my sister and my niece."

Geneva Abernathy and Esther Norcoast met at five o'clock to set up for the North Portland Community Bazaar. Geneva scanned the nearly one hundred booths in the old middle school gym. She perused the homemade clothing, wall hangings, framed photos, jewelry, you name it. Dani had brought her paintings here the last few years. Geneva had helped her in her booth. She'd also seen Esther Norcoast at her own booth last year. A few days ago Esther had called Geneva to ask for her help with her "Angel Awareness" booth.

"This is going to be so much fun," Esther said to Geneva, who looked wide-eyed at the vast assortment of products in the dozen boxes. No wonder Esther had reserved three large tables. Geneva helped Esther lay out display racks of fine silver- and gold-tone angel jewelry, pendants, lockets, and earrings. Next came angels with wings and harps, male angels, female angels, adult angels, baby angels. Geneva set up a neatly printed placard: "Little Sterling Angel with Vermeil Wings, $20.00." Another said, "Angel Surrounded by Marcasite Heart, $28.00."

Esther pointed to a gold angel necklace. "That's my daughter Katie's angel. I think about her every time I see it. She wears it all the time."

On the second table, next to the jewelry, Geneva helped Esther put up angel figurines, cherubs, seraphim, angel collector plates and ornaments, and even angelic wind chimes. Next to them sat Victorian angel photographic prints, original angel art, Christmas tree toppers, and angel music tapes and CDs. Esther turned on a portable CD player and started playing "angel music." Geneva wondered how anyone knew the music preferences of angels, but it sounded pleasant enough.

On the third table Esther laid out a supply of books, among them near-death experience accounts, including *Embraced by the Light*. Alongside these she set out *A Book of Angels, In Search of Angels, Ask Your Angels, Commune with Angels, Touched by Angels, Know Your Angels, Angel Voices,* and *The Angels Within Us*. It was an hour before they got everything set up just how Esther wanted it.

"Wow!" Geneva said. "And I thought it was just angel jewelry. You've expanded!"

Esther laughed. "A year ago I was trying to do my own handmade angel jewelry, but the life of a politician's wife doesn't allow much time." She looked at the three crowded tables. "I guess I really have branched out, haven't I? Reggie says if you're going to have a vice, this is a pretty good one."

"I've always admired your guardian angel pin," Geneva said, pointing to the winged silver emblem on Esther's suit lapel. "But I didn't realize how much you'd gotten into this. What's the story?"

"Well, five years ago my sister was dying of cancer. I really needed help and support, and I wasn't finding it in family or church. Then someone gave me a book on angels. I loved it so much I went out and got several more. The books really spoke to me, filled a void in my life. I always knew there was something more, a supernatural presence. When I got my first guardian angel pin, it reminded me of this unseen presence. It helped me make more sense of the world, made me feel good about myself. Lots of people asked me about it, and the *Trib* even did a feature story on me related to my interest in angels."

"I remember reading that," Geneva said.

"Up till a year ago I worked a lot of hours at Reggie's office, but I cut way back to give me more time with this. Last year I went to a seminar called 'Ask Your Angel,' where the leaders showed us how to get guidance from our guardians. That was a big step, because my angel went from being just a source of comfort to a source of guidance. I was facing some hard things, and it was wonderful to get the guidance I needed."

Geneva fidgeted a little. "I believe God guides his children. And I believe he sends guardian angels to them. But how do you get guidance from an angel?"

"You just ask for it," Esther said. "You talk to them, share your innermost thoughts and feelings, your emotions and your struggles. If you're wondering what to do about a problem, you ask them to draw your heart toward one option or show you another." Esther spoke in an animated voice, demonstrating this wasn't just a hobby but a passion. "I sell the jewelry as an opportunity to get out the word about angels. That's why I carry these books and pamphlets. One thing that means a lot to me is that angels never put you down. They don't make you feel guilty; they make you feel good, which is more than I can say for a lot of churches."

"Esther," Geneva asked cautiously, "do you believe in Jesus Christ?"

She hesitated. "Yes, I believe in a Jesus Christ of love."

"How about a Jesus Christ of justice?"

"Well, of course, justice. But not the negative way he's sometimes presented. I don't believe in a God who sends people to hell. I believe in compassion and comfort. That's what the angels bring us. Help and hope and guidance. You have a guardian angel too, you know."

"I believe that, though I admit I've never given it much thought. I did hear a sermon on angels once."

"Just *once*? You've been going to church for how many years, and just one sermon? Angels are so much more important than that. They have wisdom and insight people don't. Look," Esther reached over to one of the tables, "here's a couple of my favorite books and tapes about communicating with our angels. It's all very positive and encouraging. Take these with my compliments. And please, take the piece of jewelry of your choice. It's the least I can do for all your help."

"People are going crazy over you," Dani said to Torel.

"Over me?"

"Over your kind, I mean. Angels. I thought of it as a good sign, but now I'm not so sure."

"In a sense it is a good sign," Torel said. "The children of Adam feel a great need for comfort in a world that is violent and frightening. The thought of heavenly protectors working for their good is very appealing."

"Well put, my friend," Lewis said. "You must remember, Dani, that once *all* people believed in the supernatural. While having different views of God and angels, they would consider anyone who did not believe in them to be ignorant, if not insane. But the long age of supernaturalism gave way to the short age of naturalism, where men attempted to explain the universe as self-existent, coming from nothing and going nowhere. Faith in God was displaced by faith in evolution, science, man, self. None of these could bear the weight of faith. The age of anti-supernaturalism couldn't last long, for human hearts testify to a greater reality. They long to find the source of the eternal sound they now hear only in echoes."

"Yes," Dani said. "I understand that here like I never did on earth."

"They know intuitively the dark world as it now is was never meant to be their home," Lewis continued. "So they long for a better home, a true home. When modernism failed to satisfy, failed to ring true to the heart or mind, it moved to postmodernism. So, many people who twenty years ago didn't believe in the supernatural now do."

"And that's good, isn't it?" Dani said.

"Good, but only as a first step," Lewis said. "It's one thing to believe in the supernatural, another to believe in the one true God revealed in the Scriptures and the one and only Savior, Jesus Christ. As my friend Chesterton said—I must introduce you to him—'When men cease to believe in God, they do not believe in nothing; they believe in anything.' These are at once the most cynical and most gullible people who have ever lived. They are skeptical about the truth they should believe, yet gullible about the falsehoods they should question. They believe in the mystical, the occult, the New Age, anything and everything but the truth. They believe in angels because it is comforting. But the only good reason to believe anything is that it is true. And while they are correct that angels are real, they must ask the bigger question—who these angels really are. More particularly, *whose* they really are."

"So they now believe in angels," Dani said, "but without believing in the sovereign God who made those angels, the holy God who became a man and went to the cross to provide salvation for men."

"Precisely," Lewis said. "And they therefore take false comfort. For if they believed in nothing, they would likely know the crushing emptiness within and feel compelled to look outside themselves for the truth. But because they believe in the supernatural, the emptiness feels as if it is being filled. All people long to believe in the *other*, the transcendent, that which is above and beyond them, greater than they. That is why the notion of UFOs and benevolent aliens fascinates them—they offer hope and answers while not requiring them to bow the knee to the Creator and Savior who *is* the answer. Universal equality is a very wearisome and boring dogma. They long to know the superior. They long to bow the knee."

"But why would people believe in angels but not in their Maker?" Dani asked.

"Because," Torel said, "while they long to bow the knee, in their blindness they will choose to bow it to that which they should not. That is idolatry. They worship angels because they suppose angels are safe. Of course, we are *not* safe—far from it. Elyon's sword-bearing warriors are safe only to those they are sent to protect. Those who have not bowed their knee to Elyon's Son are not the friends of God, but his enemies. Still, they imagine we are safe, chubby angel babies, wish-granting genies. Belief in us gives them a link to the supernatural without having to come to grips with the frightening holiness of Elyon Almighty."

"If they seek out contact with angels," Lewis said, "without first bowing their knee to the Carpenter, they may find angels, all right, but not the ones they seek."

"You mean…fallen angels?" Dani asked.

"Yes," Torel said. "Those of my kind who rebelled against Elyon. They hate all his creation, especially the children of Adam. Sometimes they terrorize them, other times they appear to them as angels of light, disguised as if they were still servants of Elyon."

"Why do people believe them?" Dani asked.

"Because they are blind," Torel said. "Unless Elyon first touches them, do you expect the blind to see?"

"Ollie, thanks for coming. What's going on? Why are they holding me?" Clarence asked.

"Oh, I don't know. Reckless driving. Endangering pedestrians. Assault. Destruction of property. Holding a knife to someone not engaged in a criminal act. Have I missed anything?"

"Look, Ollie. These are the guys who killed Dani and Felicia."

"Did they tell you that?"

"Not in so many words. But when I asked them if they'd been to 920 Jackson Street the night of the murders, they turned tail and ran."

"And that proves they're the killers?"

"Well, why else would they run?"

"Oh, let's see. A six-four, three-hundred-pound dude with an attitude challenges them. Why *wouldn't* they run?"

"Come on, Ollie. This was the car. A gold Impala, late seventies. Two young male Hispanics. And I'm only 288 pounds."

"What color did you say the car was?"

"Gold. You remember what Mookie said."

"I know what Mookie said. But the guys you manhandled? Their Impala isn't gold. It's green."

Clarence groaned. "I was sure it was gold."

"I just went to the yard where it's been impounded. It's green. Not even close to gold. You color blind or something?"

"But—are you saying these really weren't the guys?"

"Let me say it straight out so even a journalist can understand me—*these really weren't the guys.* Based on your accusations, the police searched the car, the *green* car. No drugs. No weapons. These guys don't have a police record. They're model citizens. They work for a nursery out in Troutdale. To top everything off, they've even got an alibi. The church they attend in Gresham had a special service that night. It went late, and then they were up past midnight with each other's wives and kids at their apartments, which are right next to each other. Even the manager saw them."

"What were they doing in North Portland?"

"When you accosted them? Well, this being America and all, they really don't have to explain that. But they were looking for some repair shop with a special on front-end alignments. They had the flyer in the car. They were trying to find the place, ran low on gas, and were going to ask directions at the station when this big ugly dude confronts them like he saw their faces on *America's Most Wanted*."

"But, I was sure—"

"Sure of what? That just because they're two Latinos in a green car that looks gold only to you, that somehow they're guilty and you can chase them down like they were Charles Manson on the lam? Why don't you let the cops and the courts mete out the justice, okay?"

"Maybe because the cops and the courts don't bring people to justice."

"Your vigilante justice sure doesn't cut it."

"Better vigilante justice than no justice."

"Well, what you did was injustice, you got that? You're in trouble, Clarence. And you got the cops in trouble too. They arrested two innocent guys based on your assurances because you're a credible journalist—how's that for an oxymoron? How do you think the Portland Hispanic Council is going to respond to the cops arresting those guys? I wonder how many lawyers will volunteer to file lawsuits for these guys? By the way, you owe them a new car window. That's all they're concerned about right now. Maybe if you give them cash they won't file any charges against you."

"File charges?"

"Reckless endangerment, vehicular pursuit, destroying private property, assault with a deadly weapon. They could make a good case for calling it a hate crime too."

"A hate crime?"

"Yeah. You went after them because they were Hispanics, right?"

Clarence was released at 10:00 P.M. and got home just before Geneva came back from the bazaar. Ty had stepped out, violating his grounding, but Jonah had been watching the girls and everything was okay. Clarence decided not to mention the incident with the car. No need to upset Geneva. He had a big Band-Aid on his hand and had formulated a good excuse when she came in the door. All the kids were in bed, and he acted as if he'd been home all evening. Geneva overflowed with stories about Esther Norcoast and angels and the bazaar. He was glad to listen.

"I went to the Kims' store this afternoon," Geneva said. "I apologized for Tyrone."

"You didn't have to do that," Clarence said. "He apologized himself. Remember? I took him in this morning."

"I know. But I felt bad. We're his guardians. That makes us responsible too."

"He has to make his own choices."

"I still felt bad. Mrs. Kim and I had a good talk. I'm getting to know her. Her name's Mae."

"Uh-huh." Clarence picked up the newspaper.

"I invited them to dinner. They'll be here tomorrow night at 6:30."

"What? You invited them to dinner?"

"I think I just said that, didn't I? Hattie Burns is going to watch the kids, so it'll just be the four of us. Unless her sister comes, but Mae doesn't seem to think she will."

"But—we don't even know them."

"That's the point, isn't it? Having people over for dinner is how you get to know them."

"But, they're…"

"What? Korean? Yeah. And we're black. And Jake and Janet are white. And Ray's American Indian. So what?"

"Trying to shame me into agreeing to this, huh?"

"I'm not asking your permission, Clarence. They're coming. I hope you're here. You can hide out at Hattie's with the kids if you want to, but she'll put you to bed early. And I'll have a lovely evening with the Kims. I'll just tell them you didn't show up because the man who writes columns preaching color blindness is a racist."

Clarence glared at her. "I'm not a racist."

"Fine. Then we'll both be here for dinner tomorrow at 6:30."

"It must be hard for you living here sometimes," Geneva said to the Kims. "We've traveled overseas, but I can hardly imagine starting a new life in another country."

"Is strange place. Even now that we Americans," Benjamin Kim said. "We very scared sometimes. But we do not want to look scared, so we…what is word?"

"Compensate," Mae Kim offered. Obviously, they'd talked about it before.

"Yes. We act…in control. This make people think we aloof, hostile. But this is not so. Well, perhaps it is sometimes so."

"What do you mean?" Clarence asked.

"In Korea, there is Confucian emphasis on education. Among Koreans it created, what is word, hierarchy of skin color. When someone studies indoors all day, he has fair skin. This represent honorable life of scholar. Darker skin comes from working all day in sun. It represents lowly working-class life. So, is sometimes true Koreans keep distance from darker Americans but want to be included among lighter ones."

"One thing I respect about Koreans," Clarence said, "is you're such hard-working people."

"This come from desire to break free from centuries of poverty and oppression from Japanese."

Geneva looked surprised. "I've always thought of Korean and Japanese as almost the same," she said. Both Kims looked shocked at this statement.

"Oh, no. We very very different," Mr. Kim said. "Korean people bitter toward

Japanese because bad things they do to us. We work and work, make money, send
our children to good schools. Our students do very well academically, but sometimes
poor in relating to people. Since we are Christians, we have asked our Lord to help
us overcome this. We have prayed about it. When you invited us to dinner, it was
answer to our prayer."

Clarence nodded sheepishly, keeping his eyes from meeting Geneva's.

"I'm so glad to hear you're Christians," Geneva said. "We are too."

"Very good. We think maybe so. I wonder why black and Korean churches not
together," Mr. Kim said. "We share very much in common. We both experience
much unjust treatment. Nearly 60 percent of Korean Americans are Christians.
Many blacks Christians too, no? We latecomers to America. But we want people
accept us."

"Can I ask you something?" Clarence said.

"Certainly," Mr. Kim said.

"In your store, when you give change to black people, why don't you put it in
their hands instead of on the counter?"

The Kims looked at each other in surprise.

"Respect," Mr. Kim said. "In Korea we raised you must keep distance. We do
not put change in hands because then our hands touch customer. This not polite.
Look and you see. Never put change in hands of anyone, Korean or white or any
color. It very rude. We do not do it."

"What reason you think we not put change in hands?" Mrs. Kim asked.

"It seems like...disrespect for blacks," Clarence admitted, fidgeting. "Like you
don't want to touch us because you think we're inferior to you. I never noticed you
do the same for everyone."

"Do many blacks think this way?" Mr. Kim asked.

"Yes," Clarence said. "As a matter of fact, they do. I've heard lots of people talk
about it."

"But no one ever mention this to us," Mrs. Kim said. "Perhaps it something we
need to change."

"Very hard to change," Mr. Kim said. "Learned from time little child."

"But if it make people angry," Mae said, "we should try to change."

"Or maybe we should try to understand your culture better," Clarence said.
"Then we wouldn't be offended in the first place."

After some delicious sweet potato pie, Mrs. Kim said, "We still very sorry about
your sister and her little girl. We like them very much."

"Used to give candy to little girl," Mr. Kim said. "Felicia very happy when I give
her lunch box."

"With a giraffe on it?" Clarence asked.

"Yes," Mr. Kim said. "She like it very much."

"We miss them both so much," Geneva said.

"Is very hard to lose family," Mrs. Kim said. "We lose brother and one son." Her eyes looked terribly sad. "We thank Jesus we will see them again."

"Knowing that makes all the difference, doesn't it?" Geneva said.

They smiled and nodded. Mr. Kim hesitated, then asked, "Have police found killers yet?"

"No. I'm afraid not," Clarence said.

Mrs. Kim nudged her husband. He spoke very deliberately. "Did anyone talk about strangers in neighborhood?"

"What do you mean?"

"Night sister killed I work late. Usually lock doors nine o'clock in summer, just before gets dark. I inside cleaning up at nine-thirty. Someone drive up, and I look outside. I think if this one of my customers I will open door. But never see them before. Very fancy car, silver color. Boy comes to door, wearing red sweatshirt. One in car wearing same. He leave door open, and I see inside car. He bang on my door, and I hide inside, look through blinds."

"What did you see?" Clarence asked.

"In front seat of car big weapon."

"What color was the weapon?"

"Black. Very big. Made me decide not to open door. Then they drive off."

"You don't know where they went?"

"Headed north on Martin Luther King. Up this way."

"What did they look like?"

"One at door not too tall. Look strong. Short hair. No glasses. Boy in car, driver, not sure."

"Were they black?" Clarence asked.

Mr. Kim looked down. "Yes. Very sorry."

"That's all right," Clarence said. "Most people are black around here, the good ones and the bad ones. Anything else you remember about them?"

"Faces very hard for me." Benjamin Kim hesitated. "To us, black Americans look very much the same."

Clarence laughed. "I've always thought all Koreans look alike."

"In fact," Geneva said, "we have a hard time telling the difference between Koreans, Japanese, and Chinese." The Kims looked amazed at this.

"Police never ask me about anything," Mr. Kim said. "But when I hear big gun used, I wonder about what I saw. So sorry not mention before. Sometimes afraid to say anything. Wonder what people will think. Not want any trouble."

"Thanks for telling me now," Clarence said. As his wheels turned, Geneva picked up the dessert dishes, and they settled in the living room.

"Hattie Burns told me you had a store in Los Angeles," Geneva said. "Is that right?" Mr. and Mrs. Kim both nodded. "Is it true that your store was burned down in the riots?" Geneva asked. They nodded again. "That must have been very hard."

"Yes. Insurance only cover building. Work very hard to build up many customers. All that lost."

"Why did you leave L.A.?" Clarence asked.

"Everyone tell us same thing will happen again." Mr. Kim cleared his throat. "Hard for us to understand."

"You mean the riots?" Geneva asked.

"Yes. Had many good customers, most black. Like them very much. One Korean store owner did bad thing, shot black girl for shoplifting. She die. Very sad. But most of us have good relationship with customers. We understand white people mistreated blacks many years. Very sad. I think first decision about police who beat Mr. King not right. But I very confused. In riots, jury not hurt. Judge not hurt. Very few white people hurt. Mostly Korean and black people hurt. Our businesses burned and looted. Half of all losses to Koreans, most others to blacks."

"I can see how that would be hard to understand," Geneva said.

"Very strange," Mr. Kim said. "Black people in Los Angeles think twelve white people on jury in Simi Valley—have never been there, do not know this place—do injustice. Then black rioters punish Koreans and blacks for what twelve white people decide somewhere else. Cannot understand this. No Koreans on jury. Do you understand? Can you explain to us?"

"Sometimes," Clarence said, "people have a lot boiling up inside them because of the past. But burning your store was wrong, of course. Absolutely wrong." The expression on the Kims' faces told him they needed more explanation. "I think by always talking about racism our leaders, black and white, have made people think it's all right to hurt and destroy when they think they see racism. But it's innocent people who get hurt. And those who do the hurting aren't martyrs or heroes, they're just criminals. My father says when people of character are wronged, they never respond by doing wrong to others. Maybe the verdict showed lack of character in some whites. And the rioting showed lack of character in some blacks."

They sat quietly for thirty seconds, the issue clearly unresolved. Finally Geneva said, "Tell me about your sister, Mae. I'm sorry she couldn't come with you tonight. I always see her working in the back room, and I usually say hello to her. But she never looks at me. Have I done something to offend her?"

Mae looked down. "Oh, no. Have you not seen her face?"

"You mean...the scars? Well, I noticed them, yes. But she's still a pretty lady."

"She not think so. Does not want people see her. Is very ashamed."

"Was she born with those scars?"

"Oh, no. Happened during riots. When store burned down. She closing that night. Caught in fire. Benjamin rescue her or would have died."

"Very bad burns," Mr. Kim said. "Very painful. We just glad she live." He hesitated. "She different now. Before, friendly with customers. Now afraid."

"Is it...hard for her to trust black people?" Geneva asked. Neither of them responded.

They talked for another hour before the Kims said they needed to get home.

"Thank you very much for inviting us over," Mae said. "Would like to have you to our house."

"Under one condition," Geneva said. "That you promise to fix us Korean food."

"Oh, yes. Yes! I fix you very nice Korean meal." Mae smiled warmly as she and Benjamin backed away from the Abernathys' front door, repeatedly expressing their thanks.

The moment the door closed, Clarence's smile lost its hold.

Blacks? Fancy car? Red sweatshirts? Big rifle? What's going on?

The young man sat holding the .357 Smith and Wesson revolver, polishing its stainless steel with his mama's scarf until he could see in it his distorted reflection. He turned the four-inch barrel up and spun the cylinder, emptying all six shells on the bed. Staring blankly, he carefully reinserted one round.

Raymond Taylor, a.k.a. Gangster Cool, took out a bag of crack cocaine, already packaged for the next day's deliveries. He picked up one of the crusty rocks, smelled it, touched it with his tongue, debated whether to smoke it. Maybe it could make him forget what he could never tell his homeboys.

"They played me. Fools got it all wrong. Ain't their hood. Ain't their set. Can't tell my little homie, that's sure. What'm I gonna do now?"

He pointed the gun toward the pictures on the wall, setting his sights on people in the newspaper clippings, on one in particular. Then he slowly rotated his wrist, brushing the muzzle against the bridge of his nose, then pulled it back three inches. He peered deep into the seductive barrel, holding it so the light shone just far enough into the darkness to make him wonder what lay beyond. His trembling index finger fondled the trigger.

He felt a twinge of guilt as he looked at the double-action revolver from the front end, seeing the head of the bullet three chambers left of the barrel. He'd learned this trick on his own years ago. Because he always knew where the bullet was and which way the cylinder turned, whenever he'd played Russian roulette in front of the homeboys he'd always known he wasn't in danger. If, when he spun the cylinder, the bullet faced him from the only deadly spot—one chamber left of the barrel—he simply spun it again. None of the homeboys ever suspected. They were always amazed at how calm he was, impressed that he was the Iceman when facing death. It had built his rep. Unfortunately, that kid Jason and some others had followed his example and started spinning cylinders themselves—without knowing GC's little trick. Too bad for them.

Gangster Cool pulled the trigger, watching the chamber with the bullet move toward the barrel and hearing the click. It now sat two chambers away. He pulled the trigger again, the bullet falling into position one chamber from the barrel. He wondered if he pulled the trigger once more if he would hear the sound. His finger tensed. He'd been distressed but not suicidal when he began this little ritual. But now a voice from somewhere, whether inside or outside he wasn't sure, a distinct voice told him to do it, told him to pull the trigger, told him to do it now.

Raymond's hand jerked at the last moment, just before the explosion. The .357 round hit his forehead at an angle, breaking skin an inch above his right eye. The lead punctured his flesh and cracked his front skull, exploding bone shards into his brain. The missile hit the top of his skull with a jar that knocked him backward onto the floor. The bullet exited the top of his head, pierced the ceiling, and lodged in a rafter.

Raymond's mother heard the explosion in her son's bedroom. She ran and threw open the door, believing he'd been shot through the window by a rival gangster. She screamed at the sight of splattered blood. She saw her boy, lying in a heap, a crimson pool surrounding his head and claiming more of the hardwood floor with every second.

"My baby, my baby." She turned his head and saw his eyes open. He whispered something to her, something she didn't understand. She rushed to the phone to punch 9-1-1.

"It's my Raymond, my little boy! He's been shot!"

"Where are you, ma'am? What's your address?"

She gave the address and went running back to Raymond's bedroom, her arms flailing. She picked up his blood-bathed head again. This time the eyes didn't open. She screamed and wailed and cried out, "Oh, no. No, God, no. Not my little boy!"

Gangster Cool no longer existed. Raymond Taylor, on the other hand, merely relocated, leaving one place and arriving at another.

The woman who'd raised the boy and prayed for him, who'd invested her life in him, sobbed and held all he had left behind.

Clarence drove north on Grand, looking for the restaurant. All he saw on Grand and Estep was an old run-down bar. He looked at the undersized neon sign, faded red. *Miller's*, it said, as if anyone cared.

They probably serve burgers and chicken. To Gracie that must qualify as a restaurant.

He looked at his watch—6:15 P.M. He got out and walked in the front door, looking warily into the bar as men looked into old west saloons before pushing open the swinging doors. This wasn't really the black part of town yet. It was on the fringe—maybe 30 percent black—but sometimes that made the 70 percent white cling all the more tenaciously to their remaining turf. He saw twenty or thirty men and a few women, all white.

Clarence looked at the man tending bar. "You the owner?"

"Yeah. Who are you?"

"Clarence Abernathy. Your niece asked me to meet her here."

"Gracie?"

"Yeah. Didn't she call you?"

"But she didn't say you were…"

"What? Black?"

"Yeah."

"Well, I am."

"Yeah." He gestured for Clarence to follow to the back of the restaurant. When the owner opened the door to a private room on the right, Gracie got up immediately and grabbed Clarence's arm. He stepped back, embarrassed.

"Thanks, Uncle Willie," she said. "We need some privacy."

Uncle Willie looked suspiciously at Clarence. "You call me if you have any problems," he said to Gracie. She nodded. He shook his head in obvious disgust and shut the door.

"Hey, Clarence. You're lookin' sharp tonight. Nice suit." She touched his lapel. He backed away.

"Tell me what's up, Gracie. That's what I'm here for."

"Okay. This guy I talked to says it was a couple of Bloods."

"Bloods? What about the Hispanics that were seen driving away from the shooting?"

She shrugged. "This guy says it was Bloods."

"Which Bloods?"

"He doesn't know for sure."

"Look," Clarence said, sighing. "It's a Crip neighborhood, and the guys you talked with are probably Crips, right? Crips always blame Bloods. What else do you have?"

"What else? Isn't this a lot? I read it was two Latino bangers, maybe from the west side. Isn't that what the paper said?"

"Yeah. Anyway, what more do you have?"

"This guy knows more for sure, but he wouldn't tell me. I told him you were giving like a hundred bucks to anybody with good information. He said he could meet you after seven tonight. I told him we'd be just two miles away and you could probably meet him then. If you want to."

"Where?" Clarence looked at his watch. Six-thirty.

"At the corner of MLK and Evans, just past the Minit Mart."

"What's his name?"

"Can't tell you. That's up to him."

"What does he look like?"

"Black. Kind of short and heavy. Usually wears a dark blue stocking cap."

"What's he got for me?"

"I'm not sure. But it's about the hit on your sister, I know that. Plus," she added, "I've got another guy who knows everything that happens on the street. Everything. He's taking me out Friday night. I'll fish around. I'll call you if he knows anything."

"Uh, okay. Call me at the *Trib* if you can, all right? Not at home. You can leave a message on my machine."

She nodded and batted her eyes at him. "Look, tomorrow's my mother's birthday and I'm short on cash. So, does the hundred-dollar reward apply to me too?"

Clarence wanted to say no, but he knew Gracie's help could end up being critical. He reached into his wallet and grabbed one of the two hundred dollar bills he had left. He handed it to her and turned to head out the door.

"Thanks, Clarence. You're a sweetie. Oh, my uncle told me to have you go out the back door." She pointed to a door from the office leading directly outside. "It's the door I always use, but I forgot to tell you. He said it's better for privacy, if you don't want people to see you coming and going."

Clarence left by the back door, then drove to the corner of MLK and Evans. Seven o'clock—no one there. Seven-thirty—no one there. Eight—no one there. He waited until eight-thirty and finally gave up, hungry and exasperated. He stopped at Kim's store to get a couple of corn dogs and headed home.

Clarence and Jake sat at Lou's Diner the next day, having just polished off cheeseburgers and fries. Rory poured each of them a complimentary steaming mocha, while the jukebox played "A Bridge over Troubled Waters."

"That's a fascinating analysis," Jake said to Clarence. "Tell me more."

"Ever have a logic class?" Clarence asked. "The major premise is that all blacks who fail do so because of white racism. Of course, that doesn't explain why so many whites fail, but that's beside the point. Then comes the observation that some blacks are failing very badly. Therefore, there must be an *enormous* amount of white racism. And that means whites must transform themselves before blacks can ever succeed. So, some blacks trade on their victim status and appeal to white guilt feelings, which were far too long in coming but now are here in abundance. A lot of whites buy into this, don't challenge this faulty logic, so they can feel better about themselves, get all righteous, and strut around thinking *other* whites are racists, but not them, no sir, not them. They think they're really helping blacks, but the truth is they're just thinking about themselves—trying to shed their guilt."

"And you're saying this whole way of operating isn't solving the problem, it's making it worse?"

"Sure. Our biggest problems in the black community aren't external, they're internal. Once whites routinely did terrible things against blacks, yet despite this many blacks succeeded against the worst odds. But even though there's still plenty of racism, it isn't nearly as powerful or restrictive—whites aren't doing *nearly* as many terrible things to us now. Yet a higher percentage of blacks are failing than when racism was far worse. The opportunities and odds blacks face are much better, but for many the outcome is much worse."

"But why? I still don't really understand it," Jake said.

"In the post-civil-rights race establishment," Clarence said, "the equation is always the same. It's very simple. As Shelby Steele explains it, Black Failure equals White Guilt. So blacks who fail cannot be blamed for their failure, therefore have no responsibility for their failure, therefore have no responsibility to change or to succeed. In fact, if they believe the equation—and millions do—they're convinced they *cannot* succeed. The power over their lives doesn't belong to them. It belongs to the white racists behind every bush. It teaches irresponsibility. One day I saw a couple of black kids break a store window, and the white store owner pointed a finger at them. One of the kids said, 'You're just accusing us 'cause we're black.' See, he'd learned the game. The victim, the store owner, was now the criminal, the racist. The true criminal, the window breaker, was now the victim. Of course, boys of every race will break windows—but those that don't have the excuse of always being the victim are more likely to own up to their responsibility.

"All this leads to the dilemma of the middle-class black. On the one hand, despite his success, he may believe he's still a victim. Say he's a police sergeant—if he was white he'd be a lieutenant. Say he's a company vice president—if it wasn't for being black he'd be president. And whether or not he feels like a victim, he knows that his very success makes people see him as a traitor to the poor black. Because if some blacks are succeeding it means blacks *can* succeed despite racism, and if *that's* true, then the philosophical cornerstone has been destroyed—the supposed victim status and helplessness of blacks. So instead of being an inspiration, white-collar blacks who succeed in business—in almost any career besides entertainment, athletics, or politics—are looked at with suspicion or even disdain."

Clarence pushed back his empty mocha cup. He sighed. "Well, so much for analyzing the world's problems. I've got another funeral to attend."

Ty stared at GC's closed coffin. He couldn't believe his mentor was gone. Different emotions swirled within him, each taking turns gripping his heart. One was fear, dread, a sense he had to get away from the set. The other was a thirst for justice, a desire for revenge, a thought that he should do something to get even. But get even with whom? There was no one to take revenge on. Bloods hadn't done this. GC had done it to himself.

GC's mother was surrounded by three women—two sisters and their mother, GC's grandma. They sobbed and wailed inconsolably.

Taleisha, GC's girl, was dressed out fine. Her makeup was heavy, her diamond-studded fingernails looked like the talons of some exotic bird. Her fingers sported a cluster of gold rings, a half dozen of them on each hand, some doubled up on the same finger. Her gold earrings were miniature Cadillac emblems inlaid with precious stones. GC had bought them for her, or so she told herself. She had the look of a girl who used her appearance to get her way as GC used his street smarts to get his. Taleisha cried. Ty felt sorry for her, until he looked over and saw her in a corner looking into a mirror and putting on lip gloss.

Shadow, GC's lieutenant, stood fast, talking with no one, his granite face pierced only by two smoky gray eyes. With GC gone, he was the Rollin' 60s heir apparent. Ty looked at him in awe.

Pastor Clancy stood up front. "On days like this, you want to look for the best. But it's hard to find, real hard. If Raymond could come back here today, just for a moment, I know what he'd tell us. He'd say wake up. He'd say life is a mist, a puff of smoke. You're going to live forever somewhere, but not here. If you hang with the gangs, you may think you'll survive, but you won't. You'll end up in a casket like Raymond, dying at somebody else's hand or your own. Life is short enough. Don't make it shorter. The gangs are your enemy, not your friend. You have only today to get your life straight, and maybe not the whole day either. So better make your peace with God now. I'll help you any way I can. Ebenezer Church will help you any way we can. Come to us. Come while you still can, before it's too late."

Many of the adults cried and moaned. Most of the kids sat still, numb. The Abernathys sat together, except Keisha and Celeste, who were home with Hattie

Burns. Geneva sat by Jonah; Clarence by Tyrone. Clarence put his arm around Ty, surprised to sense no resistance. Jonah whispered to Geneva, "Mama, I don't want to die like GC. I want to die normal."

As the organ played, the ushers dismissed the attendees row by row to walk past the closed pine box up front. As he walked by the remains of a ghetto star who'd called him his road dog, Ty whispered, "You can't be dead, GC. You can't be. You weren't never gonna die. Why'd you do it? Why'd you have to play that stupid game?"

Ty felt mad at the world and mad at GC. Though it seemed blasphemy to think it, he wondered if the dude he'd been named after was the ultimate cool or the ultimate fool. He thought about Jason. He thought about how he'd spun the chamber himself, and he could have just as easily died like Jason did. He recalled the clicking sound of the firing pin. He was certain that if he ever did that again, he'd die. He felt frightened and empty.

When Ty went home, he retreated into his bedroom. He took a box out of his closet, filled with comic books. He reached down to the bottom, under all the comics, and found the nine-millimeter Taurus GC had given him. He held it in his hand, and for the first time that day, he wept.

———

"Clarence? Ollie. We're in an unusual lull. Just wrapped up two cases. In light of what Mr. Kim saw— the red sweatshirts and all—Manny and I are going back to the hood to ask more questions. We're expanding, canvassing a one-mile radius of your sister's place. It's a huge job, but we've got some time we weren't counting on. We've been to homes, gas stations, liquor stores, you name it."

"Found anything?"

"Zero. To be honest I'm not sure most of the people trust a white and a Hispanic enough to really talk to us. So I decided to split us up. Steve, one of the black detectives, agreed to join Manny for the day. I was wondering if you'd like to tag along with me. Unofficially, of course."

"Okay. I can get out of here by two. That soon enough?"

"Perfect. How about I meet you at your house at two-thirty and we go from there? We'll start with Taco Bell."

———

"I'm Detective Ollie Chandler, homicide. This is Clarence Abernathy. He's from the neighborhood."

"Herb Adrianne." The short wiry manager extended his hand. "Welcome to the world of Taco Bell."

"I'm investigating the death of Dani Rawls."

"Lady over on Jackson?" Herb asked. "Used to come here with her kids. Always wore bright colors. Seemed nice. That happened awhile back. What? August?"

"September 2. To be honest, Herb, the investigation needs a kick-start. I'm grasping at straws, wondering if anybody remembers anything about the night of September 2."

"That's been awhile. Let's see. We were robbed August 14 and September 10. Those dates stick with me. You fill out all those forms—hard to forget."

"I hear you," Ollie said. "Guess I was hoping maybe you saw somebody suspicious."

"I know the people from this hood," Herb said, "from most the hoods 'round here. They know I know 'em. They're welcome in my place, but I don't put up with any nonsense. I tell 'em this ain't Burger King—can't have it your way. No gang signs here. You flash and you're out. Some kids don't like that, but most do. It's a lot safer. Now when dudes come in from the outside, I know it's big trouble. Turf thing."

"Do you get many new faces?"

"Nope. New faces come in with old faces, not by themselves. Always watch the new faces close. Chances are they're gonna start somethin' or somebody's gonna start on them. I even watch the cars—write 'em up if I see trouble comin'."

"Write 'em up?"

"Yeah, scribble down their license number. Comes in handy when somebody takes a shot or steals somethin' and hops in their car. With all the confusion, sometimes it's too late to get the plates."

"Where do you write down the license numbers?" Ollie asked.

"Keep a ledger book under the register."

"Do you write down the dates?"

"Yeah, I think so. Usually."

"Can I take a look?"

"Sure." Herb took him back behind the register, then handed him the green-covered ledger tablet and flipped to the back. "It's all yours. Let me get on top of my crew here and I'll be back, okay?"

Ollie and Clarence scanned the various dates, seeing license plate numbers and notations, such as "tall," "muscular," "fat," "weight lifter," "White," "Mexican," "Kerby Crip," "Rollin' 60." Obviously Herb wanted to be able to describe them to the police if they ended up perps or suspects.

The records went back over a year, nearly a dozen of them each month, covering several pages. The date wasn't always clear, but could be roughly figured out by the dates it fell between. With Clarence peering down over his shoulder, Ollie scanned up to the present and slowed down as he saw an extensive notation for August 14 and again on September 10, the dates of the robberies. He looked at the ten entries in between, not expecting to see September 2.

"There it is." Clarence beat Ollie to it. "September 2—Two black males. 6'2" skinny, 5'7" stocky. Both blue jeans, black leather jackets, black caps, Jordans. Stocky guy: tough looking, shark eyes."

"It's followed by some words I can't read, then a license number," Ollie said, jotting it down: Oregon, CWR 403. "Back in a minute, Herb," he called. Clarence followed Ollie outside while Herb waved and returned to instructing a teenage employee on how to mop up spilled coffee.

Ollie unlocked the car and reached under his seat. He took out what looked like a gigantic cell phone with a full keyboard and screen.

"What's that?" Clarence asked.

"MDT. Mobile Data Terminal. Ties me into LEDS—Law Enforcement Data System. All the mobile units are hooked up to the mainframe in Salem. This'll take a few minutes. Make yourself at home. If you want a snack, you can probably find some pretty good stuff in the seat cracks. This is my stakeout car. Ever seen an evidence collection kit? Got a couple under your seat. Usually keep 'em in the trunk, but it's been leaking. Check 'em out."

Ollie typed in OR, CWR 403, and some other information. Clarence looked in the first kit. He examined the scissors, wire cutters, tweezers, pliers, knives, syringes, and a vast array of other tools, pens, paper, plastic evidence bags, a flashlight, and measuring tape. Two cameras and lenses filled another kit—one a 35 mm Nikon, the other a Polaroid for the quickies. Next was a compact video camera case. Another kit contained plaster casting, silicone rubber putty, dust and dirt hardener, oil coater, and other materials to make casts and molds. The final kit was marked, "Document evidence collection." It had transparent protective covers and paper envelopes, tweezers, and a magnifying glass. Looking over all this, for the first time in his life Clarence thought it might be kind of fun to be a cop, at least a detective.

Clarence looked at Ollie's MDT. "I've never seen one of these. The ones in cop cars are bigger, aren't they?"

"Detectives carry the smaller units," Ollie said. "You don't want the full-size computer terminals. Not conducive to undercover work. The MDT gets you everything you need. While it's processing, let's get back to Herb."

As they walked inside, Herb moved toward them, straightening a few salt and pepper shakers along the way. He pointed back at the young boy mopping the floor. "He's gonna be a good employee. Nobody taught him how to clean. Well, he's gonna learn here. You know, for kids today, it's all about 'cool' and 'party.' With 'cool' you look good rather than be good. It's all image, no character. 'Party' is do what you want, when you want. Sounds great to them, but all it creates is chaos. These kids don't know how to blush anymore. They don't know the rules. They don't have any guardrails to keep them from going off the cliff. We've got to rebuild the guardrails. Well, this is just Taco Bell, gentlemen, but it's *my* turf and in here we've got guardrails. In here my kids learn how to work and show respect."

Clarence noted the look of pride and accomplishment in Herb's eyes.

"Found an entry the day of the murder," Ollie said.

"Question, Herb," Clarence said. "You give exact figures for how tall the dudes are. How can you be so sure?"

"Take a good look at the door," Herb said, smiling broadly. Clarence looked at the door and saw the colorful lettering and red-marked design. Suddenly he realized what the red marks really were.

"A height chart," Clarence said, noticing a 6 and a 5 and one-inch increments above and below each, with wider marks at quarters and halves, like on rulers.

"Yeah. Got the idea from the 7-Eleven. The crook walks out the door, you just watch him, and you've got his height. All we need is a scale on the floor, and we'd have their weight too."

"How about a trap door?" Ollie asked. "You could push a button and drop out the bottom as they head out."

"Now you're talkin'." Herb laughed.

"There's no time indicated in your book," Ollie said. "You wouldn't know when these guys were here?"

"Well, maybe I can narrow it down," Herb said. "Got a calendar?" Ollie opened his schedule book and found one. "Okay, September 2, that was a Saturday? I only work a half day Saturdays, seven to midnight. Had to be after seven and before midnight. That help?"

"Yeah. Okay, do you remember these guys? One tall, the other short and muscular, Levis, Air Jordans? Black jackets?"

Herb looked down at his own description. "Fits a lot of dudes. Hold on. 'Shark eyes'? Yeah, it's comin' back. They looked mean, especially the shorter one. Like they'd been around the block a couple thousand times. Yeah. Thought trouble was comin' for sure."

"What are these words here I can't read?" Clarence pointed, and Herb looked closer.

"Silver Lexus," Herb said. "Sure. It's all comin' back. A '95 or '96, I think, all tricked out, those fancy wide tires with those gold zenith wire wheels, the ones that cost a couple of months' rent."

"People have been killed over wheels like that," Ollie said. "A couple dozen at least in California last year. What else?"

"Slammed down. Lower than a snake's belly. Cragared down to the max."

"Hydraulics?"

"Maybe."

"Neon lights?"

"Not sure. Don't think so. Big money though. Figured these brothas didn't win the lottery. Had to be drugs, and drugs always mean trouble. Fancy black jackets.

Gold chains, the whole deal. They just sat there pickin' at their food, seems like an hour. Thought maybe they were waitin' for a drug deal."

"Any gang indicators?"

"Nothing. That was strange too. No visible tattoos—of course they had these black jackets, kept them on even though we keep it plenty warm in here. Plain black baseball caps. The type you buy and put an insignia on, except they hadn't yet. No hand signs, no rags, no colors."

"You talk to either of them?" Ollie asked.

"I came over and asked if there was anything else I could get 'em. Nice way of saying, 'I'm watchin' you.' Gave me that cocky look, like, 'We own the place.' Decided to give 'em a few more minutes before I kicked their rears out. Next thing I know, they ghosted. Saw 'em leavin' in time to check their height. Still didn't trust 'em."

"That all?"

"No. Somethin' else. See, mostly girls work that shift. I usually send the guys out back to the dumpster, but when it's girls, I take out the trash myself. I remember I did that night because there was that silver Lexus parked by the dumpster, big as you please. Same two dudes, like an hour later. They'd just driven to the back. They were on my turf two hours. Like they were waitin' or casin' the place. Kind of spooked me."

"Look like they were slammin' or smokin' weed?"

"No. Eyes looked clear—not drugged out. I thought maybe it was a hit brewin', so when I went back in I took a good look at my nine, made sure it was loaded. Told my workers don't go out back. It was strange though, just the two of 'em in that tricked out car. Saturday night, but like they had no place to go. Just waitin'."

"You *sure* they had on black leather jackets. Didn't see any red sweatshirts?"

"No. Red would stick out here on Crip turf. You don't wear red unless you want people to know you're Bloods."

"When did they leave?"

"Don't know exactly. It was late when I took out the garbage, maybe 11:40? But I checked again before I left, at five after midnight say. They were gone. Think this means anything?"

"It could," Ollie said. "Thanks for your help, Herb."

"Any time. I'm on your side of the law, you know. Hey, how about a couple of burritos, on the house?" Ollie's eyes lit up as though he'd won the lottery.

"Cops are always welcome here. I give 'em free coffee or Cokes, toss 'em a taco or two. Figure if them bein' here stops one robbery, it pays for twenty years of free coffee."

"Yeah," Ollie said. "Caffeine's our drug of choice. Give caffeine to a cop and he'll be your friend for life. Thanks, Herb."

Ollie and Clarence walked out the door, burritos in hand.

"Clarence," Ollie asked as they settled in the front seat, "you said Mr. Kim saw two guys, both in red sweatshirts, one short and muscular, fancy car, big weapon. Right?"

"That's what he said."

"Let's go pay him a visit. I'm going to go show him a picture of a Lexus just to make sure, but I think Mr. Kim and Herb are talking about the same guys."

"So," Clarence said, "after these guys drop by Kim's store, they change from red sweatshirts to black leather jackets? Why?"

"I'm not sure. It might mean nothing. It might be the key to everything."

"But if they were the shooters, wouldn't it have been awfully stupid to show their faces and this fancy car in a Taco Bell less than a mile from where they were going to commit a murder?"

"Maybe. But don't rule out something just because it's stupid. That's how we crack cases. If people weren't stupid, we wouldn't catch them. Maybe these guys don't know a Lexus with wire wheels sticks out like a sore thumb in Portland. Maybe they had another plan to minimize their risk. Maybe they were Bloods sent to do a job, and they didn't want to look like Bloods so they changed into black leather before they did it."

"That fits with what Gracie said. That Bloods did it."

Suddenly Herb stuck his head out the door, looking around. Ollie flashed his headlights. Herb came over.

"Somethin' else I just remembered," Herb said. "I told you nobody knew these guys in the black leather. Well, it just came back to me. Somebody *did* know 'em. He came over and sat with 'em. I remember thinkin' they must be big time, because this guy was a ghetto star, wouldn't be meetin' with just anybody."

"Who was he?"

"Rollin' 60s honcho. The guy that shot himself. Gangster Cool."

———

Clarence stared at the painting on the wall. A beautiful seascape with brilliant colors, so real he could taste the salt air. He looked at the name written in the bottom right corner—Dani Rawls.

"Hello, Clarence." The man's voice sounded like a thunder clap in this small room. It seemed to bypass his vocal chords and come straight from his thick chest. Cairo Clancy was lighter-skinned than Clarence, large by normal standards, but smaller than Clarence.

"I called you here for a reason," Reverend Clancy said. "But first, I just want to get to know you." Clarence shifted uneasily. "I'm glad you've been comin' to our church. I'm sure it's a real change for you. Tell me what you like and what you don't like."

Clancy's directness took Clarence by surprise. "Well, I like the music. And I like your messages. Not used to services over two hours, though. And it surprises me some of the things you talk about."

"Like what?"

"Like reading off kids' names for their school achievements."

Clancy laughed. "Wait till honor roll comes out. I read every name. I want the kids to know that's the way to make your rep, not as a gangbanger or a dope-head. If somebody gets a scholarship somewhere, I tell the church about it. If they get a job, we tell everybody. Some people just can't see takin' church time to do that, but I can't see *not* takin' the time. The church is a family, and families talk."

Clarence nodded. "I do enjoy the church, mostly. Friendly folks."

"Before I started this church," Clancy said, "I was a young pastor at a Baptist church where folks was nice enough, but...if the 1950s ever come around again, that church will be ready."

Clarence laughed. "Yeah, I was at a church like that in the suburbs. A few years ago we got a new pastor, and he said, 'I'm going to lead this church into the twentieth century.' A couple of people caught him on it and said, 'You mean the twenty-*first* century.' He looks at them and says, 'Let's just take it one century at a time.'"

Pastor Clancy chuckled. "Some churches are like the Amish, except they set their time limits at 1950 instead of 1850. Still, you've got lots of churches so concerned about being modern and up-to-date that anything old is automatically irrelevant. All they care about is being current with the times, when what people need is to be taken back to something ancient and eternal, the Word of God. Guess we have to find a balance. So...give me some more feedback on our church."

"I like your sermons, but...they're more emotional, maybe less theological than I'm used to."

"Well, black churches are mostly in urban areas, but they've still got that rural soul. My people walk on asphalt, but their toes are more at home in red clay. Now," Clancy's eyes gleamed, reminding Clarence of his father, "the ol' black preachers never used the word *omnipotent*. They just said to their people, 'There's nothin' God can't do.' They didn't say, 'God is omnipresent.' Just said, 'God's so high you can't get over him, so low you can't get under him, so wide you can't get 'round him.'" He laughed. "Any questions about our church I can help you with?"

"I've been wondering how you handle people living in immorality," Clarence said. "At my last church, it seemed like the leaders turned the other way and ignored it."

"We don't tolerate sin here. And I don't just mean from the pulpit. Man gonna do drugs, beat his wife and children, sleep around, he won't get away with it. Not here."

"But what can you do about it?"

"Well, maybe two months ago we got a call that one of our men beat up his wife. I went over with two of the deacons, Harv Jolly and Jim Farrel. You know them?"

"Harv Jolly the linebacker?"

"Yessir. University of Washington, back in the seventies. And Farrel's a former gangbanger. Two of the most godly guys you'll ever know. Anyway, they were with me, and I warned this man, 'We'll do everything we can to help you, but nothin' can excuse hitting your wife. Nothin'. You do it again, and my deacons are gonna get you.'"

"What do you mean 'get you'?" Clarence asked.

"Well, for five weeks he didn't hurt her—turned out to be the longest he'd gone in years. But one day he hit her again, and one of our deaconesses found out. I got the call, and I sent Jim and Harv to pay him a visit."

"What did they say?"

"Didn't say much at all. Just beat the livin' daylights out of him."

Clarence looked wide eyed. "Your deacons beat him up?"

"Yessir. He repented too, once he woke up. That man's been comin' to church ever since and hasn't laid a finger on his wife for six months. Ol' Harv disciples him. They meet for breakfast every Thursday. He's comin' along, that brother."

Clarence stared at Clancy, who talked as if this was normal, as if he were talking about paving the parking lot.

"Okay," Clarence said, "since you're asking, I do have another question. The Sunday school rooms are full of posters of black history and black heroes. I see them, and they make me feel good, make me wish I knew this stuff when I was a kid. But still, isn't there a danger? Doesn't it teach our children to choose role models just because of their race?"

"I don't see it that way at all," Clancy said. "History's been edited along racial lines, and our kids need to see there's black heroes along with white ones. Last week I was talking to the children's group, and I told them about the Isonghee abacus, a bone from prehistoric Zaire with markings showing it was used for calculations. Well, that bone shows the most ancient mathematics don't come from Europe or Asia, but from Africa. Maybe you don't think church is the place for that, but I think our kids need to hear it—lots of them have been brainwashed to think they can't cut it in math class. That's why we've started the Ebenezer School of Ethnic Studies. It's not just a politically correct gimmick."

Pastor Clancy stood up and gestured dramatically. "There's a pathology of despair among our people. You know the conversations we have with each other that we don't have with white folk. You know the undertones, the history, the suffering behind it. How can we face the future, how can we face the problems of our communities unless we know what we're capable of? If a black child realizes black folk have made great accomplishments from the beginning of human history and great accomplishments in America, it gives him hope. If he thinks of black people as failures, it destines *him* to failure. I want our children to grow up believing they can succeed."

"I'm with you there, pastor," Clarence said. "I just think Afrocentrism can be as unhealthy as Eurocentrism."

"I won't argue with that—I mean, true Christianity can't be centered on any culture, it has to be centered on Christ. But Eurocentrism pervades our society. We've got to counterbalance that somehow if the descendants of African slaves are going to take their rightful place here. I teach a class called Blacks in the Bible. I open up all these passages people have never thought about."

"What passages do you mean?"

"Well, for starters, Ephraim and Manasseh are two of the twelve tribes of Israel, right? According to Genesis 41, they were the sons of Joseph and an Ethiopian woman. They were 50 percent black. The fathers of two tribes of Israel were *black*. Ever seen that in the Bible story pictures?

"Jethro was a Midianite from Southern Arabia, which was occupied by Ethiopians. He was the father of Zipporah, wife of Moses, who was a Cushite, an Ethiopian—says so in Numbers 12. Jethro's family were believers, proselytes to the Jewish faith. Moses married this black woman, and when Miriam grumbled about this interracial marriage, God gave her leprosy to teach her a lesson.

"Or how about David? His great-grandmother was Rahab, a Canaanite, from the line of Ham, father of the black race. David's grandmother was Ruth, a Moabite, another Canaanite tribe. By American standards, anyone with black blood is considered black. So, David easily had enough black blood that if he lived in America today he'd be called black.

"Solomon was David's son by a Hamitic woman Bathsheba, whose name means 'daughter of Sheba,' an African. Zephaniah the prophet was a descendent of 'Cush,' a black man. And look at the messianic line of Jesus. In his legal genealogy, through Joseph, four women are mentioned—Tamar, Rahab, Ruth, and Bathsheba. Now, *all four* of those were descendants of Ham, the black line of humanity. All of them were black! Jesus' mother Mary was also a descendant of Tamar, Rahab, and Ruth. There may have been other Hamitic blood in Jesus too, but as far as we know, there was no Japhetic blood, no white blood. Those who teach that having black African blood in you puts you under a curse must believe Jesus was under a curse—that the whole messianic line was cursed! By American standards, Jesus had enough African blood to be called black.

"This is important to me, Clarence. See, one evening when I was a young pastor I was reading the Bible story books to my daughter. She pointed to a picture of Jesus holding children in his lap. My daughter asked, 'Daddy, does Jesus love white people more than he loves black people?' I was shocked at the question. But then I realized that in the pictures, not only Jesus but all the children in his lap were lily white. I didn't even know enough then to tell her Jesus really had dark skin, Middle Eastern Semitic dark, that along with his primarily Jewish blood he had considerable African blood in him too. I really believe if the Jesus in her picture book had looked like Jesus actually looked, she would never have asked that question. Of course, if Jesus were white, he'd still be my Lord. But he *wasn't* white. And it's Eurocentrism that's remade him into a white image. I believe our children have suffered from that. No wonder the Black Muslims get away with saying Christianity's a white man's religion. It isn't, of course, but it's been twisted into looking as if it was."

"It's always struck me," Clarence said, "that the Bible tells us what's important—like whether or not a person loves God or if he worships idols. But it almost *never* says a word about people's skin color. That's a powerful statement. If skin color mattered, with all the thousands of people in the Bible surely God would say something about their skin color."

"Let me tell you something else, Clarence. It bothers me when children get taught about those primitive Africans who sometimes practiced twin murder—which was very rare, by the way—but nobody talks much about how the Romans abandoned their handicapped babies to die in the cold. People talk about those few black tribes that practiced child sacrifice, but not about the white Druids in France and Britain that sacrificed humans. What do our kids learn in school about the African kingdoms that were the most advanced in the world when Caucasians in Europe were living in caves and forests? When African countries fight, a lot of people think it's because they're just violent ignorant blacks. When Europeans fight—like in colonial wars to conquer people and take their lands and in two world wars and the Balkans and the former Yugoslavia—it's just a manifest destiny or struggle for democracy. I know people who believe Africans are violent by nature and Europeans are peaceful, when history paints a radically different picture. It shows every race has accomplished many things and every race is capable of great violence and evil. But history gets rewritten. Even in churches, our kids grow up thinking white means good and black means bad."

"How does that happen?"

"Let me tell you a story. Last summer a church youth group came in here from the suburbs to do five day Bible clubs in our neighborhoods. Great church, terrific young people and I'm glad they came. But they used what they called the 'Wordless Book' and showed our kids a black page that meant sin. They sang 'My heart was black with sin until the Savior came in. His precious blood I know has washed me white as snow.' Well, one of our kids said to me, 'Pastor, how come black is bad and white is good?'

"When you read the Bible you see both white and black used metaphorically, for good *and* for bad. Like in Leviticus, where the white spots on the skin and white puss indicate uncleanness and infection. The infected white part had to be taken care of before the person was clean. In fact, it says if *black* hair has grown in a sore, then the person is now clean, but if *white* hair has grown in it, they're still unclean. So in that case, white represents bad and black represents good."

"But the Bible *does* say God makes us white as snow," Clarence said.

"Sure. But the first time the metaphor 'white as snow' is used is where Elijah's servant sins against God and God judges him by making him leprous, 'white as snow.' So there white as snow meant diseased and under God's judgment. Of course, in Isaiah 1 it means pure and holy. My point is, white is sometimes good, sometimes bad. When Miriam muttered against Moses because he married a black woman, God judged her by making her white with leprosy. Scripture *does* talk about wearing white robes in heaven, and there white means pure and holy. But people of every color are wearing those white robes.

"Obviously God didn't create sin, but he *did* create skin. He created light skin and dark skin. He created black—black hair and black skin. If it wasn't good, he wouldn't have made it. But the way our kids have heard the Bible, they're inferior because they're black. We've got to correct that. If we don't, who will?"

"I guess kids don't always understand," Clarence said, "it's just a figure of speech when the Bible says our hearts are black with sin."

"But it *doesn't* say that. Isaiah 1:18 says, 'Though your sins are like scarlet, they shall be as white as snow; though they are *red as crimson*, they shall be like wool.' The contrast isn't between white and black, it's between white and red. Of course, even if the Bible *did* say 'black as sin,' it wouldn't bother me, any more than white being the color of leprosy and puss and infection and disease should bother white people. It's just that our children are used to associating their skin color with bad. Think about it. The Black Sox scandal. Black Death for the bubonic plague. Black market for something illegal. Black Monday for a Wall Street crash. Darth Vader was robed in black. Even had a black man's voice. We've just got to make our kids think differently about their skin color. Well, I've been goin' on. I'm sorry about that— guess you can see this turns my crank. Anything else you want to ask about Ebenezer church?"

"Here's one my wife and I have talked about a lot. Politics. White evangelicals tend to be Republican because they're concerned about biblical and family values and morality, and they're pro-life. Black evangelicals are heavily Democratic, maybe because in recent decades Democrats have been more sensitive to issues of social justice, racial equality, and concern for the poor. Now I happen to be concerned about *all* these issues, but I think Democratic policies and programs have hurt the black community. I think it's safe to say that at your church the members are mostly Democrats, right? I admit, that bothers me, especially on the abortion issue. I care a lot about those suffering children."

"In my experience," Pastor Clancy said, "Republicans tend to be more wise and less caring, and Democrats more caring and less wise. But both parties fall way short. You mentioned abortion. I know white evangelicals who can't understand why so many of their black brethren seem unconcerned about abortion. Likewise, black evangelicals can't understand why so many whites are unconcerned about poverty, drugs, crime, racism, and the deterioration of urban America. And why they seem to be doing so little to improve education, employment, housing, medical care, you name it. You and I are advocates of working hard, but we both know white conservatives who have hijacked the concept of self-reliance as an excuse to abandon the truly needy.

"To black Christians, yes, abortion should be on our list of concerns. But it has to take a number, considering everything else we've got to deal with. With the mortality rate of our already-born children dramatically higher than white children's, we tend to say let's start with the ones already born. White churches are concerned about abortion and homosexuals and feminism. We're concerned about gangs and drugs and AIDS and homelessness and jobs. Our church gets asked to participate in Life Chain every year. Some of our deacons say they feel like white evangelicals have this abortion fixation and that's all they care about. They said to me, 'These people want us to stand next to them on abortion, but they've never stood next to us on racism, social justice, unemployment, and poverty. They don't seem to care about moral issues that are important to me. Why should I care about the only one that seems important to them?' Well, I took my deacons to task on that, and we *do* join in Life Chain. But I have to admit I understand where they're coming from."

Clarence nodded. "So do I. But I still think it's essential we stand against abortion. It's not the babies' fault if white Christians haven't been consistent on justice issues."

"Okay, I'm trackin' with you," Clancy said. "But I admit I get concerned when I see flag-waving Christians whose faith in America is inseparable from their faith in God. Patriotism is fine as far as it goes, but our true citizenship is in heaven. I say, don't settle for Washington when God has called you to set your eyes on Zion. Between us, I get real discouraged by white churches sometimes. Remember a few months ago when one of the largest evangelical churches had that big 'slave auction' to raise money for a building? They couldn't understand why these oversensitive African Americans got offended. Right—what's next, they gonna do a good-natured takeoff on the Holocaust and expect Jews not to be offended?

"Got a letter from a Christian organization last week. It was all bad-mouthin' the ACLU, like everything they've ever done is from the pit of hell. Well, I disagree with *plenty* of the stuff they're doin' now, but if it wasn't for the ACLU taking up our cause, black folk would still be using separate restrooms. I wish these Christian groups wouldn't paint with such a broad brush and act like the ACLU never did anything good. The truth is, lots of white pastors wimped out on slavery and segregation and civil rights, and lots of black pastors are wimping out on Farrakhan and premarital sex and personal responsibility. Maybe both have wimped out on abortion."

Pastor Clancy looked at Clarence and took a deep breath. "Well, enough on all that. We could talk till the cows come home, and I'd like to some day. So, tell me, how's that Bible study goin'?"

"Fine," Clarence said with a tinge of guilt.

"Heard you missed the last few weeks."

Clarence sat back stiffly. "You hear a lot."

"I'm a shepherd—that's my job." He looked Clarence in the eyes and said matter-of-factly, "Go to that Bible study. You need it."

Clarence squeezed tight on the chair's arms. "You going to send the deacons after me if I don't?"

Clancy laughed. "Maybe. But in your case I might have to send a few backups." He paused. "All right, you're wondering why I called you in. It's about Raymond Taylor's mama, Andrea. She's a good woman, been part of this church since she came up from L.A. She's really broken about her son's death. But she's even more broken about his life. She's ashamed her son got hold of your Tyrone. She's ashamed to face you about that. But I think you need to talk to her."

"Why?"

"Well, for both of your sakes. Also, because she may know some things."

"Some things about what?" Clarence hoped it related to the dudes at Taco Bell.

"Some things that may help you," Cairo Clancy said. "I can't say for sure. If you reach out to her, she may choose to tell you. If not, you can just help out a woman in need. And helpin' someone who needs it is never a waste of time for a true Christian, now is it?"

CHAPTER

30

"I've got good news and bad news," Ollie said, sitting across the table at Baskin-Robbins. "Which do you want first?"

"The good news," Clarence said with imitation perkiness.

"We traced the license. Got a positive ID."

"Great. Who?"

"That's the bad news. The license belongs to a seventy-five-year-old couple in Woodburn."

"What?"

"Yeah. And either they were masters of disguise or it wasn't them Herb saw at the Taco Bell."

"Very funny. I don't get it."

"Stolen plate. Taken some time after 6:00 P.M. September 2. The old folks didn't notice until the next morning."

"Great. What now?"

Clarence watched Ollie work over a double scoop Jamoca Almond Fudge.

"Okay," Ollie said, wiping his face, "you've got two guys nobody knows sitting behind Taco Bell in a car with a license plate stolen from Woodburn, maybe three hours earlier."

"Woodburn's what, an hour round trip from Portland? You'd think they'd steal it from some place closer."

"Depends on where they came from, doesn't it?" Ollie said. "I've got another piece of news for you. That stolen plate was found a few days later—on the side of I-5 near a rest stop twenty miles south of Salem. The perps knew that even if somebody jotted down the license, we couldn't track them. They probably removed the stolen plates before they left Portland, then tossed them after going by Salem."

"But these guys weren't Hispanics, and nobody saw them at the murder scene, right? I still don't get how it fits with the guys Mookie saw. And this means the info Herb gave us is worthless. We can't trace them. They could be anywhere."

"Not worthless. See, now we know where they collected and disposed of the stolen plates. Let's put it together. You've got two guys, hardened gangsters but not local, because nobody's ever seen their tricked out car and they don't know the difference between Jackson and Jack. Let's assume Woodburn was on their way to town. That means they came from south of Portland. They cover their plates, which means they're going to pull off some job and if there's any witnesses, they don't want their car identified. They're not the only Lexus out there, even with fancy wheels, so as long as they've got the stolen plate they're safe, provided they remove it soon after the crime. Okay, they're sitting behind Taco Bell, less than a mile from your sister's. Probably just waiting for it to get later, less people on the street. They're not on drugs, if Herb was right, which could mean they're staying sharp for a hit. Say they do the hit, then they take off south, at least twenty miles south of Salem, presumably on their way home. So you tell me—where's home?"

"I don't know—someplace south of Salem."

"Well, how many black gangs would there be in central and southern Oregon?"

Clarence laughed. "Other than some students at OSU in Corvallis or U of O in Eugene, I can't think of any place south of Salem where there's enough young black men to form a gang even if they wanted to."

"Exactly. So what does that tell you?"

"California?"

"Sure. That's where I-5 south takes you. You come up north, do a job, head back home."

"Since when do California bangers drive up to Portland to do hits?"

"Since maybe the guy behind the hit has gang connections in California," Ollie said, "and doesn't want word to get out on Portland streets."

"So what hope is there of ever finding these guys?" Clarence asked.

"First, I'm going to run checks on traffic tickets issued on I-5 to California plates within twenty-four hours of the murder."

"Traffic tickets?"

"Sure," Ollie said. "You have a car like that, you don't stay behind trucks and Hyundais in the slow lane. If they're bangers, you can count on them breaking the law. It's just a question of whether they got caught. I-5's long enough that maybe they did. Then I've filed a description of the car and passengers with NCIC—National Crime Information Computer. It's run by the FBI. I could only note them as 'subjects of interest.' Don't have enough yet to call them suspects. Like you say, our only definitive suspects are two Latinos. But the NCIC should get printed out in police stations, along with a ton of other stuff that sometimes gets looked at and sometimes doesn't. Hopefully some cop will see it and contact us."

"Read about Eustace *Clarence*," Keisha teased.

Clarence also wanted to know more about the boy turned dragon. He read to the kids how Eustace tried repeatedly to peel his dragon skin off, never getting anywhere. He was still a dragon. Then Aslan, the lion who had died for Edmund's sins and come back again, told the boy he would have to let him tear the skin off with his claws. Eustace was terrified:

> "The very first tear he made was so deep that I thought it had gone right into my heart. And when he began pulling the skin off, it hurt worse than anything I've ever felt. The only thing that made me able to bear it was just the pleasure of feeling the stuff peel off.
>
> "Well, he peeled the beastly stuff right off and there it was lying on the grass. And there was I as smooth and soft as a peeled switch and smaller than I had been. Then he caught hold of me— I didn't like that much for I was very tender underneath now that

I'd no skin on—and threw me into the water. It smarted like any-thing but only for a moment. After that it became perfectly deli-cious and as soon as I started swimming and splashing I found that all the pain had gone."

"Aslan is not a tame lion," the book said again. Clarence thought about his own anger, cynicism, and disillusionment. He wondered if he should ask the Lion to remove the dragon skin. No. Putting himself in someone else's hands was too much of a leap. Especially the hands of the Lion who'd allowed so much suffering, who'd taken Dani and Felicia from him.

———————

"No calls on the Lexus yet," Ollie said to Clarence, "but I heard from a SWAT cop in LAPD. He happened to come across my old bulletin about the HK53. Told me an interesting story. In April a SWAT officer got killed in a shoot-out with a gang. This guy was in a perimeter position. When the smoke finally cleared, they found the dead officer. His weapon had been stolen."

"An HK53?" Clarence asked.

"Exactly. I'm betting that's our weapon. If it is, whoever did the hit either comes from an L.A. gang or has connections there that got him the gun."

"If they're from L.A.," Clarence said, "that fits your theory with the guys in the Lexus. Fits the license plates and explains not knowing Portland streets."

"Right. It also explains the frangibles. The cop that called me had the full SWAT report in front of him. It was a high-risk residential area, so they were using fran-gibles in their HK. The downed cop presumably had some left in his magazine. I would have thought some gangbanger would have shot those rounds off by now, but I guess if they were smart, they'd hide the weapon and not use it while it was still so hot. Nothing's hotter than a dead cop's gun. Now, once they get up to Portland, it's their big chance to use their prize. They'd never figure it'd be traced back to L.A. because they didn't know they're dealing with Lone Ranger Ollie Chandler and his faithful companion Tonto Abernathy. Plus, there's one other thing that convinces me this is our weapon."

"What?"

"Remember how McCamman couldn't understand why Mrs. Burns didn't see muzzle flashes? Well, this L.A. SWAT guy told me their cops use a special HK flash-hider attachment as a tactical move so they don't get blinded or draw attention for return fire."

"So the HK53 taken from this cop had a flash-hider?"

"Exactly. Okay, what have we got?" Ollie stood up and paced. "We've got two L.A. gangsters who were hired to come in to Portland, do a gangland hit, and hightail it back to L.A. That would explain why there's no word out on the street. The local gangsters honestly don't know who did it."

"But there's lots of Hispanic gangs in L.A., so that could connect with the guys Mookie saw."

"Except the gang that shot the cop and took the HK, they weren't Hispanics. In fact, they weren't Bloods either. They were Five Nine Hoover *Crips*."

"I'm grateful for this body, but I still don't really understand it," Dani said. "I had thought that in heaven we'd be spirits without bodies."

Torel looked at her as if this were ludicrous. "How could that be? Have you not read that Elyon created a body, then breathed into it a spirit, and only when there was both body and spirit was there a living human being? To be human is to be both spirit and body. To cease to be either is to cease to be human. That is why Jesus spoke of Lazarus and the rich man as both having bodies in heaven and in hell, immediately after their deaths. Elyon's book speaks of people in heaven before the resurrection wearing robes—robes are worn only on bodies, are they not?"

"I never thought of having a body before our resurrection bodies."

"Think of your present body as the artist's preliminary sketch out of which will later flow the masterpiece. On earth you did not long to be unclothed from your body, but to be reclothed in a superior body. Christ's resurrection body is the prototype of your own. He walked and talked and ate and was grasped and held by his disciples."

"Strange. Somehow I thought of the body as the soul's prison."

"This is the teaching of human philosophers, not Elyon. The soul without the body is not free to participate in the glories of the material worlds Elyon creates. That is why I must take on a body both here and in the dark world. But to take it on and shed it is very different than being one with it. That is why your ability to fully participate in the material world far exceeds mine. It is not disembodied spirits but fully human beings who will come from the east and west and sit at a table and eat with Abraham, Isaac, and Jacob. Until your resurrection body, this one will be sufficient for you."

"The food here is so varied and delicious and colorful and flavorful. It's as if the number of flavors has multiplied as much as the number of colors. I desire the food, I savor the smell, I relish the texture, and delight in the taste."

"Yes." The angel looked pleased. "The great banquet feast could not be more spiritual, nor could it be more physical. The two are not at odds. You are free to enjoy what you used to need—food and work and rest and exercise. Your longings on earth were the hunger pangs that prepared you to forever enjoy the feasts and delights of heaven. Your resurrection body will allow you to fully participate in it, more than even this present body. You do not become inhuman in heaven. Rather, you become *fully* human—all that Elyon intended from the beginning that you should be."

Ollie sat across the table from Clarence, more preoccupied than usual. "My lieutenant says there's some pressure being put on us to back off on the investigation of your sister's murder."

"Pressure from where?"

"Try the chief of police."

"What?"

"Well, it's not pressure *from* him, it's pressure *on* him. Your publisher could be in on it, I don't know. Somebody with some leverage."

"I can't believe they'd put on pressure to close a case."

"Believe it. Of course, you can bet they've done it in a way they can deny later. They probably said something like, 'There are dozens of other unsolved murders that deserve attention, and this one seems to have gotten a disproportionate amount. Plus, it's creating some racial tension with the cops and the Latino community, then there's this crazy journalist who commits this hate crime against two model citizens.' Something like that. By the way, those guys you assaulted never filed charges, and I hear they're not even interested in suing you—bet every lawyer in town's called them too. You're one lucky guy."

"Why don't I feel lucky?"

Ollie shrugged. "I figure the fact that someone wants us to back off shows we're getting somewhere. That we're on to something."

"Are you going to back off?"

"You kiddin' me? The chief resented the pressure. The captain told the lieutenant, and he told me, 'Don't overdo it, but give the case whatever it deserves.' Truth is, someone suggesting we back off on a case is like saying, 'Sic 'em,' to a dog. I've really got my sniffer goin' now. They say a detective has to listen like a blind man and watch like a deaf man."

"That's profound," Clarence said.

"Yeah." Ollie tore a big bite out of his hot dog, leaving a smudge of mustard on his lower lip. "I'm a class act. Sometimes I even surprise myself."

"Can I ask you something, Ollie? It's something I've been wanting to ask for a long time."

"Sure. Why not?"

"What did you think of the O. J. Simpson case?"

Ollie shot Clarence a surprised where-did-that-come-from look. He shrugged his side-of-beef shoulders. "Why do I have the feeling I'm walking into a field of

Claymore mines? Okay, I've got two legs, I can afford to lose one. Well, since I used to work for LAPD and I'm a homicide detective, I had people ask me after the verdict, 'Does that mean they're going to reopen the investigation?' I just told them, 'You don't reopen a case that's been solved.'"

"You were that certain?"

"Well, after the verdict when Simpson announced he would find the person who'd done the killings, I thought, that should be easy enough. Just find the guy with the same kind of hair, same footprint, who drives a white Bronco and left a trail of blood from the crime scene that had DNA identical to yours. Let's see, there's maybe thirty people in the world with close enough DNA for a possible match. When you eliminate the ones living in Tibet and Madagascar or who hang their laundry on the Great Wall of China and find the one that was in L.A. the night of the murders, you've got him. He wants to find the killer? Hey, it's a short walk to the bathroom mirror."

"Ollie, if you think O. J. did it, don't hesitate to come right out and say it. Seriously, though, what was your take on the racial issues in the trial?"

Ollie shrugged. "My belief is that people don't care about the color of the person who kills them, any more than they care about the color of the person who keeps them from being killed. When it comes to life and death, color takes a backseat."

"Do you think the prosecution did its job?"

"Well, yes and no. They proved their case. They made a lot of mistakes, sure. The biggest one was jury selection."

Clarence bristled. "Letting too many blacks on the jury?"

"Not blacks per se, just certain blacks. One former Black Panther was one too many. After the verdict, the guy salutes Simpson with a Black Power fist. I think maybe the prosecutors got the message then, don't you? They believed the best about America, that race wasn't a big enough issue to overshadow justice. Well, they were wrong."

"So did the verdict make you draw any conclusions about blacks?"

"Maybe. I don't know."

"Be honest with me."

"Okay. You want honest? Here's three names—Mike Tyson. Marion Barry. O. J. Simpson."

"What about them?"

"I have to draw a picture?"

"Yeah." Clarence knew where this was going, but he wanted to watch Ollie take each step.

"Okay. Tyson's a convicted rapist, and you had prominent black leaders who couldn't wait for him to get out so they could cheer him back to heavyweight champion. Barry was a convicted crack user, so he gets reelected as D.C. mayor. Simpson was a cokehead and a wife beater, at very least, even if you ignore the overwhelming evidence that he's also a vicious murderer. And what happens? Blacks say these guys were set up. They raise them up like they were heroes instead of criminals."

"Not all blacks."

"No, of course not. But lots of blacks."

"So what did it make you conclude about blacks?" Clarence braced himself, wondering why it mattered to him so much what Ollie thought.

Ollie studied Clarence's face to see if he really wanted to hear his answer. "Maybe that *some* blacks are naïve. Or don't care about moral responsibility. Or that *some* blacks have a blind loyalty to other blacks. Like they've thought so long about being victims—and yes, they really *were* victims once—they can't make moral judgments against other blacks. They feel like traitors or something. I was called in to testify at a trial of a man who was guilty, start to finish—several witnesses, unmistakable ID, the whole nine yards. But the jury let him off. I was stunned. A black juror came up to me afterwards and he apologized to me. He said, 'I knew he was guilty, but there's already too many young black men behind bars; I just couldn't put away another one.' Ironic, since the victim was black too."

"But you're not saying that happens often, are you?"

"Well, how about that Jewish scholar who was stabbed to death by the black mob in New York? He actually named the guy that stabbed him before he died. But the black jury didn't convict him. And after the acquittal, members of the jury went out partying with the defendant. It's all documented. It happened. Or what about the conviction rates for felonies? It's something like 80 percent nationally, but 30 percent in Detroit and less than that in D.C., where most of the accused and the juries are black. Or what about the black criminal law professor at George Washington University? The one who openly advocates jury nullification because the black community needs their men, even the criminals. Now that's blind loyalty, don't you think?"

"So who started the concept of blind race loyalty in American courtrooms?" Clarence asked. "White judges and juries letting off white Klansmen and winking at each other. Blacks have seen this for years. Can you understand why maybe they'd have a blind loyalty to other blacks?"

"Sure. Blacks accused of messing with whites used to be automatically convicted. It was flat out wrong. So maybe they think these black defendants are innocent and being picked on—and no doubt sometimes that's true—and when the evidence indicates that, by all means acquit them. But in lots of cases the evidence completely refutes that. I just think there are better ways to protest the system and help minorities than freeing guilty people who are just going to go out and commit more crimes, and against who? Usually the same minorities that acquit them. I understand the frustration. No, I suppose I don't. But that still doesn't make it right."

"No. It doesn't," Clarence said. "Black people are just reacting against the idea that being black means you're guilty."

"And other people are reacting against the idea that being black means you're innocent," Ollie said.

"The truth is, being black just means you're human. Which means sometimes innocent, sometimes guilty. But Ollie, you have to understand the relationship with cops these black jurors bring into that courtroom. I get stopped maybe four times a year just because I'm black. You were with me coming back from the ball game, you saw it. One time I was dropping off Jake's daughter Carly to work at a Crisis Pregnancy Center. The officer pulls me over, looks at her, and asks her if she's all right. And then he says to me, 'Whose kid is that?'"

"What'd you tell him?"

"I told him I'd kidnapped her and was going to sell her on the black market. No, I didn't—but I wanted to. He was nice enough, once I proved I was innocent. What bothers me is just that—being presumed guilty and having to prove my innocence."

"I'm not going to defend that kind of thing," Ollie said. "I can tell you that when I was a uniformed, as far as I know I never pulled anyone over just because they were black. Now I've pulled over my share of people of every race, and most the time I saw them from behind and didn't even know the color of their skin. I think the same thing goes for most cops. I agree the bozo who pulled you over coming home from Seattle was out of line. I've seen and heard enough of the Mark Fuhrman types. If the charge was racism and Fuhrman was on trial, I'd have found him guilty. It's just that it was murder and someone *else* was on trial and I think the jury lost sight of it."

Clarence shrugged. "Maybe they did. I just don't think it's that cut and dried."

"For a couple of years I had a black partner in L.A.," Ollie said. "Sharp guy, well read, articulate. Reminded me of you, but better looking. Could have been a corporate attorney or a CEO if he wanted to, but he wanted to be a cop. He's a lieutenant now. He'll make captain no problem. But the longer we spent together, the more I couldn't believe some of the things he thought. He said crack was a white supremacist plot to murder black men—he proved this by pointing out blacks can't afford the airplanes that bring in drugs. He told me all the liquor stores were deliberately set up by whites throughout the black community to dull black people's thinking and raise crime so more blacks could be killed and imprisoned. When I pointed out most of the liquor stores were owned by blacks, he said it didn't matter. He claimed government scientists created the AIDS virus in a lab in order to release it in the black community. He said AZT and other AIDS treatments were specifically designed to help white people and kill black people."

"I've heard all those claims," Clarence said, "and more."

"I wanted to stop at a Church's Chicken one day, and my partner refused to eat there," Ollie said. "He claimed they put a chemical in their chicken that makes black men sterile. I was drinking a Snapple and he points to the drawing of a ship in Boston Harbor on the label, you know the Boston Tea Party, and he says that's a slave ship. He says Snapple is made by the Ku Klux Klan and he proves it by pointing out a *K* with a circle around it, which of course means kosher. He offered no evidence for any of this, and I've heard Snapple and Church's offer proof to the contrary, but he still believed it because it was all 'well known' in the black community. To be honest, it struck me as completely irrational—even though my partner was one of the smartest guys I knew. Maybe even smarter than me."

"Now *that's* hard to imagine," Clarence said. "Okay, I don't agree with most of those beliefs, although frankly I think there may be a little truth in some of them, I'm not sure. But I can see why it's all ridiculous to you. It's because you trust the white men who own most businesses. You trust the system, people in authority. Your family has never been victimized or brutalized for your skin color. So to you, these things are unthinkable. But when you're black, you know lots of your older family members who were hurt, some killed by the Klan. You remember hundreds of incidents of prejudice and discrimination and hate against you and your family. You know your ancestors were beaten and raped and given forty lashes for learning to read or write. You've heard about the Tuskegee experiment where black men with syphilis weren't given penicillin, which would have cured them, so white doctors could study the advancing effects of the disease and watch these men suffer and die needlessly. You've heard all these stories, most of them true, so as a black you grow up being profoundly suspicious of whites. That's no mystery—it's completely understandable. If the tables were reversed, I guarantee whites would suspect black-owned companies and even black doctors of conspiring to hurt them."

"Okay, since we're being so honest," Ollie said, "can I ask you a question? If O. J. had been found guilty, do you think L.A. and say Chicago, Detroit, and Washington would have burned?"

"If they would have, the lives lost would have been mostly black," Clarence said.

"I know that. But it wasn't my question."

"I don't know," Clarence said.

"Neither do I. But I have friends who are sure they would have. And their attitude was, even though they think Simpson was guilty, the verdict probably saved hundreds of lives. One said to me, 'Better one guilty man goes free than hundreds of innocent people die in the backlash of his conviction.'"

"What's your point?" Clarence asked.

"I think you know my point, don't you? If there'd been rioting, wouldn't the black leadership have justified it? Wouldn't they have made it the fault of white America? I guess my question is, can white people *ever* be right? Can black people *ever* be wrong? Because if the answer is no, a lot of white people are going to give up trying. And if you think we've got racial problems now, look out."

"Sounds like a threat."

"Not a threat. Just an observation," Ollie said, throwing up his hands. "So what did *you* think about the Simpson case?"

"I had a lot of mixed feelings," Clarence said. "Did I believe Fuhrman was typical of a lot of white cops? Sure. Not all, but enough to pull off a small scale conspiracy, yeah. We lived with that all the time in Mississippi. My grandfather was stripped naked and tarred and feathered for no reason but to humiliate a black man. I had an uncle who was castrated by Klansmen, and the police never did anything about it. He never walked right again. He took his life a few years later. He'd fought for his country in World War II, was decorated for heroism in combat. And that's how his life ended."

"I'm sorry," Ollie said. "I really am."

"Know what black folk in most towns called the local sheriff? 'Chief head-banger.' Black men were arrested for no reason, and any time you went to jail you expected to be beaten. There were no black lawyers then, and who could afford a white lawyer? Or trust him? The cops beat the tar out of you, and the courts put you in jail. That's what I grew up thinking, because that's what I grew up seeing. So, yes, I think the police are capable of great injustice. But injustice to black men on the street is one thing. Injustice to a black sports icon who most whites saw as a hero, that's something else. It's hard to believe cops would target *this* black man who they put on a pedestal, a guy they paid big money to cheer for on the football field. And what about his commercials? Corporations paid him the big bucks because they knew he appealed to whites as much as blacks."

"I agree with you there. O. J. was a hero to me," Ollie said. "Like Hank Aaron. But remember how at first all the feminist groups hollered the police had been far too *lenient* on O. J., how they'd let him get away with wife-beating and they took too long to arrest him and all? Cops can never do it right. First, they're too lenient on a guy because he's their hero, then next thing you know they frame the same guy for murder."

"I think the real racial polarization happened," Clarence said, "when whites saw the Goldman and Brown families. It was like looking in the mirror, realizing it could just as easily be them. And when blacks saw the Simpson family interviewed, it was the same thing. They looked like their mamas and sisters and aunts and cousins and the people that live down the street and go to the neighborhood church. We iden-tify most with the people we're used to, the ones we know and love. And we don't know and love enough people of other races to identify with them. All that came out in the O. J. case. I lost a lot of sleep over it."

"But if things don't change," Ollie said, "courtroom tactics will all be centered on race, gender, economics, religion, everything that makes us different. Attorneys will appeal to the jury to decide based on things other than the evidence. A la Johnny Cochrane."

"I thought the most interesting aftermath of the case," Clarence said, "was all those calls for judicial reform made by whites. After the Simi Valley verdict that cleared the cops who beat up Rodney King, a lot of blacks brought up their usual accusations of injustice, but most whites I heard kept saying, 'We need to trust the system.' Interesting how it all got reversed when Simpson was let off. All of a sudden there were television panel discussions and letters to the editor and columns about restructuring jury selection to avoid racial prejudice. Remember?"

"Yeah, I do," Ollie said. "I called for a few judicial reforms myself. But nobody listens to me."

"My uncle Elijah made an interesting comparison," Clarence said. "He told us about a soda pop machine at Southern Pacific Railroad where he worked. It was in the management area, but everyone had access to it. Some of the executives discovered if you gave the machine a good smack in just the right place it would give you a can of pop without having to pay. Well, some of the rail workers watched the execs do this for weeks, and finally one of them tried it himself. Smack, free pop. Well, one of those same executives saw him do it. Then he said to his secretary, 'Call the vendor. We've got to get that machine fixed.'"

"And your point is what?" Ollie asked.

"The pop machine is the justice system. For hundreds of years white juries convicted blacks who were innocent and acquitted whites who were guilty of beating and lynching blacks and burning down their houses. Not many whites called for judicial reform. Then the Simpson case comes along, and a black man whites think was guilty is found innocent by a mostly black jury. So what happens? All of a sudden, white America says, 'Hey we've got to get this pop machine fixed.'"

"I never thought of it like that," Ollie said.

"Neither did the management at the railroad. When you're in the power position you're used to getting things your way."

"But two wrongs don't make a right," Ollie said. "White juries were wrong to acquit people just because they were white. And black juries are wrong to acquit people just because they're black."

"I agree with you a hundred percent," Clarence said. "I'm just saying after hundreds of years of it going one way and them doing so little about it, it's interesting what a hard time white folk have when it goes the other way." Clarence sighed. "The thing I hate is after the O. J. debacle and the Million Man March there was so much talk about racial issues, but out of it came more hard feelings than ever. It seems like dialogues of the deaf."

"Oh, I don't know," Ollie said. "We just talked about it, and you said some things that helped me. Seems like we agree on a lot when it comes down to it. I guess when I hear you say blacks are still responsible for their choices and not every problem is due to white racism, it helps me be more open to those cases when it is."

"And hearing you say you know racism is still around helps me to be able to see the other side too," Clarence said.

"I have a question for you, sort of personal," Ollie said. "As much as you know about media bias, why did you automatically believe what the *Trib* said about me brutalizing that guy?"

"Because of my experience with cops, I guess." Clarence took a deep breath. "My earliest memories of police officers go back to Mississippi. Some of them were nice. But a lot of them weren't. They'd mock us, call us names—spooks, shines, spades, jigs, coons, and niggers. They'd always intimidate black folk, I mean law-abiding folk. I could have probably gotten over that, but...there's one story I didn't tell you."

Clarence sighed, as if he needed to draw on reserves to tell his tale. "One night my daddy heard about one of my cousins, Seth, Uncle Elijah's oldest boy. He'd been hangin' around a white civil rights activist that came down from New York. All the authorities hated him. Well, word got out they arrested my cousin and this white boy and were holding them in the jail. Daddy went down to the jail with my uncle. Mama begged him not to go without witnesses, but just he and Elijah went. They got there and asked to see the boys. The sheriff was a big fat white cop."

"Like me," Ollie asked, "but not as muscular?"

"Yeah, sort of. Anyway, they ended up accusing my dad and uncle of trying to break the kids out of jail, which was ridiculous. Uncle Elijah was just like Daddy. Strong as an ox, but gentle as they come. Well, these cops decided they were going to teach those colored men a lesson. So they let out the boys and locked up the men. Then they proceeded to beat up Daddy and Uncle Elijah. They beat them with their hands and sticks and a baseball bat. They urinated on them. They tortured them by jamming a fork up their nose. I'm not going to tell you the rest, because it rips me up to even think about it. Sometimes Daddy still doubles over in pain from what they did to him that night."

Clarence tried to contain his tears, which now streamed down his face. Ollie looked stunned.

"When my cousin came to tell us Daddy was in jail, he drove Mama and me down there. We were on the outside of those thick walls, but we could hear Daddy and Uncle Elijah...they were...screaming."

Clarence sobbed. Ollie wasn't sure what to do. He sat quietly. Finally Clarence spoke again.

"Daddy was firm when we were growin' up. He disciplined us when we deserved it. But he was the kindest man. He never so much as raised his voice to us.

I know what he went through that night. And I guess I've never trusted a white policeman since."

"Your daddy's a fine man...fine a man as I ever..." Ollie's chin trembled, and he cleared his throat and wiped his eyes. "I'm sorry for what they did to him. I wish we could go back there right now, you and me. I wish we could get our hands on that sheriff, on those dirty cops."

"If we could," Clarence said, "when I was done you'd have to arrest me. I wouldn't stop until I killed them. I know. In my mind I've done it a thousand times."

―――――――

"I'm glad you came by, Mr. Abernathy," Andrea Taylor said, her eyes hanging as if heavy weights were attached. "The last years have been hard. Wouldn't have made it without Ebenezer Church, that's for sure. I'm glad you've been comin' there. And I'm sorry about...how my son influenced your nephew."

"It's all right, Andrea. It wasn't your fault. I know that."

"The hardest part," she said, "is always wondering if there wasn't something else I should have done. Anyway, I've been thinking there's something I should tell you." She looked away and took a deep breath. "One night Raymond was on the angel dust. Devil dust they should call it, that's what it is. But he was hallucinating, and I didn't know whether to hold him or slap him. But I held him in my arms, and my baby said to me somethin' real strange. I asked him about it later. He said I imagined it, but I know I didn't. He kept saying, 'It wasn't *her*; they got it wrong; that's not what I told 'em.'"

Clarence tried not to appear as anxious as he felt. "So...what does that mean?"

"Well, at first I didn't connect it with anyone. But then when my baby shot himself," she choked up, "he whispered somethin' to me just before he died. He said, 'Tell Li'l GC I'm sorry about his mama.' It didn't seem like he was just saying he felt bad for Tyrone. It seemed more like a...deathbed confession. It's been on my mind ever since. I don't know what it means, but I started thinking maybe it related to what he said before. I can't believe my boy would have hurt your sister and your niece, Mr. Abernathy. But I don't know. I just don't know. He hurt a lot of other people. I'm sorry. I'm so sorry about my boy."

"I know." Clarence came over to the couch, sat down, and put his arms around her. At first she backed away from his touch, but then she surrendered to it, leaning into Clarence and sobbing.

Clarence could blame a lot of people for a lot of things, but not this woman. After they sat for a while, she began reminiscing about Raymond.

"He kept a scrapbook, with newspaper clippings. I always wished it was a scrapbook about honor roll and sports, but it wasn't. He saved things about gang crimes and bad things. I've been thinking about burning it, once I get up the strength. I don't want it around."

"Can I see it?" Clarence asked.

She nodded. "It's in his bedroom." She got up slowly, negotiating the floor as if it were the deck of a sailboat in high winds. "You can come in if you want." Clarence followed her into the neat and clean bedroom, bed made nicely, covers undisturbed.

While she searched for the scrapbook, Clarence looked at some clippings on the wall. Most of them were from the *Tribune*. There was a story on Dani's shooting, and a later clipping of Felicia's death notice. He looked at a picture of a gang summit where gang leaders met a year before with the City Council on how to reduce violence on the streets. GC's face was prominent among the gang leaders. Clarence looked at another picture, a large one adjoining a feature story on Reggie Norcoast and his team. The picture featured Norcoast, Carson Gray, secretary Sheila, and the administrator, Karen.

Clarence sat down on Raymond's bed to read through the scrapbook. Some of the clippings contained his name, Raymond Taylor, others the names of the Rollin' 60s Crips, either in Los Angeles or Portland. Clarence read twenty clippings about various crimes. He speculated Raymond had been involved in them, most unsolved as of the dates of the articles. He flipped the page, when something dropped to the floor. It was a loose, letter-sized envelope with "GC" penciled on the front. He looked inside. Empty. There were no more clippings. The book came to an abrupt end. GC had written the final clipping by playing that stupid game, flirting with death, then being seduced by it.

Raymond clearly had a reason for saving everything in the scrapbook and on the wall. For most of the items the reason was obvious. But…Clarence looked back up on the wall, seeing the four smiling faces in Norcoast's office.

Why did Gangster Cool care about this picture? Why had he posted it on his wall?

CHAPTER

31

"We got a hit," Ollie told Clarence. "They read my description of the Lexus at a precinct roll call in southern Oregon. A Medford cop picked up on it. He called me at home, 4:30 this morning. Disturbed my beauty sleep."

"That explains it," Clarence said, looking at Ollie's unshaven mug and disheveled hair.

"Explains what?"

"Never mind. What'd he tell you?"

Ollie looked at his notes. "Officer Jim Seymour says that on September 3 at 5:27 A.M. he pulled over a Lexus that fits my description to a T. Said the wheels looked like they belonged in a display case. Driver and passenger, both young black males. He filled out a FIR on them."

"Fir?"

"Field interview report. Everything matches. Height, body build, everything."

"Why'd he pull them over?"

"Doin' eighty-eight miles an hour. Said as soon as they pulled over, their hands went straight up."

"What?"

"Yeah, said it looked really weird. It was just a speeding violation. He couldn't understand it."

"I can't either. Why would they do that?"

"Because, in my humble opinion, they're from L.A."

"How do you know that?"

"LAPD has 'em trained. In some parts of town, if you're pulled over it's assumed you're armed and ready to shoot unless you put your hands in the air. If you do, you'll be treated okay. If you don't, expect to be approached by officers with their guns drawn. You've got so many armed drivers it's a precautionary thing. I don't know anywhere else where hands in the air is routine on a pullover. Put it together with the HK53 from L.A. and heading south on I-5—I'd put big money on L.A."

"So the officer just got them for speeding? No other charges?"

"He saw a doobie pipe on the floor. Had some seed in it. Cited them for possession of less than an ounce of marijuana."

"He arrested them?"

"No. That's only a violation in Oregon. Can't arrest unless it's over an ounce. He just cited them. But he checked both their IDs."

"You mean...we've actually got their names?"

Ollie looked down at his notes. "Driver Robert Rose, passenger Jerome Rice. Officer Seymour ran checks on them. Just a few traffic tickets, but no criminal history."

"None?"

"Odd, huh? Anyway, we've got both their names, addresses, and the real license plate of the car. If they're connected to the shooting, we've got a good shot at finding out. We'll have to play our cards right because nobody actually saw them at the crime scene. We know they had a gun, according to Mr. Kim's testimony. But their car being a mile from your sister's at Taco Bell isn't enough for a conviction, unless you get a judge who really hates fast food. Speaking of tacos, I guess you've figured out we need to talk to our boy Mookie again."

"Because he fingered two Hispanics?"

"Yeah, not to mention the slight difference between a 1996 Lexus and a late seventies Impala—not that I'm a stickler for details. I mean, one wheel on the Lexus is worth more than the whole car Mookie described."

"He could still be telling the truth, though. Two Latinos could still have done the shooting or driven by just after it."

"Or maybe Mookie just saw the chance for a hundred dollars. These two new guys, Rose and Rice, they're bugging me though. No police record? Come on. I figured Officer Seymour must have missed something when he ran their names for warrants. But I double-checked and it's true. No outstanding warrants, no warrants ever. No felonies, no misdemeanors except those speeding violations a few years ago. It doesn't fit. These aren't peewees. If they're major bangers, users, dealers, who knows what else, they have to have a record. If they've got a big enough rep to pull off a hit job like that, they'd have a resume for sure."

"So how can you explain the fact that they don't?"

"Not sure. Maybe somehow they've had their records wiped clean—friends in high places or something, like maybe some mover and shaker in Sacramento? Anyway, I've got cop buddies in L.A., a couple with gang enforcement. Already called a few and asked if they recognized the names. They didn't, but there's more bangers in L.A. than there are parking spaces and usually they know them by their gang monikers, not their real names. One of my buddies is going to check out both addresses. When he finds the guys, I'm flyin' down there to chat."

"I'm impressed, Ollie. Good work."

"Hey. Even a blind hog finds an acorn once in a while."

"Clarence, what's wrong?" Geneva asked this dreary drizzly Saturday morning. Clarence was taking a break from cleaning the garage.

"What's wrong? What's right? That's a better question."

"You're so angry."

Clarence slammed his fist to the table. "Quit saying I'm angry. I'm not angry!"

"So what would you do to the table if you *were* angry?" She shook her head like someone tired of trying. "I'm going to spend the day over at Mama's with my sisters."

"Great," Clarence said. "You can join them in bad-mouthing black men. Maybe take some shots at me while you're at it."

"Don't try to take my family from me," Geneva said. "With Dani gone, they're all I've got besides you and the kids. They support me and love me. That's more than you've been doing lately."

"Right, so now I'm one of the no-goods too? Well, I'm doing everything I can. Sorry if it's not enough."

"You're doing everything you can to find Dani's killer and hang him from a tree, and who knows where you're going to end up? What good will that do your family? You're obsessed with this thing. Isn't it enough that one family got torn apart? Does ours have to go down too?"

Geneva left the room and got on the phone with her mother and two sisters, asking if she could take them to lunch. Over the years, her whole family had migrated to this area. Black women had learned to stick together. They had a closer network than white women, Geneva had always thought.

Geneva heard Clarence go back to work in the garage. She sat alone in the bedroom, wishing he'd come talk to her, say he was sorry. She thought about the family she'd grown up in. Her father had been a hard worker but was passive in the home. Her mama and older sisters and she ran the household, while two of her brothers spent a lot of time on the streets. One had come out of it and was doing well. One had gone to jail and was a lifelong addict. Daddy had passed away six years ago. The problems of their men had drawn the womenfolk closer together. It hurt Geneva that Clarence felt black women being so strong made the men feel unwanted and unnecessary. She could see his point sometimes, but given their history, black women had no choice but to be strong. It was the only way to survive.

With everything happening inside Clarence and the wall building between them, Geneva needed someone she could talk to, someone who could understand. She needed her mama and sisters—her girlfriends.

"Clarence, this is Jake. I stumbled onto something. Could be important. I called Ollie and he said we could meet at his place. Even though it's Saturday, I thought it shouldn't wait."

"What is it?"

"It's about the investigation. My friend Sue Keels will be there. It's something she knows. Can you meet us at Ollie's in an hour?"

"Yeah." Clarence got directions to Ollie's house. He hurried back to the garage to finish his cleanup project. He pulled out an old piece of canvas tucked under a storage shelf. As he pulled, one can of spray paint rolled out, then another and another. Six cans. There were several colors, mostly shades of blue. He put his finger on the tip of a shiny spray nozzle. It was still wet. He looked at the two cans that weren't blue tones. One was flat white, the other metallic green.

Dani watched as a man named Calvin Fairbank, engaged to be married, risked his life rescuing a black family from slavery. Then she watched as Fairbank served five long hard years in prison for doing the rescue. Not as much misery as most of the slaves, but then, they had no choice, Dani reminded herself. This man didn't have to do this. He could have been content to go with the flow of the times, to profit from slavery or at least to ignore it. Even if he opposed it, he could have just made speeches about slavery being wrong. There was no risk but criticism, and one could sleep better at night just mouthing the right moral position. As Dani watched, she couldn't help but feel after five years of prison, Fairbank would marry the woman who faithfully waited for his release and be content to make occasional abolitionist speeches.

Dani was shocked to watch Fairbank, after he gained release, immediately help a female slave escape from Kentucky. He was arrested again and put back in prison for fifteen years. Dani saw the young woman, Fairbank's fiancée, weeping. Years of tears. Dani felt her burden as she faithfully waited another fifteen years, twenty in all, to marry Calvin. She knew his cause was just. Dani pondered her sacrifice—waiting twenty years while her beloved languished in prison, all because he'd been compelled to help the needy in the name of Christ.

Dani watched another young man, an Englishman named William, come to faith in Christ in 1784. Immediately thereafter young William Wilberforce began his battle for the black man's freedom. She watched him as a British parliamentarian. Relentlessly, he introduced and reintroduced to Parliament motions to abolish slavery. He did so in the face of deep-seated apathy, scorn, and all the opposition the powerful slave industry could muster.

"We are all guilty for tolerating the evil of slavery," she heard Wilberforce say to Parliament. "Never, never will we desist until we extinguish every trace of this bloody traffic, of which our posterity, looking back to the history of these enlightened times will scarce believe that it has been suffered to exist so long a disgrace and dishonor to this country."

She watched as year after year Wilberforce endured sleepless nights, plagued by dreams of suffering slaves. Decade after decade his colleagues refused to pay attention to his words about the injustices of slavery. She watched in awe as in the middle of Parliament sessions Wilberforce reached under his chair and pulled out slave chains, draping them over himself as he spoke to his peers, dramatizing the inhumanity of slavery. She watched the distinguished parliamentarians roll their eyes, snicker, mock him, and call him a fool. But Wilberforce, she realized, was performing for a different audience, the audience of One. She wondered where the mockers were now. No, she knew where they were and shuddered at the thought.

Dani continued to watch the years go by. In 1807 Wilberforce finally wore down the opposition by refusing to be silent. Parliament voted to outlaw the buying and selling of new slaves. Wilberforce had overcome incredible odds. But the old slaves were not yet emancipated, and William could not rest. Dani saw him fight twenty more years, laboring to free existing slaves. She watched him in 1833, lying sick and exhausted in his bed. Then it happened—the Bill for the Abolition of Slavery passed its second reading in the House of Commons, bringing all slavery in England to its final end. Dani wept as three days later, his life's mission finally accomplished, Wilberforce died.

Dani, stirred deeply by this life of which she'd known nothing on earth, thought about many things. She pondered how one man, born in privilege, could devote fifty years of labor to being mocked and vilified in the pursuit of God's justice. She thought further, wondering what would happen if but one Wilberforce rose up in American politics today. What would happen if one representative or one senator would introduce over and over again measures and reminders of the reality that unborn babies were being killed by the millions? What if only one man or woman would pull out pictures of the unborn from under his congressional chair, would endure the ridicule and opposition, would tirelessly stand for justice, would speak up for those who cannot speak for themselves, refusing to be silent? What if just one person, relentless, would live out his convictions not for the applause of his colleagues nor the approval of his generation, but for the audience of One?

Suddenly she heard, of all things, a harmonica. She turned to see Zeke playing "Steal Away, Jesus." The clapping and singing began. Someone was strumming a Jew's harp, twanging a steady beat. It was party time. Reunion time. Laughter time. Her great-grandfather started dancing with his friend Finney. Zeke whispered something to him, and they both laughed so hard that tears flowed.

The history lesson was over, yet Dani knew it had changed her. She had labeled white people as selfish and uncaring. Yet now she had witnessed many white people who had given up their convenience and wealth and reputations and freedom, and in some cases their lives, to help suffering black people. She wondered if *she* would have had the courage to do the same for others, whether black or white. Suddenly she looked up and saw a man talking with Lewis and Torel. She stared at him in a moment of disbelief. William Wilberforce. She ran to him like an unpretentious child.

"It's a great honor to meet you, sir."

"Do not call me sir, please, my lady. I am merely Elyon's errand boy. It is I who am honored to meet you."

Dani threw her arms around Wilberforce and cried without reserve, her tears mingling with his. She'd rarely hugged a white man. In his hug she felt healing. In her hug he felt reward. In their hug both felt praise to Elyon.

Ollie's southeast Portland house was as comfortable and casual as his office, though thanks to his wife, Clarence assumed, not as messy.

Sue Keels extended her hand, and Clarence shook it. She was light skinned, blonde, petite, almost tiny. Jake looked at both his good friends, thinking the physical contrast between them couldn't have been more pronounced.

"Jake's told me all about you, Clarence," Sue said. "And Little Finn went on and on about you. It's a pleasure to finally meet you. I love your columns, especially on the pro-life issue. That one's very close to my heart." Clarence sensed her sincerity, to which he immediately warmed.

"Sorry to cut into everybody's weekend," Jake said, "but Janet and I were over at Sue's last night and the case came up. Of course, there's a lot I don't know, but both of you," he looked at Ollie and Clarence, "have filled me in on some of it. When we were talking last night one thing led to another and suddenly…why don't you fill them in, Sue? First, give them some background."

"Well," Sue said, "I'm very involved in pro-life work. I go down a couple of afternoons a week to an abortion clinic to do sidewalk counseling, you know, where I talk to girls coming in for abortions. I tell them about the baby's development, show them intrauterine photos, give them options, offer financial help, tell them about adoptions, that sort of thing. Well, anyway, in late August I was at the Lovepeace Abortion Clinic, and a girl came up by herself. That's a little unusual. Most come in with a girlfriend, boyfriend, sister, mother, somebody. Well, this girl was really broken. When I showed her the pictures of the babies, she started crying. I asked her if she really wanted an abortion. She shook her head. I invited her to come down the street and sit in my car and talk. She did. Before I go further, I should explain that normally I treat these conversations as totally confidential. But there's a reason I'm making an exception this time.

"Anyway," Sue continued, "we talked for nearly an hour, so she missed her abortion appointment. I really liked her. She was a very sharp girl. Articulate. Pretty. Poised. She said she didn't want an abortion, but she was being pressured to get it. That's common, of course. You've got a lot of girls who don't want the abortion, but they get herded in by someone who does. I asked if the pressure was coming from her parents, and she said no, they didn't even know she was pregnant. She said if they knew they'd be really disappointed in her. And she wondered how it would affect her plans to start college in just a few weeks.

"She said she'd been given the money to get an abortion, and someone had made the appointment for her. I asked her if it was the father of her child. She hesitated and didn't really answer. Later I said something about how boyfriends often push girls to get abortions, but then the girl ends up carrying most of the guilt and going through the post-abortion trauma and all that. Then she told me she didn't have a boyfriend, which I thought was a little strange. This girl definitely wasn't a hooker, and she didn't strike me as someone who would sleep around. In fact, she finally told me through tears that she'd only had sex a half-dozen times, all in late June I think. She was really distraught."

Ollie and Clarence both leaned forward, listening intently and wondering where this was going.

"Well," Sue laughed, "I guess I'm babbling on, but—"

"No, Sue," Jake said. "It's important. Tell them what happened next."

"Well, she said she didn't want her baby to suffer for her mistake, and she thanked me for talking to her. I gave her the Crisis Pregnancy Center phone number, offered financial help, told her she needed to talk to her parents and if there were any problems at home she could come stay with me, all of that. She said actually her parents had always been supportive, and she felt sure they'd stand by her after the initial shock.

"We really hit it off. She reminded me of my daughter Angela. I called her the next couple of days to check up on her. She said whoever had made the appointment for her found out she didn't show up, and now she was getting a *lot* of pressure to abort. I encouraged her again to tell her parents because they really needed to know. Actually, I was optimistic things were going to turn out okay. In fact, we were scheduled to meet for lunch that Saturday afternoon. I was really looking forward to it. Then it all happened."

"What happened?" Ollie asked.

"I'm watching the late news Friday night. The lead story comes on and they show a girl's picture. All of a sudden they're interviewing her friends, her principal, all of them are raving about what a wonderful girl she was, and they're crying. I just sat there staring at the picture." The dampness in her eyes turned to drizzle. "It was her. Just like that, this sweet young girl I liked so much, who I was going to have lunch with the next day…she was dead."

Ollie and Clarence turned toward each other and spoke the same words at the same moment. "Leesa Fletcher."

"Clarence Abernathy? This is Miles Ferguson, your brother Ellis's attorney."

"What's going on? Is Ellis okay?"

"He's fine. But they wouldn't let him call you. So he called me. He says you need to come see him. He's got some information. Says you need to talk with an inmate who goes by the name Big Dog. His real name's Ken Gold. Ellis says you should talk to him right away."

Ollie and Clarence drove south toward Salem, headed to the state penitentiary.

"We ran the plates and got some interesting results," Ollie said. "Found out the Lexus was in Sacramento the afternoon of September 3. In fact, it's still there."

"What?"

"They sold it. Actually, they traded it in for a brand new car." Ollie glanced down and caught a peek at his notes. "A Mercedes SL 500, sport model, with all the trimmings. Midnight blue. Bought by one Jerome Rice. Accompanied by a friend. No doubt our Robert Rose. And are you ready for this? They paid *cash*."

"For a Mercedes SL 500? You've got to be kidding."

"I talked to the guy who made the sale, Fred somebody. He's still pumped about it. At least, he was until he found out I'm a homicide detective. He gave them forty-thousand-dollars trade-in on the Lexus. Can you imagine that? That's what I paid for my house twenty years ago. And that was the *old* car. To get the Mercedes they produced another thirty-two thousand. All in circulated hundred dollar bills."

Clarence whistled. "Thirty-two thousand cash? Wow. I can't believe they carried that kind of money to and from Portland."

"Neither can I. So here's a thought for you. They didn't."

"But you said—"

"I said they came up with thirty-two thousand cash for a car dealer in Sacramento. That doesn't mean they had that money in the car when they came to Oregon. And they almost certainly didn't have it in southern Oregon when they were pulled over by the cop who called me."

"How do you know?"

"Officer Seymour searched the car."

"Don't you need a warrant for that?"

"Well, first he saw the marijuana pipe poking out from under the passenger seat, with the seeds in it. So, under the plain view provision he legally confiscated it. Then he asked if they had any more drugs. Naturally they said no. Then he said, 'So you wouldn't mind if I searched the car, would you?' They said, no, go ahead."

"You mean they agreed to a search? Even when they didn't have to?"

"Yeah. He asked for them to open the trunk. He said they had these smirks on their faces, like they thought he was some goat-roper cop who didn't know how to handle smart city boys. He waited till backup got there, a cover unit. Didn't want to be bending over the trunk and have the lid slammed on him. Of course, he patted them both down. They were unarmed. One had a pocketknife, that was all. He checked their wallets, escorted the passenger, the shorter guy who looked more menacing, to the backseat of his patrol car."

"They didn't seem nervous?"

"No, not at all. That tells us a lot. Number one, if they have the HK in the car or that kind of money, they don't give permission for a search. Number two, if they do, they're sweatin' bullets hopin' he won't find their secret cache. How do you hide an HK53 and at least thirty-two thousand in one hundred dollar bills—over three *hundred* one hundred dollar bills? That's a pile of money, and that's just what they spent on the car. Who knows how much more they had? But the officer said they were cool as ice water. Like they knew he couldn't get them for anything but a teensy little violation."

"I don't get it," Clarence said. "Then where was the gun and the money?"

"Well, one possibility is they're innocent and never had the gun. Okay, not entirely innocent—obviously they were up to no good to steal those plates. But maybe they didn't do the shooting. Thing is, I ran a full listing of crimes done in Portland that same night. One armed robbery, four burglaries, a rape, two car thefts, a few miscellaneous drug deals and prostitution arrests. Quiet night. Your sister was the only homicide. The armed robber was caught, and one of the burglaries and the rape happened while Herb says these two were at Taco Bell. The other three burglaries were in the middle of the night, after your sister was killed. The largest amount of cash was six hundred dollars, plus some jewelry, a microwave, and a stereo. If they hung around to do a burglary, no way they did the shooting. You don't pull off a major hit, then fool around with a dinky burglary. You get out of town pronto. Besides, you don't come to Portland to do burglaries. There's plenty of nicer homes in San Diego, L.A., and the Bay Area. I mean, we've had some guys fly in and pull off some major heists, but we'd know if that happened."

"They fly in to steal stuff?"

"Sure. They pull off their job, go straight to the airport, they're on their flight home and gone. Plus they earn frequent flier mileage. And sometimes get to see a movie. Then there's complimentary beverages and peanuts. Occasionally, a nice little chocolate. Anyway, we know they didn't do a burglary. The officer didn't find anything when he searched their car. No TV, microwave, nothing."

"So where does this leave us?"

"Well, if they stole the license plate, we know they were up to no good. If they were up to no good, the only thing we know about that they could have done was the shooting."

"But if they did it, they'd have the HK53, right? And the officer should have found it."

"You can't hide the HK in your boxer shorts, that's for sure. They could have gotten rid of it. Maybe sold it cheap to somebody in Portland on the way out of town, but I doubt it. Too much risk of being identified and traced. If I were them, I'd disassemble it and throw it out piece by piece, one section off the bridge into the Willamette, the others off I-5, maybe a hundred miles apart."

"Would they really ditch a weapon that valuable?"

"If they've got brains, yeah. Especially if they know they're coming into some really big money. Then a weapon worth a few thousand bucks doesn't mean much. Why risk a murder charge by hanging on to a fancy gun? Not when you can buy ten fancy guns and still have another fifteen thousand pocket change."

"Okay, you're saying they were paid to kill Leesa? By whom?"

"Well, it's a hunch, but right now I'm thinking this may be tied to Norcoast."

"What?" Clarence's eyebrows crawled up his forehead. "Norcoast? Ollie, I know neither of us likes the guy, but *murder?*"

"Look, whenever a pregnant teenage girl dies, there's always one big question. Who's the father? Turns out Leesa didn't have a boyfriend. And most important, Leesa and Norcoasts' daughter, Katie, were best buddies. Leesa almost lived over at Norcoasts' house, stayed overnight there a couple of times a week right up to June or so."

"Are you saying what I think you're saying?"

"Hey, I'm just saying somebody wanted to kill Leesa, and they tried it twice, assuming she didn't take up cocaine spur of the moment. The killer succeeded the second time. Whoever was behind the thing had money, connections, and a plan. Politicians have money, connections, and plans, especially if they've slept with a minor and gotten her pregnant. Hey, it's just a theory. I'm open. Do you have a better one?"

"Not offhand."

"There's more. If our boys in the Lexus did the job, they were paid big money to kill Leesa. We know they didn't have the money when they were pulled over in southern Oregon. But we know they *did* by the time they bought the car, before they left Sacramento."

"Didn't the car dealership have to make sure the title was clear?"

"Sure. Everything checked out. The dealer did the paperwork—they faxed it to me. It's standard procedure for them to photocopy the driver's license. They faxed that too, but it's real grainy." Ollie pointed to his file folder. "They're sending me a color photocopy."

Clarence pulled the fax and stared at the picture, wondering if he was looking at the killer.

"Let's get back to the Sacramento connection," Ollie said. "What can you tell me about Sacramento?"

"Capital city."

"Who lives there?" Ollie asked.

"Lots of people."

"What kinds of people?"

"All kinds," Clarence said. "Tons of political types, for one thing." He looked at Ollie. "Possible link to Norcoast?"

"Why not? There's a lot of inbreeding with politicals. May explain their mental condition. Suppose Norcoast needed somebody taken out. He's not stupid. He's so high profile and so much is on the line, he wouldn't go straight to some gang member, certainly not a local. And how many L.A. gang members would he know and trust? But he might casually mention to someone with gang connections the name and address of someone he wishes would take a permanent vacation, and then say, 'By the way, I want to give you some big money just for being my friend. No strings attached.' Then the guy knows he's supposed to call in some boys to get rid of his problem. The middle man can pay the guys handsomely and still keep a slug of the money for himself, while the guy who drops the hints can say he never ordered anything."

"You really think that's possible?"

"Of course it's *possible*. Not probable maybe, but it's a hunch. It fits a lot of the facts we know. That's what detective work is about. You keep coming up with theories that fit the facts. When more facts materialize, you revise or eliminate your theories one by one. What doesn't get eliminated is the answer. Anyway, right now I just want to find out one thing."

"What?"

"Who does Reggie Norcoast know in Sacramento?"

Ollie and Clarence walked into the prison side by side. Ellis's visiting hours were already used up, but they'd set up an official police appointment to meet Ken Gold, a.k.a. Big Dog. It struck Clarence as ironic he was about to meet a stranger with no glass divider between them, when he hadn't been able to touch his own brother for twenty years.

A guard escorted Big Dog. He was medium-sized and soft-featured, contradicting his nickname. He was young but looked like a gang veteran, with a prominent scar across his chin and a crease in his jaw that looked as if a chunk of flesh had been shot out.

"You're Ellis's brother?" Big Dog asked.

Clarence nodded. "I'm Clarence. This is Ollie Chandler. Homicide detective."

"Okay." Big Dog looked a little nervous. "I just got transferred in here a few weeks ago. Ellis has been talking about his sister. Well, I was there that night. I saw the guys that did it."

"Tell us exactly what happened," Ollie said.

"Me and my posse got down that night, done some smack, some ludes, some ice. I was on my dime speed, just kickin' it up Tenth, comin' home from Irving Park. I was almost to Brumbelow."

"What time?"

"About midnight. Heard all these pops, just a couple blocks away, toward MLK. Sounded like a war. But just one gat—no retaliation or nothin'. Like it was a big-time drive by, takin' some dude outta the box. I knew somebody sufferin', need bufferin', man, no doubt about that. Heard the tires squeal. Pulled a ghost, man, I mean they vamped outta there."

"What'd you do?"

"I hear them comin' my way, toward Tenth, man. All of a sudden they hang a right and they're just two blocks away comin' at me, crossin' Moffat. I ride up over the curb, throw down my dime and jump behind this fence on Brumbelow, by McKenney's old place. Then they fly by. See, I'm lookin' out through a crack in the fence toward the passenger side and I see this loc starin' out the window, rolled down. He had this herky rosco tucked up against the side-view mirror, pointed out at the street. At first I thought it was a gauge, but it looked more like some piece out of the movies, like Snipes or Arnold would carry. Ready to fire on someone, I'm tellin' you, finger on the trigger. Like he was expectin' a fight with 5-0 or was gonna get anybody who saw them. I was pressed up against that fence. Yo, he never saw me, or he'd a shot me, sure of that. Thought I was gonna get jammed for sure."

"What then?"

"They jetted outta the hood, the gat man and his Ace Kool—I'm tellin' you they were gone. Went down a few streets and turned out toward MLK."

"What did the guy with the gun look like?"

"Wearin' a red sweatshirt, like a Crab, with the hood down. Had a TWA and a mustache, maybe some chin whiskers. He was draped—could see gold chain on his neck."

"TWA?" Ollie asked.

"Teeny weeny afro, you know, short crop."

"You mean he was …what color was he?" Clarence asked.

"He be a brotha."

"Black?"

Big Dog nodded, looking at Clarence as if to say, Did you ever meet a brotha who wasn't black?

"You see the driver?" Ollie asked.

"Not real good, not like I seen his Ace Kool. But I could see a little from the streetlight. Had on a red sweatshirt too. And definitely a brother. No way was he a Spic." Ellis had obviously told him Mookie's story.

"Anybody else in the car?"

"Not unless they was lyin' flat."

"What kind of car?"

"No bucket, tellin' you that. Impala? Not even close. Deft, real deft. Laces, man, chrome spokes. And lifts maybe. Not so sure on that."

"Make and model?"

"Don't know my rides that well. Real fancy. Like a Beemer, but trickier."

"How about a Lexus?"

"Maybe."

Ollie pulled a Lexus catalogue from his briefcase and started flipping pages. "Look familiar?"

"Yeah. That's it! Or maybe that one." He pointed first at one picture, then at another, the LS. Ollie turned to the back and showed him a page of a dozen exterior colors. Big Dog pointed immediately at the Alpine Silver Metallic. "That's it for sure."

"You ever seen it before or since?"

"Not that one. I'd remember. Hot car."

"Why didn't you come forward with this before?" Ollie asked.

"Man, I had some outstandings. Last people I could go to was the cops. You know how it goes. You tell the cops anything and they make it like you're the one that did it and that's how you know so much. But there's another reason I'm talkin'. My life's been pretty messed up. But I got involved with Prison Fellowship in the county jail before they sent me here. And I'm a Christian now. Goin' through discipleship. And they been sayin' we should tell the truth. That God's watchin' us, even when nobody else is. So Ellis was askin' about his sister, if anybody knew anything. I did, so it seemed the right thing to do, even if it means gettin' into trouble."

"I appreciate that, Ken," Clarence said.

"Let's go back over this." Ollie sounded like a field general putting together all the reconnaissance. "You said the gun was pressed up against the side-view mirror."

"Yeah."

"What does that tell you about the shooter?" Ollie looked at Ken and Clarence both.

"I don't know," Clarence said. "What?"

"He's left-handed."

"How can you know that?" Clarence asked.

"Look. Let me draw you a picture."

Ollie drew quickly on his legal pad. Clarence looked at the sketch, impressed with the artwork. It was a man in the passenger seat, shoulders parallel to the side of the car. The rifle pointed out the car, pressing close up to the side-view mirror. It was cradled in the arm, finger on the trigger. Left arm, left finger.

"Was that how it was, the angle of the barrel?"

"Yeah. Real close anyway."

"No way the rifle could be pointed out, angling away from the front of the car, that close to the mirror, if it was cradled in the right arm. Not without the whole body lying up on the dashboard. He's a lefty, all right. Has to be."

"Yeah," Ken said. "That's right. Didn't think about that."

"There's a lot of left handers out there," Clarence said.

"Sure, but if we get close enough to narrow down the shooters, it'll help. Ninety percent of the population is right-handed. If we get it down to a few guys, or if two guys claim the other was the shooter, we'll know which one."

Ollie nailed down a few more details. "Thanks, Ken," he said, finally satisfied. "You've been helpful. Anything we can do for you?"

Ken looked at Clarence. "Send me some books, would you, bro? They have to be straight from the publisher, you know, like the ones you get sent to Ellis? Please, send me some good books, Christian books. They got lotsa garbage in here. I want to read some good stuff."

"I will," Clarence said. "I promise." He shook Ken's hand and wished him well. Clarence hesitated, then said, "Do me a favor, will you?"

"Name it," Ken said.

"Pass on this hug to Ellis for me." Clarence put his arms around Ken. The two men embraced like old friends. "And do what you can to get him to your Bible study, okay?"

As a guard escorted Ken back to his cell, Clarence and Ollie walked out of the building toward Ollie's car.

"So what have we got?" Clarence asked.

"Two black males, the shooter left-handed with possible facial hair, mustache, and goatee. Hair was a short afro then, who knows now. Probably Bloods."

"Because of the sweatshirts?"

"Yeah. We've got three sources on these guys now. Mr. Kim and Herb at Taco Bell couldn't connect them to the shooting itself. That was all guesswork. Now we've got the direct link. It's not a theory anymore. Our killers did the job, then headed down I-5. If they were Bloods out for revenge, they might have flamed on, dressed down, worn their colors. Crips wouldn't wear red sweatshirts. They'd either fly their blue or something else, but they wouldn't wear red. Besides, it's a Crip neighborhood. Makes sense Bloods would be behind the hit. That's what I figured in the beginning—until we got sidetracked by this Hispanic thing."

"Sorry," Clarence said.

"Forget it. I took Mookie too seriously myself."

"You really think he was lying?"

"Probably. I'm sure gonna find out."

"What can you do with what Ken told us?"

"Well, I'll put it into the computer under GREAT and crosslink it. Now that we've got some accurate info, that might help. Manny and I spent days pursuing this phony Hispanic connection over on the west side. We've lost valuable time. At least now we know what we're going for. Things are clickin'. I just wish I could get hold of Norcoast's phone records and explore the Sacramento connection. But no way I can make that case to a judge. If only us law enforcers weren't under the restraints of the law. Sure makes it complicated."

Clarence approached Ray Eagle after Bible study. "Ray, is there any way to get copies of phone records?"

"Well, there's ways and then there's ways. Tell me exactly what you're looking for."

"Okay, this is confidential, right? I'm looking for calls made from Councilman Norcoast's office to Sacramento, say in August and September."

"The cops are looking at Norcoast?" Ray whispered. Clarence stared at him. "Don't worry," Ray said. "I won't say a word. I've got some good phone company contacts. Detective Chandler can't pursue them without probable cause. I can. Let's see what I can turn up."

"Earth is a picture of heaven, isn't it?" Dani asked Lewis. "A poor exposure, distorted colors, grainy images, but a picture nonetheless."

"Yes, yes, exactly," Lewis said, as pleased with Dani's insight as she was. "Consider a picture of a lion. It's a two-dimensional representation that reflects certain qualities of the lion, is suggestive of the lion, makes one think of the lion. But, of course, it is *not* the lion. Earth reflects certain properties of heaven, though it reflects them poorly at best. In its best moments, earth anticipates heaven, points toward heaven. But earth is not heaven."

"And those who expect it to be," Dani said, "can never know Joy."

"Precisely, dear lady! And those who fail to look to heaven can never understand or appreciate earth. For it is heaven that gives meaning to earth. Without heaven, earth is an empty and meaningless place. As the picture of the lion is but a fraud if there is no lion, so earth would be no more than a fraud if there were no heaven. Earth without heaven would be a bad joke."

"You and Torel have taught me so much. I look at the same earth now, but I see so differently."

"The world is a book most people never bother to read," Lewis said, his voice pitched with excitement. "It sits before them calling out to be understood, but they are too busy with the details of their lives to take the time to read the book. At best, they skim it. They live lives of endless activity without bothering to understand that which gives *meaning* to activity, to happiness, to pain and struggle. Many of them die without ever understanding why they were alive. The moment after they die they will know how they should have lived, but then it will be too late. What a needless tragedy. They must learn to heed their inner ache for heaven, not dull it with earth's anesthetics. Only then can they see on earth that which will point them toward heaven."

―――――――――

"Thought you might be interested in these." Clarence handed Ollie U.S. West phone bills printed from a laser printer.

Ollie looked at them wide eyed. "Where'd you get them?"

"Never mind. I've highlighted the calls to Sacramento. Here's what I've put together. Six employees in Norcoast's office, four full time, using four phone lines. This one," he pointed to a line on the top sheet, "is Norcoast's private line. This one's Gray's private line. No other phones tie into these lines. The other two lines can be accessed by anyone—Norcoast, Gray, receptionist Sheila, office manager Karen, and two part-time secretaries."

Ollie scanned the printout, eight pages long. "Wow. They make a *lot* of long distance calls."

"Why not?" Clarence asked. "They don't pay for the calls. Taxpayers do."

"So, in the weeks surrounding the shooting," Ollie said, "we've got seven calls to Sacramento on Norcoast's private line."

"And five on Gray's," Clarence said. "Plus another half dozen on the general lines."

"Look at these numbers," Ollie said. "I'm guessing 555-1230 and 555-1237 are in the same office or department. Four of Norcoast's calls and two of Gray's are to 1237. Norcoast has one going to 1230. I'm calling it first."

Ollie dialed 916-555-1230.

"Sacramento Public Works. How may I direct your call?"

"Yeah, hi, this is…Oscar Carey calling from Portland." Ollie smiled at Clarence, who rolled his eyes. "I'm sorry, I've got a lot of notes mixed up here. I may have dialed the wrong number. Reg Norcoast gave me two numbers I could call, and I forget which is which. I think the other might be the private line: 555-1237. Is that it?"

"Yes, that's Mr. Harper's direct line."

"Yeah, of course. Let's see, I'm sort of disorganized today. I'm trying to remember why Reg wanted me to call him. Mr. Harper's the head guy, isn't he?"

"Director of Human Resources."

"Human Resources, yeah, that's it. Look, something just came up. I'll call him back in a little bit. Thanks so much for your help."

Ollie hung up triumphantly. "I love my job."

"Oscar Carey?"

"That's my a.k.a. Comes in handy when I'm on a hunt and don't want to leave a trail. Okay, Mr. Harper. I'll get his first name and run a background check on him." Ollie dialed another Sacramento number. He took the phone away from his ear, and

Clarence could hear the shrill high-pitched sound of a fax line. He dialed the first number again.

"I'm sorry to bother you again, ma'am. This is Oscar Carey, you know, the one who just called? I decided to send a fax to Mr. Harper but I wasn't sure which fax number to send it to. Would that be 555-1347?"

"Yes, that's Mr. Harper's private fax line. Or you can send it to our general fax number, 555-1798. He'll get it either way."

"All right. Oh, and remind me of Mr. Harper's first name. Matthew? Of course. I'm so forgetful. Won't bother you again. Thanks so much. Bye." Ollie hung up.

"Matthew Harper," Clarence said. "That name's familiar."

"Between the two voice lines and the two fax numbers, we've covered nearly all these Sacramento calls," Ollie said, rubbing his hands together as if he were coming off a week long fast to an all-you-can-eat buffet. "Now the thirty-two-thousand-dollar question is, who's Matthew Harper?"

CHAPTER

32

Clarence heard a light knock on the front door Saturday morning at 7:15. Surprised, he opened the door.

"Morning," Manny mumbled to Clarence.

"Something wrong?" Clarence asked.

"Just here to pick up your dad. We're going fishing."

"Oh, yeah. Sorry. Forgot all about that. I know Daddy's up. I'll get him. Come on in."

"That's okay. I'll just wait out here."

Clarence disappeared into his father's room for a moment, followed out by his daddy.

"Manuel," Obadiah said warmly. "I's movin' a little slow this mornin'. But I gots my fishin' rod leaned out by the garage door. Want to see them ol' Shadow Ball pictures?"

"Yeah. I'd love to." Manny disappeared into Obadiah's room.

Clarence considered admitting to Manny he'd been right to doubt Mookie's story about the Hispanics. But he just didn't feel up to an I told you so.

The men didn't reappear from the bedroom for a halfhour. Manny escorted Obadiah out the front door, lost in conversation.

———

Clarence sat at his desk Monday morning, looking at three-by-five cards and typing.

The body of Robert Sandifer lay in an open casket. He'd been arrested twenty-three times for felonies. At the time of his death he was wanted for the murder of a fourteen-year-old girl. He was executed by members of his own gang. He lay in the casket with his arms wrapped around a teddy bear. Robert Sandifer was eleven years old.

In the last five years violent crimes committed by juveniles rose 60 percent. The number of murders committed by minors doubled between the 1980s and the 1990s. Juveniles now account for half of all concealed weapons violations, a third of all robberies, a third of all aggravated assaults, a quarter of all weapons assaults, and a quarter of all murders. In another two years there will be a million more teenagers, children of baby boomers, in the crime-prone ages of fourteen to seventeen. Statistics indicate 6 percent of the males in this group will be chronic lawbreakers, responsible for 50 percent of serious juvenile crime. Which means that America is about to be overrun by 30,000 more juvenile thieves, muggers, rapists, and killers.

Clarence reread his first two paragraphs. Why should he write such discouraging news? Because it's true, he thought. But he didn't feel like writing anymore. He had an appointment with Ollie—and a face-off with a crime-prone-aged boy called Mookie.

———

"Well," Ollie told Clarence, "Matthew Harper has no criminal history. Went to work for Sacramento Public Works in 1994. I made a contact there that pulled his resume. Guess where he worked until 1994?"

"Reg Norcoast's office," Clarence said.

"How'd you know?" Ollie seemed disappointed.

"It came to me just as you said it. I knew the name was familiar. Red-headed guy."

"Among other things, Harper was Norcoast's financial man and his campaign director. I need to find out exactly what he did here, why he left, what his connections are."

"Ollie, this thing about Leesa Fletcher?" Clarence asked. "I don't get it.

Shouldn't the autopsy have shown she was pregnant? I mean, not even my source at the *Trib* who told me about the cocaine knew about the child."

"I'm one step ahead of you. I've got a call in to the medical examiner, the one whose signature is on this autopsy report. I want to know why he didn't mention the pregnancy."

"Do you think she went ahead with the abortion and didn't tell Sue?"

"If she did, the autopsy report would indicate the surgery. Either way, something's really fishy. We have to nail down the father of the child. If it's not Norcoast, we lose his motive, *that* motive anyway, but we might pick up a new suspect. Anyway, right now let's focus on our boy Mookie. Here's what we're going to do."

"Okay, Mookie," Ollie ushered the trembling boy into a barren room. It wasn't a standard interrogation cubicle, but an office where the walls were so thin you could hear sounds from the next room. "I'm asking your permission for Mr. Abernathy to be here, since he's the one you first talked to. This isn't an official interrogation or anything. We just want to talk. Is that okay with you?"

Mookie nodded, looking like a kid who'd rather be anyplace else in the universe.

"Okay, Mookie, we've got someone in the next room who says you lied to us. You weren't out there that night. You didn't see two Hispanic guys in a gold Impala." Ollie turned to Clarence with a smile. "Or even a *green* Impala. You didn't see anybody at all, did you?"

"Yo, man, I seen what I seen."

"Maybe you lied just for the hundred dollars. Or maybe somebody else paid you a lot more to lie. Well, that wouldn't be that serious of an offense. But then we talked with a homeboy of yours. What if I was to tell you he says you were right in the thick of this whole thing?"

"What homie? What thing?"

"We don't want to name names. But we've got him in the next room. He's been putting the finger on you, big time. Good chance we can cut a deal with him, and he'll testify against you."

"Testify 'bout what?"

"Just walk us through it one more time, okay, Mookie? Were you really out there that night when the murder happened?"

"Yeah, I was there."

"Well, that's what your homeboy says too. Except what would you think if he says the reason you were there is that *you* did the shooting?"

"Didn't do no shootin'!"

"You sure?"

"Didn't do it. No way."

"Stay here with him, Clarence. I want to check this out again with our friend in the other room."

Ollie left the room, and Mookie looked at Clarence and trembled. Clarence stared hard at Mookie, whose forehead now glistened. Suddenly muffled voices filtered through the wall, followed by a smashing impact. Voices were louder now, the words clear. "Mookie did it. Mookie shot up the house. It was Mookie!"

"No way!" Mookie said to Clarence. "No way!" he yelled at the wall.

"You killed my sister and my niece? It was you?" Clarence stood to his feet and walked toward him. Clarence gazed down at Mookie, who knew Ty's uncle's already legendary rep in the hood. He'd heard what he did to Georgie.

"No way, Mr. Abernathy. No way I shot nobody. I swear it."

"Convince me real quick, Mookie. Or maybe there won't be anything left of you to go to jail." Clarence reached out his big right hand toward Mookie's neck.

Ollie walked in. "What's going on here?"

"Keep him 'way from me," Mookie said to Ollie. "Thinks I killed his sister."

"Did you?" Ollie asked.

"No way. Who that lyin' to you? What's goin' on? I didn't do it. I swear. Shadow's over there, ain't he? He lyin' to you."

"Remember, Mookie," Ollie said, "this isn't an official interrogation. I'm not forcing you to talk. You don't have to be here. In fact, I think I'll just have Mr. Abernathy drive you back home, and you can call me sometime if you're ready to talk. Okay?"

Mookie looked at Clarence, whose stare was boring holes through his forehead.

"No," Mookie said to Ollie. "I want to talk now. I didn't do it!"

"You got an alibi for the time of the shooting?" Ollie asked.

"Yeah, yeah. Ask my mama. I was at my crib. Sick that night. Spewin' up."

"But you said you were just down the street, that you saw the shooters," Ollie said.

"GC knew I was sick. Asked me if I wanted an easy thousand dollars. Gave me this story to tell, two Spics in a gold bucket, the whole deal. I said it just like he told me. Wasn't my fault, I'm tellin' you. The homies heard you was payin' for information," Mookie looked at Clarence, "so some of the guys was thinkin' up stories. GC say nobody do nothin' without talkin' to him first. Next morning he comes to me and tells me if I say his story I'd get a thousand bucks from him and a hundred from you."

"Why would GC do that?" Ollie asked him.

"Don't know." Mookie hesitated. "GC gone, so guess it's okay to tell. I started thinkin' maybe he the shooter and wanted to cover it."

"So why should we believe you were lying before but not now?" Ollie asked.

"You realize what the penalty is for murder? You know what they'll do to somebody who killed a woman and child?"

"I didn't do it!"

"You mentioned Shadow before. Why?"

"That *is* Shadow, ain't it?" He pointed to the next room. "He knew GC talked to me. He was there. He settin' me up."

"How did GC pay you?"

"Ten hundred-dollar bills in an envelope."

"What kind of envelope?"

"Don't know. White. Dark blue inside. Thought the blue was def 'cause I'm a Crip, you know?"

"I know," Ollie said. "Anything written on the envelope? Your name?"

"No name. Just a trey."

"A tray?"

"You know, number three. In pencil. That be all, man. Don't know nothin' else."

"Okay, Mookie. Just wait here a few minutes. We'll be back." Ollie led Clarence into the other room and they sat down at the table with Manny, who was rubbing his shoulder.

"Hey," Manny said to Ollie. "Next time we do this I get to push *you* against the wall, okay?"

"You weren't that bad, Manny. There's hope for you as a professional wrestler. Mad Dog Manuel. Has a ring to it." Ollie's voice suddenly went panicky and high pitched—"Mookie did it. Mookie shot up the house. It was Mookie." The men laughed. Clarence wondered what Mookie was thinking in the next room.

"So did he talk? What did he say?" Manny asked them.

"He coughed it up all right. Gangster Cool paid him to lie. Shadow was there. Shadow probably knows more, maybe a lot more. Even though nothing Mookie said is admissible, under the circumstances, hopefully it'll move us down the road to what we need."

"He really spilled all that? Boy, that went fast," Manny said, with a look of admiration for Ollie.

"The key was when I told him I'd have Clarence drive him home." Ollie laughed. "I think Mookie would have confessed to the Kennedy assassination to stay away from Clarence. You should have been a cop, Abernathy. Talk about a thousand-yard stare. When it comes to good cop/bad cop, you're a natural."

———————

Clarence dragged himself into the Civic Auditorium to an afternoon symposium titled "Race and Ethnicity: New Perspectives." He wished he was playing tennis. But the longer he listened to the lecturer, the more intrigued he became. After the question and answer session, he sat down for the prearranged interview in a pressroom behind the stage.

Dr. Lytle leaned back and drank his orange juice, while Clarence looked back over his notes, selecting some key follow-up questions. Then he turned on the tape recorder with the round conference mike on the table between them.

"Enjoyed your lecture, Dr. Lytle. To be honest, my editor kind of forced me to be here. I wasn't really interested."

"Really? Why not?"

"Maybe because they've put me on the 'race beat.' As a columnist, I'm not used to being assigned things. I'm pretty independent. But to tell you the truth, I've thought about race all my life, and it doesn't seem to have done any good. Sometimes I just don't want to think about it any more."

"I understand. But for everyone who thinks about race all the time there are those who never do. Maybe if those who never think about it would, those who think about it all the time could relax and think about something else. Does that make sense?"

"Yeah. It makes a lot of sense. Okay, Dr. Lytle, let me get your bio straight. You're a geneticist, right? And an anthropologist? Ph.D.s in *both* fields?"

"Yes," he laughed. "When you put it that way it sounds crazy to me too."

"Maybe we should start by defining race."

"Well," Dr. Lytle said, "race is slippery, much more fluid than people think. We label it by the superficial stuff—skin color, hair texture, shape of eyes and nose and lips. Even then we don't get it right. People are called 'black' in the U.S. because they have one or more black ancestors. But the same people living in Brazil would be called 'white' because they have one or more white ancestors. Some light-skinned blacks are mistaken for Italians; some Turks look like Argentineans."

"I had a cousin so light skinned he could pose as white," Clarence said. "Now nobody mistook him for Norwegian, but he looked southern European, maybe Greek. He went away to college, and when he got home everybody asked if he'd been hassled by whites. He said, 'Nope. I fit right in, made a lot of friends.' My brother Harley pressed him on it, and finally he admitted, 'I just never told anyone I was black.' Next term somebody saw a picture of his daddy and the masquerade was over. Suddenly his relationships changed."

"Right. Race is largely a social construct," Dr. Lytle said. "We don't like uncertainty. We want things clearly defined—black and white. Historically, the emphasis on racial distinctions is a way of labeling a group by its enemies. It's like a basketball scrimmage where one team wears red and the other blue. If you and I are the same color, we're on each other's side. Of course, that's totally superficial because in terms of what matters, I'll have much more in common with some on the other side than some on mine."

"So, are you saying race is a human invention?"

"Not race per se. But the assumptions we attach to race, yes, these are mostly our inventions. They're a mixture of prejudice, superstition, and myth. It's a lever to wield power. To elevate 'our kind,' we denigrate 'their kind.' But ultimately it's very subjective. It's like gold—it's only valuable as long as people think it is. Race only matters if you think it does."

"But obviously there's an objective scientific basis for race."

"Much less than you'd think. Take Latinos. People talk as if they're a race or an ethnic group. They're neither. They're a disparate collection of nationalities descended from Europeans, African slaves, and American Indians. And you know what race East Indians, Pakistanis, and Bangladeshis are?"

"Wel...they're their own race, aren't they?"

"No. They're Caucasians." He saw Clarence's skeptical look. "Really. That's their official racial category."

"I grew up thinking there were only two races," Clarence said. "Black and white."

"Me too," Dr. Lytle said. "Never thought about American Indians, Asians, Pacific Islanders, Eskimos, Arabs, you name it. In fact, Native American is an absurd category to many Native Americans. Cheyenne and Apache and Navajo consider themselves as different from each other as blacks and whites are. And for Japanese and Koreans and Chinese to be thrown in together as 'Orientals' is insulting to them. They see obvious differences between themselves and the others. They often have strong biases against each other. The truth is, genetically we're a huge mix. It isn't just that America's a melting pot. It's that almost every American is his own melting pot. Gene research shows there's more genetic variability among the members of any one race than between the different races as a whole."

"You said that in your lecture. What exactly do you mean?"

"I mean any Caucasian will be genetically more similar to many Africans than to many Caucasians."

"I don't get it. How's that possible?"

"Richard Lewontin, a population biologist, analyzed seventeen genetic markers in 168 populations, from Austrians to Thais to Apaches. He discovered only 6.3 percent of all genetic differences between human beings related in any way to their race. He found there's more genetic difference within one race than there is between that race and any another. So if I ran tests on you and another black man we chose randomly from the street, and I analyzed both your twenty-three pairs of chromosomes, I'd find your genes have less in common with his than both of you have with a large number of randomly chosen white people."

"That sounds impossible. I can hardly believe it."

"But it's true. It's like horses—you don't separate them genetically by brown, black, and white, do you? Two white horses are as likely to have different genetics as a white and a black horse. Human genetic differences for the most part run completely independently of race. That's why 'race' isn't really an objective standard."

"But you can identify certain racial characteristics, right? I mean, black people have higher blood pressure, don't they?"

"The incidence of high blood pressure among American blacks is twice as high as among whites, that's true. But it isn't genetic. Black Africans have some of the lowest hypertension rates in the world. As for the whole *Bell Curve* controversy, the interesting thing is the genes that determine mental processes are entirely different than those that determine race. So there can't possibly be any scientific predictions about intellect based on race. The only predictors are sociological, not scientific."

"Okay, here's a question—what color were the first human beings?"

"Well, I didn't get into that today. But as a geneticist I can give you a definitive answer." He paused for effect. "They were black."

"I've heard that. But how can you be so sure?"

"Well," Dr. Lytle said, "both genetics and experience show us that dark-skinned people can and often do produce fair-complexioned offspring. However, it's genetically *impossible* for fair-complexioned persons to produce dark-skinned offspring. In other words, two black people, as dark as yourself, can have a quite light-skinned child, and not just because of white ancestry. On the other hand, two full-blooded Swedes can *never* produce a dark-skinned child. It just can't happen. Light skin can only account for light skin, whereas dark skin can account for both dark and light. Therefore, the original human beings could only be dark skinned. Of course, this fits with all the evidence of ancient people in Africa. The oldest bones, weapons, tools, utensils, and civilizations are in Africa, not in the Middle East, Asia, or Europe."

"Where do you think the human race began?"

"The biblical text mentions Eden in the east, with a river that broke into four other rivers. First, the Gihon and the Pishon. These were African rivers. The Pishon is said to wind through the land of Havilah, which the historian Pliny said was in East Africa. The Gihon is said to wind through the entire land of Cush, or Ethiopia. Then, the Tigris and the Euphrates in Mesopotamia. So we've got four rivers in relation to Eden—two African, two Mesopotamian. That's southern Mesopotamia or northern Africa. Historically, the one was inhabited primarily by dark brown-skinned people, the other blacks."

"I was fascinated by that story you told about your ancestors. Can you walk me through it for the tape?"

"Sure. My great-grandfather was a slave. After emancipation he married a white woman, very rare in those days, and they had two children. One of them married black and one married white. The white side kept it all a secret, and they kept marrying white, just like my side kept marrying black. When we were tracing our family history I heard stories from a great-aunt about this whole line of our family who had 'passed,' you know, 'gone white.' Well, sure enough, I discovered it was true. I ended up tracing down the white side and talking with them on the phone. After we connected and I convinced them we were related, I told them there was this family secret which explains why we never met."

"What did they say?"

"Well, they got real nervous and asked, 'What secret?' Like they wondered if Grandpa was a horse thief or a train robber. Actually, that news would have been a lot easier to take!" He laughed heartily. "So I looked for a gentle way to break it, and I finally told them, 'Our great-grandfather was a slave.' I made about eight of these calls to my long-estranged 'white family,' and the reaction was exactly the same from every one. 'A *black* slave?'" He laughed again, shaking his head.

"So I set up this family reunion, and I don't think it ever occurred to them that *I* would be black. They assumed I looked like them. You should have seen it. I got eight of my family members to meet with the six of them—six is all I could talk into coming. I'm a high yellow, but I have a light-skinned sister who works around whites who make racist comments about blacks, never realizing who she is. But then I've got two brothers almost as black as you. When those folks saw my brothers, they nearly fainted on the spot."

"Must've made for an interesting reunion."

"You got that right. But I'm convinced it was worth it. This one white cousin— we see each other now maybe three or four times a year—she told me just a week after our meeting some trouble broke out in the black part of town. Without thinking she said, 'There they go again.' Then she reminded herself, 'I can't say that anymore. Because they are me.'"

They are me, Clarence jotted down.

"Bad news," Ollie said to Clarence over the phone.

"What?"

"My cop buddy went to the addresses for Robert Rose and Jerome Rice. Guess what he found?"

"They moved away and nobody knows where they are. Or they were phony names?"

"Robert Rose and Jerome Rice are real guys all right, and they used to live at those addresses. We've even got their forwarding addresses. Problem is, they're cemeteries. Robert died two years ago, Jerome fourteen months. Two law-abiding black males in their twenties."

"Then how—"

"Fake IDs. Assumed identities. Our perps are well connected. If my theory about the Sacramento payoff is right, maybe the money man pulled off the ID thing with access to official records. Who knows?"

"It's not that tough to do." It startled Clarence to hear Manny's voice on the line. "The Hispanic drug lords have turned fake ID into an art form. It's done with illegal aliens all the time. Maybe some of the black gangs are getting into it." ·

"Uh, hi, Manny. So, how do you assume someone's identity and get all those papers?"

"You watch the obituaries," Manny said, "or check out fresh graves and get the name from the tombstone."

"You're kidding," Clarence said.

"Then you call in, say you're so and so, that you've had all your ID stolen, and you apply for a duplicate Social Security card."

"Social Security doesn't know when somebody dies?"

"If they're over sixty-five they usually know," Manny said, "although you still have people drawing other people's Social Security benefits twenty years after they die. But if it's guys in their twenties, it's not that hard to assume an identity. Once you've got that one card, it's your ticket to brand new photo IDs, driver's license, credit cards, everything. If you're good, you can pull off a birth certificate."

"You just have to be sure there aren't warrants out for the dead guy's arrest," Ollie said. "I knew a case where some petty burglar, a white guy, got fake ID from a dude who died in a traffic accident, then he went out and did an armed robbery. Next week he gets pulled over for a speeding ticket, thinks he's cool with his fake ID, and the cop arrests him for murder. Took this guy and his lawyer the better part of a year to convince everybody he was only guilty of armed robbery."

"We seem to keep going back to ground zero," Clarence said.

"Not ground zero. If it's a real picture on the photo ID, we've got that much. If it isn't, we know it had to be a close match, so it beats a police sketch. We've still got the temporary stickers on the new car, the Mercedes. I'm running the temps to see if our friends have racked up some more violations for us to look at. I'll let you know. Lunch at the deli tomorrow, right? Meanwhile I've got something else to check out."

Dani saw it as having the rich sense of history of a museum and the natural beauty of Victoria's Butchart Gardens, multiplied a thousand times. It was both indoors and outdoors. As she walked, she enjoyed varieties and colors of flowers she'd never imagined. She read accounts of lives lived out on earth, then watched them as they actually happened. It reminded her of a hall of fame where you press the button to see old film footage, except here she was seeing the events on earth as they actually happened.

She expected to see great historic dramas, evangelistic rallies, large stadium-packed events, well-known musicians, athletes, writers, and speakers. She saw some of those, but not nearly as many as she anticipated.

What she did see were innumerable people she'd never heard of. More than anything, she saw old women on their knees. She looked through the portal and listened to their prayers. Most often they prayed for sons and daughters, husbands and brothers and grandchildren. They also prayed for pastors and missionaries. She saw a familiar dress, a woman on her knees praying for Dani and Clarence and Marney, Harley and Obadiah and their pastor. And especially for Ellis.

"Mama!" Dani half expected the old woman on her knees to stop praying and look up at her, but of course the portal only worked one way, and it was her mother praying not now but those many years ago.

Watching her mother day by day, Dani witnessed innumerable acts of faithfulness, seldom seen and seldom appreciated, but each kept track of carefully by Elyon, the Watcher and Rewarder. She continued to walk through this place, fascinated by the people she saw. Many of these faithful old women were black. A disproportionate number, it seemed to Dani. Perhaps because these women knew how to suffer, they also learned how to hope. Perhaps because they had so little earthly power, they felt more compelled to call upon heavenly power.

———————

Clarence arrived at the deli ten minutes early, thinking that for once he'd get there before Ollie. Wrong. There he was, sitting in the corner with coffee and pastry.

"Clarence. I've just got fifteen minutes, so I'll cut to the chase." Ollie was unusually brisk. "I didn't tell you I called the four big Portland abortion clinics. They weren't very cooperative. Had to get warrants to see their records. Looked them over yesterday afternoon. Turns out Leesa Fletcher was scheduled for an appointment at the Lovepeace Clinic August 23. So I see this little notation next to her name. When I pressed them on it, I found out she didn't make the appointment herself. Someone else made it for her. From what I gathered, sometimes the girl's parent or the boyfriend or the boyfriend's mother or sister or somebody makes the appointment and tries to talk the girl into coming. Well, they couldn't tell me who made the appointment for her, except the receptionist thought maybe she remembered it was a man and assumed it was her boyfriend or father. Anyway, Leesa never showed up for this appointment—thanks to your friend Sue running interference. And there's no record she ever got the abortion anywhere else, not in this city anyway. The medical examiner who did the autopsy is out of town, so we have to wait on that mystery."

"Something else has been bugging me," Clarence said. "Let's say Harper paid these guys for the hit. First, would he really pay them before getting confirmation they'd done the job? And if he did pay them, wouldn't he demand it back when he found out they hit the wrong house?"

"The thing is, what could he do?" Ollie said. "Take them to court because they killed the wrong people for him? These are politicians, not Mafia bosses. They can't afford to demand justice from everybody. They mess with the guys they pay and maybe those guys will turn on them. Who knows? Politicians can afford to lose other people's money. But they can't afford to have the people who do their dirty work get unhappy with them. I figure they just wrote it off as a loss."

"I guess that's possible," Clarence said.

"Here's what I'm thinking," Ollie said. "The week before the murder, we've got two voice calls and one fax from Norcoast's private line to Harper's. There's no documentation of what's said in a voice call unless someone records it, which in this case is highly unlikely. But a fax, now that's worth pursuing. Where there's a fax, there's a good chance there's still a record."

"What do you mean?"

"Well, whether you print out hard copy and hand fax it or you send it directly through a fax modem, if you type it on a computer it's likely been saved to the hard disk, if not deliberately, by an autosave feature."

"I've been in Norcoast's office," Clarence said. "Don't know how much he uses it, but he has his own computer."

"Of course I can't get to it without a warrant. But I'd sure love to explore that hard disk."

"If you had access to it, what would you do?" Clarence asked.

"First, I'd look under the word processing program and see if there's a 'fax' or 'letter' subdirectory. I'd see if any letter was saved on the dates the faxes were sent, August 27 and 29. In fact, I'd check any file anywhere saved on those dates. Then I'd use a global search program. Look for all text files containing the name Harper. Then I'd search for his fax number. If that didn't turn up anything, I'd use Norton Utilities or something similar to unerase every file I could, even the partials." Ollie looked at Clarence's scribbling hand. "Why are you taking notes on this?"

"I'm a journalist. I can take notes whenever I feel like it. You're sure you can't get legal access to that computer?"

"No way I've got probable cause for the warrant. It's circumstantial evidence and hunches. That's enough in a dictatorship, but this is the land of the free. Bummer, huh?"

"I think," Clarence said, "tomorrow I'm going to pay a visit to Norcoast's office."

Ollie raised his hands in the air and stood up. "I don't want to hear anything about what you're doing tomorrow. This conversation is over. Have a good lunch." He walked away. They still hadn't ordered. Clarence had never seen Ollie turn his back on a meal.

"Councilman Norcoast's office, Sheila speaking."

"Hi, Sheila, this is Clarence Abernathy from the *Trib*. Listen, I'm wanting to do a column on some of the highlights of Councilman Norcoast's career."

"Oh, that sounds wonderful. This would be a positive column, right?"

"Oh, sure. I've been spending time with Reg lately, and I feel I owe him some good press. But I'd like this to be a surprise. Reg is out of town, right?"

"Yes. He won't be back until Saturday. Mr. Gray's with him. And Jean's at a seminar in Salem. It's kind of a ghost town here today. Just me and a part-time secretary. Do you want me to fax you some information on Mr. Norcoast's accomplishments?"

"Well, with all his accomplishments there's probably quite a bit to sort through, isn't there? Tell you what, if it wouldn't be an inconvenience, how about I just come over and look through what you have? I could bring my laptop computer and maybe work on the column there. Would that be all right?"

"Oh, sure. That would be just fine."

"Great. I'll be over in an hour. And remember, let's keep this a surprise until the column's done, okay?"

Driving from one part of the rainy concrete city to another, Clarence longed for the endless towering Doug firs of the woods, tantalizingly close to Portland, yet on busy days as far outside his reach as if he were on Mars. No longer living in the suburbs, his grandest taste of green was the cultivated park blocks of Portland, the trees and flowers here and there, tiny oases in the inner-city desert. They were reminders of a better place, but poor substitutes for it.

Clarence looked forward to tomorrow's weekly Wednesday ritual. He would put his bike on the car rack, head out to Gresham, and ride his beloved Springwater Corridor Trail.

Maybe tomorrow the dark clouds will be gone. Maybe there'll finally be some sunshine.

"Hello, Mr. Abernathy." Sheila bubbled with enthusiasm. "I've pulled a number of files. I think you'll find them helpful." She pointed to a six-inch stack.

Clarence groaned inwardly as he looked at the pile he'd have to pretend to be interested in. After a half hour of Sheila's PR efforts, he finally said, "This is great. I'll just get going on my laptop here and sort things through. You sure this isn't a bother?"

"No problem. I can't wait to see the column."

"You know what? I forgot to leave a few things my editor needs at the *Trib*. I've got them in my briefcase. Mind if I use this to send them over?" He pointed to the fax machine next to Sheila's computer.

"No problem. Help yourself."

Clarence pulled a few things from his briefcase. He positioned his body between Sheila and the fax machine, lifted the cover, took the gum from his mouth, and wedged it and a bent paper clip underneath the rollers. He closed the top and attempted to send a fax.

"Am I doing something wrong, Sheila? I can't seem to get this working."

Sheila came over and tried to get it going, without success. "Well," she finally said, "I could open up Mr. Norcoast's office, and you could use his fax."

"You don't think he'd mind? That'd be great. In fact, why don't I just bring in my laptop and set up in there, if it's no trouble. That way I'd be by the phone and fax."

"I'll be right here if you need me," Sheila assured him after unlocking the door to Norcoast's office. She kept the door wide open, Clarence noticed.

"Thanks. You're too kind." He faxed some random pages to his own attention at the *Trib.*

Before sitting at Norcoast's desk, Clarence scanned the room, not wanting to make his move too quickly. He looked at Norcoast's Hall of Fame, where the councilman was glad-handing everyone in the state with any name recognition. He looked where he'd seen the picture of him shaking Norcoast's hand. He was surprised to see it wasn't there anymore. It had been replaced. He looked around—it was nowhere to be found. Seeing it up there had irritated him. Seeing it had been taken down did the same.

Maybe I've fallen from grace with his highness. If he finds out what I'm doing now, I certainly will.

Clarence reached over and turned on Norcoast's computer. It beeped as it came on and he hoped Sheila thought it was his laptop. He moved Norcoast's keyboard over in front of his own. He felt relieved to see the familiar face of Windows 95. He ran Explorer and examined directories and subdirectories. Under Winword, he saw the subdirectory "letters." No subdirectory "faxes."

He called up the letters and was disappointed to see only a couple dozen, none in late August. Obviously Norcoast had Sheila type most of his letters on her computer.

He hit Tools, Find, Files or Folders, then chose to search the entire hard drive. Under date modified he put August 29. He ran it. Two files came up. They weren't text files, they were database files. When he opened them they showed nothing. He deleted the date designation and chose Advanced. Then in the "Containing text" box he typed Harper and clicked "Search." Immediately a dozen hits came up. He checked each of them. Nine were from two years before when he worked in this office. Three were more recent, but none was later than June. He looked carefully. Nothing.

He took a three-inch disk out of his laptop and put it into Norcoast's machine.

He then ran the program Norton Utilities—Data Recovery. After churning and whirring for fifteen seconds, thirty-eight erased files popped up on the screen. One of them had the date August 29. It was a tiny file, its condition listed as "good." He double clicked, and it popped up on the screen.

"Harper: Counting on you to do the job. Make it soon."

Eleven words. More a telegram than a fax. Seemed hardly worth typing and printing, except it had the advantage of not being subject to handwriting analysis, fingerprinting, or the easy discovery of hard copy. Whoever deleted it obviously didn't understand that nothing is unrecoverable until it's overwritten.

"The job." What job? "Make it soon." How soon? Clarence contemplated the fact that four days after this message was sent from Norcoast's office to Harper's, Dani and Felicia had been shot.

Dani saw men of all colors helping young impressionable boys. They gave them time and attention and guidance. Holding their hands, playing catch with them, eating hamburgers with them, helping them with homework, reading to them from the Bible. These men had carved out a place of eternal recognition. Their efforts with these boys had survived the Shadowlands, though their houses and jobs and bank accounts and yard work and what they had built with their hands had not.

Dani was repeatedly surprised to see so many modest earthly acts so greatly heralded. Here was a hard-working man getting up out of bed every morning at five o'clock to go to a menial job where he worked long hours to provide for his family. Day after day he did his work without complaint. Here was an exhausted young mother feeding and rocking her crying child. She was asking God for help, for strength to make it through the night, to be the best mother she could be.

Here was a pastor's wife, opening the door to someone in pain one more time when she wished she could rest and have her husband to herself. She saw a young couple who earned a Christmas bonus give it all to their church's famine relief offering. Here was a young man struggling with sexual temptation but remaining pure, drawing on the resources of Christ.

She watched a shoeshine man. Wait a minute…she knew him. Yes, it was Uncle Moses, who shined shoes in a Chicago train station for thirty years. As she watched, Moses asked God to give him just the right opportunities to share his faith that day. "God, this is my ministry. Send me just the ones you wants. Help me shows them your love."

A businessman came up to the shoeshine station. Dani somehow saw through his briefcase to the revolver inside and realized he intended to take his life. For some inexplicable reason he'd felt compelled to get his shoes shined before leaving this world.

"How's life treatin' you, sir?" Moses asked him.

"Not that good."

"I knows how that feels. But when it's not goin' so good, I remind myself how much God loves me." The man stared at him blankly.

"He proved it, you know," Uncle Moses said.

"Proved what?"

"How much he loves us. That's why he sent the very best. He sent his Son Jesus to die on the cross and saves us from our sins." The two men talked for a while. Moses gave him a booklet called *Steps to Peace with God* and walked him through each step. "I'd like to give you a Bible too," he said.

Dani watched in fascination as the poor joyful shoeshine man shared the best news in the universe with the rich miserable businessman. She wondered at how often in the Shadowlands she'd confused wealth and poverty, success and failure.

"There she is, that's my niece Dani!" This voice came not from the portal but from behind her. She recognized it immediately.

"Uncle Moses!"

"Let me introduce to you my good friend Mr. Gary Schoen." Dani extended her hand to the white man, the businessman she'd just watched her uncle share his faith with.

"A pleasure to meet you," he said. "I owe so much to your uncle."

"It's Elyon who baked the bread," Moses said. "I was just one beggar tellin' another where to find it!" He laughed from deep within, reminding Dani of her father.

After talking with them, Dani walked up to Torel, himself studying one of the acts of obedience forever enshrined here.

"I knew that once they died," Dani said, "unbelievers would have no opportunity to go back and relive their lives on earth, this time choosing Christ. But I never thought about how we believers would have no second chance to go back either. No second chance to take advantage of the opportunities, to live our lives over again, this time for Elyon's glory. I don't miss the old world. But with all its pain and difficulty, it truly was a land of opportunity. A place of second chances."

"What is your life?" Torel quoted. "You are a mist that appears for a little while and then vanishes."

"Teach us to number our days," she quoted back, "that we may gain a heart of wisdom."

"The children of God," the angel said, "have in heaven all eternity to celebrate their victories. But they have on earth only a very short time to win them."

As he did every Wednesday, Clarence arrived at the *Tribune* at 5:30 A.M. so he could get in a full day by 2:00 and head out early to make his ride on the Springwater Corridor Trail. The day was cool and overcast, with a light rain and dark threatening clouds. There wouldn't be many people on the trail, but that was fine with him.

The farther he got toward Gresham, the more he anticipated the ride. As usual he planned to ride hard the first five or six miles. Then he'd turn around, leisurely making his way back, straying off the trail to reward himself with a mocha. It was a ritual, a small but important one that helped bring order and sanity to a life that had recently been short on both.

Clarence rode hard his first leg, then headed up Eastman to Coffee's On to sit down with his double caramel mocha. After looking through the *Trib* for ten minutes, he checked his watch and realized he needed to get going to make it home in time to shower, eat, and go to Bible study. He took the coffee cup, still one-third full, and carried it out with him, riding one-handed.

He felt unusually tired. Perhaps the stress was catching up with him. He cut through Gresham Park and rejoined the bike trail. He felt funny, as if his blood sugar was dropping. Fortunately, he knew the sugar in the mocha would kick it back up soon.

Clarence rode past Hugo the Rottweiler, feeling increasingly tired, his head aching and vision narrowing. He pulled over at his usual rest stop, the trailside bench.

What's wrong with me? I feel so...

He pulled out of his bike pack a box of raisins to ward off an insulin reaction. He felt so tired, so weak. He chewed the raisins, feeling the numbness, then lay back his head on the bench.

Got to rest a little. Then I'll feel better.

He slipped into unconsciousness.

CHAPTER

33

Clarence woke up slowly, shivering, his toes popsicles.

Where am I?

It was bottom-of-the-ocean dark. He felt disoriented. Was he home napping? Wait, the waterbed must be leaking. It was hard and wet. And who opened the windows? He was freezing. He rolled to get away from the dampness and fell two feet to the ground. Where he expected carpet, he felt gravel.

He pulled himself up to sit on the wet bench and clumsily pushed a couple of different buttons on his Casio sport watch. One of them finally turned on the light—8:36. No. It couldn't be. It was…Wednesday. Bible study night. Geneva would be worried. He was supposed to be home for dinner by 5:30.

What happened?

His face was numb. An insulin reaction? He'd laid back, stretched out on the bench the way he always did on his way home. He'd eaten raisins, and besides, the mocha should have kicked in. Apparently he'd gone into insulin shock. This wasn't the first time, but it was the worst. It had never come on so suddenly or wiped him out so completely.

Clarence got on his bike, which had no light. He pedaled awkwardly down the trail, tipping to one side, then the other. This wasn't working. He got off, falling to one knee. Then he walked beside the bike, leaning on it for support, trying to remember how far away he'd parked the car. He knew he should know, but he didn't and it bothered him. Unsure in the darkness of what awaited each new step, he felt embarrassed and afraid.

What's happened to me?

He finally found his way through the spooky darkness, then leaned the bike against the car. He fumbled for his keys and eased into the front seat. He heard a groan, then realized it was his own. He practiced speaking, trying to shed the slur from his voice. Finally he reached for his cellular and dialed home.

"Clarence!" Geneva cried. "What happened? Where have you been?" Her frantic voice sounded shrill and tinny.

"I'm okay, baby. I don't know where, I mean what exactly I did. Or what happened, I mean. I'm all right, I think. I know I'm not making much sense, but I'm going to be all right."

"O Clarence, you don't sound…I'm so glad you're okay." Her voice broke.

"I'm going to drive home now and—"

"Just stay on the phone with me, Clarence. Open the glove compartment, okay? Do it, baby."

"Okay. I did it."

"Reach inside and grab one of those silver containers, you know, the glucose packets. Got it?"

"Got it. Okay, I'm tearing it open."

The orange-flavored glucose tasted flat, but he hoped it would help him think more clearly. He squeezed the packet until it was empty.

After a few minutes of talking to Geneva, Clarence said, "I'm going to open the trunk and put on the bike rack."

"Just carry the phone with you and talk to me, baby. Don't cut me off. If you have to set it down, okay, just keep talking to me."

"Okay." He got out of the car, put the phone in his sweatshirt pouch, took his key ring, and floundered trying to find the trunk key. Finally he opened the trunk lid. He removed the bike rack, closed the trunk, and strapped on the rack. He heard Geneva's muffled voice crying out to him from his pouch. "I'm okay baby," he called to her. He tried twice to lift up his bike to the rack, bashing his knuckles in the darkness. Finally he got it on and started to strap on the bungee cord.

"What's that?" For a moment he thought he saw a light shining behind him. He whirled around and peered into the darkness of the bike trail. "Who's there?"

He heard Geneva's muffled shriek, then removed the phone and put it up to his mouth. "It's okay, baby—thought I saw something, but it was nothing, all right? I'm going to drive home. I'll call you back in a while, okay?"

"Promise me you'll drive safe, baby," Geneva said. "Real slow, okay?"

"I promise." He sat at the wheel for a few minutes. Just as he was about to start the engine, a car pulled up behind him, its bright lights intensifying his headache. He felt tense, stiff, and defensive. Was this a cop? Somebody was coming toward him, now tapping on his window.

"Clarence, is that you? It's me. Ray Eagle."

"Ray. What are you…?"

"Geneva came to Bible study and asked us to pray. Then we went out searching for you. I figured I could pray while I drove. We combed North Portland and down by the *Trib*. Geneva said maybe something could have happened on your bike ride. She told me you usually park out here. Man, am I glad to see you're okay. What happened?"

"I don't know. Maybe an insulin reaction."

"Yeah, Geneva said that. I've got some orange juice and a Baby Ruth bar. Help yourself."

Clarence opened the candy bar and self-consciously chewed it, bits of chocolate falling on his lap.

"I'm just glad to see you, brother." Ray extended his arm through the window, putting his hand on Clarence's shoulder. Clarence felt embarrassed, but strangely comforted. "Have you called Geneva?" Ray asked. Clarence nodded. "Good. Look, you ride with me. You're in no condition to drive."

"No. I can drive. No problem. I'm much better now."

"Well…then I'm following right behind you. Drive slow. If you feel funny, pull over, okay? You hear me honking, that means you pull over, all right? I'll call Geneva and tell her I'm with you—you keep both hands on the wheel, okay?"

"Okay," Clarence said. The drive took longer than usual. He finally got home at 10:05. Ray jumped out of his car and escorted him to Geneva's waiting arms.

"We were praying for you, Daddy," Keisha said, hugging him tight. "We prayed God's angels would protect you."

Jonah and Celeste hugged him too. After taking his blood sugar and finding it was 288, way too high, Geneva helped Clarence take some insulin, pampered him, washed him up, and put him to bed.

———

The alarm sounded at 5:45 A.M. Geneva turned it off immediately, irritated she'd forgotten to disarm it. She told Clarence there was no way he was going to work. He insisted he had to go, to get off a column.

"I feel fine," he lied. He promised he'd come home early and rest. He popped a couple Advil, shaved and showered while Geneva fixed him oatmeal. She clung to him tight before letting him out the door.

Clarence drove into work bleary eyed, his head throbbing, still embarrassed that Ray and the whole Bible study group went out searching for him. He'd had three cups of coffee—two at home and a third from a drive-through espresso station. It still wasn't working.

It was just getting light, one of those dreary November days where the sky looked as if it had been rubbed hard with a dirty eraser. The air was heavy with the feel of a rainstorm threatening to cut loose.

Clarence pulled into the Fifth Street parking garage and passed by open spots on the second and third floors to circle up to the fourth floor to his favorite parking place, right by the elevator in the corner closest to the *Trib*. It was still early enough that there were only a half-dozen other cars up there. Clarence got out and pulled on his overcoat, taking his time, his muscles feeling old and tired.

Somebody else pulled in beside him. He had on a business suit, looked like an attorney. He went to the elevator and held open the door for Clarence.

Clarence nodded his thanks. The man leaned toward him and reached across to press the first floor button. When he brushed up against him, Clarence moved back. His personal space meant even more to him the way he felt now.

"Miserable day, huh?" the man asked.

"Yeah," Clarence said.

You don't know the half of it.

———

"Clarence? Good news. Got another hit on our guys, this time with the Mercedes temp plates."

Even Ollie's raspy voice sounded loud to him. Clarence held the phone two inches from his ear.

"I figured these same two guys with fake IDs buy a fancy Mercedes in

Sacramento and they've got to test it on the highway. Sure enough, they got a ticket doing ninety-four in a sixty-five. I've got to test drive one of those babies myself."

"Where were they?" Clarence asked.

"Just south of Buttonwillow."

"Where's that?"

"Way down I-5, a little more than two hours north of L.A. Well, less than an hour and a half if you're traveling 94. Nothing in Buttonwillow but a Motel 6, maybe a McDonald's. But that's where CHP nailed 'em."

"Did the cops search the car?"

"Nope. They pulled over and cooperated. No mota pipe, no reefer. Valid ID, valid title to the Mercedes, no outstanding warrants. No basis to detain them. Just one mama of a speeding ticket. But it's what we needed. They were way past San Francisco and Oakland, way past Fresno, past the turnoff to Bakersfield. They were headed to L.A. or San Diego, no doubt about it."

"You're still talking huge areas, thousands of gangbangers," Clarence said. "So can you put out word there's a couple of Bloods using fake ID and driving a seventy-thousand-dollar Mercedes?"

"Not sure they're Bloods."

"But the red sweatshirts. You said—"

"Yeah, but stack that up against the fact it was Crips who shot the cop with the HK53. And remember the color of Mercedes they bought? Blue. Doesn't sound like a Blood's color preference to me. Maybe they were Crips wanting anyone who might have seen them in Portland to think they were Bloods. Except when they were in Taco Bell, but that's a Crip hood and the red sweatshirts would draw attention. Anyway, Blood or Crip, there's lots of high rollers with nice cars. It's not the only blue Mercedes around. But these temporary licenses are only good so long. And they had to give a valid address."

"Why?"

"You can give a fake address buying a used car. But when you get a new car you get the temporary license, and in a couple of weeks they deliver permanent plates by mail—to whatever address you put down. If it's a fake address, you don't get your plates. I've put in a request to get the address both at the car dealership and the motor vehicles department. The car people are dragging their feet, and the DMV's government. So we'll see what we get. Oh, one other thing on Leesa Fletcher. Dr. Canzler, the medical examiner who did the autopsy, he's out of the country for another ten days. We're going to have to wait to find out why his report doesn't say she was pregnant." Ollie paused. "Hey, Clarence, you okay?"

"Yeah. Why?"

"I don't know. You don't sound yourself."

"Had a rough night."

_____

Clarence got his second cup of *Trib* coffee, his fifth of the day, and sat down to edit the column he'd rough-drafted the day before. He was grateful for the head start. A dull brain could handle revision better than creation. He absentmindedly ran his finger beneath his right ear.

> I'm convinced Charles Murray is wrong and there is no genetic cause for black failure. But many liberals quietly suspect he's right. They think blacks *can't* succeed if placed in equal competition with other races. This makes them exactly what they call everyone else—racists.
>
> People once believed blacks were inferior and couldn't compete with whites in athletics. Nobody says that any more. Black athletic success has disproved the thesis. Likewise, black academic success will accomplish far more for our children than endlessly repeating the mantra 'No more racism.' Heaping all the blame on racism has fostered failure by distracting the black community from raising our competitive standards.
>
> We have endless campaigns against white racism. We have mandatory sensitivity classes and campus multiculturalism lectures. We have speech codes and hate crime laws. Racism has become the windmill in a quixotic crusade. Liberals are redoubling their efforts to topple racism, while we neglect the *real* solutions of raising the standards of two-parent families, lasting marriages, moral training, discipline, and academic excellence.
>
> According to its admissions application test scores, if University of California at Berkeley were to admit students on merit, few Hispanics and blacks would qualify. So how have we dealt with this problem? By working to raise the academic standards in schools attended by blacks and Hispanics? No, instead we implemented racial quotas. Ironically, most of the black and Hispanic students admitted to Berkeley under this camouflage flunk out. The tests don't lie, and students with lower scores *cannot* compete with those who score higher. They flunk out of Berkeley, when they would have succeeded at any number of other colleges. Under quotas, blacks and Hispanics become failures—dropout statistics—when if they'd gone to a college where they were admitted on test scores, they would have succeeded. Ironically, many will believe they flunked out of college because of racism, rather than because they entered a college for which they weren't qualified.

We must make a concerted effort to strengthen black families and improve black education, to raise the bar instead of lowering it, to transform inner-city schools back into true institutions of learning, and to assist black families who want their children in private schools.

We *cannot* succeed at eliminating racism. We *can* succeed at fostering discipline, determination, and self-improvement. And that is our young people's true ticket to success.

Harley won't speak to me after this one.

Joe, the *Tribune* security guard, looked respectfully but uneasily at the blue-and-black-uniformed policeman who walked in the lobby of the *Trib.* Joe's eyes focused on the prominent gold badge, a slightly rectangular shield, directly above the officer's left pocket.

"May I help you, officer?" Joe asked, in his most professional, we're-law-enforcement-colleagues tone.

"Officer Guillermo Rodriguez." He handed him a business card. "I'm here to see Clarence Abernathy."

"Anything I can help you with?"

"No."

"Okay. Well, uh, can you please check in at the receptionist's desk over there?" The officer went to Elaine's desk. She'd been listening to the exchange.

"So," Elaine said, choosing her words carefully, "Mr. Abernathy is expecting you?"

"No, he's not," Rodriguez said.

"All right, well, let me call him and ask him to come down."

"Actually, I'd rather go up and see him unannounced. What floor?"

"Fourth floor. But if he's not expecting you—"

"Please don't call him. I'll find him myself. Thanks."

He placed his handcuffs and gun on Elaine's desk, walked through the metal detector, picked them up on the other side, and went to the elevator.

Clarence sat in his cubicle, trying to cut through the fog of his migraine and revise the column staring back at him from the terminal. He was finally making progress when suddenly, despite his earplugs, he sensed a presence behind him. He turned quickly, to see a uniformed policeman. His heart raced.

"Clarence Abernathy?"

"Yes?" He heard the blunted voice and fumbled to take out his earplugs with some appearance of dignity.

"Officer Guillermo Rodriguez, Portland police."

The officer didn't extend his hand. Clarence's eye went not to the officer's badge nor the radio positioned near his shoulder, but to the huge black belt housing handcuffs, asp baton, pepper-spray, and a large 9 mm Glock, along with two extra magazines.

"What do you want?"

"I need to talk with you. I've discussed it with Mr. Foley, and he said we could use that room over there." He pointed to an editorial conference room.

"I'm busy. Need to finish up a column."

"I can wait. A little. Ten minutes?"

"Fifteen or twenty."

"All right." The officer's politeness didn't cover the fact he wasn't pleased at the delay. "Come in as soon as you're done."

Between the hammer beating on his brain and the uniformed officer pacing in the conference room, Clarence's revisions went nowhere. He made a few cosmetic changes, pressed the send button, and delivered to Winston his premature and underweight column, still sixty words short.

Clarence cleared his throat and went to the conference room. There the officer was studying several white report forms and a yellow notepad. He looked like a journalist prepping for an interview. Except journalists don't carry weapons and handcuffs.

"What's going on here, officer?" Clarence asked.

"I'm here to get your side."

"My side of what?"

"You've been accused of some serious crimes."

Clarence stared at him in disbelief. Was Pete getting back at him for all those practical jokes? But this didn't feel like a prank. "What crimes?"

Officer Rodriguez looked down at the papers. "Possession and use of a controlled substance, that's a class B felony. Delivering a controlled substance to a minor, that's a class A felony."

"Drugs? You're accusing me of doing *drugs*?"

"And rape three—contributing to the sexual delinquency of a minor. That's a class A misdemeanor. Statutory rape."

"My wife's the only woman I've ever had sex with. And she's not a minor. What are you talking about?"

"I'm talking about you having sex with a seventeen-year-old girl."

"You've got the wrong man, officer. I don't do drugs, and I never touched a girl. I don't know what you're talking about."

"The girl's name is," Rodriguez looked down at the sheet, "Gracie Miller."

"The nearest telephone pole always looms largest to them," Lewis said to Dani and Torel. "It becomes their reference point, so the newest so-called 'truth' is the most popular."

"My brother talked about political correctness," Dani said. "Is that what you mean?"

"Often, yes," Lewis said, "although sometimes what is politically correct is also true. Usually, however, it is simply the latest in an endless string of wrong perspectives, each of which seems right for the moment because of its newness. Of course, silly things said now are as silly as they would have been if said long ago. But in the Shadowlands, men live by the myth of moral progress."

"What do you mean?" Dani asked.

"They regard failure to change moral standards as stagnation," Lewis said, hands clasped behind his back, pacing in professorial style. "The old fashioned becomes synonymous with the bad, the new synonymous with the good. But the square of the hypotenuse does not become outdated by continuing to equal the sum of the squares of the other two sides. An unchanging standard is not the enemy of moral progress. On the contrary, it is the necessary condition for it. If the destination is as mobile as the train, the train can never arrive."

"But some of the old standards *were* wrong," Dani said.

"Of course. But the *oldest* standards are Elyon's, and they are always right. Certain old standards of men were wrong, such as slavery and oppression and the doctrine of racial inequality. Other old standards were right, such as the sanctity of unborn human life and the wrongness of sexual immorality. To progress, you must change the old that was wrong by conforming instead to that which is older still, the ancient and eternal truth of God. But you must not change the old that was right. To do so is not moral progress but moral disintegration. What they see as lack of progress is often moral permanence. They fail to realize truth can be discovered on earth, but it can only originate in heaven."

"That's always been the message of prophets, hasn't it?" Dani asked.

"Exactly," Lewis said. "The prophet is not the revolutionary he appears. He does not call people to what is new, but to what is old. Not to human prejudice but to eternal values, which are always right. Prophets resist the current of their time by holding to the truths of eternity. They take us forward by pointing us back to truth we have departed from, truth just as true now as it always was. Ironically, the beliefs of the present age that take pride in not being old fashioned, tomorrow *will* be old fashioned. Truth, however, never goes out of date."

Dani and Torel sat listening attentively while Lewis paced as if standing in front of a Cambridge lecture hall. "They talk about human progress as if technology improves morality. They see men as the solution rather than the problem. They look at the third millennium after Christ, and they predict great progress. But if man were making moral progress, the twentieth century would have been a step toward utopia, would it not? Yet that century of technical progress was the century of genocide. More human beings, born and unborn, were murdered in that century than in all previous centuries combined."

The words stunned Dani. She'd never thought of it in those terms.

"Of course, the Evil One has been active throughout human history. But had Elyon given him only one century in which to work, the evidence would point to the twentieth century. They speak piously about the horrors of previous generations while they have blinded themselves to the horrors they commit daily, routinely—horrors we see so clearly from here. Their lifetimes have been characterized by hatred, oppression, race wars, and holocaust, yet in their self-aggrandizement they believe their generation can bring peace on earth. Theirs is the height of human arrogance. For the power to tame man's self-destruction resides not in them but in Elyon. Only the church of Christ has within it the life-changing power of God, and only that power enables change. Man is the problem; God, the solution. Men who try to solve the world's problems without God are destined to failure."

As Lewis spoke, behind him the portal opened and Dani saw what appeared a multimedia presentation of colleges and universities, the oldest with church steeples and crosses long ignored except as relics.

"Their universities were once built on Truth. Now they dispense their home-grown truths in plastic wrappers, like little slices of processed cheese. They are the most dangerous kind of sinners—sinners who no longer believe in sin, addicts pronouncing themselves free while everyone else can see they are pitifully enslaved. Deprived of joy, they reduce life to the pursuit of pleasures. But without Elyon there are no pleasures. The pursuit of pleasures without the giver of pleasure can never end in heaven, only hell. Refusing to anchor their lives in the bright sacred mysteries, they turn instead to the dark evil mysteries. Denying Elyon, they turn to the demon Moloch, for man is made to worship, and if he will not worship the true, he will worship the false. Hence a generation that prides itself on uplifting peace and caring for the earth and rising above barbarity daily offers its children in sacrifice to Moloch."

Torel nodded his head slowly, as one who had long contemplated this reality. "In ancient times," he said, "and I speak as one who was there, men were led astray by false gods, but they never were so foolish as to believe there were *no* gods. Educated western men put themselves in the place of God. They affirm themselves as the rule-makers. Men work together to create a moral tower of Babel, reaching to the skies. Since they think they make the rules, they feel free to break them and change them to conform to their whims. Morality becomes whatever they wish it to be. Of course, their minds have no power over reality. Truth no more cares about their beliefs concerning it than the sun cares whether people believe it will rise in the morning."

"Let's get the facts straight," Officer Rodriguez said. "You met with her at Jefferson, right?"

"Yeah. In the principal's office. He set the whole thing up."

"Right. That's what he told me this morning. But when I asked him if he noticed anything strange between you and Miss Miller, he said he walked in on you after the appointment was supposed to be over. He said he thought the two of you were discussing personal things."

"Did he accuse me of something?"

"Actually, no, he thinks highly of you. But when I told him what Miss Miller said, he looked back and was afraid maybe something happened that day. He was really sick about it, felt guilty he set the thing up and that it happened right in his office."

"*What* happened? Nothing happened!"

"I don't mean something happened then. Just that it turned into something later."

"Nothing happened then *or* later."

"Do you deny calling her at home the night of," he looked at one of his papers, "October 29?"

"No, I don't deny it. I was just returning her call."

"Why was she calling you at home? If it was business, wouldn't she call you at the paper?"

"Yes, usually, but this was different."

"Yeah," Rodriguez said. "Obviously."

Clarence's eyes registered fury.

"Her father tells me he didn't appreciate you calling her at home. Said you gave a phony last name and he thought it was a new boyfriend the way she ran off to her bedroom and shut the door. Do you deny giving her your home phone number?"

"She asked me for it."

The officer removed from a bag Clarence's business card with his handwritten home phone on it, holding it by its edges and showing it to Clarence. "Do you normally give out your private home number to high school girls?"

"Not normally," Clarence said, "but she said she could only call me in the evening."

"Do you deny meeting her at a bar last week?"

"It was a restaurant! I mean, okay it was a bar, but she told me it was a restaurant."

"And you couldn't tell the difference? You spent a couple of hours with her, just the two of you, in a back room at a bar she wasn't old enough to legally enter?"

"I wasn't there more than thirty minutes. Maybe twenty."

"Not according to witnesses, including her uncle. I talked to half a dozen people who say they saw you come out from the back room with her two hours later."

"What? That's impossible. They're lying!"

"Six people telling the same lie?"

"Yeah, if that's what they really said."

"Oh, that's what they said all right. And a couple of them say after you went out the front door, they looked out the window and saw you kiss her."

"You can't be serious. I didn't even go out the front door. And I never touched her!"

"The witnesses say otherwise. And her uncle says Gracie told him that night you got frisky with her in the back room. He was ready to come after you with a shotgun, but she said she was as much to blame as you. Told him there was a chemistry between you."

"He's lying. She wouldn't say that."

"Oh, but she would. And she did. I wouldn't be here if I hadn't talked to her first."

"This is a setup. Why would she do this to me?"

"I can't think of a good reason, can you? Anyway, you say you left after half an hour? Okay, so you have an alibi for that next hour and a half, right?"

"Yeah. Let's see. I was gone by 6:45 at the latest, and then—"

"And then what? You went home? Your family can back up your story?"

"Yeah, they were home. But…I wasn't."

"Oh?"

"Gracie, Miss Miller, she said a kid wanted to meet me at MLK and Evans, to talk about something."

"Okay. So what's the kid's name?"

"I don't know."

"You met with a kid and you don't know his name?"

"I didn't meet with him." Clarence heard the hollowness of his own voice. "He never showed up. I waited there an hour and a half. He never came."

"Did you tell your wife how you were spending the evening?"

"No. Just told her I was working late."

"Yeah. I'll bet."

"I *was* working late."

"Whatever you say. People define work different ways. Most would probably say spending the evening with a gorgeous young blonde in the back room of a bar is stretching the term *work.*"

Clarence's hand instinctively darted across the table, his index finger poking the officer in the chest. "Watch your mouth!" Clarence shouted.

"You watch your finger, Mr. Abernathy," Rodriguez grabbed his hand and flung it back at him. "You go for me again and you'll have a barrel in your mouth. Now cool your jets, big shot!"

Clarence restrained himself, waiting for the officer to imply again something about a black man going after a white girl. If he did, he decided he'd take him down, jail or no jail. After a few moments, though, he got ahold of himself.

"All right," Clarence said. "I'm sorry. I'm kind of stressed out. It's not what it seems."

"For your sake I hope not." Rodriguez looked down at the papers. "Okay. Do you deny you were with Miss Miller in Gresham yesterday afternoon at 5:30 P.M.?"

"What are you talking about?"

"She says you told her to take MAX out to the end of the line in Gresham, and then you picked her up there."

"She's lying."

"Then all you have to do is give me your alibi. Where were you?"

"I was—I was unconscious on the side of a bike trail."

"What?"

"It's a long story."

"I'm sure it is. But you don't have to bother constructing it, because the MAX driver said he saw you pick her up there. I showed him her picture and yours. He remembers seeing you both. Gracie says you took her to a motel in Troutdale, that you did drugs and…plenty of other things. I went to see the manager an hour and a half ago. I showed him your pictures. He confirms you checked in. Obviously you used a different name. They always do."·

Clarence felt numb. He thought of Geneva and the children. He thought of his father beaten and tortured in that Mississippi jail. He thought of an uncle who'd been castrated and his father's cousin who'd been hung by the Klan for being accused of less serious crimes than these.

"What happens now?" Clarence asked weakly.

"If I thought you posed an immediate threat I could arrest you here. I'm not sure that's necessary, although you assaulting those two guys in the Impala and putting your hands on an officer makes a good case for your being a loose cannon. I could send my report to the sexual assault division and they could take over the investigation. If I think there's sufficient evidence, I can turn it over directly to the district attorney's office. That's what I'm probably going to do."

"How can you do that to me?" Clarence asked. "What's your evidence?"

"We don't have physical evidence, of course. She's taken a shower since then. The motel sheets had already been washed, so no semen stains are left for DNA tests."

Clarence felt sick just hearing the words.

"But I've got the girl's testimony and a bunch of witnesses that dispute your testimony, not only yesterday but last week at the bar. Even what you admit to is bad enough. You admit giving her your phone number, calling her at home, meeting her alone in the back room of a bar. You have no alibi for that night and none for yesterday afternoon. Then there's the drug charges."

"I don't use drugs."

"You've never used drugs?" The officer stared at him.

"Look, I tried pot in the sixties, okay?"

"Didn't inhale, huh?"

Clarence glowered at him.

"You say you're not a user. The rings around your eyes say otherwise."

"I'm telling the truth."

"The eyes don't lie." He studied Clarence's eyes as if he were an optometrist. "Your pupils don't say meth or crack—they say heroin. They look like you haven't slept, like you've been on the nod. Heroin's what the girl said, and your eyes say the same. You still deny it?"

"*Of course* I deny it. I've never touched heroin in my life."

"I'd run a toxicology test on you, but heroin would be out of the system by now. Cocaine would still be there. Maybe I should have brought you in right after the girl talked to us this morning, but I wanted to do my homework first. I was hoping you'd fess up. Guess I should have known better."

"I'm innocent."

"Uh-huh. So's everybody. Our prisons are full of innocent men."

Clarence wanted to jump across the table at him. He knew he could take him in a fight, but there were a few problems. The Glock in the officer's holster was one. The long-term consequences were another, although right now by themselves they weren't enough to restrain him.

"Mind if I search you?" Rodriguez asked.

"Go ahead."

"Stand up." The officer stood behind Clarence, sticking his hand first in his right coat pocket, then his left, then his front pants pockets, then his back. Clarence felt violated, but what was the alternative? To act guilty?

"Satisfied?" Clarence asked.

"Can I check your inside coat pocket?" Clarence nodded. Rodriguez stepped around front and checked the coat and shirt pockets.

"Looks like you're clean," Rodriguez said. "Of course, I wouldn't expect you to carry it here."

"Where's innocent until proven guilty?" Clarence asked. "Or don't you believe in that?"

"What I believe doesn't matter, Mr. Abernathy. Can I search your desk?"

"Fine! Search my desk. Search my overcoat. Come search my house. Bring a bunch of your storm trooper buddies with you. But when you're done searching, you leave me alone. Got it?"

Clarence saw the officer looking over his right shoulder out to the newsroom. About ten people stood frozen and wide eyed, gazing into the editorial office. One of them was Jess. Clarence realized he'd been louder than he intended.

"Calm down, Mr. Abernathy," Officer Rodriguez said. "If you're innocent, you've got nothing to worry about. Let's go to your desk."

Clarence led the way. Rodriguez opened the desk while Clarence looked around at a dozen reporters who pretended not to notice his work station was being searched by a uniformed police officer. The officer fumbled around in his desk, then pointed to the orange capped needle.

"It's an insulin needle," Clarence said. Rodriguez looked skeptical. "You know. Insulin-dependent diabetic? We have to take shots. There's millions of us."

The officer picked up the needle on the capped end.

"Can I take this?"

"Yeah. In fact you can stick it—" Clarence caught himself.

"You wear an overcoat?"

Clarence led him to the coatrack near the elevator and removed his overcoat from the hook. The officer put his hand in one pocket, then the other. He pulled out an insulin bottle and another needle. Suddenly he stopped. He drew out something in his hand, a tiny little clear glass vial. It was about an inch tall, half an inch wide, with thick glass and a black cap. Inside was white powder.

"What's that?" Clarence said.

"Can I open it up?" Rodriguez asked. Clarence nodded. The cop smelled it.

"Heroin. Okay, Mr. Abernathy, you're under arrest. Turn around and put your hands behind your back."

Clarence stared at the people around him, now nearly twenty of them. More crowded up, as the frozen images attracted attention in a newsroom that was normally endless motion. The officer chose his hinged handcuffs with no connecting chain, clamping them firmly on Clarence's wrists.

"You have the right to remain silent."

This isn't happening.

"Anything you say can and will be used against you in a court of law."

O God, don't let this be happening.

"You have the right to consult with an attorney..."

What will Geneva and the kids think? What will Daddy think? What will everybody think?

"If you cannot afford to hire an attorney..."

A man's reputation is all he has.

"Do you understand each of these rights I've explained to you?"

Clarence nodded and Rodriguez escorted him to the elevator in full view of three-dozen *Trib* employees. Once on the ground floor he walked him out to his patrol car. The officer pushed his head down for the tight squeeze into the car, just like the cop had done to Ellis twenty years ago—the last time Clarence had touched his brother.

Out of the corner of his eye, Clarence saw someone running up to the car with camera in hand. She focused and started to take the picture, then realized who was in it. Carp lowered her camera and stared wide eyed at Clarence. Another camera clicked. As Clarence rode off he thought he saw Carp grab the camera from the other photographer. He wasn't sure because the restraints kept him from turning and seeing what was really happening.

CHAPTER

The officer drove Clarence to the Justice Center, pulling into the secured underground area. Clarence thought about all the time he'd spent in this same building, meeting with Ollie. But this time he would end up on one of those floors where the public elevator didn't stop—lockup.

At an intake station, Officer Rodriguez removed Clarence's handcuffs and the Justice Center guard put on the county handcuffs, equally uncomfortable.

Rodriguez handed the intake officer his booking sheet. The woman made copies and returned the original to Rodriguez. They chatted pleasantly, as if Clarence didn't exist. They took his watch, keys, wallet, pocket change, insulin and needles—everything but his clothes—and bagged them up.

Another guard led Clarence through a door and said, "Stand there on the red X." Clarence stood. In front of him were three heavy steel doors. It felt like a bizarre version of *Let's Make a Deal*. Which will it be? Door number one, door number two, or door number three?

A security officer made the choice for him. Door number one. He escorted him into a large, poorly lit cell smelling of vomit and urine. The predatory expressions of some of the room's inhabitants instantly changed when they saw Clarence's imposing physique. Everyone moved back from him except one high-strung guy whose pupils looked like pinpoints. Clarence plopped down on the stark metal bench, staring at the twelve-inch grate in the middle of the floor.

"Well, look what we got here, boys," the addict said. "We got ourselves a nigger."

Clarence looked around the holding cell, doing some quick math. Three white guys, including the addict, one other black, and a Latino.

"Yeah, he's a nigger, all right," the addict said. "What you doin' in here, boy?"

Clarence looked at him with disgust. He wouldn't let this guy push his buttons. He wasn't worth it.

"I seen yo' mama, black boy. She was sellin' herself over on Third Street and I had me a—"

Clarence's right fist smashed the man's nose, knocking him across the room. One of the guys beat on the door and called for a guard. Two guards rushed in and saw Clarence hovering over the man with the bloody face. One of them jumped on Clarence. Thinking he was another inmate, Clarence threw the officer against the wall.

"Stop or I'll shoot," the second officer yelled. Clarence turned and looked down the barrel of a Colt Police .45. He raised his hands. They handcuffed him again and escorted him to a private cell. The officer he'd thrown against the wall gave him a shove for good measure. At least this cell didn't smell of urine. He sat there, index finger brushing against the scar under his right ear.

Later, whether fifteen minutes or two hours Clarence didn't know, a guard escorted him to the photograph and fingerprint processing section. "We've got your fingerprints on file, I'm sure," the man said.

"Never been fingerprinted," Clarence said.

The man gave him an unbelieving look. "We've got to determine your classification. Decide how to house you. What's your record? What aliases have you been arrested under?"

"Never been arrested," Clarence said. "Just pulled over for speeding."

"Well, we'll just take your prints here, and it'll run out your record for us." Clearly this was a man used to being lied to.

A guard escorted Clarence to medical intake, where he explained to the nurse his diabetic condition, and that he took four shots a day. "While you're in here, it'll just be two shots," she said gruffly. "Nurses come into the population twice a day, that's all."

Clarence didn't bother arguing. After a few minutes, they escorted him to a room with eight other men, including three from his original holding cell, all of whom backed away.

"Take off your clothes. All of them." With two armed guards looking on, the officer gave directions like an exercise instructor. He told them to bend over and do humiliating things to prove they weren't hiding something. Clarence had never been strip searched until now. He felt like an animal. He felt like what his ancestors must have felt. The smirk on one of the guard's faces chilled him.

"Okay, fellas. Now we dress you for success." The officer guessed at their sizes and passed out faded blue pants and smocks. For Clarence he didn't have to guess. Extra large.

The men were escorted through another security area. Clarence was put in a little cell by himself, equipped only with a small cot and a metal toilet, which stunk. The bars went from ceiling to floor, so his most private actions were not private at all, but completely visible to anyone in the corridor.

An hour later they escorted him out for dinner. The man next to him said, "Trade my ham for your roll."

"Okay," Clarence said, making his first jailhouse deal. He ate quickly, as he had as a child when food wasn't plentiful. He looked around the eating area and stood up at the table. A guard tensed, stepping toward him.

"Can't I call my wife or my lawyer or somebody?" Clarence asked him.

"Phone privileges are at seven. Another hour and a half. You haven't called a lawyer?"

"No," Clarence said. The man left to check out Clarence's story. He came back in five minutes. "I'll take you to the phone."

Instead of dialing his lawyer, Clarence called Geneva. "Hey, baby, it's me."

"Clarence, where are you?" Her voice sounded shrill. "Jake called and said you'd gone off in a police car. I've been worried sick. Where are you?"

He heard the panic in her voice. "I'm...I'm in jail." The smelly phone mouthpiece was suddenly flooded with hot tears.

The guard felt sorry for Clarence and let him make another phone call. This one wasn't to his attorney either. It was to Ollie. He promised Clarence he'd check on bail and get hold of his lawyer for him.

"It's wonderful you're still a teacher here," Dani said to Lewis.

"Elyon's gifts are irrevocable. We do not set them aside here, we develop them further. Our service on earth was preparatory to our service here. I'm still writing. I've completed a number of volumes since I arrived. I've just finished a children's series. I'll pick out a book for you—I've got just the one in mind."

"Please! Writing and reading in heaven? Books in heaven? I never imagined it."

"The Bible itself talks about the books in heaven kept by God—the book of remembrances, the book of life, the books of man's works on earth. He even keeps a book of the laments of the righteous in the Shadowlands. His Word says, 'Record my lament; list my tears on your scroll—are they not in your record?'"

"Still, I've never thought about people writing new books here."

"If Elyon had some of his people teach and write and speak and compose songs on earth, why would he do otherwise here? If we learned about him through books on earth, why would we not do so here? If we took joy in reading on earth, why would that joy cease here? Wouldn't we expect more of what brings joy rather than less? Does life stop here or does it commence? Does life contract here or does it expand? You were an artist on earth, were you not? Does it surprise you to be an artist here?"

"Yes, it did at first."

"But why? Life here is a continuation of life there," Lewis said. "It is not a new volume, not even a sequel, but the next chapter. Granted, the setting has changed dramatically, but the children of God are the same characters, the plot of the unfolding drama of redemption continues, and the theme is still the glory of God. You bring here the same desires, knowledge, and skills. The difference is those desires are fulfilled in all the right places, and your ability to learn is far superior. Knowledge here is not merely isolated facts, pearls without the string, but facts held together by perspective. And as for your skills, your creative gifts, your artistic talent, they were given you by Elyon, were they not?"

"Yes. Of course."

"And is he one who takes back gifts he has given? Or is he rather one who gives ever more opportunity to use those gifts? How could anyone imagine that in heaven Elyon would remove the knowledge and gifts he gave us and cultivated in us on earth? How strange it would be for him to take away the abilities he gave us now that we can finally exercise them without impediment."

"Professor Lewis is correct," Torel said. "Earth was far more closely connected to heaven than most there ever imagine. And for those who do not bow their knee to Elyon, earth is far more closely connected to hell than they imagine. Every day on earth, every choice you made influenced your life toward eternity."

Torel pointed to a large building with inscriptions written in many languages. "Let us go to the Hall of Writings. It is filled with writings done on earth that are still read and studied here—words that outlasted the dark world because they derived their perspectives from this world."

"I've been here many times, Dani," Lewis said. "It's one of my favorite places. May I show you around?"

"That would be wonderful." She took his arm and they walked, Torel beside them. "I'm sure you have many writings here, Lewis," Dani said.

"You have some as well," Torel said to Dani.

"What? I never wrote a book. Not even an article."

"Do you think it had to be *published* to qualify?" Lewis laughed. "Most of what is published does *not* qualify. And much qualifies that was read only by a few, some read by none but Elyon."

"But what did I write that could be here?" Dani asked.

In the gigantic Room of Letters, they showed Dani letters of love and encouragement she'd written to her parents and Clarence, letters of devotion and direction she'd written to her children, evangelistic letters written to Harley and Ellis, letters of moral concern written to school principals and newspapers, letters of thanks written to many others. Finally, there were letters of praise she had written to Elyon.

"Most of these I'd forgotten," Dani said.

"But Elyon does not forget," Lewis said.

In the midst of this engaging tour, Dani felt a sudden tug toward the portal. She rushed to it, Torel and Lewis behind her. She saw quickly what had transpired over the last hours on earth. Clarence was in trouble.

She looked at the throne, toward the Carpenter, her heart pleading, then fell to her knees to intercede. Lewis and Torel followed her lead.

Clarence kept thinking maybe they'd come and escort him out, apologizing for the mistake. Or at least that they'd let him out to visit with Geneva or somebody. But nothing happened. He felt as if everything he'd worked for, everything he'd earned, his character, his reputation, suddenly meant nothing. He told them he needed more insulin, that he needed to check his blood sugar, but guards and nurses alike seemed to assume he was lying, that he was trying to get away with something. It seemed not to occur to them that he might be innocent.

They let him out of his room at 7:00, just for an hour. He looked at the books on some makeshift shelves. Most of them were trashy. He found a Bible. He devoured it, reading the Psalms. He asked if he could take it back to his cell. The guard wouldn't let him.

He lay in the bed, cold and shivering, a frightened child lying in the darkness. He remembered what they'd done to his daddy in jail and wondered if this was punishment for what he'd done to that boy in the projects. He wanted to sleep until the nightmare was over. He didn't.

After breakfast the next morning, at which Clarence traded sausage for pancakes, a guard ushered him into a room where Ollie and Jake came in to meet with him, they on the free side of the thick glass, he on the captive side. He instinctively placed his hand on the glass. Jake put his up to it.

"How are you, brother?" Jake asked, eyes red and wet.

"Been better. The food's not Lou's, that's for sure. You'd starve, Ollie."

"I had to pull in some favors to get in here with Jake," Ollie said. "We don't have much time. I've been talking to everybody since you called last night. It doesn't look good."

"You've got to believe me," Clarence said. "I didn't do it!"

"I know you didn't do it, Clabern," Jake said. "We're doing everything we can to get you out."

"Ollie, why would somebody do this to me?" Clarence asked.

"I'm not sure. Maybe it means we're getting close. Maybe it means they wanted to get you off track or undermine your credibility. If they can make this thing with the girl stick—or even if they can't—who's going to confide in you? People back off from anyone involved in a scandal. When I was accused, even after I was cleared, people wouldn't trust me. Maybe they're trying to dry up your contacts. Obviously they see you as a threat."

"I don't feel like much of a threat."

"The good news is I pitched a case to the lieutenant this morning. I convinced him you're being framed. Well, *maybe* being framed. He thinks I'm a good judge of character. He's always thought that since I lobbied for him to get his promotion. Anyway, I sold him on the idea that whoever did this to you didn't want you nosing around about your sister's murder. So if we can find who framed you, we may find out who killed your sister."

"Hadn't thought of that."

"You've had other things on your mind. Anyway, I've got some latitude to look into Gracie Miller's case against you. Maybe I can help clear you *and* we can find whoever's behind the murders."

"When can I get out of here?"

"They're raising bail right now. Unfortunately by the time people found out yesterday, banks were closed. Hopefully you'll get out today. I've made some calls on your case. I've talked with several people and looked at the reports. Wednesday night the Miller girl was definitely picked up at the Gresham end-of-the-line MAX station by a big black guy in a suit who checked into the motel with her. Last week she definitely left her uncle's bar with a big black guy in a suit, presumably the same guy. People noticed they were…familiar with each other."

"But it wasn't me. Can't you just show them my picture?"

"I did. I even went to the bar last night. Talked to the girl's uncle and two barflies. They all looked at the picture of you and said the same thing. 'Yep,'" he put on his best redneck bar voice, which wasn't that far from his own, "'that's him all right. Like we said, he's a big black guy.'"

"What did you say?"

"I said it doesn't matter that he was a big black guy, the only thing that matters is whether he was *this* big black guy. They insisted he was, but I could tell they weren't sure. Problem is they say they are. Now, this blonde girl they could pick out of a lineup of twenty blonde girls the same size. But you put twenty big black guys in a lineup and they'd maybe narrow it down to fifteen. Same with the hotel manager. He looked at the picture and of course he said yes. What else would he say?"

"My brother Harley says white folks are descriptively disadvantaged about black folks."

"Yeah. And it sure made it easy to set you up. This big guy dresses like you, shows up in a shadowy bar, then he walks out with the girl and kisses her under the streetlights. You didn't help things by writing out your home phone number on your business card. You really called her at home?"

"I know. It was stupid."

"Yeah. But stupid isn't the same as statutory rape and drug abuse."

"No. But who's going to believe it isn't?"

All three knew the answer.

"Clarence," Jake said, "I want to pray for you now." He put one hand up to the glass, Clarence matched his hand to it, and Ollie sat uncomfortably while Jake prayed aloud.

At noon, twenty-one hours after he'd been arrested, Clarence was escorted out of his cell and taken through out-processing. Forty minutes later he walked out the door into the Justice Center lobby, into Geneva's arms. They held each other for a long time.

They walked out the front door, past the Justice Center cornerstone with its prominent quote above the name Martin Luther King—"Injustice anywhere is a threat to justice everywhere."

Geneva drove Clarence to the law offices of Bowles and Sirianni.

"How much did it take to bail me out, Grant?"

"For the three charges it was going to be thirty-one thousand, so 10 percent was thirty-one hundred."

"Going to be?"

"Well, you managed to pick up a few more charges. Try Assault 2. Class B Felony. Something about 'Intentionally causing serious physical injury.' Ring a bell?"

"You mean the crankster in the holding cell?"

"Yeah, for starters."

"He kept calling me nigger and then he dissed my mama."

"There's no law against that."

"There ought to be."

"Clarence, the guy's a career felon arrested for armed robbery. What do you want them to do? Add 'using the n-word' and 'saying naughty things about somebody's mama' to armed robbery and assault and battery charges? Did you have to hit him?"

"I guess I was a little upset. It'd been a bad day, all right?"

"Remind me to stay away from you on a bad day. You broke his nose."

"Yeah. I thought I heard something crack." He looked at Geneva out of the corner of his eye.

"Your final charge was assault on a public safety officer." Clarence looked surprised. "Two officers claim when they came into the holding cell, you tossed one of them against the wall."

"I didn't know it was an officer. I thought it was one of the other creeps in the cell."

"Well, you've made things complicated, to say the least. Final bail was sixty thousand, so we had to pay six."

"Where'd you get six thousand dollars?" Clarence asked Geneva. "We've got just two thousand in the bank."

"Now it's fifty in the bank," Geneva said. "Jake and Janet came up with another two thousand. Pastor Clancy threw in eight hundred from the church. Our Bible study group came up with the rest."

Clarence lowered his head, saying nothing.

"Okay, we need to talk strategy," Grant Bowles said. "Nick checked into your arrest. There were some procedures we can challenge. We can say the officer was out of his league, should have turned it over to the detectives and the sex abuse experts. It's a judgment call, but we'll argue it was a bad one. Also, he failed to give you a drug test and didn't get the girl to the med school for the semen examination. Has to be done within forty-eight hours. We're lucky he blew that one."

"Why?" Clarence asked. "If he'd done it, it would've cleared me." He looked uncomfortably at Geneva, sitting quietly beside him, her arm in his. "There would have been no drugs, and no semen, or it would've been someone else's, not mine. Right?"

"Sure. Whatever." Clarence looked at his attorney long and hard. For the first time it occurred to him that he didn't believe him.

"Look, Grant, I didn't do this. No way. If you don't believe that, I want another lawyer."

"Clarence, it's my job to defend you, and that's what I'm going to do. But if you're sure you're innocent, you can take the polygraph test and that will help us."

"If I'm sure? Of course I'm sure. I didn't do it!"

"Okay. Then we'll submit to a polygraph test. It's not admissible, but it makes a strong statement to the prosecutor. The DA's looked over the officer's interview notes, and he's taking it to a grand jury so they can determine whether there's probable cause."

"So I'll be able to tell them my side of the story?" Clarence asked.

"No, you won't. It doesn't work that way. They just hear your accuser. They aren't giving a final verdict, just determining if there's probable cause to take it further."

"And if there is probable cause?"

"The DA puts out a warrant for your arrest. Then you go through booking. But you've already done that. So you'd just show up at the arraignment."

"When's that?"

"Tuesday, 2:00 P.M., Room 3 back at the Justice Center. There's just one arraignment hearing a week. Lots of other people will be there."

Clarence remembered that the *Trib* had a reporter assigned to the weekly arraignment. As a respectable citizen with no record, and as a fellow reporter, surely Dan Ferrent wouldn't put his name in the paper. Especially not with a minor involved. Would he?

His heart sank. He kept thinking of his children, especially Jonah. And what people would be thinking and saying.

"Manny talked with the officer who arrested you," Ollie told Clarence as they sat in his living room. "They're buddies."

"That figures," Clarence said.

"What figures?"

"That they're buddies."

"Why? Because they're both Hispanic?" Clarence didn't respond. "Well, I've got a lot of white friends," Ollie said. "You got a lot of black friends?"

"Yeah."

"Then don't make something of it because Hispanics have Hispanic friends, okay? What's good for the goose is good for the gander. Anyway, Manny asked him why he chose to follow through on the case rather than hand it over to the sex abuse detectives or the CAT."

"Cat?"

"Child Abuse Team. He said he likes to follow a case through. That's okay, it's his call. Manny asked him why he cuffed you, given your history as an upstanding citizen and all. I'm sure he checked and saw you didn't have a record. He said the reason he did it was you were so hostile with him. Of course, I didn't realize you would be so incredibly stupid as to actually lay a hand on him."

"It was just a finger."

"Finger's on your hand, right?"

Clarence looked down at his hand. "Yeah."

"The officer felt you were a risk since you were agitated and you're so big."

"Or since I'm so black?"

"You know, Clarence, you're not a fun guy to try to help. Anybody ever tell you that? Manny and I, we're both concerned for you so we try to get some info that might be helpful, while you just make it worse for yourself by justifying your stupidity."

"I didn't do it!"

"Didn't do *what*? Mess with the girl? Do the drugs? I believe you. But did you yell at the police officer? Poke him in the chest? So what do you expect? He told Manny at first he was going to cut you some slack. Till he saw how you acted and he found the stuff on you."

"He arrested me."

"He was doing his job. If you'd cooperated, there would've been no handcuffs and you could've just walked out the door with him. But that was too easy, huh? Well, let me welcome you to the slow cogs of American justice," Ollie said, getting up to leave. "I hope they move faster for you than they did for me."

"Ollie, wait," Clarence said. "I'm sorry. I really appreciate your help. Look, sit down, would you? Talk to me. Is there anything more on Dani's case? Like with the license plate?"

"Motor Vehicles got me the address where the license plate's being sent." Ollie took out his notepad and flipped a few pages. "To a Mr. Rafer Thomas in L.A. One of my cop buddies down there went and checked him out. He was real cool. Said there must be a mistake. Doesn't know anything about a Mercedes. The guy has a Crip history, and you can bet he's a friend or relative of one of our guys. I sent down a PI to check out his family. Ray Eagle."

"You sent Ray?"

"Yeah. He does a good job, ex-cop you know. But he's the one that called me. He's doing it for free."

"For free?"

"We can't afford to hire PIs. But since Ray volunteered to help you, I said sure. He flew down this morning. Motor Vehicles is going to send the plates through to Rafer Thomas. Ray's going to be on surveillance, watching the mailbox. When the plates come, wherever Thomas goes, Ray goes.

An official-looking, brisk-walking woman escorted Clarence into a plain, colorless room. It was quiet, deathly quiet, conspicuously lacking life's background noises. Only one door came into the room. There was no other way to get out. On one wall was a mirror. Clarence supposed it was a two-way mirror. He wondered what invisible eyes were watching him.

Nick Sirianni, Grant Bowles's young partner, sat in a chair off to the side. Nick seemed nervous, his eyes darting around the room. Clarence wondered if this was the right move after all.

"Please be seated, Mr. Abernathy," a middle-aged, accountant-like man said. Clarence sat uncomfortably in the chair. It seemed fashioned for a five-foot four-inch, 120-pound woman. The man started to strap a tube around his chest.

"What's that?" Clarence asked.

"A pneumograph tube."

"What does it do?"

"Just relax, Mr. Abernathy. It monitors your breathing."

A female assistant put a blood-pressure cuff around his right arm. She pumped it, and he felt it close in around him.

"Turn your hand up, please." She put electrodes on his fingers and the surface of his hand. He felt like a serial killer about to be electrocuted.

They set up a microphone in front of him. He wanted to ask if this was going to be taped, but he didn't want to sound defensive.

Why is it so hot in here?

He wiped his face with a handkerchief, self-consciously, feeling as if he was being studied like a lab rat. At an overly neat desk sat a white man with the calm measured voice of a scientist studying a specimen. "What is your name?" he asked him.

"Clarence Abernathy." He paused just before he said it, afraid that by saying it wrong he would appear to be a liar. It was irrational, he knew. But it was as if he were on trial for every black man who'd ever lived. If they thought O. J. got away with something, they'd make sure he didn't.

The man asked him question after question. "Do you know Gracie Miller?"

"Yes." Why did he feel guilty? Of course he knew her. He met her on assignment.

"Did you give illegal drugs to Gracie Miller?"

"No, I didn't."

"Have you taken drugs in the last week?"

"No," he said, but then he realized the man hadn't said "illegal" this time. He thought about his insulin. Was that considered a drug? Should he qualify his answer? Too late. His interrogator had moved on to another question.

Several other questions followed and then, there it was. "Did you have sexual relations with Gracie Miller?"

"No!" He said it louder than he meant to. He felt agitated at this whole process. He wanted to be done with this nonsense and get out of this cage. Without showing any expression the man at the neat desk studied the physiological changes as they were transmitted through a small panel unit and into the synchronized readings on the moving graph paper. Later he would take these parallel graphs and correlate and interpret them to determine whether Clarence was lying. But already he was drawing his conclusions, Clarence felt sure.

The interrogator repeated several earlier questions, including whether Clarence took drugs and had sex with Gracie Miller. Half an hour later, they unhooked him from the devices.

"You're free to go now, Mr. Abernathy."

Clarence walked out with his lawyer. "That was so weird," Clarence said to him. "I just told the truth, but I feel like I blew it."

"You did fine," Nick said. "Don't worry about it."

"They sit in judgment over truth," Torel said, "but Elyon alone knows everything, sees every heart, records every action. He is the rewarder of those who embrace truth and the punisher of those who embrace falsehood. Truth brings its own rewards, sometimes in the Shadowlands, but always in heaven."

"I realize now," Dani said, "sometimes I put more value on the rewards in that world than those reserved for this one."

"Earth's treasures are easily destroyed," Torel said. "If a person's treasures are on earth, death is the ultimate tragedy, for it separates him from his treasures. Every day brings him closer to death, and therefore every day moves him farther from what he treasures. Jesus said to lay up your treasures in heaven, so that every day on earth, as you get closer to leaving that world, you are headed *toward* your treasures instead of away from them. He who is headed away from his treasures has reason to despair. He who is headed toward his treasures has reason to rejoice."

Dani nodded. "No wonder so many there live lives of despair instead of joy."

"Do you recall the story Jesus told," Torel asked, "about using your resources on earth to gain friends in heaven so that when your life there was done you would be welcomed into eternal dwellings? What you did during your life on earth made special friends for all eternity, friends eager to open their homes to you in heaven. People you helped and discipled and shared your faith with, they will invite you to their dwellings in the heavenly city. You will share meals together, make music and celebrate, and tell great stories of old."

"I can hardly wait for that, Torel."

"There will be others too you still haven't met. Those you influenced without even knowing it by your godly example, by your letters, your phone calls. Those you reached through your art, the lives you touched in your church and Bible studies, and the lives in turn that they touched, lives you don't even know yet. Those to whom you brought the truth—like when you gave a book to one person who passed it on to another, and she to another. There are people you talked to on a bus, waitresses, a woman who cut your hair. The child of the woman who cut your hair. The friend of that child. There is an effect like dominos falling, one touching the next, which touches the next, and so on. When you gave your time and money to the poor and to reach people with the gospel, these were investments that will bear eternal returns. Here you will always be thankful for every minute of worship, every hour of prayer, every dollar you gave to further the cause of Christ. People will come to your home and say 'thank you,' and they will open their homes to you, and you will hear their stories. Perhaps you may go back over time and space and relive their adventures with them."

"If only I'd understood this on earth. It would have been a great motivator. It would have changed the way I lived."

Clarence arrived at Bowles & Sirianni at ten the next morning. He sat down in the office of Grant Bowles.

"I'm sorry to have to tell you this, Clarence."

"What?" Clarence caught his breath.

"You failed the polygraph," Grant said. Clarence sat motionless, staring at nothing. "The examiner says your responses indicate you weren't telling the truth. At least not on the key subjects of doing drugs and having sex with Miss Miller."

"But I *was* telling the truth. I'm innocent!"

"Clarence, listen, I'm your attorney. It's my job to defend you, and I'm going to do everything in my power to get you off. Anything you say to me is entirely confidential under attorney/client privilege. I cannot, I will not divulge it to anyone."

"Why are you saying all this?"

"Because I have to ask you. Are you *sure* you never did heroin or had sexual relations with Gracie Miller?"

Clarence stared vacantly into his attorney's eyes. He got up, walked out of the room, and headed for the elevator, ignoring the voice behind him. "Clarence, we're not done. We have to talk."

Clarence drove straight to the Justice Center. As he went up the elevator, for the first time he knew exactly what was going on in all those floors where the elevator wouldn't stop. He sat down with Ollie and told him about failing the polygraph.

"I wish you'd told me this before," Ollie said. "I never recommend taking a polygraph."

"Why? I wasn't lying."

"I know that. But the lie detector has a basic flaw—it doesn't detect lies. It detects stress. It records blood pressure, pulse rate, respiration. That's not the same as recording truth and lies. I rarely use polygraphs anymore. I've seen people I know for a fact are guilty pass them. I've seen people I know are innocent fail them. They're right the great majority of the time, of course, but that's no consolation when they're wrong."

"But...I don't understand," Clarence said. "I thought they were reliable. Obviously, my lawyer thought so."

"He's probably only had good experiences up till now. He'll think twice next time."

"He said if I'm innocent I should take it, if I'm guilty I shouldn't. If I didn't take it, I'd have looked guilty." He wondered if his voice sounded as pathetic to Ollie as it did to him. "Your reputation is all you've got, Ollie. I felt like I had to take that test to save my reputation."

Ollie looked at him. Neither of them had to say it. If Clarence's reputation was all he had, then now he had nothing.

Clarence put the girls to bed. He tried to explain to Jonah what had happened, embarrassed both by what he'd been accused of and that he'd failed the polygraph test. After an awkward conversation, he left Jonah's room and went out to join his daddy and Geneva, who sat in the living room in front of the fire, Obadiah on a rocker and Geneva on the couch.

"I was just talkin' to Geneva about your mama, Son. Some days I miss her so bad it hurts. You should have seen her when I first did. Um, um. She was so pretty, uncommon pretty. Like my daughter-in-law here. She could cook up gumbo by the bucket like nobody you ever seen. When we was courtin', we used to sit on that ol' Mississippi porch countin' cricket chirps. And later when we was married, we'd put you kids to bed and we'd lay out a blanket and get on our backs and count the stars. We got up to a thousand one night. Well, yo' mama's on the other side of those stars, lookin' down. Not that long I'll be lookin' down here too. And when I do, I want to see my son tellin' his chillens about the God who created those stars."

"I've lost everything," Clarence said. "You work so hard, and then someone takes it all away with a lie."

"You hasn't lost everything, Son," Obadiah said. "The things most important are the things only God can see. Ain't nobody can take those away. Only God knows what's truth and what's lies. He separates the grain from the chaff. Don't matter what men think. Only matters what God thinks. If the world thought you was innocent and God knowed you was guilty, you should be shakin' in your boots. If the world thinks you're guilty and God knows you're innocent, then what the world thinks don't matter a hill of beans, now does it, boy?"

"Do you know what they're sayin' about me, Daddy? I could go to jail for this. Lose my job. A man's reputation is all he's got."

"No, a man's character is all he's got. And his God's all he's got."

"And his family," Geneva added.

Obadiah nodded so hard his old neck creaked. "We're still here for you, Son. Your family loves you. You got the best woman who ever walked God's green earth, save your mama and your sister." He smiled and nodded at Geneva. "We know they's lyin' about you. I been lied about myself. I knows what it's like. But see, character, that's what a man is in the dark, where only God sees him. You're in a trial right now, Son. You gots to make sure you're lettin' the good Lord build his character in you. You gots to entrust yourself to the God who judges justly. That's what you gots to do."

"I don't understand why he'd do this to me."

"Clarence, you remember that time in Mississippi, just before we moved north, when I told you to haul in the hay before the rain come? 'Member what you said to me?"

"Yeah. I said, 'I don't feel like it.'"

"And what did I do?"

"You took off your belt and told me, 'Son, I can change the way you feel.'"

"That's what you needed. We all need it, Son, even when we don't realize it. You ask me why your Father's doin' what he's doin'. I don't know the answer for sure. Maybe it's discipline, maybe it's to change your priorities, maybe to make you more like him. Maybe he's just tryin' to get your attention. Maybe he's decided to change the way you feel."

"I just can't take this," Clarence said, leaning against Geneva on the couch. "I'm at the end of my rope."

"Maybe, Son, that's just where he wants you."

———————

Dani gazed through the portal. "Daddy's right," she said to Torel. "It was Elyon's appraisal of my life on earth that mattered, and only his."

"That is true," Torel said. "I do not understand how anyone could think otherwise."

"In the Shadowlands I wanted other people to like me," Dani said, "to approve of me. And sometimes I held back from doing what Elyon might want me to because I didn't think others would understand or approve. Now I realize it didn't matter. Only the Carpenter's approval matters. I wish Antsy could see that."

"Your brother does not realize men make a poor audience, for they do not see or hear clearly," Torel said. "They can applaud what is ugly and wrong. They can deplore what is beautiful and right. Elyon is the Judge. He is the audience of One. He knows men by their character, not merely their reputation."

Dani looked at her brother, head in his hands, depressed and disillusioned and inconsolable. She prayed he would learn that what mattered now was exactly what would matter always—God's appraisal of his life.

———————

Clarence got up from the chair, seeing the light still on in Jonah's room, knowing he was working on a project. "I need to be with him," he said to Geneva. She smiled and nodded. Clarence knocked on his door. Jonah opened it, surprised to see his father.

"This is your project for the science fair, right?" Clarence said. "What are you workin' on?"

"Nothin'."

"What do you mean, nothin'? Tell me. I really want to know."

Jonah looked at him as if he wasn't sure. He went over to his desk and got a round dark plastic object about a foot long, with an attached electrical cord and a three-inch metal point coming out the end. The point looked like a giant nail.

"What's that?"

"An induction coil," Jonah said.

"What's it do?"

Jonah plugged in the cord to the wall outlet. He reached the point out and touched Clarence's arm. An electric arc looking like a miniature lightning bolt jumped out, and Clarence's arm flexed out of his control. The surprise made the shock seem much stronger than it was.

"Whoa! What is that thing?"

Jonah smiled. "Fifty thousand volts."

"Fifty thousand? Isn't that…a lot of volts?"

"It's low current. That's why it doesn't kill you."

"So, what's your project? The electric chair?"

"No. We're doing a unit on electricity. At first, my project related to lightning. I was going to do a paper on it and use the induction coil to model lightning. But then I got these spectrum tubes." He picked up one of three thin glass tubes about ten inches long. "This tube contains neon. The others are mercury and hydrogen."

He put the induction coil up to about half an inch from the wire at one end of the tube and the miniature lightning struck it. Suddenly the tube glowed a reddish orange.

"Wow," Clarence said. "What makes the color?"

"It's the true color of the gas. The charge just brings it out. Every element has its own color fingerprint. That's what my project's about."

He touched the induction coil to the mercury tube and it turned violet. "You take this spectroscope," Jonah handed it to his father, "and it shows you the exact signature." Clarence looked through, seeing a violet line to the inside, a yellow line to the outside and a green line in between.

"That's the true color of mercury," Jonah said. "Each element is different. The induction coil lets you see things as they really are."

"I'm impressed." Clarence reached for the induction coil.

"There's an on/off switch on the power supply," Jonah said. "You—"

Clarence reached it up Jonah's loose T-shirt, just above his bottom, and flipped the switch.

"Ow! Hey!" Jonah grabbed it back and shocked Clarence a few times. The father wrestled it out of the son's hand and unplugged it. They scuffled on the bedroom floor, wrestling, giggling, and laughing, then finally embracing.

Geneva stood outside the room, peeking in the cracked door. She smiled and wiped her eyes. It had been a long time.

Clarence read the expression on Jake's face as his friend handed him the open newspaper. Clarence looked fearfully at page seven of the Metro section.

> North Portland resident Clarence Abernathy has been accused of statutory rape—having consensual sexual relations with a minor—as well as substance abuse and delivering a controlled substance to a minor. The teenager's identity is being withheld because she is a minor. A grand jury is considering whether there is sufficient evidence to bring the case to trial. Abernathy is a columnist for the *Oregon Tribune*.

There was no byline, but Clarence knew who covered the police beat and hung around the precinct like a vulture, circling the press board. Dan Ferrent hadn't even waited for the arraignment to get out a smear job on his colleague.

Clarence marched toward Metro, Jake half skipping to keep up with his long strides. Reporters moved to the side as if they were the Red Sea and Clarence was Moses.

"What's with this?" Clarence asked Ferrent, slamming down the newspaper and pointing at the article.

"Hey, I'm just doing my job."

"A hack job, you mean."

"The *Tribune* pays me to do this. I'm assigned to the press board at the precinct. When a police report is complete, it becomes public knowledge. It's fair game for the press. That's why they call it the press board."

"I know why they call it the press board, *Ferret*." Clarence enjoyed mispronouncing the name. "But it doesn't mean you *have* to print whatever you see up there."

"Look, Abernathy, I have nothing against you, but this is what we do for everybody, doesn't matter who. I don't think we should play favorites. Frankly, by making it so short and putting it on page seven, we did you a favor."

"A favor? Why didn't you ask me about the charge? Give me a chance to defend myself. Isn't that standard journalistic practice?"

"Not in this case. It was just a brief factual report of the charges, that's all. It didn't seem the time or place to get into counter-charges. Besides, I assumed your lawyer wouldn't let you talk. They usually don't."

"Factual? The accusation's a lie. And it's not your job to assume anything. I would have talked. No matter what my lawyer said."

"Besides," Ferrent continued, "I ran it past my editor and he got it cleared at the top. So your gripe is with the big boys."

"Berkley? He approved this?"

"Don't say I said that. Somebody up on top. I just know it went through."

"You've tried and hung me. Whatever happened to innocent until proven guilty?"

"It still holds. That's why the article says 'accused.' It doesn't say 'guilty.'"

"Nobody remembers your fine little distinctions. They just remember the paper links me with statutory rape and drugs."

"That's not my problem. Hey, if the mayor was accused of rape or murder, don't you think the paper would cover it?"

"So all it takes is one person, one messed-up high school girl, and she can bring down anyone in this city?"

"Not if they have an alibi."

"You still like to go fishing by yourself out on the Deschutes, Ferrent? Then what's your alibi for all the crimes going on in the city? You have no alibi. That doesn't make you guilty, does it?"

"Face it, man," Ferrent said, "you admit you took a teenage girl to a bar?"

"I didn't take her to a bar. She called me, said she had to talk. We didn't drink, eat, or socialize. And I never touched her."

"Hope you can prove that."

"How can I prove what *didn't* happen? It's impossible. Bet you can't prove to me you didn't do the hit and run over on Alder yesterday, can you? In fact, bet you can't prove you didn't do the shooting that killed my sister and my niece."

"Relax Clarence, you're getting agitated—"

"Agitated? You don't know agitated. This is nothing. You keep pushin' me, man, you're gonna see agitated. What do I have to do, hire someone to tail me everywhere so I can prove I'm innocent of everything some jerk might accuse me of? What communist country do you live in, anyway? I thought this was America!"

"Look, Abernathy, the whole thing does sound pretty bad, you have to admit."

"You're pathetic," he said to Ferrent. "I think I'll write you up in my column. I'll call your ex-wife. Bet she can give me some juicy stuff. And you know what you can use this article for."

Clarence slammed down the newspaper and turned around. He saw dozens of people staring at him. He felt certain he knew what they were thinking about him.

Jake led Clarence to the lunchroom, over to a corner. He'd never seen his friend so agitated.

"Jake, I can't believe this is happening. It only takes one person, one accusation, to ruin your life. I'll never be able to prove I'm innocent. No one will ever believe me."

"Geneva believes you. Your kids believe you. Janet and Carly and I believe you. So does everybody who really knows you."

"But I've worked so hard to build my reputation. And overnight, it's gone. It's just gone. People aren't ever going to trust me. I can't understand why they'd believe accusations against a man just because they're in a newspaper."

Clarence suddenly thought about Ollie. He had believed *exactly* what the *Trib* said about Ollie. He felt like vomiting.

Clarence drove home with none of the anticipation of the weekend he usually carried on Friday afternoons. He pulled into his driveway and sat in the car, trying to regain composure before seeing Geneva and the kids.

He opened the front door and a flushed Geneva came out to him. "I'm so sorry," he said. Clarence put his arms around her, his large body drawing strength from her small one. "Thanks for standing by me."

"Of course I'll stand by you. Always. We're in the hard part. It'll get better, baby. It has to." She sighed. "Bad as it is, I'd rather have it like this and know you need me than have it like it was and know you didn't."

She felt him shaking, and somehow it both comforted and frightened her.

"Let's go to the Bible study potluck tonight," she said.

"How can I face them? You should see how everybody looks at me now."

"They helped raise bail for you," Geneva said. "You owe it to them to be there. Besides, you belong with your Christian brothers and sisters. You need them, whether or not you know it."

Clarence walked into the living room and saw Jonah doing his homework. He didn't look up. Ty walked in the front door and went to his room. No eye contact. The weight on Clarence's shoulders felt even heavier.

Everyone at Bible study was friendly but unusually quiet. The laughter was subdued. John Edwards sat next to Clarence on one side, Geneva on the other.

"Well," John said, "there's no use pretending this is a normal evening. Our brother Clarence and sister Geneva are here. We've been praying for them. I'm really glad they came." Heads nodded, and Clarence heard many expressions of agreement. "I said it to you personally, Clarence, but I want to say it in front of the whole group. I'm with you. I believe you. You can count on me."

"Me too," said Bill, the white southerner, Maggie nodding. "And us," Sal said. "Same here," said Duane, Karen indicating her agreement. Ray's wife nodded, her husband's absence a testimony to their commitment to Clarence.

He looked around the room as if he couldn't believe what he was hearing. "I... want to thank you for raising money to get me...out of jail." His internal dam managed to hold back the tears. "I've lost my sister and my niece. And now...I feel like I've lost everything." Clarence leaned forward. Geneva rested her head on his bowed back.

"You haven't lost us," John said. "I want to say something to the whole group. When Clarence was released from jail yesterday, I went over to his house to see him. I asked myself what I'd want people to do if I was accused of something like this. First, I'd want them to ask me straight out, so there were no doubts lurking in their minds. So I asked Clarence, 'Brother, did you make any sexual advances to this girl?' He said, 'Absolutely not. God is my witness.' Well, I believe him. Everything I know about him makes me accept his word.

"Now, I'll say this too. If Clarence had told me he was guilty, but repentant, I would have stood by him too. Sure, he'd have had to face the consequences, but he'd still have needed our forgiveness and support. But he's not guilty. And that money we helped raise for bail, that was an investment in our family. You're part of our family, Abernathys. That's what the church is all about."

"And there's more where that came from," Bill said. "If this goes to court you'll have a lot of legal fees. Maggie and I have talked about it. If you end up needing the money, we can take out a second mortgage on our house. It was Maggie's idea."

Clarence excused himself and went to the bathroom. He sat on the edge of the bathtub, his face buried in his hands, trying not to make any noise. Finally, he forced himself to get up, wash his face, and go back to the living room.

"This week I wrote down all the racial stereotypes I learned as a kid," John said. Obviously they'd decided to move on, and Clarence was grateful. "Maybe you heard colored people all had big feet and were great dancers. Well, here's some of what I heard. Mexicans all carried switchblades, Indians were born alcoholics, Irish were drunks with bad tempers, Germans were stubborn raw-meat eaters, Catholics never took baths and were to blame for all the world's problems because they never practiced birth control. Japanese were squinty-eyed devils, Jews were just out to rip you off and those dirty Hebes actually started World War II so they could control the army surplus business after the war. Chinamen came with a laundry basket attached to their navel, and Swedish people had hollow skulls but were strong and more honest than most whites."

"Well, at least you got it right about the Swedes," Sal said, pointing at Duane. Everybody laughed, especially Duane.

"I guess my point is," John said, "maybe some of you grew up hearing the word nigger. Well, in my hood we not only called each other nigger, but I heard people called wops, dagos, micks, kikes, shvartzes, harpies, krauts, nips, japs, chinks, you name it. Nobody's got a corner on racism—everybody doles it out and everybody gets hit with it. True, when you're not in the power position—as minorities aren't—your racism can't have as detrimental an effect on society. But it can sure destroy you and your family.

"Tonight we're going to study John 4. If you did your background reading, you know racial hatred was as common in the ancient world as it is today. The Samaritans were half-breed Jews who intermarried with heathen people the Jews thought were inferior. Jews detested Samaritans, and Samaritans detested Jews. In John 4 Jesus steps over on the wrong side of the tracks and reaches out to a Samaritan woman, who had a bad reputation. If you don't know somebody, you assume the worst about him—especially if you've been told the worst. But when you reach out to someone, like Jesus does, you get to know him. You love him just like Jesus loved this woman. You talk honestly to people you love, and you do whatever you can to help them."

While everyone else looked down at their Bibles, Clarence looked up at all the faces in the room. As bad as he felt, he knew Geneva was right. This was where he belonged.

"Ray?" Ollie asked. "Listen, Clarence is sitting here. I'll punch on the speakerphone. Okay, we can both hear you now."

"How are you, Clarence?" Ray asked.

"Okay," he lied. "Missed you at Bible study."

"Yeah, I missed you all too. Here's the scoop. I was there at 12:30 when the license plate was delivered to the Rafer Thomas home. Mr. Thomas took it inside just for a minute, then headed out to his car with the unwrapped plate in hand. I followed him to a street corner store in South Central, and I knew I was in trouble. There was heavy foot traffic. Dozens of people coming in and out every five minutes, half of them carrying sacks. I got out and went up to the front door. Everyone stared at me like I was Sitting Bull in war paint. Not effective undercover work, so I went back to my car and studied the situation from there.

"I kept watching the streets for a jazzed up midnight blue Mercedes SL 500. Saw a good share of Mercedes, but not that one. These guys are smart, or they're lucky. It was half an hour when Mr. Thomas comes back out of the store. He's carrying a sack. So do I follow him or stay put? He might have the license in his sack and be heading to where these guys hang out. I followed him. We go a few miles, and it's obvious he's headed back home. By the time I turn around and get back to the store, any one of a hundred black males could have made the pick up, or they could have done it while I watched. Who knows? Our perps could have sent their mother or their girlfriend. Short of holding everyone at gunpoint and checking their bags as they left the store, there's nothing I could do. Sorry."

"That's okay, Ray," Ollie said. "At least we've gotten as far as a store in South Central. There's a good chance their hood is nearby, so it's still a help."

"This is definitely Hoover turf," Ray said. "It's just that it's one gigantic territory. I'll keep cruising and looking for the Mercedes and do some digging. I'll keep you posted."

"Hey, Ray?" Clarence said, throat clutching a bit. "I want to thank you for going down there for me. It means a lot. Just don't go risking your life, okay?"

"No problem. That's why God gives us brothers, huh? Listen, one other thing I've been thinking about, and I want you both to hear it. I'm in a tough position here because I don't want to violate client confidences. I know you've been investigating Councilman Norcoast, though I don't know the details. Let's just say I have some info on Norcoast. It may not be relevant, but it could be."

"What do you mean?" Ollie asked.

"Look, Ollie, if you can get a court order against me to divulge information, I'll do it. Frankly, you may know about it already or it may not be worth your trouble, but it could be, I don't know. I just want you to be aware I'll bend if you can hit me with something official."

"I'll keep it in mind. One other thing. After you turn over some more rocks down there, I could really use you in Sacramento. Let's stay in touch, okay?"

Ollie hung up the phone and shuffled through some papers. He looked at Clarence. "This morning I talked with the principal at Jefferson, Mr. Fielding. I asked him about the girl."

"Gracie?"

"I'd get in the habit of calling her Miss Miller. Anyway, he told me he was really surprised she'd volunteered for the interview with you. He has a feel for who volunteers for stuff like this. She isn't the type. She's a regular crack user and sometimes crank. Fielding said he wished he had the power to take control of the drug situation there, but thanks to the ACLU, he has no freedom to search lockers."

"Okay, so she's a druggie. What else did he say?"

"Hangs with a bad crowd. Shoplifter. Petty thief. Looks for the quick buck, needs it for her crack. Hangs with the gangs. Rollin' 60s mostly, but has contacts with three or four different Crip sets. She's an oddity, not a full gang sister who hangs with the girlfriends, but she's popular with the guys for other reasons."

"I'll bet."

"The principal also said she has no respect for authority. Zero academic interest. Never does her homework. In the old days that would mean she'd flunk out. Now it just means she's not valedictorian. She even managed a few Ds and an F, which Fielding says is almost impossible if you've got any brains at all, and he says she does. He told me one other thing I found very interesting."

"What's that?"

"With all her lousy grades there wasn't a single B, but there was one A, and her teacher says she's a natural at it."

"What class? PE?"

"Nope. Drama."

Ollie walked into McDonald's. He perused the tables for a blonde girl who looked like she wanted attention. He intended to give her the kind she didn't want.

"I'm Detective Ollie Chandler," he said, holding out his badge.

"I'm impressed," Gracie said, batting her eyes with practiced effect.

"You're not really impressed," Ollie said, "but you will be. I'm thinking of offering you a deal."

"What do you mean?"

"Well, here's how I size you up. Besides being a crackhead, you're a miserable student who got an A in drama, and your teacher says you're one heck of an actress. Congratulations. Maybe after you get out of jail, you can get a bus ticket to Hollywood."

She flinched, but only slightly. "I don't know what you're talking about."

"You working more than one scam, is that it? Okay. Clarence Abernathy. Now do you know what I'm talking about?"

"Look, I liked the guy. I didn't turn him in. It was my uncle."

"Yeah, after you told him you slept together. Played that pretty cool, didn't you? Whoever hired you as an actress for this little B movie thought statutory rape and a drug charge would bring him down, huh? Well, maybe Clarence has an alibi you don't know about. And maybe you're in big trouble for framing a man, lying about him, and giving false testimony to officers of the law. Want to go off to one of those creepy jails for minor girls, Gracie? The ones where the wardens are as weird as the inmates? See, we know who hired you for this job. We know who paid you off. Now I might be willing to make a deal to get them. Or I could offer *them* a deal and go after you. How about it? Feel like talking?"

"Not really," she said, coldly but with noticeably less confidence than she'd had a minute earlier.

"Here's my card," Ollie said. "No, I won't be writing my home number on it, thank you. Just call me at the office if you change your mind. I wouldn't wait too long, though. Somebody'll take me up on the deal if you won't. You're expendable, Gracie. Remember that. When push comes to shove, they'll sell you out. Your only chance is to sell them out first."

Gracie watched Ollie walk out the door and drive out of the parking lot, talking on his phone as he drove. She tugged on a quarter wedged tightly in her jeans. It popped out like a yanked tooth. She walked hurriedly to the pay phone in front of McDonald's, peering down the street to make sure Ollie was out of sight.

Ollie turned and drove down a side street, then circled around. He parked a street over from the McDonald's, where he watched her through his binoculars, still talking on his phone.

"Got it? Yeah. She's at our pay phone now. Same one she kept using yesterday. Just punched in a number and hasn't said anything. Must be listening to a message, waiting to talk. Wait, no, now she's punching in another number. Hold on, she just hung up. Obviously not enough time for a trace. Barely enough time for a busy signal. Wait a minute, I think she dialed a beeper number and entered in the pay phone number for the return call. My bet is, Mr. Beeper's gonna call her back right there at Ronald's."

Ollie smiled broadly as he opened up his first of two Big Macs. "I love this job," he said aloud. He continued to watch Gracie, who looked impatient and agitated, shivering in the cold. Suddenly she picked up the phone. On his cellular he said, "Okay, she's on now. You've got it, right?"

He kept rooting for her to stay on the line longer. Seven minutes later she hung up.

"Yeah? Terrific," Ollie said. "The Delores Williams residence at Twelfth and Switzer? Wait a minute. I think I know her son. Davey Williams. Better known as Shadow."

"Okay, Sheila, remember, this is confidential police business, all right? It's not to be shared with anyone else in your office. Understand?"

"Yes." Sheila sounded nervous over the phone. "I won't get in trouble for this, will I?"

"No," Ollie said. "Now, you're sure no one else is in the office? And if a call comes in and gets picked up on the private line answering machines, you'll know?"

"Yes, I'll know."

"All right. Call me back as soon as you hear something, just like we talked about, okay?"

"Okay."

Ollie put down the phone and picked up a laser-printed page that read, "Harper: Counting on you to take care of the job. Make it soon." He put it in the fax machine. "I've deleted our return number in our fax, so it won't show up on his printout," he said to Clarence. "I've also got a blocker on this line, in case he has caller ID. He won't know where the fax is coming from."

Ollie dialed, pressed "Start," and watched the paper pull through. He waited about a minute, pressed "Redial," and ran the same page through again. He waited another minute, and did exactly the same thing a third time.

"What do we do now?" Clarence asked.

"We wait."

"I'm puzzled," Dani said to Zeke. "As I've studied you on earth, despite all that was done to you, I saw no bitterness. How could you forgive people so easily?"

"'Member the Carpenter's parable of that man forgiven a huge debt by his king?

Then the man refused to forgive someone who owed him far less."

"Yes, I remember."

"Well, great-granddaughter, I reckon that's one of those passages you should go back and study. You haven't learned its full meaning yet. The Carpenter was sayin' our debt to God is infinitely beyond our capacity to repay. He was also sayin' our debt to God is infinitely greater than any person's debt to us, no matter how cruel or unjust they've been. Compared to our sins against God, anybody's sins against us is small potatoes. He was also sayin' that when we experience God's forgiveness, it changes us into forgiving people. Jesus said, if you're forgiven you *must* forgive others. Once you understand our sins against him and his forgiveness for us, how can you *not* forgive others?"

"I guess I sometimes saw the worst in people," Dani said.

"There's plenty of bad to see, that's for sure," Zeke said. "The answer isn't to pretend people don't do bad things, but to realize God sees us at our worst and still loves us. And by his grace he helps us to see others at their worst but still love them. No sinner is beyond his reach, chile. Bitterness, that's just a self-imposed prison. It's a terrible cost to yourself and your loved ones. It's a cost I wasn't willin' to pay. Bitterness never relieves suffering, it only causes it. I used to pray for the overseers and masters who beat me. I knew they wasn't beyond God's grace because I wasn't. One of the slaves, ol' Elmo, he used to say the massas didn't deserve forgiveness. I said, "Course they doesn't deserve forgiveness, Elmo. No man does. If you deserved forgiveness, you wouldn't need it.'

"Elmo says to me, 'I just wants what I deserves. I wants what's comin' to me.' I said, 'Don't go sayin' that, Elmo. If we gets what we deserves, then all we gets is hell.'"

"I knew that," Dani said, "but somehow I never experienced it at the depth you did."

"I remembers one ol' hound named Rosco. You gived Rosco a bone and he'd bury it. Then he'd always dig it back up just to be sure it was still there. When he was still a pup, every day he made his rounds. He'd go to twenty or thirty places, bury his bones, but he'd never let them lie. He'd just keep diggin' 'em up again. That's how peoples can be. They maybe bury sins a little bit, say they've forgiven, but they never forget where them ol' bones is. They always go back, dig 'em up again and again. So they can still wallows in their pity and comforts theirselves by thinkin' how they's victims. As if that made 'em righteous. Sad thing is, by pushin' away God's grace to others, they push away his grace to them."

———

"Detective Chandler? This is Sheila." Ollie pressed the speakerphone.

"Did Mr. Harper call?" Ollie asked.

"He sure did. Just like you said. He sounded really upset."

"Good. Who did he ask for?"

"No one," Sheila said.

"No one?"

"He said somebody was sending him a bunch of nonsense faxes and I should tell whoever it is to knock it off. Mr. Harper was moving out of here just when I got hired, so I didn't know him well, but I sure never heard him this upset. He asked me who was sending the faxes. I said I really wasn't sure."

"Perfect, Sheila. You've done your job. Treat yourself to a Dove Bar or something."

"Oh, I couldn't." She laughed. "I'm on a diet."

"Okay. I'll have one for you. Remember, this is police business. Confidential. Can't tell Norcoast or Gray or anybody, right?"

"Right. One other thing—before he got off, Mr. Harper asked if Jean, our office manager, was back from a conference in L.A. He didn't say he wanted to talk to her, but if she'd been here I think he would have. I'm not even sure how he knew she was in L.A."

"Jean, huh? Are they friends?"

"They worked together closely when Mr. Harper was in our office. That's all I know."

"Okay, thanks again, Sheila." Ollie hung up the phone and smiled at Clarence. "Now we know for sure the original was faxed from Norcoast's office to Harper's, because that's where he assumed it came from today. I'm disappointed he called the main number rather than Gray's or Norcoast's private line. I was hoping he'd show us exactly which of them sent the fax. Granted, you got it off Norcoast's computer, so it was probably him, but probably isn't good enough. Anyway, at least we know we're on the right track."

"That fax doesn't say what the 'job' is," Clarence said. "But Harper had to know *exactly* what it meant, right?"

"Right. And that had to be stated in some previous voice conversation, probably one of those phone calls from Norcoast's office. No one would be stupid enough to put any specifics in print. We can't prove exactly what was said, when, and by whom. We certainly can't prove someone told Harper to send up some hit men to 920 North Jack Street. But this," he held up the paper he'd faxed to Harper, "is our cash cow. We've got to milk it for all it's worth."

Clarence sat down in Jess Foley's office, along with Winston. "Look, Clarence," Jess said, "This morning I met with Raylon and one of the *Trib* attorneys. As you can imagine, we're in a very difficult position with the charges brought against you. We want to make a proposal."

"Let me guess, a leave of absence? Or are you asking for my resignation?"

"If you resign, that's your choice," Jess said. "It might be best for you and your family, I don't know. Personally, I hope you don't. But meanwhile we're offering you a paid leave of absence. Winston and I have discussed it, and we can fill your slot with other columns until this thing gets resolved. What do you think?"

Clarence looked at Winston, who didn't return his gaze. Then he looked at Jess, who was clearly less comfortable doing this than editing a newspaper.

"What I think is that neither Raylon nor you nor any of the *Trib* attorneys has even asked me if I did anything wrong. Maybe it's because you're assuming I did. Well, I didn't. And maybe what matters to you isn't whether I'm guilty, but just that I've been accused. Well, I'm innocent, and if it makes the *Trib* look bad because somebody lied about me, too bad for the *Trib*. To walk away would be to say I was guilty. It would be just what whoever set me up wants. I'm staying, and I'm going to keep writing. Of course, you can fire me. But if you do, tell Raylon when I prove I'm innocent, I'm going to sue the *Trib*. Maybe even a class-action suit—discriminating against a minority employee. Yeah. Tell Raylon to chew on that for a while."

Clarence marched straight to his desk, choosing the column subject he considered most likely to infuriate Raylon Berkley and Reggie Norcoast. He pulled out a file full of notes and typed emphatically, pounding his fingers on the keys.

> The Center for New Black Leadership's board members—including Shelby Steele, Glenn Loury, and Phyllis Berry Myers—say the time has come for emphasizing black self-reliance, economic power, and social stability. They maintain that calling for personal responsibility must no longer be caricatured as "blaming the victim." They say, "We will promote and celebrate black achievement as evidence of our humanity, rather than lament and advertise black failure as evidence of our victimization."
>
> The Center is part of a ground-swell movement most readers haven't heard of, since it receives so little media attention (due to journalists' annoying habit of considering liberal extremists the only "real blacks").
>
> But clearly, a new day is dawning among black Americans. I find it both refreshing and hopeful. I call upon the *Trib* and other media to give this important new movement the coverage it deserves. I for one will be featuring the efforts of some of the leaders in this movement in future columns.

"Ready for this?" Ollie asked Clarence. "I think we've traced bank account records from Norcoast's office to Harper's."

"You can do that?"

"It wasn't official," Ollie said. "I was just talking about the situation with Ray in Sacramento, and bang, next thing I know I get this fax." He waved the paper. "Some interesting transactions. Like, thirty-five-thousand dollars wired from Norcoast's campaign account to Matthew Harper's personal account. The date was September 2."

"Same day as the murder."

"I might have expected it the next day, after the job was done, but apparently they jumped the gun to make sure he was ready with the cash when our perps showed up in Sacramento. Of course, if the payoff had been a day later, the money probably wouldn't have been wired at all, once they knew the shooters blew the hit."

"This is a lot of speculation, Ollie."

"Yeah, but take a look at this." He showed him another account from U.S. National Bank of Sacramento. "Harper withdrew the thirty-five thousand two hours after it was wired. And see this notation?" Clarence nodded. "That means cash. Thirty-five thousand in cash. If he was going to buy a boat, make a down payment on a house, whatever, he would've written a check. When you take out that kind of cash, it means you don't want a paper trail linking you to whoever you're going to hand it over to."

"But Norcoast's office has to have financial records. They've got to be able to explain the thirty-five thousand."

"No doubt they *can* explain it. Harper does political consulting on the side. He might have even made a phony billing sheet for his time. But no matter how they explain it, I say it's no coincidence the shooters came up with thirty-two thousand in cash to get that Mercedes. How many people besides Harper and our perps do you suppose were walking around Sacramento with that kind of money?"

"What next, Ollie?"

"I could go a couple of directions. One, keep working behind the scenes, building the case, and go for Harper in one fell swoop. Two, contact Harper, ask him some questions, see if I can get him nervous and flush him out."

"Which are you going to do?"

"My gut tells me I should send in my dogs and see if I can flush this bird out in the open." Ollie picked up the phone and dialed Harper's private line, pressing the speakerphone for Clarence's benefit, and turning the volume on low.

"Yeah, Mr. Harper, this is Ollie Chandler, Portland Police. I'm calling to ask you a few questions about a case I'm working on."

"What can I do for you, officer?"

"Detective. Homicide detective."

"What can I do for you, detective?"

Ollie listened carefully for any cracks in the voice. So far, none.

"We're checking out some phone calls and faxes made between your office and

Reggie Norcoast's office in August and early September."

"Why?"

"Oh, we've got our reasons. What were these phone calls about?"

Harper hesitated. "I do political consulting for Mr. Norcoast and a half-dozen other politicians. We often talk campaign strategy. I used to work for him in Portland."

"How many hours did you put in for Norcoast this summer?"

"I don't know, off hand. How is this relevant to your investigation?"

"I suppose it must have been a lot of hours for you to be paid thirty-five thousand in one shot. And such a nice even number too. Let me ask you, Mr. Harper, did you have any visitors the day of September 2?"

"How should I know? You want me to check my Day-Timer? Okay, fine. Here it is. Looks like I was in the office all morning. A few appointments, phone calls, it's all here. In the afternoon I had lunch, worked out at the health club, came back to the office for a few more appointments and a staff meeting. Satisfied?"

"Do you happen to remember how much money you were carrying that day?"

Long pause. "Who knows? What's that got to do with anything? I usually carry maybe a hundred dollars in my wallet. I don't know. I don't have to answer any more of your questions. If you want to speak further, you can call my attorney. This conversation is over. Good-bye."

Ollie put down the phone, then rubbed his hands together like a master chef mixing his ingredients. "Okay," he said to Clarence. "It's hit the fan now. I sent the message we're onto him. If he's smart, he knows I'm still fishing, that we don't have enough to nail him. It's risky, because he may try to cover his tail. On the other hand, often that's what gives people away. Telling me I'd have to talk to his attorney was a dumb move."

"Why?"

"Too defensive. At first, he was trying to sound casual, like a guy who had nothing to hide. But the more I showed him our hand, the more afraid of self-incrimination he got. Why should he care if I ask him about legit political consulting and a thirty-five-thousand-dollar fee? When I asked him what he was doing September 2, so what? Unless September 2 means something to him. I ask him how much money he was carrying, and if it's the usual hundred bucks, it's just an irrelevant question. If it's thirty to thirty-five *thousand*, he has reason to get edgy. He sounded edgy. I didn't accuse him of anything. I'm a detective—most the people I talk to aren't suspects, they're innocent people who may have info pertaining to the case. But he *assumed* I was accusing him. People assume that for a reason. Often because they're guilty."

"Why didn't you say anything about the fax?" Clarence asked.

"That's still my ace in the hole. I'm waiting to play it."

"What next?"

"I don't know," Ollie said, grinning, rubbing his hands together again. "But whatever it is, it's gonna be fun."

At his Tuesday afternoon arraignment, Clarence sat in a courtroom full of the accused. Most of them, he assumed, were guilty, which reminded him that everybody else must assume he was guilty. What made him think he was the only innocent person here?

Clarence was formally charged, and a court date was set for February. That meant it would hang over his head another two and a half months while the DA's office prepared their case against him. Meanwhile, everyone would have it permanently cemented in their minds that he was guilty.

The *Willamette Post* printed a feature subjecting Clarence to ridicule as another one of those conservative family values hypocrites. He'd often taken on the liberal weekly and mercilessly lampooned its terminal political correctness. This was their perfect opportunity for revenge. They made the most of it, printing a terrible, hard-edged picture of him. He wasn't even sure where they'd gotten it. He looked so enraged in the photo it made him wince. Then there was a demure picture of Gracie, looking the young innocent Anglo exploited by the big bad black man. Under normal circumstances the *Willamette Post* would never portray a black man like this. But Clarence was an outspoken conservative. The most brutal treatment is reserved for traitors.

Ollie sent three more faxes a minute apart, just as he had the day before. He waited a few minutes, then called Matthew Harper's private line.

"Mr. Harper, this is Detective Ollie Chandler. I talked with you yesterday, remember?"

"Are you harassing me, detective? If you are, I could take you to court."

"Excuse me? This is just the second time I've called. How am I harassing you?"

"Are you the one who keeps sending these…"

"These what?"

"Never mind. What can I do for you?"

"Well, there's a document that's come to our attention. It was faxed to you from Councilman Norcoast's office on August 29."

"What document?"

"It says, 'Harper: Counting on you to take care of the job. Make it soon.' Sound familiar? Now, what job would that be talking about?"

"I don't know what job. Not sure I ever received a fax like that in the first place. If I did, it was probably about a consulting job. Remember, I told you I do political consulting for the councilman."

"Are you saying the councilman sent you that fax?"

"I didn't say that. You're the one that's been sending me that fax, aren't you?"

"Is there something about that fax that bothers you?"

"No. I've just had a half-dozen copies of it sent to me in the last two days. I don't understand. What's going on? Where did you get this fax?"

"Where do you think I got it? From the same person who sent it to you August 29, where else?"

"No...I don't believe you."

"Well, suppose I told you he says he was referring to something else, but he's afraid you flipped out on him and you did something he never intended."

Harper laughed. "Nice try, detective. What am I supposed to do now, say, 'Tell him he's not going to get away with it'?"

"Get away with what?"

"Setting me up for the fall."

"What fall would you be anticipating?"

Harper hung up on him.

"The fish has bit," Ollie said. "But there's one thing I don't get."

"What?" Clarence asked.

"He seemed to know immediately I was bluffing when I told him the guy who sent him the fax claims he meant something else. Obviously I have the fax. Why wouldn't he believe I've confronted Norcoast or Gray with it, and whichever of them sent it denies its real meaning? What tipped him off?"

Clarence shrugged.

"If I could inflate this evidence," Ollie said, "I could argue probable cause to a judge to get my hands on Harper's phone records. But it just isn't enough. We know he got that fax at 3:32 P.M. on August 29. What I want to know is, who did he call then?"

Ollie looked up a number on his Rolodex, then dialed it quickly. "Ray? Ollie Chandler. How's things in Sacramento? Listen, I've got something else I need you to do."

————————

"All right, let's try it again," Ollie said to Clarence. "Anybody at all who could have planted the heroin in your overcoat?"

"I'll tell you once more, Ollie. The coat's in my closet at home Wednesday night, right? I get up Thursday with my hangover. It's raining. I wear it to my car, then take it off and lay it over the seat. I don't put it back on until I park my car. I get in the elevator at the parking garage, go to the ground floor, walk to the *Trib*, come up the elevator, hang up my overcoat, and go to my desk. It's that simple. I don't see how anyone could have planted it until I got to the *Trib*."

"Okay, then someone at the *Trib* planted it while the coat was on the rack. Who?"

"Everybody there has security clearance. These aren't criminals, these are journalists." He looked at Ollie. "Don't say what you're thinking, okay? Yeah, I guess somebody at the *Trib* could do something like this, but I really doubt it. My conservatism isn't popular, but they don't hate me that much. At least, I don't think they do."

"I'll have Manny check into vendors, custodians, computer technicians, anybody that had access to the coatrack Thursday morning."

"There is someone else who could have planted the powder," Clarence said.

"Who?"

"Rodriguez."

"The officer? Come on, Clarence."

"We've been over this before, Ollie. To you it's inconceivable a cop would do that. To me it's a real possibility. He could have easily pulled it out of his pocket and planted it in my coat during his search. Be open-minded."

"Okay." Ollie sighed. "Let's get back to whatever knocked you out for four hours on that bench. Is there anything else you ate or drank, anything that could have been poisoned?"

Clarence thought hard. "Yeah. That green powder stuff Geneva mixes in my orange juice."

"The health food? Yeah, I hear you. But we can probably rule out Geneva as a suspect."

"Well, she swears she'll never divorce me, but more than once she *has* threatened to kill me."

Ollie looked at his notes. "Breakfast was heated Grape Nuts with a packet of Equal, toast, and coffee. More coffee at the *Trib*. Sandwich at the deli for lunch. But nobody else at the *Trib* or the deli passed out later in the day. You sure you didn't stop for a doughnut?"

"I'm not a cop, Ollie, I'm a journalist."

"You are what you eat, isn't that what they say? Journalists must eat a lot of bologna. Come on. You're a big fellow. What else did you eat?"

"Ollie, that's it, I'm telling you. Maybe it really was insulin shock. But it's never come on so suddenly or put me out so long."

"If it was insulin shock, it was an incredible stroke of bad luck for you and good luck for Gracie and whoever else wanted to take you out on the abuse charge. I'm not a big believer in luck. They knew you were going to be out of commission on a remote part of a bike trail on a dark rainy day. If they didn't know, they wouldn't have had your impostor posing with Gracie."

"But I still don't see how they could have knocked me out like that."

"I've done my homework." Ollie flipped his yellow pad furiously, finally land-ing on a page full of pen scratchings. "Called an anesthesiologist, Dr. Randy Martin. I described what happened. He said if this was a knock-out drug, he'd go with one of three candidates. First, fentynl." Ollie looked at his notes. "High potency narcotic, puts you to sleep for two hours, maybe more. Used in hospitals for surgery."

"Hospitals? You think I was drugged by a doctor?"

"No. Stuff gets stolen from anesthesiology carts. I've got a call in to see if we can find out what's been stolen lately, in case there's a connection. Second drug is keta-mine. Primary use is anesthesia. Dr. Martin says it induces a zombie-like effect for two or three hours. There's a teenager lives next door to me. I figure he must be on ketamine."

"Zombie? I was out cold."

"Third candidate is sufentynl. Most potent narcotic around. He told me about a cousin of this drug called…" Ollie looked down. "Carfentynl. It's used as a military weapon. Dr. Martin says a Q-Tip of this stuff touched to the nostril of a moose will knock it to the ground, out cold."

"Why would anyone want to do that to a moose?"

"Don't know," Ollie said. "Seems like if you got close enough to put a Q-Tip to the moose's nostril, you'd just shoot the sucker and save yourself some trouble. Anyway, obviously it isn't the carfentynl you got or you would have been knocked out right when you ingested it. Technically, you may be slightly bigger than a moose, but still. Now with this sufentynl, Dr. Martin said the right dosage could put you out four hours."

"You said the tests showed my insulin was clean. But even if something was mixed in my food, wouldn't I have tasted it?"

"Depends on what the something was and how strong the food or drink it was mixed in. Dr. Martin said the only other possibility that fits the symptoms is a street drug, an opiate."

"Opiate?"

"Yeah, specifically morphine or heroin. I wish we'd gotten you in for a test ear-lier so we'd know what was in you, but it seemed like an insulin reaction then. All right, let's go over it again, from the top. Wednesday. You left the *Trib* a little after two?"

"Right. Parked by the bike trail maybe around three. We've been over this, Ollie. Too many times."

"But we're still missing something." Ollie sighed and tossed his notes in his briefcase. "Okay. You up for some male bonding, big guy? I think it's time you and I went for a bike ride."

36°

Clarence sat uncomfortably in his cubicle on Monday, noticing all the stares, including some that weren't there. Those who didn't come talk to him he felt certain believed he was guilty. Those who did come to him he assumed were putting on a cloak of civility when inside they despised him for what they thought he was.

He tried to push these distractions aside and focus on the column he had to deliver to Winston in a little over two hours.

> If the grand imperial wizard of the KKK was determined to destroy black America, he couldn't have come up with a better plan than the welfare system that offered financial rewards (including housing) for not working and for having children outside of marriage.
>
> Welfare to give temporary aid to get someone back on his feet or help him acquire job skills, that's reasonable. (But whatever happened to help from family and church and neighbors, instead of government?)
>
> For thirty years, Uncle Sam has been a surrogate father, and everybody, including real fathers, started asking, 'Who needs Daddy after all?' Every day the moral chaos of our culture screams the answer to that question.

Around two o'clock, he walked out of the *Trib* to meet Ollie and drive to Gresham to reenact his Wednesday bike ride when his life had come unraveled.

Clarence parked the Bonneville in his favorite little patch of roadside grass and gravel near the Springwater Corridor bike trail. He took two bikes off the rack, his eighteen-speed Cannondale mountain bike and Ollie's Sears three-speed beater from the Eisenhower era. Clarence put the rack in the trunk, and he and Ollie mounted their bikes.

"The things I do to keep this city safe," Ollie said.

"Just don't fall," Clarence said. "Don't want you to squash the wildlife."

"Very funny. Catch me if you can." Ollie's big legs churned, and he took off in a flash of spitting gravel. Clarence stared at Ollie, amazed again at the deceptive strength of this cop who looked like a giant marshmallow in pants but could head butt you into tomorrow.

Clarence rode up next to Ollie. It seemed strange to have company. He'd gotten used to traveling this path alone. He slowed to a stop after a quarter of a mile and pointed to a bench on the right. "That's where I conked out."

"We'll check it out on the way back," Ollie said. "I want to do everything just like you did on Wednesday. Talk to me as we go. Tell me what you saw."

They passed by the Rottweiler on the left, who barked like crazy. "See you on the way back, Hugo," Clarence called. They crossed under Hogan Road, close up against the gently flowing creek. The next few minutes both men admired the sounds and sights and smells. Clarence took strange pride in it, as if it were his turf. It felt like showing off his clubhouse to a friend.

"Okay, I'm starting to get winded," Ollie admitted when they got past Main Street Park. They pulled over at the cemetery, its plush green grass and ordered tombstones suggesting death was less senseless and traumatic than it seemed.

"You didn't get any Kool-Aid or anything from somebody on the trail, right?"

Clarence shook his head.

"Okay. Let's go back and look at that bench."

When they reappeared twelve minutes later, Hugo did a double take, looking surprised to see Clarence again so soon. When he saw Ollie he started barking. Clarence pulled over and petted him, then removed a milk bone from some foil in his bike bag and gave it to him through the cyclone fence.

"Did you know dogs are color blind?" Clarence asked. "Maybe you and I don't look all that different to him."

"Two handsome studly men, that's all he sees?" Ollie said. They rode just a little farther before coming to the bench. "Okay. Show me exactly what you did."

"Put my bike over here on this side, just like always." Clarence pulled over to the right, parking his bike beside the trail.

"What do you mean, just like always? I thought you stopped because you weren't feeling well."

"I *wasn't* feeling well. I could hardly wait to get here. But it's where I always stop. It's part of my routine."

"You really *are* predictable, aren't you?"

"Sue me," Clarence said. "I like things to be orderly. I always pull over here to stretch out and rest a few minutes, soak in the smells of the outdoors. Spend a few extra minutes before I head back to the cold cruel world."

Ollie leaned down next to the bench. He inspected it closely. He pointed his right index finger down into the gravel and pushed it around. "It was raining Wednesday, right?"

"Yeah. Rained almost the whole ride. The weather was getting worse all the time, dark gray clouds. Too bad, because as remote as this part of the trail is, even in November you'd still have a dozen people easy come by on a decent afternoon. Somebody would have seen me on the bench."

"Maybe somebody did."

"I doubt it. It's a fair-weather trail. When I ride in the rain I rarely see anybody this far out."

"I called your doctor about insulin reactions," Ollie said. "He told me sometimes after hard exercise they can come on pretty fast."

"Yeah, they can. That's why I always stop for a mocha. That keeps my blood sugar up and—"

"What did you say? A mocha? What mocha?"

"At Coffee's On—espresso place on Eastman. Oops. Guess I didn't mention that, did I? I always swing up there before I head back toward Main Street Park. It's so routine I don't even think about it."

"Oops? I ask you to tell me everything you do, list everything you ingested, and you leave out a stop and a beverage consumption, and all you can say is oops?"

"Okay, sorry. Don't get cranky on me. So, what do we do now?"

Ollie smiled. "We go get a mocha."

They pedaled the remaining quarter of a mile to Clarence's car, strapped on the bikes, and headed to Coffee's On. They pulled up to a space right in front of the door.

"Where do you park your bike?" Ollie asked.

"Right here." He pointed to a wooden bench anchored into the concrete. "I lock it up. Used to be you didn't have to lock things up in Gresham. Times have changed."

"All right. Now do exactly what you did Wednesday."

"That's easy. It's always the same. I walk in and order a double caramel mocha." Clarence opened the door and stood behind the six people in line.

"Double shot of coffee plus a flavor?" Ollie thought about it. "That might be strong enough to cover the taste of a knock-out chemical. Go ahead and order."

"You want anything?"

"When we're done," Ollie said, the consummate professional.

"Double caramel mocha," Clarence said to the smiling girl whose name tag read Jessica. She obviously recognized him. "Usually just see you on Wednesdays, don't we?" she asked.

Clarence smiled and nodded, relieved she hadn't been reading the newspaper or watching the news. He did feel the stares of several others sitting around the tables. He paid for his mocha and took a seat, Ollie following him every step.

"Is this exactly where you sat?" Ollie asked.

"No. It was busy. All the tables were full. I sat over there at the counter, by the window."

"Then sit there now." Clarence did. "Okay," Ollie said, "so you just drink your mocha?"

"And read the newspaper. After I go to the restroom."

"What?"

"The restroom's back there." Clarence pointed to the far end of the coffee shop. "I always drink a lot of water before I bike. Don't want to get dehydrated."

Ollie looked at him skeptically.

"What? It's no longer a crime for a black man to use the restroom, remember?"

"You're saying you go to the bathroom *after* you buy your coffee?"

"The coffee's hot. I like to give it a couple minutes to cool down."

"You're telling me you just leave it out here on a table?"

"Yeah, with a newspaper so nobody takes my spot."

"Lid on or off?"

"Off, so it cools faster."

"How long are you in the bathroom?"

"I don't know. Not long."

"Go to the bathroom. Take the usual amount of time."

Clarence rolled his eyes self-consciously and headed to the back. Ollie clicked on the lap timer on his wristwatch. He clicked it off when Clarence reappeared.

"Three and a half minutes," Ollie said. "Do you always take that long?"

"I guess so. Didn't seem long to me."

"While you were in the bathroom," Ollie said, "I could have put strychnine in this thing, changed my mind, dumped it, ordered a new one, sat it back down, and filled it with rat poison. And still have time to read the sports page."

"You really think somebody tampered with it?"

"If it wasn't an insulin reaction, it was a chemical, right? We checked your water bottle, we tested your insulin. Clean. This was the last place you drank anything, right? Unless you've also forgotten to tell me you make another stop for a Chablis. Anybody who follows you just a few times sees this incredible routine. Precisely the same. Every Wednesday you come out and park your car in that same place and go for your bike ride and even lie down and rest in the same place? How hard would it be to follow you on a bike, see exactly where you go, and make a plan?"

"Isn't this a bit elaborate? And all pretty iffy too? What if someone had seen me on the bench? If it hadn't rained, they probably would have."

"Ever hear of a weather forecast? Criminals can watch them too. 'It's going to rain tomorrow, so nobody's going to be out on that trail—hey, what do you say we drug the big guy at the espresso bar where he leaves his drink out for anybody to contaminate it?' You're usually at the *Trib* surrounded by people or at home with your family, right? If they tailed you, they probably saw this as their best chance. The only time you're off the beaten path, away from people long enough where you could be put out for hours and not have an alibi. And even if their plan didn't work, they could just sit on it and do it again another day."

Clarence finally took a drink of his mocha. He looked surprised. "It's really sweet."

"That's because I mixed in three packets of sugar."

"Why'd you do that? It's plenty sweet as it is."

"To see if anybody noticed. Nobody did, of course. I put in sugar, but I could have just as easily put in crushed up sleeping pills, poison, you name it."

Ollie went up to the side of the front counter, showed Jessica his ID, and asked her if she'd noticed anyone hanging around Clarence's coffee the other day. She hadn't. It was a long shot.

"Look, Jessica," Ollie said, "could you give me a triple mocha with a double shot of almond and a single shot of coconut?" Clarence raised his eyebrows. "It's a suped-up Almond Joy. I usually get two shots of coconut, but I'm on a diet. Come to think of it though, I've been riding a bike. Jessica? Make that two shots of coconut, would you?"

They sat and talked while Ollie savored his coffee. "Okay, Clarence, so you're done with your coffee. You toss the coffee cup over there," he pointed to the waste-basket built in under the counter, "or leave it on the table or what?"

"I toss it. Well, *usually* I toss it. Except when I'm in a hurry. Then I take off before I've finished. Carry it with me. Yeah, that's right, on Wednesday I knew I had to get home and shower to make it to Bible study. So I had to rush. I still had prob-ably a third of a cup of mocha left. After hard exercise, I need the full amount of sugar to ward off an insulin reaction, so I took it with me."

"On your bike?"

"Sure. I just ride one-handed. No problem as long as the cup's not too full."

"So what did you do with the cup?"

"Tossed it when I was done, I guess."

"Don't guess. Tossed it where? On the side of the trail?"

"I don't litter." Clarence sounded as if he'd been accused of armed robbery.

"Sorry, for a moment I forgot I was dealing with Captain Responsible. It won't happen again. So, what did you do with the cup?"

"I must have dumped it in one of the trash cans on the trail," Clarence said. "Yeah, right, I took my last sip then crumpled it up. I think it was just after I tied in to the trail at Main Street Park. So it was probably the first wastebasket I got to on the trail."

Ollie asked Jessica for a phone book. He looked in the blue pages, pulled his cellular phone out of his suit pocket, and dialed.

"Hello, this is Detective Ollie Chandler, Portland Police. I need to talk to some-one, maybe in your parks or sanitation department, whoever would know about waste disposal pickups on the Springwater Corridor Trail. Gresham Parks and Recreation? Yeah, sounds like she may be the one. Sure, I'll hold."

Ollie took his last swig of coffee and eyed the pastries up on the counter. "Detective Ollie Chandler here. I'm investigating a case and need some information.

Can you tell me when the waste is collected from the trash bins on the Springwater Trail? No kidding? Great. Yeah, that's good news. Thanks."

Ollie put up his right thumb. "Waste is collected on Tuesdays, every week through October, but every other week starting in November. Tomorrow's the day. You're in luck. I've got an extra pair of gloves in the car. And I've got a job that's right up a journalist's alley—sorting garbage."

———

Dani gazed at the Carpenter, seated at the right hand of the throne. He looked and listened attentively as a woman finished reading the Scriptures. She read the last words and looked toward him, then bowed her knees. He smiled approvingly. Now an old man—or was it a young boy; he seemed both at once—walked forward and began reading the words where she'd left off.

As he began to read, behind him Dani saw a panorama of injustice upon earth. People enslaved and unjustly imprisoned, churches attacked by governments and burned by bigots, schools told God's Word could not be read or posted there. Children abused, wives beaten, men cheated of their wages, people robbed of their rights, their freedom, and their lives. Dani realized the injustices she saw, now going on in the Shadowlands, were the backdrop to the words about to be read by the boy-man. Dani looked at the throne, gazed into the kind eyes of the Lamb of God, and saw him nod to the reader, who began to speak the eternal words, as scene after scene of horrible injustice flashed behind him from places where most imagined no one saw nor cared.

> "I saw heaven standing open, and there before me was a white horse, whose rider is called Faithful and True. With justice he judges and makes war. His eyes are like blazing fire, and on his head are many crowns. He has a name written on him that no one knows but he himself. He is dressed in a robe dipped in blood, and his name is the Word of God. The armies of heaven were following him, riding on white horses and dressed in fine linen, white and clean. Out of his mouth comes a sharp sword with which to strike down the nations. 'He will rule them with an iron scepter.' He treads the winepress of the fury of the wrath of God Almighty. On his robe and on his thigh he has this name written: KING OF KINGS AND LORD OF LORDS."

Dani looked at the throne again, trembling as she saw the fiery eyes of the Carpenter. He looked no longer a Lamb, but a Lion, roaring and prowling, ready to make prey of the arrogant and unjust. Those same warm and approving eyes she'd seen so often burned with a fire fueled by unspeakable holiness and immeasurable power. The man read another passage.

See, the LORD is coming with fire, and his chariots are like a whirl-wind; he will bring down his anger with fury, and his rebuke with flames of fire. For with fire and with his sword the LORD will execute judgment upon all men, and many will be those slain by the LORD.

She could feel the hot anger in the Lion, sense the smoldering wrath waiting to be unleashed. For a moment it terrified her. She had to remind herself she was no longer the object of his wrath, that the Lion had become Lamb and paid an eternal price to deliver her from the inferno of his holiness.

Still, even as she saw the Lion's intensity, she sensed his patience. Every moment that he held back his wrath was a gift of opportunity to those in the dark world to fall in repentance before him. And in the midst of the scenes of oppression and injustice from the Shadowlands, she saw this very thing—not only the persecuted turning to him and crying out to their Redeemer, but now and again the persecutors turning from their evil and throwing themselves upon his forgiving grace. The wrath in the Lion's eyes held steady, but he restrained his urge to make all things right once and for all. He determined to give those in the Shadowlands just a little more time—a window of opportunity in which they could bow their knees to the King of the universe, from whose judgment there can be no appeal.

After putting on their gloves and dumping out the garbage on the side of the trail, Ollie found a green and white cup from Coffee's On.

"Don't think that's mine. I always crumple them up," Clarence said.

Ollie looked at it closely. "Plus, I don't think you were wearing lipstick that day, were you?" Ollie pointed to the quarter moon red mark. "Besides, this isn't your color."

They continued to search. Clarence pointed to another green and white cup, this one wadded up. Ollie picked it up carefully, opened it just enough to peek inside, smiled his approval, and lifted it into a big plastic evidence bag. He sealed the bag and marked it with a heavy black pen. "In five or six days we should know something," he said.

"Ollie, this is Ray Eagle, calling from Sacramento."

"Yeah, Ray, what's up?"

"How's this? I've got a phone call made on Harper's private line to Los Angeles at 3:41 P.M. August 29—eleven minutes after he got the fax. It's just a one minute call. To the home of Rafer Thomas."

"Bingo," Ollie said. "Our license plate man. He's the contact. Thomas must have gotten the message to the perps to call Harper. I don't suppose they called him back collect?"

"Nope. Nothing on the phone records. I'm working on Harper. He was involved in L.A. politics big time before going to Portland. He was a key player in organizing a couple of gang summits there. And the politician he worked for in L.A. hired gangbangers to hand out political literature. Sound familiar? Once you hire known criminals to do one thing, why not another?"

Clarence sat reading the *Trib* this quiet Saturday morning. He heard his father rustling in his bedroom.

Spike the bulldog came up, Charlie Chaplain style, nuzzling Clarence's feet as if it was the world's greatest privilege. A slipper and faded green tennis ball propped open his gargoyle mouth, the ball stretching his upper lip to its limits. His tail rotated like a helicopter blade.

Clarence smiled. "I've been neglecting you, haven't I, boy?" The hound scrunched up close, eyes soulful.

Until they'd gotten Spike a few years ago, Clarence hadn't been around dogs since the hounds in Mississippi. They'd had a cat for a while at Cabrini Green, but it ended up serving as target practice for local hoodlums. He mysteriously disappeared one night, never to be seen again. Daddy'd said, "He's Jimmy Hoffa's cat now."

Clarence held Spike's face squarely toward his own, as if the dog might understand better if he gave him a clear shot at lipreading. "Hate to tell you, boy," Clarence said, "but Mama asked me to give you some ear medicine." He took the little tube off the table, held it in his hand, and watched the dog's eyes get even bigger and his big overhanging lip quiver. With a flair for the dramatic, he fell on his side, submitting himself to the treatment.

"You don't like this, do you, boy? Well, sometimes what doesn't feel good is still best. Your master knows what he's doing. Trust me on this. You'll get your reward. The pizza bones are waiting."

Spike dutifully submitted to the unpleasant and incomprehensible treatment. Soon it was over. Even as he shook his ears at the discomfort, he raced ahead of Clarence to the refrigerator, eager for the payoff.

"Got the tests back from the lab," Ollie said to Clarence Monday morning. "It was your cup, all right. A couple of fingerprints, yours. There were a few drops of fluid inside plus a crystallized residue. It was heroin. As in double mocha, double heroin."

"Heroin?"

"Yeah. The good thing is, heroin isn't that popular these days. Cocaine's taken over. So a heroin purchase could be easier to track. Gracie told the cops you gave her heroin, so it was a solid setup if they drug-tested you. My first thought was tar."

"Tar?"

"It's heroin that looks like little brown tar droppings. It's brown because it's been cut, you know, diluted with chocolate or coffee grounds. Blends right in with a mocha. It would have to dissolve, though, so we're not talking real tar. But the guys who cut it to tar start with raw heroin, the pure stuff. It's powder, super strong. Every once in a while some gets out before it's been cut, and three or four addicts die the same day before somebody figures it out. I've got a guy I think might be able to help us. Want to get in on it?"

"Sure. Thanks, Ollie. How about two o'clock?"

Ollie drove Clarence down a southeast Portland residential street. He went up to the door and knocked. The dark brown man who answered the door looked to be fifty.

"Clarence, this is Pepe." The men shook hands, Clarence noticing the needle tracks on his arms. "Pepe got addicted to heroin when he was injured in Nam, and he's been on it ever since." Ollie's directness didn't seem to offend him. "Pepe, how much heroin would it take to knock a man Clarence's size out for four hours?"

"Depends on how pure."

"The purest stuff you can buy on the street."

"You can get forty or fifty percent pure, China white, they call it. Regular user?"

"Never," Clarence said.

"First time, on China white? A thirty-cent bag would kill him. Even a twenty might kill him."

Clarence looked confused. "Cent means dollar," Ollie said. "A twenty-cent bag costs twenty dollars." Now Pepe looked confused, as if he could hardly believe someone could be that ignorant.

"Put him out four hours?" Pepe asked. "Okay, ten or fifteen cents of China white."

"How much would that be?"

"Maybe a fifth of a gram."

"Show us how much."

Pepe reached for the cupboard and grabbed a sack of mashed potato flakes.

"This isn't the real stuff, is it, Pepe?" Ollie asked.

Pepe laughed. "No." He took a spoon, turned it upside down, and used the back of the handle to measure a very small amount of the flakes.

"This much would put him out."

Clarence could hardly believe it. It was less than half a little packet of sugar.

"Even after you woke up, this would bring on the nods," Pepe said.

"Yeah, I was nodding all right," Clarence said. "Light-headed, groggy, sleepy."

"Dizzy?" Pepe asked. "Turned green? Diarrhea? Vomiting?"

"Yes."

I can't believe I'm talking with an addict as though he's my doctor.

"At first you can't hold down food when you're on the drug. Then you can't hold down food unless you're on it. It's a demon," Pepe said matter-of-factly.

"Would you be able to taste it in a cup of coffee?" Ollie asked.

"Small cup?"

"Big. Sixteen ounces."

"Weak or strong?"

"Double coffee, chocolate, caramel flavor, plus milk."

"Heroin is sour, but in something that big and strong? Probably wouldn't notice it."

"Where would you get China white around here?"

"Chinatown. Or on the east side, on Eighty-second, at a Chinese restaurant."

"You can buy it at a restaurant?"

"Not every restaurant. I know which ones." He wrote down two restaurant names.

"Take care of yourself, Pepe. You're not slingin' on me, are you?"

"No. Not slingin'. Usin' sometimes, but not slingin'. Been takin' my grandkids to church."

"That's good. Just make sure they don't lose their grandfather."

"Okay, Ollie." The two Vietnam vets shook hands. As Ollie went out the front door, Pepe saluted him. Ollie made a call while he drove Clarence toward Chinatown.

"Officer Wong in Narcotics please. This is Detective Chandler. Yeah, hey Joe. Listen, I'm trying to trace a sale of China white. Can you point me to the highest volume dealer in Chinatown?"

"You armed?" Wong asked.

"Yeah. But I'm not after the dealer. I just want info on a customer."

"China white? There's not that much of it in Portland anymore," Wong said. "More of an East Coast thing. People here have graduated to crack and zip. Lots of tweakers around. But a little China white still gets imported for the long-time addicts. They get it from just one source, and he gets it from the East Coast. His name's Lee. He's got a little knickknack shop on Third Street, called Lee's Curios. You can't miss it. Tell him I sent you or you won't get a word out of him."

Ollie turned right on Second Street, under the colorful archway covered with artwork denoting the entrance to Chinatown. Clarence looked at the guys sitting on the streets. He noticed the tattoos. One had a prominent eagle on his arm, another high on his chest, his shirt unbuttoned. He saw large tattoos of knives and swords and dragons.

"I think the dragon is for martial arts," Ollie said. "Not sure about the other stuff. A lot of these guys are professional criminals. Auto theft, burglary, shoplifting. The more serious ones are into armed home-invasion robberies, loan shark collections, prostitution. Even murder for hire."

"No kidding?"

"Look at that young guy." Ollie pointed to a short muscular Asian with a New Wave hairstyle and clothing. "If he was dressed differently, he'd look like a college student. He could be. Some of these guys go back and forth. They come here, sell drugs and steal to finance their education. It's weird."

"What's with the round marks on his hands?"

"Cigarette burns. You find them on lots of the Asian gang members. Self-inflicted. They show bravery. Filipinos have quarter burns."

"Quarter burns?"

"They get a quarter hot in a fire, then press it on their skin. The hotter the quarter and the longer it's on the skin, the better you can see President Washington's head. The clearer the image, the braver the image bearer. See that guy? Going on the nods? Scratchin' himself? Heroin. The amount he's on right now would probably kill both of us." They swung up to Third Street and found Lee's Curio Shop.

Clarence and Ollie walked in together, feeling as if they'd entered another world. The smell of incense, the products being sold, everything was alien. Either man by himself would have stuck out. Together they were as noticeable as men from Mars.

Ollie showed Lee his badge and ID. "Officer Joe Wong sent me. I'm not after you, Lee. I just have a few questions. What can you tell me about a customer, maybe a new customer, recently buying your product? And I don't mean incense or chimes."

"Most my customers regulars," Lee said. "Know them well."

"We're looking for someone intending to use China white to knock somebody out. Don't suppose they would have told you that, though."

Clarence thought he saw a light turn on in Lee's eyes. "Few weeks ago man never seen before ask me about pure China white. Ask if I sure it would dissolve."

"Dissolve?"

"Yes. In coffee. Could not understand why mix heroin in coffee, but he was white man. Sometimes have strange ways."

"Anything else you can tell me about this man?"

"Only that he was with another man. Very unusual."

"Unusual in what way?"

"Other man was black. Very big. Look like this man." He pointed to Clarence.

"For moment, I think was him. Very strange to see black and white man together. People stay with own kind." He looked uncomfortably at Ollie and Clarence, who stared for a moment at each other. Ollie jotted down as much descriptive detail as Lee could give.

"Strange, isn't it?" Clarence said as they walked toward the car. "You've got white, black, Hispanic, and Asian addicts. You've got white, black, Hispanic, and Asian pushers. You've got white, black, Hispanic, and Asian officers and detectives and pastors and businessmen and you name it."

"Yeah," Ollie said. "It's almost like we're all part of the same human race, good and bad."

Clarence caught a sudden sidelong glimpse of piercing color. "Look at that, would you?" He pointed to the sky.

It was a spellbinding rainbow, not the ethereal shimmering type, but the carved out solid sort that look as if you could get on top and slide right down, skidding back and forth from one color to the next. The flaming red ribbon moved into a glistening orange, a brilliant yellow, then green and blue. The blue receded into the blueness of the sky, reappearing when set off by the browns and greens of Portland's west hills. Clarence had never seen glistening violet like this. Dani would have loved it.

What did Dani used to call rainbows? God's promise of hope? This rainbow, though, ended not in a pot of gold, but in the dull gray grime of littered streets. Clarence looked around and saw some kids walking. Several of them saw him and Ollie looking up and followed their gaze. They looked quickly back down at the street, the sky holding no promise for them. But Clarence watched two teenage boys on the corner stop dead in their tracks and gaze at the rainbow, captivated by it. Seeing those two boys somehow gave him hope.

"I've been doing a lot of thinking, Clabern," Jake said to Clarence after they watched the Packers play the Bears on Monday Night Football.

"That can be dangerous if you're not used to it," Clarence said.

"I...want to ask your forgiveness," Jake said.

Clarence sat up. "For what?"

"For my part in the hurt you and your family and your forefathers experienced."

"And your part was...what?"

"Okay." Jake took a deep breath. "I've been thinking this through, so here goes. I know if my grandfather stole from your grandfather it isn't my fault. But if my grandfather used that money to buy a house and send my father to college while yours couldn't go because he didn't have money that was rightfully his, then not only did your family suffer from the stealing, I benefited from it. Without realizing it, I've been the beneficiary of the exploitation of slaves and sharecroppers. Their loss has been my gain."

"Then it's their forgiveness you need, not mine," Clarence said.

"If I could apologize to them I would. But they're not here. You are. And you've lost an economic and educational heritage you could have had if they hadn't been enslaved. You're an extension of them, just like I'm an extension of my forebears. So it comes down to me and you, because we're the ones here. I really feel like I should ask your forgiveness."

"Jake, I'd forgive you for any wrong you did to me, you know that. But I still don't see how you can repent for sins you didn't commit."

"I've been talking with my pastor, and he showed me some verses in Daniel 9. When Daniel talks about his forefathers' sins against God, he keeps saying 'we' have sinned and done wickedly. Here's a man who will go to the lions rather than disobey God. Yet he confesses the sins of his fathers as his own, even though he didn't do those sins. Same thing with Nehemiah. He weeps over and confesses the sins of his fathers. There's no indication Nehemiah personally did any of these sins. There's every indication he didn't. Yet he took ownership of his forefathers' sins. He considered the sins of the nation, the sins of his forefathers and his brothers, as *his* sins. He took responsibility for them. He confessed them and didn't expect God to answer his prayers until he did. I've been praying for racial reconciliation for a couple of years. But I don't think I can expect God to answer my prayer and bring a solution until I confess my part of the problem."

"I don't know what to say, Jake."

"My pastor's been mulling this over too. There's another verse he gave me. Luke 11:47. Let me read it." Jake pulled out his pocket Bible. "This is Jesus talking to the religious leaders, and he says, 'Woe to you, because you build tombs for the prophets, and it was your forefathers who killed them.' Then he says in verse 50, 'Therefore this generation will be held responsible for the blood of all the prophets that has been shed since the beginning of the world.'"

"What does that mean?" Clarence asked.

"I'm not sure I completely understand it. But obviously if a man is held accountable for the blood of prophets shed by his forefathers hundreds of years earlier, there has to be some kind of transgenerational responsibility. A man is responsible for the sins his forefathers committed against others. It sounds strange, but that's what it says. Here's another passage." He turned to a page marked with a yellow Post-it note.

"Exodus 34:7 says God does not leave the guilty unpunished—he punishes the children and their children for the sin of the fathers to the third and fourth generation. It may seem unfair, but when you consider that the descendants of the victims are suffering, which isn't fair either, the fact that the descendants of the oppressors suffer maybe shouldn't be so surprising. My pastor says that maybe the only way for the descendants of oppressors to get out from under the curse is to face up to their ancestor's sins, repent, and seek forgiveness from those they've wronged."

"I hear you, Jake, but it's a pretty radical concept, taking responsibility for your ancestor's sins."

"Yeah, and the Bible's a radical book, isn't it? It says we all sinned in Adam, right? Well, that's going all the way back to our most remote ancestor, and we're held responsible for *his* sins. It seems like the closer in time to us it was done, the more a sin is linked to us, but if we're responsible for Adam's sin, obviously we're responsible for our grandfather's. It's as if we white people sinned in our American ancestors who enslaved your ancestors. I'm seeing it everywhere now. I was reading in Hebrews where it connects Abraham's actions to his great-grandson Levi long before Levi was born because Levi was 'still in the body of his ancestor.' That's a genetic connection. Even though I don't understand how it works, I need to accept my responsibility by faith. That's why I'm asking for your forgiveness."

"I've never felt you were a racist, Jake. Maybe racially unaware or insensitive sometimes, but certainly not a racist."

"The more I've prayed about this, the more the Lord has brought things to my mind, things I'd forgotten. I remember once when times were hard and my dad was laid off. Finally, he got a job with a delivery company, which was a switch for a Harvard grad. There was a guy who'd been working there twenty years, who taught him the ropes. Dad figured he'd eventually work up the ladder from loader to driver, one step at a time, but the next thing you know, my dad was given a job as driver. The other guy had to tell Dad where to go, how to get places. He was obviously more qualified for the job. Dad as much as said so. But that guy was black. I never thought much about it. Maybe just thought that's the way it was. Now I look back and I realize Dad made more money, I got more advantages. We profited from racism. We didn't mean to. I'm not heaping false guilt on myself or my father. I'm just saying I was the beneficiary of racism, of injustice.

"And that's not all, either. Twice I can remember, when I was young, I made fun of two kids, one a little Chinese girl and the other a black boy. I called her chink, and I called him nigger. I'm ashamed to admit it. A few days ago I was reading James 3:9. It says, 'With the tongue we praise our Lord and Father, and with it we curse men, who have been made in God's likeness.' It says that's evil. And I realize that whenever I've insulted someone because of his race, I've insulted the God who made him that way. That applies to my private thoughts about them too."

"You really have given this a lot of thought, haven't you, Jake?"

"There's more. One day a few years ago I was downtown near the *Trib*. I set a bag on a park bench while waiting for the bus. Next thing you know, I turn around and a couple of black kids grab it and run. I remember thinking, 'That's a black kid for you.' Of course, I was a good liberal then, I took pride in not being a racist, so I would never have admitted that's what I thought. But it is. The sad thing is, just a few weeks before, I had my bike stolen by a white neighbor kid and some mail stolen by a white man in the apartment complex. And never once did I think, 'That's whites for you.'"

"What did your pastor say when you came to him about this?"

"He said he hasn't thought much about it until recently. But he said he believed the church's biggest sin was silence. That Bible-believing churches didn't stand up against slavery and segregation and unfair treatment. And God was grieved by it. And we're still paying for that sin in ways we don't even understand."

"He actually said that?"

"Yeah. He said in America we see ourselves as individuals, disconnected from the past. But we aren't. We're connected to the sins of the nation. And to the sins of the church. What the nation did against blacks is a load we carry until we confess and repent of it and work alongside our black brothers to help make things right. In the church we bear responsibility for what we did and what we failed to do. Sins of commission and sins of omission. And one thing he said really hit home—I can't get it off my mind. He said for years he's been praying for revival. But lately he's been thinking revival can't come as long as the church fails to stand up against injustice—racial injustice, killing the unborn, mistreating the elderly, and all that. He said he used to believe if revival came it would take care of all that stuff. Now he's thinking maybe we have to address those things first before God hears our prayers for revival."

Jake never remembered Clarence looking so surprised. "I'll ask you again, Clarence. Do you forgive me for my part in being linked to and benefiting from the exploitation of your ancestors?"

"Jake, I don't know what to say. Of course, I forgive you. But...you know, nobody's ever said anything like this to me. I've had a lot of white people—including Christians—say, 'Slavery was an evil thing, but of course I had nothing to do with it.' What I've always heard when they say that is, 'It wasn't my fault, so just take care of your own problems, stop whining, and leave me alone.' I admit it's hard for us blacks to deal with our own responsibility and our need to repent and forgive when we feel like whites won't accept responsibility for what they've done."

"Remember when we were at Promise Keepers in Seattle?" Jake asked. "Remember when they asked everybody to stand up if they'd been guilty of racism? Well, I wanted to stand up. God knows I've been guilty of most other things. But I didn't. Sure, I heard a lot of racist talk when I was a kid, but I really didn't think it affected me. I still don't know how much it did. But I've come to realize a lot of things. And if I was asked again today, this time I'd stand up."

"Maybe I should have stood up too," Clarence said. "To tell you the truth, I wasn't thinking about my attitude toward Asians and Hispanics and whites, but I've been thinking about it lately. Racism is racism. It doesn't flow just one way. I see my daddy's love and it convicts me. I see Ty's racial hostility and it scares me. I guess I have something to confess too. I used to really resent white people. Sometimes I still do."

"I can understand why," Jake said.

"No. Don't justify it. It's wrong. But you know, it's a lot easier for me to say that to you after what you said to me. And I also want to tell you I really appreciate how you've stood by me after all these accusations."

"I've never been really close to a black man before," Jake said. "Maybe because I didn't understand or didn't think I could understand. But anyway, being your friend has meant a lot to me, Clarence. It's helped me understand the body of Christ. You miss a lot when you only spend time with those most like you." Jake cleared his throat. "Anyway, all this is leading up to something."

"What do you mean?"

"I've got a favor to ask you."

"What's that?"

"Janet and I are getting married. End of December."

"Hey, that's great. I'm really happy for you, man." He slapped Jake on the back. "So, what's the favor? Need a chaperone for your honeymoon?"

"No. I'd like you to be my best man."

Clarence stared at Jake in disbelief. Finally a big smile broke across his face, a smile that looked remarkably like his father's.

CHAPTER

37

"Dr. Canzler, glad you're back," Ollie said to the medical examiner. "Hopefully you can clear something up. Do you remember doing an autopsy on a girl named Leesa Fletcher? She died September 8."

"Sounds familiar, but I do lots of autopsies," he said. "Refresh my memory."

"Eighteen years old, African American. Lived in North Portland, on Jack Street. Media said she died of a congenital heart condition."

"Of course. That one I remember. Weird."

"Weird?"

"The family said she had this heart condition, and it was true. I talked to her doctor. It all looked pretty straightforward. I ran routine toxicology, blood tests, and all. Thing is, we don't get those back until a week later. That's when I found out she had enough cocaine in her blood to stop two or three healthy hearts. You know that, right? You read my report?"

"Yeah, I did. I've got it right in front of me. You said probable cause of death was cocaine overdose. But why wasn't that reported in the media?"

"Ask them. I can guess. Autopsy reports are confidential—no media privilege. But under public information access laws, we're required to tell them cause of death. Well, they always ask cause of death right after it happens, naturally. So I told them it looked like heart failure, presumably due to this congenital heart condition. It was a week later before I got back toxicology and knew about the cocaine, two weeks before I finished the report and filed it. If cause of death is doubtful, the media sometimes check back. But it didn't appear doubtful this time. We don't call the media if we come up with a different cause of death. When I got back toxicology, I just called her parents. They were really broken, could hardly believe it. I doubt they told anybody."

"You didn't call homicide?"

"For a drug overdose? You guys want me to call every time somebody ODs? I don't think so, detective. You've got enough work to do already, don't you? Just looked like a naïve first-time user who took too much."

"So," Ollie said, "anything else you remember about the girl?"

"You mean, besides the fact she was nine or ten weeks pregnant?"

Ollie tensed up, then looked down at the papers in front of him. "Why didn't you say anything about that in the autopsy report?"

"What are you talking about? I did."

"I've got the report right here. It doesn't say a word about her being pregnant."

"Are you crazy? I filed the report. I know what I said."

"Look, can I fax this to you?" Ollie asked. "I want you to confirm whether it's your signature."

"Yeah—555-5787. I'll be waiting."

"I'll call you back in five minutes, okay?" Ollie ran the three-page document through the fax machine. He leaned backward and closed his eyes, doing a detective's primary job—thinking. A few minutes later he called the medical examiner back.

"Dr. Canzler? Well, is that the report you filed?" Ollie asked.

"That's my signature, all right. But the report's been tampered with. I want to see the original."

"Well, this is the copy of the report I requested a few weeks ago. What's wrong with it?"

"It seems to be all here except my report on the amniotic sac and the fetus. I know I mentioned the pregnancy. I had to. Positive." He sounded as though he was trying to convince himself. "Look, I keep my own copy of every death certificate and autopsy report I file. I'm going to pull them from my files right now. I'll call you back, okay?"

"I'll be waiting."

Ten minutes later Ollie's phone rang. "Have you gotten my fax?" Dr. Canzler asked.

"No. Hang on a second." Ollie walked over to the homicide fax machine and retrieved the three-page report addressed to him.

"Okay, I've got it." It appeared identical to the report he already had.

"Look at the bottom of page two," Dr. Canzler said.

Ollie read a full paragraph describing Leesa's pregnancy, the amniotic sac, and the preborn child, a ten-week-old male. He grabbed his copy from the coroner's office and compared the two.

"Somebody blanked out that whole paragraph," Ollie said. "Yeah, you can see how the bottom margin is bigger than on the first page. It's a white out. So, when I called the ME on duty that day, she must have sent me an edited copy."

"No," Dr. Canzler said. "I went to the original too. It looks just like yours. It wasn't a copy that was tampered with—it was the original. Somebody whited out that paragraph so neat and clean I wouldn't have known if I hadn't typed the original myself."

Clarence tried to keep out the distractions that warred for his attention, ranging from his legal nightmare to more problems with Ty. He turned his fingers loose on the keyboard.

> Affirmative action was an attempt to counteract a proven history of racial discrimination. I believe it was a noble effort in its time and gave a needed boost to get many minorities into the workplace and initiate some upward mobility. But thirty years after the laws were changed, the question is whether counter-discrimination is the solution to discrimination. Or does the lowering of standards for minority groups ultimately doom them to live under the assumption of inferiority—the very shadow that caused discrimination in the first place?
>
> If all people are equal, then shouldn't all be held to equal standards? And if the past discrimination against some has made it harder for them to achieve these standards—and clearly it has—isn't the solution special help to *raise* their performance rather than lowering it by telling them they can get by at a substandard achievement level?

Imagine Alex Trebec saying, "Today on *Jeopardy*, our contestant of color, Robert Smith, will begin the first round with $2000 so he can have a chance against our white contestants." What an incredible insult that would be to minorities. But if we mandate that minorities get jobs and promotions and college entrance with lesser skills and lower test performances, isn't that what we're doing? And ultimately, aren't we just adding fuel to the fires of racism by fostering the very stereotypes we're trying to avoid?

"Okay," Ollie said to Manny and Clarence. "Let's do some brainstorming. Suppose our worst suspicions are right. What if Norcoast did get Leesa pregnant? He could pull some strings on the autopsy report, maybe. But let's go back. Would he really pressure her to get an abortion?"

"Sure," Manny said. "That baby would be leverage. Leesa didn't have a boyfriend, remember? When her parents find out she's pregnant, they can count backwards and ask where she was hanging out ten weeks ago. Plus, once the baby's born, he's likely to be light skinned. They're going to take one look and ask, okay, what white man was our daughter spendin' time with?"

"Or," Clarence said, "she might come right out and tell her parents or sister or a close friend who the father was. If it was Norcoast, he couldn't take that chance. Even if she said she wouldn't tell, there's a never-ending potential for a slip-up or even blackmail. This is our next mayor, a man who wants to be governor or senator. Everybody says he's the brightest political prospect in the state. Careers have ended with smaller scandals, that's for sure."

"But there's one more angle that caps it all off," Ollie said. "DNA tests can be run to prove paternity. But if mother and child die in one act before people know there's a child, suddenly you've got no mother to make the accusation and no baby to prove who the father was. All the potential embarrassments are swept aside. No doubt about it, if he was the father, Norcoast had a powerful motive for Leesa's murder."

"What's up?" Clarence asked, surprised to see Ollie at his door Saturday afternoon. "Something happen?"

"No. I'm here to see your father. I brought him my Hank Aaron autograph." Ollie lifted up an old Milwaukee Braves program, Aaron's autograph dark and prominent.

"Daddy?" Clarence knocked on his door. "Detective Chandler's here."

"Ollie? Is he now?" Clarence could hear the same sparkle in his father's voice that animated his eyes. "Send him in. Send him in!"

"Hello, Mr. Abernathy. How are you?"

"Fine as frog's hair, sir, fine as frog's hair. Just taking my blood pressure." He unfolded the arm wrap and put it down, then shook Ollie's hand. "Don't want to get in trouble with my doctor or my daughter-in-law."

"I came to take you up on your offer," Ollie said, "to see some of your old baseball pictures. Manny said I shouldn't miss them." Obadiah's eyes lit up. "And I thought you might like to see this." Ollie proudly handed him the Braves program.

"Well, I declare, son. It's Henry's signature all right." Obadiah sat down on the bed gingerly, studying the program and naming other players he knew.

Clarence made a few phone calls. Then, he sat in the corner of the living room closest to his father's open door.

"See these pictures?" he heard Obadiah say to Ollie. "It was blacks who made the first street sweepers, corn harvesters, fountain pens, clothes dryers, sugar refiners, typewriters, shoe makers, lemon squeezers, pencil sharpeners. Look at this." Clarence knew his father was showing Ollie his picture book on black patents Clarence had gotten him last Christmas.

"I never knew all this," Ollie said.

"Well, I'll tell you one that ain't in this book. You know who invented the first shin guards? A black catcher. White players was always spiking him, so he taped pieces of wood to his legs to protect them. Pretty soon all the catchers was doin' it."

"I love that picture of Jackie Robinson," Ollie said. "Once he broke the color line, it wasn't long before lots of other blacks came in, was it?"

"No sir, it wasn't. All the teams learned real quick that if others was gonna do it, they better. You know ol' Bear Bryant, when he was coachin', he got asked why the University of Alabama was finally letting blacks on the team. Know what his answer was?"

"No," Ollie said.

"To catch the ones on the other teams." Obadiah and Ollie both laughed hard.

Clarence inspected his aquarium controls, then leaned back again and heard his father speaking. "We was sharecroppers in a bitty Mississippi town, so far down they had to pump in the sunshine. We built our little house after the old one burnt down. It was three years 'fore I could afford to get doorknobs and locks. Didn't matter none. Nobody stole from you back then.

"But it seemed like them days some white folk would sooner strangle a colored man than talk to him—exceptin' they'd have to touch him to do it. It was gettin' worser and worser in some ways. Lots of folks still couldn't get used to the idea we was somebody. Back when I was fightin' that goosesteppin' lunatic for my country, if you'd relied on them newspapers you'd have thought coloreds wasn't born, 'cause the papers didn't report it. You'd have thought we didn't finish school, 'cause they never printed our honor rolls or graduations. You'd have thought we didn't get married, 'cause papers didn't print our wedding announcements or pictures of black brides and grooms cuttin' cakes. You'd have thought coloreds didn't die, 'cause they never announced our deaths or covered our funerals. Had to start black newspapers to do all that. After a while, a man gets tired of not bein' treated like a person."

"I can't imagine what it must have been like," Ollie said.

"Sharecroppin' was a far cry better than slavery, but we still didn't own the land and we didn't get wages—just the promise of sharin' profits. Well, promises get broken. One year Mr. Banks, the landowner, told me I wasn't goin' to get nothin' 'cause he had to send his boy to college. I told him, I has to feed my chillens, so he give me just a little, and I believe he thought he was generous to do it. Decided then we had to leave.

"So in '64 we moved on out for Chicago. Yessuh, Mr. Ollie, I could hear them train whistles blowin' all the way from ol' Miss. But too many of us heard the same whistles, I reckon. In twenty years after the big war, somethin' like five million black folk moved from the South to the North. We thought the North was the promised land. We went up eager to work, many of us with cotton-bailin' hooks still in our pockets.

"Thing is, we was all farmers. Knew how to work the land hard, but not much else. Weren't suited for the cities. My third-grade education wasn't enough to get me a job at a bank! So work was in the plants and odd jobs and clean up. Well, the South broke its promises, and the North didn't live up to its promise, and that's just how it was."

Clarence listened to the silence and wondered what would come next.

"Now, Ollie, maybe you notice some of our black folk just try to get by, to make do. You ask 'em what's up and they say, 'Jus' tryin' to survive, that's all.' Well, that comes from slavery and sharecroppin'. Lots of our folk didn't have great dreams like white folk because most everybody told 'em the dreams wasn't possible. Success was just makin' it to the next day, just survivin'. See, your labor always went to somebody else. No matter how hard you worked or saved or planned, you could never be white, so lots of coloreds thought they could never succeed."

"That must've been hard," Ollie said. "But when you went up North, didn't you find there was less prejudice?"

"Well, see, in the South, Negroes was always low, but white families was sometimes real fond of 'em. White chillens loved their colored mammies. Maids and gardeners could get close too. Even back in the old days some of them slaves lived in the big house, under the same roof as the massahs. But they always knowed their place, and if they forgot they got reminded real fast. Now when we moved up North, we saw blacks who'd worked their way up in businesses. They succeeded, got educated, had real nice homes. But blacks and whites never lived together; the neighborhoods was always separate. And they didn't socialize. Kept their distance. In the South most whites knew some blacks, but in the North most didn't. So you had more opportunity in the North, but not more relationships. Maybe less. The way I sees it, in the South, white folk didn't care how close we got as long as we never got too high. But in the North, white folk didn't care how high we got as long as we never got too close."

Clarence tilted his head, straining to hear every word.

"I ain't complainin' now," Obadiah said. "Never been one to whine and make excuses. But it's hard for peoples to be motivated to self-improvement when all the benefit goes to someone else. It's hard to pull yourself up by your bootstraps when you feel like somebody nailed your boots to the floor. That's why the sharecroppin' cabins of the South become the ghettos of the North. Well, nowadays the opportunity for black folks is here, opportunity I barely dreamed of. And lots of them has grabbed on and made somethin' of their lives. But other folks is still in chains in their minds. My daddy used to say, 'We's a stolen people.' When someone steals your property, that's one thing. But when he steals you and turns you into property, it does something to a man that's impossible for free folk to understand. It changes the way you look at yourself, and it gets passed on to your chillens and their chillens. See, when you're a black man, you start thinking there's nothin' lower than you but the ground itself, and one day even that's gonna be over you. So some folk just passes the time until they go to the ground or they start lookin' to put other people under them. Well, Mr. Detective, what do you think of all this ol' man's ramblin'?"

"I think you're a wise man, sir."

"Well, that's right kind of you, sir, 'cause the older I gets, the more days I has where not all my dogs is barkin', if you follow me. I tell you what I learned when I went north, Ollie. I learned there's no Promised Land in this world. I made the mistake of thinkin' any place out of the South would be heaven. I was wrong. It wasn't. Yessuh, the only train whistle that's goin' to take you to the Promised Land is the glory train. And when I hears *that* whistle, ol' Obadiah Abernathy's gonna get on board. I'm gonna make it to that Promised Land. But not till then."

Obadiah laughed heartily and went straight into singing in his thin voice, "Git on board, little children, git on board. De gospel train's acomin', git on board."

The phone rang. Clarence went to it, reluctantly breaking from his eavesdropping. When Clarence came back a few minutes later, the men were still in Obadiah's room. He'd heard lots of laughing, but it was quiet now. He strained again to hear his father's voice.

"So, that's what Jesus said, Ollie. There's just two places we can go. Heaven or hell. Every man's gonna end up in one or t'other. It's our choice. To accept Jesus is to accept heaven. To reject Jesus is to accept hell. All you has to do is confess your sins and bow your knees to Jesus and accept his dyin' on the cross for you. Then you can knows when you dies you'll go to heaven. How 'bout you, son? What choice you made?"

"I don't think I'm ready to make a choice right now, Mr. Abernathy," Ollie said. "But thanks for telling me this. I really do appreciate it."

"Just one beggar tellin' another beggar where to find bread," Obadiah said. "That's what my brother Moses always used to say. But don't forget now, Mr. Ollie, you don't never know how much longer you gots left to make that choice."

Clarence felt guilty that in all the time he'd spent with Ollie he hadn't shared his faith with him. Daddy's faith was so real it overflowed him. He envied that.

After another hour's visit, Clarence walked Ollie out to his car, a brown '82 Malibu with missing hubcaps and lots of dents. It made Ollie's old precinct car look fancy.

"Never seen this one before," Clarence said.

"Beaut, ain't she? You think she's a prize now, you should have seen her before she hit 250,000 miles." Ollie peered in the driver's side window. "Shoot. Locked my keys in the car."

"Need a clothes hanger?" Clarence asked.

"Nah. Got a hidden key. Hope it's still there, anyway." Ollie walked to the back of the car and reached underneath, groping up into the undercarriage. Finally he retrieved a grease-smeared metal case, removed a key, and held it up. Ollie opened the door, put the key back in the case, and returned it to its hiding place.

Clarence read aloud the four bumper stickers plastered on the car's rear. "Save the Males. Visualize Whirled Peas. Legalize Lutefisk." He leaned over to take a close look at a badly faded sticker. "What does this one say? Okay, I got it. Save the Planet: Kill Yourself."

Clarence looked at Ollie and shook his head.

"Hey," Ollie said, shrugging his shoulders, "everybody's got their causes."

The phone rang late Sunday evening, and Clarence jumped up to get it.

"Take a deep breath," Ollie said.

"Why? What happened?"

"Just got some bad news."

"What?"

"It's Gracie Miller."

"What about her?"

"She's dead."

"Another key witness dies. And another drug overdose?" Ollie threw up his hands at their Monday morning meeting. "Leesa and Gracie might have been our best shots at breaking this thing. I think I was really close to cutting a deal with Gracie. Three drug overdoses if we count yours, and two of them fatal. Drugs seem to be the weapon of choice here."

"Even though she set me up," Clarence said, "I really feel bad for Gracie."

"Gracie? Her type's always expendable. Like the girls that go to L.A. to become movie stars. Most of them end up hookers, beaten up by their pimps and their johns, dying from bad needles and God knows what diseases. Gracie died in Portland. Saved her the drive to Hollywood." Ollie looked at the floor. "Yeah. I feel bad for her too."

"Where does this leave us?" Clarence asked.

"We got clearance to check out Gracie's room where her father found her body," Manny said. "I came across this envelope," he held it up for Clarence to inspect, "on her dresser, under a makeup stand. Still had some cash in it. Twelve fifty-dollar bills. Don't know how much was in it originally."

"You think it was a payoff?" Clarence asked.

"Notice the blue lining in the envelope," Ollie said. "And the penciled number two on it. What does that remind you of?"

"Didn't Mookie say something about an envelope?"

"Yeah, with a blue lining and a penciled number three." Ollie said. "Makes you wonder if there was a number four, doesn't it? But one thing we know for sure."

"What's that?" Clarence asked.

"There had to be a number one," Manny said.

"I figure number one dealt directly with the payoff person," Ollie said. "He might have been the go-between from the money man to Gracie and Mookie. No way the big guy would deal directly with them—too high risk. So number one could be Gangster Cool or Shadow, maybe both working together. Since Gracie called Shadow when I told her I knew who hired her, five's got you ten he's her contact. She suddenly overdoses and she's conveniently out of the way. And since everybody knew she was a user, it's not even suspicious. Everything's pointing to Shadow right now. With Leesa and Gracie and Gangster Cool all history, Shadow's our link to the big fish, the Norcoast connection."

"But Shadow won't be easy to get to," Manny said. "The guys I've talked to on the Gang Enforcement Team say Shadow's tough, maybe as hard as GC. Everybody knows Shadow killed that kid Sylvester on MLK—and Raphael, the Woodlawn Park Blood. But there's no proof. He might not ever break."

"No fingerprints but Gracie's on the envelope," Ollie said. "Was hoping there'd be one on the stickum, but nothing. I did have them scrape the gummy seal at crime lab. They found some DNA."

"DNA?" Clarence asked. "You mean, from the person who sealed the envelope?"

"Who else? It wasn't Gracie's saliva, we know that," Ollie said. "It was whoever licked the envelope."

"Saliva? But isn't it all dried up?"

"Hey, they've run conclusive DNA matches from the backside of a forty-year-old postage stamp."

"No kidding? Saliva has DNA just like blood?"

"Not exactly. Saliva has skin sluffage in it, and that carries DNA."

"Skin sluffage?"

"Yeah, skin from the inside of the mouth. It leaves a nucleated discharge."

"You sound like a scientist, Ollie."

"Yeah, well, you have to know all sorts of things to be a good detective, and I don't just mean who serves cherry pie after midnight, though that's important too. DNA testing is all about nucleated cells. Red blood cells won't do; you need white blood cells, which aren't just in blood, they're in skin. When we get a warrant to go after somebody, we take them to a medical facility, or if they're in jail, the nurse takes two vials of their blood and swabs their mouth with a Q-Tip. Then they air dry it, and you've got your saliva match as well as your blood match. It just gives you something extra."

"Are you saying we can trace down who licked this envelope?" Clarence asked.

"Theoretically, yes," Ollie said. "Practically, no."

"Why not?"

"Except for sex offenders, we don't routinely keep DNA files on people. It's not like fingerprints. I mean, even fingerprints, we only have people who've been booked, right? But DNA? We don't have much to test it against. Just for the heck of it, I ran our results against what we've got on computer, but nothing came up. I would have been shocked if it had."

"But couldn't you get an order to take a sample from a suspect?"

"Only if there's probable cause, which has to be proven to a judge, who has to issue a warrant. Same old deal. We'd want to test Norcoast and Gray, right? But what's our evidence? We don't have anything close to probable cause. 'Yes, your honor, I was hoping to get two blood vials from Norcoast because, well, in my humble opinion he just seems to me to be oozing with slime.' Trust me, they won't buy it."

Manny excused himself, and Ollie took a call. Five minutes later he got off.

"Question, Ollie," Clarence said. "If a private citizen was collecting DNA samples, just as a hobby or whatever, all he'd have to do is get something with a person's blood, right?"

"Right."

"Or something that's been in contact with an open mouth, with saliva, even if it's dry, right?"

"Right. But it would have to be done carefully."

"Like put it in a baggy or something?"

"Yeah. But the private citizen would have to act on his own," Ollie said. "If the police initiated it, it would be inadmissible."

"But even if it was inadmissible, it could still be helpful, couldn't it?"

"Yeah. And it would probably be admissible as long as the police didn't suggest or initiate anything or give approval to it."

Clarence packed up his briefcase and headed for the door. "Later, Ollie."

"Hold it, Clarence. I hate to say it, but this whole thing with Gracie..."

"What?"

"Police and everybody else are going to ask who had the most to gain through this girl's death. Obviously, you're near the top of the list. With her gone, the DA might consider dropping the case. But whether or not he does, some people are going to think you were involved. I've heard it already."

"It happened last night, right? I was home with my family the whole evening. They can all testify to that."

"Yeah, that's good," Ollie said. "But with Gracie overdosing, people are still going to wonder if you were behind it. Going to think you're the one who got her on drugs or whatever. I'm just trying to prepare you for the critics. I know a little bit about it. Lots of people still believe I'm a brutal racist."

———

Clarence walked the Portland streets during his lunch hour, thinking about Gracie and her short life. His mind drifted back to the projects. He was playing basketball as a fourteen-year-old, watching out of the corner of his eye as the hoods stood on the side and shot craps, played the dozens, and intimidated the meek. He remembered all the admiring females watching them and how it spurred them on. He remembered how the guys acted around the girls, all the posturing and showing off and saying, "Gimme yo' phone number, baby. Please. I'll *die* without yo' phone number." Rappin' to babes was a ritual, an art form.

One girl came to mind—Tisha. At first he'd thought she was very pretty, a black version of Gracie. But Tisha was easy, and the guys used her up like a carton of cigarettes, disposing of the carton when they were done. After a while her eyes went vacant. A couple years after moving, Clarence heard from his cousin Franky that Tisha had committed suicide. Tisha. Gracie. Tisha's image had always haunted him. He considered the different ways black men and black women had suffered.

Clarence walked back toward the *Trib*. He went down a couple of streets and sat on a bench by a patch of grass, watching the city go on around him.

He loved the sights and sounds and smells of the city. The aroma of Vietnamese food, of Thai and Chinese and Creole. The sounds of shop bells ringing as customers entered. The bustle, the activity, the smorgasbord of endless variety. The libraries, the art and culture, the communication, the exchange of ideas.

He hated the sights and sounds and smells of the city. The abandoned businesses, broken windows, graffiti, stolen and beaten-up shopping carts, the incessant honking, the sirens, the pungent smell of uncollected garbage and urine on alley walls. He hated the flashing lights of porno shops that stripped and sold paper women, reminding him how his great-grandmother was sold to the highest bidder. He hated the city that had taken Dani and Felicia from him and now had stolen his hard-earned reputation. The city that killed kids with so much potential, kids like Robby, Leesa, Jason, Raymond, and Gracie.

He remembered visits to his cousin in Jackson, where on hot days they put the big wrench to the fire hydrants and kids played in the spurting water. He could still see the market where fruits and vegetables lay out in stands on the street. People dropped their money in little wicker baskets and made their own change, and at the end of the day the shopkeeper had just the right amount of money or maybe a little extra. Now everything of value was locked up, with huge steel bars and security cameras and alarm systems. Cars had the Club and those obnoxious alarms that went on for hours. The city was no longer community. It was chaos, physically and morally dirty.

This part of downtown, where he now sat, was city at its best. Where he was living, in Dani's place, felt sometimes like city at its worst. Life got compressed in the city. Children looked like teens, teens looked twice their age, people in their thirties and forties who in the suburbs would have been playing golf and dressed in jogging suits looked old and worn and beaten up, deep furrows cutting across their faces. The people aged with the neighborhoods, and the neighborhoods dried up like fruit long ago fallen from the tree.

Portland's newer houses, the nice ones, were gradually becoming their own walled cities. They had security entrances, bars keeping out unwanted vehicles, security guards, special passcards. They reminded him of a military compound. Only authorized people could even take a walk in the area. Almost all were white, Asian, or Middle Eastern. Very few were black, Hispanic, or American Indian. It was more of a wealth divide than a racial divide—rich blacks and Hispanics could live up there too. But those outside the walls were at the bottom of the food chain. And the bottom feeders were the ones those inside the walled cities feared most.

The city seemed to Clarence a house whose foundation was collapsing, chipped away and eroded for too many years. It seemed beyond repair. Today he had no hope for the city.

———

Dani gazed intently at the great city, so high that even with her enhanced vision she couldn't see the top. The city was still being built, though it looked nearly complete. Many of Michael's legions came and went from it on missions of delivery and construction, she supposed. She longed to see it up close, as one longs for a new house to be finished so she can walk through it at last. In this case the anticipation was even greater because she'd never even seen the floor plan. She knew the Carpenter was supervising the building project, though, and that knowledge thrilled her.

Standing there she understood as never before that she'd spent her life on earth in a rented room, on borrowed time. With less than her new world she could never again be satisfied. The only good reason for loving the old world was that sometimes, in its grandest moments, it seemed a little like this one.

The New Jerusalem, the city of God before her, called to her as only home can.

"How can a place be home when I've never set foot there?" She spoke aloud to Torel and Lewis, then smiled and answered her own question. "When your beloved has promised he is preparing it for you."

Dani remembered Clarence once telling her how the idea of heaven being a city left him cold. She had no answer then, but she did now. He was thinking of the only cities he knew, with their pollution and dirt and crime and poverty and noise and conflict. She realized now this heavenly city would have the freshness and vitality and openness of the country—all the things for which Clarence loved the country— with the vibrancy and interdependence and relationships of the city. And with none of the divisions, racial and otherwise, that marred both city and country in the Shadowlands.

Lewis put his hand on her shoulder. "Elyon's Book says his people spent their lives in the Shadowlands longing for a better country—a heavenly one. Elyon says that in the dark world his children do not have an enduring city but are to look for the city that is to come. Tell me, what is a city?"

Dani thought about her tutor's question. "A place of many residences close to each other. Where the inhabitants are under a common government. A place of varied and bustling activity, communication, interaction, jobs, duties, creative expression. Art and music and drama."

"Yes," Lewis said. "Elyon says that the patriarchs did not gain on earth what God had promised them. But that was all right because they looked forward to the city with foundations, whose architect and builder is God. Whether or not Adam's race knows it, until they at last enter its gates, they will *always* be looking for the city that is to come. Man's first emptiness is for a person, the person of Christ. His second emptiness is for a place, the place Christ prepares for him. Those who do not understand this waste their lives in the Shadowlands trying to fill the emptiness with anything and everything but the one person and place that can truly fill it."

"I know the city will be wondrous," Dani said, "but I can't imagine anything greater than this place we stand in now."

"That is the nature of heaven," Torel said. "You always experience what is beyond your imagination. But once you experience it, your imagination is stretched farther. Instead of imagination always surpassing reality, as it did on earth, here reallty always surpasses imagination."

"It seems too good to be true."

"In Elyon's realm, everything that is good *is* true," said the angel. "You are in the perimeter of heaven, having just stepped inside. You stand in the foyer of heaven's auditorium, the entryway to the city. If the foyer is so wondrous, what do you think the auditorium will be? If the gateway is so grand, what do you think the city will be?"

"I knew he promised a place for us. I just couldn't imagine it would be so… extraordinary."

"As you prepared a room," Torel said, "for each of your children—I was there when you did, you know—Elyon's Son prepares a room for each child that arrives in his world. The quality of the room you prepared was limited both by your abilities and your resources. Elyon lacks neither. The great city will one day be moved to the new earth, and at last you will enter the place he has made for you."

"Somehow I never envisioned this city as an actual place. I thought the descriptions were figurative."

Torel looked perplexed, while Lewis smiled. "What does a figurative place look like?" Torel asked. "How do you eat a figurative meal, drink figurative water, walk on figurative streets, or sing figurative songs? I do not understand the human compulsion to reject the plain meaning of Elyon's Word."

"But," she said looking at the city, "it's so *huge*."

"It is exactly the size Elyon told you it would be," Torel said. "Did you not read Elyon's Book where he laid out the precise measurements of the eternal city? I am confounded at all the things your people were plainly told in Elyon's Word but which you act amazed about when you get here. Will you also be amazed to find flowing water, trees, brilliant jewels, and golden streets polished to appear like transparent glass? I can understand why *seeing* such things would amaze you. But to be surprised at their very existence when Elyon revealed them to you is beyond my understanding."

"This whole place is beyond my understanding," Dani said, laughing. She looked through the portal at Clarence, sitting sullenly on a city bench. "Yet I understand so much more than my brother does. It's so hard for him. Why must he go through this? Why is Elyon permitting him to suffer so much?"

"Imagine a man shut up in a dark room with no windows," Lewis said. "He has only a few oil lamps. The comfort they bring keeps him in the room, grasping on to their tiny flickering light which cannot satisfy and cannot last. To experience the full light of day, the man need only walk out of the dark room, go to the front door, open it up, and step out into the sunlight. But as long as the flickering light of the oil lamp is there, he will not leave it, he will cling to its meager light. If you loved such a man, if you wanted the best for him, what would you do?"

"I'm not sure," Dani said.

"You would blow out the little man-made lamps," Lewis said. "Once he was free from their hold, you would lead him through the darkness and toward the door, so at last he could behold the light of heaven."

"Hello, Mr. Abernathy. How are you?" Sheila's upbeat voice convinced Clarence she wasn't thinking ill of him.

"Well, things are a little tough right now, but I'll make it. Can I speak to Reg Norcoast, please? Or if he's not available, Carson Gray?"

"Mr. Gray went home sick. He's been coughing and sneezing all day. I believe I can get Mr. Norcoast for you."

Norcoast came on the line. "Clarence, I'm really sorry about all the trouble you've been having."

"Yeah. Well, none of it's true and I'm going to be cleared, but sometimes it takes awhile. Listen, you've been saying you wanted to play tennis again. I've got a court at four-fifteen today."

"Hey, tennis sounds great. Normally I couldn't—I've got a standing appointment with Carson Thursdays at four-thirty. But he went home sick. Poor guy was coughing and sneezing and hacking and I said, 'Go home before you get us all sick.' Four-fifteen out at Cascade Athletic Club on Division?"

"Yeah. Court three."

"Super. I'll see you there."

Clarence had expected Norcoast to say no. Politicians don't like to be seen with people in trouble. He flipped open the Ebenezer Church directory and looked up Harold Haddaway.

"Harold? Clarence Abernathy. You working at Councilman Norcoast's office tonight? Can you do me a favor? It's a little unusual. Could you let me into the office for just a few minutes tonight? There's a good reason, believe me. You can stay right next to me the whole time, okay? Really? What time do you come in? Everybody gone by then? Great. Be there by seven-fifteen. And do me a favor, okay? Don't mention this to anyone. And don't dump the garbage until I get there."

Reggie Norcoast served right on target, pounding Clarence's backhand. No time for a backswing. Clarence could only block the ball and rely on the pace generated by Norcoast to get it back. The councilman's service routine was exactly as Clarence remembered. He rubbed his left sweatshirt cuff across his mouth. Then he bounced the ball twice, went into his high toss, and brought down a powerful serve, mixing in a few heavy spin serves to vary the pace.

Clarence lost the first set 4-6 and won the second 7-5. That was the first set he'd won off Norcoast, but it took everything he had. They didn't have time or energy for a third set, so they went to a twelve point tie-breaker, which Clarence lost 5-7.

They shook hands and walked to the locker room to shower. They tore plastic bags off the roll dispensers and put their tennis clothes and sweatbands in them. They sat in the hot tub, showered, returned to their lockers, got dressed, and started to walk out, each with his own duffel bag. Norcoast paused, double-checking inside the locker and his bag.

"Did you see my sweatshirt?" Norcoast asked Clarence.

"No. Are you sure you put it in the locker?"

"I thought so. But if I left it out, somebody might have thought it was his. Lots of gray sweatshirts. No big deal. Hope they get good use out of it. Have time for dinner, Clarence?"

"No, thanks. I've got a few things I've got to do back in town tonight."

"Yeah. I promised I'd be home all evening with Esther. Thanks for the match. It was fun."

Clarence rushed home, energized but tired and hungry. Geneva reheated the roast and potatoes in the microwave. He'd opened some of his mail at work but had put the rest in his briefcase so it wouldn't distract him from his column. He started opening it now. A few of the dozen personal letters were complimentary and supportive. Some were neutral. But three letters stuck with him as if they were the only ones:

"Can't stay away from white girls, huh? Better watch your back, nigger."

"You can take the boy out of the jungle, but you can't take the jungle out of the boy."

"We have always enjoyed your column, but your recent behavior has left us in shock. We've thought of you as a true Christian standing up for conservative values in the midst of a biased liberal media. But now you've betrayed us all by doing these horrible things. Your column and Jake Woods's were two of the very few reasons we even subscribe to the Trib. Now we'd just as soon never see your name in print again. Shame on you."

Clarence pushed back his plate, dinner uneaten.

The same people who whine about how biased the Trib is turn around and believe everything the Trib says.

"What's wrong, baby?" Geneva asked "Didn't like the roast?"

"No, it's fine. I'm just not hungry. And I've got something I have to do."

Clarence walked out the fourteenth floor elevator to the detective department carrying a brown grocery bag that looked out of place with his tailored suit. After he waited five minutes, Ollie came barreling out and shook his hand.

"We've got to stop meeting like this, Clarence. Our wives may get jealous. What's up?" Ollie held open the door and beckoned him into the office area.

"No time to come in. Got to get back to the *Trib* and polish off a column. Just thought I'd drop these off for you." He opened the bag so Ollie could peer in.

"A gray sweatshirt in a plastic bag? Smells ripe."

"I think you'll find that the left sleeve, especially the cuff, has a healthy sampling of saliva from the mouth of one Reggie Norcoast."

"No kidding?" Ollie pointed in the bag. "And what's in these little baggies?"

"Four still-moist tissues from the wastebasket of one very sick, coughing, and hacking Carson Gray."

"Nasal discharge? Gag me. Well, we'll see. It might do the trick."

"As a backup, I scraped off two globs of chewing gum from under Gray's desk." He held up a baggy. "Didn't touch it. Used my pocketknife."

"Gray sticks chewing gum under his desk? Amazing the dirty little secrets you find out about people. Chewing gum, huh? Never used it for a DNA test before. I read in a journal it's been done, though. Let's see what the crew in criminology can do with it. If nothing else, it looks like it's good for a few more chews. DNA testing usually takes weeks, but I'll put a rush on it."

Clarence headed to the elevator. "I never asked you for this, right?" Ollie asked.

"Nope. It was 100 percent my idea, start to finish."

————

"What's your column tomorrow?" Jake asked Clarence as they sat at Lou's Diner.

"Winston says with the latest O. J. controversy, it's time for another go at 'the great racial divide.'"

"The O. J. thing's never gonna go away is it? The case that never dies."

"October 3, 1995—I remember the exact day of the acquittal, can you believe it? Ollie and I had a long talk about it. Interesting."

"You and I never talked much about the trial when it was going on, did we?" Jake asked. "I guess I wasn't sure how to bring it up. But I know it bothered you."

"Sure it did. When O. J. was accused, I felt like I'd been accused."

"Why?"

"Because I'm a black man."

"But that doesn't—"

"I know, I know. It sounds irrational. One day I overheard two rednecks at a lunch counter, talking about O. J. One guy said to the other, 'What'd you expect from a nigger?' I wanted to put his face in his mashed potatoes, but then he probably would have just said, 'What'd you expect from a nigger?'" Clarence laughed, but not convincingly. "You know what I thought about, Jake? Something I never told a white guy before, but I sure brought it up to my black friends."

"What?"

"I thought about how nearly all serial killers are white. Manson. Son of Sam. Bundy. Dahmer. Gacy. All those guys. But when Dahmer sexually abused and murdered men and cannibalized them, did anyone say, 'What'd you expect from a white man?' Did anyone even think of saying that? Of course not. When Aldrich Ames betrayed CIA agents in the Soviet Union for a maroon Jaguar and a nice house, and twenty people were murdered as a result, did anyone say, 'That's a white man for you'?"

"Race has nothing to do with it," Jake said.

"Unless you're a black man and it's a black criminal. See, when a white man does something wrong, he's just another bad man. But if Dahmer had been black, the whole equation would've changed. He wouldn't have been just another bad man; he'd have been another bad *black* man, a *black* murderer, a *black* cannibal. Every black man feels the weight of that—at least, I do."

"It really affects you that way?"

"Look at the stereotypes. Black men have illegitimate children and don't raise them or care for them. That's what people think. Well, how many centuries did white men rape their black slave women, get them pregnant, refuse to acknowledge the children as their own or raise or care for them? How many black men have been accused of 'having a thing' for white women? How many black men are automatically viewed as potential rapists of white women, when for hundreds of years it was routine for *white* men to rape *black* women? But do white men feel everybody's viewing them as rapists? No. Black men do."

"Well," Jake said, "white men do have to live with the stereotype of being racist oppressors. Sometimes you feel like everybody's loading guilt on you. It really gets old."

"I hear you. But what about the 'Blacks are violent' stereotype? I heard people in the sixties point to marches and demonstrations and riots to defend that thesis. But look at organized labor in this country. White workers marching, rioting, and burning before the civil rights movement even existed. Look at history. For three hundred years whites steal, whip, torture, rape, brutalize, and murder their black slaves. The vast majority of those blacks never fought back, never returned violence for violence. You could make a great case for American blacks historically being the least violent people in the world, obviously a great deal less violent than the whites who whipped them. After all that, now you've got some black criminals rioting and shooting each other and everybody thinks, 'Yeah, those black people are just violent by nature, aren't they?'"

"I don't think that way, Clarence."

"Maybe you don't. But haven't you heard people talk about Africa? Idi Amin and what he did in Uganda. The civil war in Mozambique. The slaughter in Rwanda.

They think it's because blacks are violent—I've heard it said, Jake. I'm sure you have too. And I say, look at the bloodshed in the Middle East. So that makes Arabs and Jews violent by nature? Look at the wars and murders in Central America. Hispanics are violent by nature? Look at the bloodshed in China—Mao killed what, five times the number Hitler did? And Pol Pot—Asians must be violent by nature. And Hitler, he was a Caucasian, right? So were all the soldiers who did the killing. And how about Stalin's Caucasian Russians murdering starving children in the Ukraine, millions of them? And what about the Bosnian Serbs? More Caucasians. Look at Ireland. They're white as they can be, religious church-goers, too. But does anybody say, 'See that proves it—those whites, they're just violent by nature'? Of course not."

Jake felt Clarence's frustration and didn't know how to respond.

"Know what it all tells me, Jake?"

"What?"

"Not that blacks are violent. Or Hispanics are violent. Or Asians are violent. Or whites are violent. Just that all of them are people and it's *people* who are violent. Color doesn't matter. Like Pastor Clancy says, 'It's not a skin problem, it's a sin problem.'"

"I'm with you there, brother," Jake said. "And I've got another example for you. Think about Bobby Knight and John Thompson. Knight grabs players by their jerseys and screams and swears at referees and throws chairs. Thompson's a controlled disciplinarian who treats his players with respect. But nobody looks at Bobby Knight and says, 'Just another out-of-control white man.' And they don't look at John Thompson and say 'There's another cerebral, thoughtful, disciplined black man.'"

Clarence looked at Jake with surprise. "Careful, bro. You almost sound like a black cat. Like you're starting to see through different eyes."

CHAPTER

Blacks are lazy. There's a stereotype few people say aloud anymore. Like most racial prejudice, it lingers barely beneath the surface. And like most, it is also irrational. Consider the historical facts. A culture of white people enslaved blacks to do their menial labor for them. For hundreds of years blacks worked sixteen hours hard labor a day so whites wouldn't have to wash their clothes, cook their food, tend their animals, or raise their crops. Yet somehow the belief surfaced that it's *blacks* who are lazy. The truth is, of course, there are lazy whites, blacks, Latinos, Asians, and Native Americans. There are also hard-working whites, blacks, Latinos, Asians, and Native Americans. The fact that I even have to make what should be a self-evident point demonstrates the depth to which we are permeated by racial stereotypes.

After finishing his column, Clarence started opening the day's mail. He braced himself. The first letter was printed crudely by one of those adults who still write like a second-grade boy who'd rather be at recess. "So you played around with the white girl, nigger? Got the jungle fever? Bet it felt good. And now you killed her. O. J. got away with it, but you won't."

Clarence's index finger rubbed against the leathery patch an inch below his right ear. He opened the next letter, this one on letterhead from a Gresham businessman.

"Though I've never written you before, I've always enjoyed your columns. Just wanted you to know I believe in innocent until proven guilty. Unless you are proven guilty in a court of law, I'll continue to believe you when you say you didn't do these things. If I was in your position, I'd want others to assume my innocence, and Jesus said, 'Do unto others as you would have them do unto you.' Keep writing that column, Clarence, and know a lot of us still trust you. Respectfully, Jim Riegelmann."

Letters such as this, and he'd gotten several others, moved Clarence deeply. Encouraged, he decided to open one more.

"Nigga: why you messin' with white trash in the first place? Sisters ain't good enough for you? I'm glad she's dead. You deserve to die too."

The whole Abernathy clan gathered at Clarence and Geneva's house December 12 for a combined Christmas and Kwanzaa event. As they had the past few years, they met two weeks before the first day of Kwanzaa in deference to Harley's family's custom of preparation for their holiday.

Before dinner Harley set up a red, black, and green flag. He stood before the family and spoke in solemn and heartfelt tones.

"Habari Gani. This is the Bendera Ya Taifa, the flag of the black nation. The red stands for blood, because with blood we lost our land and without blood we cannot acquire land. The black stands for our proud identity as African people. The green stands for our land, which we have lost but which we must regain, for without a land of our own we can have no freedom, justice, independence, or equality. We gather today to begin our preparation for Kwanzaa. We give thanks for being part of a black family."

After Harley's wife and children said a few words about the meaning of the Kwanzaa season, Obadiah opened a Bible and read the Christmas story from Luke 2. A family feast followed that went on for two hours, punctuated by stories, laughter, and animated discussions.

"Geneva, honey," Obadiah said, "I swears that's the best sweet potato pie this old soldier's had since my Ruby used to make it."

Geneva got up and hugged her father-in-law. "Now *that's* the greatest compliment I've ever gotten, Daddy. Nobody did tater pie like Mama."

"Nobody," Obadiah agreed, "but yours is as close as they come, I reckon." He looked at all the children. "If your grandma could see you now...I expect she can. Some of you didn't ever get to meet her here, but you'll see her on the other side, if you loves Jesus like she do."

"What was she like, Grampy?" Keisha asked, as the family retired to the cramped elbow-brushing living room.

"She was an Aunt Jane if ever there was one," the old man said as soon as he was seated on the couch. "A Miss Sally through and through." The children looked confused.

"Aunt Jane and Miss Sally," Clarence said, "were nicknames they used for a few older women in each black church. They were always highly respected women. Usually didn't have much education, but lots of homespun wisdom and God-given common sense. They were especially close to the Lord."

"Close to God, my Ruby was. And even closer now," Obadiah said. "My own mammy was an Aunt Jane. Mammy used to ring that ol' bell on the porch, she did. Meant it was supper time, time to come home. Sometimes this ol' boy hears the bell a ringin'. Time to come home."

Obadiah tilted his head, listening intently. A few family members felt embarrassed, as if this old man belonged in a place where people who hear voices are kept from hurting themselves. Obadiah went right on listening to the music no one else could hear. In moments such as this, when his old age was most obvious, Obadiah looked most youthful, boyish, as if running unrestrained through the meadows of childhood. Was he remembering childhood or anticipating it? How could it be that the older he got, the younger he appeared? After listening to the music in silence, the old man joined it with a dilapidated voice that nonetheless rippled with enthusiasm.

"Oh Freedom, Oh Freedom, Oh Freedom over me. And before I'll be a slave I'll be buried in my grave, and go home to my Lord and be free.

"Git on board, little chillen', git on board. De gospel train, she's comin', git on board.

"Amazin' Grace, how sweet the sound that saved a wretch like me; I once was lost, but now am found, was blind, but now I see."

Most the family joined in now, though Harley seemed uncomfortable and buried his nose in a newspaper he'd picked up from the coffee table. They sang four verses, Obadiah knowing every word of every verse, though nowadays he often couldn't remember what happened that morning. Clarence could tell how far back his father's mind went by the way he pronounced the words.

"When we been dere ten thousand years, bright shinin' as da sun, we've no less days to sing God's praise, dan when we first begun." The tears poured down Obadiah's cheeks as he stared out the window. Clarence followed his daddy's gaze. He could see nothing.

"Merry Christmas to my family," Obadiah said, bouncing suddenly back to the moment, lucid and sharp, as if his empty tank had been refueled. "And Happy Kwanzaa too," he added, looking at Harley, who still gazed at a *Tribune* article.

"These Republican crackers won't be happy until they crush the last black man," Harley said, throwing down the paper. "White devils."

Geneva glared at her brother-in-law for ruining the mood.

"There's some white devils all right, brother, and some black devils too," Clarence said. "How many whites you seen comin' in here from the suburbs to blow black heads off? Most of our crime is black on black, and you know it."

"And I know who it was," Harley said, "that taught blacks their lives were worth nothin'. I know who robbed them of their African heritage and taught them to hate what they are and to hate each other. Whites poured toxic waste into our black sea for hundreds of years, and if some of them don't dump quite as much waste on us now, that doesn't do anything to clean up the toxic mess they made. You don't have to pull the trigger to be responsible for a death."

Obadiah held up his hands, and Clarence and Harley restrained their tongues. "Both of you has a point. Trouble with you, Son," Obadiah said to Harley, "is when you trace your roots back, you stop too soon."

"What do you mean?"

"You go back to Africa," Obadiah said. "Well, Africa ain't far enough. Keep goin' back, back to Noah and his sons, back to Adam and Eve. Go back to where we all come from the same stock, whatever color their skin was, and I don't care if Adam was green and Eve was purple. It's right there in Acts 17 and 26: 'From one man God made every nation of men.' We're the same race, human race. We got the same problem, sin. We got the same solution, Jesus. Black Republicans, White Democrats, Hispanic Chinese American Indian Independents, it just don't matter. Sin's sin and the Savior's the Savior. Your generation seems to always forget that."

"All due respect, Daddy," Harley said, "but my generation didn't roll over. If we hadn't fought for our rights, we wouldn't have any. When it comes to racial justice, we were the pioneers."

"No, Son, you weren't," Obadiah said, determined to stack up his third-grade education against Harley's Ph.D. "Harriet Tubman was takin' three hundred slaves to freedom a hundred years before you was even born. Sojourner Truth was refusin' to leave white streetcars a hundred years before Rosa Parks. Frederick Douglass was writin' books about justice and gettin' stoned by crowds who thought he was an uppity nigger. And a lot of us in betweens was doin' all along what we thought we could. So don't act like black folk didn't do nothin' till you smart young blacks come along in the sixties. It just ain't so."

"One thing's for sure," Harley said, "your conservative churches weren't the solution, they were the problem. They let Bibles and prayer in their schools, but they wouldn't let black children in. Don't forget, Sophie spent six months at one of your evangelical colleges. She heard them talk about 'Martin Luther Coon.' Tell them, Sophie." Clarence braced himself. He knew what was coming—he'd heard the story before, though not for years. He didn't want to hear it again and especially didn't want his children to hear.

"We were watching an old black-and-white TV in the dorm lounge." Sophie's voice was reserved and hesitant, like someone having to open an old wound. "That's when the newscaster said, 'Martin Luther King has died in a Memphis hospital.' All of a sudden a bunch of the students clapped and cheered. Those white Christians celebrated when they heard Martin had been murdered. Next day I left that school, and I never looked back."

Clarence always found it easier to battle ornery Harley's anger than sweet Sophie's pain.

"You knows how sorry I is for that, Sophie girl," Obadiah said. "Breaks this old man's heart what happened that day. No excuse for it. But it wasn't the spirit of Jesus you saw, it was the spirit of the devil, and he can get admitted to any college."

Obadiah hung his head, as if groping for what to say next. "Well, family, now's not the time for such words. I thanks God for every one of you. Pray with me, will you?" He bowed his head and nearly all the family followed his lead. "Tonight, Lord, as we celebrate your Son's birthday—and our African heritage—touch the hearts of everyone in this great family. Show 'em how much you love 'em. Teach us how much we needs you. And Father, tell your son Jesus 'Happy Birthday' from Obadiah Abernathy and his kin."

Harley and Clarence went into the kitchen to get seconds on tater pie. Keisha and Celeste and two of their cousins, Marny's girls, came up to Geneva and whispered in her ear.

"The girls want to sing for us," Geneva said. The four girls stood out in the middle of the living room. With exuberant faces they looked up toward the ceiling.

"Happy birthday to you, happy birthday to you, happy birthday, dear Jesus, happy birthday to you."

Dani, Ruby, and Felicia looked on. They'd heard every story and every argument and sung along with every song. Now as the Christmas dinner faded from the portal, Dani hugged her mother and daughter tightly. They all three felt the joy of seeing their family and the pangs of missing them. They felt an incompleteness made sweet by anticipating the Great Reunion.

Dani now sensed two hands on her shoulders. She turned around. "It's you," she said. "You knew and you came." Without reservation, she and Ruby and Felicia threw open their arms to welcome him into their hug. They cried together, all four of them, until the tears ran their course into smiling and laughter, which was always the other end of tears in this country.

While keeping her arms around him, Dani loosened them just enough to lean back and look him in the eyes. She smiled broadly and said, "Happy birthday."

The children had the day off from school due to teachers' in-service, but Celeste was at afternoon kindergarten as usual. Geneva, Jonah, and Keisha sat down to lunch together. Before praying over the meal, Geneva said to the kids, "We need to pray for your father." Jonah nodded.

"What's wrong with Daddy?" Keisha asked.

"You know how he hasn't been himself since Aunt Dani and Felicia died. And now that people are saying…some bad things about him, well, he just really needs our prayers."

"What bad things are people saying about my daddy?" Keisha asked.

"I'll try to explain, honey, but it's hard. Anyway, right now could we just pray for Daddy?"

The mid-December cold became a dense choking fog on Portland's streets, swirling, clinging to the skin. The fog climbed up railings and stole into homes through window cracks, as if in Dickens's London. It tingled the spine and took the breath away not to know, even in mid-day, who might be standing in an open alley only ten feet from you.

"It's time we paid a visit to Shadow," Ollie said to Manny.

They arrived on Moffat Street at one in the afternoon. Shadow's mother came to the door. "Davey's not here now. Don't know when he be back. Comes and goes as he pleases." Her eyes looked vacant.

"All right, Mrs. Williams," Ollie said. "We just want to talk with him, that's all. We'll be back."

Ollie and Manny returned to their unmarked precinct car.

"Okay," Ollie said. "Let's check out the crack house over on Robins."

"The abandoned church?" Manny asked.

"Yeah. Gang division says Shadow spends a lot of time there."

Ollie and Manny drove the four blocks to Robins and pulled over to the curb in the low fog. They watched the building a minute but saw no activity. They got out of the car, both looking like well-worn professionals, suits wrinkled. They knocked at the door of the old church, most of its windows boarded up. No response.

"Police," Ollie said. "We want to talk with Davey Williams—Shadow."

A rapid sequence of explosions erupted from within. Splinters flew off the front of the door, one of them gouging Manny in the cheek and drawing blood. Ollie and Manny ran from the line of fire, pulling their weapons from their shoulder holsters as they ran, and ducked into a three-foot crawl space behind a dumpster.

"You okay?" Ollie reached out to his partner's bloody face, from which Manny was extracting a piece of the door. "They must think it's a drug bust. We need the SERT boys for this one."

"They'll ghost by the time we get SERT here," Manny said.

"That cell phone's just sittin' in the front seat, right by the radio," Ollie said. "I've got to get to the car. Cover me."

Just as he was about to start running, the muzzle of an automatic weapon poked out between two boards over a window of the old church. Twenty rounds flew off, making wild popping noises as they ripped into metal. The rear window of Ollie's car exploded, and both tires on the passenger side gasped out their air in unison. Ollie retreated behind the dumpster. The partners crouched next to each other, talking strategy in high-pitched tones.

"What's going on?" The loud deep voice came from behind, catching both cops by surprise. They whirled around, instinctively training their weapons on the intruder.

"Clarence? What are you doing here? Get down," Ollie said.

Clarence hunched low next to them. "I was headed home on MLK and thought I saw your car pull up by the crack house. I turned around to see what was up. Then I heard the gunfire. What's happening?"

"Just paying a little social visit to Shadow," Ollie said. "The homeboys acted like we were invading Cuba or something. Criminy. Man, they're packin' heat today!"

Ollie was bundled up thick for the cold weather, looking even more rotund than usual. Crouched down, he cut a memorable image—the Pillsbury Dough Boy in a dark-blue snowsuit. In other circumstances Clarence might have laughed.

"We need backup," Ollie said.

"What do you want me to do?" Clarence asked.

"There's a Dunkin' Donuts around the corner." Ollie pointed back toward MLK. "Go get me three or four cops."

"Very funny, Ollie."

"I just need to get to a radio or a phone," Ollie said.

"I've got my phone in the car," Clarence said. He pointed back fifty feet down the street, now wondering if he'd parked too close to the war zone.

"All right," Ollie said, speaking in machine gun staccato. "All the shooting's come from the front of the building. I can't tell if they're looking through those boarded windows on the side. If they are, I don't want to give them two targets. Both of you stay put. I'm going to run for your car, Clarence. It's unlocked, right?"

The detective half stood to get circulation back in his legs. Then he ran from behind the dumpster, his back to the crack house. Six rounds burst from the lower side window. Clarence watched in horror as Ollie flew forward, as if released from a slingshot, then lay motionless on the concrete, twelve feet away.

"Ollie!" Clarence yelled and ran toward him.

"No, Abernathy, stay down!" Manny said it too late.

Shots rang out at Clarence, and Manny opened fire on the window. He heard Clarence groan and saw him reach for his shoulder. Manny gambled, running out to Clarence, whose left cuff was already red, blood dripping down his arm from the shoulder wound.

Clarence dragged Ollie backward toward his car, his hands locked in the detective's armpits. Manny tried to lift his partner's legs to help carry the load, but Clarence was hauling the 260 pounds so quickly Manny couldn't grab hold. Clarence stared at the two bullet paths ripped through the back of Ollie's suit and shirt. One looked like a lung shot, the other appeared close to the heart. Either looked fatal; together they left little room for hope.

"Get him in the back," Manny said as he ripped open the front door and faced the crack house, establishing a shooting position behind the door.

Clarence laid Ollie on his stomach in the backseat, while Manny jumped in the front, picked up the phone, and called 911. "Emergency, Code zero. Police officer down. Need ambulance at 540 North Robins. This is Officer Manny Domast. Detective Domast. I have no access to police radio. Repeat, 540 North Robins, the crack house, the old church. Repeat, 540 North Robins. Officer down."

Manny punched in a direct call to the sergeant's desk in uniformed where he'd worked until ten months ago. By force of habit he spoke as if on radio rather than phone.

"This is Detective Manny Domast. Code zero, officer down. Detective Chandler has been shot. Need EMT. Dispatch SERT unit to 540 North Robins. Gangsters, heavily armed, firing from crack house." Clarence heard something unfamiliar in Manny's voice—panic.

"Ollie. Ollie!" Clarence begged for response, but none came. Clarence's hands fell on Ollie's back, now soaked with blood. Manny's voice faded to the background as Clarence's fingers reached to Ollie's wrist and groped for his pulse. He couldn't feel anything.

Dani watched from above, seeing fallen angels surrounding the crack house, bombarding young men with images of madness and evil. She watched the boys mindlessly loading and shooting and congratulating themselves for the pandemonium. She witnessed an ancient evil using these boys to act out his blasphemy, intoxicating them with a primordial lie he used in corporate boardrooms, on college campuses, and on the street—a false claim of dominion, the belief that they could be as God.

She watched righteous angels courageously wield their swords, fighting to regain turf that had once been theirs, twenty years ago before the inner-city church closed its doors and moved to a nicer part of town. The angelic presence had once outnumbered the demonic here. But not in recent years.

Dani watched and prayed as Ollie was shot and slammed to the ground. She watched as Clarence charged out from behind the dumpster and a bullet headed to the center of his back. She anticipated rushing to the birthing room to greet her brother. But as she watched, the sword of Clarence's guardian took on physical properties just for an instant, visible only to those who see with the eyes of eternity. The sword caught the bullet in midair, only three feet from Clarence's back, deflecting it so it only grazed his left shoulder.

The portal closing off, Dani gazed across a great gulf, seeing in the far distance a surreal world of gray—the fringes of hell. It struck her that as heaven was better than the most wonderful dream, hell was worse than the most horrible nightmare. Heaven was the city of God; hell, the trash heap of man. She did not find herself wondering how God could allow people in hell. That was obvious. It was exactly what all people, including herself, deserved. What struck her as amazing was that God could allow people in heaven.

She saw on earth people living between Eden, a world that had ended, and Jerusalem, a world that had not yet begun. As she saw the events on the city street, she understood with breathtaking clarity that earth is the walkway between two kingdoms, heaven and hell. Earth's most wondrous dreams were of heaven; its most horrible nightmares, of hell. Hell was the worst of earth multiplied a thousand times; heaven, the best of earth multiplied a million times. Earth was a place to preview both, to sample each, and to make the final unalterable choice between them.

"Heaven and hell were both at my elbows every day," she said to the Carpenter, who sat on the throne far away, yet whose undivided attention was upon her now. "Every choice on earth casts a vote for heaven or for hell. How clear it all is now. How cloudy it often was there."

Clarence had been detained only an hour in the hospital emergency room. His injury was superficial. It had drawn a lot of blood and still hurt, but they'd patched him up and let him go. He was glad Geneva was at her mom's for the day and didn't need to know till later what had happened. He'd dropped by the house to pick up a few things. Now he sat in his car three houses down and across the street from Shadow's, waiting and watching.

He saw Shadow arrive at his crib with two homies. Clarence studied Shadow. His hair was cornrowed to the back, with some nuclear waste thrown in, and over it a blue bandanna. He wore gray work gloves that sent a message, "Don't mess with me. I mean business." Shadow slapped hands with his homeboys, and then they disappeared around the corner, leaving alone the new leader of the Rollin' 60s.

Shadow sauntered up to his porch, looking at a magazine that had come in the mail, while Clarence got out of his car and approached him briskly from behind. The young man heard Clarence's footfalls on the stairs. He spun around, and his eyes dared Clarence to make the next move.

"Hey, Shadow," Clarence said. "Don't reach for your heat or you're history, you hear me?" Clarence lifted his right hand from his suit pocket, showing Shadow his Glock 17. He tilted the gun up slightly, the red light focusing on Shadow's chest, causing him to freeze. Clarence walked behind Shadow and yanked a Sig Sauer 9 mm out of the gangster's waistband.

"Chill out man," Shadow said, scoping out the hood, hoping some 60 would see what was comin' down.

"You're going to take a ride with me." Clarence forced Shadow toward the Bonneville. When they reached the car, Clarence searched him, removing a knife from inside his right sock. He shoved him into the passenger seat.

Clarence pulled out into the street, heading to MLK, where he turned south toward I-84. "You killed my friend," Clarence said, "the cop who came to see you at the crack house. Yeah, that's right, I know it was you. He just wanted to talk to you, and you killed him. And I think you killed my sister."

"No man, didn't kill her. I swear it."

"Dani Rawls. September 2. Forty rounds. My five-year-old niece too. Comin' back to you now?"

"Heard about it. Didn't do it. No reason to kill your sister, man."

"But you did pay off Gracie Miller to lie about me, didn't you?"

"No way, man. Wasn't me."

"Well, we're gonna find out. I've got a friend who has a nice little cabin twenty miles outside the city," Clarence said. "I know where he keeps the key."

The farther Clarence got outside the city, the more disoriented Shadow became. This wasn't his turf. After a forty minute drive, silent and tense, Clarence turned down a long winding dirt road, ten miles past Gresham on the way to Mount Hood.

They drove up to an isolated cabin, buried in thick Douglas firs. Clarence got out of the car and took a box from the trunk. Had this been Shadow's turf, he might have ducked and run, but he didn't know where to go and he had no allies here. Clarence opened the passenger door and herded Shadow inside with the Glock.

"Sit down." Clarence pointed to a sturdy old chair at a table, then took a tow-rope out of the box and tied Shadow's waist to the chair. "Stretch your arms out on the table."

"Whatchu doin' man? Whatchu doin' to me?"

―――――――

"Too many black folks has forgotten," Zeke said to Dani, "our struggle was never to get independence from God. It weren't a struggle to be out from under lordship. It was a struggle to be under the *right* lordship. Freedom isn't being out from under authority. Freedom is being under the right authority. God's."

Dani nodded, watching the images forming in the portal. A plantation master was speaking to a group of slaves, one of them Zeke.

"When old Ned died last week," the Sunday-suit-wearing master said, "there was some grumblin' 'cause he weren't buried in the ground. I say he was a nigger so it don't rightly matter. I can't afford to waste a perfectly good box every time a nigger dies. But to show you I's a kind Christian man, I's gonna give you materials to build your own coffins, but only on your own time. You can't go stealin' your time from me; that's breakin' God's law. Hear me?"

"Yes, Massah Willy," Zeke said. Dani then watched Zeke, bone tired from his all-day labors, using saw, hammer, and nails to build his own coffin under moonlight. After the job was done, Zeke wrote on the side of the coffin with a piece of coal.

"Not bad for an old slave that taught hisself to read and write from that old Bible I hid under my bed." Zeke read the words aloud: "Psalm 16:11—In thy presence is fullness of joy; at thy right hand there are pleasures forevermore."

Dani saw the master come up to Zeke's coffin, squinting at it. "Who wrote those words? Wipe 'em off. I should whip you for writin', and I would if I weren't so full of lovin' kindness."

"As I wiped off each word," Zeke said to Dani, "I recited it as a prayer to Elyon. See, the massahs could control our bodies, but they couldn't control our minds. My body was enslaved, but my heart was free."

Dani hugged him, then reached to his face and wiped his tears. "Ironic," she said, "how that man who claimed to believe God's Word couldn't stand to see you write it on your coffin. What was going through his mind?"

"Don't rightly know, but I expect slaves readin' and writin' reminded Massah Willy we was real men. See, they'd say we was just like cows or mules, but I never seen a cow readin' or writin'. Me writin' Scripture reminded him I was a spiritual being, God's chile. Cows and mules don't pray and sing and worship neither. Now, hearin' too much Bible reminded Massah Willy he'd has to stand before God for everything he'd done. What brings comfort to those who suffer injustice brings terror to those who commit injustice. Buildin' that coffin and writin' those words was a labor of love. For me the promise of bein' in God's presence was joy. For him the promise was terror."

"I guess we can't know exactly what he was thinking, can we?" Dani asked.

"Often I looks through the portal and wonders what people was thinkin' when they said and did things," Zeke said. "Sometimes I knows I'll be able to ask them. But I can't ask questions of Massah Willy. He just ain't here to ask."

Clarence removed Shadow's gloves and took another rope, tied it around his wrists, and pulled it across the table. Then he tied it to the table legs underneath on the opposite side so Shadow's arms were stretched tight.

"Why you doin' this?" Shadow's voice cracked.

"Ever take a lie detector test?" Clarence asked.

"No. My lawyer say not to."

"Smart man," Clarence said. "I'll have to get his name from you. Well, Shadow, today's your chance to try out the lie detector. Got me a polygraph test right here. It'll tell me when you lie. We're going to use the three strikes and you're out rule." He held up the Glock 17 in his palm. "You lie three times, I put a bullet through your head."

A look of horror shot through Shadow's eyes. He'd heard this big dude's rep, what he'd done to Georgie.

Clarence took his father's blood pressure unit out of the box, wrapped it around Shadow's right arm, and pumped it tight—too tight. Then he took out a length of clear surgical tubing he'd gotten off the shelf of a medical supply store less than two hours before. He tied it tight around Shadow's chest. Finally, Clarence plugged into the wall outlet the electrical cord running from the power supply of Jonah's induction coil. He positioned the thick metal nail-like end an inch from the crook of Shadow's left arm. Shadow's eyes got big as he looked at the imposing piece of metal.

"You lie and I'll know it. Three lies and you're dead. Got it? First question—what's your name?"

"Shadow."

Clarence moved his finger on the power supply, sitting on his lap where Shadow couldn't see it. A bright arc jumped to Shadow's arm, which involuntarily flexed upward, abruptly stopped by the tension of the rope. He screamed, eyes wide. Clarence switched the unit off.

"What's happenin', man?" Shadow shouted. "You tryin' to fry me?"

"It's just fifty thousand volts. That's strike one. Shadow isn't your real name."

"Davey. Davey Williams. Everybody call me Shadow. That don't count."

"It counts. Strike one. Now, are you a Crip or a Blood?"

"I be Crip, man. Rollin' 60s, do or die. Hate Bloods."

"Well, you're telling the truth there," Clarence said. "You deal drugs?"

"No." He tensed up, then quickly added, "Wait, yeah, sometimes."

"Almost strike two. Good thinkin', Davey. Keep telling the truth, and you'll keep breathing. Okay. Did you kill Sylvester over on MLK back in June?"

Davey's eyes looked wild. "No way, man." The arc jumped to his arm, which twitched and flexed.

"The machine knows you did it. Strike two." Clarence picked up the Glock 17 and with a dramatic flourish racked the slide to chamber a round. He thought about Tommy Lee Jones in *The Fugitive*. "One more lie and your brains are wallpaper," Clarence said. Davey let out a low moan.

"You also killed Raphael, the Woodland Park Blood." Davey looked horrified, yet he didn't deny it. "But I'm not going to give you a chance to lie about him, because next lie I have to shoot you. See, I'm not here about those boys. Now—do you know who gave Leesa Fletcher the cocaine that killed her?"

Davey looked down.

"Answer me. Now."

"Yeah. GC do it."

"She wasn't a user. He forced it on her, didn't he? And you were with him, weren't you?"

"We cased her crib. Witch's parents drove off, we come to the door. Said we wanted to talk. GC offered her coke. She wouldn't take it. He had me make up this heavy mix. I hold her down, and GC shot it in her arm. Witch went quick."

"Who told you and GC to do this?"

"Nobody." Beads of sweat stood out on his head. He watched the induction coil as if it were a rattlesnake. "I mean, everything come by envelopes. Think it's the same dude. Can't be sure. We'd do the job, money just showed up. That's all I know, man, I swear."

"Did you do the same thing with Gracie? Force an injection on her?"

"Didn't have to force Gracie. She be a base head, crack witch."

"How'd you get Gracie to OD? The truth." Clarence laid the point of the coil on the hinge of Shadow's arm.

"Gave her some pure stuff, uncut. She took it and just ghosted right out of this world."

"Who put the heroin in my coffee?"

"White? In yo' coffee? Don't know whatchu talkin' about." Clarence picked up the Glock and squeezed the handle. The red light shone in Shadow's eyes. "Tellin' the truth, man," Shadow said. "Don't know nothin' about no white or coffee."

"Did you pay Gracie to say I sexually abused her?" Silence. "Answer me!"

"No," he whispered, as if he hoped the machine might not hear him. A one-inch arc leapt to his arm. The electricity stopped for a moment, then arced again. It happened a third time. Shadow's arm showed a big strawberry splotch. Terrified, he twitched and wrestled with the rope that held down his arms. He looked up frantically at Clarence, staring into a ruby red light.

"Too bad," Clarence said. "Now I pull the trigger."

"No, wait! Don't do it, man. You can't shoot me!" Shadow saw Clarence's finger turning white on the trigger. "Okay, I gave the money to Gracie. But GC sent me to do it!"

"But whose idea was it to set me up? This is your last chance."

"Okay. Chill. Be cool, man. It was that guy from the councilman's office. The little guy."

"Gray?"

"Yeah, Gray, that's the dude. That be him."

"How do you know Gray?"

"Met him and the councilman at the gang summit last year. You know, where the bigwigs, they bring in gang leaders for a powwow."

"Has Gray ever hired GC or you before?"

"No. Wait. Yes. Couple of times.

"What did you do for him?"

"Passed out stuff."

"And?"

"Just some bitty favors, that's all. We did a few things for him, gave him some names, talked to some people. He put in a word for us with the DA on some charges. That's it."

"What would your gang think if they knew you and GC were gettin' paid by the Man?" Clarence asked. "Okay. Here we go. Did you shoot up my sister's house?"

"No way, man, no way." No arc. No shock.

"Now think carefully before you answer. Did you or GC meet with some guys from out of town that did the hit?"

Shadow looked down. "GC met a couple of dudes at the Taco Bell. Gave them an address. They got it wrong. Wasn't his fault. I didn't have nothin' to do with it—straight up, man. Don't even know who sent GC down there. He wouldn't tell me. Same guy, Gray, I guess, but don't know for sure."

Clarence took a tape recorder out of his pocket. "If I decide not to kill you, Davey, here's what I'm going to do. I'm going to take this tape recording and put it in a safe deposit box with a written record of what you've confessed to—the murders, the setup, the payoff, everything. And if anybody comes after me or my son or wife or nephew or anyone I know, then there's a detective named Manny who's going to get this. And no lawyer's going to save you. The cops will nail you for sure. So pass the word. It better be safe for my family or you're history. Got it?"

Shadow nodded. Clarence took off the surgical tubing and the blood pressure unit, then untied him roughly.

Neither said a word on the drive back to North Portland. Clarence pulled up across the street from Shadow's house. "Get out of my sight. Remember, anybody in my family gets hurt, you pay." He pushed Shadow out the passenger door, not bothering to return his Sig Sauer or his knife.

"Now, chillens, I been hearin' some talk I want to set straight. I wants you to understand not all white folks is bad. There's plenty of good ones, and don't let nobody tell you different." Obadiah spoke to his grandchildren, gathered at his request in the living room late in the afternoon. Ty sat there under protest, but Granddaddy had insisted.

"I was thirty-five when I joined the army because I wanted to serve my country. There was a private named Mike Button, from Texas. One day we was doin' field maneuvers in ninety degree heat. So we takes a break. I's standin' under a shade tree, and ol' Mike, he comes up to me and says, 'Forgot my canteen. Mind if I have a drink, Obadiah?' I reached to get my cup to pour him some water, but Mike just slaps the cup away and grabs the canteen. Then he pulls it to his mouth and takes a long draw. Well, them days whites didn't never drink from the same bottle as blacks. I knowed it weren't no accident. Mike did it on purpose. That was the beginning of a fast friendship. We wrote each other letters every Christmas until five years ago when he died. I still writes to his widow, but my hand's so shaky don't know if she can read it. One day I'm gonna see ol' Mike again because he loved Jesus and so do I. My black hand's gonna grip his white hand. And it's gonna be a strong grip then. All hell won't be able to break apart those two hands." His right eye grew heavy. He reached to it, and a big tear cascaded down his cheek.

"Tell us about the Depression, Gramps," Jonah said.

"Well, now, them were some days, I'm tellin' you. My brother Elijah, he traveled with me then. We couldn't find no work in Mississippi, so we took to ridin' the rails. We'd get off town to town, search for work all day. Most nights we was outside. We'd find some newspaper, lay it over us, and put our arms around each other jus' to keep from freezin'. Loved all my brothers and sisters, but none like ol' Elijah. And I think he'd say the same about me. One time me and 'Lijah, we was in Detroit. We was kickin' ourselves for ridin' the rail so far north, it was so cold. We was huddlin' up for the night in a back alley, and in the dark I hears someone amoanin'. So Elijah and me, we moves over to this poor man, stiff as a board. I gets on one side and Elijah on t'other, and we puts our arms around him.

"He was scared at first. Can't blame him." Obadiah laughed. "We got out of him his name was Freddy. That's the only thing he said all night. 'Frrrrrrrrreddy.'" He laughed again. "Cold as ice. But after thirty minutes of his face buried in my ol' sweater, his mouth thawed out. We gived him our last piece of bread. He needed it more than we did. 'Lijah was singin' the ol' spirituals, and another hour or so Freddy got warm enough and Elijah's lullabies put him to sleep. No one could sing like Elijah. Well, come just after dawn, Elijah sings 'Amazin' Grace.' He wakes ol' Freddy up. Of course, by then we knew Freddy was white. You should've seen the look on his face when he realized he'd spent the night as lunch meat in a Negro sandwich!"

"What did he do then, Grandpa?" Jonah asked.

"Well, he stayed right there. And we got to talkin'. When it warmed up to about forty degrees, we got up and looked for work together. Became good friends. And for almost a week ol' Freddy spent the nights in that same Negro sandwich!"

"Frrrrrrreddy," Obadiah said again, laughing so hard it took his breath away. "I hasn't told you the best part, chillens. Freddy asked us why we cared enough to keep him warm. Me and 'Lijah, we told him the reason. It was Jesus. We went our separate ways after that week, 'cause Detroit was home for him, but if we was goin' to sleep outside, me and 'Lijah preferred Mississippi!"

"What happened to Freddy?" Keisha asked.

"Don't rightly know. Never saw him again. But one thing we learned. There's two times when color don't matter. One's when you're cold and hungry. The other's when you know Jesus."

Dani looked through the portal, watching Freddy sandwiched between her daddy and Uncle Elijah. She looked as the three men said their good-byes, then was startled to see Freddy suddenly disappear. Simultaneously, in the same spot, she saw an angel appear in the invisible realm.

A look of shocked realization swept across Dani's face. "Freddy was an angel?"

"Yes," Torel said. "Some of us Elyon sends as guardians. Others he sends to test his children and to teach them lessons. Adam's race is unaware of who these are. You encountered such messengers yourself, dozens of them. Freddy tested your father and uncle, gave them an opportunity to care for a needy person in the name of Christ. They passed the test. Great reward awaits them."

"What kind of reward?"

"That is not mine to say. But it will involve the angel himself, the one they helped. And it will involve the Master, who takes personally the help given in his name to the needy, as if it were done directly to him. Those who help the needy he repays lavishly, beyond the dreams of men."

"You said I met such messengers myself. Did I pass the tests?"

"Sometimes you did, sometimes you did not. For those you did not, of course, you will receive no reward, nor will you have opportunity to earn that reward now, for earth was the land of opportunity. But you will be taken back, shown those opportunities again, so you can learn here the lessons you failed to learn then and there. As for those tests you passed, you will learn of these too. You will meet those messengers you helped. From their hands and Elyon's you will experience reward richer than I could describe. I will say no more about it now."

Clarence came in and sat next to the hospital bed. "How you feeling?" he asked.

"For a guy with a couple of broken ribs, I'm feeling pretty good. The doctor says it's blunt trauma. The force of the impact came through the body armor even though the bullets didn't. By the way," Ollie said, "thanks for bleeding all over my suit."

"With those bullet holes, your suit was a goner anyway," Clarence said. "I might just buy you a better one at the Goodwill. I thought you were history, Ollie. I really did. I thought it was your blood, not mine. I couldn't even feel a pulse. I guess my fingers were too numb from the cold. I never knew you wore body armor till Manny told me in the car. You could have saved me a lot of sweat if you'd told me."

"I usually don't wear it, but when we go into any potentially dangerous situation, it's policy for detectives to put on the armor. It's pretty lightweight these days. Saved my skin, that's for sure. Anyway, the lieutenant tells me by the time SERT got to the crack house, the homeboys had scattered out the back. We can't even prove Shadow was there. No positive ID on anybody. Can you believe it? They shoot up my car, open fire on me, ruin my shirt, wing you, and they get away with it. Shadow's out there laughin' at us right now."

"I don't think he's laughing, Ollie."

"Why's that?"

Clarence told him the story of the phony lie detector test. Ollie listened intently, raising his eyebrows and trying not to smile.

"You scare me, Abernathy. You shouldn't be doin' stuff like that." He tried to look stern. Then he said, "You really told him he'd killed me?"

"Sure. If he thought he'd killed my friend, it made it more believable that I was willing to kill him."

"You told him I was your friend?"

"Hey, maybe I exaggerated, I don't know. I've got the tape. Want to hear it?"

"I'm not sure. No matter what we try to get Shadow on, his lawyer's going to demand that tape. You might want to destroy it before it becomes trial evidence and it's too late. I better not hear it. We'll go after Shadow, all right—awfully creepy to kill those girls. Still, he's not the big fish. The marlins I want to reel in are Norcoast and Gray."

Three days after the crack house shooting, Ollie called Clarence at the *Trib*. He spoke cryptically, inviting him to go for a drive in the afternoon. "I've got a surprise for you. Somebody I want you to meet."

"Okay, give me two hours to finish my column." Clarence didn't feel like being surprised or meeting anyone, but he agreed.

Clarence disciplined himself not to open his mail until he wrote his column. He'd learned that the hard way the last few days. He read through a story on the front page of the *Tribune*: "Racist Drug Prosecutions Provoke Lawsuit." He shook his head in amazement at what the article seemed to be saying. Some of his best columns were backlashes to headlines. He started typing.

> Yesterday another lawsuit was filed by a bevy of civil rights organizations claiming that the disproportionate number of blacks prosecuted for using and dealing crack cocaine proves racial bias.
>
> I have in front of me information *not* presented in this article—the racial breakdowns of defendants for every type of drug-related offense. Did you know 63 percent of powder cocaine defendants are Hispanics? Or that most heroin prosecutions are of Asians? Or that whites constitute two-thirds of all marijuana defendants and over 85 percent of all LSD defendants, and that a disproportionate number (by 10 percent) of whites are arrested for dealing methamphetamines?
>
> In regard to this civil rights lawsuit, the question is, why are a disproportionate number of blacks being prosecuted for crack cocaine? Dare I suggest a simple and obvious answer—crack cocaine is used and sold by a disproportionate number of blacks!
>
> What's the solution to this statistical inequality? Well, we could let 95 percent of blacks who sell crack go free, just to even things up. They could go right on inflicting untold suffering on the black community. (By the way, for those who complain about longer sentences for crack dealers, ask law-abiding blacks if they want them back on the streets.) Or we could recruit more whites to sell crack so they can go to jail in equal proportion to blacks. Of course, to be consistent, we'll also need to recruit more blacks to sell meth, LSD, and powder cocaine, more Hispanics to sell heroin, and more Asians to sell crack. Equality—isn't it grand?

"Where exactly are we going?" Clarence asked as Ollie drove into Gresham, glancing down at written directions resting on his left thigh.

"You'll find out," Ollie said, wincing from his sore ribs. He navigated onto some remote back road Clarence didn't even know existed. They came to a long driveway, lined with thick trees that seemed somehow familiar even though Clarence knew he hadn't been on this road.

"Hey," Clarence pointed to the cyclone fence on his left. "We're on the other side of the Springwater Trail. That's Hugo's place, isn't it?" Just as he asked, he heard the Rottweiler barking.

Ollie drove up and parked. "Hi ya, fella," Clarence called as he got out of the car. Hugo stared at him, head tilted. An old man in a thick flannel shirt, with disheveled white hair, walked out of the dilapidated house.

"You must be the detective," the man said, looking Ollie over as if he was expecting someone more impressive. "I'm Floyd Kost." They shook hands, and Ollie introduced him to Clarence.

"Well, Floyd," Ollie asked, "is this the man?"

"Yep. No doubt about it."

"What are you talking about?" Clarence asked.

"Well," Ollie said, "I had Manny get me the names and phone numbers of the half-dozen houses nestled back near this section of the bike trail. I called each of them and asked if they remembered seeing some big lunk laying on a park bench three sheets to the wind. No luck in the first five calls. Floyd was call number six."

"Come on in," Floyd said. If Clarence had entered this room under other circumstances, one look would have convinced him the house had been robbed and the frustrated perpetrator hadn't been able to find what he was looking for. Magazines and junk mail, both opened and unopened, were strewn around the living room. Clarence sat on the edge of an old couch. He looked at the date on the sun-bleached *Reader's Digest* next to him. September 1988. Clarence had the impression they might be Floyd's first visitors since this *Reader's Digest* arrived. He looked out the window and saw Hugo. Beyond him was the bike trail. It seemed odd seeing something so familiar from an unfamiliar perspective.

"The detective tells me you call him Hugo," Floyd said, pointing at the Rottweiler. "His name's Sergeant. I've seen you feed him scraps before. Next to me, I think you're his best friend. You're the only other person who pays him any attention. I'm a hermit, I guess—lived here alone since my wife died eight years ago."

"So," Ollie said, "you can pinpoint the exact time it happened?"

"Well, sure. Peter Jennings comes on at six, and it was just before then."

"Perfect," Ollie said. "So walk us through what happened two weeks ago Wednesday."

"Well, Sergeant was barkin' up a storm, more than usual I mean. It was odd because there was no traffic on the trail, see—the weather had turned bad and it was almost dark. Finally I bundled up in my yellow raincoat, and Sergeant was pullin' on me like he was a sled dog, flyin' down that trail like a bat out of hell. I figured he'd caught the scent of a coyote or something. But we come to the bench and there was this big fellow," he pointed at Clarence. "Mr. Abernathy, was it? The detective tells me you're some big-shot reporter or something, but I don't read the newspaper anymore. Peter Jennings and Oprah and Geraldo and them tell me all I need to know. Anyways, I've seen you stretchin' out on that bench before, but I thought it was downright peculiar to see you out in the rain like that. Ol' Sergeant runs right up to you and sniffs you like you're real familiar. That's how I was sure it was you, because he treats strangers different. Anyways, he goes right up and licks your hand, then he goes to your bike pack and sniffs for the goodies. He got pretty upset when you didn't wake up. I didn't know what to do."

"What *did* you do?" Clarence asked.

"Well, I was afraid to touch you. Figured you'd just fallen asleep and if I shook you, you might jump up and attack me, like one of those crazy Vietnam vets—I saw a movie about them."

Clarence smiled and pointed to Ollie. "He's the crazy Vietnam vet. I'm just a normal guy."

Floyd eyed Ollie suspiciously, then continued. "Anyways, I just came over and saw you were breathin' fine, chest movin' up and down. And you were all bundled up in your sweatshirt and pants and a windbreaker. I'm one to mind my own business, so I just turned around and went home, got in just when Peter Jennings came on. Well, I watched local news at six-thirty, then *Jeopardy* and *Entertainment Tonight*—I'm not a big *Wheel of Fortune* fan, see—then *Seinfeld*, and by that time it was eight-thirty." Floyd stopped talking and just looked at his guests.

"And...then?" Ollie asked.

"Well, by now Sergeant was getting hoarse, poor fella. He'd just kept barking like Lassie when the farmer's trapped under a tractor. The thought kept naggin' at me that maybe you were still out there and really in trouble. See, dogs know things people don't. So I thought before the nine o'clock movie comes on, I better see if you were still out there, because if you were, I was gonna try to wake you and if I couldn't, I'd call 911. Maybe make it on that 911 television thing for saving your life, who knows?

"So, anyways, I finally went out with my flashlight, but without Sergeant this time because he was just throwin' a fit. Well, I got to the bench and you weren't there, but I thought I heard something up ahead. I walked farther toward where the trail crosses the road. I shined the flashlight just a little, didn't want you to come after me. I saw you liftin' your bike up to your car. Kind of scared me, because I could hear you talkin' to yourself. Like you had mental problems or something. Saw somethin' on *Sixty Minutes* about people like that." Floyd's voice rambled to a stop.

"What time was that?" Ollie asked.

"Well, I went out maybe fifteen or twenty minutes before the movie. Guess I probably saw him at his car ten minutes before nine."

"Yeah," Clarence said. "Yeah," he said it with more enthusiasm. "I thought I saw a light, just for a second. I turned around and it was gone. Freaked me out a little. Geneva too. I wasn't talking to myself, that was my wife. I was on the phone with her. She was kind of frantic, wanted me to keep talking to her."

"One of those new-fangled phones you don't plug in the wall, huh?" Floyd asked. "Seen those on TV."

"So, Floyd," Ollie said, "you're absolutely positive this man was the same one you saw that night? And you'd tell that to a district attorney or a judge?"

"Well, I'm 99 percent sure. But the other witness, now he was 100 percent sure."

"The other witness?" Clarence asked.

"Sergeant. Dogs know these things. He knows your scent from all the times you've stopped and petted him and given him treats—spoiled his dinner more than once, but I won't blame you for that. Yeah, Sergeant knew it was you and nobody else. I could see that. Some district attorney or judge has some doubts? I'll bring him in and show him how Sergeant reacts to strangers and then how he reacts to you. Won't be any doubt then."

"Well," Ollie said, "hopefully we won't need to subpoena Sergeant. But if we do, tell him there's a steak in it for him." He looked at Clarence, smiled, and stuck out his right hand. "Congratulations, big guy. You've got a Rottweiler for an alibi."

Two days later a sworn statement from Floyd Kost, complete with copious references to television programs and how dogs know things, was submitted to the district attorney, with a copy going to Ollie.

"What happens now?" Clarence asked.

"If they believe Floyd and Sergeant are reliable, it establishes an ironclad alibi for you—from 5:40 to 8:50. That's all you need. It proves Gracie was lying."

"But what about the witnesses who say they saw me with Gracie at the light rail and the hotel?"

"Well, your alibi proves it wasn't you. Hopefully the DA will realize they all just saw a big black man. None of those witnesses had actually seen you before. Floyd and Sergeant had. They knew what you looked like. And smelled like, in Sergeant's case. The DA's office will talk to Floyd, if they can pry him away from the tube. They'll decide from there. We'll just have to wait and see what happens."

Ollie and Manny walked the back parking lot of the Taco Bell on MLK, Ollie chomping on a Double Decker Taco Supreme. When he finished, he opened the dumpster and dropped in his trash. He got down on his hands and knees to look under and behind the old brown dumpster, its paint scratched and peeling. Then he joined Manny in studying the old wooden fence, top to bottom.

Most of the graffiti was typical, the same stuff all over North Portland—tags from various Blood and Crip sets. "What's with these?" Ollie asked, pointing to a couple of Hispanic gang tags. "This isn't Latino turf."

"Hey," Manny said. "It's Taco Bell. TB's like the Mexican embassy."

Ollie and Manny ended up studying the same piece of dark-blue graffiti. It was only five lines. The letters intersected each other, beautifully, but they were unintelligible, except the fifth line, which appeared to be a backward P-187.

Manny tried to translate, while Ollie went back inside.

"Herb, when was that back fence last painted?"

"We spray it over every couple of months to discourage all the taggin'. Let's see, I'd have a copy of the work order in my files. You want the exact date?"

"Yeah, please." Ollie eyed a stray burrito sitting on the rack.

"Help yourself," Herb said, tossing him the burrito and heading to the back room. He reappeared as Ollie took his last bite. "Last painted August 28. We're overdue. I'll have to get on it." He got Ollie a large Diet Coke.

"Thanks, Herb. Hey, hold off a little on that repaint for me, would you?" Ollie asked. He went out to his car, pulled a kit from under the seat, and took out his 35 mm Nikon along with a Polaroid. He shot a half-dozen pictures of the wall with the Polaroid, a dozen with the Nikon, most of them of the blue five-lined tag. As he and Manny drove off, Ollie picked up the phone and called gang enforcement.

"Lenny? I want the best, most experienced tagger you've got. Preferably a Crip. I've got some hieroglyphics I want him to translate."

Clarence saw the light on in Jonah's room and knocked on the door at ten-thirty in the evening. He heard a muffled voice and stuck his head into his son's room.

"What are you reading, Jonah?"

"*Huckleberry Finn.*"

"Read it aloud to me. You can work on pronunciation."

"I don't want to."

"You're a good reader. I want to hear you."

"I don't think I like this book," Jonah said.

"Why not?"

"Huck keeps trying to decide whether to turn in the runaway slave."

"Jim?"

"Yeah. Jim. He says he thinks if he turns him in he'll go to heaven, but if he helps him escape he'll go to hell. That's what his Aunt Sally and the church people told him."

"Well, they were wrong, weren't they?"

"I guess."

"Here. Let me just pick a section and you read it. Okay? I want to hear you read."

"Okay." Jonah began to read, reluctantly at first, but his voice got more and more animated as the story picked up. He read a couple pages before coming to Huck telling his aunt Sally about a steamboat accident:

"We blowed out a cylinder-head."

"Good gracious. Anyone hurt?" Aunt Sally asked.

"No'm. Killed a nigger."

"Well it's lucky, because sometimes people do get hurt."

Jonah stopped. "Daddy, why does it say that?"

"You mean nigger? That's what they called blacks in those days. Huck was just ignorant. He shouldn't have said it, but back then people just did."

"But what about Aunt Sally? What did she mean? A black person got killed, but she says it was lucky nobody got hurt."

"Well, I guess she just didn't think of black folk as people."

"But Aunt Sally was a Christian. That's what the book says. We're Christians, aren't we Daddy?"

"Yeah, Son. And many of the slaves were Christians too."

"But if she was a Christian, why would she say that?"

"Well, not everybody who claims to be a Christian is. And not everyone who is a Christian thinks the right way. Why don't you just keep reading?"

Jonah put down the book. "I don't want to read anymore."

———

"As you know," Cairo Clancy said to his congregation, "this morning our guest speaker is Pastor Ben Schaffer from First Church, just a mile and a half down the road from us. I've told you before I've been meeting weekly with Ben for nearly a year. We've talked about things that, very honestly, I've never talked about with a white brother before. I've invited him to speak in our pulpit this week, and he's invited me to their pulpit next week. Please give a warm welcome to my friend and brother, Ben Schaffer."

The two men embraced long and hard, and as the embrace lingered, the applause intensified. Clarence sat between Geneva and his father. Next to Obadiah on the other side sat Harold Haddaway.

"It's a great privilege to be in this pulpit," Pastor Schaffer said. "I can't express what my friendship with your pastor has meant to me. More about that later. I want to start with Ephesians 2:13, where God is talking about the racial divide between Jews and Gentiles. He says, 'Now in Christ Jesus you who once were far away have been brought near through the blood of Christ. For he himself is our peace, who has made the two one and has destroyed the barrier, the dividing wall of hostility.'"

"Uh-huh!"

"Say it now."

"Hallelujah."

Pastor Schaffer looked surprised but energized by the commentary from the congregation. "Folks, the biggest racial divide in history was between Jews and Gentiles. And if that barrier is broken down in Christ, so is *every* racial barrier. This passage says that because of Christ's work on the cross, we're all part of the same family. Like it or not, we share the same Daddy, and that means we're family. Now I, for one, like it. I like it very much. But it's something we have to think through because this verse tells me that if I stand at arm's length from brothers and sisters of another color, I am opposing nothing less than the finished work of Christ."

"Amen."

"Yessuh!"

"Preach it, pastor."

"God's Word tells us nations and people reap what they sow. Well, this country sowed a poisonous crop called slavery, and we're reaping the consequences even today. Look at verse 15. It says Christ's 'purpose was to create in himself one new man out of the two, thus making peace.' He has made Jew and Gentile one man, and he has made black and white one man. Now, I'm going to ask you something I've already asked my own church. I'm asking you to please forgive me for my ignorance and silence on matters of racial justice. Please forgive me for never having asked your pastor to lunch until a year ago. Please forgive me."

The congregation was suddenly quiet, at a loss, taken aback by Pastor Schaffer's directness. But one deacon sitting toward the front said, "We forgive you," and one by one people across the congregation echoed the words.

"Look at our two churches," Ben Schaffer said. "Our facilities are only a mile and a half apart. But we've been *worlds* apart, haven't we? I've been a pastor at First Church for fifteen years, and I'd never been inside this building until ten months ago. Your pastor hadn't been in our building until that same day. See, that day, after having lunch, we took each other on tours. And we met each other's staffs and some church folks, and we walked in each other's neighborhoods. And that's when Ebenezer Church became real to me—something more than just a name on a sign— a real part of the body of Christ. It's like I was the left arm becoming aware of the right arm for the first time."

"Glory."

"Well, well."

"Hallelujah."

"See, Cairo and I got to talking one day. Turns out both of us had been to huge Promise Keepers events. I'd attended one in Portland with thirty thousand men. And he'd gone up to Seattle a year later where there were sixty thousand. He told me how much it touched him to see black speakers along with the white and to see all those white men applauding blacks—not just black entertainers and athletes, but black spiritual leaders. To hear resounding applause for the idea of racial reconciliation moved him. Then he told me Promise Keepers sponsored a racial reconciliation seminar in Portland and only twenty-five men showed up, eight blacks and seventeen whites. It was a powerful time, Cairo said, but the tiny numbers reminded him how distant the dream still was. Well, both of us have been praying that we can move closer to that dream.

"I've got something more to confess to you. I'm part of a denomination that, like many others, once supported segregation. I'm ashamed to say I went to a seminary that in those days, the early sixties, didn't allow black people to attend. Over the years I've bragged about that seminary, given it credit, and there were many good things I learned there, many things I have reason to be proud of. But for its decades of practicing segregation, I only have reason to be ashamed. Racial prejudice is a contradiction to the gospel of Christ. It's heresy. So I ask you to forgive my seminary."

"My Lawd."

"Yes, we forgive."

"Glory."

"In the last number of months, God has broken my heart over this. And I'm convinced there can be no revival until we're broken about the racism that has been a cancer both in our country and our churches. It gets even closer to home. Six months ago Kathy Ward, our church historian, was doing some research for our hundredth anniversary. She discovered a piece of history that some of you at Ebenezer may not know. I certainly didn't. In its early days, at First Church colored people were allowed only in the balcony. They couldn't mix with whites on the church floor. And there were two separate drinking fountains, yes, even here in Oregon. Finally, since they were being treated like second-class citizens of God's kingdom, the black Christians left and started their own church down the road. I sure can't blame them for that. Back then the new fellowship was called Second Church. In 1920 the name was changed to Ebenezer."

Nods and grunts of realization rippled through the congregation.

"The truth is, in this country black and white Christians operate in two separate worlds. Yes, they're voluntarily separated, but separation is separation, and it hurts us and our Father who wants his children to know each other and love each other and enjoy each other's company. It's been said that eleven o'clock on Sunday morning is the most segregated hour in America. That's not just a tragedy. It's a sin. It's a sin that my ancestors are largely responsible for, and I have to take responsibility for it—if I don't, who will? It's a sin for which I repent. I'm not going to flagellate myself with guilt, because that's not going to help anybody. Just feeling guilty doesn't solve any problem. I want to be part of the solution.

"Cairo and I have talked and dreamed of having church services together in the future. Maybe joint church dinners and retreats and youth group gatherings, maybe start a ball team together. I know you don't need patrons, you need partners. So do we. Who knows, maybe our two churches will someday merge into one again. Now I know black churches aren't waiting anxiously to get involved with whites, because usually blacks end up getting swallowed up. Well, I don't want it to be that way. I don't know if our churches could ever be one church, but I do know we can be one in the Spirit, and I'd sure like to build the kind of relationship where we could explore the possibilities together."

"Hallelujah."

"You said it, preacher."

"Now, I also believe that true repentance involves more than saying you're sorry. When Jacob wanted to reconcile with Esau after stealing his birthright, he knew he had to give his brother justice. He did an act of restitution that owned up to the original sin. Only then were he and his brother reconciled. Zaccheus said to Jesus he would repay four times over what he had stolen from people. That was restitution. I suppose some people think all the social programs and affirmative action are restitution, but it seems to me they haven't worked very well. Maybe that's because they were attempts to throw money at a problem and get rid of guilt feelings without personal involvement. I think there's been half-hearted attempts to solve problems without true repentance. And Cairo reminds me that sometimes there's been true repentance by whites, but some blacks have refused to forgive them."

"Uh-huh."

"That's true, pastor."

"Restitution should have come along with emancipation, but it never happened. And now in America we're generations removed from slavery and thirty years past segregation. It's hard to know how to do restitution or even who to do it to. It certainly can't be paternalism or just handing out money to ease consciences. That doesn't overcome bitterness, it just fosters it. Cairo and I really believe what we need to do is learn to work side by side as brothers and sisters in Christ to help each other deal with the problems we're facing in our city."

"Amen to that."

"Maybe that's going to stretch all our comfort zones, but it sure needs to happen.

I heard a brother from India say that Hindus and Muslims in his country can duplicate every miracle, every sign and wonder produced by Christianity, except one—the miracle of unity between people of different races. I want to be part of that miracle. Maybe you noticed your pastor is wearing sandals this morning. We've got a basin up here because I've asked to do something. Frankly, it's something I've never done before. And I can't say I'm all that comfortable, but I know it's right. I'm going to do a foot washing. I'm doing this because Cairo Clancy is my brother, I love him, and I want to be his servant. I hope and pray this will be a symbol of a newfound commitment to brotherhood between our two churches."

Pastor Clancy sat in a chair in front of the basin. Pastor Schaffer got down on his knees and took off Clancy's sandals. He picked up a nearby towel and soaked it in the basin. Then, as a breathless silence descended on the church, he began washing Clancy's feet. Clarence heard sounds around him, sounds of purses opening and tissues being used. Sounds of crying. As Pastor Schaffer looked up at him, Pastor Clancy whispered words heard only by the two men and an audience invisible to the congregation.

After a few unforgettable minutes, Pastor Schaffer stood and addressed the church once again. "You've probably noticed some white faces up in the front row you've never seen before. Well, these are the members of our church board. We've met with your church board three times now, and our men have asked if they could come wash the feet of your board members."

Seven black men and seven white men walked up from the front rows, while ushers lined up seven chairs on the platform and brought in seven more basins. The Ebenezer deacon board sat down. The seven deacons from First Church removed the shoes and socks of those from Ebenezer Church and washed and dried their feet. Some of the men sitting and some kneeling seemed to enjoy this, some seemed less comfortable, but all seemed determined and purposeful.

Clarence sensed something powerful in the congregation, something he'd never felt before. He heard around him moaning and weeping and cries of hallelujah. He saw in his father's eyes that other-worldly look. Geneva squeezed Clarence's hand, and he met her eyes. He saw her tears, then reached up to wipe his own. He thought about Jake.

The choir sang, "Red and yellow, black and white, they are precious in his sight, Jesus loves the little children of the world." The people joined in, the words never having meant so much.

"One more thing I want to tell you today, my brothers and sisters," Pastor Schaffer said. "Our board has talked a great deal in the past four months about our church name. Very frankly, we've grown uncomfortable with the name First Church. In many cities across the country there are churches of the same denomination named First Baptist and Second Baptist, First Presbyterian and Second Presbyterian, or whatever. Often the First Church is white, the Second Church black, and usually the reason for the Second Church forming was they weren't welcome in the First. Well, we've come to think that our name might imply some sense of superiority that is untrue and unchristian. So we appointed a committee to come up with some alternative names. And in our hundredth anniversary celebration next month, we'll be officially changing our name to Church of all Nations. Our prayer is that we will truly become that. We look forward to having Cairo Clancy, your pastor and my dear friend, bring God's Word to our church next Sunday. Thank you for opening your hearts to me today."

Rousing applause permeated the building; hallelujahs and amens rippled across the congregation. Many people stood to their feet and raised their hands in worship. Pastor Clancy hugged his friend on the platform and closed the service in prayer, his voice breaking repeatedly.

When church was dismissed, Clarence looked at his father and Harold Haddaway. He saw tears and wonder in both men's eyes. They sat speechless, not moving.

"Now, wasn't that somethin'?" Obadiah finally said.

"Never seen nothin' like that," Harold said. "Never thought I'd live to see nothin' like that."

Clarence looked at Harold, suddenly noticing his burgundy tie. It was unique, covered with identical black-lined designs of various sizes, like irregular triangles, with the lines on the right side thicker than on the left, making it seem as though the tie was leaning off center.

"Harold, where'd did you get that tie?" Clarence asked.

"Well, you won't believe it, but it was throwed away. Some of my nicest things come from them garbage cans I clean out. I find boxes of donuts they just toss, as if you can't eat 'em after five o'clock. This tie's good as new even though it was in Mr. Norcoast's trash. Nobody'd know it even belonged to nobody else unless they read the lettering."

"Lettering?"

Harold turned the tie so Clarence could see the back side. Sewn into it with white thread were the words, "From Leesa, With Love."

"Harold," Clarence said, "can I borrow this tie from you?"

"Well, sure." Harold laughed. "I'd give you the shirt off my back. I reckon I can give you the tie off my neck!" Loosening his tie, Harold smiled at Obadiah, as if to say, "You never can tell what crazy things these young people are going to think of next."

"Here," Clarence said, taking off his blue-and-black Wembly tie and handing it to Harold. "This is for your trouble."

"Well, I'll be," Harold said. "Never have swapped ties in church. I reckon this is a day for things that's never happened in church before!"

Many warriors did battle in the North Portland church, as a great cloud of witnesses watched and interceded concerning the events they saw through the portal. Evil spirits whispered accusations to some at the service, brought up old grievances to others, and suggested to still others all this was unnecessary or token or meaningless. The fallen angels said to some the white pastor hadn't gone nearly far enough and to others he'd gone too far. The foot washing was a cheap throwaway gesture, a slap in the face. How dare he act as though white offenses were forgivable? How dare he imply centuries of exploitation could be neutralized by a mere apology? To the whites at the service, the whispers were different—how dare he lay guilt at the feet of whites who'd done no wrong? Hundreds of attacks, each tailor-made to the prejudices of the individual, were launched during and after the church service. Some of them succeeded. Most did not.

Invisible forces of righteousness fought valiantly against the evil warriors, and they prevailed. The Spirit of the living God touched hearts. The warriors-on-leave in heaven and the graduated saints of God looked at the church service with awe and approval. At points during the service they burst into spontaneous applause. Near the end of the service when Ebenezer Church stood up and clapped, a deafening noise shook the far reaches of the cosmos, a sound so great that all heaven seemed to tremble. The sound came from the throne. It was the sound of two disfigured hands, omnipotent hands, meeting each other. For despite all the injustice and hatred on earth, at this moment, in this place, among these people gathered in the Shadowlands at a church called Ebenezer, injustice lay broken, hate trodden down, truth uplifted, and love celebrated. It was a foretaste of a day and place yet to come. The audience of One shook the cosmos with the applause of heaven.

"Hi, Harley."

"Clarence?" Harley's voice halted. "Is Daddy okay?"

"Sure. He's fine." Clarence felt embarrassed he called Harley so infrequently that his brother had assumed it must be an emergency.

"What's happening, bro?"

"You remember the kente cloth you wore at the family get-together at your place a few months ago? The brown-and-yellow cloth?"

"Sure. What about it?"

"There was a design on it. It's like a triangle with one side thicker than the others. Does that design mean anything?"

"Sure does. It's an African symbol for masculinity."

"Okay, thanks, Harley. That's all I needed."

Clarence showed the tie to Ollie.

"When I did the background check on Leesa," Ollie said, "I talked to a few of her close friends." He rummaged through his notes, found a number, and made a call.

"Megan? Detective Ollie Chandler. I spoke to you about Leesa before, remember? Listen, I've got another question. Did you ever know about Leesa making a tie?"

"Yeah, sure. We were in the same home ec class. We had a sewing unit. Mrs. Green made all of us sew a tie. Most of us gave them to our boyfriends or our dads. Mrs. Green had some materials somebody donated. Leesa picked an African design, I think."

"Do you know who she made it for?"

"No," Megan said. "I assumed it was for her father. But she said it wasn't. I figured maybe her brother or uncle or somebody, but I couldn't understand why she wouldn't tell me. It wasn't like her. She used to tell me everything. Anyway, she really got into that tie. Even worked on it after school."

Clarence walked into Norcoast's office complex for their appointment. He caught a cold glance from Jean the administrator and a warm one from Sheila the receptionist. Norcoast invited Clarence into his private office, then grabbed a quick phone call. Clarence reached in his briefcase and removed something. While Norcoast talked and looked out the window, Clarence replaced one eight-by-ten picture on the wall with another. He put the original in his briefcase and closed it. Just then, Norcoast hung up.

"I see you have a picture of the two of us," Clarence said, pointing at the wall. Norcoast's brow furrowed. He walked over to inspect the picture.

"Let's see," Clarence said, "that was at the Fight Crime rally, wasn't it? Nice tie you had on. Don't think I've seen it on you since. Actually, I've never seen a tie quite like that."

Norcoast stared at the picture in disbelief.

"Where'd you buy it? The tie, I mean?"

"Oh, I don't know," the councilman said weakly. "Maybe Nordstrom."

"Doesn't look like any tie I ever saw at Nordstrom. What are those little designs?" Clarence pointed. The tie's designs appeared much more prominent than Norcoast remembered them. They jumped off the picture.

"And look, the tie's flipped over here at the bottom," Clarence said. "Something's written on it. You can just barely read it. Let's see, what does it say? 'From... somebody with love.' What's that name?"

Norcoast grabbed the picture off the wall. The muscles beneath his left cheek twitched.

"Hey," Clarence said, "I'd love to get a copy of that picture. Can I just borrow it and make a copy on your machine?"

"Not right now. Maybe later." Norcoast clutched the picture frame to his chest. "Listen, Clarence, something's come up. I can't meet right now. I'm very sorry. I'll call you later." Norcoast ushered him out of the office, quickly closing the door behind him.

Clarence walked out to the reception area and sat down in a chair off to the side. He sat there five minutes. Suddenly the fire alarm went off. Norcoast stuck his head out his door and said to Sheila, "No problem. Don't worry, just a little accident. I've opened my window. No damage."

A little smoke wafted out of Norcoast's office. He turned from Sheila and saw Clarence. He quickly closed the door, harder than he intended.

Ollie stood behind Taco Bell and sized up the short wiry young man dressed in an oversized plaid Pendleton shirt. The dark-blue shirt with its long sleeves seemed to envelop him more like a bedsheet than a shirt. Around his neck, hanging outside the flannel shirt, was a black woven cross necklace.

"So, Eddie," Ollie said, "you're a Four Trey East Coast Crip, that right?"

"Yeeeah. Four Treys forever, man."

The gang detectives had told Ollie that Eddie Pearl, street name Picasso, was probably the most experienced graffiti artist—or vandal, depending on one's perspective—in Portland. He'd come up from L.A. two years ago.

"So, what do you make of this, Picasso?" Ollie pointed to the five lines of blue text on the fence. Manny hovered over the boy's shoulder as if he were an eager apprentice.

Eddie studied the composition like a master analyzing the work of another master. He looked at it from a distance, then up close. Moments of appreciation were punctuated by moments of puzzlement.

"This be fresh, 'round here anyway."

"You mean this particular tag?" Ollie asked.

"Yeah, tag's def. Nobody around here do this tag. But I'm sayin' the style's fresh."

"Style?" Ollie asked.

"Every tagger gots his own style. Like the shape of the letters, you know? Some circles, some squares, some diamonds. Some loopy, some wavy. Printed blocks, those easiest to read."

"Some of these letters are completely separated," Ollie said, pointing to the tag. "And some barely touch each other, but a lot of them overlap so much I can't distinguish the letters."

"Yeeeah. Hardest be overlapping wavy ones, like these. Problem is, it be a mixed style. See," he pointed at another piece of graffiti, "this one's Four Seven Kerby Bloc. It all be backwards, so it's easy to read. But this one just has *some* letters backwards, and they overlap. It's wavy. Not a full diamond style. Called half-diamond. See the diamond above the i?"

"Barely," Ollie said. "Can you translate this piece? In the last line, *P* is for Piru, right? Blood."

"Yeah. And you know 187."

"Section 187, California penal code for murder. He's a Blood killer, so obviously he's a Crip. But that's all I can make of it."

Picasso nodded. "Next line up is Sur." It looked to Ollie like a single broad letter, but as Picasso ran his finger over it, he could now see a backward *S* with a *u* and *r* stemming from it.

"What's Sur mean?" Ollie asked.

"Southern California," Manny said. "It's Spanish. You see it all the time in Latino graffiti."

"That's right. I forgot. But…the guy isn't Hispanic, right?"

"No way, man," Picasso said. "He be Crip. Lot of Crips and Bloods pick up stuff from Spic gangs." He looked at Manny tentatively after saying Spic.

"How about the third line?" Ollie asked, looking at several letters hopelessly overwritten.

Picasso stared long and hard. "Okay, got it. *HC. C's* backwards over the *H.*" As soon as he lined it out with his finger, it became obvious, like one of those images you can't see until someone tells you how to look at it, and then you can't understand why you didn't see it all along.

"So what's HC?" Ollie asked.

"Hoover Crip," Picasso said. "He be a Hoover."

Ollie wrote it down.

"Second line be Nine Deuce."

"Of course," Ollie said, seeing the backward two over a forward nine. "A Nine Deuce Hoover." Ollie and Manny exchanged glances. Both were thinking of the SERT officer's HK53 lost in the L.A. battle with Five Nine Hoovers, an allied set.

"Okay, what's the first line?" Ollie knew what was often on first lines. If he were a praying man, he'd have been praying right now.

"First line be OG, Original Gangster. Then be his name."

"His name? What is it?"

"Sniper. No, wait." Picasso ran his finger over the jumbled mass of lines. "Spider. Name be Spider."

"Spider," Ollie said with a gleam in his eye, writing it down. "Now, Eddie, there aren't any Nine Deuce Hoovers in Portland yet, are there?"

"No way, man. He be from L.A. No doubt."

"So...you're telling me the guy who wrote this is an L.A. Nine Deuce Hoover who goes by Spider?"

"That what the soldier say. Art don't lie," Picasso said.

"Eddie," Ollie slapped the master on the back, "it's all the Taco Bell you can eat, on me."

Clarence lay sleepless again. Unfortunately, he couldn't sleep without shutting his eyes. And every night lately, lying in wait for him on the back of his eyelids was a boy whose name he didn't even know.

Fourteen-year-old Clarence was hanging with Rock and Shorty in Cabrini Green. His father didn't think they were good influences and told him to stay away from them. So he had to steal away to meet them over by the junkyard, which made the friendship as tasty as forbidden cookies.

"Say, you look at that? Tell me what you see." Shorty's voice was young and cocky.

"See a white boy," Rock said in a steady measured tone, "wanderin' where he don't belong."

Young Clarence followed their gaze. Sure enough, there was a white boy, maybe twelve or thirteen, riding his beat-up red Schwinn, a confused and frightened look on his face.

"I think honky's wantin' to get licked," Rock said.

Before Clarence could say anything, Rock and Shorty were running full out toward the intruder. Clarence looked behind him. No one else was around. He looked ahead to see his friends overtaking the white boy. In an instant he made the decision that would haunt him. He ran to join them. They'd just rough up this boy, teach him a lesson.

The boy lay frozen on the ground. Rock was stretched out on top of him, letting spit dribble from his mouth onto the boy's forehead.

"What's wrong, white boy? Too scared to fight the niggas?"

Rock punched him hard in the side. Shorty let loose with a short kick. Unsatisfied with that, he moved back like a field goal kicker and ran at him five feet before he let one loose. Clarence thought he heard ribs crack. The boy choked and grimaced.

After a few more blows, the shellacking got too boring for Rock. He looked at Shorty and Clarence and said, "Let's take him to the dump."

When Rock told him he'd urinate in his mouth if he didn't, the boy marched in front of them like a prisoner of war in the Bataan Death March.

Run, white boy, Clarence kept saying inside himself. He'd seen Rock and Shorty feisty before, but never so mean. He kept thinking what his daddy would say.

He knew he should go home or talk the other boys out of it or get help. But he couldn't do that. These were his friends. This was their neighborhood. White people owned the whole rest of the world. They needed to stay away from here. Besides, Clarence had vivid memories of black boys who'd wandered into white neighborhoods. They'd come back beaten and cut up, sometimes with broken bones, hanging their heads like little whipped dogs, recounting stories of humiliation. Maybe this white boy had beaten up black boys. Maybe he deserved this.

By now the boy was sobbing, and he couldn't get out a full sentence. He kept saying, "I'm sorry," and "I just got lost." Rock came to an old bedspring propped up on its side. He tucked the boys hands into the big coils, and then tucked his feet in too. The boy couldn't pull out his hands without cutting them. His eyes were full of fear.

Rock punched him in the groin like he'd seen in some movie. When the boy cried harder, Shorty got in on it, taking a swing at his face. Clarence felt as though he was going to throw up. He saw his friends looking at him. It was his turn. Suddenly he did something he would rehearse every day for the rest of his life. He jumped up a little and kicked the boy in the stomach. A karate kick, like on TV. Then he jumped and kicked him again. He yelled obscenities at him, any one of which his daddy would have whipped him for and washed out his mouth with a bar of soap.

But Daddy wasn't there. No one was watching. Just he and his friends. Clarence kicked the boy first because he was probably a rich kid, although his bike wasn't very fancy and his clothes looked kind of poor. He kicked him because he was probably a nigger-hater, although he hadn't called them any names. He kicked him again just because he was white. And that much was undeniable. He kicked him again because they wouldn't let his daddy play in the majors. Again, because his favorite aunt had died after she'd been turned away from a white hospital in Mississippi. Another kick because he had to live in the poor part of town while this boy probably lived in a big mansion with colored house help. He kicked him again even harder, because of those Mississippi white boys who pummeled him and Dani with the broken beer bottles, leaving scars on both of them. He kicked him again because the Mississippi cops tortured his daddy. He kicked him again because his mama cried when they wouldn't let her family into the restaurant. And again and again and again for a hundred other reasons, running out of kicks long before he ran out of reasons.

Clarence didn't know how many times he kicked the boy, but he heard Shorty and Rock calling his name. "Clarence! Stop it, man. He's out. He's out. Okay?" It was Shorty, looking scared, glancing every which way and saying, "Let's get out of here."

Rock and Shorty took off. Clarence was left alone, collapsed now from exhaustion and dizziness. He looked at the boy just hanging there limp, a red spot in his side growing bigger and bigger on his stained white T-shirt. He looked like a religious icon, as if he'd been crucified. The longer Clarence looked at him, the more he saw just a boy. Clarence started crying. He gently touched the boy's face.

"Come on, white boy. Wake up, now. We was just scarin' you, that's all."

He carefully removed the boy's hands from their bedspring prison, cutting them a little as he pulled them out. It bothered him about the cuts. The boy was dead weight. Clarence lowered him to the ground, clearing away junk so he could lie flat. He bent over the still body. He thought he saw the boy barely breathing, or maybe it was just the wind rustling his T-shirt. It scared him worse than anything had ever scared him. The boy lay beside an old refrigerator, butted up against the bedspring.

Suddenly Clarence stuck his head in the refrigerator and vomited. He looked every direction. He took off running and didn't stop until he came to his house. He knew he should tell someone, get help for the boy, but he was afraid of what they'd do to him, maybe put him in jail for the rest of his life.

To this day he didn't know who the boy was and whether he'd lived or died. For the last thirty years, he'd relived those memories while taking a bike ride or seeing a bedspring or opening a refrigerator. Frequently the boy came to him at night when there was nothing to keep him away.

Clarence had always been taught God could forgive everything anybody ever did. All his life, he'd believed this was true for every sin he could think of. Every sin except one.

CHAPTER

A man's skin color is no more a predictor of his character than is his height, his blood type, or his cholesterol level. Racists exist in every group in America. Some whites who pride themselves on not being prejudiced against blacks can't stand Hispanics. Some blacks who pride themselves on not being prejudiced against whites can't stand Asians. So it goes. Prejudices aren't a function of skin color but of small minds among men of all colors.

Clarence's telephone rang at the *Trib*, answered by the machine. "Mr. Abernathy? This is Ranae Maddox, assistant district attorney."

Clarence picked up the phone immediately.

"Yes, Mr. Abernathy, I just wanted to inform you that I followed up on the affidavit filed by Floyd Kost. I interviewed him personally, and even though he's a bit quirky, I'm convinced he's telling the truth. Based on that, and on the fact that our case hinged primarily on Gracie Miller, our office is dropping all charges against you."

"You mean," Clarence spoke the words slowly, "I won't have to go to court?"

"No, you won't. And we're sorry for any inconvenience this may have caused you."

Inconvenience? Try humiliation.

Clarence called Geneva, just getting out the news before he choked up.

"I'm so happy, baby," Geneva said. "Let's go out with Janet and Jake tonight and celebrate!"

"That sounds great," Clarence said. "And thanks again for...standing by me."

"I'd never consider doing anything else. I think there was something about that in our wedding vows, wasn't there? I love you, baby. Get home early as you can, okay?"

Clarence felt deeply thankful for the news and for Geneva. But it'd been so long since he'd thanked God for anything, he felt as if he'd forgotten how.

Clarence went to Dan Ferrent's desk, taking with him the names and numbers of Ranae Maddox, Floyd Kost, and Ollie Chandler. He wanted to make sure Ferrent wrote a follow-up story on him being exonerated. Even so, he knew many people would never read the follow-up and some who did wouldn't believe his alibi. They'd always believe he'd gotten away with something.

The reputation he'd worked so hard to build was no longer under attack. Yet it would never be fully restored. Like the tide coming in and out, his emotions vacillated between relief and resentment.

Clarence walked the sidewalk, bundled up heavily. All the shops were decorated for Christmas, and holiday music permeated the city. He entered the Justice Center, realizing for the first time in his life he no longer felt nervous being in a building filled with cops.

"You really think the killers would leave graffiti behind Taco Bell?" Clarence asked Ollie. "Wouldn't that be incredibly stupid?"

"To us, maybe," Ollie said. "But the key to solving crimes is to stop thinking like yourself and start thinking like the perps. Put yourself in their place. Assume they're from a heavy gang area in California, where graffiti is everywhere. It gets crossed out and painted over all the time. They rarely get caught, and even when they are, they never get more than a hand slap. You always keep spray paints in the car. Tagging becomes a habit, like spitting on the sidewalk. A guy does it long enough, he does it without thinking. Taco Bell's a mile from what's going to be the crime scene. They figure nobody'd recognize their tag up here. And even if they did, so what? Where's the link between a Taco Bell wall and a shooting a mile away? What's the risk?"

"More than they realized, obviously," Clarence said.

"These guys don't think about tomorrow," Ollie said. "They think about the moment. They're killing a few hours by a Taco Bell dumpster in a strange city, waiting for witnesses to get off the streets and the intended victim to be in her bedroom. They can't do drugs, because they want to be sure they're sharp for the hit. They get bored, real bored and jittery. So one of them pops the trunk, takes out a spray can, and lays a little tag on the wall. Why not?"

"So what can you do with Picasso's translation?" Clarence asked.

"I've linked in with the L.A. gang cops and their network. I've asked for any info they've got on a Nine Deuce Hoover named Spider. They'll come up with something."

"But a Nine Deuce? Didn't you say the HK53 was taken from the cop by Five Nine Hoovers?"

"I figure the Five Nines thought the cops would put the pressure on them, look for any excuse to search their cribs, even their safe houses. In fact, one of the L.A. cops told me that's exactly what they did. Never found the HK. My guess is whoever nabbed it originally either sold it or traded it for drugs or weapons. And who would they deal with? An ally. The Hoover sets are confederates. A lot of Five Nines and Nine Deuces are going to know each other."

Ollie's phone rang. He answered, "Ho Ho Ho…Homicide. Ollie." Clarence rolled his eyes.

"Oh, hello lieutenant," Ollie said, feet suddenly shifting as though he needed to go to the restroom. "Yes, sir. I agree, sir. No, it certainly wasn't appropriate. I'll get the word out to the guys. Yes, public image is important, sir. We have to keep that in mind. No, not a laughing matter. I should say not, sir. Yes, sir, I'll take care of that for you. Merry Christmas." He put down the phone.

"How do they put up with you?" Clarence asked.

"I don't know," Ollie said. "Sometimes I can hardly put up with myself. But then I take a good look in the mirror and remember what an amazingly handsome fellow I am."

"I have a suggestion, Ollie."

"What's that?"

"Get a new mirror."

———

He had no name here. No new name, not even the old names. Not Raymond Taylor. Certainly not Gangster Cool. There was nothing to distinguish him from anyone else. In fact, there was no one else at all. He felt like an isolated piece of litter blown helter-skelter on the fringes of a dump. His existence was arbitrary and pointless now. The rep he'd worked so hard for meant nothing here. It was no longer a reward, but a punishment.

"Where is everyone?" He heard the loneliness in his voice, and it frightened him. Where were his homeboys who'd died—Buzzard and Stick Man and Li'l Capone and the rest? He knew they must be here, but where? What about his brother and cousin and grandma? They too had left the old world, but he knew instinctively they were not in this one. They'd chosen a different path while in the land of choice and opportunity. He would never see any of them again.

I'll never be able to touch Mama, he thought, locked behind the invisible bars of eternity, serving an eternal life sentence. He could see occasional images, catch fleeting glimpses across the divide to the old world. He could see his mama's tears, her grief, but also her faith in God. Seeing it did not comfort him.

Segregation ruled here. Not just segregation of the races, but each man eternally segregated from all others. Isolation. Loneliness. Parched and barren souls living alone, separate, unable to communicate with each other.

"What have I done?" Raymond clenched his teeth, hurting the inside of his mouth. He waited for the taste of blood. There was none. He was a bloodless man, able to feel pain but not able to destroy the body he'd be trapped in forever.

There was no family here, no gang, no hood, no turf. Only unending nothingness. Uninterrupted boredom. The tedium crushed him already, though he'd been here only a short time. What would a million years of tedium do to him?

At first he tried to rehearse his deeds that earned him his rep, his Original Gangster status. He now saw them for what they were—pathetic self-indulgent attempts to get recognition. No one was here to listen. Even if they had been, they wouldn't be impressed, only absorbed in their own self-centered misery. The things he'd done and boasted of he was now being punished for. He had planted on earth. He was reaping the harvest here.

"What's that?" Raymond cried out, cowering in fear at a horrid sight. He caught just a glimpse of a face, a terrifying face. Somehow he knew that in another place that same face brought endless delight, for it smiled with approval on its inhabitants. But here it brought unmitigated terror. He who by his presence made heaven heaven, by his absence made hell hell. And yet, somehow he must not be entirely absent, for his untempered holiness was the burning fire, his attributes the sulfuric air that caused Raymond to choke. In a moment of insight, he realized the Holy One had actually been here once, been here for him so he would not have to be here. Yet here he was.

He saw the haunting image of the Terrible One, and caught a glimpse of ugly scars on his hands and feet. They repulsed him. The thought of touching those hands or being touched by them appalled him.

He remembered Pastor Henley's assurances in Los Angeles that everyone was good by nature, that people were not responsible for the bad things they did, that the fire and brimstone message of the Bible literalists was not from God, not Christlike. "God is love, and therefore there is no hell," the pastor had said. "You and I would not send people to hell, and God is surely more merciful than we." The words had sounded so reassuring. But it was all a lie, Raymond realized with startling clarity.

He cried out for the rocks to fall upon him, to obliterate him. But there were no rocks here. There was nothing here. Nothing familiar. Nothing comforting. Nothing at all.

Here there was no opportunity to kill, no opportunity to die, no one to dare or boast to, no one to jive or hustle or con or steal from, no one to seduce, no one to tell stories to, no loved one to embrace. He no longer had dominion. Perhaps he'd never had it, perhaps his sense of control over turf had been an illusion all along. Perhaps true dominion belonged only to one, the Terrible One with the monstrous scars.

His mother had warned him. She'd told him about Jesus. He'd never really rejected him, not in words anyway. When his life was in danger, he'd even prayed to God. But he'd never followed through on his vows made in moments of crisis, never accepted God's one and only provision for his rescue.

There was no color here, no texture, no richness, no variety. The utter isolation meant there could be no culture here. Hell was not multi-cultural. It was non-cultural.

Across the far reaches of this nothingness, others he'd known on earth now existed as shriveled souls, husks of humanity. On one of these desert islands of misery, a pathetic nameless man once known as Pastor Henley engaged in an unceasing litany of telling God that hell was a violation of his love, that he had been a man of God, that he had preached a message of love and acceptance, and God had no right to keep him here.

The smell was horrible. Raymond's stomach turned in revulsion. It was as if he were immersed in hot excrement, the sewage of sin and self. It was putrid. He wanted to vomit, but could not. He was held captive to the moment before relief. There could be no relief here. Only endless self-preoccupation, self-hatred, self-everything, and therefore nothing. Self stripped of its one reference point, the God of the universe, and therefore stripped of its worth, stripped of its humanity. The vomit continued to build within, but it could never be released.

Was hell God's fury exploding upon him? Or was it his own fury imploding within him? He felt himself shrinking, the ever-narrowing man. In heaven, he somehow knew, his brother Jesse was the ever-broadening man. Jesse had been right. Raymond had been wrong.

"Too late. It's too late!" he cried, hoping the words would travel far enough to be heard by some other soul, someone else to join the company misery loves. No.

There was unlimited misery here. But there was no company.

The fires of blame and excuses and rationalizations and justifications scorched him. He experienced the corroded metallic taste of life without God. No, not life. Mere existence, stripped of purpose. No work here. What he would give to be able to perform even the most menial task, even to flip a burger. It would give some semblance of meaning. No rest here. How he longed to sleep. No rules here. A structureless hell in which there was no hierarchy, no baby gangsters, no lieutenants, no generals. All eternal wannabes without hope of advancement.

"I had a choice!" he screamed at himself in rage and horror. Why had he chosen what any sane man would not? Why would he live forever, paying for his sin, when there was one who had already paid for it? The utter insanity of sin gripped his soul. The Governor's pardon had been offered repeatedly, every year and every day and every hour of his life on earth. Now it was too late to receive it. Eternal condemnation. No reprieve. No hope. Eternal regret. Everlasting stagnation. Unending despair.

His circle of influence had shrunk to nothing. His life had gone into eclipse for all eternity, erased as if it were no more than a stray pencil mark. He had no turf, no dominion. Those he'd ridiculed as church-going wimps, he knew now, would reign over the universe, participating joyously in the one true dominion.

"I should have listened," he yelled, hearing not even an echo. "I should have listened to Mama and Jesse and Pastor Clancy."

He heard a horrible nightmare of a scream. It sounded like a crazed animal crying out in agony as it is riddled by the lead of a shotgun. Terrified, he realized the bloodcurdling scream was his own. More horrible still, he realized no one else would ever hear it.

Clarence answered his home phone during dinner. "Good news," Ollie said. "We've got a DNA match with Gracie's envelope."

"Norcoast or Gray?"

"Can't talk about it over the phone. Let's save it for tomorrow. I'll be out most of the day. How about four o'clock tomorrow afternoon?"

"Ollie, you can't string me out like this. Can't you just give me the bottom line?"

"No can do." Ollie sounded like a man who enjoyed holding the cards.

"Okay." Clarence sighed. "Jake told me you could be a pain in the neck, Ollie. Well, he didn't tell me the half of it. I'll be there at four."

Clarence, Obadiah, and Geneva attended the evening community meeting at Mount Olivet Church. The neighborhood association chairman, Rod Houck, took the floor and pointed to a table. "We've got some handouts for you related to discouraging drugs and promoting abstinence. There's also a sign-up sheet for a new twenty-four-hour hot line and prayer chain through the churches."

"Amen" and "Hallelujah" surfaced among the nodding heads, reminding Clarence that here, in contrast to meetings he'd attended in the suburbs, a religious consciousness spilled over openly into community affairs.

"First, the bad news," Rod said. "I'm reading from this yellow sheet called Gang Trends. It gives us predictions based on statistics over the past years. It says, 'Gangs will become more violent, using military weapons and killing more police officers. They will continue to use and exploit juvenile members to commit crimes due to the more lenient juvenile justice system. They will continue to fund their crimes through expanded drug trafficking. Female gang members will increase. More gang members will become career criminals—less will outgrow or escape gangs. Some gangs will evolve into organized crime groups. Jails will be overcrowded with gang members, and gang assault on jail personnel will increase. Due to budget restraints, some jurisdictions will be forced to limit their efforts to prosecute hard-core gang members for the most serious and violent crimes. The crime level will outstrip the community's ability to deal with it—courts will be gridlocked with gang cases. Probation officers and parole agent caseloads will increase to the point where supervision of gang members will become superficial and meaningless.'"

Groans surfaced across the auditorium.

"Now I know that's a tough way to start," Rod said, "but maybe if we realize what we're up against, it'll motivate us to do whatever we can. It may sound hopeless, but I'm convinced we can turn this thing around. We can't turn it around by ourselves; we need each other. Well, this is a community meeting. Who wants to speak up?"

"I say the gang problem is only as big as we let it be." It was Frank, Clarence and Geneva's next-door neighbor. "Everybody these days is sayin' what we need in this country is more tolerance. I say what we need is *less* tolerance. We've tolerated all this gang foolishness, and now it's killin' us. Me, I think my New Year's resolution is going to be less tolerance!"

Laughter and applause.

Jami Lyn Weber from Atkins Street stood up. "Well, here's one thing we *can* do. You all know Stoney's is the store that sells most the ball caps and T-shirts in our hood, including most the gang stuff. Stoney's takes drug money to sew on Crip killer and Blood killer insignias as if they were school mascots. I've bought gifts there for years, and so have most of us. Well, last week I told them they weren't getting my business anymore until they stop working for gangs. They just pushed me off. So I'm asking you, how about a boycott, Dr. King style? They won't listen to me, but they'd *have* to listen to all of us or they'd go broke."

Lots of handclapping and amens.

"Dr. King used to say," Jami Lyn continued, "if a man has to choose between parting with his prejudices and parting with his money, usually he'll part with his prejudices. So how many of you will agree to boycott Stoney's until they stop the gang stuff?" Almost every hand in the room went up. "All right, then. Call Stoney's, drop by and explain, or send them a letter. I happen to have their address and phone number right here." She held up a half sheet of paper, handwritten and photocopied. "I'll pass these out, and you pass them on to all your neighbors."

"That's a good start, Jami Lyn," Rod said. "Who's next?"

"How about we do the same thing at Boyd's Music?" a man asked. "You listen to that gangsta rap they sell? If I took the words from those songs and said them to a girl on the street, I could be arrested. But the boys listen to this stuff all the time, callin' girls these terrible names and treatin' 'em like dirt. You think it doesn't make them disrespect women?"

"Same with Smitty's Video," a woman added. "They carry all this sex and violence crud, and our kids end up watching it. Now I know the main responsibility is ours as parents, but we can sure reduce the temptations by cleaning up these stores. How about a boycott on Smitty's too?"

"I'll pass around a sheet of paper," Rod Houck said. "Sign it if you want to tell Stoney's and Boyd's and Smitty's they've got to get rid of their garbage if they want our business. We're on a roll. Who else?"

Jay Fielding, principal at Jefferson, walked up front and took the microphone, his wife Debbie beside him.

"Debbie and I have been talking and praying about this. Let me put it real simply—we lose the next generation and we've lost our country. These kids need a bigger cause. Instead of doin' battle against each other, they need to do battle against evil, gangs, drugs, selfishness. And not just against something, *for* something. For God. For family. For country. For their children and grandchildren. We can't let them run wild—that's giving up on them. We've got to set limits. Can't let them stay out to all hours unsupervised on the street. What happens on the street, 90 percent of it, is bad. We can't let them wear gang clothes. And we've got to take charge when it comes to their friends. When I was growin' up, my parents always had veto power when it came to my friends. I say we've got to reclaim our children."

The clapping began, and several people stood to their feet. Then everyone stood, applauding both the man and his words.

"No offense to the principal," one man said, "but some of you know a group of us have been working on starting a charter school. Now I've always been a supporter of public schools, but I think things have gotten out of control and we need a fresh start—a place where kids are taught to respect teachers and each other, a place that's safe, where there's no drugs and weapons, where learning is *cool* instead of lame.

Now they've got these schools in some parts of the country and they're so popular, black folk are getting on the waiting list the week their child is born."

"Just want you to know," Jay Fielding stood back up and said, "I'm all in favor of anything that helps our children. If a charter school does that, God bless your efforts—and maybe it'll help give us leverage to reform our public schools too. I say, go for it." Heavy applause.

"Now, I'm going to read you a few more statistics," Rod Houck said, "that reinforce the importance of everything you've been saying. Listen to this. African Americans are 12 percent of the population, but 44 percent of all homicide victims in America. Nearly 95 percent of black homicides are committed by other blacks. Half of all children born with AIDS are black. Our infant mortality rate is twice as high, not counting abortions, which are also twice as high. Our unemployment rate is twice as high. Two out of three black children are born out of wedlock, three times the national average. Black children are four times more likely to live in poverty, six times more likely to be on public assistance. A man living in Harlem is less likely to reach age sixty-five than a man living in Bangladesh. But here's the one that most hits home to me. In the ten largest cities in America, the high school dropout rate for black males is 72 percent."

A united groan rose from the room.

Reverend Clancy took the floor again. "There's something else we need in the city, and I say without it *everything* else will fail. We need the church of Jesus Christ."

Amens and hallelujahs shot up from everywhere.

"Jesus didn't say the gates of hell wouldn't prevail against the Democratic Party or the Republican Party or the NAACP or schools or drug rehab centers or recreational programs. He did say the gates of hell wouldn't prevail against his church. Now I say the churches have dropped the ball. We used to be the center of the community. Well, some of our churches are trying to be that again. There's a couple of churches in the suburbs partnering with us. We're taking kids to parks, museums, the beach, the mountains, on camping trips. We're getting them into summer camps. We've got some classes to teach you to communicate with your children, to talk with them about their futures and drugs and sex and standing up for what's right. Brother Jim from Teen Challenge sent over some information on helping kids off drugs and evangelizing and discipling them in the process. Now I want Brother Don Frasier to tell us what Bridge Ministries is doing."

"Well, we've got some lofty plans," Don said. "Mel Renfro's developing a top-notch recreational facility. We're starting a family counseling center and organizing clerical support for our smaller churches. After-school tutoring programs. An African American Christian arts and entertainment center. A vocational teaching center. A coffee house. A Christian bookstore. A rehabilitation center for social offenders. Eventually we want a K-12 Christian school. We've already started our mentoring program where men work with boys and women with girls. We know all this is ambitious. We're going to need lots of help. But we believe God is big enough to bring us that help."

"Amen."

"Yes, Lord. Do it, Father."

"There's some great things going on in inner cities around this country," Clancy said, "and we can do them here too. Church-sponsored thrift stores, where folks get good clothes at great prices and people learn to work. Low-cost health clinics, law offices, classes to help people get their GEDs, volunteer tutoring, Crisis Pregnancy Centers, Big Brother programs, job hot lines. There's two churches in the suburbs that have started feeding us info on job openings. But all these programs won't matter unless we come back to truth, a moral foundation for families and communities to live by. We've got to unleash the truth on the streets, shine some light in the darkness. The heart has to change. Not just the outside, but the inside, and then the outside will follow. These kids don't just need to be taught math and to put down needles and guns. They need Jesus. Without Jesus our cities are doomed, and so's our whole country. In 1900 less than 10 percent of the world lived in cities. Now it's 50 percent. If the church doesn't claim the cities, it's going to lose the country and the world."

"Amen."

"You said it, preacher."

"These kids have strong loyalties," Clancy said, "but to the wrong things, the wrong people. You turn that loyalty toward Jesus and you'll see somethin'. You make them see their enemy's Satan. Show them their family's the family of God, their turf is God's kingdom. Help them build their rep as followers of Christ. Teach them Jesus is worth livin' and dyin' for, and you'll see things happen like this city's never seen."

"Glory."

Clarence stood up, his voice its own built-in microphone. "I've lived in this neighborhood less than three months, so I'm no expert. But I know this. One of the things we've got to do is take on the drug dealers. If a man breaks into my house and points a gun at my children, I'm gonna take him down." Clarence spoke with the fervor of a preacher. "Well, that's just what the drug dealers have done. They've broken into our neighborhoods, and they've pointed the gun of crack cocaine at our children. We've got to take them down before they take our children down."

The room erupted in applause. It startled Clarence. He didn't remember the last time he'd felt his voice had been so well received.

Rod Houck took the mike again. "Most of you know a group of us have been working on Neighborhood Watch Patrols. You've seen these orange hats, right?" He put one on his head. "Well, to get one of these cool hats, all you have to do is sign up. We go in groups of five. We just carry flashlights and walk around. Hang around the drug dealers and the hookers, drive away business just by being there. We write down license numbers of the johns and drug buyers. Sometimes we take pictures. We see people casin' out a house or hangin' in the shadows, we scare 'em off. We tell the young kids to get home before we call their parents."

"Isn't that dangerous?" a voice asked from the back.

"How much more dangerous can it get?" Rod asked. "Actually with five of us in a group we haven't gotten pushed around or shot at once yet. I heard about this woman down in L.A., South Central. She's got one block; they call it Mama's Block. She gets out there with a broom in the morning. She sweeps stuff up, tosses the garbage, harasses the drug dealers. She has this slogan—'Not on this block.' It's working. And we can do it here, block by block."

This went on for another hour. Afterward people stood and talked and shared their vision with fervor and excitement.

When Clarence escorted Geneva and Daddy onto the street, he saw in the moonlight leafless trees, too few of them—stark, barren, lifeless. This part of the city wasn't upbeat yuppie flower boutiques and espresso bars, but cold merciless pavement. Under the streetlights, the asphalt looked bleak, gray, and colorless, like hardened layers of addiction, abandoned enterprise, crime, and hopelessness.

As Clarence walked, still hearing the voices spreading out from the church back into the neighborhoods, block by block, he stopped and pointed out to Geneva and Obadiah the oddest thing with his flashlight, right there on the side of the street. First, one strand of grass, then another, then a few inches away a whole patch of grass, living and vibrant, growing up right through the asphalt, breaking it apart, threatening to take over. The patch of grass grew stronger the more territory it claimed, becoming more entrenched by the day. How could these living blades of grass grow up through what appeared an impenetrable surface in an inner-city winter? Yet here they were, doing exactly that.

Before meeting with Ollie, Clarence popped two Advils. He hadn't slept again. The boy in Cabrini Green wouldn't let him sleep.

"Your evidence gathering was a nice piece of work," Ollie said to Clarence, "for a journalist."

"Thanks. I think."

"The DNA in the envelope's saliva matches perfectly the DNA in the tissues you gave me. And the gum to boot."

"Carson Gray?"

"Yep. He's our man. Of course, Norcoast is probably in on it too, but the trail leads right to Gray at least. He made the payoffs. Probably didn't hand deliver them, of course. Too smart for that. Bet he never thought licking an envelope would nail him."

"So what happens now?" Clarence asked.

"Well, unfortunately we can't hang him just for sticking gum under his desk. There's no law against being tacky or Gray would have been arrested years ago. All we can prove is that a girl who died of a drug overdose had some money she kept in an envelope that had once been licked by Carson Gray. It makes a connection, it gives us a little leverage, but it doesn't give us enough for a murder charge, not even close. But at least it tells us we should put the bead on Gray."

"So," Clarence said, "Carson Gray *was* behind Gracie's attempt to frame me. That fits with what Shadow said."

"On Gracie, yeah, but what about Leesa? Don't forget the fax was on Norcoast's computer. Why wouldn't Gray use his own computer? But if Shadow's telling the truth, Gray called for the hit on Gracie. If he did that, he was capable of calling the hit on Leesa that killed Dani and Felicia. In any case, Carson Gray stinks more than this lousy sweatshirt and these disgusting tissues." He handed Clarence a very worn and gamey brown paper bag. "I think it's time we paid a visit to Reggie Norcoast."

"Hello, Clarence...Detective Chandler." Norcoast smiled warmly, extending his hand to Clarence. "I'm so glad you've been cleared." He looked uneasy when Clarence didn't offer his hand in return.

"Councilman," Ollie said, "I'll get right to the point. What if I told you Leesa Fletcher died of a drug overdose?"

"Leesa? But...I thought it was heart failure. She had a disease, didn't she?"

"It was heart failure all right. Take enough cocaine and any heart will fail."

Ollie and Clarence both studied Norcoast, trying to detect if this was old news to him.

"Something else you should be aware of, Councilman. We know you had sex with her."

Norcoast sat quietly, measuring his response. "That's not true. And you can't prove anything."

"What if I told you Leesa kept a diary?" Ollie asked. "And that it says you had sex with her?"

Clarence stared at the nervous twitch of Norcoast's left cheek.

"There must be some mistake. I mean, she was my daughter's friend, close to our family. Maybe she was just using her imagination. Adolescent girls do that sometimes, you know." Norcoast wiped away a bead of sweat.

"What if I told you," Ollie said, "that when she died she was carrying a baby?"

Norcoast flushed, his facial expressions wavering between anger and fear. He said nothing.

"And what if I told you," Ollie said, "that you were the father?"

"You can't possibly know that," Norcoast said.

"Apparently you aren't aware, Councilman, that when an autopsy is done and the woman is pregnant, they always do a DNA test on the baby in case paternity becomes an issue, for instance as a homicide motive. So we have the baby's DNA. All you have to do is submit to DNA testing and you can prove the child wasn't yours. It's that simple. What do you say, Mr. Norcoast? We can all go down together to the lab, and you can give the blood sample so you can clear your name on the spot. Or I can even have someone come here right now and take the sample. That way we'll know conclusively if there's a DNA match. How about I just make a call and order a medical tech?" He reached for the phone on Norcoast's desk. The councilman put his hand on the phone, holding it down.

"No. I need to talk to my attorney."

"All right, you do that," Ollie said. "But I've got some other things we need to discuss. Like the fax you sent to Matthew Harper."

"Harper? What fax?"

"This one." Ollie handed him the fax. Norcoast looked at the words: "Harper: Counting on you to take care of the job. Make it soon."

"What job?" Norcoast asked.

"We thought you might know," Ollie said, "since you're the one who sent the fax."

"Me? When? I don't remember sending a fax like that, to Harper or anyone else. If I did...I don't remember."

"It was composed on your computer and sent to Harper from your fax machine on August 29."

"How do you know that?"

"It's my business to know things," Ollie said. "Four days after you told Harper to take care of the job, two Los Angeles gang members he hired came up to murder Leesa Fletcher. But instead of hitting her house, on 920 North Jack Street, they hit Dani Abernathy Rawls's place on 920 Jackson Street."

"What are you saying, detective? You can't possibly be accusing me of attempted murder."

"Not *attempted* murder, Councilman," Ollie said. "Murder."

"This is outrageous," Norcoast said. "It's not true. You can't prove anything. It just didn't happen. Please...do you know what a false accusation like this could do to my reputation?"

Ollie and Clarence looked at each other. "Yeah," Ollie said. "I'd say we both have a pretty good idea what false accusations can do to reputations. Now I don't know how much of what you're telling us is true, Councilman—probably not much—but your relationship with Leesa is enough to end your career. So you might want to consider cooperating with us. We have proof Carson Gray made payoffs to people for dirty tricks, including Gracie Miller, who set up Clarence. And we can also link him to Gracie's murder."

"Carson? I don't believe it. He's tough, sure, but he'd never do anything like that. And he'd certainly never put me at risk. I trust him. He's too loyal. No way. I'm going to talk to our attorney."

"Good idea," Ollie said. "But you might consider getting a different attorney than Mr. Gray's. And tell both of them to cancel their vacation plans. They're going to be real busy."

———————

"I didn't know Leesa kept a diary," Clarence said to Ollie as they walked out the door.

"She didn't," Ollie said.

"But you told Norcoast—"

"You weren't listening. I never said she kept a diary."

"And what about the DNA? Can you really prove whether Norcoast was the father? How come you never mentioned that? I didn't know they ran a DNA test on the unborn child."

"They didn't. I never said they did. I said, 'Apparently you're not aware' they do. Well, the reason he's probably not aware of them doing a DNA test on unborn babies is because, unless the death is suspect, they don't. But none of that really matters. Because now we don't *need* a DNA test, do we?"

———————

Clarence went to bed that night, telling himself he finally had reason to sleep through the night. But being cleared of the charges, seeing the investigation progress, experiencing the encouragement of the church service and the community meeting—none of it was enough. None of it brought back Dani and Felicia. None of it brought back his tarnished reputation. None of it gave him confidence that justice would ever be meted out to the killers. Norcoast and Gray and Harper, and maybe the shooters too, would be protected by layers of lawyers having civil discussions and making backroom deals. He couldn't stand the idea. His thirst for justice was becoming insatiable. He felt little hope justice would ever be satisfied by a corrupt and incompetent legal system.

———————

Ollie flew into LAX four hours after getting the call that LAPD had found a Nine Deuce Hoover named Spider who currently drove a tricked-out blue Mercedes.

When he arrived at his old precinct, LAPD Lieutenant Tucker escorted Ollie into a dark, empty observation room with a view through a two-way mirror into a holding room. Ollie studied the young man seated alone in the room. He appeared to be in his early twenties. He wore a black Raiders jacket. Hanging out from under it was a knit shirt buttoned to the top, draping down a foot over his creased Levi's. He wore Air Jordans with Crip-blue shoelaces, unlaced and dangling. His hair had a fresh fade cut, a highly styled flattop with geometric designs etched into the sides.

"That's Spider," Lieutenant Tucker said. "More a.k.a.s than you can shake a stick at, but the fingerprints tell us the real name's Earl Banks. Here's his rap sheet."

Ollie looked over both pages and whistled. "What's he doing walkin' the streets? Sorry," Ollie said, seeing the pained look in the lieutenant's eyes. "I know I'm asking the wrong guy. I really appreciate your cooperation."

"We're on the same team, detective. I'd do this for you anyway, but the possibility you could link us to the cop killer who stole the weapon makes me feel even more hospitable." He gestured at the window. "He's all yours. Let me know if we can help. Think I'll stay and watch you work awhile."

"No problem." Ollie smiled, welcoming the chance to perform for an audience. He walked out in the hallway and down to the holding room. He stepped in and made himself at home in the chair across the table from the contemptuous gaze of Spider.

"Hey, Spider, what's happening?"

Spider wasn't talking.

"How's the Mercedes runnin'? Like it better than that dumpy old Lexus you traded in?"

No response.

"I'm down here from Oregon just to see you, Earl. Nice part of the country, Oregon, isn't it?"

"Never been there."

"Really? Never stolen a license plate from Woodburn? Never hung out at a Taco Bell on Martin Luther King? Never met with Gangster Cool of the Portland Rollin' 60s? Never wear a red sweatshirt so you'd look like a Blood instead of a Crip? Never pulled over for speeding by a cop in Southern Oregon on your way down to Sacramento where you got your Mercedes?"

"Never."

"What's with the false IDs, Spider? Robert Rose and Jerome Rice? You and your buddy assumed the identities of dead guys. How come?"

Spider shrugged.

"We know where you were midnight September 2—920 Jackson Street. You thought it was Jack Street, didn't you? Well the sign had been graffitied, and you got the wrong street. You shot the wrong people. You killed an innocent woman and a five-year-old girl. Nobody's happy with you, Spider. I think they're all turning on you. You shot up a Crip family. Took all that money from the guy that hired you, but you wasted the wrong people."

Spider stared at him blankly.

"What if I told you we found the license plate you stole, the one you tossed over to the side of the road near Salem?"

Nothing.

"What if I told you your fingerprints are on that license plate?" Spider's eyes darted.

"Or that your prints are on a disassembled part of the murder weapon we found?"

Ollie studied his eyes, looking for uncertainty. He thought he saw some.

"Tell you what, Spider. Let me get you a soda or something. Does a Pepsi sound good?"

Spider nodded, looking at Ollie with surprise, as if he wasn't used to this kind of treatment. Ollie went to the door and called out to the hallway. "Hey, bring Earl a Pepsi, would you? And maybe a donut or something." In a few minutes a Pepsi and donut showed up at the door, and Ollie set them down on a small table in front of Spider.

"Here. Relax. I'll be right back."

Ollie returned a few minutes later carrying a boom box. "I know you've been cooped up in here for a while. Thought you could use some tunes. Go ahead, choose your favorite station."

Spider flipped the knob, found some music incomprehensible to Ollie, and turned it up loud. Ollie reached for the volume and turned it down.

"You can rock out on it later. Right now let's keep it at background level, okay?" Ollie smiled. He took a packet of colored markers out of his briefcase and chose a dark blue. He went to an erasable wallboard and started writing. First line: "Fingerprints on license and murder weapon." Next line: "Positive ID on Lexus and Mercedes." Next line: "Testimony of Medford police officer."

"Now, I'll throw in a few more. I haven't got the results of the print they took of your shoes a couple hours ago, but I'm betting it's a perfect match with the shoe print at the murder scene. Wear size eight and a half Air Jordans, don't you?" He wrote, "Matching footprint."

"And then we have a convenience store owner who saw you come to the door, saw your face close up and even saw the gun in your car because you had the door open. Remember the store you went to, the one that was closed, before you went to Taco Bell? He was looking out the shades." Ollie wrote "Positive ID from: store owner, Taco Bell manager, eyewitness at the scene."

"Whatchu mean, at the scene?"

"We've got you from every angle. A witness saw you screeching away from the murder scene. Even know the guy that paid you thirty-five thousand, give or take a few bucks, in Sacramento. Matthew Harper. Ring a bell? Now, Spider, lots of guys have had their lights put out for half the evidence we've got against you. What we've got so far could earn you, oh, about seven to ten years on the electric chair."

Spider unconsciously wrung his hands and glanced side to side.

"Just one more thing, some friendly advice. I guess you know the weapon you used in Portland was the same one stolen from an L.A. cop in a street battle last spring. And of course, LAPD figures whoever had the rifle—that would be you—also killed the cop. If I were you, I'd talk to *me* since I'm an amiable Oregon cop and all the fresh air up there makes us generally nicer than L.A. cops. I'll be headed home before your lawyer gets here. If you don't talk to me, once I leave, you're in the hands of LAPD. And I can't vouch for them being nice—especially since they think you're a cop killer."

Ollie turned his back on Spider for a moment and looked toward the mirror, winking at the lieutenant he assumed was still on the other side. He turned back toward Spider.

"I'll let you think about it, Earl. Anything I can get you? More Pepsi?"

Spider shook his head. Ollie started to go out the door, packet of markers still in his hand. He turned around. "I know it's got to be boring in here. I'll leave you these." He tossed Spider the markers, noting he caught them in his left hand.

"Don't draw on the walls, but feel free to use the boards up there." Ollie pointed to the erasable wallboard he'd used, and a blank one next to it. "Make yourself comfortable. I'll check back with you one more time. In case you want to talk with me before LAPD takes over."

CHAPTER

41

Lieutenant Tucker took Ollie across the street to a sandwich shop. "It's official," Tucker said. "Spider's footprint's a positive match with the copy of the cast you brought us. Just like you said it'd be. Still no lead on Robert Rose's real ID. Thought it'd be easy to nail him—assumed he'd be Spider's close friend, but looks like he's not even in the same set. Maybe that was deliberate, so if one got caught the other wouldn't go down with him. Sure wish we could get Spider to cough up his name."

Tucker handed Ollie a family Christmas photo. "This is Rob Tallon, the SWAT officer who was killed—the one whose HK53 was stolen." Ollie's eyes went to

Tallon's wife and three children. They appeared an idyllic family, whose lives, Ollie knew without asking, had been shattered.

"We've passed out dozens of these photos. A lot of us keep them at our desks next to our own family pictures. Reminds us Rob's killer is still out there. Here, you can keep this one."

"Sure hope Spider leads us to him," Ollie said, carefully putting the picture inside his suit pocket. "Speaking of which, we better get back. You can't hold Spider much longer before attorneys storm the precinct. And I want to see if he's done any artwork."

They went back to the dimly lit observation room, where a man in plainclothes with a notepad in front of him peered into the holding room.

"Detective Chandler," Lieutenant Tucker said, "this is Greg Suminski, our resident handwriting expert, the one I told you about." Ollie shook his hand, then looked in on Spider. To his delight, he saw a number of scribblings on the board. Spider was just now finishing off the last line in a five-line composition. He was writing with his left hand.

Ollie pointed at the photo sitting in front of Suminski, an eight-by-ten of graffiti on the Taco Bell fence. "Okay," Ollie said, "was this written by the same guy?"

Suminski looked down, then held the photo up in front of him, juxtaposed to the board. His eyes went back and forth methodically, checking every letter of every line.

"Absolutely," he finally said. "No doubt."

"You're saying," Ollie mouthed it slowly, "you'd testify in court that these were written by the same guy? So Spider would have *had* to be in Portland, less than a mile from the murder scene?"

"The guy in that room who just wrote on that board is the author of *this* tag," Suminski said, pointing to the photograph. "Count on it. But you better get in there before he erases it. You'll need a decent photo for a courtroom blow-up."

Ollie went to Spider with a uniformed officer, bringing him another Pepsi and escorting him and the boom box to another interrogation room. Then Ollie returned to the original room with his camera to take some pictures of Spider's handiwork. He asked the lieutenant if an LAPD photographer could take some as backups, which he did.

When he finished taking the pictures, Ollie decided to reward himself. He went in search of a jelly donut.

———

Ollie and Spider met back in the original interrogation room, where the temperature had been turned up to 78 degrees at Ollie's request.

"I need to take off soon, Spider, but I've got something you should hear first.

What if I told you your guy in Sacramento, Matthew Harper, is selling you out? What if he says he hired you just to make a delivery and you did the murder completely on your own?"

"He don't say that." Spider tried to sound certain.

"How do you think we found you if Harper didn't give us Rafer Thomas?"

Spider looked around nervously, unable to answer.

"And Rafer Thomas will be the next to turn on you. He won't be willing to go down as an accessory to murder. He'll deal. How do you think we found out where you live if Rafer didn't tell us?"

Spider wiped his forehead.

"Then there's your driver for the Portland hit, a.k.a. Robert Rose. What if I told you we met with him an hour ago and he wants to cut a deal? Suppose he's willing to testify you were the shooter, so you'll fry and he won't. Suppose he says it was all your doing, that you told him the two of you were just goin' up there to do a couple of burglaries, that he never knew you intended to shoot anyone until you did it?"

"He say that, he be a liar."

"I'm afraid there's a lot you don't know about this soldier—not your Road Dog, is he? Goes by all kinds of a.k.a.s. He sure fooled you, Spider. Bet you a hundred you didn't even know his real name's Jimmy Tennesen, did you? You probably know him as Michael Bock."

Spider's eyes got big. "Sailor's name not be Michael or Jimmy. It be Allen."

"Allen Jones?" Ollie smiled knowingly. "Yeah, that's another one he uses."

"Not Jones. Ivester."

"Ivester, yeah, he goes by that one too." Ollie turned and winked at the two-way mirror. Allen Ivester, a.k.a. Sailor. Pay dirt.

"Thing is, it looks really bad for you, Spider. You're the one we can positively ID, the one the witnesses saw, the shooter. And since it was your gun, LAPD knows you killed that cop in April."

"Didn't even have that piece in April." Spider's voice trembled.

"Only one way to prove that," Ollie said. "You'd have to tell me who did have it."

Spider said nothing.

"Okay, Earl, if you're done talking with me, I'll head off now. You can take this up with LAPD." Ollie walked to the door and opened it, then turned around and said, "I wish you luck."

"Wait," Spider blurted out. "Monk have the piece. Got it from Monk."

"Who's Monk?"

"He Nine Deuce. Traded him for it." Ollie thought he heard a noise from the adjacent room, like a muffled cheer.

After a few more minutes, the well ran dry.

"I think they'll be bringing charges against you, Earl," Ollie said. "Better talk to your lawyer. Just knock on the door and ask one of the officers. They'll take you out to make the phone call."

Ollie walked out, heading to the observation room doorway twenty feet away. Lieutenant Tucker and a gang detective stepped out into the hall to greet him. Tucker smiled broadly and gave Ollie a high five.

"Monk! Nice work, Ollie! And Spider's driver was...Allen Ivester. Brilliant! The dominoes are falling."

"I can't believe you got him to finger Monk," the gang detective said. "I know him. He's minister of defense for the Nine Deuces. We thought he was in that gunfight, but we couldn't prove it. This is just the break we needed."

"As we speak," Lieutenant Tucker said to Ollie, "one crew's going to find Allen Ivester and another's going to arrest Monk on suspicion of murdering Officer Tallon. We owe you big for this one, Ollie!"

———

The faint pneumatic sigh of the oil furnace expressed its bewilderment as to whether it was supposed to come on again after having been off so short a time.

Clarence lay shivering in the waterbed, reaching through the darkness blindly toward the dial to turn it up another notch. He pulled over his feet the Green Bay Packer stadium blanket he'd put on top of the covers. This was Geneva's job, freezing on a winter night. But she lay there under her two extra comforters, sleeping soundly. How many nights without sleep would this make for him? He'd lost track. He felt punchy and disoriented, tossing and turning like a rotisserie minus the heat.

He couldn't remember the boy on the bike coming to him so many nights in a row. He couldn't remember ever feeling there was so little purpose in going to work in the mornings. He couldn't remember it ever being so dark and cold.

———

"Wait a minute," Clarence said to Ollie, after Chandler recounted to him and Manny his adventures in L.A. "I didn't know you got Spider's prints off the license plate. And the gun? You never even told me part of the gun was found."

"There *weren't* any clear prints on the plate, unfortunately," Ollie said. "It was out in the weather too long. I never told you I said there were prints, did I Manny?"

"No." Manny smiled. "You just told us you said, 'What *if* I told you we found your prints on the plate?'"

"Same with the HK53," Ollie said. "We never found the gun, and I never said we did. Since they didn't object to the car search in Medford, I knew they'd ditched it. No time or place to deal it after the hit. I figured they disassembled it and disposed of it piece by piece—that's what I would have done. I gambled Spider would buy we wouldn't know that unless we'd really found a piece."

Clarence looked at Ollie. "You've played some poker along the way, haven't you?"

"Comes with the territory. Got a message from Lieutenant Tucker saying they arrested Allen Ivester last night. But I'm not optimistic about either of our Crips handing over Harper. They probably see him as someone who can help them behind the scenes, but only if they don't betray him. We'll try to get Harper from this side, through Gray and Norcoast. See if we can turn them against Harper and Harper against them, Harper against Spider, Spider against Harper, Ivester against Spider, Spider against Ivester. And throw in Rafer Thomas too, he's a wild card. If they think the ship's goin' down, pretty soon they're fighting for the life rafts. We'll see. I tell you, Clarence, you would have been really impressed with LAPD."

Clarence was expressionless.

"Very professional, very helpful," Ollie said.

"Yeah," Clarence said, rubbing his red eyes, "I suppose they're cooperative when the victim's one of their own."

"You mean when a cop is killed? Or when they're after a black man who killed a white cop. Is *that* what you're thinking?"

Clarence didn't respond. Ollie reached into his briefcase and took out a picture of a husband and wife and two daughters and a son, ranging from ages four to nine. It was a beautiful family, in front of a fireplace at Christmas time.

"Who are they?" Clarence asked.

"That's Officer Tallon," Ollie said. "He was the murdered SWAT officer, the one they took the HK53 from."

"You never told me he was black," Clarence said.

"I didn't know he was black until they gave me this picture. But it really doesn't matter." Ollie looked at him. "Does it?"

"No," Clarence said, his throat dry. "It really doesn't."

"If it means anything—and apparently it does—Lieutenant Tucker's black too," Ollie said. "Those guys were pros. Start to finish."

"Ollie's been full of himself since he got back from L.A.," Manny said to Clarence. "He's even harder to live with than usual."

"Hey, don't either of you guys mess with me today," Ollie said. He picked up a long black leather case leaning on his desk. "I'm carrying heavy metal, packin' major heat. I checked out this HK53 from the department for a few days. Taking it home tonight."

"Why?" Clarence asked.

"I do it every once in a while when there's some loose ends. Sometimes just living with a piece of evidence or a weapon, just having it around, triggers something I haven't thought of. Maybe I'll lean it on my nightstand and it'll whisper secrets to me in the night."

"Maybe I better call your wife and warn her," Manny said.

The low gray sky seemed as hard and impenetrable as it was dark and foreboding. Winter's long bony fingers gripped the city, having already stripped bare the trees, leaving everything a lackluster gray. Clarence Abernathy scraped just enough ice from his windshield to allow him to see straight ahead, but not up or down or to the side. He didn't care.

Clarence found himself longing for the past, nostalgic even for Mississippi. Geneva kept telling him he should just be grateful the charges against him had been dropped. But they'd been unjust charges, and his reputation would suffer from that injustice the rest of his life. How good could he feel about that? Having lost his reputation, he now cared less about trying to uphold it than he ever had. It would be like guarding the jewels after they'd already been stolen. What did it matter what he did any more? How much worse could people think of him?

He didn't share Ollie's jubilation at the progress in the case made down in L.A. Sure, Spider would probably go to jail eventually, provided he faced the right judge and jury and his lawyer wasn't too good. Shadow might go down too. But Clarence seriously doubted those who pulled the strings and set up the murder would be put away. Harper would come up with some angle, and Norcoast and Gray would worm their way into lesser charges. Even if Ollie could come through with his mountain of circumstantial evidence, would it be enough? How much of Clarence's own amateur sleuthing, right down to the tissues from Gray's garbage can, would prove inadmissible? On finding corners had been cut, would some liberal judge drop the charges entirely?

How many men had weaseled their way out from under evidence that should have nailed them dead to rights? Men such as Norcoast and Gray and their high-priced Ivy League lawyers always had some technicality, some way of getting off the hook. They were above the system, like the politicians and cops in old Mississippi. In the end, Clarence told himself, they would get off—but Dani and Felicia would still be dead. There would be no justice. It gnawed at him like a nagging ulcer. It produced ever bigger and darker clouds in his mind, each new cynical thought seeding them with rain.

Clarence's sleeplessness and fatigue were compounded by severe blood-sugar swings. He hadn't told Geneva, not wanting to worry her. He felt on the edge, tired of playing games, tired of waiting for justice that would never come.

If it's justice I want, maybe there's only one way to get it.

"The longing of your brother's heart is for something further back," Lewis said to Dani. "For Eden. And for something further forward. For heaven. Limited to the horizons of that world, his thoughts can only remind him of what is not. Out of that can only come despair. Men are born with a longing for Eden, Elyon's garden, and a longing for Jerusalem, Elyon's city. This longing creates the pain of separation from what is good and the hope of experiencing the good as it was meant to be. When we were in that world, our hearts could never fully rest. Sometimes the turmoil was overwhelming, as it is now for your brother. He's like a man without eyes, groping along the wall in search of justice in a world of injustice."

"He's totally disillusioned," Dani said. "I wish I could go tell him there's so much more happening that he can't see."

"Elyon has told him that already, in his Word. He must find it there himself, learn to believe and trust what the Sovereign One has said to him." Lewis paced again in his inimitable professorial style. "Your brother is right to be disillusioned with that world. He does not belong there. No one does. Only the ungodly could be content with a world so dark, and even they are never truly content. Clarence's error is in being disillusioned with what is true, for truth is just as real now as it was before the tragedies he's endured. That he is so disappointed with the failings of the dark world shows he put too much hope in that world. Only *this* world can bear the weight of his highest expectations. Only *this* world can fulfill his deepest longings."

"Can we pray for him, Lewis?" Dani asked.

They bowed their knees toward Elyon's throne, lifting up one still living on the planet of pain.

The man reached underneath the worn brown Malibu, just below the Visualize Whirled Peas bumper sticker. He groped around, finally fingering a greasy little container. He removed the key and opened the trunk. He looked both ways, then removed the long black leather case, shut the trunk, took it to his own car, and drove away.

"Sheila? Hi, this is Clarence Abernathy."

"Hello, Mr. Abernathy. Say, I've been wondering when we'll see your column featuring Mr. Norcoast's career. Don't worry, I haven't spoiled the surprise!"

"Uh, well, I'm still working on it, but I'm sure you'll be seeing the councilman's name in the paper real soon. Listen, speaking of surprises, I heard Reggie's birthday is Sunday."

"Yes. He'll be forty-five!" Sheila was as effervescent as always.

"That's great," Clarence said. "Listen, there's five or six of us, friends from his district, and we were wondering if maybe there'd be any time tomorrow when we could drop in as a surprise, bring Reggie a cake and some presents. Just for forty minutes, maybe? Hopefully Mr. Gray could be there too. Any possibility you could help us pull this off?"

"Oh, that sounds just *wonderful*," Sheila said. "I love surprises. Let me check everybody's schedule. Jean's gone tomorrow, and neither of the part-timers work Fridays. Yes, Councilman Norcoast and Mr. Gray have a breakfast appointment out, then they've got a telephone conference with Congressman Sparks from ten-thirty until eleven. Then both of them have an hour open until they'll need to leave for a lunch appointment. Sounds like eleven would be perfect!"

"Wonderful," Clarence said. "How about you write me in for an eleven o'clock appointment with Mr. Norcoast, but just tell him it's an interview, okay? He won't know the others are coming, all right? Don't tell Mr. Gray either. I've got a little plan I won't bore you with, but we need to be with just Reg for a while, then we'll call in Carson. All right?"

"Certainly," Sheila said. "I *love* this kind of thing! The councilman will be *so* surprised."

Yes, he will. More than you can possibly imagine.

"Antsy is stuck in the present," Dani said. "His eyes are closed to the past, in which Elyon has proven himself faithful, and closed to the future, to his promise that all wrongs will be made right."

"Your brother sees himself as the main character in life's drama," Lewis said. "He demands the script be written to his liking and he storms off the stage when it isn't. He resents Elyon directing the drama as he sees fit."

"He's so angry and desperate. More than I've ever seen him."

"His anger and despair are like a compass that points to true north," Lewis said. "They are a reminder there's a right direction, and the whole earth is headed in the wrong one. Hell is automatic. Heaven's values, however, are a choice against the grain, a choice he needs to make. Your brother's disillusionment is valid, but he must not allow it to control him. He must let it direct him toward heaven."

"I'm afraid he's making the wrong choices," Dani said. "He thinks he can't wait for justice, yet final justice won't come until the last day."

"You are right, my sister," Lewis said. "Life in that world never fulfills God's perfect design or man's deepest longings. At its best, it hints of them and kindles longing for them. Your brother longs for what will be. But if he takes things into his hands now, his attempt to accomplish God's justice will be an act of injustice. If your brother's pain leads him to look to Elyon for healing, the pain will serve him well. If he allows his pain to become his master, it will destroy him—and perhaps others."

Clarence drove out east of Gresham, down a deserted back road leading into a thick grove of trees. He took out the HK53 he'd taken from Ollie's trunk. He inserted into the standard magazine twenty-five .223 rounds, then aimed toward a prominent marking on a tree and pulled the trigger.

The weapon fired, but only once. The shell casing didn't eject. He removed the casing manually and got set to practice firing again.

At 10:50 A.M. Friday, Clarence walked into Councilman Norcoast's office with a cake box in his left hand and a long black leather bag slung over his right shoulder. He walked in with six other men, four black and two white. A couple of them Sheila recognized. She noticed none of them seemed in a party mood.

"Hello, Mr. Abernathy. Gentlemen." She waited for introductions, but Clarence didn't oblige.

"I've kept the secret," Sheila said. "I have to take off in just a few minutes myself. You'll never believe it," she said to Clarence. "A photographer from the *Tribune* called me this morning and she wants to take some pictures of me, for a possible feature of a Portland working woman. Can you imagine that? She asked me to meet her at Pioneer Square at eleven-fifteen. So I'll need to leave you gentlemen here. Mr. Gray's in his office. He and the councilman are on the same conference call. As soon as you see the light go off on line two," she pointed to the phone, "you can just knock on Mr. Norcoast's door. I told him I'd be leaving just before eleven, and he's expecting you."

Sheila turned on the answering machine, got together a few things, and headed out the door. The six other men sat quietly while Clarence positioned himself by the desk, waiting for the light to go off.

As soon as Norcoast put down his phone, the men walked in his office door. Clarence stood behind them, and under the distraction of their movement, he took two objects out of the cake box and affixed them to the wall.

"Gentlemen." Reg Norcoast appeared slightly flustered. "What a pleasant surprise. I knew I had an appointment with Clarence, but...Mr. Fletcher, hello, good to see you." Norcoast extended his hand to Leesa's father. He didn't reciprocate.

"What's all this about, Clarence?" Norcoast asked.

"I was just admiring some of your pictures, Councilman." Clarence pointed to a couple of pictures on the wall. Norcoast walked a few feet closer and stared, red faced.

"Which one are you looking at?" Clarence asked. "The picture of you and me with that tie of yours? Or the one right next to it? The one with your arm around Leesa Fletcher?"

"No. No." Norcoast looked at Leesa's father. "That's not true. I mean...where did that photo come from?"

Clarence pointed now to the photo of himself standing next to Norcoast. The councilman remembered how that photo had reappeared before. He remembered taking it out of the frame and burning it. This was the same picture, but...what was that shadow on his forehead?

"Nice tie, Reg," Clarence said. "Neat little symbols there. Say, Harley, isn't that the African symbol of masculinity?" His brother walked closer.

"Yes, it is," Harley said in the murky tone of a hanging judge.

"And what's this tattoo on the councilman's forehead?"

"That's the African symbol for justice," Harley said.

"Well, Norcoast," Clarence said. "That's why we're all here this morning. We've come to get justice."

Norcoast's eyes shifted wildly around the room.

"You know Mr. Fletcher, Leesa's father," Clarence said, gesturing, "and I think you've met Leesa's older brother Solly." From the way he filled out his Georgetown letterman's jacket, the boy had obviously pumped his share of iron. "And, of course, you know Pastor Cairo Clancy from Ebenezer and Jake Woods from the *Trib*. You remember my brother Harley here, the professor at Portland State? And you haven't met Stu Miller, father of Gracie Miller. Name ring a bell? See, Leesa's gone from this world, and so's Gracie and Dani. So *we're* here on their behalf."

"Tell me what's going on," Norcoast said. "I don't like your tone. What's happening here?"

Harley glared at Norcoast. "It's an African tradition that the male family members of female victims privately face the man responsible for the crime. The Qur'an says it is honorable to be the tool of justice."

"Now wait a minute," Norcoast said to Harley. "You're still chairman of the black studies department at PSU, right? I helped fund that department. I've gone to bat for it several times. We're on the same team. We're—"

"We're what? Brothers?" Harley spit on the floor. "That's what I think of you, *brother*."

"But you can't just charge into my office and threaten me," Norcoast said to him. "You'll be fired. You'll—"

"Nah, I've got tenure. Wouldn't expect you to understand this justice stuff, Norcoast. It's a black thing."

Norcoast turned back to Clarence. "Have you gone crazy, Abernathy?"

"Well, maybe I have," Clarence said. "But some of us here have lost faith in the justice system, with people like you using it for your own purposes. So before you go to court, we want to get in some old-fashioned country justice."

"Woods," Norcoast looked at Jake. "For crying out loud, talk some sense into him."

Jake shrugged. "These men have some very serious charges against you. If they're right, you've done terrible things to their families. Clarence is my friend, and he asked me to come here today and stand with him. I don't know exactly all he's got in mind, but I trust him."

"Reverend Clancy," Norcoast said, eyes pleading. "Tell them this isn't the place for justice. We have laws and courts for that. Tell them!"

"I think justice belongs everywhere," Clancy said. "I'm a Christian Bible preacher, not a Muslim, but it's hard to argue with the Qur'an on this one. Or with African tradition. See, justice is part of every religion and culture. Eye for an eye; tooth for a tooth."

"You can't let them hurt me," Norcoast said to the pastor in a frenzied voice.

"Dani Rawls was a good friend, a wonderful sister," Clancy said. "She was a sheep in my flock. And so was Leesa Fletcher once. I baptized that girl. You led her astray, Councilman. You're a wolf in sheep's clothing. My own deacons do some disciplining from time to time—so don't you tell me what I can and can't do. Seems to me you could use a little disciplining."

Norcoast searched the other eyes, from Leesa's father to her brother to Gracie's father. He found even less sympathy.

"What do you want from me?" Norcoast asked Clarence.

"The truth," Clarence said. "Telling us the truth is your only hope. First, did you sleep with Leesa Fletcher?"

"No. No!" he said. Clarence stepped toward him. The councilman put up his hands. "Okay. Yes, yes I did. I'm sorry. I'm so sorry." He looked at Leesa's father and brother, backing away from them until he hit the front of his desk.

"And were you the father of the child Leesa was carrying?" Clarence asked.

"Yes. I think so. That's what she said anyway."

"Did you have her killed with the drug overdose?"

"No! I'd never do anything like that. I'm no killer. I swear it!"

"You think you can pull our chain," Harley said, taking a step toward him, "like we're a bunch of dumb shoeshine boys?"

"No, no. I don't. I don't think that."

"Did you order the hit on Leesa's house that ended up killing Dani?" Clarence asked.

"No! I've never tried to hurt anybody. Not Leesa, not anyone."

"Did you put Gracie up to framing me? Or did you have somebody give her bad crack to kill her?"

"No. Never!"

Clarence moved up within inches of Norcoast and put his hands on the councilman's suit lapels. "I don't think I believe you. How about the rest of you?" He turned and looked at the faces, either angry or stoic. "Maybe we should start off getting some justice for what he did to Leesa."

"Okay, Norcoast," Clarence said fifteen minutes later. "Call in Carson Gray."

Norcoast, trembling, pressed his intercom. "Carson, I need you in my office. Yes, well, tell him you'll call him later. Get in here. Now."

Twenty seconds later Carson opened the door and entered Norcoast's office, then stopped dead in his tracks, surveying his surroundings like a second lieutenant walking into a room full of majors and colonels. He looked at his boss, who was disheveled and agitated, dripping with sweat.

"Carson," Norcoast said, "tell them everything you know about Leesa Fletcher. Everything."

"What's going on here?" Gray asked.

"These," Clarence said, hand outstretched, "are the family members of Dani Rawls, Leesa Fletcher, and Gracie Miller. We're here to get justice." Gray's eyes moved slightly, just a little twitch. "We know about how you paid off Shadow, Gracie, and Mookie," Clarence said.

"I don't know what you're talking about," Gray said.

"We know everything," Clarence said, borrowing a page from Ollie's book.

"Then you don't need me, do you? If you have something to say, say it to my lawyer. You're not getting anything from me."

"Okay," Clarence said, "let me put it another way. Tell us everything, or I'll kill you and your boss."

Gray's eyebrows rose half an inch. "*Kill* us? You're too funny, Abernathy."

Clarence reached over to the long black leather case, unzipped it, and took out the HK53. He cradled it in his arms and stared at Gray. Jake and Clancy exchanged glances, looking shocked and uncertain. The ante had suddenly upped. Jake stepped toward Clarence, then hesitated, stopping still five feet away.

"This," Clarence said, "is the weapon the thugs you hired planned to use on an eighteen-year-old girl."

"My daughter," Mr. Fletcher said, eyes steely.

"But the morons got the wrong street, as you know, Gray. So they used this weapon," Clarence turned the HK53 three-quarters of the way toward Gray, "on my sister and my five-year-old niece."

"I didn't have anything to do with that." Gray looked around the room, his suit fitting even more awkwardly than usual, since his entire torso was in retreat.

The agitated faces of the big men clearly unnerved Gray, especially Harley's face, framed by his thick black Malcolm X glasses. Gray's eyes darted away from Clarence to the other men, then back toward him. He looked like a scared rabbit trapped under the gaze of a pack of hunting dogs.

"Gentlemen, please," Gray said, "there's obviously a misunderstanding here." Harley stepped toward him and Gray jumped back. "Wait. I'm a member of the

NAACP. The councilman and I have a long history of supporting civil rights."

"I'm impressed," Harley said with a growl. "Tell me you give to the United Negro College Fund, and I'll dance a jig and shine your shoes, you little pip-squeak."

"We want to hear you talk, Gray." Clarence pointed the barrel toward him only a moment, then fixed it on Norcoast. "But let's finish with your boss first. He's already admitted to sleeping with Leesa Fletcher and getting her pregnant. Haven't you, Reg?"

"Yes." Norcoast hung his head.

Gray looked at Norcoast in disbelief. He felt unable to swallow as he watched Clarence point the weapon at his boss, his finger now on the trigger.

"If I killed you here and now," Clarence said to Norcoast, "it might be the only chance of getting any real justice. For what you did to that girl you deserve to die."

"Come on, Clarence," Clancy said, stepping forward, sounding nervous. "He's not worth it. Just call a press conference and hang out their dirty laundry. Don't go to jail for it."

"The Councilman's holding out on us," Clarence said. "There's more he needs to confess. Okay, Mr. Norcoast, I'll give you to the count of three." He held out the rifle in shooting position, pointing it straight at Norcoast's chest. "One."

"No," Norcoast said, voice cracking. "Please. There's nothing else."

"Clarence, what are you doing?" Jake Woods stepped toward him, his hands extended. "Come on, brother. You promised no serious injury, remember? Let's think this over, okay?"

"I *have* thought it over," Clarence reached out his long left arm and pushed Jake hard. "Stay back, Jake. Two."

"Please, don't." Norcoast sounded pathetic.

"Three." Gray and Norcoast and several of the other men looked at Clarence Abernathy in horror. Fire seemed to burn in his eyes. His finger turned white on the trigger. Everyone watched breathlessly, frozen to the floor. Suddenly the trigger gave and a hail of gunfire rang out.

The huge rifle jerked in Clarence's hands, and a wide-eyed Norcoast fell backward, landing flat and motionless behind his desk. Clarence had fired six rounds in the second before Jake and Cairo tackled him. They wrestled him down, trying to pull the gun from his arms. Finally they pried it loose, and Jake pulled out the magazine.

Norcoast's body lay in a crumpled heap back of his desk. Carson Gray was moaning, face drained of color. His knees buckled. He fell to the ground like a monk falling to prayer at the appointed hour. He looked up in disbelief.

Jake rushed behind the desk, stooping low over Norcoast. He put his fingers first to the wrist, then frantically to his neck. "Nothing," Jake said. "Nothing!" He turned to Clarence, a look of betrayal on his face.

The roomful of men stood motionless, no one looking sure what to do next.

"I'm calling 911," Jake said, stretching his hand to the phone on the desk. Clarence yanked on the phone, ripping it from the cord and dropping it on the floor. He reached into his suit pocket and pulled out his Glock 17. He only half pointed it at Jake, as if he didn't want to.

"Stay where you are, Jake. All of you. Look, I don't want to hurt any of you. It'll all be over in a few minutes. You didn't do this, I did. I'll tell the cops I misled you all. I'm just not going to let Gray get away with it." He stared at Gray, his eyes looking as fearsome as the gun barrel. "I've already killed one man. Won't make any difference if it's two."

He stepped toward Gray and pointed the Glock at his forehead. "Talk now, Gray, and I *might* let you live."

"Grab him, stop him," Gray said. "Please. Somebody help me."

Jake stepped toward Clarence again.

"Get back, Jake, I mean it. I'm turning myself in when I'm done. But first I finish with Gray."

Clarence squeezed the handle and the red light appeared on Gray's forehead.

"Clarence, don't," Clancy said. "Let the law take care of him."

"Stay back, Pastor. The law doesn't take care of them, you know that. There's no justice anymore. Well, there's justice here today."

"No, no, wait, don't," Gray begged.

"Clarence, let me talk to him." Clancy stepped boldly into the line of fire. He whispered to Gray, "Tell me the truth. I'm not talking as a reverend, I'm not asking for a religious confession. I'm telling you if you give me the truth right now, I'll walk you out of this room and you can call the police and get some protection. Tell me who did it and they can go after them. Give me some names. But if you don't…well, you're on your own."

"But I'm innocent. I never did anything," Gray said. "It was all Norcoast. I'll testify against him. I will."

"I've seen enough," Clancy said. "I'm out of here." He walked for the door.

"You can call the police," Clarence said, "but by the time they get here Gray'll be dead."

"No, Reverend, you can't leave." Gray moved a foot toward him, then suddenly stopped when he saw a red beam out of the corner of his eye. "I've always supported you. I've always thought the world of your church. Our office donated that memorial bell, remember?"

Clancy looked at him with disgust. He walked out the door and closed it behind him.

Clarence trained the red dot back on Gray's forehead. "You've got till I count to five to confess your sins. No, you've got a lot of sins. How about I count to ten? If I don't think you've confessed everything, I pull the trigger. One."

"You can't let him do this," Gray said to the men, most of them backed against the wall, ten feet from Clarence.

"He's got the gun, we don't," Harley said.

"Two."

"Wait, Mr. Abernathy, no, please," Gray said.

"Three."

"Yes, okay, all right," Gray said. "Norcoast told me he got the girl pregnant. I set up an appointment for her abortion and sent her directions to the clinic, with a thousand dollars for the abortion and some extra to take care of her. That was only right."

Leesa's father looked at him with eyes that could kill, but weren't going to have to.

"Four."

"Wait! I'm telling the truth," Gray said. "I don't know anything about your sister and your niece, Mr. Abernathy, I swear it. I never hired anybody to kill the Fletcher girl. I thought she just died of heart failure—that's what I was told. Okay, I started to wonder about it when I heard the autopsy said drug overdose. I thought maybe Norcoast had her taken care of. Maybe he did. I got somebody to…adjust the autopsy report. I'll give you the name, I'll tell you who, okay?"

"Five," Clarence said. "What about Gracie?"

"I contacted a gangbanger—Shadow—I paid him to get some girl to set you up. I didn't want to know who it was. I *didn't* know who it was until it happened. I paid somebody to follow you and put you out of commission so you wouldn't have an alibi. But I specifically told him *not* to kill you, okay?"

"Six. Who did you pay to put drugs in my coffee? I want a name."

"Harry Belle," Gray said quickly. "Lives in Vancouver. He's kind of a PI, but…he does other stuff too. He followed you, put the heroin in your coffee—not enough to kill you—remember, I told him not to kill you. He told me he put the heroin in your overcoat the next morning in the parking garage elevator."

"Seven. Who's the big black guy who looks like me, the one at the bar and at the hotel with Gracie?"

"Don't know his name," Gray said. "I swear it. Only saw him once. He's an associate of Harry's. I'm telling you, Harry set that whole thing up. I didn't know the details. I was out of the loop."

"Eight. Who'd you hire to kill Gracie?"

"Nobody!" Gray sweat profusely, staring at Norcoast's motionless legs poking out from behind the desk. "All I did was tell Shadow to make sure Gracie didn't talk, that's all. I didn't mean for him to kill her. Never said anything like that. It just got out of hand, that's all. It wasn't my fault."

"Nine. One more chance to tell the truth about the hit on Leesa Fletcher."

"I didn't have anything to do with that. Nothing! I really didn't," Gray said.

"Please! You've got to believe me."

"Ten." Clarence paused a moment, then pulled the trigger. The hammer dropped.

Gray stared, eyes bulging.

Nothing happened.

"All right, gentlemen," Clarence said. "Thanks for your cooperation. I think we can leave now."

Gray stood speechless for five seconds. "But...what? You can't just...What about the councilman?"

"What about me?" Norcoast asked in a tone of disgust, getting to his feet.

Just then Ollie Chandler barged in the door. "What's going on here, Clarence?" Ollie looked around the room. He saw the Glock 17 lying on the desk, and then his eyes landed on the HK53.

"I looked everywhere for that rifle," Ollie said, red spreading up his neck from the collar. "I reported it stolen this morning. I'm in the doghouse at the department. You've got some explaining to do, mister."

"Sorry, Ollie. I asked Clancy to call you when our drama was nearly over, but I couldn't risk telling you earlier." Clarence reached into his coat pocket, from which a little black wire ran to his tie. He took out a micro tape recorder, popped out the tape, and handed it to Ollie. "You'll want to listen to this. It's all here. After his confession about Leesa, Norcoast agreed to cooperate with us to get a confession out of Gray."

Gray glared at Norcoast. Norcoast stared back at Gray and imitated his voice: "I'm innocent. *I* never did anything. It was all *Norcoast*. I'll testify against him."

"I thought you were dead," Gray said.

"So you figured you'd just smear my reputation?"

"You managed to do that yourself, Councilman." Mr. Fletcher looked at him with disdain.

"Wait, Reg," Gray said. "They *forced* you to set me up and they *forced* us to confess to things we didn't do. That's how it was, and that's completely illegal. It'll never hold up."

"Actually, when I found out how you betrayed me, betrayed this office, used your position to frame an innocent man and to *murder* a girl...I decided to go ahead and play along. They didn't force me."

"I demand to see my lawyer," Gray said, looking around the room, hoping to find a sympathetic eye. He didn't.

"You must have some beautiful sisters, Gray," Ollie said. "Looks to me like you used up all the ugly in the family. Go call your lawyer—nobody's stopping you. Just don't leave the building." Gray straightened his shoulders, as if to affirm his indignation at being mistreated.

Norcoast looked again at the pictures on the wall. He was standing with his arm around Leesa, and they were looking into each other's eyes like an adoring couple. Was this a nightmare? Who'd taken that picture? He knew he'd been more discreet than that. He'd never posed with her. Or had he? Pictures don't lie. Do they?

———————

Clarence met Ollie in his office at four that afternoon.

"I listened to the tape," Ollie said. "I can't believe you convinced those upstanding citizens to be in on this charade. They were really taking a risk."

"I called them all last night and we got together. I lobbied them," Clarence said. "When I told them about Norcoast and Gray, they all wanted to see them go down. Like me, they didn't have much confidence the truth would come out in the legal process. When I explained my idea about loading the HK with blanks and using the unloaded Glock, they bought it.

"Pastor Clancy and Jake were the hard sells. They must have asked me ten times if I was absolutely *positive* they were just blanks. I don't think the other guys would have felt bad if there was a live round or two in there. We all met together again this morning and went over the plan. Some of them had to do some acting—Jake and Cairo especially. Now, Harley, he wasn't acting." Clarence laughed and shook his head.

"Anyway, Ollie, you can see why I couldn't let you in on it. You would have told me not to and you'd have been in big trouble just knowing about it. I wanted to take the risk myself. If something went wrong, it was just me stealing the HK."

"Which isn't going to go over very well at the precinct," Ollie said. "I still can't believe you got Norcoast to play along."

"Plan A was based on hoping Gray would crack just being confronted by all the men, but he was too cool. That's why we had to go to Plan B—taking out the HK and firing the blanks. My gut told me the councilman would agree to nail Gray once he understood he'd framed me and pulled off a murder or two out of his office. I've gotten to know Norcoast pretty well the last couple of months. I knew he'd feel betrayed by Gray and that he'd want to distance himself from him. Speaking of acting, Norcoast did all right himself. And with no rehearsal."

"Where'd you get the blanks for the HK?"

"Sergeant McCamman put me on to that. A military surplus store. He said the army uses them for training with M-16s. Two bucks per twenty rounds of .223 blanks. Needless to say, the sergeant knew nothing about me borrowing the HK53 from your trunk."

"Blanks don't fire as loud," Ollie said, "but I guess that close indoors, most people wouldn't notice."

"Gray was the only one who had to believe it, and to him I'm sure it sounded like dynamite."

"How'd you manage to fire more than one blank?" Ollie asked. "There's nothing to cycle the action, so usually blank rounds won't eject. You have to remove them manually."

"You knew that, huh? I sure didn't," Clarence said. "I found out when I tried it yesterday. I wanted the full effect of an automatic, so I called McCamman and he told me HK makes a blank adapter for their weapons. It does something to the gasses or the pressure so the action cycles perfectly, just like the real thing." Clarence pointed to the HK. "Notice anything different?"

Ollie picked up the gun and looked at the silver-colored fixture.

"Wait a minute. There's no hole in the end."

"That's the adapter. I called a dozen places in town, and one guy actually had an HK blank adapter," Clarence said. "I never pointed it directly at Gray for more than a moment, for fear he'd notice there was no place for a bullet to come out. Once I showed Jake and Cairo there was no hole in the muzzle, no chance for an accident, they calmed down. And Jake checked my Glock twice this morning just to make sure it was empty."

Ollie shook his head. "I tell you, Abernathy, you scare me. So what's the deal with the photos on Norcoast's wall? Where'd they come from?"

"Those were Carp's work, you know, my photographer friend? Mr. Fletcher gave me this playful looking pose of Leesa from her senior pictures. I told Carp what I wanted, and early this morning she scanned it in along with a picture of Norcoast and manipulated the image into this seamless picture of them as a couple. Remember, she did that work for me earlier, taking that photo of Norcoast and me and putting in the message from Leesa on his tie. For an added touch, this time I had her put the African symbol of justice on his forehead. Just wanted to disorient him, throw him off guard, make it look like we could prove more than we could. Like something you'd do."

"Now the DA's going to have to figure out which confessions are admissible and which aren't," Ollie said. "But since it was a bunch of civilians that set it up, most of them family of victims, at least it might get some sympathy, and it doesn't make the cops look bad. They can't get us for entrapment. It doesn't make my evidence inadmissible. I'll tell you, though, Clarence, for a minute there you had me scared. I was afraid maybe you went off the deep end, turned vigilante on me."

"The thought occurred to me. But I kept thinking about Geneva and the kids and my dad. And Mama and Dani and Felicia. No way I could do that to them. It's like I felt them all praying for me to do the right thing."

"Weird," Ollie said.

"Maybe not," Clarence said.

"One thing I still don't get," Ollie said. "Between Norcoast, Gray, and Shadow, we know who killed Leesa and Gracie and who set you up. And we know Spider and his buddy were hired by Harper to do the hit on Leesa that killed Dani and Felicia. But we still don't know who was behind the main event. If Norcoast or Gray didn't set up the murder with Harper, who did?"

42

Clarence went out from the garage to look at the roses, his blue jeans stiff from the cold. The denim rubbed hard against his frigid legs. He rolled out some twine to tie up the roses a bit closer, to protect them from the winter ice.

He looked at the shriveled-up buds, marveling that they still had life in them. He imagined what they'd look like in the spring, beautiful and colorful again. Maybe in the spring he'd plant more roses. Maybe some petunias and marigolds and primroses. With Dani gone, this place needed more color.

"Hang on," he said to the barren roses. "Your time will come. You can make it through the winter." Just then Jake and Janet pulled into the driveway.

"What are you two lovebirds up to?" Clarence called.

"Some last minute wedding details," Jake said. "And we've been looking at houses. At first we'll be in Janet and Carly's place, you know, but we're thinking we'd like to start over in a new place. Since we'll be young marrieds and all—Janet and I and a nineteen-year-old and a one-and-a-half-year-old, I mean." He put his arm around Janet, who smiled broadly. Geneva came out the front door, and the women threw their arms around each other, though it had been only two days since they'd seen each other.

Clarence pointed to a house across the street and two doors down with a For Sale sign out front. "Won't find a better deal in Portland than that place. Just needs some fixin' up."

"Looks like a pretty decent structure," Jake said.

"I'd help you work on it," Clarence said. "We could be neighbors." Geneva and Janet caught each other's eyes.

"I thought you were movin' into that place out in the country," Jake said.

"Changed our minds. For now, we're staying here." Clarence pointed again at the house for sale. "How about we take a look at it right now?"

"Why not?" Jake said.

As they crossed the street, Clarence wondered if his dreams of a beautiful place in the country would ever materialize. Maybe they'd just be postponed. Or maybe they'd be fulfilled in another world.   •

Clarence handed Ollie a year-old *Trib* article. Ollie looked at the headline: "Gang Summit to Curtail Violence." The article spoke of gang leaders meeting with the Portland City Council on how to reduce street crime. A photo of attending gang leaders included both Gangster Cool and Shadow. Clarence had highlighted one line in yellow: "Councilman Norcoast and three members of his staff attended the gang summit."

Clarence gave Ollie another article, a feature story on Reggie Norcoast and his staff. There was a picture of Norcoast, Carson Gray, Sheila, and Jean.

"Where'd you get these?" Ollie asked.

"From Raymond Taylor's bedroom wall," Clarence said. "I saw them there when I talked with his mother. I went over last night and asked her for them. I could understand the photo with GC and the article on the gang summit. But Norcoast's staff picture didn't make sense. Now it does. He knew them, and he did more than pass out campaign literature."

"This photo's good timing," Ollie said. "Want to join me on a fishing expedition?" Clarence sat by Ollie's phone as the detective pressed on the speaker and dialed a Sacramento number.

"Harper," the tired voice said.

"This is your old buddy, Detective Chandler. What would you say if I told you now we've *really* nailed the person who sent you the fax? Of course, it wasn't Norcoast or Gray. But what if I told you our lady insists you misconstrued her message, that you came up with some far-fetched scheme to kill somebody when she intended no such thing."

Clarence looked at Ollie in surprise. What was he saying?

"She said that?" Harper asked. "No way. That's not how it was and she knows it. She was trying to blackmail me."

"Blackmail you? How?" Ollie asked. Harper hung up.

"She?" Clarence asked Ollie. "Who is 'she'?"

"I don't know," Ollie said. "But remember how Harper seemed to know immediately I was bluffing when I hinted I'd talked with the guy who sent him the fax? That's bugged me ever since. When Gray and Norcoast both denied it at gunpoint after confessing everything else, it dawned on me how I tipped off Harper. I said 'guy.' If Harper had been contacted by a woman, he'd know I was bluffing. So I just bluffed him again, but this time I was holding the right cards. It was a woman, all right."

"But," Clarence said, "besides two part-time secretaries, Sheila and Jean are the only women who work in that office, right?" Ollie nodded. "Well, I can guarantee it's not Sheila. Miss Bubbly Perkiness isn't the type. Jean, on the other hand, has ice water running in her veins. I could see her being involved."

"People aren't always what they appear," Ollie said, now lost in thought.

"What are you going to do?"

"Well, I might start by meeting with Sheila. I could hand her the fax, ask her what she'd say if Matthew Harper claimed she called him, set up the hit, and sent the fax. See how she responds. What's the worst thing she could do? Reach in her purse and spray me with mace?"

"Trust me, Ollie," Clarence said. "Read my lips. Forget about Sheila. Go after Jean."

Clarence and Ty sat on the couch.

"Listen, Ty, I went down to the Teen Challenge center, and they walked me through their program. They really know their stuff. They can help you with this drug problem, and they can disciple you too, really get you into God's Word. I'd like you to come with me, at least check it out and see what you think."

Ty nodded. In the last three weeks, and especially the last two days, his relationship with the gang had come crashing down on him. Shadow's arrest and his uncle's role in it had put Ty on the outs with the 60s. He felt betrayed by GC's role in his mother's and sister's deaths. And he was tired of pretending he liked what the crack was doing to him. Gangs and drugs were starting to seem like nothing more than broken promises.

Clarence and Tyrone talked for a while about many things, when suddenly Ty started to cry. Clarence put his arm around him. "What's wrong, Ty? Things are finally looking up now. It's going to be okay."

Ty wouldn't talk for a while. He tried to leave the room, but his uncle insisted he stay with him. Finally Ty choked out, "If it wasn't for me, Mama and Felicia wouldn't have died." The tears flowed now, mystifying Clarence.

"That's nonsense, Ty," Clarence said. "What are you talking about?"

"The street sign. Jackson. I'm the one that tagged it. Made it look like Jack." He stared at Clarence, desperation in his eyes. "It's my fault they died."

Clarence held him tight. "No, Ty. It wasn't your fault. It was other people who set it up. It was other people who did it. It wasn't you." Ty melted in his arms, a rag doll. Clarence sensed he had more to tell and determined to stay with him until he did.

Finally Ty said, "I shot somebody."

"Who? When?"

"Awhile back. GC gave me a sawed-off. Shot a Blood in a gang war. Name's

Donnie. Had him in a math class at Tubman. He…gave me his cookies." Ty sobbed.

"Did he…die?"

"No. But he hasn't been back to school. Heard he's had lots of problems." Ty's voice cracked. "Got his stomach stapled up and stuff."

"Okay," Clarence said. "We'll go to the police and you'll tell them what happened. Then we'll go to Donnie and his family. You can ask their forgiveness. We'll offer to help them any way we can. I'll be there with you the whole way, son. All right?"

Ty looked scared, but he nodded, clearly at the end of himself. Clarence could see the weight of guilt on his shoulders. It was a guilt he understood.

After a quiet few minutes Clarence said to Ty, "God can forgive us no matter what we've done, because Jesus paid the price for us. And if God can forgive us, we can forgive ourselves." Clarence paused, then sucked in air. "I'm going to tell you something I've never told anybody, Ty, not even Geneva and your grandpa." The boy looked up. "When I was your age, your mama and I lived in the projects in Chicago. One day I was with my buddies Rock and Shorty. We were just hangin'. Then we saw this white boy ridin' in on his bike…"

Thirty minutes later, Ty got up from the couch, went to his closet, reached deep into a box of old comics, and retrieved a 9 mm handgun. He looked at it, weighed it in his hand, and took it to the living room to give to his uncle.

"Ray? Ollie Chandler. Listen, we've got some stuff on Norcoast, pretty serious stuff, but there's some major holes that have to be filled in. I don't think I can get a court order for you to talk to me unless I've got some idea what you may know."

Ray Eagle sighed. "Okay, Ollie. Just promise me you'll forget everything that's not relevant to your case. Here goes. In June, Norcoast's wife hired me to follow him and watch for…indiscretions. She wanted photos, had to see exactly who it was. One night after he left his office I followed him to a hotel. He didn't check in, but went right up to a room, as if he had an appointment or something. I managed to get in the elevator at the same time. I walked ahead of him, pretended to be outside my own room, fumbling for my passcard. He knocked on a door behind me, and someone let him in real quick, I couldn't see who. In an hour he left the room by himself. I kept watching the door. Ten minutes later the woman came out, and I managed to get a few discreet pictures. I gave them to Mrs. Norcoast. Gee, Ollie, I hate to even admit I do this kind of thing. It sounds so sleazy, but it was work and I knew Mrs. Norcoast would pay the bill."

"When you gave her the pictures, what did she say?"

"Nothing," Ray said. "She was pretty detached. Obviously she suspected or she wouldn't have hired me. She paid me cash on the spot and said she wouldn't need my services any longer, which was fine by me."

"I know you've told me more than you wanted to, Ray, and I appreciate it. I assume you keep your negatives. Could you get me a picture of this woman?"

"Can you honestly tell me it might be critical to your investigation?"

"Yes."

"Well," Ray said, "I'm in this deep, I may as well put my whole head under. I can have it for you in a few hours. I'll bring it by your office."

After putting the children to bed and praying with them, Clarence sat down with Geneva and Daddy, who was coughing and seemed particularly frail.

Clarence told them about Ty shooting the boy and tagging the street sign. After they discussed this for half an hour, Clarence said, "There's something I need to tell you both. It's not going to be easy."

Slowly, painfully, he told them the story of the white boy he'd beaten up thirty years ago. Both sat spellbound, amazed that this could be surfacing after all these years.

When he finished, Clarence wiped his eyes and rested his head on Geneva's shoulder. She hugged him tight and whispered, "It's okay, baby, it's okay. I'm so glad you told us."

After gaining his composure, Clarence looked at Obadiah. "I'm so sorry, Daddy."

"You held on to that all these years, Son?" Obadiah said, his eyes weighed down. "You done your share of sufferin', that's sure. But Jesus already did the sufferin', see, the only sufferin' that sets things right. He wants us to accept the atonement, not repeat it. Has you talked to God about this?"

"Yes," Clarence said. "Finally."

"Then he'll take care of it now." Obadiah thought for a moment. "That white boy you beat up? Was he ridin' a red bike?"

"Yeah. Why?"

"This all happened at the dump, right by the junkyard, right? He was left layin' by an ol' refrigerator, wasn't he?"

"How'd you know that?"

"A neighbor, ol' Ron, he told me he found the boy. People was scared 'cause a white boy got hurt and nobody knew who done it. Well, ol' Ron showed me right where he found the boy. Could still see the blood. See, Ron drove him to the hospital hisself. He kept track of that boy. Talked about it the next few weeks. The boy was in the hospital a few days. Had some broken ribs, if I recalls right. But he ended up okay, I knows that much. Told your mama all about it, but for some reason I never told you kids. Guess I should have. He turned out okay, Antsy, he turned out okay.

Now why didn't you never tell your daddy about this?"

"I was so ashamed." Clarence hung his head, then looked up at his father. "You're not foolin' with me, are you Daddy? You're sure the boy was okay?"

"God is my witness," Obadiah said.

Clarence broke into tears again, his hands holding his head as if his shoulders had no strength in them. Geneva drew him close. Finally Clarence said, "I'll bet you to this day that boy hates blacks."

"We all carries lots of memories, lots of scars," Obadiah said. "Like that one there under your ear. But I just hopes that boy found Jesus—'cause there's some scars only he can take away. I knows," Obadiah said, nodding. "Believe me, I knows."

Clarence escorted Sue Keels up the aisle, passing by Jake on their right, then parting at the bottom of the church platform stairs. Sue ascended the stairs to take her place as maid of honor, and Clarence ascended to his place as best man.

Clarence looked down the aisle and watched Geneva being escorted by Ollie, looking in his tuxedo like an overstuffed penguin. The big guy grinned up at him. But it was Geneva's eyes Clarence met. He didn't remember her looking so beautiful since…their own wedding twenty-one years before.

Clarence looked at his daddy, sitting next to Jonah in the second row, each of them watching out for the other. Obadiah caught Clarence's eye, then smiled and whispered something to Jonah, who also smiled, both of them looking up at Clarence.

Janet walked in wearing a striking white wedding dress. She was escorted not by her father, who had passed away, but by her daughter, Carly, pale and walking very slowly, leaning on a thin petite cane. Despite her deteriorating health, Carly was all smiles, and she and her mother whispered and giggled the whole long walk up the aisle. This was the second time Janet had been given away in marriage, the first thirty years ago. Two weddings to the same man. But a different man, Clarence knew. He'd seen close up the last two years of Jake's life.

"I Jake, take you Janet to be my wife."

Jake and Janet looked like kids again.

"Jake, what symbol of your love and commitment would you share with Janet?"

Clarence untied the ring from the pillow held by the most excited ring bearer in the history of the universe, Little Finn. Clarence handed the ring to Jake, not sure whose grin was bigger, Jake's or Finn's, not realizing his own might have outdone them both.

"In accordance with the laws of the state of Oregon and by the authority that is mine as a minister of the gospel, I now pronounce you husband and wife. What

God has joined together—again—let no man dare to separate. Jake," the pastor paused for effect, "you may kiss your bride."

Jake and Janet kissed now, understanding a great deal more about love than when they'd kissed at that wedding thirty years ago. The entire church erupted into applause, long and heartfelt.

At Clarence's request, in the recessional Ollie and Sue joined arms, and Clarence escorted out Geneva. When they locked arms, he kissed her cheek. "You look beautiful," he whispered as they walked down the aisle.

"You ain't mulch on the flowers yourself, baby," she whispered back. When they got to the rear of the auditorium, Clarence took her aside.

"I want to get away with you, baby," Clarence whispered. "Maybe a second honeymoon or something. What would you think of us renewing our wedding vows?"

Geneva looked shocked. "That sounds...wonderful." Her eyes watered, and he surrounded her in a hug. They finally released each other just in time to hear a loud voice say, "Wow, Mr. Abernassy, you and Mrs. Abernassy really knows how to do a *big* hug!"

Obadiah had sat down, looking weary, but assuring everyone he was fine. Clarence kept glancing over at him. Suddenly he saw him slump over in his chair. Clarence ran to him. His daddy had already lost consciousness.

Clarence picked him up while people scrambled to find a phone. Ollie waved to Clarence as he went for the front door. "I've got the precinct car. I'll pick you up out here. Faster than an ambulance."

Clarence nodded as he walked toward the door, people crowding around son and father, father looking remarkably childlike in his son's huge arms.

As Clarence got his daddy in the backseat, Ollie grabbed the magnetic cherry top, popped it on top of his car, and turned on the siren. He pulled out of the church parking lot and wove through traffic, speeding toward Emanuel Hospital. When they pulled up by the large Emergency sign, Clarence threw open the door, picked up his father, and ran inside.

"Hello, Mrs. Norcoast," Ollie said, admiring the mansion's beautiful decor. "Thanks for letting me come over to meet with you. I'll get right to the point. I'm sure you know about your husband's involvement with Leesa Fletcher."

Esther Norcoast, dressed impeccably, turned frigid. She moved only her right hand to reach up and finger the angel pin on her blouse.

Ollie handed her the fax sent to Matthew Harper. She looked at it.

"Where did you get this?" Esther asked.

"Well, let's just say we know you typed it on your husband's computer and sent it to Mr. Harper on his fax machine. We've been in contact with Harper. What would you say if I told you he saved the fax in case something went wrong? As you know, as a result of this fax, Leesa Fletcher ended up dead."

"I thought she died of heart failure."

"Yes. From a drug overdose. But she was the real target in the shooting that killed Dani and Felicia Rawls. The guys Harper hired for you got the wrong house. You knew that, didn't you?"

Esther teared up. Ollie had been groping in the dark, preferring not to mention Ray's photo of Leesa Fletcher. He suspected now he'd pushed the right button. "What did you have on Harper, Mrs. Norcoast?"

Esther sat quietly a long time. "He worked for my husband. I used to spend a lot of time in the office, until the last year when I really got involved in my angel business. Three years ago I was going through the books and saw some things I didn't understand. I started watching Matthew, then I caught him manipulating figures on the computer. He'd been embezzling. I told him I'd give him a few months to return all the money, but then he'd have to resign. I said if he did, I wouldn't tell anyone. Even Reg and Carson didn't know, still don't. But I kept the records proving Matthew's guilt, just in case."

She seemed to be organizing her thoughts as if this were an after-dinner speech.

"When I found out about...Reggie's involvement with the girl, I confronted him. He broke off the relationship, but the next thing I knew I overheard Carson telling someone the girl was pregnant and he'd given her money to get an abortion but she hadn't done it. I realized that if she gave birth to...his baby, everything we've worked for could crumble. She'd tell someone, and next thing you know there'd be a scandal, which would cost us the mayoral race, ruin everything. Besides, I couldn't live knowing he'd had a baby by another woman. I thought about it. I knew Matthew had some...connections. I called and reminded him he owed me a big one, and if he did a job for me, I'd turn over all the records I had on him and pay whatever was necessary to get the job done."

"Thirty-five thousand dollars," Ollie said.

"Yes," Esther said, surprised Harper had divulged all the details. "I still go over the office books once a week. Nobody else pays much attention to them. Matthew's done plenty of consulting work for us. And we've had a lot of generous contributors come through for us the last six months, everyone from Raylon Berkley to the former governor—Reggie's very popular, you know—so I knew we could cover it. After I sent the fax, Matthew called me and said they could come up here that Saturday night. We wanted to make sure they found the right house, but of course I couldn't talk to them directly."

"So you went to Gangster Cool," Ollie said, chilled by how controlled and at ease Esther appeared to be. "I read three members of your husband's staff attended the gang conference with him. I checked the records and found out you were one of them. Is that where you met Gangster Cool?"

"Yes. Raymond—that's how I knew him—he'd done some campaign-related work for us. He'd done a good job. So I asked him to meet with the boys Matthew was sending so he could give them the address and directions to…the girl's house.

"The next morning when I saw the paper, I was shocked. When I read the headlines about Dani Rawls, I kept looking to see if there were any other shootings. Then I realized it was all a terrible mistake." A single tear dropped from her left eye, and she caught it gracefully with a tissue.

"Once you found out they'd killed the wrong person, what did you do?"

"I contacted Raymond and told him he needed to do whatever it took to take care of that girl. The next weekend I read she'd died of this heart condition. I hoped that's all it really was. The hardest part was having to go to the funeral with Reggie and Katie. I didn't want any of us to be there. But the important thing was, she was gone."

Ollie stared at this woman, sitting there in all her elegance talking about murdering her daughter's best friend.

"I'm sorry, detective. I never wanted to hurt anybody but that black girl and her bastard baby. I opened my home to her, gave her some of my clothes and a beautiful gold angel pin. How *dare* she spite me like that? How dare she seduce my husband and try to ruin everything we've worked so hard for? She had the nerve to make him this miserable tie that said 'Love, Leesa.' And he had the gall to wear it in public! When I saw it at the Fight Crime rally, I was so angry I almost ripped it off his neck. I told him I never wanted to see that tie again. I saw a picture in his office of him with that tie. I got rid of it on the spot."

"What made you think Harper would cooperate with you?" Ollie asked.

"Matthew's a dependable man. He's helped a lot of people. He cares about his career. I knew he wouldn't take the risk of his reputation being ruined. Besides, I made it easier for him. I told him the woman was a hooker—that she entrapped Reg and was trying to blackmail him."

"You said that about Leesa?"

"It sounded…better. And it was kind of true. Not the blackmail part. Maybe she wasn't a hooker, but she had a hold on him. And she was ruining our lives. I had to stop her. You understand that, don't you? I'm sorry other people got hurt, but I *had* to stop her. Reggie does too much good for too many people to let one person ruin him like that."

"You came up with all this on your own?" Ollie asked. "Didn't work with anyone but Harper and Gangster Cool?"

"Well, of course I couldn't have done it without Sartol."

"Sartol? Who's Sartol?"

"He's the one who came up with the idea. I was so confused. I needed guidance. He gave it to me."

"Mrs. Norcoast, who is Sartol?"

"Why, he's my angel."

Ollie stared at her.

"I asked for his help with this whole dreadful problem. Then Matthew Harper popped into my mind. I knew he was the solution. And then Sartol reminded me of Raymond and helped me work out all the details. It was a perfect plan—I never could have done it on my own. Sartol's my guide. I ask my angel about lots of things. He's never failed me yet."

"How are you, Daddy?" Clarence asked his father, who looked small and frail in the hospital bed.

"If I was a hoss, they'd a shot me already." Obadiah chuckled feebly. "But I's *not* a hoss—so don't go and shoot me, all right? Older than dirt, but I's still a man."

"You're the best man I've ever known," Clarence said.

"You should get around mo', Son. Meet mo' people."

"I mean it, Daddy. You were always a hard one to disobey, but you've been everything I could ask for in a father. If I could be to my children what you've been to me..."

"Give 'em your time, Son. No substitute for your time. Learn those younguns God's ways. Teach 'em who they is—chillens of the King. Some man treats 'em like a dog, that's his problem. He gonna have to face their Daddy the King. Chillens grows up real quick, Son. I knows. Don't miss the chances you got now. Won't get 'em again."

Clarence nodded. "I called Uncle Elijah. He's concerned about you. Wanted me to tell you he was prayin' for you."

"He's a good brother, 'Lijah. Best friend a man could ever have. Went through the hard days together. Kept each other warm those cold nights. Had us some fine times, we did. A true brother. I wish you and Harley could—"

"I know." Clarence choked. "I'm sorry we never got to Cooperstown."

"It ain't too late."

"What do you mean?"

"I mean, I wants you to take Jonah and Ty and Geneva and the girls too, if they wants to go. And ask Harley too. You can do it. They gots some old Negro League pictures, you know. Look for me. Twenty-two years in Shadow Ball, your old daddy's gots to be in some of them pictures."

"But it's you I wanted to go with, Daddy."

"Don't worry none about me, Son. I's goin' to the *real* Hall of Fame." He laughed and looked at Clarence with those soulful eyes, the light inside flickering with the winds of eternity. "Remember, Son, God sees around the corners, even if you can't."

Clarence noticed someone at the doorway.

"Manny? Come in."

"Mr. Manny? My detective friend?" The old man reached up his hand. Manny walked in and took it. "Tell you what, Son," Obadiah said. "Let me talk to Mr. Manny awhile. Got some things I wants to tell him, 'portant things every man should know. You go get you some coffee or something. Maybe some fresh air."

Clarence nodded, walking out of the room, knowing what his father meant by important things.

When Clarence returned to the room forty-five minutes later, Obadiah had fallen asleep, and Manny was standing there holding his hand. Manny turned away a moment, then walked past Clarence, nodding respectfully but saying nothing.

Clarence hovered over his father, wanting to protect him, unaware that someone much bigger and stronger than he stood beside the bed, sword outstretched toward heaven, prepared to give everything in defense of this one old man, from whom he had learned much and to whom he had become loyal beyond measure.

Clarence called Ollie from the hospital to update him on his father.

"You won't believe this," Ollie said. "Norcoast is in the hospital. He attempted suicide."

"What?"

"His wife's confession devastated him," Ollie said. "He knows he's ruined politically, of course, and he's never done anything else but be a politician. The papers, TV, radio, they're all over it. He loves his wife and feels guilt over his affair with Leesa. I've heard his daughter won't speak to him for what he did to her mother and her best friend. Plus, he feels like he betrayed everybody. I found out it was Gray who asked Raylon Berkley to stuff the story on Leesa, didn't give him the real reason for asking of course, but now Berkley's embarrassed and keeping his distance from his old friend Norcoast. I guess it was all too much to handle—Norcoast lost his image, his job, his family, and his friends, so he took a bottle of pills. He's not out of the woods yet. He may still die."

"What hospital, Ollie?"

"Right where you're calling from—Emanuel."

Clarence went to the front desk to get Norcoast's room number. He'd just been moved off critical condition and out of ICU but was still under close monitoring. Clarence went to his room on the fourth floor and stood over him. The councilman was drained of color, pale and pasty. Unconscious, he lay very still. Clarence stood over him for ten minutes before Norcoast started to move. He shuddered and trembled. He started mumbling, appearing to be seeing things and hearing voices.

"O God, they're trying to get me." Clarence backed away from the tortured voice. "Monsters, demons attacking me." His arms flailed. "It's so hot. Hurts so bad. No. Stay away. Don't hurt me." After a few minutes of incoherence, he calmed down a little, then spoke again, eyes closed. "Gone now. Where is everybody? I'm so alone. I'm burning up! Help me!" He screamed out, writhing, soaking himself in sweat, casting the sheets to his side and bumping against the bedrails. Two nurses ran into the room.

Clarence backed out of the room, shaken. He went directly to the hospital chapel and prayed fervently for his father, but even more fervently for Reggie Norcoast.

The next morning Clarence came early to the hospital, first visiting his father, who was unconscious. Then he went up two floors to visit Norcoast. The door was closed. A nurse told him the councilman had had terrible hallucinations all night, but he was now awake and out of trouble.

Clarence peeked in the door. Norcoast, usually vibrant and healthy, looked pale and peaked, like a man who'd been through a wringer. Clarence knocked lightly on the doorframe.

"Hello, Reg, can I come in?"

"Clarence?" Norcoast looked down. "I can't tell you how sorry I am about Esther and Gray and everything." He lay there looking dejected and pathetic. Clarence pitied him.

"Reg, I need to talk to you about some things. I know I've never talked with you about my faith before, but I feel it's—"

"Clarence, something wonderful happened last night." Norcoast suddenly sounded euphoric. "I was just about to die—in fact I think I may have died, really. I was walking down this shining corridor and there was this magnificent angel of light. It was so beautiful. The angel assured me there's a special place in heaven for me. He said I just needed to get in touch with myself, live a good life, and do the best I could to love others. It was so real. I was on the verge of heaven, and I didn't want to come back. But I realize I was *sent* back for a reason. To tell people about God's love and acceptance."

Clarence looked at him, slack-jawed. "Reg, I was *here* last night. I heard you crying out to God and screaming and talking about demons attacking you. You felt like you were on fire, then you talked about being all alone. You weren't on the verge of heaven. You were on the verge of hell!"

"What are you talking about?" Norcoast said. "No, you've got it all wrong. I remember it clearly. A bright angel, a beautiful home, peaceful feelings. Serenity. It was the most wonderful place I've ever been. The most extraordinary experience I've ever had. I've lost so much that's dear to me in the last few days, but this is a great comfort. I've made contact with my angel now. Esther says eventually I'll learn to talk to him and get his guidance."

Clarence stared at him, at a complete loss for words.

"How is he?" Harley asked Clarence as the brothers stood outside their father's room.

"Not good. Still unconscious," Clarence said. "The doctor doesn't think… there's very much time."

Harley nodded, removing his glasses and rummaging in his pockets. Clarence handed him an extra handkerchief.

"Look, Harley," Clarence said. "There's something I need to say to you….I'm sorry I've got such a big mouth sometimes."

Harley looked at him somberly. "What do you mean, 'sometimes'?"

They both laughed and put their arms around each other in a long embrace for the first time either could remember, maybe the first time since Mama died. Suddenly they heard the sound of faint singing. They both rushed into Daddy's room. The words were barely audible, the tune broken but recognizable.

"O Freedom, O Freedom, O Freedom over me. And before I'll be a slave I'll be buried in my grave, and go home to my Lord and be free.

"O Canaan, bright Canaan, I'm bound for the land of Canaan.

"Amazin' Grace, how sweet the sound that saved a wretch like me, I once was lost, but now am found, was blind, but now I see." His voice whispered, but with surprising intensity.

"Someday when I his face shall see, someday from tears I shall be free. Somebody's callin' my name. Git on board, little children, git on board. De gospel train's a comin', git on board."

Clarence and Harley stood over him, Clarence's arm around his brother. Daddy's eyes were open, but they seemed to be looking somewhere beyond the room.

"I hears that whistle blowin'," Obadiah said. "Train's a comin'. Folks a gatherin'." His whisper gained strength, energized by something the brothers couldn't see. "Who's dat walkin' beside me now? Tall as an oak. These ol' legs don't feel so sore. Who's dat up ahead? Whose face I see? O, my sweet Jesus. It's you. It's you."

Obadiah grew suddenly quiet, his eyes staying open, not blinking, but watering up. Clarence wiped away Obadiah's tears with a tissue. After a minute the old man suddenly started talking again.

"Who dat, now? Daddy, it's you, ain't it? O Daddy, what you told me was true, and here it is. And…O Mama, yes, me too, Mama." Silence again. "Moses! How are you, brother? How long's it been now? And where's my Dani? There she is! O Dani,

I hadn't stopped cryin' for you yet, little girl. And who's this one? My little Felicia, that you? O sweet Jesus, sweet Jesus. I never knowed such joy. Thank you, my sweet Jesus."

Clarence and Harley stared wide eyed as the tears streamed down their father's face. "He's hallucinating," Harley said. Clarence nodded. The brothers stood shoulder to shoulder, leaning close over their father, wanting to hear every word as his voice faded in and out.

"My oh my, and who's dat woman? Uncommon pretty, she is. I missed you terrible, Ruby. Gets lonely countin' cricket chirps and watchin' stars all by yo'self."

Clarence looked at Harley. He wondered whether...

"Wait a minute, there." Obadiah said, "Mike? That you, ol' soldier? Now there's a grip. Been waitin' a long time to shake that hand again. Hold on. Who dat behind you? Elijah? Where you come from, brother?"

No, of course not. It was all just a hallucination after all. Amazing what the mind could do. The old man's body jolted with a spasm of pain.

"You all come out to get me, didn't you? Well, don't want to stay out here, that's sure. I hears that ol' porch bell a ringin'. Time to come inside, ain't it? Time for me to cross dat ol' Jordan. Time to come..."

Obadiah's eyes grew big and his pupils contracted as if seeing a bright light. Then his eyelids fell over them as if they were blinds suddenly tugged shut. Obadiah Abernathy gasped his last breath in one world and his first in another.

The body lay abandoned. Clarence and Harley looked at each other in disbelief. It seemed impossible that only an instant before this empty shell had still contained a man.

"O Daddy," Harley sobbed.

Clarence fell to his knees, laying his head on the bedspread. "We gonna miss you, old man," Clarence said, choking out the words. "We gonna miss you terrible."

Several minutes later, Harley and Clarence helped each other up and walked out into the hall.

"Antsy?" Clarence hadn't heard Harley call him that for twenty years. "For just a moment, I thought maybe Daddy was really...I don't know. Did you think...?"

"Yeah, I did," Clarence said. "Up until he thought he saw Uncle Elijah. I just talked to him last night. 'Lijah's still in Mississippi."

"And if anything's for sure," Harley said, "it's that Mississippi and heaven aren't the same place."

That evening, at Keisha and Celeste's insistence, the family sat down to read. Clarence, Geneva, Jonah, and Ty all gathered close to the girls in the living room, sitting on the floor, propped up against the couch and beanbag chairs.

"Before Granddaddy read to us, he always sang a song," Keisha said.

"What did he sing?" Clarence asked, figuring he knew the answer.

"'Amazin' Grace.' And a bunch of others. He said some of them were slave songs."

Clarence's low voice rumbled up slowly, as if climbing stairs. "Amazing grace—how sweet the sound—that saved a wretch like me! I once was lost but now am found, was blind but now I see." He continued verse by verse, climaxing with, "When we've been there ten thousand years, bright shining as the sun, we've no less days to sing God's praise, then when we'd first begun."

"You're a good singer, Daddy," Keisha said.

Clarence cleared his throat, searching for a slave song. "Someday when I his face shall see, someday from tears I shall be free. Somebody's callin' my name. Git on board, little children, git on board. De gospel train's acomin', git on board."

Geneva closed her eyes as Clarence sang. She absorbed the sound of her husband's soothing voice, which resonated into her soul. It had been so long since she'd heard him sing like this.

"Swing low, sweet chariot, comin' for to carry me home, swing low, sweet chariot, comin' for to carry me home." The more he sang, the more Clarence felt like they weren't alone in the room. The music linked them to other voices far away and yet very near. For a moment he sensed a voice that had been very thin when he'd last heard it this morning, but was now full and robust. It struck him as eerie, like hearing the whispers of eternity. He didn't understand that the songs shared by earth and heaven sometimes create a momentary bridge connecting the two worlds.

The phone rang. They'd had calls coming and going from relatives all day, so Geneva reluctantly got up to answer it.

In a few minutes she returned. "It was your cousin Jabo in Jackson," Geneva said to Clarence. "I left him the message about Daddy earlier. He called about your Uncle Elijah."

"I suppose he's taking it pretty hard," Clarence said. "They were so close."

"It's not that," Geneva said. "Uncle Elijah passed away."

"When?" Clarence asked.

"Ten o'clock this morning, Mississippi time. Jabo said he was sorry he didn't call earlier."

"He died three hours before Daddy," Clarence said. He put his big hands on his face and tears overtook him again. Geneva and the children put their arms around him and each other, there on the living-room floor.

After a few minutes of reminiscing about his father and uncle, Clarence led his family in prayer. Then he picked up the last Narnia book, opening to the bookmark at the beginning of the final chapter.

"Uncle Antsy," Celeste said, "what does it mean when it keeps saying Aslan is not a tame lion?"

"Well…" Clarence hesitated. "Maybe that he's good, he's faithful, but he's not predictable. He doesn't always do things the way we want him to. He's not a genie you can call out of a bottle to do your bidding." He saw the children weren't quite following him. "You know how a lion tamer is a man who makes the lion do what he wants? Well, God isn't a tame lion. We can ask him for what we want, but we can't make him do it. He's the King, we're not. He calls the shots, we don't. We have plans that make sense to us. He has better plans that make sense to him. No matter what happens, we need to learn to trust in his wisdom, not our own."

After reading twenty minutes to an unusually attentive audience, Clarence turned to the final page of *The Last Battle.*

"Only one more page?" Keisha said. "I don't want it to end."

"I hope C. S. Lewis writes more books," Celeste said. "Then we can read those too."

"C. S. Lewis is dead," Geneva said. "Sorry."

Celeste and Felicia looked very disappointed.

"Okay, girls, here's the end of the book." Clarence read the final section heading, "Farewell to the Shadow-Lands."

> "There *was* a real railway accident," said Aslan softly. "Your father and mother and all of you are—as you used to call it in the Shadow-Lands—dead. The term is over: the holidays have begun. The dream is ended: this is the morning."
>
> And as he spoke he no longer looked to them like a lion; but the things that began to happen after that were so great and beautiful that I cannot write them. And for us this is the end of all the stories, and we can most truly say that they all lived happily ever after. But for them it was only the beginning of the real story. All their life in this world and all their adventures in Narnia had only been the cover and the title page; now at last they were beginning Chapter One of the Great Story, which no one on earth has read; which goes on forever; in which every chapter is better than the one before.

ABOUT THE AUTHOR

Randy Alcorn is the founder and director of Eternal Perspective Ministries (EPM), a nonprofit ministry devoted to promoting an eternal viewpoint and drawing attention to people in special need of advocacy and help. A pastor for fourteen years before founding EPM, Randy is a popular teacher and conference speaker. He has spoken in over a dozen countries and has been interviewed on over two hundred radio and television programs. He has taught on the part-time faculties of Western Baptist Seminary and Multnomah Bible College, where he teaches contemporary social ethics. Randy lives in Gresham, Oregon, with his wife, Nanci, and daughters, Karina and Angela.

Randy produces the quarterly issues-oriented magazine *Eternal Perspectives.* He is the author of seven previous books, including *Money, Possessions and Eternity; Christians in the Wake of the Sexual Revolution; Pro-Life Answers to Pro-Choice Arguments;* and, co-authored with Nanci, *Women Under Stress.* Randy's bestseller *Deadline* was his first novel.

Inquiries regarding publications and other matters can be directed to Eternal Perspective Ministries (EPM), 2229 East Burnside #23, Gresham, OR 97030. EPM can also be reached by e-mail via ralcorn@teleport.com. EPM's homepage on the World Wide Web is http://www.epm.org/~ralcorn or http://www.teleport.com/~ralcorn.

READERS RESPOND TO RANDY ALCORN'S
BEST-SELLING NOVEL *DEADLINE:*

"This is the finest work of fiction I have ever read. And I read a lot of fiction!"
—BATH, NEW YORK

"*Deadline* is without a doubt the best Christian fiction I have read. The characters are well developed and the plot is excellent. For three days I rarely put the book down." —BLAIR, NEBRASKA

"I've never read the Bible, but *Deadline* really made me think about my life. It moved me in an unfamiliar way and also left me with a new thirst." —MOSES LAKE, WASHINGTON

"This was the finest book I have ever read. Not only was it a heart-stopper and heart-breaker, it was also a heart-changer. The Holy Spirit really dealt with me through this book. This old boy was changed—you'll never know how much, at least not until we get on the other side." —FREDERICKSBURG, TEXAS

"I just finished reading *Deadline*—what an intriguing, stimulating book! I absolutely loved the mystery and the challenging thoughts. I'm encouraging my friends to get a copy. I hope you'll be writing another novel soon!" —SAUGUS, CALIFORNIA

"I just finished reading *Deadline* and had to write to you to tell you how much I enjoyed it. It was almost impossible to put down. I couldn't wait to see what happened next." —FOND DU LAC, WISCONSIN

"I am compelled to write in response to your book *Deadline*. I have not read it once but twice, and plan to keep it in my treasure of books that are to be reread and savored anew each reading. Never have I read fiction that touched me in thought and spiritual contemplation. I must say this is the best book I've ever read." —GARLAND, TEXAS

"*Deadline* was one of the most powerful, eye-opening, stop-and-make-you-think books I have ever read. This is one book I'll be recommending to all my friends. I sure hope there will be a sequel to *Deadline*. I'll be watching the shelves." —SACRAMENTO, CALIFORNIA

"I've had *Deadline* two days. I am up, sleepless and absorbed into the morning hours. It's now 1:57 A.M. I have to get up in three hours. I want to buy a carton of *Deadline* novels and rave about it with family, pastors, friends, etc. Thank you! I continue to laugh and cry through this book." —CORVALLIS, OREGON

"I am most impressed with *Deadline*. It is the best piece of fiction I have read. I have been in the Christian bookstore business for fourteen years and am thrilled to introduce readers to your book. I am currently featuring it in the store." —MARYSVILLE, WASHINGTON

"I have just finished reading Randy Alcorn's *Deadline*. What a brilliant and beautiful book!" —HAKODATE, JAPAN

"Two days ago I finished reading *Deadline*. Never have I been so impressed by such a book. I just want you to know that you have touched my life with *Deadline*. I will never forget this book." —BOSTIC, NORTH CAROLINA

"Bravo! Bravo! Just finished reading *Deadline* and enjoyed it thoroughly. Hope we don't have to wait too long for another novel!" —MERRITT ISLAND, FLORIDA

"What a terrific book. It had more twists than a screendoor spring! We were on vacation and I was so engrossed I almost resented having to leave the book long enough to go look at scenery! It was pure genius the way you wove the story around biblical truths without sounding preachy!" —SANDY, OREGON

"I'm actually almost at a loss for words as I write this note. This is one of the most thought-provoking books I have ever read." —GRESHAM, OREGON

"I could not put this book down. I am a bookworm and seldom find reading material which captures me as this did. I intend to reread it shortly as I am sure I did not even scratch the surface of what it contains." —FT. WORTH, TEXAS

"I just finished reading Randy Alcorn's book *Deadline* and was completely taken by it. It is a book that must be read widely." —SEATTLE, WASHINGTON

"I have worked in two libraries and read many works of fine literature. But I can honestly say that with the exception of God's Word, I have never read a finer book than *Deadline*. The suspense, the humor, the spiritual insights were refreshing and inspiring. I no sooner finished the book than I wanted to read it again and get it to everyone I know." —BRIDGEPORT, WEST VIRGINIA

"I am a fussy reader, but *Deadline* was a fantastic story! I couldn't put it down. My husband and daughters are happy to finally have me back with them. I'm checking the bookstores looking for another one!" —WYOMING, MICHIGAN

"*Deadline* was wonderful! I'm a cross between Jake and Finney—but the book caused me to rethink my positions. I laughed and cried all the way through the book." —WASHINGTON, INDIANA

"*Deadline* is GREAT! I didn't want it to end. Thank you for such an insightful novel. What's next?" —WRIGHTWOOD, CALIFORNIA

"I am an eighteen-year-old soldier. I just finished *Deadline*. It had a profound impact on me. I face the same moral dilemmas Jake did, and seeing what happened to him brought me to some startling realizations about myself. Thank you for the impact *Deadline* has made on my life." —FORT GORDON, GEORGIA

"Yesterday I finished reading *Deadline*. I enjoyed it so much I couldn't put it down. When is the next book coming out?" —HILO, HAWAII

"Wow! *Deadline* is an awesome work—it affected me tremendously. I will never have the same view of heaven again. Reading this book started as a high school assignment for a book report , but it turned out to be so much more!" —LITTLE ROCK, ARKANSAS

"Thank you for *Deadline*. It was fantastic. It is definitely one of the best books I have ever read. I loved it! Two nights ago I woke up at 3:30 A.M. thinking about the story, and finally just got up so I could keep reading. My family is happy I finished it though, so I can get back to being a wife and mom. I'll be looking forward to any more of your novels. Maybe a sequel?" —STEVENS POINT, WISCONSIN

"Last night I finished reading *Deadline*, with much regret. It was one of those books you don't want to end. I felt like I knew personally the characters. They were so real. I will look forward to reading any other novel Randy Alcorn writes." —MILLSTATT, AUSTRIA

"*Deadline* is a great book. Fantastic! Any more in the making? Don't stop now!" —BALDWIN, FLORIDA

"Thought I'd let you know how wonderful I thought your book *Deadline* was. Absolutely the most awesome novel I have ever read! I have not looked at things the same since. Thank you, thank you, thank you!" —PORTLAND, OREGON

"I just finished reading *Deadline*, almost nonstop. I found it exciting, thought provoking, challenging, and most of all hopeful." —SHELBY, MICHIGAN

"Well, here I am traveling in the Crimea, a borderline insomniac, and it's all your fault. I've devoured (not once but twice) your delectable novel *Deadline*. The book really is a grabber. Thanks for working hard at weaving your biblical convictions into a format that makes this a terrific evangelism tool!" —ATLANTA, GEORGIA (Vice President, Walk Thru the Bible)

"I just finished reading *Deadline* and felt compelled to write you, even though it's midnight. Few books have touched me the way *Deadline* has. The book does something I've yet to see credibly portrayed in fiction—human contact with heaven. As a college professor I, and many of my colleagues who study the rhetorical implications of mass media, find evil is colorfully portrayed in horrific detail, while good is always something vague and beige. Thank you for bridging this gap. *Deadline* has been reorienting my thoughts toward heaven." —SAN MARCOS, CALIFORNIA

"This note is to tell you how much my wife and I enjoyed *Deadline*. The story line is great and your presentation of truth throughout is powerful and seamless. Your description of heaven, especially as a realm of endless discovery and wonder, has caused me to go back to familiar passages with a new sense of excitement." —ANAHEIM, CALIFORNIA

"*Deadline* was excellent! I'm a pastor and my copy circulated until it fell apart. Thanks for displaying so many critical biblical values in such a creative and readable format." —BROOMALL, PENNSYLVANIA

"I'd like to thank you for the countless hours of research and writing you did on your novel *Deadline*. Reading it was such a blessing, challenge, and inspiration, I stayed up till 3:30 A.M. to finish it. A friend let me borrow it and I've been able to do little else but read it since. It really spoke to me and refreshed my spirit." —CLUJ-NAPOCA, ROMANIA

"I am writing to commend you for one of the best Christian novels I have read. *Deadline* challenged me to view this world differently, from a much more eternal outlook while at the same time proving to be very entertaining and captivating." —ELLICOTT CITY, MARYLAND

"I have just finished reading *Deadline*. This book is absolutely wonderful. I love getting my hands on a book I can sink my teeth into. I'll share it with my friends, churched and unchurched." —VANCOUVER, WASHINGTON

"I just finished reading *Deadline*. It was marvelous! I had a hard time putting it down. I am a pastor and will recommend your book to my congregation. I hope to see your next novel soon." —KIRBYVILLE, TEXAS

"I was very impressed with this book. It would make a great movie. The research in journalistic circles is very thorough and convincing. I think many agnostic and atheistic people can relate to Jake." —SAN FRANCISCO, CALIFORNIA

"I find most Christian novels trite and predictable and their characters one-dimensional. I was surprised to find this book none of the above. It was insightful, unpredictable, and a real page-turner. It is powerful and morally stirring without being preachy. I have never made notes in the back of a novel before, but my back pages are full in this book. We're now selling *Deadline* at our church book table. This book is making a difference and is a breath of fresh air in a fairly stale market."
—EUGENE, OREGON

"I am only seventeen, but many times while reading about *Deadline's* characters I was moved to tears, deeply touched. Then I laughed from genuine joy, deep inside. I really needed that. Thank you for *Deadline*." —RIPON, CALIFORNIA

"I just wanted to tell you how much I enjoyed reading *Deadline*. It was a gripping story with great characters and a powerful message. I was hooked from the beginning! The book was totally enjoyable." —GRESHAM, OREGON

"I immediately purchased *Deadline* on seeing it was written by the author of *Money, Possessions and Eternity*, one of the most profound books I have in my library. *Deadline* is the first fiction I've read that I profusely highlighted. I ran out today to purchase four more copies." —SAN ANTONIO, TEXAS

"Just finished reading *Deadline* and WOW! Thoroughly enjoyable. Now, if you could just get it faithfully adapted to film." —KOKOMO, INDIANA

"I enjoyed this book immensely. I sat down and savored it. The juxtaposition of the temporal and eternal held my attention. Thanks for a wonderful story."
—TULSA, OKLAHOMA

"I thought *Deadline* was one of the best novels I've read in a long time. I hope you will be writing more in the future!" —FRESNO, CALIFORNIA

"I just finished your book *Deadline* five minutes ago. I had to write you a thank-you note before I went to bed. I have few memories of ever being so moved by a book. I was often frustrated that I could not read the words on a page through the tears in my eyes. You have created characters so believable that I almost look forward to seeing them on the other side. If this is what your readers get for a first novel, I can only eagerly anticipate what is upcoming." —HILLSBORO, OREGON

"*Deadline* was a gripping and transfixing novel, and I found it difficult to put down." —AUSTIN, TEXAS

"I just wanted to thank you for your latest book *Deadline*. I usually steer away from Christian fiction, but found this book really captivating. I recommended it to many friends and describe it to them as a murder mystery with a beautiful glimpse of heaven and eternity. Although I have been an active and growing Christian for over 25 years, I feel as if this is the first time I have actually begun to look forward to heaven." —FAIR OAKS, CALIFORNIA

"I have never read a modern work that so powerfully blends, defines, and clarifies earthly and eternal perspectives! Jake's struggles helped to define the parameters of my own struggles. I want to personally thank you for writing *Deadline*." —WATONGA, OKLAHOMA

"I normally don't write letters to authors, but this is an exception. *Deadline* was excellent. I read it several times months ago and still can't get the story out of my mind. The characters were alive. When I finished *Deadline* I felt a real sense of loss. Jake and Finney and their families had become family to me. I hope—I pray—you will consider writing a sequel to *Deadline*. It's a story that should go on. I will in great anticipation watch the bookstore shelves!" —CLAIRTON, PENNSYLVANIA

"*Deadline* touched my life! Last night while reading it I cried and cried and finally had to force myself to put it down and go to bed at 2:30 A.M. But not until I had taken a good hard look at what had happened to my spirit in the last 29 years." —SALEM, OREGON

"I have just finished *Deadline*. I bought it for my husband for Christmas when I saw it on the top ten bestsellers display. I cried most of the way through the book. It made me come to terms with my complacent Christian life. I have a renewed longing to get to know my Savior better. I want my life to count for Him. This letter does not do justice to how much *Deadline*, with God's help, has changed me. I am a different person than I was before." —LARGO, FLORIDA

"I just finished *Deadline*, and wanted to write and thank you for such a fantastic book! I've been reading it over the last two months and cherishing my time with this book and not wanting it to end. Reading it was a joyful slow process as I would read a few pages, talk to God, cry tears of thankfulness to God, and then begin to read again. This was the most meaningful fiction I've ever read, and I read a lot of books from Christian bookstores. I hope you are in the process of writing many more novels." —SAN DIEGO, CALIFORNIA

"As the editor of a major daily newspaper, I wanted to express my appreciation for your excellent work in your book, *Deadline*. I enjoyed the story very much. The plot was exciting and the characters are very well developed. I thought you did a masterful job of capturing the atmosphere of the newsroom and the thinking of so many in our business through the character of the columnist. It was very well done." —INDIANAPOLIS, INDIANA

"I was up until 2:00 this morning reading. That is not an unusual occurrence of late. The reason is that I have been absolutely enthralled with your book *Deadline*. I am not a great fan of novels, particularly Christian ones. They usually strike me as particularly insipid and poorly written. Your book was a marvelous exception. I have never written to a novelist before. But I felt compelled to let you know how much I enjoyed your work, including the realistic conversations, the frightening description of Hell, and the descriptions of Heaven. Thank you for the marvelous gift you have given to the Christian world." —CALGARY, ALBERTA, CANADA

"I finished reading *Deadline* about ten minutes ago and I am still smiling. I have read literally thousands of books. I can say with honesty and true conviction that the effect your book has had on my life is surpassed by only one other book—God's Word. I laughed out loud while reading it; I also cried and found myself talking to the air at times. Your writing has deeply affected my spiritual, emotional, and physical life. I hope to never lose the freshness of spirit that I feel right now. Since starting *Deadline* I have enjoyed a more fulfilling spiritual life and prayer life. I am crying while writing this letter. They are tears of joy and tears of gratitude." —BRIDGEWATER, NEW JERSEY

"It hasn't been more than two minutes since I finished *Deadline*. What an incredibly touching book. I cried my way through it, as almost all of the issues you dealt with really hit home for me. This was such an inspiring book." —SURREY, BRITISH COLUMBIA, CANADA

"I just finished *Deadline* last night and I had to write you a letter to thank you for writing it. Not only was it enjoyable fiction, but I truly believe it changed my outlook on life. Thank you for a wonderful book. I borrowed it from a friend, but I will now buy my own copy and treasure it for years to come." —LOUISVILLE, KENTUCKY

"I am writing to let you know how much I truly enjoyed and was inspired by your book *Deadline*. Through your marvelous work I learned valuable new lessons. And being very new to living in God's Word, I found it fuel to continue in my battle against Satan and the darkness I once lived in. This book made me laugh and cry, but best of all it made me think." —OREGON CORRECTIONAL FACILITY

"I have just finished reading your book *Deadline*, and all I can say is WOW!

Reading about Finney and his experiences in Heaven brought chills and tears. Especially touching to me was Bobby's entrance into heaven. You see, Mr. Alcorn, I have cerebral palsy and earnestly yearn for the day when I can walk and say 'It doesn't hurt anymore,' as Bobby said. I look forward to seeing you at our Home in Heaven."
—CASANOVA, VIRGINIA

"*Deadline* is fantastic, one of the best books I've read in years. My daughter and I thoroughly enjoyed reading this book!" —ARLINGTON, TEXAS

"*Deadline* is very exciting and enthralling. But most of all it made us think in a way we never have before." —WESTMINSTER, CALIFORNIA

"*Deadline* was a fascinating, intriguing, and thought-provoking book, written in a manner where I really did not want to put it down." —CARLETON, NEBRASKA

"By the time I read the words 'Well done, good and faithful servant,' tears were streaming down my face." —INDIANAPOLIS, INDIANA

"Thank you for your novel *Deadline*. I have problems with my eyesight. I do feel your novel was touched by His Spirit. It is treasures like this book, after my Bible reading, that I want to have stored in my mind should my sight totally fail."
—FORT MYERS, FLORIDA

"I have read many books and have never before written to an author. But I just finished reading *Deadline* and wanted to say thank you! It moved me. I was very blessed reading it. I will recommend it to all." —HOPKINS, SOUTH CAROLINA